A M Y:

OR,

LOVE AND MADNESS.

𝕬 𝕽𝖔𝖒𝖆𝖓𝖈𝖊.

LONDON:

PUBLISHED BY E. LLOYD, AT THE OFFICE OF THE " ILLUSTRATED EDITIONS
OF STANDARD WORKS," 12, SALISBURY SQUARE, FLEET STREET.

1847.

AMY;

OR,

LOVE AND MADNESS.

A DOMESTIC STORY OF THE HEART'S TEMPTATION. BY THE AUTHOR OF "THE WIFE'S TRAGEDY," ETC.

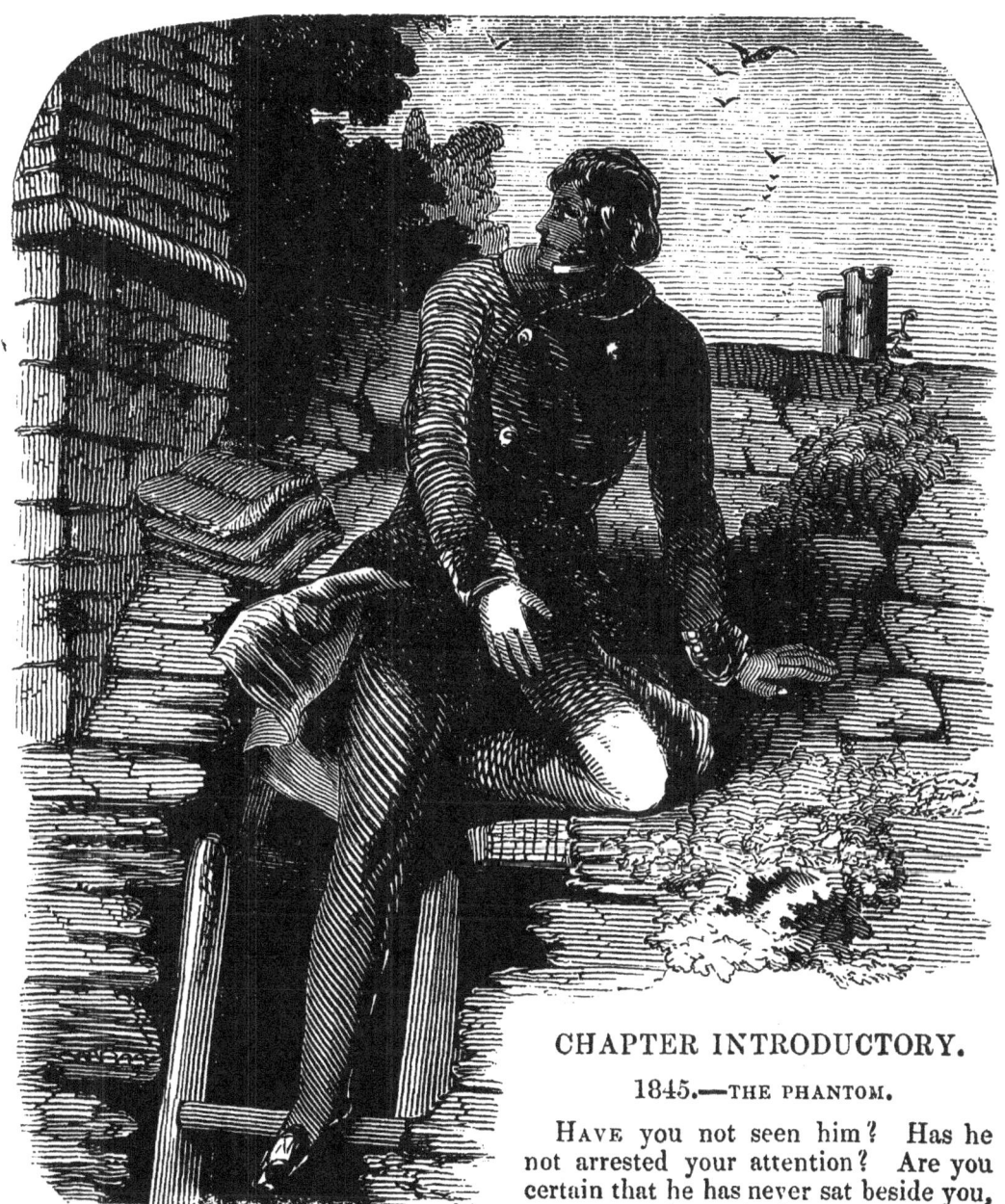

CHAPTER INTRODUCTORY.

1845.—THE PHANTOM.

HAVE you not seen him? Has he not arrested your attention? Are you certain that he has never sat beside you, never stood beneath the same roof with yourself? In all your walks and wanderings about and around London, have you not met him—has he not rushed by you—have you not looked round and wondered who he is, and why he is ever restless, ever moving?

He is an old man—so old, that one might suppose him to have seen a hundred summers. His form is gaunt, thin, lank, and shrivelled ; his white hair, of which he has abundance, flows down his shoulders, and floats on the breeze as he passes quickly by. Pale as that of a spectre is his face, yet his eyes are dark, and bright, and of a fearful expression. Those eyes are never turned towards you, never regard you, yet they glare at some visionary object which always seems to glide on before, and which is invisible to myself and to you.

Wrapped up in a dark-coloured and threadbare cloak, he pursues his way through crowded streets and narrow lanes. He speaks to none—he asks questions of none.

You would think that man to be engaged on business of importance, so quick are his movements, so fleeting are his footsteps. Nevertheless, he is not known to trade with any, nor have I met with one individual who can aver having touched his hand, or entered into his acquaintance.

I have a propensity to inquisitiveness—my curiosity amounts to a passion. It is my delight to unravel mysteries, to ferret out secrets, to discover the why and the wherefore of everything that is strange, and wild, and wonderful. In deserted, musty chambers it is my delight to make my home ; and where other and more timorous people fear to tread, it is my love to ramble. Every eccentric individual who walks the streets is known to me—every personage presenting the least appearance of singularity has been an object of interest to me. There is only one exception—only one solitary exception amidst the many, and that one is the man whom I have alluded to.

Times without number has the question been put to me, " Can you tell me who that man is ?" I have shaken my head in reply, for I had no answer to give.

Even to the children who throng the streets of the metropolis, is that man a mystery, and a source of inward dread. As he passes by, they shun him ; when they see him coming, they raise an alarm, and flee away to hide themselves.

Maidens fear to encounter him in the thoroughfares. Aged people shudder when he meets their gaze, and offer up a prayer to Heaven for one of whom they know nothing.

There is but one name which he is known by, and that is—" The Phantom." I have named him " The Phantom of London."

Years ago I first saw that man. I remarked him as he passed through the streets ; his bright, piercing eyes hidden beneath his dark and beetling brows ; his white hair long and streaming ; his head projecting forwards ; his shoulders inclined, like those of one ever ardent in the pursuit of some wished-for object. I was struck by the peculiarity of his gait, by the wanness of his countenance, by the abstractedness of his air. He has been a mystery to me from that moment.

I have met him in the thronged and noisy avenues of the city, stalking onwards, neither looking to his right nor to his left, not heeding the jostling crowds, but gliding through them with the same spectre-like step, with the same quick and continuous motion.

I have watched him also, in the more select and retired parts of the town—in the large squares, the fashionable streets, and the broad-paved places. There, as elsewhere, he flits onwards with the same noiseless, gliding motion, more like a being from another world, than a habitant of our own. I have seen the rich and the stately look out at their carriage windows to gaze at him ; and I have noticed the servant-maid to rest her pitcher, and the errand-boy to put down his basket, in order to fix their wondering eyes upon the phantom-figure who was advancing up the street.

In the country I have seen him also. Walking along at a smart pace over Barnes Common on a summer's evening, I heard footsteps behind me. It was near dusk, and there were but few passengers on the road. The sound of footsteps grew more distinct. They advanced nearer—nearer still. I turned round to see who was behind me. Suddenly, a figure swept by so swiftly, that I fancied it was borne by the wind. This figure was enveloped in a dark cloak. There was no mistaking it—no guessing a second time ; I knew at one glance who was the owner of that cloak—I knew him to be the phantom-mystery.

Impelled by an irresistible impulse, I followed the fleeting shadow with what swiftness of speed I could command. In vain my efforts ; he was lost in the gloom ;

he was so far ahead, that I could not perceive his form; I could not hear his footsteps.

Yet it has not been always under such circumstances that I have met with him. I have seen him at rest as well as in motion; I have seen him beneath a roof, as well as in the open air.

Chance led me to the gallery of the Italian Opera. That night was destined to be an unforgotten one to many, for it was that on which the voice of the divine Malibran resounded within those walls for the last time. The crowd was very great, and it was with much difficulty that I succeeded in getting within the doors. Just as I was turning round one of the angles of the staircase, I espied a figure half way up the stairs before me. He was almost hidden by the crowd which hemmed him in on every side; but I knew him on the instant. With great perseverance, and at the expense of some rough usage, I endeavoured to force my way through the crowd, that I might reach the step on which he stood. All my struggles were in vain. Those behind bore me onwards and upwards, but they also accelerated the ascent of the man beside whom I longed to stand. I saw him mount higher and higher; I saw him hold out his hand to the money-taker, and then pass onwards; I could not discern that he paid down any money. Only a few minutes after him I also reached the pay-place. I threw down the price of admission, and, nearly forgetting to take up my check, hurried onwards. When I reached the gallery, I glanced round to discover where the object of my pursuit had posted himself; before I could make that discovery, the hand of an official was laid upon my shoulder, and I was told, in a rough voice, to sit down. The opera commenced; Malibran exerted herself to the utmost, and the whole house was enthusiastic in its applause. After the green curtain had fallen, the beautiful prima-donna came forward to bid her last farewell; every one arose; hats and handkerchiefs were waved. In a seat below me there was one individual who had not risen, and who did not bestow one cheer. It was he—the man whom I had strained my eyes in search of. I could not get near him, and I lost him in the crowd when making my exit.

At another time I was in the pit of Drury-lane Theatre, when a cry of " fire!" arose. I turned round to make my escape. Before me I saw the old man with the white hair; he also was hurrying out, and in his arms was a young girl who had fainted when the alarm was first given, and who narrowly escaped being trodden to death. The old man eluded me again, and the young woman I could not find.

Not in the theatre only have I met with that man, but I have been near him when within the walls of a church. I have seen him in Westminster Abbey, and once I was but a few inches from him in the cathedral of St. Paul's. I must relate the incident of my meeting with him there. After having seen the whispering-gallery, the model-room, and the clock, I expressed my desire to the guide that he would show me to the ball and cross. There is something connected with that glittering ball, perched as it is so high up above the city and its throng, that to me is a source of strange, indefinable feelings, when I turn my gazing eyes towards it. I had never ascended to it it—never been within it. An opportunity now presented itself, and I determined to avail myself of the privilege, and make the ascent. Onwards we went—onwards, up amidst stones, iron-work, and rafters; up staircases that were narrow, and to look down from which made the poor faltering brain to swim; up ladders that were hung in darkness, where the spider made his home, and cobwebs hung like folds of drapery—upwards till we stood beneath the ball.

Arrived at this altitude, were two or three other individuals who had been escorted thither by another guide; one of these was already upon the ladder which leads up into the ball. I at once attempted to follow him.

"Stop!" cried the guide; " stop till he has landed."

I could not wait—I could not linger behind. The place was very dark, but I rushed forward and planted my feet upon the ladder.

The person above felt the sudden motion occasioned by my stepping upon the frail machine. He turned round and looked down; a ray of light fell upon his countenance, and I knew him—I knew him.

It was he—it was the old man with the white hair—it was the phantom which I had encountered so often.

Whether it was this sudden discovery, or whether the height to which I had ascended was the cause, I know not, but a feeling of faintness came over me ; my brain reeled, a dizziness of sight followed, and I knew that I was about to fall.

I was caught in the arms of the guide—borne by him down the ladders, and along the galleries into the body of the church. I felt myself to be very ill, and desired to be taken home.

The idea was a strange one, nevertheless, it was one which continually haunted me, and which haunts me now. I believe that I am destined to become acquainted with that unknown and wondrous man ; I believe that, at some future time, I shall learn his history and his secret. I have a belief, which is still more strange, and for which I cannot account—it is, that I am destined to be of service to that man.

Although I have met him in a variety of places—although I have encountered him under a variety of circumstances, I have particularly observed that there is one class of situations in which he is most likely to be found.

Wherever there is much excitement—wherever there is noise and tumult— wherever there is matter to divert the senses and to distract the mind, there may you meet with him—there does he love to be present.

I made one of the many gazers on the occasion of the last coronation. Amongst the crowd I saw that white-haired old man ; but I stood upon the bare ground, and he occupied a place upon a stand.

Again, I was an on-looker when the loyal inhabitants of the west-end illuminated their houses in honour of the royal nuptials. Amidst the multitude who then thronged the streets, I discerned the same old man.

I was present at the burning of the Royal Exchange. My eyes wandered continually from the burning building to the figure of an individual who, like myself, was a spectator of the scene of devastation. It was he—it was that old man.

Last spring I paid visits to Ascot and Epsom. At both of those places I obtained a glance at the phantom form which haunted me wherever I went, yet always fled from me whenever I endeavoured to approach.

Once, however, I made one at a great assemblage, where that man was not present. It was on the occasion of an execution at Newgate. I had never before been witness to a similar scene ; I am ashamed of myself for having been present then ; never more will I so degrade myself. The crowd was a large one ; but, though I looked eagerly and expected to behold him, I could not discern that man —that phantom.

Whenever there is a royal procession, whenever some great star makes his or her first appearance at the theatres, it is an easy matter to obtain a glance at the man of whom I write.

Often and ardently have I longed to unriddle the mystery of that man. What is he ?—whence did he come ?—of what nature is the secret which he evidently bears about in his breast ?

I have had and have many conjectures concerning him. Can it be that he has committed some great crime ?

I have applied to my friends for their opinion. They shake their heads, and return me no direct answer ; yet, from their manner, I plainly perceive that they conceive my white-haired old friend to have sold himself to the evil one. Perhaps they are right, but I do not think so myself.

Do you wish to know the guess which I have made concerning him ?

Circumstances prove him to be a seeker after excitement ; yet does he seem to seek that excitement more out of some irresistible impulse than from any love of the excitement itself. Mark you, I have never seen him laugh—never seen a smile upon his countenance.

Why should a man seek after excitement if he has no real love for it ? My answer is, he may do so to drive away or to forget pain.

It is probable—indeed, I think it is very likely, that this mysterious old man is haunted by the recollection of some fearful deed which he has either witnessed, or in which he has played a part. What that deed may have been—what may have been its dreadful nature, I know not ; I wish I could find it out.

A fortnight ago I was tormented by that wish ; my conjecture had become conviction, and it drove away sleep from my pillow. I could neither write nor read on account of the distraction which it caused in my thoughts.

They asked me why I refused to eat—why I put the food away from me ?

I could not answer them ; I did not like to tell them of the horrible conjectures that haunted my mind—that wrested from me repose, and destroyed all appetite.

"Do not ask me," I replied, testily ; "I cannot eat."

I put on my hat, and sallied forth into the streets. After wandering about for an hour or two, I reached Holborn. There was a disturbance in the middle of the road. I stepped up to ascertain its cause ; it was but a trifling matter, and was soon brought to a termination. I turned about to depart ; as I did so, my eyes rested on the figure of the white-haired old man—the phantom.

I saw his face for a moment, and, so much did that sight overpower me, that minutes elapsed before I could move from the spot. The countenance of the old man had become so pale, of such a blue-grey paleness, that to me it seemed as the face of a corpse. His eyes had sunk deeper in his head, and they glared with more than their wonted ghastly brightness.

Presently I summoned up courage.

"Now," said I, "I will settle my doubts ; I will satisfy my mind. I will follow that man, go he where he may ; and, if I peril my own life in doing it, I will wrest from him the secret of his existence."

I looked around, and saw the old man at some yards distant.

The chase commenced. I knew that he was fleet of foot, and I resolved to be so likewise. Whether my speed could equal his own remained to be determined by the trial.

Onward—onward ! Up Holborn to Chancery-lane. Still he was as far from me as before.

Down the lane ; through Temple-bar, and round St. Clement's church. I had lessened the distance between us by one-third.

Onward—onward !—fleeter—faster !

I jostled through the throngs on the pavement and in the road with difficulty ; but he glided through them with ease, like a skilful skater, who cares not for those who stand in his way.

Onward—onward, along the Strand ! I had reached Somerset-house, and he was but a score of yards in advance.

"I shall have him now," said I ; "it is impossible for him to escape me."

We kept up the chase with spirit. Whether he knew that I was following him, I cannot say. Onward we went ; I caught sight of his dark cloak only a dozen yards before me.

On a sudden, he turned out of the Strand, down a short street which leads to a dark, subterranean arch. I followed him ; he entered the arch ; he was lost in the darkness.

Probably you know that arch ; it leads to a gloomy series of passages which run beneath the terrace of the Adelphi. There are lamps here and there, at certain distances apart, but the faint light emitted by them only serves to make the gloom more gloomy.

For one whole hour I searched those passages ; but, though I searched narrowly, and, as I thought, examined every hole and corner, I found not the man—the phantom.

A fortnight has elapsed since then. Every day I have walked the streets of the metropolis, and every evening I have visited some one or other of the places of assembly. My object has been to meet the old man again.

I have not met him. All my endeavours seem useless ; I cannot meet with him. And why should I wish to do so ?

It is because I still have the belief that I am to learn his secret at last, and that I am destined to be the minister of comfort to him.

Oh, joyous—joyous thought! should he prove to be some repentant transgressor whose wish is to unburden his mind—should it be that he longs for some kind hand to moisten his lips while he tells the tale of joys and sorrows past—should it be that he desires Heaven to send him some one to be his consoler in his hour of death—to stand beside his bed—to minister to his wants—to listen to his requests—to support him on his pillow—to close his eyes when all is over, and all his weary life come to an end;—should such prove to be the case, and if it shall happen that I am destined to be that person, how happy I shall be in having rendered such service—in having done such a deed!

But why do I talk thus? I have not seen him for a fortnight. Perhaps he is dying, or he may be dead.

CHAPTER I.

1846.—THE RIVER BY MOONLIGHT.—THE HAUNTED HOUSE BY THE WATER-SIDE.

HE is dead.

I know it all now; I have learned the whole story. The mystery is mine—the mystery is mine!

The mystery, did I say? Ay; the fearful mystery.

Listen! would you know it—would you know what I have learned, how I came to learn it, and what it has to do with the old man whom you will never again meet in the streets—never, never more? Then, listen.

If there be one pleasure which I love more than any other, it is the singular one of being on the water at night.

How beautiful it is, on a mild evening, to cast yourself in your boat, and venture out on the river or the lake, by the light of the moon. All the world cannot furnish another such source of delight. Beautiful is it to watch the silver beams dance upon the ripples, as though the surface of the water was studded with diamonds; beautiful is it to float away from the noisy resorts of men to some silent spot, where the only sound is that of the ripples' play, and the only objects in sight, the moon above you, the majestic trees around you, and the beautiful water upon which you move. The more turbulent passions then fade away from the mind, and the soul seems to soar above this common earth, seeking for itself communion with the spirits of other worlds.

I had been engaged in the city during the day, and had become exhausted and feverish through the excitement of business. It was a lovely evening, for there were only one or two white clouds in the sky, and the moon was at its full. I felt no inclination for sleep, and accordingly wandered out to seek refreshment in the coolness and quietude of the hour. Before me lay the river Thames; and a boat, which I could at all times command, rested upon the sands at some little distance. The night was certainly very cold; but I cared not for that, having taken the precaution to wrap myself up in a large Petersham coat. A desire seized me to go upon the water. For the moment it seemed to me a frantic wish, but the impulse grew stronger, and I knew that when I should come to take the sculls in my hands, I would soon warm myself by rowing. On the water I determined to go, and on the water I went.

The tide was flowing up, and resting upon my sculls, I allowed the boat to be carried on by the water.

It was a late hour of the night, and all sounds were hushed. No boat seemed moving upon the water except my own. One by one I watched the lights pass away from the windows of the houses that were stationed by the water-side. I passed by the old palace of Lambeth, and saw the moonlight falling upon the Lollards' tower. I turned my eyes towards the prison on the opposite bank of the river; but a cloud obstructed the moonlight from falling upon it, and the dark walls were wrapped in gloom. My boat shot between the piers of Vauxhall bridge, and a few minutes after I turned round my head, thinking that I heard the descent of some substance from the bridge into the river; whether such an event happened, I know not, though I could perceive a series of circular ripples upon one spot of the stream, and fancied, perhaps wrongly, that I could distinguish the tips of white fingers appearing above the water. Still my boat floated on, and in a few minutes I was some distance from the spot.

So blue was the sky, and so clear was the air, that every star seemed to shine with double brightness. I had heard a report that there was to be an occultation of one of the planets that evening, and in my curiosity to witness such a phenomenon, I guided my frail vessel till it had passed beneath Chelsea bridge, and then, wrapping my coat tightly around me, I threw myself along the bottom of the boat, that I might have a clear view of the heavens.

The occultation took place. The planet disappeared, was lost, and then returned again. After having witnessed the occurrence, I arose and looked around me to see where my boat had been carried to.

I was in the middle of the river, and on each side of me the banks were open and unbuilt upon. A few tall and dark trees here and there swayed their large branches to the breeze as though they had life, and were the only living things around me, at least, within sight.

Suddenly, the heavens became overclouded, the moon was hidden; only two or three stars were visible. The light breeze had increased until it had become a keen wind, and the heavy branches of the trees groaned as they moved to and fro. No longer did the ripples dance in the moonshine—no longer could I feast my eyes on sights of quiet beauty, nor discern those distant hills which a few minutes before had been illuminated by a soft and silvery light. Even the silence was no more; for the surface of the stream was broken by splashing waves, and I heard the wind moan, and whistle, and creak, and sigh, as it swept across the open country, putting all things into agitation as it passed.

The night had become much colder, and it was evident that a storm was gathering. I resolved to row back to one of the bridges with all possible speed.

I seized hold of the sculls, and was about to make the first strike. Just then I discerned something which caused me to pause in my intent.

What was that something?

On the bank to my right, I discerned a lone and desolate house. Its walls had long fallen to decay, its doors bore the appearance of not having been unclosed for half a century. I knew immediately whereabouts I was by the glance which I had of that lonely ruin.

And I knew that ruin. I knew it well. It was *the haunted house by the river side*.

'Everybody knows it—everybody has gazed at that old house, and wondered why it stands there as it does; why its walls have been suffered to fall to decay, and why its history is unknown.

I had often passed by that house in the daytime, stopping often to look at it, and to remark its singular appearance. Apparently, it has been at some distant day the residence of those who were well-to-do in the world. Its owner may have been some rich merchant on the Exchange, or some titled individual whose fancy it was to have his dwelling by the river. Perhaps the laugh and the song have resounded within those walls; perhaps the foot of beauty at one time trod upon its floors; but all is quiet, all is desolate now. I had stood in my youthtime in the fields beyond, and longed to break into that old house—longed to ramble over its rooms and scale its rotten staircases; but the doors were fastened up, and I had not the courage to make the attempt. To confess the truth, I had made myself a coward in the matter by conjuring up a variety of conjectures concerning the history of the old ruin, and the cause of its being suffered to fall to pieces without any one interfering to prevent its farther decay, or to clear it from the ground. I had fancied that murder had been committed there; then came the questions—of what nature was that murder? —how was it committed, and who was the murderer, and who the victim? I had never been able to obtain an answer to any one of these questions, nor could I perceive any direct method by which I might satisfy my mind on the subject. What was more curious still, no one could tell me, though I had often inquired, who the old ruin belonged to; and if I put any farther queries concerning it, the only and the invariable reply was,—it is the haunted house.

Now, anything that is reported to be haunted, is invested with peculiar interest to me, and because report attached the accusation of being haunted to this old house, I felt all the more anxious to learn the secret concerning it—all the more anxious to know the why and the wherefore of its having been so condemned.

Every report has some kind of a foundation in truth; so I said to myself when I thought over the mystery of the haunted house. After much considera-tion, I came to the firm conclusion that murder had really been committed there; and having so concluded, it became an easy matter to fancy that the spirit of the murdered one still haunted the apartment in which the deed of blood had been done.

No one had been seen to enter the doors of the haunted house for many years; no one expressed a desire to enter within its doors.

I had that desire.

Before telling what occurred on the night when I sat in my boat, it is neces-sary that I relate an incident which took place two summers before.

It was the evening of what had been a sultry day. By chance I was led to ramble in the fields which adjoin the haunted ruin.

As the shadows of evening descended, I turned my eyes towards the old house. On an instant I was seized with a desire to break into and make an examination of its interior. The desire was irresistible. I ran towards it, and looked about to see in what manner I could make my entrance. I tried the door—that would not yield—the shutters, they were closely fastened. Casting a glance upwards, I saw sundry projections in the outer wall, which I knew would facilitate me in an attempt to ascend to the roof. To the roof I determined to climb. I looked around me—no one was near—no one could I see upon the river or in the fields. Addressing myself with great zeal to the task, I soon scaled the wall, and stood upon the roof. What was to be done now? There was no trap-door, no inlet by which I could descend into the interior. Once I thought of the chimney, but I soon abandoned the idea of making an entrance in so perilous a manner. I looked about me for a moment, and then fell to work to remove the tiles. Having done so, I squeezed myself through the aperture which I had thus formed, and groped about in the darkness until I found the top of a ladder, down which I descended into one of the upper rooms. The last rays of the setting sun shed their mellow light into the apartment, and, as I trod upon the floors, a feeling of dread came over me; so solemn seemed the silence of the place.

I passed from room to room, but there was nothing which appeared to hold out any hope of my obtaining a clue to the mystery. In one of the upper rooms there was some straw upon the floor, which seemed to have been put there recently; there was mystery in that. In the same room there was also a large oak chest, which I tried to open, but could not. Having searched the upper apartments, I descended to the lower.

I walked into what had once been the drawing-room. A shattered and antique chandelier was still pendant from the ceiling, while sconces that had long ago lost their polish were affixed against the walls. In this room, mirth and jollity had once been; gaiety had there dispensed its smiles, and beauty had displayed its power and its charms.

Still I found nothing that recompensed me for the trouble which I had taken. There was a back room, the door of which opened out of the drawing-room. This door I attempted to unclose; time and the action of the air had rusted the hinges. With difficulty I pulled it open.

Through the apertures in the shutters the beams of the setting sun fell into the old room. Much old furniture was there remaining, and cobwebs were hanging like vallances around a bedstead which stood at one end of the apart-ment. I was struck with surprise when I beheld these things, and wondered why all had been left in its present state—untouched—unmoved.

See p. 18.

I entered the apartment, and cast a glance at the various articles which it contained. Suddenly my gaze was arrested by one particular portion of the wall, being that on which the beams of the sun fell. The wall itself had at one time been painted of a light colour, but that particular spot was dark. I was puzzled to account for such being the case.

With a presentiment that I was about to learn something fearful, I advanced towards the dark spot. I examined it. Could I—could I be mistaken?

Great Heaven! how I trembled!

I took my knife from out of my pocket, and scraped this dark portion of the wall. On removing the mere surface, I found the dark mark to have a reddish tinge. I scraped still deeper; and, as I scraped, I gazed.

My suspicions ripened into conviction. I felt myself competent to swear to it as a fact—those dark marks were *the marks of blood!*

Of what blood?— of whose blood?

Ah! I could not answer those questions—I could not reply to the interrogations which I involuntarily put to myself.

I stepped back, and folded my arms, to gaze upon the dark stains. While I was thus gazing, the sun suddenly sank beneath the horizon, and the apartment became enveloped in gloom.

Oh! what fancies thronged through my brain, then! what fearful phantoms, on a sudden, presented themselves to my view! I rushed out of the apartment—flung to the door—hurried up the staircase—mounted the ladder—made my way through the roof—scrambled down the wall—leaped upon the ground, and made off with speed from the place of horror.

Weeks and months passed, yet I could not summon up sufficient courage to enable me to renew my search. I communicated what I had seen to some of my friends, and urged them to co-operate with me in a farther investigation; but they shrugged up their shoulders, laughed at my entreaty, and told me that the place was haunted.

"I will allow that such is the case," said I, endeavouring to persuade them into a compliance with my wish; "but is that any reason why we should decline paying it a visit?"

"What would be the use of our doing so?" asked one.

"I do not see the necessity for going," observed another.

"Gentlemen," said I, "I hope that I have no cause to impugn your courage; I hope you are not afraid."

"Afraid of ghosts?" they replied —"ridiculous! all the ghosts departed the land when railways were first invented."

It was useless to attempt persuasion with them; none of them would accompany me, and I dared not enter that house again by myself.

Let me return to the night when I was in my boat upon the river.

I had taken the sculls in my hands, to retrace my way down the stream. On casting a glance towards the haunted house I saw that which caused me to hesitate, and to pause.

It was strange!—it was very strange!

I stood up in my boat to look; for a moment I could not believe my own eyes; yet there could be no mistake—there could be no deception.

There was a light in one of the windows of the haunted house! For a minute—for only a single minute—I debated with myself as to what I should do. My resolution was soon taken, and throwing myself upon the seat, I took up the sculls, and rowed towards the bank.

The hour was midnight, and all around was dark and gloomy; yet, like a beacon, shone that light from the window of the old ruin.

"It is a signal for me,—it beckons me to come!" I exclaimed, as I redoubled the rigour of my strokes.

Swiftly my boat sped across the water; I flung my sculls into it, and leaped upon the bank.

The spot of ground upon which I now stood was immediately in front of the old house. I looked up, and still I saw the ray of light shooting out through the hole in the window-shutters above me.

There could be no doubt but that there was some one inside the haunted place; who that person was, or what business he or she had there, I could not tell—I could not guess.

"Perhaps," said I, to myself, "it is some curious person like myself, who is searching as I once searched there." But then came the question, why should he have chosen midnight as the time for his search?

I meditated for a moment, and became convinced in my own mind that the individual within had not been led thither out of mere curiosity, but was some one who was acquainted with the fearful mystery of the place.

Stealing up to the door, I applied my ear to the woodwork, and listened. I could not hear any noise—all seemed silent. Could the light be supernatural? Was the place haunted, as it was said to be?

I rushed back to the river-side—my boat had got entangled among the weeds, and had not floated away. Snatching up one of the sculls, I strode towards the old ruin, fearless of ghosts, and of all things ghostly. All seemed silent still.

I uplifted the scull—I dashed it against the door; a second stroke, and I was in the house—in the deserted hall.

The staircase lay before me; I hesitated ere I ventured to ascend. So high had grown the tempest outside, that the noise made by the wind was sufficient to drown any other sound.

When the wind had ceased howling I listened.

It was not improbable that my ears deceived me, still I thought otherwise. I thought I heard a groan.

Emboldened by the feat which I had already performed, I prepared to grope my way up the staircase. Before I had ascended half-a-dozen steps, I thought I heard the groan repeated.

Onwards and upwards I went. Presently I stood upon the landing next to which was the room where the dark stain was upon the wall, but the light which I had seen on the outside I knew to be in a room that was higher yet.

I was still upon the staircase—I ascended the next flight, and stood where, through the crevices of a door, a pale light streamed out upon my face.

I shuddered for a single instant.

"What is that light? What shall I behold if I open that door? Strength! strength!"

I was strong enough then for the performance of any feat. I thrust the door open, and ——

CHAPTER II.

THE GIRL IN THE HAUNTED RUIN.

I THRUST the door open.

Ha! it was he!—it was this man whom I had so long sought to become acquainted with, whose secret I had so longed to learn.

The room was the same one in which I had seen the straw strewed upon the floor. There, and upon that straw, lay the old man with the white hair—the phantom, whom I had so often followed through the streets.

Still standing at the door-way, I gazed at the pale, ghastly figure before me. Not a muscle could I move, not a step could I advance.

The old man turned his hollow eyes towards me, and a smile seemed to pass over his countenance.

"Is it you?" he faintly asked.

"It is I," I replied.

"I am glad you are come—very glad," he ejaculated.

Glad that I was come to visit him—that I had found him out at last! What could he mean?

I stepped up to the side of his couch of straw. For the first time in my life I touched those lank and shrivelled fingers. A strange thrill shot through my heart, and, in a weak tone of voice, I asked,—

"Do you know me?"

"Well," was the feeble reply.

Never in my life have I been more disconcerted than I was at that moment. Here was an individual who had been a mystery to me for years—who was a mystery to me now; one whom I had hunted through the metropolis, and exerted myself to the utmost in order to win his acquaintance; a mysterious personage who flitted from place to place, and yet was to be found everywhere—more like a spectre than a man; one whose very name I did not know, to whom I had never spoken, whose voice I had never heard; here was this very individual replying to my question, and asserting that to him I was well known. I started back—I gazed at him—I thought him to be a maniac.

As I continued to gaze I observed that his lips had turned of a bluey paleness, and that his fingers were employed in picking the threads of his garments. These I knew to be the signs of approaching death.

What was I to do? already was he exhausted—already was death in the room with him. He might die before I had learned his secret, and with him the mystery of his existence might perish!

I again took his hand, and kneeling down beside him, asked him if I could render him any assistance—if I could procure anything for his use that he might desire.

He stretched out his lank finger, and pointed to a bottle which stood upon the oak chest that had before excited my curiosity on the occasion of my former visit to the same apartment.

I thought he wished me to procure him some stimulus.

"It is night," said I, "and this house is so remote from any place where ——"

He pointed again to the bottle, and interrupted me by moving his lips.

I relinquished my hold, and grasping the bottle, found, to my surprise, that it was filled with some cordial, which, from its odour, I judged to be brandy.

Again I knelt beside the old man, and applied the bottle to his quivering lips. He clutched it with his bony fingers, and drank eagerly.

"Does that revive you?" I asked.

"Yes; I—I am better now."

"It has given you strength?"

"Yes—strength—I shall not die yet."

"I hope not," said I,—"I hope not. It is fearful to think of death in this lonely place."

I could not understand the cause of the look which he then threw at me. It was a look of horror! Presently his countenance was again lighted up by a faint wan smile, and, grasping my hand with a convulsive grip, he ejaculated,—

"I am glad you are come. Oh! how glad am I that you have come at last!"

"I!" I exclaimed. "My good friend, you are mistaken. I am not the person you take me to be."

He shook his head, and again attempting to smile, said,—

"I mistake not. He is you, and you are he."

"He! do you really know me, then?"

"Prop me up—prop me up, and I will talk to you."

There were no pillows in that chamber—there was nothing which I could place beneath his head. In vain I glanced into every nook and corner. I sat down, and gently raising him up, placed my arm around his emaciated body, and pillowed his head against my shoulder.

"More brandy!" he ejaculated—"more brandy!"

Again I lifted the bottle to his lips, and again he drained the inspiring draught with eagerness.

The silence was dreadfully solemn; there was no sound except the hissing noise of the burning oil in the wick of the lamp, which stood upon the chest by my side.

I and the dying man were alone in that room together—alone in that fearful house!

"Listen!" said he, grasping my hand as he spoke.

"I am listening now. Speak—tell me who you are—tell me why I have found you here?"

"Not yet, not yet," was his reply.

"But you say that you know me—you say that you expected my coming."

"I did."

"Nay, you cannot have had that expectation; for it was by mere chance that I was led here this night."

"Chance!" exclaimed the old man.

"By nothing but chance."

The dying man turned his ghastly eyes towards me, and, looking me in the face, said,—

"There is no such thing as chance; we are the puppets of destiny. Do you believe in chance?"

I stammered in endeavouring to reply, for I suddenly remembered the strange ideas which had possessed my own mind concerning this man; how I had believed that at one time or another I should penetrate the mystery which seemed to enshroud him—how I should at length win his acquaintance—how I was destined to be near his bed of death—how I should be called to close his eyes, and perform for him the last services awarded to the dead! I had believed in these ideas, I had put faith in them, and allowed them to grow up as articles of belief in my mind, and now all had come to pass—all was as I had believed it would be. Here was I in the haunted house; here was I beside the bed of the dying; here was I about to hear the mystery, and here was the old man, whom I had sought London through to find, with his head pillowed against my own shoulder.

He looked me in the face, his sunken eyes brightened, and, with an expressive gesture, he put to me the question,—

"Answer me; you do not believe in chance?"

"Not now, not now."

"It makes me happy to hear you give me that assurance. There has been a time when I believed in chance, and nothing else besides—that time is past now."

"Tell me," said I, "why did you expect me?"

"Because I have believed in your coming; because I have seen you, in my dreams, sitting beside me, even as you are sitting now."

"But me—how did you know me?"

"I put a like question to you; how did you recognise me when you entered at that door?"

"Because—because I have observed, watched you, wondered who you were, and in what place you dwelt."

"And I have watched you."

"Watched me!"

"Yes; I was in this house when, two summers since, you made your entrance after the fashion of a burglar. It was in the gloom of the evening, and you saw me not."

"In this house?"

"Ay; and I saw you enter the room which is beneath the one in which we now are."

"That room?"

"Yes; the room wherein is the stained wall, where you made the discovery—where you scraped the dark mark and found it to be blood."

"Then, you know it—then ——"

"I can tell you how that blood came there."

"And whose it is, and why ——"

"Everything."

"Haste, then—haste!"

"Do not be impatient. There is not much life in me now; but this is not death yet. I have waited for your coming that I might tell you all."

"But I have sought you ——"

"I know it. You followed me through the city and the Strand."

"Ha! did you know I was behind you?"

"I did."

"Then why did you escape me—why did you not confide what you have to say to me, then?"

"Because it was not time."

" Then you will tell me now—I am to hear it now ?"

" That depends on one condition."

" And what is that ?"

" I will name it presently. Give me drink—more drink."

I once more placed the bottle to his lips, and draining off the draught he looked in my face, and said,—

" It wants drink, good drink, to die like this."

" To die !" I exclaimed.

" Yes, presently ; not now ; I am not to die until I have told you all—until I have performed the task."

" Hasten, then, hasten ! your strength is almost gone—it will go before you have time to tell the story."

He grasped my hand, and fixed his gaze upon me. There was a strange un-earthly light glistening in his dark eyes, which caused me to tremble.

" Why are you afraid ?" he asked.

" I—I am not afraid. Tell me—tell me all, there will not else be time."

" There will be time," he replied, in a hollow voice, the tone of which was im-pressively solemn. "See, you ; fourteen days and nights I have lain upon this bed of straw. My strength has been passing away every hour of that time. I am an old man, and have lived more years than are commonly allotted to the life of mortal man. Know you why I have lingered so long—why I have walked the earth so many years ?"

" No."

" That the torture might be longer—that I might drink deep of the cup which I had filled for myself."

" Ah ! then you have been——But tell me, you are growing weaker, much weaker."

" I shall not die till I have told you all. Day after day, for weeks, my strength has lessened ; yet still I have had the assurance that you would come at last. Look you at that window ; those holes have been boarded up for years, so that the light of this lamp has not been visible on the outside. This night, only an hour ago, that board fell down without being touched by human hand. Know you why it fell ?"

" I cannot guess—I cannot say."

" It was that the light should shine forth—that it should be a beacon to you —that it should beckon you hither."

" It did so."

" I know it ; and when you burst open the lower door, I knew that it was you."

" But that knowledge ——"

" Came not by chance, my friend. Why is it that I have been told of your coming in dreams—that some unseen being has whispered it in my ear while I slept ? Why is it that I have been taught to wait your coming, if, now that you are come, my strength should fail me before I had told you everything ?"

" It may—it may."

" Not so ; it will not. There is more than an hour's life in me yet. How fearful is the agony of that hour to be !"

" Say you that you are in pain ? Is there no remedy—no anodyne—no medi-cine at hand ?"

" None but the drink ; and I must drink—drink to drive away the thoughts— the forms. Ha ! do you not see those forms ?"

" I !—forms !"

" Well—well ; mind me not—mind me not, when I seem mad. I want no medicine for the body—nothing that will keep away death. It is not body or brain ; but soul and heart—in them it is—the agony is in them."

" But can I not relieve you—cannot I do anything that may soothe ?"

" What would you do ?"

" I know not—anything."

" Go, then, to that chest—go ; take the lamp, and place it upon the ground."

I did as he desired me.

"Now, this kerchief, untie it, and take it from off my neck. Have you done so? Now, unroll it—unroll it carefully. There is a small key within it. Have you found it? Now open the chest with the larger key, which you will find beneath it. Throw back the lid. That which you will find inside, is placed there for you."

The chest was a large oaken one, and was fitted up with many drawers. I drew out each of these drawers one by one, but found nothing in any of them.

"There is some mistake," said I; "the chest is empty."

"Not so; take out the small drawer at the bottom, which is to your left hand."

"I have done so; but I see nothing."

"Look well, and you will perceive a key-hole—a small key-hole. Have you found it?"

"Yes."

"Use, then, the lesser key. The wards may be somewhat rusty; but use patience."

"The bolt will not yield."

"Try again."

"I did so; and managed to turn the key round in the lock. Still I could see no door or drawer, which held out a promise of yielding up the treasure of which I was in search. Indeed, the lock itself seemed to be inserted in the board, which formed the bottom of the trunk.

"What am I to do, next?" I asked, putting the question in a manner which betrayed my impatience.

"Pull the key—pull it upwards."

I obeyed the command, and found, to my surprise, that the chest had a false bottom. On lifting this up, I discerned two rolls of papers, both of which were tied round with string, and sealed with many seals.

"Am I to take possession of these papers?" I asked.

"Bring them to me," was the reply.

I took the two packets, and presented them to the dying man. One of them was very bulky, and was sealed up with more seals than was the other.

"These papers have been reserved for you. They have been locked in that box till your arrival to claim them."

"I claim them!"

"Yes; all that you wish to know is here, in this larger parcel. The mystery house, and the mystery of myself."

"And the other, the lesser ——"

"Concerns you also; but not so intimately; yet it will be committed to your keeping."

"Give them to me," said I, eagerly; "they shall be rightly valued by me."

"That value is great."

"I feel it to be so."

"You would have them now?"

"Yes. I wish to know about this house—about myself; I wish to know the secret of ——"

"Stop!" cried the dying man.

I held out my hands to receive the papers; but he put them away from me, and made a gesture to signify that they were not yet to be mine.

"But will you not tell me—will you not ——"

"Stop! there is the condition. Did I not say that there was one condition which you must attend to before you can become possessed of the knowledge which you wish to gain?"

"And that condition is—what?"

"Listen. Know you any maiden who is young, and good, and very beautiful?"

"I do."

"Does she reside near this place?"

"I could reach her home in less than a quarter of an hour."

"Is she fair?"

"Very so."

"And you know her to be good—you know her to be untainted by the crimes and follies of the world?"

"Certainly from the crimes—as for the follies, she, of course, inherits her natural share."

The face of the dying man became lighted up with a smile, as I replied to his last question. He motioned me to kneel beside him; then, taking my hand, he said,—

"You may deem me to be a madman; you may imagine that I am not possessed now of those faculties which I enjoyed in my youth—if you think so, you think wrongly. Mind my words! These papers will not be yours, unless you bring that maiden to me."

"To you!—here!"

"Go; I give you one hour—there is an hour's life in me yet. Use all despatch, and fetch the maiden—bring her hither."

"Into this place I cannot."

"Then the secret which you wish to learn you will never know."

"But how is it possible I can comply with your request? It is the dead of night —the maiden is my cousin, but she has gone to rest many hours ago; this house is an object of dread—you may be dead before I get back."

"No; I am not to die yet. I shall live till you return."

"But the girl—she will not accompany me—I could not persuade her."

"Go and make the attempt. I cannot die unless she be brought to my bedside."

"Great Heaven! you cannot mean it—you are but in jest."

He turned his eyes towards me, and looked me in the face.

"Is this a place for jesting?" he asked. "Look you; I shall never see the light of another sun; I shall never witness the dawning of another day. It is already early morning; and my hours—my minutes are numbered. You know not the agony which at this moment causes my heart to feel as if it were in flame, and my brain as if it were molten lead; you cannot comprehend the nature of the torments which make the present hour worse to me than an eternity in hell. If you would do me a service—if you are willing to soothe my tortured mind, and alleviate the pangs of death, go, fetch me the girl you have spoken of—fetch her instantly."

I hesitated, and knew not what reply to make, nor what course to pursue. The request was so strange, so really horrible, that I could scarcely bear to meditate upon the means to be made use of in effecting compliance with the demand. He saw my hesitation, and, gasping for breath, said,—

"You will not do so for charity; do it, then, for your own sake; do it that your curiosity may be gratified."

"But the girl ——"

"She shall not see me die, only let her be brought here."

"What can be your object?"

"You will know when you return. If you are not back in an hour, I shall light these papers at that lamp, and they will be lost to you for ever."

"And with them the mystery?"

"Yes; irretrievably lost, and you know not yet how great that loss would be."

I gazed at the dying man, and thought on the fearful words which he had uttered, and the more fearful request which he had made. I know not what possessed me; but I suddenly came to the resolution to do as he had desired. At that moment I was desperate enough to do anything to obtain possession of those papers; so desperate, indeed, that, while now writing, I wonder at myself, that I did not wrest the coveted parcels from him to whom they belonged, and make off with them, leaving the old man to die with no one by his side. Yes; I was fearfully desperate.

"It shall be done," I cried. "I will bring her into this room—I will force her to accompany me, despite any resistance which she may make!"

"She will not resist—she will not refuse," said the dying man; "yet tell her not to what place she is coming— tell her not what scene she is about to witness. Bring her hither, and, in your way back, get some man to come along with you; but leave him without—leave him within call."

"I will do all—everything!" I exclaimed.

"Go, then—go; the hour will soon be past."

In accordance with his desire, I placed the bottle which contained the cordial beside the dying man, and, having done that, I hastened out of the room, rushed down the staircase, and made my way across the fields towards the residence of my friends.

My cousin is a light-haired, fair-cheeked girl, of little more than ten years of age. I need not detail the lie which I invented, and the persuasions which I used to induce her to accompany me. Greatly to my surprise, she made but few objections, and attiring herself as quickly as possible, contrived to slip out of the house without letting her friends know of her departure.

Along the road and across the fields we hurried. It was wondrous that we were not stopped—that no one arrested us, with a desire to know where a man so wild-looking, and a girl so young, were hastening to at that hour of the night. My cousin believed that she was on her way to visit some relative who was suddenly taken ill. I urged her to put forth what little strength she possessed, that we might arrive in time. Onwards—onwards we went. I encountered a man who was journeying to his home; I stopped him—I forced him to accompany us. Again we fled onwards, and, before the hour had expired, we stood at the door of the haunted house.

" Where are you taking me to ?" asked my cousin.

" Never mind where; you will see presently; you will know soon."

" It is so dark—so dismal. I will not follow you."

Frantically I snatched her up in my arms, and carried her up the stairs. I thrust open the door—I saw that he was not dead—I placed my cousin beside him.

" There," said I, " is the maiden. I have complied with your request—I have satisfied your demand, and now—I call upon you for the reward."

" It shall be yours."

My cousin placed her hands before her eyes, and endeavoured to escape. I held her firmly, despite all her remonstrances.

" And is she, too, afraid of me ?" asked the dying man.

" No—no," I replied; " not of you—the place—the scene."

The old man attempted to raise himself up, and, looking piteously at me, he said,—

" Tell her not to fear—tell her that I will not harm her. I know that I am hated by her; and well do I deserve to be hated by all who are good and fair as she is. But I have something to say to her; let her come nearer."

" And now," said I, " let me have possession of those papers, according to your promise."

" You shall—you shall."

" But now. The condition is complied with—the maiden is here."

" Yes; thank God—thank God !" ejaculated the dying man.

He beckoned to me that I should approach him. I did so; I threw myself on my knees; I held out my hands.

" The papers—the mystery !"

" Place the light nearer to us both."

I did so.

He took the larger packet of the two, gave one look at it, and, putting it into my hands, said,—

" The revelation of the mystery is contained in that which you now grasp. Everything connected with the story of this house, and the more fearful story of myself, is detailed in those papers. Be careful how you read them, and do not doubt the truth of what you read;—it is all too true—would to Heaven that it were but fiction !"

" And am I to keep the secret—am I to destroy them ?"

" Read and consider. They are yours to do with as you please. The tale which they tell is one of blighted hopes—of misguided passions—of wicked devices—of too deep love of woman—of deeds which in your wildest dreams have had no parallel. You will shudder at some passages—you may glow with delight over others; in some you will meet with illustrations of human nature in its loftiness, and in its beauty; in others you will be made acquainted with some of the darker chambers of the heart, and learn realities which have been, alas! too real. There is a deep moral contained in the whole; and a lesson is taught which it were well should be communicated to all. Do then with the story as you please. It is right that the world should hear it at last; it is right that my fellow-men should be made acquainted with the history of one who was once a man like themselves. Yet be careful how you trust it in the hands of timid woman."

" Careful !"

" Yes ; but my strength is leaving me. Take it—the packet is yours."

He gave me the packet, and I clutched it as if it were some precious treasure.

Reader, the following pages contain the story which I found narrated in the contents of the packet. Unfortunately, the manuscripts were written in such a disjointed manner, and so little art had been used in the relation of the various incidents, that I found it to be necessary that I should re-write and re-arrange the whole. This I have done ; and all which follows is the same in substance with what I read in the mysterious papers, though, in transcribing and arranging, I have availed myself of the licence of my art.

Nights and days I pored over those manuscripts. The impression which they made upon my mind will never pass away ; the incidents will never fade from my memory. I shuddered as I read them over—I shudder as I think of them now. Yet do I remember with pleasure, certain portions of the strange tale—certain portions which continually recur to my mind, and which, on account of their beauty, and on account of their connection with all that is most lovely in the display of human affection, will live with me as treasures for ever.

What the dying man wanted with the maiden ; what were the contents of the other sealed packets ; and how the scene in that lonely chamber was brought to a conclusion, must not be told of yet ; but will be revealed in the course of the story.

The story is one of mystery—of passion—of pathos—one both of the heart and home.

CHAPTER III.

1778.—THE FEAST AND THE PHANTOM.

On the western coast of England, and near to the sea-side, stood a small cottage sheltered by a range of hills. This cottage was neat in design, rustic in its construction, and English-like in its white walls. Apparently, it was the residence of some person whose position in society was a very humble one ; yet there were evidences of its being also the dwelling-place of those whose eyes could appreciate the beautiful, and whose hearts were gentle and kind ; for the manner in which the little cottage was externally decorated, told that the inmates were lovers of beauty, while the care displayed in the tying-up of the delicate flowers which bloomed in the small parterre in front, told, also, that the hands which tended them were gentle hands, and that they belonged to those whose hearts were kind, affectionate, and loving.

It was the evening of an autumn day. The sun was setting, gilding the surface of the ocean with a golden glow, and illuminating the windows of the little cottage which stood by the sea-side. At one of those windows was a beautiful girl, engaged in playing with a bird, whose cage was half hidden amongst the clustering flowers which trailed up over the front of the cottage. Merriment was depicted on the countenance of this girl ; yet was her appearance more that of the coquette than of the gentle siren. Her features were well formed and expressive ; her complexion was of a dark rich tint ; her eyes were large, jetty, and beautifully bright, while her lips were small and of the deepest vermillion hue. On each side of her neck hung tresses of shining chesnut coloured hair, which were not tied up in any formal manner, but descended in rich profusion upon the shoulders of the beautiful brunette. She was a maiden of, apparently, some twenty years of age, and one whose rare beauty would have done honour to a court. Playfully she dangled a small flower before the cage of her favourite bird, and laughed at the vain attempts which the little creature made to obtain possession of the annoying object.

Deeper sank the sun in the distant sky, until it almost touched the surface of the water. The beautiful girl left off playing with her bird to gaze upon the magnificent scene which lay outspread before her—the ocean in its vastness glowing as if it were one wide extent of liquid fire, and a vessel passing along in the distance, its sails glistening in the ruddy light. No wonder that the maiden gazed, no wonder that she thought she had never before seen so beautiful a sunset.

And still the sun sank deeper, until it seemed like some huge ball of fire floating upon the distant wave. The maiden clasped her hands in admiration, and ejaculated,—

" How magnificent—how very magnificent !"

Just then, a fair, white, and delicate hand was laid upon her shoulder, and a sweet-toned voice said—

" It is indeed glorious, Kate. How seldom do we witness such bright evenings as this !"

" Oh! Amy, you frightened me," exclaimed the beautiful brunette, turning round, and putting on a look which was intended for sudden fright.

" I, Kate—I frighten you ?"

" Yes ; how should I know who was behind me—how was I to know whose hand it was that touched me ?"

" Not a very rough one, Kate—not a very rough hand ; and as for the naughty person ——"

" Say no more, Amy—say not another word till yonder beautiful sun has passed from sight. It were profanation not to watch him to his rest, when he departs so gloriously, and in such magnificent splendour."

The two girls placed themselves at the window to admire the gorgeous scene. One arm of each was twined round the neck of the other, and tress intermingled with tress.

Presently the dark-eyed girl cast a glance at her companion, and perceived that she was not looking at the setting sun, but apparently buried in a fit of musing.

" Why, Amy, what can be the matter with you ? I thought you loved to gaze on glorious objects."

" And so I do, dear Kate."

" And where would you find a scene more magnificent than the present one ?"

" Nowhere—nowhere."

" Then, tell me—but gracious Heavens, Amy ! your cheeks are of as deep a red as yonder crimson sky."

Amy turned away her face.

" Come, come, sister Amy," said the handsome Kate ; " you have some secret—some little secret of which I am entirely ignorant."

" I, Kate ?"

" Yes ; you naughty, dear little sister ; I am sure there must be something which I know nothing about—something very extraordinary to draw away your eyes with such a beautiful scene before you, and to bring such a blush upon your cheek. Come, tell me, Amy, what is it—what is the naughty thought ?"

Amy was silent.

Kate took the hand of the blushing girl in her own, and endeavouring to obtain a view of her countenance, said,—

" I think you've done something wrong, Amy ; your hand feels so warm, and your cheeks and your forehead are so very red."

Amy still continued silent.

" Come, you naughty, wicked little sister, do tell me. I am sure you have done something wrong. Let me know what it is."

" Nothing, Kate—nothing."

" Oh, yes ; I'm sure you have. Let me see what you can have done that would be wicked ; you haven't been writing a letter to your sweetheart, have you ?"

" No, Kate."

"Then I must guess again. Perhaps you have received a letter from him?"

"No, Kate—no."

"Why, what can you have done that would be more wicked? You haven't given up poor Ernest, and made love to some one else, have you?"

"Oh, no! indeed not, dear sister!"

"If you had done so, Amy, I should never speak to you again; for poor Ernest will return soon, I am sure."

Amy made no reply to this observation.

"Come, sister," said Kate, "I cannot guess—I cannot unriddle your secret. If you wish to keep it from me, I will not press you to disclose it; only assure me that you have not wronged poor Ernest."

Amy turned round and threw herself upon the bosom of her sister.

"Kate," said she, "dear Kate, do you believe me capable of so doing? do you think that I could prove false to Ernest?"

"I could not, Kate, I could not!"

"You would be a most wicked little Amy, if you did."

"I could not—cannot—will not."

"Those are warm words, and they seem to come from your heart, Amy. I am glad to hear you make such a promise. But am I not to know, my sister, the little secret which you possess?"

"What secret, Kate?"

"Oh, you naughty Amy. Just as if you had no secret—none which I do not know."

"And have I?"

"Why do you act as you do? Why are you ashamed to show your face? and why does your cheek absolutely burn my shoulder? Come, Amy, you have a secret, and am I to know it or not?"

Amy uplifted her head, and, looking confusedly at her sister, said, in a laughing manner,—

"Only wait, Kate—only wait till to-night."

"Till to-night!"

"Yes; only for three hours more."

"And what, then, Amy?"

"You will know all; you will not want to ask me for my secret, then."

"Why, what is to happen?"

"Oh, I cannot tell you. You must wait—you must be patient."

Kate looked archly at her sister, and with a smile upon her countenance, said,—

"I think I can guess, Amy."

"No, I'm sure you cannot."

"Yes, but I think I can; I think I have guessed rightly, already."

"Tell me, then, what your guess is."

"Not so, you unfair dealing Amy. Let you know my guess, indeed, when you will not tell me your secret!"

"I cannot tell you, Kate; but you will know by-and-bye. Come, you must assist me in getting up a little entertainment."

"An entertainment, Amy!"

"Yes; for one of father's friends, whom he expects will pay him a visit this evening."

"Are you sure it is one of father's friends, Amy?"

"Oh, yes, Kate; one who is a friend to father, and to—to ——"

"Well, Amy?"

"To all of us, Kate—a very dear friend."

Kate looked at her sister with a roguish smile glistening on her countenance. Amy blushed and bent down her head.

"Oh, my dear little Amy," exclaimed the laughing Kate, "I am so glad—so very glad."

"Glad of what, sister?"

"To see you looking so well. Here have you been pining and pining away, your cheeks growing pale and fleshless, your eyes sunken and dim, your beautiful hair losing all its gloss, and you yourself looking like a poor, miserable nun."

" Kate, Kate, oh, what nonsense you are talking."

" It is all truth, Amy—all sad truth ! you may deny it, if you please, but I have seen it all, and so has everybody else ; and, what is more, everybody has guessed the cause ——"

" The cause, sister ! what cause ?"

" Oh, you dear little deceiver ! Don't you know that there is only one cause for pretty girls becoming lean-cheeked, downcast, and hollow ? Don't you know that when people see a pretty little beauty—such as yourself, Amy—walking about the house, moping and getting ill, and wanting the doctor, and talking about dying, and wishing themselves dead, and all such nonsense as that ; don't you know that everybody sees at once what is the matter, because the kind of disease is so very general ?"

" I really don't know what you are talking about, Kate."

" You ought to know, Amy. I've been telling you how naughty girls behave when they are in love."

" But love is happiness, Kate ; at least, I have been taught to believe that the two words mean the same thing."

" And so they do, Amy, according to young ladies' dictionaries ; not that I know anything of such matters myself. It was, however, of young maidens, whose sweethearts happen to be far away from them, that I was speaking. Poor Ernest, now ——"

" I wish you would leave Ernest alone, Kate."

" Leave Ernest alone, Amy ! Why, I wouldn't rob you of him for all the world, though I must confess that I like him very much."

" Do you like Ernest ?" asked Amy of her sister.

" Yes, indeed, I do ; but you need not be jealous because I have made that confession. It makes me very happy, Amy, to see that your love for Ernest is as great and as deep as it should be. Poor fellow ! he don't give you credit, I dare say, for one half of the sighs and good cryings that you've had on his account while he's been away. I would wager my pretty bird, which I love very much, that Ernest don't think how you have been pining away because of his long absence, and how sister Amy has lost her appetite, and her good spirits, and all her merry humour, merely because her sweetheart has been away just nine months longer than he promised he would be. Amy, you've taught me a lesson which, I hope, I shall not forget, when I, too, come to have a sweetheart of my own ; and as for Ernest, if he dares to return with a blooming face, and a bright eye, and a light step, I shall take care to give him a good chiding for his unfeelingness, and tell him how you have behaved, and how you have moped, and pined, and become most affectionately ill, all on his account ; and ——"

" Kate—dear Kate, how foolish you are talking !"

" You may say so, Amy ; but I shall do as I promise."

Amy looked seriously at her sister. and, in a grave voice, put the question,—

" How do you know, Kate, but that while you are talking in this light manner, poor Ernest may be dead ?"

" Why should I think that ?"

" Consider the dangers of the voyage, sister ; consider what a terrible climate that is to which Ernest went ; consider all the chances that there are of his having been shipwrecked, or taken off by the fever, or made a captive by pirates, or murdered on the African coast, or ——"

" That will do, Amy. Rest assured, my dear sister, that lovers don't go off in that way. Then, for my own part, I should like to have a husband who had gone through a few hardships, and witnessed a few scenes of danger. Oh, the romance of wedding a man who had fought with savages, and had nearly been eaten by cannibals, and had been shipwrecked and had been left upon a rock, and had swam across the sea, like a Leander, careless of all danger for the sake of seeing his Hero. For my own part, Amy, I shall expect my sweetheart to perform some such feats, in order that I may have something to love him for. Only think, now, if your Ernest has lived through a desperate attack of African fever, and comes back most interestingly thin and sickly ; only think, sister, how much more you will love him than you ever have done yet."

" You cruel girl !" ejaculated Amy, bursting into tears.

Kate perceived that she had said more than she ought to have uttered. Being kind and loving at heart, she was grieved to see the effect which her words had wrought, and immediately exerted herself to heal the wound which she had inflicted.

" I did not mean to hurt your feelings, Amy," said she, caressing her sister most tenderly. " Forgive me, if I have done so. I am a foolish girl to talk such nonsense."

" You speak, Kate," said Amy, sobbing, " as if I were destitute of all affection, and as if I cared nothing about Ernest, or ——"

" You are mistaken, Amy ; you have misinterpreted my words. But, come, do not let us quarrel. I will help you, dear sister, in the preparation of this feast which you have mentioned, and the nature of which you seem so much inclined to keep in the dark. Do you know, sister, it is my belief that you have received a letter from Ernest."

" I, Kate !" exclaimed Amy, blushing, as she spoke.

" Ah ! you naughty little deceiver," she exclaimed. " Well, Amy, if I am not to be told ——"

Amy took her sister by the hand, and drew her towards the door.

" Come, Kate," said she, " you must not be inquisitive. I will tell you all that I know before to-morrow morning."

The two girls left the room. The sun had sunk in the distant ocean ; the bird had gone to rest upon its perch. Some four or five hours had passed away, and now the curtain draws up, disclosing another scene.

In the largest apartment of the cottage appeared all the preparations for an approaching feast. A table had been laid out with great care, and garnished with many of the niceties of the season. Flowers had been appropriately disposed about the room, and the various articles of furniture had been arranged so as to produce the best effect. Amy was busying herself to get everything in order, and Kate was watching the behaviour of her sister, while she was also assisting in completing the various arrangements. Not a word was spoken by either for some minutes, till at length Amy glanced at the old-fashioned wooden clock, and observed, in an undertone,—

" Dear me !—they ought to have arrived."

" Who, Amy ?" inquired Kate, touching her sister on the shoulder.

" Why—why, father—father and brother Frank, Kate ; I expect them here very soon."

" Where have they gone, Amy ?"

" Not far—not far. Hark ! I think—I think ——"

" What, Amy ? Gracious me, how you are blushing !"

Amy threw down the article which she happened to have in her hand, and hastily pulling her little kerchief over her shoulder, passed by her sister, and entered the adjoining apartment. Kate waited her return for a few minutes, but finding that she came not back, curiosity tempted her to ascertain in what it was she was engaged.

Stealthily, and on tiptoe, Kate crept into the room ; all was perfectly dark, but the window was open, and Amy was looking out, as if desirous of discriminating some object in the gloom.

" Why, Amy, what is there upon the sea, to-night, that you risk taking cold to watch it ?" asked Kate, stepping noiselessly up to her sister, and tapping her on the back.

" Look, Kate !" said Amy ; " tell me what you see."

" There is nothing to be seen, my sister ; all is dark and very gloomy ; we shall have a thunder-storm in a few hours."

"In less time than that, Kate. See! was not that a lightning-flash? But, look, Kate—look down towards the shore."

"Well, Amy, I am doing so; but I cannot see anything. What is there to be seen, my sister?"

"To the right, Kate; look to the right."

Kate fixed her gaze in the direction indicated by her sister, for a few moments, and then exclaimed,—

"I think I see something—something dark."

"Does it move, Kate?"

"Yes, it is moving now; it must be a boat; and it is near, very near the beach."

Amy clapped her hands together in delight, and exclaimed, in a rapturous manner,—

"It is them! It is them!"

"Who, Amy? Is it father and brother Frank?"

"Yes. Run to the door, Kate. It is very dark, so take a candle, and hold it up to show them the path. Make haste, dear Kate; do make haste!"

"Why, Amy, I never saw you so excited before. What can be the matter?"

Amy made no reply, but ran again to the window, and listened attentively. The sound of distant voices fell upon her ear, and she could distinguish the grating of a boat's keel, as it struck upon the sands below.

"Now, Kate; the light—the light!"

Posting themselves at the door of the cottage, the two maidens waited the approach of some persons who were now ascending the steep path, which led upwards from the seashore to the eminence on which the cottage was built. Footsteps sounded in the distance, and Kate heard the voices of persons engaged in conversation.

"Where has father and brother Frank been to, Amy?" asked she.

"You will know soon, dear Kate. See! can you not discern them on the left side of the path?"

"I see something moving—but—hark! It is Archy; he is hastening towards us with all speed."

"Poor foolish Archy!" said the younger sister.

In another minute a boy, of apparently some twelve or fourteen years of age, bounded up to the door of the cottage, and grasped the hand of Amy. The face of this youth wore a peculiar expression; for though delight was pictured on his features, there was a look of vacancy in his countenance which was at once distressing and touching. His eyes were of the mildest blue; yet they seemed destitute of animation; his hair was of a pale, golden colour, but hung about his temples in wild disorder. He seized the hand of the maiden with fervency, and laughed as he looked up at her flushing face.

"Who is coming, Archy?" asked Kate—"where have you and father been?"

"To the ship—the big ship. The man's a-coming—the man who talks of Amy!"

"What man is that?" demanded Kate.

"The sea man—the man who came here two nights ago."

"Came here!" ejaculated Kate, in astonishment. Then, casting a glance at her sister, the puzzled Kate perceived that Amy had turned aside her head. Before she could ask any more questions, she obtained the solution of the riddle by the arrival of her father and brother in company with a young man, who was dressed in seafaring attire.

"He's come, sissy Amy—he's come!" cried Archy.

In another second the sailor had caught Amy in his arms, and clasped her to his breast. Amy had laid her face upon his shoulder, and Archy, the poor idiot-boy, was dancing and skipping around them both, exclaiming in his wild manner—

"He's come—he's come! we brought him from the big ship; and he's come to see sissy Amy!"

Yes; it was Ernest who had returned, and who now folded in his arms the form of her who had loved him so long and so truly. Two years had passed since they had last met, but Amy had not forgotten Ernest in his absence; nor had Ernest in that absence proved untrue to the maiden by whom he was so tenderly beloved. Oh! what pleasure is comparable to that, when, after being tossed for many nights and days upon the stormy ocean, when, after having buffeted many a tempest, and weathered many a gale, the mariner sees the shores of his native land, knowing that one loving heart waits to welcome him there, and finding, after a few hours have passed away, that the lips, which he pressed so fondly at the last parting, breathe the softest tones of joyful affection at his return! What is home to the sailor, unless that home contain some one fond heart which he believes is beating truly for him?

"Amy, sweet love!" exclaimed Ernest—"I have kept my promise."

"You have, dearest Ernest. I am glad that you left the ship so early, for there are many black clouds over head, and much do I fear that we shall have a storm in a few hours."

"And what of a storm, Amy? Have I not witnessed many since I parted from you down on yonder beach, just two years ago? You spoke of storms then, but I told you I should weather them all in safety; and so I have—so I have, Amy, nor cared for one of them, because I knew that you were praying for me, and because in the lonely night watch I have seen in my fancy a form standing by my side, which I knew to be yourself. You have taken part in all my dreams, and have been ever in my memory. Now, sweet Amy, I have returned to kiss again those sweet lips, and to tell you that I love you even more than when we last parted."

"For shame, master Ernest!" exclaimed Kate, who had been a silent witness to this scene. "If I were sister Amy, I would cuff your ears for talking in that manner, when people are present to hear every word you say."

Ernest turned towards the beautiful brunette, and rudely snatching a kiss from her lips, endeavoured to apologise for not having behaved as he should have done.

"Forgive me!" said he. "Next to seeing Amy herself, the most gratifying sight after a long voyage is to look upon the countenance of Katherine Heyton."

"Katherine Heyton, indeed! There was a time when Mr. Ernest Morden used to speak in rather more friendly terms."

"Well," exclaimed Ernest, laughing, "let it be Kate, then—dashing Kate Heyton, as I used to call you, when every eye was fixed in admiration on you at the fair."

Kate blushed, and laughed heartily at this reference of an old friend to days that were passed away. She then took the hand of Ernest, and, pressing it kindly, said—

"How glad—how very glad I am to see you back again! It is well that you have come back as you have, or you would have lost Amy, who, truth to say, has very nearly sighed herself away into a skeleton, under the belief that she was forgotten and deserted by her faithless Ernest."

"Did Amy say so—has such been her belief?"

"Don't believe that wicked Kate, dear Ernest," said Amy. "I am sure that I have never told her a word of what she now tells you—not one word."

"But your looks have said as much, Amy," observed Kate.

Ernest smiled upon the affectionate girl who stood by his side, and pressed her fair white hand fondly to his lips.

"Let Kate say what she pleases, dear Amy. That you have not ceased to love me I readily believe; and if you have at any time doubted my constancy, it is I who am to blame for having been so long absent."

"I have never doubted, Ernest—never, I assure you."

"You would have done me wrong if you had, Amy. But, come, your father and Frank have gone into the cottage, and here stand we in the open air. Kate and I are old friends, or I should not forgive her for what she has said concerning you. There is a long story for me to tell, and no doubt there is much which I have to hear from yourself and from Kate. Come, dearest, let us in."

The happy pair entered the cottage together, Kate following at a short distance behind, engaged in whispering questions to Archy, with a view to extracting from him the particulars of Ernest Morden's arrival. Archy, though an idiot, was not wanting in shrewdness, and the replies which he made to the interrogations of Kate were such as called up many a smile upon the countenance of the maiden.

An hour passed away, and how under such circumstances an hour would pass the reader may readily conceive—when Amy's father took Ernest by the hand and invited him to partake of the feast which had been prepared in expectation of his arrival.

"Ernest Morden," said he, "in years gone by, I and your father were friends; I knew him in his youth, though I was not permitted to be with him in his last days. There is nothing which I more earnestly desire, than that his son may continue that friendship between the Mordens and the Heytons, which has already existed so long and so happily."

"We need not fear but that Ernest has a like wish to your own, dear father," remarked Kate, casting, as she spoke, a glance at her sister, who was standing beside Morden, holding him by the hand.

"Kate is jealous of Amy," observed Frank Heyton. "In order to preserve happiness between all parties, I think I must exert myself to find Kate a husband."

"I can dispense with your services in that matter, brother Frank," replied Kate, in a tone of assumed haughtiness. "There are some giddy girls who are obliged to seek sweethearts for their amusement; and to such end, that they may play off tricks upon those who ought to be considered their friends. I trust that I am grown too old and too wise to commit myself after that fashion."

Amy rose up, and threw her arms around the neck of her sister.

"Forgive me, Kate—dear Kate!" said she; "I know why you use such hard words—it is because I have kept up this little deception, and not told you that Ernest was to arrive this evening."

"And what do you suppose Ernest is to me?" asked Kate. "Trust me, sister, I have no desire to interfere with your gallants or your love-affairs. Yet you might have abstained from telling an untruth."

"An untruth! Kate?"

"Yes; did I not guess that you had received a communication from Ernest, and did you not affirm that my guess was positively incorrect?"

"If Amy did say so much she said the truth," interposed the elder Heyton. "The ship which has brought Ernest to us again, anchored in the roadstead two days ago. No sooner had the vessel been made fast, than Ernest rowed hither to ask after his old friends, and, of course, to pay his compliments to Amy. On that night, as you well know, Kate, both you and Amy were from home. Ernest told me briefly the various particulars of his voyage, and would fain have stayed under this roof until both of you returned, had it not been that he was obliged to go back to his ship. In two days, he told me, the free leave to quit the vessel would be gained, and I therefore advised him to keep quiet until then—until to-night I mean; when he could come upon you and create a little pleasant surprise."

"But Amy, father—she knew that Ernest was returned."

"She learned it, Kate; but neither from Ernest nor from me."

"Then who could have told her?"

"No less a person than Archy, who is by no means so much of an idiot as we suppose him to be. The conversation which I had with Ernest in this room, was overheard by master Archy, and told by him to Amy."

"Come here, Archy," said Kate, beckoning to the fair-haired youth, who had taken a seat at the opposite side of the apartment, and whose gaze was intently fixed upon Ernest Morden—"come here, Archy, and tell me why you told the secret to Amy and not to me?"

The idiot boy looked at his beautiful questioner, but refrained from making any reply.

"Will you not come, Archy?"

The boy approached the maiden in a reluctant manner. Kate again put the question to him—"Why did you tell to Amy that which you told not to me?"

Archy smiled, "I know," he replied—"Archy knows."

"But tell me, why."

"Because sissy Amy loves me, and because I love sissy Amy."

Frank and his father burst into a loud laugh.

"Beware, Ernest," said Frank; "see you not there is a rival in the field already?"

Ernest and Kate both joined in the laugh, fixing at the same time their gaze upon Archy. Strange it is, that in those ill-fated individuals in whom the intellect knows not life, the feelings should be developed above the ordinary degree; yet, such is the fact; in them the mind sleeps, but the heart has its sway; their feelings are often deeper than those of their brethren and their sisters, and they too often indulge in dreams—in fond dreams, which in their very wildness necessarily engender woe. Thus it was with poor Archibald, the idiot boy of this our story; and when he saw that every eye was fixed on him, and that those around him were indulging in laughter at his expense, he hid his face in his hands and burst into tears.

"Come to me, Archy; why are you distressed?" asked Amy in her kind, gentle voice, as she drew the idiot boy towards her, and patted his cheek with her soft and delicate hand.—"Tell me, Archy—what is the cause of your grief?"

Archy looked up and whispered in her ear,—

"Why do they laugh at me—what have I done to make them laugh at me so?"

"Nothing, dear Archy. Sister Kate is jealous because you told the secret to me and not to her."

"And why should she be angry with me because of that? The seaman is your friend, and not hers—isn't he?"

Amy blushed, and scarcely knew how to reply to this interrogatory.

"He is the friend of all of us, Archy—he will be your friend if you behave well to him."

"He is a good man and I like him; but I thought you cared more about him than sissy Kate does; so I only told you what I heard."

"That will do, Archy—that will do," said Amy, turning away her face from the observation of her sister. "Go, they shall not laugh at you again."

The maiden wiped the wet eyes of the poor idiot boy, and told him to go to his amusements, but Archy drew his stool towards the chair which Amy occupied, and seated himself by her side. Little did the maiden think what deep emotions—what wild fancies—what more than madman's dreams were generating in the soul of the simple youth who nestled then beside her—little did she dream of the part which Archy was to play in the drama of her young life; wedding together the stories of love and idiotcy, and weaving therein the wildest of all wild tales.

Happily—how happily did the hours flit away. Amy's cheeks, which had hitherto been pale, now glowed with a tinge brighter than that of health, while her sparkling eyes told to the gazer of the deep joy of her heart. Many were the gallant things which Ernest said to her, and many a time had she to turn away her head to hide her blushing face. Kate also joined in the merriment, and exerted herself to tease her sister. Their father and Frank were not behind hand in adding to the mirth of the evening; and never before, beneath the roof of that cottage, had the sounds of joy risen more merrily, nor the bursts of laughter rang more freely.

"And now that Ernest has returned, it will not be long, I suppose, before we have a wedding," observed Kate, who was resolved to provoke her sister to the utmost.

"Amy is too young, and Ernest will not be so cruel as to take her away from us yet," said Frank. "Doubtless, though, my pretty sister thinks very lightly of the objection, and wishes to avail herself of the opportunity."

"Let them laugh, Amy—let them laugh," said Ernest, patting his intended bride on the back. "We will keep to the compact, let them say as they please."

"The compact, Ernest!" exclaimed Kate.

"Ay, my pretty sister that is to be. It was settled before I went this last voyage that Amy should be mine on my return. Look you, too. I am not the poor fellow that I was when I went away. I have done my duty to King George, and am Lieutenant Ernest Morden, at your pleasure."

"Lieutenant, Ernest!" exclaimed the astonished Kate.

"Yes; Amy is not to wed a poor midshipman. I have won one prize on the sea; there is another prize which I covet still more, and which I have yet to win on land."

"And that is—what?" demanded Kate.

"No less an one than your own fair sister," replied Ernest, placing his arm around the neck of Amy.

"Then you are not to go to sea again till ——"

"Till I have robbed you of your companion, sister Kate."

"Sister Kate, indeed!"

"Yes; and ——"

The elder Heyton filled up the empty glass of Ernest, and rapping the table, said, in a half-angry tone,—

"A truce to your quarrelling, children. Amy is betrothed to Ernest; and Kate, my girl, you must be content to seek out some other young master for your husband. The wedding was a settled affair two years ago, and in a very short time Amy will leave us to seek some other home. Lieutenant Morden stays with us to-night; therefore, away, and provide what accommodation this humble place will afford."

Kate rose up to obey her father's command. Mr. Heyton invited Ernest to draw nearer the table.

"This love-talk," said he, "is fit enough for boys and girls; but have you nothing to tell of your voyage—no adventures on the sea—no escape from ship-wreck—no boarding of pirates—no weathering of storms? Come, there is still wine remaining in the bottle, and Amy will not be displeased to hear of what you have seen and encountered since you left this coast two years ago. Have you nothing to tell?"

"I have, and I will ——"

"Hark!" exclaimed Amy; "the storm has began. Mercy me! how loud the thunder is!"

Ernest patted the rosy cheek of his betrothed, and said,—

"Come, Amy; a sailor's bride must have no fear of storms, nor yet be afraid to hear the popping of thunder."

"I am not afraid, Ernest. I—I ——"

"You tremble, Amy!"

"Yes—no—I feel—I feel ——"

"Do you feel ill, dearest?"

"No, no; not ill; but a sensation—a feeling ——"

"A feeling of what?"

"Of—— But look at Archy; he, too, is frightened. What is it the boy sees?" asked Amy, timorously.

Poor Archibald was seated on his stool, with his eyes fixed upon the window; an expression of surprise and terror was visible upon his countenance, and his face had suddenly become blanched to a perfect whiteness.

"What are you frightened at, Archy?" asked Frank Heyton, placing his hand on the shoulder of the idiot.

Archy made no reply, but lifted up his finger, and pointed towards the window. As he did so, his teeth chattered.

"Is it the thunder, Archy? Are you afraid of the thunder?" asked Ernest.

"The shadow—the black man!"

"What man—what shadow?" exclaimed Frank Heyton.

Amy rushed to the window, and, drawing the curtains more open, looked out. Suddenly she shrank back, as the figure of a man, darkly habited, passed by the window.

"What do you see, Amy?" asked Kate, who at this moment re-entered the room.

Before the terrified Amy could reply, a knock was heard at the door of the cottage.

"Hark!" cried the elder Heyton. "Surely, there is some one applying for admission; but who is there that would think of visiting us at this unseasonable hour?"

The knocking was repeated.

"Shall I open the door?" asked Frank.

"No—no," ejaculated Amy, faintly.

"Why not, dear sister?" inquired Kate.

"Because—because—I am afraid."

"Afraid!" exclaimed Ernest. "Amy Morden must not be a coward. Even if it be a smuggler-captain, and the whole of his crew, I think we are strong enough to give them their deserts. Say the word, Heyton, and let me open the door."

"Do so, by all means," replied the father of the maidens.

The cottage-door was quickly opened, and an old man, coarsely attired, with a staff in his hand, presented himself, and asked for admission.

"I have yet a long journey to make, and the weather has become very tempestuous," said the applicant. "For the love of Heaven, give an hour's shelter to an aged and infirm traveller!"

"Come in, my good friend—come in," said Heyton. "The storm is a sharp one, as you say, but it will not last long; meanwhile, rest yourself here, and partake of the few refreshments which we happen to have in store. The Heytons never yet shut their doors against those who were in distress."

"Well said!" exclaimed Ernest. "Come in, good master, your garments must be pretty well soaked; but there's worse weather than this at sea."

"Ay, and worse things happen there," replied the stranger, in a peculiar tone of voice.

Ernest Morden took the hand of the aged traveller, and helped him over the threshold of the door. As he entered the apartment in which the maidens were, Kate Heyton suddenly started, and turned round to address her sister. To her surprise, she saw that the countenance of Amy was pale, and expressive of terror. Kate hesitated for a moment, then, casting another glance at the stranger, she hastened to render aid to her sister.

"You are ill, dear Amy—you tremble in my arms!"

"I am not ill, Kate; but faint—very faint."

"What is the cause; what can I do to relieve you?"

"Nothing, dear Kate." Amy pointed with her finger towards the stranger. "Do you not see?—the dream—the picture!"

"Yes, yes, dear sister; I see—he is very like; he—but come, Amy, you will cause Ernest to believe that you are really ill."

Kate led her sister to a chair, and entreated her to rally her spirits. Every time, however, that she glanced at the stranger, a shudder passed over her frame, which was perfectly involuntary, and which she could not resist. Her father and her brothers were busily engaged in conversation with the traveller, and some minutes passed before Ernest noticed the apparent illness of his betrothed.

"Amy!" he exclaimed; "you, surely, are not frightened because of this little squall. The thunder has ceased, and the lightning flashes are not so vivid as they were."

Amy reclined her head upon the arm of Ernest, and faintly answered,—

"It is not the storm—not the storm, dear Ernest; I am not afraid of the storm."

"Then what has made you ill?"

"I am not ill—I—dear me, Ernest! I am very foolish to behave in this manner. You must pardon me. I am a silly girl, and my fancy causes me to appear very ridiculous. I am well enough now, Ernest—quite well."

The maiden rose from her chair, and endeavoured to force a laugh. She was in the act of moving towards her father, when her glance again lit upon the stranger; she started, shuddered, and springing forward, clutched the arm of Kate with a nervous grasp.

"Do not, Amy—do not be frightened."

"I—I am not frightened, sister; but he is so very like."

"Like what, Amy? Like a figure of the imagination, and nothing more; fancy made the form, and fancy is working out the resemblance."

"Yes, sister, yes; but ——"

"Come, Amy, come; take you a seat beside me, and Ernest shall sit on the other side. We are not children to be frightened by a fancy-freak."

Amy made no rejoinder to the words uttered by her sister; but, allowing herself to be led to a seat, desired that her chair should be placed near the window.

"Are you not afraid of the lightning, dearest Amy?"

"No, sister Kate—not of the lightning; there is nothing to fear in that."

The timid and affrighted maiden had not assumed her seat at the window many minutes, before Archy, the idiot boy, stole towards her, and nestled by her feet. His face was pallid, like that of the fair girl, and, like her, he glanced frequently and suspiciously at the stranger.

"Why look you at that man, Archy?" asked Amy, bending down her head, and whispering in the ear of the idiot boy.

Archy did not answer, and the maiden felt that he trembled as she touched his shoulder.

The stranger had taken a seat beside the table, and had entered into conversation with the elder Heyton, and with Ernest Morden. Apparently he was a man of some seventy or eighty years of age; one who had seen much sorrow, and had worked his way through many hardships; his step was feeble and tottering; his hands shook as he seated himself in the chair which was offered to him by his host. He rested his hands on his staff, and bent down his head. His hair was long, trailing, and of a perfect whiteness; but a red flush was upon his cheek, and his eyes glistened more brightly than the eyes of decrepid age are generally wont to gleam. The garments which he wore were of the commonest description, and were old and tattered—a coarse, grey cloak was wrapped around him, and a hat, which had suffered much rough usage, was drawn over his forehead, so as almost to conceal his eyes. Worn and weary, he truly seemed to be; and seeming to be such, he readily obtained admittance into the cottage of the kind and benevolent Heytons.

It was strange and mysterious that the entrance of this individual should have had such an effect upon the two sisters and the idiot boy. Ensconsed in her retreat by the window, Amy paid little heed to the storm without, but kept her gaze steadily fixed upon the aged stranger. Kate, also, as she moved about the room, could not refrain from stealthily regarding the same object, and at every glance she clasped her hands, and compressed her lips, as if she beheld that which caused her astonishment, perplexity, and surprise. There was nothing in the mere outward appearance of the stranger which could be accounted as a just cause for his behaviour on the part of the maidens, and there had been nothing in anything which he had said or done, since first entering the cottage, which was apparently calculated to strike the most timid with affright, or to awaken distrust in the mind of the most imaginative; yet, strange to say, Amy, her sister, and the idiot boy, each regarded the unknown with a feeling of undefined fear, and shuddered, and turned pale, as they involuntarily directed their eyes towards him.

"Have you journeyed far to-night?" asked Mr. Heyton, addressing his guest.

"Only from the village, on the other side of the hills."

"And whither are you bound, my friend?" inquired Ernest Morden.

"To the next town, Darlingham, I believe you call it."

"Darlingham!" exclaimed Frank Heyton—"why, that is five miles distant; you will never be able reach there to-night."

"I care not, so long as this heavy rain becomes abated. The distance is not so fearful; for, though old, I am not altogether disabled from journeying. A pleasant walk on a summer's night has its attractions for me yet, as it had years —long years ago."

"I am afraid that there is but small chance of your having a pleasant journey on such a night as this," observed Mr. Heyton. "Let me persuade you to stay beneath our roof till the morning. What accommodation we have is in a very humble style; but even shelter may prove acceptable."

The stranger mused over the offer which had been thus generously made; his deliberation was a protracted one, and he appeared irresolute whether to accept or refuse the proffered kindness. Amy had trembled as the proposal which her father had made had fallen upon her ear; she now exerted herself to speak, though her tongue seemed to cleave to her mouth, and to resist the attempt.

"We have not room, father; you forget."

"How, Amy? Yes; we will contrive to find room, if our friend consents to stay."

"That you may do with ease," exclaimed Ernest Morden. "There is the bed which you have prepared for me. We sailors care little about your blankets and your down; and I am a few years younger than our good traveller here. Give him the bed, and oblige me with half-a-dozen of your best chairs."

"No, dear Ernest," cried Amy, springing up, and clinging to the arm of Morden, "that must not be."

"Not be, Amy? Do you think, dearest, that I could sleep in peace in my bed this night, if I knew that this aged man was traversing along the coast, exposed to the storm, and the cool, raw air. No, Amy, no; you mistake Ernest Morden, if you think that of him."

"No, dear Ernest, I am not so ungenerous."

"If you were, Amy ——"

Before Ernest Morden could finish the sentence, he was interrupted by the stranger, who arose, and placing his hand on the arm of the sailor, said,—

"Trouble not yourselves on my account, good people; I have already resolved to hasten on my way, and wait only for the rain to cease from falling so heavily. But—excuse me for asking—is that fair girl your sister?"

Amy shrank back trembling as she heard the stranger make this unexpected reference to her.

"No, good friend; she is the daughter of our host; and, as I'll wager, a fairer maid than any whom you will find in the town of Darlingham."

"Fair she is, young man, and goodly too; but it seemeth to me that she is some relative of yours, because of the warmth of your speech."

Ernest Morden laughed.

"Not yet, my good friend—there is no relationship yet; but ——"

"Are you sure there is no relationship?" asked the stranger, in a deep and thrilling voice.

"If you will be accurately answered, my friend, know then that this same fair maiden will, in good time—and short time too, I trust—become a sailor's bride."

"Have you chosen her for *your* bride, Ernest Morden?"

Ernest started.

"You know my name, I perceive," said he. "I was not aware that we had seen each other before."

The stranger's face was directed downwards, but Ernest fancied that he heard a chuckling laugh proceed from the unknown, who, after a pause of a minute, fixed his dark gleaming eyes upon the countenance of Ernest, and said,—

"I know you, Ernest Morden, and I know your secret."

"Me!—My secret!"

"Ay; thinkest thou that thou speakest truly, in saying that thou wilt wed that maiden?"

"Who or what shall prevent it?" exclaimed Ernest.

"I will."

"You?"

"Ernest Morden, we have known each other for years—we have shaken hands with each other in happy hours, when we dreamed not of such a meeting as this. I have loved you, for I thought you to be brave. I deemed you to be generous and true; brother never loved brother more kindly, more affectionately. My hope was to see you become the husband of my sister; for, in that event coming to pass, I fondly and—as it now seems—foolishly believed that the happiness of Amy would be completed. And all this time I was deceived, and was deceiving myself. While you were no more than a common seaman, you loved my sister; now that you have gained advancement, you look with disdain upon her poverty, upon my father's poverty, and your wish has been to shake off Amy as an incumbrance, as ——"

" Stop, Frank Heyton !" exclaimed Morden. '· The God above us witness to the falsity of what you say. Two hours ago my love for Amy was as great, as strong—ay, more strong, Frank Heyton, than it was when we parted on yonder shore two years from this time."

" Because it was deception then, Ernest Morden."

" Not so, Frank ; there never was love on this earth, if I loved not your sister then. With absence that love grew deeper, and with the passing day it strengthened. Do I not assure you that, only two hours ago, I loved Amy—I would have made her my wife."

" Only two hours ago, Ernest ! and could real love change in so short a time ?"

" It has not changed, Frank Heyton."

" Say you so," cried Frank, taking the hand of his companion. " Then what am I to understand from the occurrences of this night ? Are you still willing to marry my sister ?"

Ernest Morden turned away his head.

" I may not—I cannot," said he.

" And for what reason, Ernest Morden ?"

" Because the obstacle which prevents me, is one that I have not the power to remove—is one that is for ever insuperable."

" And what is that ?"

" Ask me not, Frank Heyton. Go, ask those who are at home. Would to Heaven that I had known of its existence before."

" But you are glad at the discovery, Ernest Morden; it has infused pleasure into your soul."

" Not so ; the knowledge which I have gained within the last hour has proved to me the greatest misery, with one exception, that I have ever known ; yet, had I remained in ignorance, my misery would have been greater still."

" I do not understand your words, Ernest Morden ; their meaning is beyond my comprehension. I am Amy's brother, and I have a right to make the demand which I now make. Tell me on what ground, and for what reason, you have acted as you have done."

" I may not, Frank ; I dare not tell you now. Let us descend from this place ; the night air from the sea is bleak, and I have that to do which must be done soon. Let us descend."

Heyton held back his companion by the arm.

" We go not down yet, Ernest Morden. Once more I ask of you—will you explain the occurrences of this evening ?"

" Not here—not now."

" Yes, here and at this time. There is no necessity for trifling, and I am no playfellow in this matter."

" I cannot tell you more, Frank Heyton ; I cannot at the present moment enter into an explanation of the mystery."

" You will not ?"

" Nay, I dare not."

Heyton uplifted the weapon which he held in his hand, and grasped more firmly the arm of his companion.

" Only now, Ernest Morden—only a minute ago you called me Amy's friend ; why you used the term I know not, but I am that friend, and she is my sister. The subterfuge which you have endeavoured to use has failed you. I am not blinded by your words, and it is difficult for me to keep down the impulse which urges me to slay you where you stand. I am armed, Ernest Morden, and you are not. What is there to prevent me from committing murder at this moment—at this place ? Two things only—you have been accounted by us as a friend, and our fathers were friends together before us. Therefore, Ernest, let the contest be fair. This quarrel will not pass away without the expiation of blood. Come you with me where we can procure a weapon to match—a bright, a strong weapon; and then, let Heaven favour him who has done the least wrong."

A minute passed before Morden gave his reply.

"No, Frank," said he, "I fight not with you, for you have not done me harm. Put up your weapon, and if you desire enlightenment in the matter of this mystery, let your inquiries be made at your own home."

"This is evasive—this is juggling, Ernest Morden. You would obtain a delay in order to effect an escape. I knew not that I should have to call you coward as well as knave."

The blood involuntarily rushed to the cheeks of the young sailor, and a tingling, burning sensation in his fingers caused him suddenly to clench his hands. With some difficulty he overcame the suggestions of his less gentle nature.

"It is useless to provoke me, Frank Heyton; you and I have been friends too long; with you I will not fight."

Heyton flung away the cutlass, and rushing forward, seized the shoulders of his companion.

"We are equal now, Ernest Morden. Ha! ha! there is no longer an excuse. You part not as you would—you go not hence as you came. See you this cliff? You asked me why I brought you here. Look you down—look you down on that beach, and on those points of broken rock. It would be death to him who should fall from where we now stand to where we now look, and thither must one of us fall. Step back, Ernest Morden—step back, and let the struggle be fair. Hand to hand we grapple each other, and one of us must fall from the peak on which we stand. Nerve yourself, Ernest Morden; it is no child you play with now; nerve yourself, for the passion—the impulse within me is deadly. Ha! ha! no swords are wanted here—no fire-arms we need. There are points below us—sharp, craggy points, and the brains of him who falls will be scattered for the birds to pick. To the struggle, Ernest Morden—to the struggle, if you have a wish to live."

With the savage grasp of a madman, Frank Heyton seized the shoulders of Morden, and commenced the struggle. Nature had given strength and power of limb to the young sailor, but the excitement of passion lent vigour to the arms of Heyton.

Fierce and furious was the conflict. Ernest exerted himself to get free from the madman whose grasp detained him, and whose savage gestures told of the vengeful feelings which urged him to his desperate attack. Both had youth and activity of limb; both had muscles that were well strung, and sinews to which exercise had given strength. There, in the dark night, at the midnight hour, on the summit of the Eagle's Altar, they struggled. Fearful was the position selected for the contest; had the foot of either slipped, both would, in all probability, have been precipitated—both would have descended fathoms deep, where the pointed crag would have received them; or where, upon the pebbled shore, they would have been found the next morning by the fishermen, mutilated, shattered, lifeless!

And still the struggle continued; Heyton endeavouring to fling Ernest over the precipice, and Ernest only striving to get free of his assailant. They bent, they writhed, they intertwined, arm was interlaced with arm, and foot was planted against foot. They turned round as upon a pivot, for nothing more than a mere pivot did the peak upon which they stood appear. Their chests heaved, their eyes gleamed, their teeth were set, their hair floated upon the midnight breeze; not a word was spoken, not an exclamation escaped their lips. Nearer to the edge of the precipice they drew, nearer—nearer still. Both could perceive a faint light which shone upon the dark waters below; both heard the rumbling of the surge upon the deserted shore. One minute—a single minute, and their feet might have slipped—the strugglers been at rest for ever. One minute only, and, had a few inches of chalky rock given way, the summit of the Eagle's Altar would have been deserted and desolate as before. High swelled the blue veins like ridges on their foreheads, loudly and quick beat their hearts, heavy and deep were their respirations. And now the struggle was nearly at an end, for both were becoming exhausted—both were fast losing their strength. For the first time since the commencement of the contest, the lips of Heyton opened.

"Ha, ha, ha!" he laughed; "ha, ha!" and he drew Morden to the very verge. "Ha, ha!" and he attempted to take him in his arms, to enfold him in his grasp, to lift him aloft, to fling him to the depths below.

The sea-birds heard the wild laugh, and flew around the combatants, wondering why man fought with man ; the cormorant and the crow hovered over them, waiting for the expected feast.   The brink was near, the foot was planted ; Ernest Morden was in the grasp of Frank Heyton. and at that moment the clouds in one portion of the heavens separated, the light of the moon broke through, illuminating a narrow strip of land.   By that light Ernest Morden discovered a moving object in the distance ; by that light he saw something, the sight of which gave him a wish to live.   Gathering up his remaining stock of strength, and concentrating the little power which he had left, by one vigorous effort he contrived to free himself from the clutch of his foe, and to cast Frank Heyton upon the ground.   Not pausing a moment, he caught up the sword which his opponent had thrown aside, brushed with his swollen hand the sweat-drops from his brow, took one deep-drawn hearty inspiration, and then, darting down the narrow path by which Heyton had ascended, was soon lost in the surrounding darkness.

CHAPTER V.

THE BLOOD MARKS IN THE MOONLIT GROVE.

DREADFUL was the position in which Frank Heyton lay ; the peak was narrow at its apex, and the head of the fallen struggler hung over the verge of the precipice. Out broke the beauteous moon to shine upon the Eagle's Altar, to illuminate the up-turned countenance of the prostrate and insensate man.   How solemn was the scene ! moonlight, in its beauty, falling upon the features of him who had striven with his friend ; upon those features which, though now devoid of movement, told of the terrible emotions to which they had given expression.   Below was strife—above was serenity ; on the rugged stone lay anger, vengeance, and wrath ; above, in the now unclouded heaven, smiled the orb of beauty, telling only of calmness, love, and peace.   It was a suggestive scene, for it pictured the coming of that day—that glorious day when strife and enmity shall cease through the world for ever ; when man shall take the hand of man, caring not for difference of country, faith, or custom, and war shall be among the things that were—the recollection of it, a relic of the days gone by.   Even now, the advent of that day is near.

Yes ; the moonlight kissed the face of him who was a murderer in intent ; it revealed the deep, dark hue which was settled there ; it gave to view the teeth that were locked together, the eyeballs that were starting from their sockets, the hands that were clenched so firmly that the nails had pierced the flesh ; it illuminated the place of contest, and fell upon the Eagle's Altar, like a light playing round the victim which had been laid there for sacrifice.   It were easy to fancy that the bright moon itself laughed then at the folly of quarrelsome, impotent, and puny man.

A few minutes passed away, and then Frank Heyton felt his senses returning to him again.   His lips unclosed, his eyes moved, his power of respiration was regained.   He attempted to raise himself up, and, as he did so, he saw, or thought he saw, a human form, which glided from his side, and stole quickly away.   Consciousness had returned.   He sprang up, he darted forward ; his hand grasped the form which, but a minute before, he had seen flit from him, and hide itself in the shadow of the cliff.

"I have not lost you, Ernest Morden ; ha, ha ! my hand is on you, again.   Over the height, now ; over to the depth and to the death !   Over, over, over !"

Frantically he dragged forward the object which he had grasped ; he knew, he felt that it was flesh.   One image alone was present to his mind, one object engrossed all thought.   Madness blinded his eyes, and he saw not the face which was directed towards him in terror.   Frenzy had taken possession of his soul, and he heard not the piteous supplications which were now being addressed to him.   With the strength of a giant, he uplifted the human being whose life was in his clasp ; with the hellish grin of a demon he advanced towards the fearful brink.

"Ha, ha ! you have not escaped me ; you would not fight, you would not

Struggle; but I will destroy you now. To the deep you go; to the deep, Ernest Morden, to the deep. Ha, ha! the brother is the sister's friend!"

Aloft he swung the body—aloft, in the moonshiny air; he heeded not the cry, he listened not to the supplication. Firm was his clutch, frantic were his movements, feeble was the form which struggled in his grasp. He stood upon the brink, his feet trod the very verge; he uplifted the living object, he held it out over the precipice. One moment, and it would have descended, one moment, and the murder would have been done! His fingers loosened their clasp, the grin was still upon his countenance, the body was about to fall. Just then the face of the struggling being was illuminated by the moonshine; just then Frank Heyton saw that face; he started back, he staggered, he relaxed his hold; it was well for him, and for the one by his side, that he had still sufficient strength remaining to move from the verge of the precipice.

"Merciful Heaven!" he exclaimed, "what was I about to do?"

There was the human being before him—the human being whom his own hand had nearly slain. The form was one which he well knew—the face, one which he had often gazed upon. Pale, terrified, trembling, and speechless, stood Archy the idiot boy.

Frank Heyton enfolded his arms round the neck of the poor youth. Tears, scalding tears, coursed down his cheeks, and, with quivering lips, he exclaimed,—

"God pardon me, Archy! I was about to murder thee—to dash thee upon the pointed crags. Forgive me, my boy!—forgive me!"

Archy burst into tears.

"You will not forgive me, Archy!—you will pardon me for the deed which I did unwittingly! Have I harmed you?—have I done you harm?"

"Frank would not harm Archy," replied the idiot.

"He would not—he would not, poor boy! It is madness which is on me, and I knew not what wickedness my hand was about to commit."

"Don't weep, Frank; Archy is not angry with you. Archy is an idiot, and you would not harm an idiot."

"Ay, boy, thou talkest of idiots; but there is one here who is madder than thou. Dost thou know what I mean?"

"Yes, Frank—dear Frank; you are hunting—hunting on the cliffs by moonlight—the bright moonlight."

"A right term, boy—it has been a hunt, as you say; know you whom I hunt?"

"It is Ernest—Amy's Ernest."

"Say not so, boy; speak not the two names together. Saw you that which took place in the cottage?"

"Archy saw—Archy saw Ernest, and Archy saw the dark man; Archy knows what he saw."

"But why have you followed me—what has brought you to this place, boy."

"Archy came to watch, and to tell you what he could see. He has seen more than you have."

"Have you been here long—did you see the struggle on this place."

"Archy saw all."

"And where is he—which way did he go?"

"Does Frank mean the dark man?"

"The dark man, boy!—which speak you of?"

"Of the man who wore the cloak—the man whose eyes are dark and very bright—the man who told Ernest of the mark on Amy's neck."

"The mark!—saw you such mark, boy? What do your words imply?"

"Let Frank go home to Amy, and he will understand what Archy means."

Frank Heyton clenched his hands and ground his teeth.

"No, boy—no; not home—not back to her until I have caught him—until I have struggled with him once again. Tell me—tell me quickly, did you see which way he went?—do you know which path he took?"

"Archy saw, and Archy knows."

"Then, quick, boy; tell me, point me the way. Let me be on the hunt again."

"On the hunt for Ernest?"

"Ay, for him."

"And what would Frank do if he caught Ernest?"

"Kill him—kill him, boy, for the deep insult which he has given to us all, and for the deeper wrong which he has done my sister."

The idiot turned away his face, and attempted to move from the spot.

"Archy cannot help Frank to do murder," said he.

"That would not be murder, boy; there would be no crime in such a deed."

"Does Frank's heart tell him so?"

"It does, boy—it does!"

"But Archy's does not tell the same. To kill Ernest would be to do murder."

Frank Heyton grew impatient.

"Away with your childishness, boy! It is not in my mind to harm thee; but I might do so, if you say not, quickly, which path Ernest Morden took. Speak, boy—speak!"

Archy paused for a minute. Then, looking up in Heyton's face, he made the inquiry,—

"Will Frank promise not to harm Ernest, but only to make him tell why he did wrong to Amy?"

"Yes, boy, he shall tell that. I will make you the promise."

"Archy agrees; let Frank follow him."

This conversation passed in less time than it has taken the pen to record it in. The idiot-boy sprang forward, and led the way down the cliff. Frank Heyton followed him, and in a few minutes both stood together in the open country below.

"Which way, Archy—which way?"

The idiot hesitated for a moment, and then struck off down a narrow lane which was garnished with hedges on each side, and embowered overhead with tall and outspreading trees. Along this lane the pursuers journeyed for about a mile, Archy going on before, and Heyton following. Presently they turned into a meadow on their right, and after proceeding across it at full speed, gained the high road. Broad streamed the paly moonlight upon dusty foot-path, grassy field, mouldering stone, and leaf-clad bough. The night had suddenly become beautiful as the day; and every surrounding object—tree top, twig, and lonely dwelling, was glittering in silver sheen, and decked with pearly spangles. Cattle were quietly reposing in the fields on either side, and the drops of rain falling from the swaying bough, and pattering upon the sod beneath, seemed to be the only sound which disturbed the stillness of the hour.

Yes, there was another sound—the sound of footsteps and quick breathing— the sound of one hastening to shed blood, and another who led the way, unwitting to what he was becoming the leader. The pursuers stood in the open road; no human being could they see before them, no moving object was visible in the rear. Heyton turned to the idiot, and grasping him by the shoulder, said,—

"Whither now, boy—whither now?"

"Archy knows."

Darting aside, the idiot boy plucked a stake from the hedge, and returning with it to the middle of the road, planted one end on the ground, and applied his ear to the other extremity.

A minute passed by. Frank Heyton was becoming more and more impatient.

"What means this foolery, boy? Wilt thou lead me as thou promised, or must I go alone?"

Suddenly the boy flung away the stick, and cast himself upon the ground. Bending his head downwards, he placed his ear upon the road.

"Dost thou hear them, Archy—dost thou hear aught?"

Up sprang the idiot; his pale blue eyes sparkled in the moonshine, and the moonbeams played upon his flaxen hair.   A smile of joy was upon his countenance, as, nodding his head, he replied,—

" Archy hears."

" Is it them, boy—is it him ?"

" Let Frank follow Archy."

The road was of an equal breadth, so far as the gaze of the two pursuers could reach.   Low hedges, with here and there a tall tree, bounded it on each side. Gradually it ascended towards the top of a hill, some mile-and-a-half distant. All was clear, and void of traveller, beast or rider ; from the spot whereon the idiot and the avenger stood, to the summit of the hill, no fugitive was to be seen—no re-treating forms were visible.   Still the boy had heard a sound, and still was Heyton sanguine that he should overtake.

" Let us on, Archy—let us on !"

And onward they sped ; till, after coursing along the road for some two or three hundred yards, Archy turned aside into a shaded lane which stretched downwards to their left.

" Why this way, Archy—why not gain the hill ?"

The idiot stopped and laid his finger on his lip.

" Hist !" said he ; " Archy reads right."

Imitating the manner of his guide, Frank Heyton glided onwards, stealthily and without noise.   As they proceeded, the lane became narrower and darker.   Flowers of a thousand brilliant hues were flowering on each side, and the ruts, grown over with grass, told that it was not an oft-trodden path.   There bloomed the evening primrose, giving to view its yellow blossoms, which appeared almost white in the lunar ray ; there slept the lesser convolvulus, which had closed its cups, and gone to rest, to wait the breaking of another morn ; there trailed the bindweed, twining upwards, caressing the trunk of the stalwart tree, and throwing out its spiry tendrils, and flaunting its white and purple cups, like some wily leman wooing to her arms a sturdy knight of old.   Everything told of beauty and repose.   Well might Frank Heyton doubt of his having any business there.

" This is the wrong path, Archy," said he ; " this will only lead us into the wood—the dark wood."

" Archy knows.   The dark for the dark—the guilty to the gloom."

" But the men, boy—the men we follow ?"

" Does Frank wish to catch them ?"

" You know it—I have told you so ; and you are leading me wrong."

The idiot grasped the hand of his companion, and looking him in the face, said,—

" Why does Frank say that Archy is not keeping his word ?"

" Because, boy, you promised to show me the way which Ernest Morden had taken ; and you now lead me along a path which will only conduct us to a wood."

" The dark to the dark," replied the idiot boy again.

" But Ernest, boy—he has not gone this way ?"

Archy pointed with his finger towards the green turf which lay before them.

" Let Frank use Archy's eyes, before he blames Archy," said the idiot.

Softly slept the moonlight on the grassy sod.   Frank Heyton stooped down and glanced in the direction indicated by Archy's finger.   To his surprise he saw the print of footsteps on the down-pressed grass ; they were the foot-prints of a man. A little further, and there were marks of a like description, but they were not cor-respondent in size. On the grass, on the moss, on the earth, these marks were every-where visible.

" Two men have passed this way," said Heyton, addressing his companion.

" Archy knows."

" Then are they not far, boy.   Softly—softly ; See, the path winds down into the wood."

It was as Heyton had said.   The lane now dwindled down into a mere green alley, leading into the very centre of a wood.   Every one is familiar with the cha-racteristics of the green woods of merry England ; every one knows how cool and sheltering they are when the burning sun of summer throws his rays upon the outspread landscape ; how they invite the weary traveller to step aside into their pleasant recesses, where he may hear the birds sing, the springs bubble, the leaves rustle, and the insects chirp ; where, upon the stump of some old tree, he may take his seat, and make his footstool a bed of flowers—his pillow, a turf of moss. Just such a wood was the one into which the avenger and his idiot companion now entered. High over head towered the eternal trees, which had swayed their boughs there when earth was some centuries nearer to its youth ; their entertwined and verdant tracery formed a roof which canopied the intruders from the falling moonbeams, and hid them in a solemn and an antique gloom. Here and there were open spaces, through which, in the blaze of summer noon, the sunbeam might be seen to leap, and down through which the silver light now faintly fell. Far away, in the remotest depths, were shady nooks, wherein the axe of the woodman had never rung, and where man had yet refrained from defacing the sublimities of nature—those spots exist not in the day in which we write. The flowers bloomed, but Frank Heyton stayed not to pluck them ; the nightingale sang, but the pursuer lingered not to hear those notes which smoke-dried townsfolks have been taught to regard as melancholy, but which the true observer of nature knows to be the sweetest, softest, and loveliest in the realms of song. And still pressed the pursuers into the heart of the wood.

" Are we going right, Archy? Can you see the track? Do you hear a footfall ?

Stopping for a single moment, the boy knelt down upon the sod, and gazed along the vista formed by the trunks of the trees. Then, starting again to his feet, he took the hand of Heyton, and drew him onward.

The wood was still around them. A canopy of leafy verdure still hid from their view the starry sky, and deprived them of the moon's soft light. Upon their ears fell the hum of a thousand sleeping things, and upon their hands descended the pearly drops detached from the breeze-moved bough.

Presently a scene of gorgeous splendour opened suddenly to their view. The path through the wood led upwards ; and before them was a long grove of trees, arched above and open at the farther end, where it terminated upon the brow of the hill. Like some glorious work of giant architecture did it appear—vast, elegant, majestic, and sublime. As the two pursuers approached, it broke upon them like the nave of some huge gothic cathedral, the tall trunks resembling the columns, the twined boughs the pointed arch, and the altar-piece formed by the bright moon itself, which was seen through the opening, sailing in her beauty along the unclouded sky. Storm and darkness had disappeared ; the eve of gloom had changed into the night of splendour—changed as by an enchanter's touch.

" Where now, Archy ; there is none here save ourselves ?"

Again the idiot lifted up his finger to command silence.

" Hist !" said he ; " hist !"

Archy hastened on before, and Frank Heyton followed, keeping sharp watch about him as he went. On a sudden, the idiot-boy started, moved a few paces back, and laid his hand upon the arm of his friend.

" What have you seen, Archy ?"

" Hist ! follow—follow !"

" What have you to show me—have you discovered him ?"

Without replying to this question, Archy drew Frank Heyton onward, treading lightly upon the turf as they went. Not many steps had they taken, before the idiot suddenly stopped, and pointed with his out-stretched finger towards a bright object which glittered upon the moon-lit turf.

" See, Frank ! Archy has not led you wrong."

Heyton stooped down and picked up the object to which the boy had directed his attention.

" Ha !" he exclaimed ; " what is this? my own weapon—the one which I flung from my hand not an hour ago. How is this, boy—how is this ?"

Frank Heyton said truly ; the weapon was the same which he cast from him when preparing for the struggle on the Eagle's Altar.

The idiot again laid his hand upon the arm of his friend, uttered a short exclamation, and pointed to one particular portion of the turf.

"What see you now, Archy?"

Where the finger of the idiot indicated, the pursuer gazed; and there, upon the green turf, glittering as a liquid mirror in the dancing moonshine, was a pool of blood—red blood, clotted, gelatinized and quivering. Where it had fallen it had dyed the petals of the wood-flowers and had changed white blooms into scarlet blossoms.

"Does Frank see?" asked the idiot.

"Yes, boy—yes; but the meaning—how came this blood here?"

"Let Frank look at the sword which he has found."

Frank Heyton did so, and found the blade of his cutlass to be smeared with blood.

" It has been used, boy; but upon whom? And by whose hand has this blood been drawn?"

" The dark—to the dark," replied the idiot-boy once more.

Doubtless there was meaning in the saying of the wild and mindless youth; which meaning, however, it required more penetration than Frank Heyton possessed to fathom. The present was no time for framing riddles, nor for solving enigmas. A combat had taken place—the combatants were not far distant; could there be any doubt as to who these combatants were? One of them was certainly Ernest Morden, for none but he could have obtained possession of the weapon which Hey- ton had thrown from his hand not an hour before. This weapon had evidently been used, and, in all probability by Ernest. But with whom had he fought? Whose blood was it which there stained the earth? Whom had Ernest Morden quarrelled with in that secluded place? Could it have been the stranger—the mysterious old man of the cottage; and if so, why should Ernest have fought with him, and where had the wounded fled? Arousing himself from the abstracted state into which he had been thrown by this last discovery, Frank Heyton turned to the idiot-boy, and addressing him, said,—

" It is Ernest Morden who has done this. Twice on this night has he been victor, and he must yet struggle again. Canst tell me, boy, where to find him?"

The idiot returned no answer.

Heyton repeated his inquiry.

" Have they gone far, Archy—have they fled far?"

Hesitating for a few seconds, the idiot bent down, and dipped his forefinger in the pool of blood; then, looking at his companion, he said,—

" While the blood is cooling there is but short time for flight. Follow before it is cold."

" What mean you, boy—is the blood still warm?"

" Archy leads—let Frank follow."

CHAPTER VI.

THE MAN AND THE PHANTOM ON THE TOWER BY MIDNIGHT.

EMERGING from the grove, the pursuer and his companion stood upon the brow of the hill. A beauteous prospect met their view. Above shone the bright full moon; on their right lay the sea, glistening in a wide tract of silverly light; far away to their left, stretched a wide and beautiful country, clothed with verdure, and dotted here and there with massive mansion, smiling cottage, and sequestered home. Wide meadow uplands slept in their quiet beauty, surrounded by dense masses of deep and leafy shade. Circling the vast panorama was a range of hills which commenced at the sea-coast, and stretched away inland until they were lost to view in the distance. Frank Heyton and the idiot surveyed the scene, but the tumult of passion in the breast of the former prevented him from appreciating its beauty.

There was one object by the sea-coast which stood out prominent from the rest. It was an old and ruined fortress, of Roman construction, which had been a strong- hold in the time of the Normans. Standing, as it did, upon an eminence, the moonlight fell upon its castellated keep, and made its battlements visible to the eyes of the distant beholder. Between the base of the hill on which the pursuer stood, and the moat which surrounded this fortress, meadow and woodland intervened.

Heyton paused for a moment to examine his weapon, and to discover, if possible, what work it had executed. Then, turning to address his companion, he was surprised to find the idiot-boy upon his knees.

" Up—up, Archy! What foolishness seizes you now?"

The face of the idiot was turned towards the moon; his hands were uplifted as if in prayer, and tears were trickling down his cheeks.

Heyton shook him by the shoulder.

" Arise, boy! Is this the time for indulging your madness?"

" Archy is praying to the moon," replied the idiot ; " the moon is Archy's friend."

" But Ernest Morden, boy ——"

" Hist—hist !" cried the idiot, suddenly springing up. " See, Frank—see !" and clinging to the arm of Heyton, he pointed in the direction of the old fortress— " The moon has answered Archy's prayer."

" What would you have me to see, boy? There is field, wood, and castle ; what besides ?"

" Look—look to the meadow beyond the farm."

" I see it ; there are cattle sleeping on the grass."

" Now to the right—the little clump of trees to the right."

" Yes, boy, yes. Ha ! there is a man ; I see him stealing along in the shade. Is it not so, boy—is it not so ?"

" It is he—it is the phantom," replied the idiot.

" What mean you, Archy? Is it Ernest, think you ?"

" The shade—to the shade ! The dark—to the dark ! It is the phantom !"

Flittingly, as glide the shadows of a dream, stole the form of a man around the little knot of trees which Heyton had descried. Very evident was it that this man was endeavouring to conceal his flight, keeping as he did in the shadow cast by the trees. Whether or not he was Ernest Morden Frank Heyton had no means of knowing ; and the conjectures of his companion were useless, owing to the mystical manner in which he gave his replies.

" Tell me, Archy, think you it is *he* ?"

" Archy knows it is the dark man ! Archy knows it is the phantom !"

" Follow, boy, follow."

With mad speed Frank Heyton rushed down the hill, and directed his companion to hasten after him. Onwards he went ; neither hedge, fence, nor rivulet impeded his course. Over mound and meadow, over stone and flower, through bush, through brier he sped his way. In his right hand he carried the blood-stained weapon, with his left hand he beckoned his breathless companion to keep close to his side. Panting and exhausted, they arrived at the clump of trees.

" Hold back, Archy ; let the shade hide us both. See you him now ?"

The idiot boy crept along in the shadow of the copse, but presently drew back, and motioned Heyton to approach him.

" Does Frank see ?" he asked, as he pointed to the retreating form of the man visible at some hundred yards distant.

" Yes, Archy, yes ; he is hastening towards the castle. We must overtake him before he reaches the moat."

And again the pursuers sped onwards, continuing their chase regardless of any obstacles in their way. The distance between them and the object of their pursuit decreased ; every moment they gained upon him, every moment gave him with more distinctness to their view. Suddenly a rise in the ground interposed between him and them.

" On, Archy, on. We are almost upon him now."

They increased their speed—they gained the top of the mound. Bright shone the moon upon the green sward which intervened between the spot where they beheld the figure of him whom they pursued.

" Stop, Ernest Morden. It is Frank Heyton who calls upon you to stop."

Startled by the shout, the fugitive paused, glanced behind him, saw that pursuers were on his track, and then hastened on again with increased speed.

" Darest thou to face me, Ernest Morden ? Darest thou to face thy foe ?"

The fugitive returned no answer, but directed his course towards the castle. Heyton increased his speed, and was but some twenty yards in the rear, when he suddenly stopped, and seizing the arm of Archy, whispered in his ear,—

" Are you sure that it is he, boy? I thought I saw the grey hair of an old man."

" Let Frank follow the phantom," replied the idiot, urging Heyton onward.

And still they continued the pursuit, still they followed the retreating form ;

nothing intervened between it and them, except the level sward upon which they trod. The shadow of the pursued stretched out in the moonlight to meet the steps of the pursuers.

"On, Archy. The clouds are again gathering over head ; and, see ! he is rounding the postern to reach the castle where it fronts the sea. On, Archy, on."

The moat was gained—was crossed ; they trod over the falling fragments of the ruin, they turned round the abutting postern, and before them, only five yards in advance, was the figure which they followed.

"If thou art Ernest Morden, turn, and face me ; if other than he, I demand thy name."

Not the least attention was paid by the dark figure to Frank Heyton's challenge. In vain did the pursuer repeat his words ; in vain did he call upon the fleeting form to stop. Entering by a low door in one of the angle towers of the fortress, the fugitive vanished from the sight of those who pursued him.

" Be wary, boy, be wary. He may conceal himself, but he cannot escape me."

Heyton, with his cutlass drawn in his hand, pushed forward, and followed the figure through the door by which he had passed from sight. Archy shrank back as he approached the gloomy wall, but Frank took him by the hand, and drew him within the building.

" Hist, boy ! See you where he has hidden ?"

Scarcely were the words spoken, before Heyton heard footsteps upon the old stairs which wound up through the tower inside which he stood. The steps were broken, and crumbled beneath the tread ; yet did not the pursuer hesitate, but springing forward, clambered up the dark, dangerous way, regardless of the gloom and the desolation.

And still he heard the footsteps of one ascending the stairs above him—still he heard the rustle of garments, and the quick breathings of the retreating form.

Suddenly the steps terminated in a kind of corridor, from which a distant view of the surrounding country was gained. As Frank Heyton felt the cool air blow again upon his face, he saw the dark figure pass into the tower, at the opposite extremity of the place on which he stood.

Again he rushed forward, and again he had to climb steps which were more broken, and more perpendicular than those of the other tower. From loopholes in the wall he could glance at the scene without, and through arch window-holes he could look down upon the interior of the ruined keep. He looked up, and saw the dark garments of him whom he pursued only a few steps above him.

"You cannot escape me, Ernest Morden. I will hurl you from these stairs ! I will hurl you from the tower top !"

One step more and his hand touched the garments of him whom he pursued ; another step, and he stretched forth his fingers to grasp the dark object above him.

Just then the loose stone upon which Frank Heyton trod gave way, and bounded downwards to the bottom of the tower. The next, and the next followed, as the weight of the pursuer rested upon them. Dreadful was the position of Frank Heyton—he trod upon air—his feet swung in the darkness ; with his hands he clutched the projecting stone which formed the next of the series.

Awful thought ! had the hand of the rash man relaxed its hold he would have fallen through the darkness, and been shattered on the ruins ; had the stone to which he clung broken off from its point of attachment, Frank would have rolled with it to the abyss, where none might seek him—where his remains might never be found !

He clung—he clung in mad desperation ; the brittle stone to which he clung was all that intervened between him and death !

Through the darkness he heard a laugh—a laugh of some one who exulted in his misery, who was rejoiced to know that Frank Heyton had ventured where death loomed upon him, and where his grave was likely to be. That laugh proceeded from above—that laugh came from the dark figure which he had pursued. Could that figure be Ernest Morden—Ernest, who had been regarded by the Heytons as a friend ?

Maddened and reckless, Frank Heyton grasped the stone firmly, and made a spring. Happily for him his strength was not wholly exhausted; the point was won—his knees rested upon the solid step—he was saved from the threatened destruction.

Without casting a look behind him, without turning round to gaze upon the danger which he had escaped, the adventurous youth hurried onward, impatient to seize the object of his pursuit. They would meet now; there was no chance of escape. On the top of that lone tower was another struggle to take place?"

"Ay, laugh, if thou wilt, Ernest Morden; Frank Hayton is not gone to his grave yet!" exclaimed the pursuer, as he rushed up the remaining steps of the tower, and stood upon the battlements.

Had his senses deceived him, or had he followed a dissolving form? On the battlements he stood—on the lone and dizzy height; he looked around; he ran from side to side; no living being stood there except himself. Crumbling and moss-covered ruins were around him, but no figure like to that which he had pursued could he now discern.

The tower was high, and isolated from the rest of the building. There appeared no other way of ascent or of descent than that by which, at such perilous risk, Frank Heyton had reached the summit. Whither had the dark figure gone? how had it disappeared?

The pursuer listened, but no foot-fall met his ear; no sound of breathing, no rustle of garments, nothing that might indicate the proximity of living thing.

Had Frank Heyton been deceived?—had he ascended by one staircase, and the figure which he had missed by another? No; such could not be the case, for he had seen the dark garments flit on before him, and he had touched with his own hand the heel of the fugitive.

Had he been mistaken concerning the laugh? No; for he had heard it, clearly and distinctly. It had proceeded from above, and was hoarse and muffled.

What, then, was Frank Heyton to suppose?—where was he to look for his foe? There was no place for concealment—nothing but grey old battlements, crumbling in the midnight air. Where he now stood, the sentinel in days gone by had kept his watch, and from the moss-covered terrace where he trod, the archers had once poured their arrows, thicker than a hailstorm, down. There was nothing behind which to hide, no niche in which to couch from sight.

Opening on the battlements was the small door through which Heyton had passed, and which led to the staircase by which he had ascended. There was no other door, no other staircase.

He looked from where he stood to the ground below. The height was fearful, and there was nothing by which to effect a descent, nothing to cling to, nothing to plant the foot upon, nothing for the hand to grasp.

Exhausted and powerless, Frank Heyton seated himself upon the battlements, and gazed around him. His senses were confused, his brain was bewildered. The perspiration hung in large drops upon his forehead, and his hand shook as he raised it to his brow.

From where the youth sat, he saw the hill upon which he had stood half an hour before—the hill on which was the grove, wherein he had regained his sword, and where he had seen the pool of blood. Nearer still he saw the clump of trees, in the shadow of which he had first discerned the dark figure that he had pursued. Beneath him was the green sward, on which the shadow of the tower was boldly projected in the moonshine; and close to the wall of the fortress ran the moat, which opened into the sea, and the drawbridge which he had crossed in his pursuit.

Where was the figure he had followed, and how had it contrived to escape him?

Frank Heyton thought of the mysterious words which had been uttered by the idiot boy; he remembered that Archy had spoken of a phantom, and he doubted whether it had been aught else than a phantom which he had followed.

But the rustling garments—the heel which he had touched—the laugh which he had heard;—must not that have been a living thing which had uttered sounds of laughter, and which had proved solid to the touch?

Frank Heyton arose, and again examined every nook and corner of the tower-top. His search was in vain; the fugitive had eluded his pursuit.

"God knows what I have pursued this night!" he ejaculated, and he leaned against the crumbling wall. "Ernest Morden has escaped me; but whether it was him or some unreal form which I have followed to this height, it is not for me to say."

Baffled in his endeavours to obtain a second meeting with his foe, and growing somewhat timid from the mysterious nature of the event which had just occurred, Frank Heyton turned about to descend and seek his companion. To his consternation he perceived that so many of the steps in the tower-staircase had given way, and fallen to the bottom; that a wide gap now existed, over which it was impossible to pass.

Now, indeed, was the position of the pursuer a fearful one—on the top of the old tower, and no means of making a descent! Clouds, also, were again passing before the moon, and indications of another storm became apparent.

The youth rushed to the top of the staircase. Through the loop holes streamed the faint moonlight. Above were the steps upon which he trod—below were those by which he had ascended, but separated now by a wide chasm which yawned between. More fearful still, the very stones on which his feet rested trembled beneath the weight of his body, and his head turned giddy as he gazed into the darkness below.

Suddenly he determined upon calling the idiot boy to his assistance. His tongue seemed to adhere to his mouth, and his lips quivered as he uttered the cry. Again and again was that cry repeated, but there was no response from below.

Where was Archy?—had he, too, disappeared; had he met with danger or with death?

For the twentieth time Frank Heyton called out the name of the idiot boy. By the walls of the old ruin was that call echoed and re-echoed, but no answer came from Archy.

"Is it all a dream—a fearful dream; or am I left here to die?" ejaculated Frank Heyton, as he clasped his hands to his ice-cold brow, and gnashed his teeth in the madness of his despair.

CHAPTER VII.

THE MYSTERIOUS PORTRAIT.

LEAVING Frank Heyton on the summit of the old tower, and not pausing to inquire what had become of the idiot boy, we go back to the cottage, in which lights were still burning, though the hour was long past midnight, and all things were silent and sleeping around.

After the departure of his son in pursuit of Ernest, Mr. Heyton turned towards Kate, and desired her to assist him in conveying Amy to her own apartment. As they proceeded to raise the insensate girl, her eyes opened, and with a countenance expressive of terror, she clung wildly to the arm of her parent.

"Do not let him come near me, father; do not let him come near me!" she exclaimed.

"Be calm, my Amy; there is no one present except Kate and myself."

Amy raised her head, and parted with her fair hand the hair from off her brow. Pale was her countenance, and bloodless were her lips. Her eyes, which had become supernaturally bright and shining, surveyed the apartment with a wandering yet vacant gaze. Her delicate frame shivered and trembled as if stricken with sudden cold, and the grasp with which she clung to her father's arm was like that of a drowning person clutching the rope which is thrown out as a means of escape from the watery tomb which yawns to receive another habitant.

"Why look you so, my poor Amy?" asked her father, patting with an old man's fondness, the cheek of the fair girl, and pressing her throbbing temple against his breast—"Why are you frightened, dearest?—what see you to cause you fear?"

"Is he gone, father—is he really gone?"

"Do you mean Ernest, my child?"

"No, father, not him—the other."

"The old man—the guest to whom we gave shelter?"

"Yes, father, him." Then suddenly starting up, Amy fixed her bright eyes upon her father's countenance, and demanded with much earnestness,—

"Why did you do so, father—why did you admit him beneath this roof?"

"The laws of hospitality commanded me to do as much, my child. Will you blame your father for having shown kindness to a stranger, albeit that kindness has been ill-rewarded?"

"No, father, no ; but to him—that man—Kate should have warned you."

"Kate warned me!" exclaimed Mr. Heyton, in surprise ; "did Kate know him?"

Mr. Heyton glanced at his elder daughter, and saw that she was leaning against the mantel-shelf, her whole frame agitated by some violent emotion.

"There is mystery in this!" exclaimed the parent. "Come hither, Kate ! Let me know the meaning of your sister's words."

Vainly did Kate endeavour to move towards her father. As she did so, a feeling of faintness came over her, and her limbs failed her, so that had she not again grasped the mantel-shelf, she would have fallen on the cottage floor.

"Do not speak harshly to sister Kate," interposed Amy. "It is but little which she knows."

"Kate!—Kate knows!" ejaculated Mr. Heyton, in amazement. "What secrets are there that ye have hatched, and kept between you?"

"None, dear father—none !" cried the beautiful Kate, rushing forward, and throwing her arms round the neck of her parent.

"Then, what does Amy mean?"

"She means," replied Kate, with much agitation, "she means that he—that the stranger was so like, so very like the portrait."

"What talk you of, girls? And you, Kate—what portrait is it of which you speak?"

Kate was silent. The dark, rich blood had vanished from her cheeks. She shivered, as trembles the leaf of the aspen-willow, in the breeze of an autumn evening.

The father looked upon his children in mute astonishment. There was something in the demeanour of each which he could not understand, and which he had never before remarked in either. Kate glanced at her sister—their eyes met—they trembled—their cheeks turned deadly pale—there was a sudden tremor observable in each ; and then, both turned away their eyes, as though each had committed some terrible crime, and could no longer gaze undauntedly upon the other.

Every action, every change of countenance in the two girls was attentively observed by their parent ; and, as he gazed upon them, his own countenance also underwent an alteration. At first, the flush of anger gathered on his cheeks, when, from the behaviour of his daughters, he supposed that they had played partners in the committal of some fearful misdeed which they had hitherto kept concealed from him. But, when the father saw how each of his children fixed a gaze of terror upon the other—how, when their eyes met, their eye-balls glared—how, in each look was told the story of some terrible mystery, which each knew, but of which both dared not to speak—how they could not look each other in the face, as they had done of old—how they feared to sit side by side—how their lips quivered, their limbs shook, the heart of the parent became touched, and his own face became pale as theirs. Over his own frame came a trembling—a difficulty of respiration—a wild, chilly feeling—a sinking of the heart—a lessening of the pulse—a creeping, freezing sensation, like that felt by those who enter unhallowed and hideous places at the midnight hour. From the countenance of the parent, anger had disappeared, and the expression of fear—fear for the tender beings who then crouched beside him—for the children of his love—was depicted on every feature. The thought, the terrible thought suggested itself to his mind, that, by those upon whom he gazed, a sin had been committed, for which there was no atonement, and which involved in its consequences immediate danger to the transgressors. No data had he from which to guess what this crime might be; but the mysterious behaviour of Ernest, and the words uttered by the stranger, coupled with the knowledge which Kate and Amy seemed to have of that stranger, and the present demeanour of his two children, caused many sad and gloomy conjectures to arise in his mind; and he had a foreboding of some terrible revelation which he believed it was his destiny to hear revealed.

Had it not been for the quivering of their lips, the palsied-like motion of their limbs, the three living figures in that room would have seemed more like statues than human beings. Silence—the silence of death—reigned in the apartment. Amy was clinging to the arm of her parent, and the gaze of that parent was directed towards the maiden; the eyes of both fixed, the look of each expressive of anxiety and fear. On the other side stood Kate, her hands resting upon the shoulder of her father, her face hidden in her hands. Dreadful was the very silence, for so deep was it, that not a breath was audibly drawn, and each heard the beating of his or her own heart.

Starting from his statue-like state, Mr. Heyton took the arm of his eldest daughter, and in a hollow, faltering voice, addressed her in tones of the tenderest parental fondness,—

"Tell me, Kate—tell me, my child—what have you done, and why do you tremble when I look upon you?"

"Pardon us, father—pardon us for concealing it from you," implored Amy, still clinging to her parent, as if she desired his protection to shield her from danger.

"What have you concealed, child? Your father listens—let him hear all."

"I—I have not strength—I dare not—I ——"

Poor Amy was so agitated that she was unable to reply to her parent's interrogation. Mr. Heyton clasped her fair white wrist, and in a voice of agony, repeated her words,—

"Dare not!—dare not, Amy!"

"I cannot, father—it is too fearful."

"Fearful, child! Good Heaven! what meaning is there in your words?"

"A meaning, father, that—that—I cannot—dare not—tell you."

"Amy, let your confession be what it may, it is fit that I should hear it, and that it should be told to me now. Ernest Morden has offered an insult to each and all of us this night, which insult must not be passed over, nor lightly forgotten. There may be that in which you have to say—that in the confession which you have to make, which will explain the mysterious occurrence of this night. Tell me, child; is such the case?"

"Yes, father, I ——"

"Do not pause, child; do not hesitate."

"There is, father—there is an explanation of—of——"

"Of the cause of Morden's behaviour. Is it so, Amy?"

"No, father, no; I said not that."

"You said that you could explain why he acted as he did this night—you have avowed that much."

"No, father, indeed not—indeed not!"

"Then to what do your words refer, child?"

"To him, father—to him!"

"Ernest Morden, mean you?"
Amy faltered in endeavouring to reply. The secret which she possessed, was one which she had not sufficient physical strength to reveal. Again a tremor passed over her body; again she clasped her parent's arm with the tight, spasmodic clasp of a person convulsed; again she turned away her eyes, yet nestled close to her father and her sister, as though she feared the presence of some evil spirit waiting to seize her, and snatch her away.

"Do not trifle, Amy," said Mr. Heyton, in a sterner voice than he had yet spoken in. " Even now your brother is in pursuit of Ernest ; and, if they meet, there may be murder done. It is in your power, perhaps, to prevent bloodshed, and, it may be, to prevent harm from being done to an innocent man. Calm yourself, child, and let me hear the revelation, whatever its nature may be."

Tenderly, fondly, affectionately, did the parent caress his child. There was the frail girl, clinging for protection to the strong man ; but the strength of the man was failing him fast, and the weakness of the maiden took from her the power of utterance. Like some fair form about to be dissolved, lay she there in her father's arms. You might have deemed that death was with her—that the once warm heart was cooling within ; for death-like was her look, and death-like were the hollow tones in which her broken sentences were muttered in the ear of her parent. Amy was very beautiful, though her's was not the dazzling beauty of her sister, but the beauty of attraction which wins you, you know not why. Kate was like the full-blown rose, challenging you to admiration ; but Amy was the quiet violet, luring you to its lowly shade. You might have fallen into extacies while gazing upon the one ; but the countenance of the other was calculated to awaken in the mind of him who looked upon it, the holiest feelings of the heart—the purest emotions which arise in the bosom of man. What wonder, then, that the parent looked upon his child with fondness?—what wonder, then, that the tears were in the father's eyes when he beheld his daughter's misery? Age looked upon youth, and the sorrows of youth stole from age its sternness, made the bold to fear, and brought the strong man to the earth, that, weak himself, he might sympathise with woman's weakness.

Once more Amy attempted to answer her father's question, but her lips quivered and her tongue refused to articulate the words which she wished to speak.

"Take courage, my Amy," said her parent. "Speak, dearest, speak !"

"Not now, father, not now."

"Why delay, child? If you have aught to tell which concerns your own happiness, it equally concerns mine, and it is right that I should know it."

Amy pointed to her sister, and, in a scarcely audible voice, said,—

"Kate will tell you, father. Ask sister Kate."

Mr. Heyton turned towards his elder daughter, and waited for an explanation from her; but Kate appeared to be as much affected as her sister, and, like her, incapable of holding conversation on the subject.

"Children, what have you done?" exclaimed the parent. "Kate, will you not perform this task for your sister, or are you both implicated in this mysterious secret?"

Kate sank upon a chair, cast a glance at the window of the apartment, then covered her eyes with her hands, and was silent.

For a moment, Mr. Heyton stood as if stupified ; his hand was clasped to his brow, his eyes were fixed upon his elder daughter, and he drew his breath with quick, irregular, and fitful acts of respiration.

"Take me, father—take me away; lead me into the next room," supplicated Amy.

The parent placed his arm around his daughter, and supported her, as with feeble footsteps she moved into the adjoining apartment. There, casting herself upon the bed, she waved her hand to her father, and implored him to leave her to solitude and silence.

"Why leave you, Amy? I have yet heard no word of explanation from your lips."

"Kate must tell you, dear father. Kate must tell you all."

Mr. Heyton hesitated, doubting whether it would not be imprudent for him to leave his daughter alone. Unfortunately, their old servant, Madge, had obtained leave of absence for a few days, and was now on a visit to a friend, at some distant part of the country. There was no one in the cottage except himself and his two daughters.

"I wish that Archy had not gone out," said Mr. Heyton ; "if he were here, I could send him in search of assistance."

"I need no assistance, dear father. But where is Archy gone?"

"He has followed your brother Frank."

" And Frank, you said ——"

" Has gone in pursuit of Ernest."

Amy looked at her father inquiringly, and demanded,—

" Are you sure that Archy has gone in company with Frank ?"

" It is my belief that he has," returned Mr. Heyton.

A smile of satisfaction passed over the face of the maiden, as she ejaculated,—

" I am glad of that—very glad of that !"

" Of what, Amy—of what are you glad ?"

" That Archy has accompanied Frank ; said you not so, dear father ?"

" He has, child."

" And they have gone to seek Ernest ?"

" They have."

" That is fortunate ; oh ! that is very fortunate !"

Mr. Heyton was again puzzled to account for the fervency with which Amy uttered this interjection.   Perplexed more and more, he took his daughter's hand, and begged her to be more explicit."

" Answer me, my dear child : why do you congratulate yourself on the circumstance of Archy having followed Frank ?"

" Followed him, father !   I thought you said that he had gone with him ?"

" They did not go out together ; but, doubtless, Archy has overtaken Frank."

" I hope so—I hope so !" ejaculated Amy, clasping her hands together and breathing more freely.

" But what cause have you to be rejoiced, my child, at such an occurrence ? Archy has been denied by nature those faculties of mind which your brother possesses, and he can, therefore, be of little assistance to him."

" Yes, yes, dear father, he may be—he may be !"

" How so, Amy ?   I do not understand you.   Every word you have spoken is full of mystery.   Why do you feel happy to hear that Archy is absent with your brother ?"

" Because—because Archy knows—Archy can tell ——"

" Ha !" exclaimed Mr. Heyton, suddenly starting up ; " have you told your secrets to that idiot, and kept them hidden from me ?"

" Not told him, dear father ; oh, no !   I dared not to tell him ; but he knows—he has seen ——"

Amy shuddered, and could not bring the sentence to a conclusion.

" And what has Archy seen—what does the idiot-boy know ?   Strange that secrets should be kept hidden from me which are known to him."

" No, dear father, not known—not *all* known."

" All !—all, Amy !   Are they then so many ?"

" You have not heard, father, and I—I have not strength to tell you now.   But, leave me, leave me, and go to Kate.   Do not let her stay in that room alone."

" But, the confession, my child—the ——"

" Kate must tell you.   Kate is stronger than I am, and it does not concern her so much as it does me.   Go—ask her ; she will tell you everything—everything that is known to her and to me."

Reluctantly Mr. Heyton quitted the bedside of his younger daughter to seek her sister in the outer apartment.   As he had left Kate so he found her—seated on a chair, her back turned to the window, and her face hidden by her hands.   She started as he re-entered the room, and exclaimed,—

" Ah ! it is you, father—it is you.   Thank Heaven it is only you !"

" Why thank Heaven so fervently, my child ?   Why are you startled ?"

" Because—but it is nothing, father.   I was frightened—I—forgive me, I am a very silly girl."

Mr. Heyton took a seat beside his daughter.

" Kate," said he, addressing her in an earnest manner, " there is something— some deep mystery, known to you and to your sister, but which you have hitherto kept concealed from me. Whatever its true nature may be, I know not, but I have the evidence before me that it is a secret which deeply affects you both.   For your own peace of mind I pray you to make every disclosure.   We are alone, there is none to overhear us, none to listen to a child's confession to her parent. Come, then, my Kate, do not be afraid, do not hesitate to do that which is right, and which is required of you in the fulfilment of your duty as a daughter. Amy has expressed her wish that you would do this in her stead, and her wish, in this matter, corresponds with my own. Come, Kate, I listen."

" Not here, father—I cannot tell you the story now."

" Why not, my Kate? What time or place more fitting ?"

" It is night, father—it is midnight, and we are alone."

" Alone ! and wherefore fear you because of that? To none but the guilty is there aught that is fearful either in night or loneliness. Once more, Kate, I entreat you—I entreat you because I love you—because both you and Amy are dear to me, that you confide to me this secret. It is nothing hard that I ask—nothing more than it is my duty to require. I have never been a stern father to you. Neither you nor Amy can reproach me with hard-heartedness, cruelty, or over-strictness. Your happiness is bound up with my own, and everything which tends to work woe to Amy, or to you, exerts the same tendency towards myself. You cannot deny this, Kate—you cannot deny that I have been kind to you, that I have loved you ——"

Kate rose up, and cast her arms around her father's neck.

" You have, dear father—you have loved us both, and you love us now. I know it—I am sure of it."

" Then why, child, refuse me this one request ?"

" I do not refuse you, dear father. I will tell you all—I will tell it you some other time."

" Some other time, Kate !"

" To-morrow—to-morrow morning, perhaps."

Again the maiden sank back in the chair, and her father, taking her hand in his own, allowed the compassionate emotions of his bosom to give way to a feeling of anger. His tone was no longer that of entreaty—no longer that of one who supplicated the grant of a favour.

" Hear me, Kate Heyton !" he exclaimed ; " you are my child, and if you have forgotten your duties to a parent, it is necessary that I recall them to your mind. Years ago, when your mother died, you were left to my sole care. That mother's charge on her bed of death was, that I should protect and cherish the child whom she the most dearly loved. I have not failed in the performance of that duty, as you well know. Amidst the wreck of my affairs, I was not forgetful of your sister or of you. Then it was that I strove hard to keep you from poverty—then it was that I made an effort, for your sakes alone, to secure some little sum, to subsist on in future days. I have toiled for you, I have striven for you, and I claim for my reward, not your love, but your respect. In this matter, I also lay claim to your obedience. If wrong has been done by either your sister or yourself, confess it, and you shall be pardoned. No matter how much you have erred, I still promise you forgiveness."

" Father, dearest father !" cried Kate ; " you misunderstand—you do not comprehend the meaning of my words."

" Explain them to me, my dear Kate."

" Not to-night, father. I cannot to-night. Wait—wait."

Mr. Heyton could not withhold his anger.

" No, Kate," said he, " there must be no delay. I should not be acting as a parent ought to act, were I to permit you to have your way in this business. Only just now, when I looked upon your sister as she lay on the bed, I feared for her. I feared that not only was her peace of mind destroyed, but her health of body also. It is right, therefore, and it is requisite that you give an immediate explanation. It may be—Heaven forfend it should be so !—that Ernest Morden has acted the villain's part beneath the roof of his father's friend ; if such be the case, he shall not escape with impunity. But it may be that you—that my own children—that those whom I have loved and cherished, have done some great wrong, have been partners in some great wickedness ; if that be the fact, it is still more incumbent on you that you delay not to confide everything to me openly and at once. Your so doing may save bloodshed—it may save murder ; the innocent may escape accusation, and the really guilty be pardoned. I do not ask you, then, to make this explanation, but I command you—I insist upon your doing it. I should render myself highly culpable were I to admit of any excuse, or sanction any delay. Kate Heyton, your father desires you to confess to him the cause of your own and your sister's uneasiness. You will not, unless you are much changed of late, so far forget yourself, as to disobey."

Kate lifted up her head ; tears were flowing down her cheeks and a mingled look of terror and distress formed the expression of her countenance. Glancing round the room before she spoke, and lowering her voice almost to a whisper, she replied to her father's solicitation.

" You have wronged me, dear father—you have wronged poor Amy and myself. The darkness and loneliness of the hour oppresses me, and takes away my strength. Yet, rather than you should again say such words as you have already spoken, I will make an effort to tell you the secret, although the mystery of that secret will probably be only increased by that which I am about to communicate to you."

" Even your words, child, are full of mystery."

" And so will be my story. Draw your chair close to me, dear father ; let me feel the touch of your hand, and know that you are sitting beside me."

" Kate, my child ! what mean these preparations—why this dread ?"

" Listen, father ! have you at any time heard of a picture being painted from the fancy only—the picture of an individual, father, whom the artist had never seen, who had never been described to him or her, and of whose real existence that artist was totally unaware ; and then, father, that after a time, the individual should himself appear, that the artist recognised him, that his picture was at once a portrait ; know you of any such case ?"

" None, my child. The picture to prove a portrait, say you ?"

" Ay, and not a mere portrait of the features only, but an accurate representation of every particular ; of the dress, the expression, the characteristics, the minutest points both of colour and of form. Still more more wonderful, father, that the portrait should be unlike any other ; that it should be peculiar and unique ; that features should be limned there which do not commonly exist together in the same countenance ; that even the carriage, the attitude of the person should be pourtrayed ; heard you ever of any such performance ?"

" Never, Kate. But what certainty could there be of the truth of the artist's story ?"

" The greatest of certainty, father —the artist's own certainty."

" He might have seen, child, and forgotten ; the individual might have met his eye long years before, and the image have slept in his brain ; such is very possible."

" But how, father, if in the portrait the individual was delineated as he at length appeared ! If it had been but a recollection of some figure which had floated before the eyes in days long past, then would the picture have shown the person represented as he appeared at that period ; allowance would not have been made by the artist for the effects which time had wrought in the years intervening between the seeing of the object and the painting of the portrait ; yet, I have said that as the picture represented him to be, so stood the person when he came—the same in feature, form, and characteristics, dressed in the like garments, habited after the same fashion, accompanied by all the auxiliaries ; the resemblance not imaginary— not in the *tout ensemble* only, but in the minutest part. Once more I ask you, father, have you seen or heard of such a picture ?"

" Never, my child. A performance of such a character would rank among the mysteries which have ever puzzled the human intellect ; and which still remain unexplained and seemingly inexplicable."

" You have said rightly, father ; the picture was a mystery, as you say."

" But there cannot be such a picture, child."

" Nay, father, such a picture exists !"

"You know it?"

"I have seen it."

"And the artist ——"

"Was myself!"

"Kate!" exclaimed Mr. Heyton, starting up from off his seat, "Kate, girl! I asked you not for a tale like this, but for an explanation of this night's mystery."

"And with the mystery of this night, father, that picture has much to do."

"Much to do, child?"

"More, father, than perhaps either you or I imagine."

"But, Kate—child—daughter, this portrait is ——"

"You shall see it. Follow me."

"Where would you lead me?"

"To Amy's room; the picture is there; it is in her possession."

Kate moved towards the door which led into the adjoining apartment, but her father placed his hand upon her arm, and endeavoured to detain her.

"Go not in, Kate; your sister sleeps, perhaps; and it would be unwise to disturb her."

"My sister has desired me to relate to you that which she fears to relate herself. I cannot comply with her request, unless I have the means of entering fully into the explanation."

"Do so here, Kate—do so now."

"I will make no further delay; but you must see the portrait; you must look upon it for the first time."

"Gently, then—tread gently."

Kate Heyton turned the handle of the door, and entered the room; she was followed by her father, who placed his hands before the candle to shield the light. All was still and quiet. They moved towards the bed, on which lay the younger maiden; but Amy had drawn the bed-clothes over her face, and her position and appearance caused those who looked upon her to suppose that she had fallen into a gentle slumber.

"Softly, Kate—softly; she sleeps."

Strange was the scene in that small and silent apartment. On the bed lay a youthful maiden—the contour of her form dimly apparent through the light coverings which she had drawn around her. By the bedside of the sleeper stood two figures, an old man and a girl, the one passing onward to the grave; the other just emerging into womanhood; but the faces of each were pale, the limbs of both trembled. They stood by that bedside, and the world knew them for sister and father, yet seemed they more like robbers—like guilty persons who had stolen thither to commit a crime, and who were unnerved, through a consciousness of being engaged in an evil deed. The candle shook in the hand of the old man; the fingers of his companion played with a tremulous motion, indicative of the agitation of the inward heart.

"Kate, why do you pause?"

The maiden hesitated for a moment, and eyed every corner of the apartment suspiciously. Then, summoning up her strength, she stepped forwards and placed her hand on a small box, which stood upon a table, near the head of the bed.

"Is it there, child? have you the portrait there?"

"It is here," replied Kate, in a whisper.

"Quick, then, and show it me, that we may leave the room."

"Be patient, father, the secret is here."

"The secret, child?"

"Yes; the secret which we have hitherto kept hidden from you."

"Did you not bring me here to show me the portrait?"

"I did; and with the portrait the secret is connected—in that portrait the mystery lies. It is here."

Opening the box, Kate took out a small, square packet, carefully done up in paper. With trembling fingers she unfolded the envelope; and, having done so, paced in the hand of her father a small drawing.

"Know you the original, father? do you recognise the resemblance?"

Mr. Heyton started, and gazing fixedly at the picture, exclaimed,—

"It is he! it is the traveller who asked for shelter!"

At that moment Mr. Heyton felt the pressure of a soft hand on his shoulders, while a voice from behind, said,—

"That is the man—that is the mystery!"

Mr. Heyton looked round and saw that his younger daughter had arisen, and that she was again gazing at her sister with a fixed and meaning look.

"Amy, my child," exclaimed the parent, "I thought you to be asleep."

"Sleep, father? No, no; there is no sleep for me this night—no sleep for me again."

"Why, Amy, why talk you so strangely?"

"See you the picture, father?"

"I have it in my hand."

"And you know whom it is like—you know the person whom it resembles?"

"The resemblance, child, is that of the old man who asked for admittance at the door of this cottage little more than an hour ago. The likeness is life-like; there are the same dark eyes, the same grey, straggling hair, the same sharp, well-defined nose, and the same carriage of the head. Kate must be an excellent artist to have produced such a portrait."

"But know you, father, when, how, and from what copy the portrait was drawn?" asked Amy.

"Your sister has told me that she had not beheld the original of it until——"

"Hush, father!" cried Amy, "say no more."

"I have promised to tell father everything relating to this picture, sister," said Kate; "shall I tell it to him in this room?"

Amy hesitated for a few moments, and then replied,—

"Yes, Kate, yes; tell it to him here; tell it to him aloud, that I may know whether you tell it correctly."

"By your bed-side, Amy?"

"Yes; take this chair. Now, father, listen! I will cover my head with the bed-clothes while you go on with the story, sister."

Kate took her father's hand, and, placing the picture on the small table by her side, commenced the explanation.

"Understand me, dear father; the mystery of this night's occurrence, the behaviour of Ernest Morden, the fear which has seized my sister and myself, have all to do with the strange man who is represented there. Both I, and sister, father, shuddered when we heard the knock at the door; we shuddered when you gave the traveller leave to enter; we shuddered, father, when we saw him, and we shuddered when we felt that his dark eyes were fixed upon us. All that has happened this night you know already, and everything which has occurred resulted from the entrance of that man. Beautiful was the early evening, dear father, and happy were we both when gazing upon the sunlit waters, and dreaming of the years to come. Amy had not told me of the coming of Ernest, but I had guessed as much from the unwonted gaiety of her behaviour. We stood by the window of the front room, father, and gazed upon the beautiful scene before us. I was glad to see Amy looking so happy, for prior events had cast a gloom upon her countenance for some days before. Amy knows that I love her—that I love her dearly, and that I would make any sacrifice to promote her happiness. It did my soul good to see her so smiling and so merry as she was some eight or ten hours ago. We stood by the window, father, the little bird was singing in its cage, there was the rippling of the waves as they washed upon the shore below. All was still, all was summer-like, all was beautiful. How glorious did the red sun rest upon the ocean! how majestically did he sink into the gleaming waters! But when he was gone, father, when he *was* gone, and the clouds, and the breeze, and the evening shadows came, I felt a sensation of gloom, I felt a presentiment of something sad about to happen; I felt as if some dear friend had bade me a fare-well for ever. On the countenance of my sister I also remarked an expression which caused me to believe that similar emotions to mine own were felt by her. I laughed, I made merry with Amy, I drove away the heavy sensations, I talked of pleasant things—of coming joy—of future happiness. Thus passed the evening away; thus made we merry until Ernest came. Doubtless sister was overjoyed, then, and so was I, father—so was I; for I knew that his coming was delightful to my sister, therefore was it a source of pleasure to myself. Ernest, dear father, was the sun—the bright, beautiful sun; but the other—the man who asked for admittance—the traveller was the shadow—the shadow of the evening. My blood ran cold in my veins when I heard that man cross the threshold—I was not in the room at the time—I saw not who it was; but something told me whom I was to see. I saw him, father—I knew him; I saw him for the first time ——"

"The first time, Kate?"

"I had never seen him before, father."

"But the portrait—you say that you knew him."

"I did, father. To you he was a stranger, but to me he was as one whom I had been in company with before—with whom I had become familiar; and yet, dear father, I had never seen him—never heard his voice till then."

"Your words are mysterious in themselves, child," replied to old man. "But the portrait"——."

"It is that which forms the chief mystery; and yet are there other mysteries connected with it. Listen, father, and I will tell you in what manner this portrait came into existence."

"Quickly, child—tell me that quickly!"

"Nine mornings ago, father—nine mornings from this present one, I heard the strangest story that ——"

Kate was here interrupted by her sister, who arose, and placing her hand on the arm of the elder maiden, said,—

"Do not tell the story in the dark, dear Kate; do not, I pray of you, tell it in this dark room."

Mr. Heyton interfered.

"The room is not dark, Amy," said he; "we have lights, and I will fetch another candle if you wish it."

"No, father, no; candles are useless; they only throw some places into the shade. See, father—see those dark corners! what may there be lurking there, what may be hidden in that gloom?"

"My child!" exclaimed the parent, feeling a sensation of dread come over him; "what fancies possess you? what strange ideas haunt your imagination? There is no one in the room except ourselves."

"I do not know that, father; I am not sure of it."

"How shall I convince you, my child?"

"The moon is up, father; the storm has ceased. Open the window, draw aside the curtains, and let the bright moonlight look in. I shall feel safer—more secure, father, if I can see the moon as I lay."

Such was the position of the apartment in which the parent and his children now were, that from the small window a view could be obtained of the sea, and the surrounding scenery. The edge of the cliffs could be discriminated for the distance of some four or five miles, and a jutting promontory gave to view the sandy beach, and the boatmen mending their nets. Such was the prospect in the daytime, such was the scene, and such the objects discernible from that small window when the sun was up, the day bright, and the wind sleeping in its cavern-dwellings.

But it was night now; yet at night the scene, as viewed from that window, was still beautiful.

"Open the window, father; the air is close and sultry in this small room. Draw the curtains aside, and let me gaze upon the lovely moon."

Mr. Heyton rose to comply with his daughter's request. He moved towards the window, he drew the curtains aside, and then—

Suddenly Amy sprang from off the bed—rushed towards her father—grasped him by the arm—threw up the window, and wildly exclaimed—"See, father!—see, dear father, see!—there is Ernest Morden and the dark man. There will be death upon the Eagle's Altar!"

Broad streamed the moonlight on the Altar; and the strugglers, where were they? "There has been murder," again exclaimed Amy.

And with a shriek that woke up the echoes of the else-silent night, the terrified Amy fell back into her father's arms. Her eyes were fixed and glaring wildly; her mouth was open; her lips were colourless; her cheeks were paler than the pale moonlight that stepped in at the window to kiss them. In that one moment she seemed to have made a fearful transit—the transit from life to death!

" Take her—take your sister," said Mr. Heyton, as he gave the insensate Kate ; " be careful with her, be very careful ! "

" Father, would you leave me ; where are you going ?"

" To follow Frank, child—to climb the Eagle's Altar. How know you not that your brother lies not murdered there ? "

CHAPTER VIII.

THE WELL ROPE.—THE DANGLER IN THE SHAFT.

Frank Heyton was alone on the tower of the old fortress. Hitherto the moon had given him light wherewith to make a survey of his position, and of the objects around him ; but now dark clouds again began to float upwards from the sea and to steal along the sky. Another storm might come on—a storm as wild and as fearful as the one which had occurred within the last two or three hours ; what was Frank to do? There was no place in which he could seek shelter, no roof under which he could hide his head. Might he not, exposed as he was, be struck dead by a lightning-flash ; or, might not the old tower, which was already tottering to its fall, be thrown to the ground by a thunderbolt, or shattered by the fury of the elements? A stouter heart than that of Frank Heyton's would have quailed under such circumstances ; stronger limbs than his would have become unnerved. Adventurous as he was, he could not but contemplate his situation with a feeling of dread, enhanced by the memory of those mysterious occurrences which had happened within the last few hours.

How, and by what place of exit, had the phantom-form which Frank Heyton had followed, disappeared ? he had pursued it through the castle, he had touched its garments and its foot when ascending the tower staircase, and he had seen its dark figure on the steps above him, when the stones gave way beneath his tread. The figure could not, if mortal, have sprung from the battlements ; their height was such that to have leaped from them would have been sure and sudden death. He could not have escaped by climbing down the outward wall, for that would have been a feat which a cat or a monkey would have hesitated at attempting to perform. There was no visible door by which any other part of the building could be entered, and the top of the tower itself was isolated from every surrounding structure. Where then could the figure have gone, how had it disappeared.

Frank Heyton thought—was the figure which he had pursued, that of the person whom he had taken it to be—was it Ernest Morden ? a little reflection caused him to doubt this having been the case. When he struggled with Ernest on the cliff, the sailor wore only his common dress—the close-fitting dress of a navy lieutenant ; but the individual whom he pursued into the castle, seemed to have been attired in a loose dark garment ; then, if he had not been mistaken, he had observed the fugitive to have grey hair, while the hair of Ernest Morden was of the richest and deepest brown. Suddenly, it occurred to his mind, whether he had not made a mistake, and whether the person whom he had pursued was not that same man—that weather-beaten traveller who had applied for admittance at the door of his father's cottage. Frank called to mind the strange sayings of the idiot boy ; he remembered that Archy during the pursuit had spoken of the fugitive as ' the dark man.' Could it be, that this conjecture was the right one ? No, it was impossible ! for age and tottering infirmity had characterized the applicant at the cottage-door, but quick had been the movements and fleet the feet of him to whom Frank Heyton had given chase. Old age could not have made such speed, the toil-worn traveller could not have used such alacrity.

Yet, as Frank Heyton meditated, and as he recalled the several attendant circumstances to his mind, it seemed wondrous and unaccountable to him that the figure should have fled from him as it had done, if it had not known him—if it had not been afraid of being overtaken. Had he not distinctly challenged it—had he not challenged it by the name of Ernest Morden? and had it not turned round its face, had it not glanced backwards, had it not thrown a look at its pursuers, and then fled onwards as before? If the fugitive had not known Frank Heyton, he would have stopped, and have desired to know what business he had to pursue him; had he not feared Frank Heyton, he would not have made such efforts to escape being captured. After all, however, he might have been some robber—some common thief, whose guilty conscience caused him to fear pursuit of any kind, and whose hiding-place by day might be among some of the old ruins which environed, and which adjoined to, the old castle. This conjecture, however, did not solve the mystery; for, allowing the fugitive to have been a robber, how had he contrived to disappear?

Had the fugitive been that of living mortal—was that a human being which Frank Heyton had followed? Frank shuddered as he put the question to himself. Could breathing, substantial flesh and blood, have vanished as this form had vanished? could it so suddenly have passed from sight as this figure had passed? No, it could not be; no solid thing of human shape could have disappeared so strangely—so miraculously. "It was a phantom—an ignis fatuus," exclaimed Frank Heyton; "and I have been deceived in following it hither."

So Frank Heyton thought; but he could not drive away from his mind the fact—the strong fact, that he had touched the foot of this fleeting form, and found it to be solid—that he had grappled its garments with his fingers, and had heard them rustle in the breeze which haunted the lonely ruins. "Can sight, touch, and hearing, all have deceived me?" he exclaimed; "can every sense have played the traitor?"

When, after being silent for a few minutes, he replied to his own interrogatory, by exclaiming—

"No; one sense was true—one sense did not deceive me. Sight, sight—there was sight! Archy beheld the man whom I pursued—Archy saw him as I followed him over yonder green sward—as I pressed upon him when he crossed the drawbridge on which his foot marks still remain!"

But now came another question—where was Archy himself? He had accompanied Frank to the castle-entrance; he had stood by his side at the bottom of the first staircase. Loudly did Frank Heyton vociferate the name of the idiot-boy; loudly did he call upon him to come to his assistance, and to render some description of help. Every call was in vain. The name of "Archy" was echoed and re-echoed by every tower, wall, and buttress of the old ruin; but there was no reply—no Archy responded to the call.

"This is fearfully strange," ejaculated Frank; "whither can Archy have wandered? God grant that nothing evil has happened to that poor boy."

And now the heavens put on a still more lowering aspect. Large drops of rain began to fall upon the old moss-covered battlements, and to patter in the moat below. Low in the distance sounded the hoarse rumble of the thunder, and afar upon the sea were dark shades cast by the lurid clouds which were congregating in the heavens above. Frank Heyton saw the impending danger, and became desperate as he reflected upon his own folly in having scrambled up the ruin as he had.

No coward adventurer, however, was Frank. He saw that something must be done—some way of escape contrived; and he forthwith fell to work to do the best that was in his power. Once more he advanced towards the top of the staircase by which he had ascended, and once more he wondered at his own daring in having reached the height where he now stood.

He looked downwards, but saw no means by which he could descend. There was the wide gap where the steps had broken away, and that gap was too wide for him to attempt at spanning it. Lower still, he could perceive other steps, but they wound down spirally, and to have dropped upon them would have been a fearful risk; for the sudden weight would, in all probability, have detached them also from their holdings, and have toppled them and their burden into the depth and the darkness below.

Frank Heyton was still peering downwards through the gloom, when something met his eye which caused him to start, and he exclaimed joyfully,—

"Ha! the discovery is made—the mystery is explained ; I have not ventured the ascent in vain !"

What was that which Frank Heyton saw?

Below him, in the wall which formed one side of the stair-case, and turning off from the very next step which over-hung above the gap, he descried a small door-way, so hidden in an angle that he had not observed it before ; and so obscured by the gloom of the place, that, from the position which he occupied, it was but barely discernible.

A gleam of triumph lit up the face of the adventurer. No doubt had he that within that door the figure which he had followed had sought concealment ; though, upon reflection, he remembered having seen the form stand upon a more elevated portion of the stair-case. His resolution was taken. Once more he uplifted his stained weapon in the faint moon-shine ; and once again he started in pursuit of that object which had eluded him in a manner so mysterious.

There is an old proverbial couplet which asserts that—

> " His step must wary be, and slow,
> Who hath a slippery path to go."

And so Frank Heyton found ; for the steps quaked beneath the super-imposed weight, and the crumbling mortar fell in dust upon the ruins beneath. Those steps were of more recent erection than the other parts of the castle ; for the mortar which the Normans used was of a kind which endures when the stones which it cemented have mouldered and decayed. The Keep of Rochester Castle, for instance, furnishes an exemplification of the truth of this fact.

Cautiously and gingerly had the adventurous youth to retrace his steps down the hanging fragment of the old stair-case. Clutching with his fingers every projection in the wall, he at length stood upon the step which was above the gap—the one step which alone intervened between himself and destruction.

Frank had not mistaken ; there was a door in the wall—a small, low door-way, through which he squeezed himself with difficulty. Having done so, he cast a hasty glance around, and discovered that he was in a dark chamber of very limited dimensions, which received no light except that which passed through a narrow loop-hole in one of the walls. He uttered an exclamation as he passed through the door-way, and uplifted his weapon, expecting to encounter the individual whom he had followed through the ruin.

The pursuer was disappointed. There was just light sufficient to make the walls of the apartment visible ; but that apartment was tenantless, except by him who had so recently intruded.

"Still he must have entered here," said Frank to himself, " in no other place could he have effected concealment."

But the dust lay thick upon the stone floor of the vaulted chamber ; and, at every foot-step which the intruder took, he brushed away the webs of spiders, and frightened birds from their nests, causing them to fly away through the narrow loop-hole.

" There must be some other door—there must be another way of exit from this place," said Frank ; and he at once proceeded to a careful examination of the stone walls by which he was surrounded. No door, however, could he find ; none, save that by which he himself had gained entrance.

Again did Frank Heyton find himself at fault. He had made sure that his search was at an end, and that the fugitive was at length within his grasp ; but he now gave himself up to despair, for there was nothing to indicate the proximity of him whom he had sought, and though he had obtained shelter, he saw no means of escaping from his unenviable situation.

The adventurer was still engaged in his examination of the room, when his eyes were suddenly attracted by an object in the centre of the apartment.

" What is this ?" cried Frank, as he approached the object, and scrutinized it narrowly.

From the vaulted roof of the chamber depended an old rope, which was passed over a pulley. There were two holes in the floor, and through these the rope was also passed.

"What can this be intended for? And why is it hanging here?" said Frank; as, stooping down, he examined the floor through the holes in which the rope passed to some place below. To his surprise he found the central portion of the floor to be of wood; and, setting to work to examine it more accurately, he discovered the existence of a trap-door, which after some difficulty he forced open, and at once looked down into a dark abyss beneath. Into this abyss the rope descended—in the darkness below it hung.

"Ha!" exclaimed Frank, "I have it! By this rope he escaped, by this rope he has descended to some secret hiding-place!"

Elated by his discovery, the adventurer was also about to make a descent by the same means which he supposed the object of his pursuit to have adopted. Frank had taken up his sword preparatory to this bold adventure, when his eye caught sight of something which caused him to waver in his intent, and which also excited his astonishment.

Stealing in through the loop-hole, a bright ray of moonlight fell upon the old rope as it hung in the silent gloom. How great was Frank Heyton's surprise to behold the rope covered with mould—with damp green mould, which apparently had grown upon it for many years, the rope during that time having been allowed to hang undisturbed.

"This is strange!" cried Frank, "can I, can I be mistaken?"

He stretched out his hand—he encircled the rope with his finger; when he removed his hand, a spot was left where no mould was visible. The certainty flashed upon him—no hand but his own had touched that rope within the last hour—probably not within the last twelve months.

Once again, then, was Frank Heyton foiled. He had congratulated himself on having discovered the means by which the mysterious one had disappeared, and he now found that he was as far off as ever in his knowledge of how that disappearance had been effected. Chagrined at the disappointment, and nettled at having been so completely outdone by the individual whom he had pursued, he threw himself upon the floor in one corner of the chamber, and drooped his head, moodily on his chest.

The rope which had excited Frank Heyton's expectation so sanguinely was one that had been used in former days for the purpose of hauling up water, bread, and other provisions from the lower apartments of the fortress. Such contrivances were very common in the days of the Normans, and are often to be met with in their architectural remains as presented to our inspection at the present day. A similar contrivance is still visible in the old fortress of Norwich, another in one of the towers of Carnarvon; and another, in that superb ruin, the Keep of the Castle at Rochester.

It would be idle to attempt an analysis of the feelings of Frank Heyton's mind as he meditated by himself in that gloomy place. Every occurrence of the night passed in review before his half-closed eyes; and though but a very limited portion of time had elapsed since his leaving the cottage in pursuit of Ernest, yet so many had been the adventures he had met with, and so multitudinous had been the thoughts which had agitated his mind, that it appeared to him as if days must have rolled by to have allowed him time sufficient for the performance of all in which he had been engaged.

"It is a dream," he soliloquised, "it is some fearful dream, and I cannot now be awake."

Just at that moment a cloud passed before the moon and the light suddenly ceased to fall through the loop-hole. So solemn was the momentary gloom, that on the return of the light Frank involuntarily started to his feet, determined at all hazards to attempt an escape from a place beset with so many horrors.

For a moment, Frank Heyton paused, a thought struck him. He again bent down and peered into the blackness of the deep hole, in which the rope swung to and fro when agitated by his hand.

Nothing could he see—nothing discriminate. He heard the other extremity of the rope knock against some solid body at a great depth, and that was all. Again he arose, and again he meditated.

"If it be strong enough," said he, "if it be but strong enough."

He pulled the old rope with his main strength, but it yielded not to the effort ; he shook it smartly, and to his satisfaction found that it still retained somewhat of its primal strength.

"Joy, joy!" he exclaimed, "it is not rotten—it will bear my weight."

He clenched the old rope firmly and swung himself to it—swung himself over the gloomy abyss. It did not give, it did not stretch to its hanging weight.

Once more Frank Heyton stood upon the floor of the vaulted chamber. After musing for a few moments he took his resolve.

"To remain in this place," said he to himself, "were folly. Some risk must be dared, some plan of escape attempted ; I will descend by this rope ; to what place it may lead me I know not, but at any rate I shall be nearer the ground, and shall have a better chance of gaining the outside of the fortress."

He took the rope in his hand—he gazed once more down the darksome depth. Few could have dared the attempt which he now meditated ; few are there whose eyes would not turn dizzy, whose brains would not reel, whose frame would not shudder, and their blood fail from trickling in cold streams through their veins, were they compelled to perform so dreadful a task. The adventurer was ignorant of what horrors that gloom beneath him might contain ; he knew not into what place he was about to descend. Others might have hesitated and conjured up 'unreal mockeries' to increase the hazard of the attempt. Not so Frank Heyton. Boldly he clasped the rope, boldly he swung himself over the murky pit, and boldly he directed his eyes upwards to the pulley from which the rope was suspended ; for, in good truth, he feared to look downwards lest he should be suddenly overcome and fall headlong—it might be, fathoms deep.

Cautiously he entwined himself around the rope, cautiously he let it glide through his hands. Downward—downward he slid. The gloom increased and thickened around him ; the rope still swung loosely in the depth beneath.

Hark! was that a snap? horrible supposition, should the rope break before the landing was gained !

Frank Heyton still gazed upward—still slid downward, cautiously and slow. The depth seemed more than he had supposed it to be ; so faint was the light that he could not discern the objects amongst which he swung.

Downwards—downwards—downwards still !

Hist! surely there was a snap, the sound of something giving way, of something breaking from its hold above.

Frank Heyton was brave, Frank Heyton was not one to make his own phantoms ; still he slid downwards, and still he placed hand beneath hand, then hand beneath hand again.

Frank Heyton was brave, but what was that ?—what meant that sudden jerk ? Ha! there was no mistaking its meaning, no building on false hope. The rope was breaking—had broken. It creaked—it gave—it yielded ! One by one the suspended man heard the strands above him crack asunder, and at every snap he knew —he felt that he was by that much nearer to his doom. His very heart quailed within him ; the perspiration exuded from every pore, sweat-drops stood in clusters upon his brow, he had no hand by which to dash them off—by which to keep them from falling into his burning eyes. Crack again went the old rope, snap went another strand, and another jerk told its fearful tale. Ha! what was the man to do? how was he to save himself from the death which yawned and opened upon him ! Crack, crack ! the strain is great. Snap, snap ! and two other strands are gone. There cannot be many more, there can be but a few threads remaining— a few threads between the life of fear, and the fearful death !

The young man did not reproach himself—did not blame himself for his hardihood in having undertaken the terrible venture. He thought of his sister—on that gentle, that loving Amy ; visions of times gone by flitted with rapidity before his sight. These were visions that made him long to live—these were thoughts that made life then appear all precious to him. Snap went another strand, and fearfully loomed the threatened death upon him. Oh ! if he could then start aside—if he he could but now effect a landing ! He dangled his legs in the gloom ; he made one sudden effort to throw himself, he knew not where, and then—the rope broke—the man fell ; there was one dull heavy sound, and all was perfect stillness !

CHAPTER IX.

DEATH LOOKING AT THE MAN IN THE GLOOMY DUNGEON.—WHAT WAS SEEN, AND WHAT WAS FOLLOWED.

FORTUNATELY for Frank Heyton, the fall was not one which deprived him of life. After lying stunned for some twenty minutes, his senses returned to him, and he became conscious of his position. He cast a look upwards, but a faint glance—a dusky mellowed light was all that he could discern. There was nothing by which he could judge how far he had fallen ; though from the little inquiry which he had received, he concluded that his fall had only been through a short space. How far above him the top of the tower might be, he knew not ; and at what depth he lay he had no means of telling.

Endeavouring to rise, he found that his limbs were sore, and that he had sustained some slight bruises in his fall. To his great joy, however, no bone appeared to be broken, and he could limp, though he was unable to walk or move with his wonted alacrity.

After gazing upwards till he was tired of so doing, Frank Heyton set himself to work to reconnoitre his position ; height there was none, and whatever objects there were around him, were perfectly invisible to his sight. He felt the floor upon which he had fallen, and found it to be composed of stone, though in one spot, immediately beneath the well-hole, the stones seemed supplanted, and their place supplied by a quantity of loose rubbish. On some of this rubbish, the back of Frank Heyton had found a resting-place.

From looking up at the light, and examining the structure of the floor, Frank passed on to ascertain the character and formation of the apartment in which he now found himself. In his present situation, eye-sight was useless, and he, therefore was compelled to supply its place by exercising the sense of touch. Groping his way round about, he found his new lodgings to be of very circumscribed dimensions, with walls of rough stone, which felt damp as he laid his hands upon them. Greatly to his relief, he at last discovered a door ; but to force this door open, was more than he had strength to perform. Vainly did he exert himself—vainly did he put forth all his remaining strength to push open this portal, that he might thereby effect his exit. The door was apparently locked or bolted on the other side, and all his efforts to break it open by the exertion of main strength proved futile, and resulted in disappointment.

From using his arms, hands, and feet, Frank proceeded to make use of his voice. He called loudly, but no one replied ; he hallooed for assistance, but his own voice sounded strange to him in that strange and caverned place.

Frantic and excited he again had recourse to his feet and hands, with them he beat upon the door and kicked it till he could move his legs no longer. Mad folly ! the door remained firm as ever, and no one seemed to hear the uproar, none approached the prisoner to set him free.

Foiled in his attempts to open the door, or to obtain assistance, Frank Heyton immediately applied himself to the discovery of other resources. The exigency of the situation seemed to develope fresh energies—energies which till then he had never dreamed of possessing. There was the hole in the room above, the hole through which he had fallen. If he could but reach that, if he could but grasp the margin of that, the means of escape might be at once attained. This, however, was not so easily to be accomplished. He endeavoured to reach that roof, to touch it with the tips of his fingers, but although he outstretched his arm to the utmost, and stood on tip-toe till his feet ached, his fingers wandered in darkness, and the roof was higher —higher still. What was he to do? he searched the chamber for some box, or plank, or barrel upon which to stand, but none such could he find, no article of any description met his touch. Making a further examination of the walls, he found that the roof was arched like that of the chamber above, and that it arose in dome fashion, the hole through which he had fallen being in the centre of the dome.

Here was a terrible predicament, here was an awful situation. Well might Frank Heyton now reproach himself for having ventured on the rope; well might he give himself blame for having descended without having a knowledge of the place to which he was about to descend. His situation now was, if possible, worse than it had been, when on the summit of the tower he feared the coming storm, and marked the gathering of the thunder-clouds in the distant sky. What if the lightning now struck the building? what if it became shattered beneath the stroke, where would Frank Heyton be then? who would even find him? the ruins would immolate him in their fall, and build a mausoleum over the place of his tomb ; but, none— no, not even the raven nor the vulture would seek him out, and those who loved and cared for him would mourn for his return in vain.

He listened, but no sounds of voices nor of footsteps fell upon his ear. If the wind were howling without, he heard it not; if the thunder rolled along the heavens, he knew not that the storm was exercising its fury.

And again he laid his hand against the wall of his prison, again he found that wall damp to his touch, and in some places covered with oozy slime. He rapped his knuckles against the stone work ; but it was firm and solid, returning a dull sound to the feeble stroke.

" Merciful God ! " he exclaimed as he fell upon his knees, " into what place have I descended, in what place am I know? Is it—is it some fearful dungeon—some lone, forgotten dungeon, buried deep in the bowels of the earth? and am I, too, buried, never to look upon the sun again? Oh! agony! agony! agony! "

With the actions of a maniac, Frank Heyton now beat his head against the stony wall. The air of the place was foul, and he feared speedy suffocation. He clutched every salient point with the wild grasp of a convulsed and torture-wrung person ; he dug his nails, into the interspaces of the stone flooring, and caused his hands to bleed in vain attempts at breaking open the door. Exhausted, powerless, without hope, without aught to inspire consolation, he threw himself upon the pavement of the cell, and resigned himself to that which he supposed would inevitably be his fate, starvation, asphyxia, death !

Moments passed, but they were those moments which produce the effect of years —moments which appear to lengthen out into hours, and to be of ceaseless duration. And again, as when he clung to the rope—again, as when death loomed upon him before, the visions of his boyhood—his bright, his dreaming, his once-pleasant boyhood, floated before the prisoner's eyes. Beautiful figures which had haunted him in his early day-dreams came back to taunt him now ; fairy forms which had flitted by his side in the stilly summer evenings, came back to taunt him now ; imaginary sounds of the music of bees, and birds, and happy things, rang in his ears, and came to taunt him now. No longer looked he upon death as something remote—something which he knew must come, but would not arrive yet—no, already had he and death shaken hands—already did he fancy that he heard the foot-fall of death in the dungeon by his side. A dizziness and stupor came over him, his nerves vibrated sensibly, the whole place seemed in motion, dancing fires frisked before his eyes, and the noise of bells and cymbals sounded in his ears. He gasped, he turned faint —sickly faint, and again he fell upon the stone flooring, motionless and insensate.

The place into which Frank Heyton had fallen, was a chamber situated beneath the fortress, and intended for the storing up of provisions in case of a siege. By means of the rope, articles of any description might have been hauled up to those

who were above ; and, in the centre of this dungeon, a quantity of loose and mouldering rubbish concealed the entrance to a deep and capacious well.

Time elapsed, but whether it had been minutes or hours, Frank Heyton knew not. Once again his senses returned to him. He lifted his hand to his brow, but so cold and clammy felt his own skin to his touch, that he drew his hand back again, as if he had found himself in contact with a corpse. He endeavoured to take a deep respiration, but his chest seemed as if bound down with leathern thongs, or under the pressure of a heavy weight. There was a creeping sensation of his extremities, as if worms were crawling over his limbs. The feeling of suffocation became still more unendurable, and his mouth was parched to perfect dryness.

"Great heavens !" he mentally ejaculated, "this is—this must be death ! What is the phantom which I have followed here ?"

Hope was gone, the prospect of escape was gone, life began to fade from the eye —to grow dim and dream-like in the distance. Gone were the fairy visions—forgotten the days of the once-bright past ! Frank Heyton resigned himself to his fate, and fell upon his knees to die as a man should die—bravely, on the field of battle—calmly, on the bed of death.

Shapes and shadows—shapes and shadows, dim and gloomy flitted before the eyes of the hopeless man. They were not shadows of this world, but of the next— the fearful, spirit-daunting next.

His head droops, his heart beats slower, feebler, fainter. And was he to die— he who had risked death to save a sister's honour ? Alas ! who was there to save him ? Who was there to interpose between him and death ?

He must die !

Hark ! a sound—a sound of a distant foot-fall. The dying man heard it. He started at the sound. Again—again he heard it ! He became maddened with joy. He crouched—he listened. Ha ! the sound was more distinct. There was the tread of feet, the measured tread of some one advancing cautiously. Nearer and nearer the sound came—nearer to the prisoner in his cell—the dying man in his dungeon. Frank Heyton endeavoured to rise, but his limbs failed him ; he made an effort to cry out, but his tongue adhered to his palate, and the cry died away in his throat. What, if the person so near should pass on—should fail to enter the dungeon—should, unknowingly, leave the captive to his fate ?

Again burst the perspiration from Frank Heyton's brows, and his forehead burned beneath his touch. His agony was more intense than it had been within the last hour, and hope and fear mingled as they now were, constituted the most exquisite of tortures.

List ! list ! was the man departing ; were the footsteps becoming more remote ?

No, they approached, they came onward ; already were they in the very vicinity of the dungeon.

Now was the moment of anxiety—now was the crisis of fate.

Ha ! the foot-steps were near—quite near ; they came to a pause behind the very door of the vaulted cell. Bolts were drawn back—rusty bolts which creaked and whined in their unwillingness to be disturbed.

"Joy ! joy !" thought Frank Heyton ; but his limbs were paralyzed ; his tongue refused to speak.

The door grated upon its hinges—it turned back—it opened. A man appeared without, holding a lantern in his hand.

The man gazed upon the prisoner, and Frank Heyton uttered a faint cry.

Ah ! there was no mistaking him—there no confounding that man with any other person. Frank Heyton knew him at once—knew him at one single glance. It was the phantom which he had pursued—the traveller who had gained entrance to his father's cottage.

And the dark man seemed to recognize the prisoner. For one moment he gazed, then started—drew back—closed the door, and spoke not.

"Mercy ! mercy !" shrieked Frank.

But the bolt—one bolt only was shot to ; yet that bolt excluded the prisoner from the world without.

"Mercy ! mercy ! leave me not here to die !"

The footsteps sounded in the distance—they grew fainter—they were lost.

One vigorous effort, and Frank Heyton started to his feet. That light, that one gleam of the lantern had revealed a prize which had hitherto escaped his search.

Groping his way towards one of the angles of the dungeon, he laid his hand upon a wooden beam which rested against the wall. It was of some weight, and he had before passed it over as constituting some part of the vaulted chamber. His hand closed upon it with a nervous grasp ; he exerted his feeble strength, and lifted it from its position. Valiantly he advanced towards the door, he shook it, but the bolt was firm.   Aloft he raised the beam ; with frantic force he dashed it against the door.   Again—again—again he repeated the blow. The hinges groaned, the wood-work crashed and crumbled at every stroke. Would it never yield ? was the material too firm, the carpentry too good ?

Once more—once more ! Ha ! it gave —it gave ! another stroke, and the bolt flew from its fastenings, the door swung back with a start.

" Victory ! victory !   Freedom and life are won !" shouted Frank Heyton, as he flung down the beam, and rushed out from the gloomy dungeon.

He found himself in a passage—a narrow passage, where light was not.   The air, however, felt cooler and fresher to him than that of the place which he had just quitted.   His blood again ran freely through his veins, owing to the excitement occasioned by his recent exertion.   His mind brightened, despair fled away, hope revived, and lived again.

But where was Frank Heyton now, whither was he to direct his way ?   All was darkness, all wore the appearance of continual night.   Was he daunted ? No ; for though he was a prisoner still, he experienced the delight of not being limited to space, of having somewhere to roam, some new discoveries to make.

Cautiously he stole along the passage, and presently he found himself in a large apartment.   Feeling round the walls, he met with another passage, down which he bent his way, reckless of whither it might lead him.   He listened— no sound could he hear ; he strained his eyes—no glimpse of light could he discern.

Onwards he went, and now he stood in a large room, which, apparently, had pillars that supported the roof.   Overhead was an opening, through which he looked up and saw the moonlight streaming down an old shaft.   How pleasant was the sight !

He paused,—he had made up his mind to attempt climbing one of the pillars, and escaping through the opening, when he suddenly thought that he heard footsteps behind him.

He turned round, but all was gloom ; yet in that gloom he fancied that he could discern some darker figure flitting in the darkness.

Ha ! had he found the phantom again, was it so near him ?

He rushed forward, and perceived something to pass into the passage which he had just traversed.   He followed it—he stretched forth his hand, and in his grasp was flesh—warm flesh—flesh that was not his own !

" Speak !—tell me who thou art ?

PART VIII.

CHAPTER X.

THE SOLITARY STUDENT.—AN ALARM AT MIDNIGHT.—THE INEXPLICABLE
OCCURRENCES.

THE reader having been thus far introduced to the family of the Heyton's, and having been made acquainted with the mysterious events which occurred to that family on one single evening, must now for a short time take leave of Amy and her friends, to be presented to new characters in a new scene, accompanied by an increase of mysteries.

It was night—the same fitful, stormy, moonshiny night on which the events detailed in the former portion of our story occurred.   Broadly swooped the silver beams over forest, field, and fell—over grass-green glade, and leafy, sombre foliage.   Here and there the sky was visible between the clouds, and little joyaunt stars could be discerned looking down at the earth, twinkling with merriment in their own excelling brightness. The storm had passed away, the thunder cloud had vanished from the sky; the ocean was again sparkling with its myriads of ripples, as they danced beneath the light of the high-throned, pale-rayed moon. Borne on the gentle breeze, the odours of a thousand beautiful flowers floated along; grass, trees, and flowering shrubs, all alike exhaled some delicious scent—all alike contributed to make the air redolent with perfume.

Such was the time; the place has yet to be described.

Follow with your mind's eye, reader, as we point out to you that scene where the following events occurred. Picture, first, to yourself the moonlight night; then the quiet, serene beauty of the earth as it appeared after the cessation of a storm. Come, it is an easy matter to accomplish—easy to point out to the imagination a broad landscape, gently undulated, and made up of meadows, corn-fields, and groups of clustering trees, with cattle sleeping in the pastures, and a dreamy stillness thrown over the whole. There! Do you not behold it? Has it not a visible existence to you? This much accomplished, and all that follows may be readily delineated by the same magic power.

High up, on the side of a gentle rise, stands a quaint old mansion, fashioned after the style of a baronial hall. Though it is placed at a considerable elevation, and overlooks much of the surrounding country, yet, as you may perceive, it is half hidden from the view of the distant spectator by being embosomed amidst thickly-clustering trees, their dense foliage screening it alike from the sultry sun and from the northern blast. Let us pass onwards, and, journeying through the wood, approach nearer to the olden, noble-looking building.

Be wary! The wood is dark and closely set. Those same trees nodded their heads to the breeze a century ago; they swayed their boughs to the breath of spring and groaned in the storm of autumn, when not one of the many living millions of this land had his being or had known his birth. Gently, then, through the old wood, for the whispering leaves seem to tell weird-like stories—stories of those who once trod these shady paths, but who have long since mouldered away amid dust and darkness; their shouts of laughter ceased—their names forgotten as if they had never been.

And now the ancient mansion stands before you. It is a large, extensive pile, built perhaps before the reign of Richard Cœur de Lion, or before the first of the Plantagenets sat on the throne of England. There are its turrets and battlements, its twisted chimnies and its projecting bows. Still, as in the olden days, the moonlight looks down upon the court-yard wide, and the turret lone; now, as then, the shadows of the frowning towers lie lazily upon the ground, and the nests of the sparrow and the marten cling to the mimic macchiolations. This is one of those castellated residences, of which so many specimens still remain to tell of the wealth and magnificence which characterized our ancestors in an age that has long past away.

How quiet and solemn is everything connected with the old mansion. No shouts of noisy laughter are heard within; no bustle of moving attendants, no ringing of bells, no patter of feet upon the oaken staircases. One sound alone breaks the sleeping stillness; it is that caused by the old fountain, as the water wells up out of the dolphin's mouth, and silvered by the moonbeams, trickles into the moss-coated basin beneath. The heron, on its one leg resting, stands dozingly beside the old pond; while on the silent water floats the queenly lily reclining in her vessel of broad green leaves.

Nothing to tell of noisy life, nothing to disturb the wrapt imagination of the gazer as he contemplates the majestic building. No lights flit before the windows, no doors are heard to creak upon their hinges. Deep and dark is the shadow thrown by the old porch, and deeply sunken in the wall are the narrow casements through which the pale light now passes into the ancient dormitories. The footstep of the armed guard clanks no longer in the court-yard; nor does the mailed warrior now bend his knee on yonder terrace to kiss the hand of his lady love, and to receive from her that pledge of her affection which was to be borne in his bosom to the distant battle fray. Such a scene had been witnessed in the days of old at Warrenton Hall, and such scenes were connected with every pleasant recollection of the antique building as it had been in the time of its early glory.

All is calm, and quiet, and dream-like; the long crimson curtains have been drawn aside, and through the bay-window the moonlight now streams into the tapestried hall. Warder—if warder there is—now slumbers at his post; and beauty lulled to sleep by innocence, is reposing in the olden chamber.

See you that oriel window? It was at that the lady looked out and waved her scarlet scarf to her gallant knight, as mounted on his destrier, he parted from her to seek a noisier scene; it was at that she fell upon her knees every night to pray Heaven that it would protect him in the contest; and at that she strained her eyes every morning waiting and watching for his return. The window is now closed; the knight has mouldered to dust upon the field whereon he fell, and the lady, her eyes having grown weak with weeping, rests in the chapel holy, with her scarlet scarf still clasped in her once soft and lily hand.

No more the clarion rings; no more the banner flies. The steed rests in his stall; but he bears no warrior in his saddle. Beauty still strolls upon the terrace at eventide; but her fingers play not with a helmet's plume, nor tighten the jesses of her favorite falcon.

Warrenton Hall stands grim and gloomy; time has tampered with its architectural beauties, crumbled a battlement here, and thrown down a cornice there. The ivy has crept over the buttress, and the moss has grown in the figures on the dial-plate. Generations have been born and lived, laughed, talked, wept, and died within its walls. In the same court where the child pursued the butterfly, that very child, grown up to man's estate, mounted the steed, and again, in the after-time, hobbled on the oaken crutch. The picture of the child, and the picture of the old man, hang together in the long gallery; and the garrulous housekeeper will tell you—"That was Sir Robert when very young; and that, Sir Robert just before he died;" but, ask her who Sir Robert was? and she shakes her head and tells you "that she does not know, but believes that he was a great man who once lived in the hall!"

It is the midnight hour, and the inhabitants of the antique mansion have retired to woo sleep in those chambers, quaint and gloomy. Heavy is the slumber of stalwart manhood, and gentle and calm the sleep of youthful maidens; dreams of ambitious struggles haunt the couch of the one, and pictures of love and happiness flit before the eyes of the other. Stand beside the bed of man or maiden and watch if the slumber be easy, if the countenance be calm, and you have then the best opportunity for learning the inward workings of the heart.

Stilly is the hour, and silent is the scene; but look you! what means that strange appearance.

In one of the windows of Warrenton Hall is seen a light; it burns steadily, fixedly; it has burned there for the last hour.

Why is the light burning in that one apartment when all seem to have sought repose, and when no sound, no step is heard?

There is a large library—a large, gloomy-looking library; rows of dusty books stand on shelves affixed to the walls, and busts in bronze of the classic authors of old, arranged upon marble pedestals. Between the book cases hang ancient suits of armour, the rust having long since taken up its abode on the helmet, the cuirass, and the coat of mail. Grimly does some sword-dented casque loom through the darkness, the spider having woven its web from the chain to the plume and sought a retreat in one of the eye-holes of the fallen vizor.

Not a sound disturbs the silence of the old library; so profound is that silence that, if you listen, you may hear the bubbling of the oil in the burning lamp, and the low hum of the spider as he busies himself in weaving his web.

The lamp stands upon an antique table! and at that table is the form of a man.

He is a young man, whose age, apparently, does not exceed one or two-and-twenty, he has a pale, thoughtful countenance, his hair is clustering and dark ; while, from beneath his massive and projecting brows gleam a pair of black eyes, which glitter with radiance more than common.

Watch you how he is wrapt in thought over that old, worm-eaten book ! His lean and hollow cheeks rest upon his hands, and his elbows find their support upon the oaken table.

The student has no companion in his study, no one with him in that gloomy library, nothing to tell him of the world without, except the solitary moonbeam which steps through the stained window and lazily extends itself on the table beside the student's arm.

That student is none other than the brother of Ernest Morden. It is Gervase Morden whom you recognize in that pale-faced, bright-eyed individual.

Let us look over his shoulder and see what book it is which so thoroughly enchains his attention.

It is one of those weird and wondrous works, relating to the most mysterious of all philosophies—that of the Rosicrucians. It tells how Rosencreuz travelled to the east, and won from the Arabian cabalists those secrets which he taught to his followers under a solemn engagement that they were to keep them secret for one hundred years. It tells also of other mysteries ; how Albertus Magnus was known to possess the secret of human life, and how by the might of his wisdom, he clothed his garden in winter with all the beauty and vegetation of spring. In the same book you may read how Arnold de Villeneuve was said to have the power of conferring immortality ; and how Bernard of Treves found out the secret of alchemy at the hour in which he died. But the passage over which the student pores, tells the following story :—

" Lone and disconsolate was the Emperor Maximilian when the cruel hand of death took from him his wife, the beautiful Mary of Burgundy. Her image was ever present to her mind ; the recollection of her gentleness ever besieged his thoughts. Through the bright days of summer, and the chill nights of winter, he missed his early idol ; and, sad unto very sadness, was the heart of the chivalrous emperor. To Heidenberg of Trittheim—Heidenberg, the renowned sage, he went,—' Canst give me back her whom my soul adoreth ? O necromancer !' ' Nay, I cannot give thee her back,' replied the sage ; ' but, if thou so wish, she shall arise to comfort thee.' ' Let me behold her, good Heldenberg—let me behold her, and thy reward shall be beyond whatever thou desireth !' Then did Heidenberg of Trittheim appoint a place and an hour for the emperor to meet him again. Maximilian came ; and, in a small dark room, the spirit of her whose memory he loved rose again to his sight. The gentle Mary stood once more before the lord of her soul, and the emperor stretched forth his arms to clasp his beloved one to his breast. But Heidenberg of Trittheim had told him that his wife could not be given back to him, seeing that she had passed into the other world, but that he should behold her according to his desire ; so, as long as the emperor gazed, Mary of Burgundy showed herself unto him, but when he endeavoured to touch her with his hand she passed away into nothingness."

Gervase Morden closed the book.

" And have I read truth ?" he exclaimed, " come back the dead to haunt the earth again ? No ; it is a delusion—it is the vagary of the insane mind. The belief in ghosts is the belief of the vulgar—is the belief of those who imagine only, but never reflect."

At that moment Gervase Morden turned his eyes towards the door of the room, and suddenly started.

Slowly was the door opened ; and, in the dusky gloom, the student perceived the outlines of a human figure gazing at him. Apparently this figure was clothed in garments of a light colour, and the countenance was of a pallid hue.

Gervase Morden felt awe-struck. The book which he had been engaged in reading seemed to swim before him ; the nature of its contents had predisposed his mind to be acted on by fear, for it was but during the last five minutes that his thoughts had been employed on the subject of spectral appearances, and the feasibility of individuals receiving visitations from the inhabitants of another world.

"Not a limb—not a finger could the student move; all power seemed to have been suddenly reft away from him, like as though he had been stricken with paralysis in the chair whereon he sat.

And still he gazed, still he fixed his eyes upon the half-open door and the figure standing there. He could not speak, he dared not withdraw his gaze.

The door opened wider, the figure stole across the library towards him.

He shuddered; a sensation of coldness came over him, and involuntarily he closed his eyes.

At the moment when he closed his eyes, the lamp, which had been gradually burning dimmer and dimmer, gave one flicker and then went out. The faint, yet sharp, spirting sound with which the light expired, caused the student again to start, and to be terrified by that which was nothing in itself.

And once more he started; for he heard the tread of the figure on the floor beside his chair, and suddenly a hand was laid upon his arm.

"Mr. Morden!" said a faint, hollow voice.

The student moved not; but a cold shiver again passed over him, and the perspiration burst out upon his brow.

"Mr. Morden," said the voice again, "are you asleep?"

Gervase started; for there was something familiar to him in the tone by which he had been addressed. Opening his eyes, he perceived a female standing by his chair, whose form was but dimly visible in the moonlight which now alone lit the apartment.

The hand which was laid upon his arm held him with a tremulous grasp, and he could hear distinctly the quick, fitful beating of a heart which was not his own.

"Mr. Morden, are you awake?"

"Good Heaven!" exclaimed the student; "is it you, Martha? Why did you steal into the room in such a manner?"

"Pardon me, Mr. Morden! I was afraid—I thought you were asleep—I—you looked so dreadful—so very dreadful."

"But what want you with me? Why are you not a-bed?"

"I cannot—I dare not go to sleep—I—"

"Martha!" cried the student, rising up from his seat; "what has happened to you? Why is your face so pale? and why do you tremble?"

"I—I cannot tell you in the dark. Have you no other light, Mr. Morden?"

"None; but here is the moon. Come to the window, and I will draw the curtains wider apart."

Gervase Morden led the young woman to the window; and, having placed her on a seat in the recess, he threw aside the crimson drapery, and allowed the moonlight to stream through till it illuminated the apartment with a pale and silvery splendour.

Martha Watson was the confidential servant of the lady of the mansion. She was a young and delicate-looking person; but, to the acute observer, there was much that was disagreeable in her countenance. Her features being sharply cut, her eyes restless, and her lips thin, pale, and drawn inwards, as if submitted to continual biting by their owner.

The student and the maid seated themselves before the window, and involuntarily turned away their eyes from gazing into the recesses of the room, to look out upon the court-yard and the distant park which surrounded the hall.

"Why have you come here, Martha, and what is it that agitates you?"

"I—I am afraid—I—you will forgive me, Mr. Morden, for coming to disturb you?"

"Yes; but why have you come, and why do you shake and tremble? Have you been frightened?"

"Yes, and —— Hark! did you not hear a step?"

"Not I. Who should be moving about the house at this time of night?"

"I know not; but—but—are you sure there is no one in this room but ourselves?"

Gervase Morden glanced round the apartment almost expecting to behold some mysterious form seated in the chair which he had just vacated. So excited had his imagination become, that the very suits of armour which were suspended against the walls seemed to move as he looked upon them. The plumes on the ancient casques appeared to nod, and the banners hanging up over the book cases to wave, as though agitated by something which passed suddenly and quickly along the room.

"There is nothing, Martha. Wherefore have you come here? why have you sought me?"

It was some moments before the young woman could summon up sufficient strength to reply.

"I have come to consult you, Mr. Morden," said she, "I thought that I should find you up, but when I opened the door, you stared at me so strangely, that I was afraid to say a word, and I hardly dared to enter the room."

"But what have you to say now, Martha?"

"I have come to ask you—to ask you whether you believe in ghosts?"

"In ghosts! Why so strange a question?"

"Because, Mr. Morden, it is my belief that there are ghosts in this house, though I am afraid to tell my lady that I think so."

"She would treat it as very ridiculous, if you did. Tell me, however, what reason, have you for entertaining this belief?"

"Because I have heard them."

"Heard what?"

"The—the—"

"Is it of the ghosts you are speaking?"

"Yes; I am sure there are some in this old house, though what they want here, I do not know. I have come to you, to ask you if you are aware of any one having been murdered, or died in any strange way in this hall?"

"Good heaven, Martha!"

"I thought you would be likely to know, Mr. Morden."

"I! But—but why such a question?"

"Because, Mr. Morden, if there had been, then——"

"If there had been what?"

"A murder!"

"Well?"

"Then there would be a cause at once for what we have heard and know."

"Are there, then, others besides yourself, who are infected with this foolish fancy, Martha?"

"It is not a fancy, Mr. Morden; we have all heard, and we all believe."

"But who are all? and what have all heard? and what do all believe? and what, in fact, is the meaning of that which you are now talking about?"

"The noises, Mr. Morden—oh! those noises."

"What, good Martha—what noises?"

"I will tell you, Mr. Morden—I will tell you as well as I can. Our sleeping rooms, you know, are in the gallery, which opens at the foot of the staircase that leads to the great hall. It is very dismal to sleep so far away from the bed-chambers of the family, and I feel it the more, too, because, before my lady was married to Sir Thomas, I used to sleep in the same room with her; and, indeed, I ought to be nearer to her now, considering the service I——"

"But the noises, Martha?"

"I am coming to them, Mr. Morden. We sleep, as I have said, in the long row of rooms in the gallery that turns in from the grand staircase. Well, nine nights ago—I remember the night very well, for it was on a Tuesday, and my poor old mother had been to pay me a visit in the afternoon. She is a good old soul, and is very fond of a strong cup of green tea; so that when she comes——"

"I thought, Martha, you had something to tell about noises and ghosts?"

"Yes, Mr. Morden, and I'm telling you about them now. Nine nights, as I have said—on the night of the afternoon that my mother came to see me—I, and Margaret, and Cicely, and Susan, had all gone to bed. We had been up rather

later than usual, and as Susan and I sleep together, we fell a talking after we had gone to bed. It wasn't about anything very frightful we were talking, for it was only about Susan's getting married—which, you know, is soon to happen. Well, from talking about that, we began to talk about Mr. Newland, —Mr. Newland, you know, is the young man whom Susan intends to make her husband. Then we talked about Mr. Newland's father, and then how Mr. Newland's father had once seen a ghost, and then——"

Martha broke off abruptly in her relation.

" And what then, Martha ?"

" Do not speak too loud, Mr. Morden. After Susan had told how the old Mr. Newland had seen a ghost, we —we —"

" You did not see one, too, did you ?"—" We heard one.''

" What ! a ghost ?"

" Yes ; but do not say so here—not in this dark room."

" To your story, Martha.   What was it you heard ?"

" First of all, I must tell you that there are store-rooms behind our sleeping apartments, and that those store-rooms are always kept locked up.   Well, when all was quiet, and when everybody had gone to bed—I had heard you leave the library and go up in your own room—there was a noise, all of a sudden, like—like —"

" Like what, Martha ?"

" Just like as if some one was walking in the rooms behind us.   We could hear the footsteps quite plainly ; and then, presently afterwards, we heard somebody breathe.   Neither Susan nor I could say a word to one another, but we both heard, and we both thought, that robbers had broken into the hall."

" Were the sounds very distinct ?"

" So plain, Mr. Morden, that we could both swear to there being footsteps, if we were on our death beds ; and then, what was more horrible than all, we could hear the very breathing of some one in the room behind us."

" And what else happened during the night, Martha ?"

" Nothing.   In the morning we told what we had heard to Mr. Thwaites, the steward, and he unlocked the doors, and examined the store-rooms ; but it did not seem as if any one had been in them, and nothing had been moved from its place."

" Well, Martha, doubtless, after all, your fright was occasioned by some one of the male servants having stayed up later than yourselves, and had occasion to go along the gallery in which your sleeping chambers are situated."

" No, Mr. Morden, it was at the head of our bed we heard the noise, and it is the foot of the bed which faces the door that opens into the gallery."

" Still it must have been one of your fellow-servants moving about at that late hour."

" I and Susan have asked them all, Mr. Morden, and they all say that they were a-bed and asleep."

" It was a strange occurrence, certainly ; more especially so, because both you and Susan heard the same noise.   And what is the conclusion that you come to, do you believe it was a ghost ?"

" I don't know what to think or say ; but there was one strange thing—one very strange thing."

" And what was that, Martha ?"

" It was told me by Mr. Richard, the butler, and he took both me and Susan to show us the place —."

" What place, Martha, and what was that which was shown to you ?"

" Why, there is a very long passage, you know, which runs along from the bottom of the kitchen stairs to the wine-cellars.   Mr. Richard had been to the cellars, in the evening, to fetch some wine, and coming back, he happened to spill some of the oil out of his lamp upon the stones in the passage.   Being in a hurry, he could not step to clean it up, but sprinkled a handful of sand over the place, and there left it.   The next morning he went down again, and the very first thing he saw, was the print of a man's foot on the sand, which he had sprinkled down."

" His own, probably.   What more likely than that he should have trodden on the sand after he had sprinkled it on the oil spot ?"

" Yes, Mr. Morden, we thought of that directly, but we soon found it to be a wrong conjecture."

" How made you that discovery ?"

" The foot-print was not the size of one made by Mr. Richard's foot."

" Indeed ! but might it not have been the foot-mark of some one other of the servants ?"

" We tried it with all, and it was smaller than any.   Besides, no one but Mr. Richard, and Sir Thomas himself, could have got into the passage."

"How are you so sure of that ?"

"Because it is only Mr. Richard, and Sir Thomas, who have keys to the door, and Mr. Richard had locked the door, and taken the key with him to his own room."

"And is there no other way of entrance ?"

"None."

Gervase Morden meditated for a few moments, and then inquired of his still trembling companion,—

"Are you sure that the foot-mark was not that of Sir Thomas himself? May he not have gone down to the cellar after Richard left ?"

"We thought of that, and we got one of master's shoes, and measured it, but master's foot is rather larger than Mr. Richard's; so, it is very plain, that it could not have been him."

"There is mystery in this matter, Martha," said the student after a pause; "so long as there was nothing more than the mere sounds, which you and Susan believe you heard, the affair might be resolved into a mere instance of the fallaciousness of our senses, but when the more extraordinary circumstance of the foot-mark, which you speak of, is brought into account, it becomes an occurrence which demands some investigation. Why have you not told me of all this before, Martha, and why have you chosen to tell the story now ?"

The young woman trembled, and hesitated in making her reply. "Because, Mr. Morden, we have all heard those sounds again."

"When Martha, when ?"

"To-night."

"Say you so ? tell me what sounds you mean."

"We were sitting in the kitchen before the fire, talking over what I have just told you. All of a sudden we heard the tread of somebody in the passage which leads to the wine-cellar, and which runs along under the stones of the kitchen. We all became quiet, and the tread of feet in the passage beneath us could be heard distinctly. It was some time before any of us could move, but when we did, we ran immediately to seek for Mr. Richard, and finding him in the garden, we told him of what we had heard. He came back with us and tried the passage door, but it was locked as he had left it, and the key was in his own pocket. There was nothing to be seen and nothing more to be heard. Mr. Richard took some more sand and strewed it over the middle of the passage. Then locking the door, we all returned to the kitchen."

"And heard you anything more ? "

"Nothing."

"Then why have you come to me ? "

"Oh, I daren't have come up to the library alone, Mr. Morden. We have been sitting in the kitchen for the last hour talking over the circumstance. Not one of us dare go to bed, and Mr. Thwaites says, it would be proper to wake master and tell him what we have heard, because some one might be robbed and murdered, and we should get all the blame. But Mr. Richard advised that I should go up and consult you before we went to master's bedroom; so, as I was afraid to come by myself he offered to accompany me."

"And where is he now ? "

"Waiting in the passage outside."

Gervase Morden arose, and walking to the library-door, called to the butler that he should enter.

"Your pardon, Mr. Morden for disturbing you; but we did not know exactly what to do."

"Tell me Richard — what is the meaning of all this disturbance in the house ? "

"God knows Mr. Morden what it all means, but it's very certain that some one is moving about the old hall whom nobody knows anything of. If our ears have deceived us, our eyes can't have done so; and then, there's not one of us but has heard or seen something."

" And what is your guess about the cause of this mystery ? "

" Guessing's no use, Mr. Morden. I've lived in Sir Thomas's family for six and thirty years, and during all that time, I've never been so puzzled in my life, as I have been during the last fortnight. Iv'e heard tell a good deal about ghosts in my younger days, but I never gave much credit to such tales, and I don't thoroughly understand how ghosts can do the things that people say they have seen them do. I've talked to people who have sworn plump down that they'd looked at ghosts with their own eyes, and I've known others who have said their solemn oath that they'd heard ghosts speak ; but I never knew anybody to say that they'd seen a ghost's foot-mark, there's Cicely, our cook, and Martha here, who say it must be a ghost that is walking about this house ; they may think so, but I cannot think with them, and I shouldn't be half so much frightened if I thought it was nothing but a ghost after all."

" Nothing but a ghost—oh, Mr. Richard, how dreadful ! " ejaculated Martha, who by no means approved of the butler's heretical opinions on the subject.

" Am I to understand that you wish me to render you my assistance in the unriddling of this mystery ? " demanded Gervase Morden.

" We did not know what to do, Mr. Morden ; and that is why I proposed that Martha should go and see if you were still up, and ask your advice about the matter. Very likely you have read in some of those large books how such things happen, and what ghosts really can do, and what they can't."

The student smiled.

" My knowledge on the subject, Richard, is slight—very slight indeed ; but I also have somewhat to tell you concerning this very mystery about which you are now puzzled."

" Mercy on us, Mr. Morden ! you haven't seen the ghost, have you ? " ejaculated Martha.

" I have seen nothing," replied the student, " though I have heard more than I know well how to account for."

" Heard, Mr. Morden ? mercy me ! have you, have you !

" Peace, Martha. This library you are aware adjoins the great hall. Four nights ago while sitting at the table reading, and after the turret clock had struck the hour of twelve, I heard footsteps in the great hall. As the circumstance was of unusual occurrence at so late an hour, I felt somewhat surprised. Hearing, however, nothing more than the sound of footsteps, I came to the conclusion that some one belonging to the house had business there, and therefore I gave no further thought to the matter,"

" Mercy on us, Mr. Morden ! that must have been the ghost you heared," exclaimed Martha.

" Did you say that it was after twelve, sir ? " asked the butler.

" The turret-clock had struck about half-an-hour before."

" Then it could not have been any of the household, sir ; for Mr. Thwaites keeps the keys of the great hall, and takes care to see the doors locked every night ; and Mr. Thwaites, to my certain knowledge, has been in bed every night by eleven o'clock for the last three weeks."

The student deliberated for a few minutes, and then said,—

" Well, there is something which is at present inexplicable in these occurrences. I will go with you down stairs, for I should much like to examine the passage leading to the cellars, as it is probable that some one may be concealed therein."

" Oh, do come down, sir ! Cicely and Susan will be so glad to hear what you have to say about the ghosts," exclaimed Martha, crouching beside the butler, and accompanying him and Gewase Morden as they descended to the lower apartments of Warrenton Hall.

CHAPTER XI.

THE EXPEDITION TO EXPLAIN A MYSTERY.—HOW FOOT-MARKS WERE SEEN AND NO
FEET TO MAKE THEM.

ROUND the fire-place in the large antique kitchen of the old mansion, were gathered some ten or twelve persons, conversing together in low voices, and nestling near to one another as if each was afraid of being suddenly snatched away by some grim and grisly form. Men and maidens were alike congregated together, each having some anecdote of wonder to relate, and some mysterious circumstance to add to the general stock of marvels.

"I never could go to sleep in this house again, not if master gave me fifty guineas to do so," ejaculated Susan, the maid who had heard the sound of foot-steps in the store-room.

"Nor I either," added Margaret, the pretty pantry-maid. "Goodness gracious me! the old house is dismal enough of itself, without having ghosts and all such like creatures walking about the passages in the middle of the night."

"So say I," subjoined Cicely, the stout cook. "Who knows but what one of the ugly things may come and take us out of our beds while we are asleep?"

"Lor' Cicely—good mistress Cicely, don't talk like that," ejaculated the game-keeper's wife, "if I thought such a thing as that would ever happen, I shouldn't get a wink of sleep again as long as I live."

"Well, it's very likely; there's unlikelier things than that come to pass," rejoined the cook. "It's what I'm now expecting every night."

"And do you go to bed at all?" inquired the gamekeeper's wife.

"Why how can I stay up? There is work enough for me to do while the sun is shining, and when the stars come out it's a blessing to go to bed; for its about the only happiness that I know of now."

"Still to think of ghosts coming into one's bed-room, especially when one's eyes are shut, and one can't see what they are going to do with us—oh, its perfectly awful!"

The gamekeeper jogged his wife by the arm, and with a smile upon his coun-tenance, said—

"There's no cause for you to be fearsome, Joan—you that have got a husband to take care of you; but it's something frightful enough to these poor women who have to sleep all alone by themselves."

A burst of merry laughter followed the gamekeepers's remark; but silence was soon induced, through the sound of footsteps in the distance.

"Hist!" cried Susan.

In a few minutes Gervase Morden entered the kitchen, accompanied by Martha and the butler. Rising up from their seats, each of the servants made an obeisance to the pale, dark-eyed student. Then gathering around him, they immediately proceeded to narrate the cause of their alarm, and to request that he would assist them in elucidating the true nature of the mystery. Turning towards the porter who stood aloof from the rest, he desired him to approach.

"Jeffery," said the student, "who has passed through the hall gates to-night?"

"Not a living body, sir, since the hour of ten."

"And who entered or departed then?"

"Miss Ismay, sir, returned from the park, along with Robert, her servant."

"Have the gates been locked since then?"

"They have."

"Are they locked now?"

"Yes; and here, sir, you may see the keys. The key of the great gates, and the key of the hall-door have not been out of my hands since ten o'clock."

"That will do, good Jefferys. And now about the noise which I believe many of you are said to have heard within the last few hours—whence did the sound appear to proceed?"

"From the passage which leads to the wine-cellars, and which runs beneath the kitchen where we are now standing."

"How many of you can positively say that the sound was heard by them."

"All of us, Mr. Morden," replied a stout burly man, who, dressed as a gardener, stood holding a mattock in his hand; "we were all in the kitchen at the time, except Jarvis and Mr. Richard, who had gone out to the court-yard a few minutes before. I'm not a man to be easily frightened, nor I don't say that I'm frightened now, but there did sound something very terrible-like in the tread of those feet; they weren't like the steps of a christian."

"That, indeed, they weren't, as we all know," remarked the laundry-maid, "I never heard a tread that was anything like it."

Gervase Morden surveyed the faces of the group assembled around him, with a view of ascertaining whether any trick was being played by some one of the party; there was nothing, however, in the countenance of any one of them to justify or strengthen this suspicion.

"It is my impression," said he, after a pause, "that people are concealed in this house for some bad purposes, and it behoves us accordingly to do our best towards searching out the real secret of the matter. Collect, therefore, what arms you have at hand, and you, that are bold enough to do so, may accompany me in the investigation which I am about to make. Richard, have you the key of the door opening into the cellar passage?"

"It is here, Mr. Morden, and it has not been out of my hand during the last four hours."

"That is well; now tell me, what other entrance is there to that range of apartments, now used as wine-cellars?"

'None other, sir; at least, none that I know of."

"And you are sure that the door was locked when you went down some two hours ago?"

"Quite sure, sir; I had to open it with my key, and Jarvis and Jefferys here, saw me do so."

"Well, what did you find?"

"Nothing, sir; there was nobody to be seen, and we could, hear nothing stirring."

"You then locked the door after you?"

"I did, and the key has been in my hand ever since."

"That will do. Now then, take you a lantern, Jefferys, and you, Richard, go before with the key. There is a gun hanging up over yonder door, give me that down, and let the gamekeeper bring his also. I intend that the cellars shall be searched thoroughly; those, therefore, who wish to be satisfied on the subject, may join with me in the search, while those who are too timid for the venture, may stay here and wait till our return. Are all ready?"

In a single minute every male domestic had armed himself with a weapon of some description, the gamekeeper seized his gun, the porter grasped his blunderbuss, the gardener shouldered his mattock, and Richard, the butler, equipped himself with one of the long spits, which he took down from its resting place, over the mantle-shelf. The expedition was arranged, and the departure was just about to take place, when it received a check from the female servants, who, one and all, solemnly protested that they would not be left in the kitchen by themselves. After much squabbling and contention, it was finally settled that they also should form a portion of the party, and follow as a kind of rear-guard, to act only in an emergency. Pokers, broom-handles, and ladles, were now called into request as implements of female warfare; and thus armed and appointed, the whole body set forth to discover the cause of their alarm. Gervase Morden led the way, while immediately behind him followed the old porter, and the butler with the key clenched firmly in his hand.

Arriving at the bottom of the staircase, Morden paused, and the butler pointed out to his notice a quantity of sand, which he had strewed outside the cellar-door.

"I did that," said he, "that we might see in the morning whether anybody had opened the door; and I have again sprinkled a good bucket of sand over the middle of the passage, to mark the footstep of any one who may tread upon it."

"Wisely done, good Richard; and, as you perceive, the sand which is outside the door has remained without foot-mark. Let the key be now placed in the lock, and be every one prepared to follow me to the cellars."

Agreeably to Morden's order, the butler stepped forward, and was about to unlock the door, when his arm was suddenly grasped by the gamekeeper.

"Hist! Mr. Richard," he exclaimed in a loud whisper, "I thought I heard something move inside. There! did you not hear it?—did you not hear the tread of a foot?"

"Mercy, me!" cried the cook, turning very pale, "if it should come out upon us all of a sudden?"

"Quick, open the door!" commanded Gervase Morden.

The butler attempted to turn the key in the lock, but just at that moment, a faint sound was heard to proceed from the inside of the passage and his fingers became suddenly paralysed. Morden pushed him aside and turned the key. The door opened—the passage was dark and silent.

Again, at that very moment, he fancied that he heard the tread of a foot in the darkness before him.

"Give me the lantern," he cried, "let the cowards stay behind, let those who are brave follow me."

Animated by his example and urged by one common impulse, the whole of the party rushed into the narrow passage. Nothing was there to be seen, no ghost or living form presented itself to their view.

"Let us on," cried Gervase Morden, "every cellar shall be searched, every avenue examined."

"And onward he hastened, followed closely by the butler and the gamekeeper; on a sudden he came to a pause.

For a single second Gervase Morden ceased to breathe; then holding up the lantern, he pointed with the muzzle of his fowling-piece to the sand which had been strewn upon the floor, and uttered the one word:—

"Look!"

Each of his companions cast a glance in the direction indicated, and immediately their cheeks became of a deadly paleness.

There were the foot-prints of a man in the loose sand.

"Let us follow," exclaimed Morden. "Some one is within this place, and there can be no escape."

He was again about to rush onward when he was detained by the grasp of the gamekeeper.

"Look you, Mr. Morden," said he, "the foot-marks are not those of a man who has fled that way; they are those of some one who has come up the passage."

"Right," cried Morden, "then they must have gone out at the door."

"If you recollect," observed the gamekeeper, "the sand outside had no mark of foot upon it."

Gervase Morden started.

"This is strange!" he exclaimed. "Here is evidence that a person has passed up the passage, and here, also, is evidence that those steps have not been retraced, for the toe of every foot-mark is directed this way. Yet, is no one to be seen, and the door has not been opened. What path, good Jeffreys, can have been taken?"

"There is no path, sir—there is no other door; we are between stone walls; there is only the entrance to the cellars before us, and the door-way by which we came in, at our backs. Let us leave this place, for God A'mighty only knows what sort of things there may be round about us."

"No, Jeffreys, no," returned Morden, "I will not quit it, until I have unravelled this mystery."

"But the foot-marks, sir—"

"Well, Jeffreys—well?"

"Some one, you see, has come up the passage, and not gone out at the door, yet, nobody is to be seen, and the sand shows that the same person never returned by the way he came."

"It is as you say, Jeffreys; nevertheless, we will make an examination of the cellars, for there may yet be some one hidden there."

The old servant drew back.

"Why do you flinch, Jeffreys—why will you not follow me?"

"If it was anything human that had to do with this matter, I would; but, I wouldn't go any further now for the worth of a world."

"Tush, man! Give me the lantern. Ghosts, or house-prowlers, it matters not which, they shall find that they have not terrors to deter me from seeking them out."

Morden's arm was grasped by the butler.

"Do not be too rash, good sir!" he implored; "we are convinced now that it is no man like ourselves, who has been in this passage to-night. Let us wait till to-morrow, and then we can tell the whole affair to the chaplain."

"Unhand me! let me go!" exclaimed Gervase Morden. "Am I to be fooled by the fear of something which I have not seen?"

"For the love of heaven, sir, be not so rash!"

"Cease! unhand me! Follow those who dare."

Gervase Morden freed himself by a vigorous effort, from the grasp of his terrified companions; his eyes flashed fire; his cheeks were flushed; he was resolute in his determination to unravel the mystery. For one moment—for one single moment only he paused, to examine the priming of his fowling-piece; then, placing the lantern between his arm and his chest, he made one step forward to pierce the darkness before him.

One step, and then he paused.

A shriek—a shrilly, thrilling shriek, sounded through the old mansion. Gervase Morden heard it, and so did every one of those who stood in the passage with him."

"Good heaven! what was that?" he exclaimed.

All turned pale—paler than they already were; the hair on the head of some began to bristle and stand on end, while others in their fright let the weapons with which they had armed themselves fall from their hands.

"Hark!" cried Gervase Morden—"hark!"

Scarcely was the word out of his mouth before the shriek was heard again. This time, it was less loud than it had been before, sounding like the exclamation of a person overcome by and fainting under some sudden fright.

"God help every one of us!" ejaculated poor old Jeffreys, dropping on his knees, and clasping his quivering hands.

"Up, man—up!" cried Morden—"whence did that sound proceed?"

"From Miss Ismay's room, I think," replied one of the servants.

"And was that Miss Ismay's voice?" cried Morden.

"I think so—I—Lor' have mercy! Suppose the ghost should have got into her bed-chamber!"

"And have run away with the young lady," added another of the frightened throng.

Gervase Morden dashed through the group, rushed out of the passage, and sprang up the staircase, which led to the upper portion of the hall,

"Follow!" he cried, "follow, if you would prevent robbery and murder!"

CHAPTER XII.

THE MAIDEN IN HER CHAMBER.—GERVASE MORDEN AND CONSTANCE ISMAY.

THE shriek of woman heard in the hour of midnight, when everything around is quiet, and sleep has won the world to its soft embrace, has a fearfulness about it, which causes it to thrill to the heart of the hearers, and immediately to awaken their sympathy and their apprehension. More fearful by far is such a sound, when heard in a large and lonely house, echoing through vaulted gallery, and bannered hall, coming upon the silence of the night, like some herald from the dead, to warn the listeners in their beds, of the approach of unexpected woe —to tell them of death itself—to notify that a soul has departed to its bourn in another land.

Awful is the midnight shriek! it tells of things which the ear listens to with horror. Perhaps the miser is dying, and his heart is torn with a sudden anguish, as his fingers, involuntarily, loosen their grasp of the money-bags, which he loved so well; perhaps, a faithless maiden repents her at the moment of her dissolution, that she has wronged one who loved her, and was deceived. It may be, that an old man—some aged child of earth—with his grey hairs clustering o'er his brow, wakes suddenly in his bed, to find the life of time fading from him like a dis olving view, and the future eternity looming upon him with all its horrors. Then, perhaps, he lifts his paralysed arm; then, the visions of a man-hood spent in crime, flits before his eyes; then, he prays for the first time, to a God whom he ever despised—and then, one loud and piercing shriek breaks from his lips, telling the sadsome story that a mortal, like ourselves, has recoiled on his bed of death, from meeting with that Judge, before whom we shall all in like manner have one day to appear. Terrors, such as these, are told by the midnight shriek; therefore, does it ever bear fearfulness in its sound, and ever cause the blood to trickle coldly in the veins of the affrighted hearer.

The shriek which Gervase Morden heard, while standing in the haunted passage, was heard by others as well as by himself. It was heard by that trembling throng which cowered around him; it was heard by the stalwart knight, and his loving lady, while the eyes of both were closed in slumber; it was heard by the aged crone, startling her from her toil-won sleep; it was heard by the maiden, whose dreams were then of bowers lonely, and of lover's vows; it was heard by the priest, as he knelt in the pale moonlight, to offer his midnight prayers; and it was heard by the watchman at his post, causing him to turn sharply round, and to whistle to his dog, who, with head averted, and ears erect, was listening for a repetition of the sound.

As Gervase Morden reached the long gallery, immediately above the great hall, he was met by Sir Thomas Warrenton himself. The knight was stricken with sudden fear, on seeing the armed group, which now followed the student, and stepping forward, attired, as he was, in his night-clothes, he exclaimed,—

"Morden—Gervase Morden, what was the meaning of that cry?"

"Heaven knows, Sir Thomas. My belief is, that it proceeded from Miss Ismay's room."

"From Miss Ismay's?"

"From her, herself."

"God keep us! What can be the matter!"

Without pausing, or wasting more time in conjecture, the whole of the party rushed at once along the gallery, towards a small staircase at the further extremity. Ascending this, they stopped before the door of a chamber, and listened attentively.

No sound, no breathing could be heard.

"Did I not say so?" observed one of the servants to another, "did I not say, as we came up the stairs, that we should find her taken away?"

Sir Thomas rapped the door with his knuckles.

"Constance!" he cried, "Constance, dear, are you awake?"

There was no answer.

He repeated the application, and listened again. Faintly and low, a moan, as if of some one in distress, fell upon the listener's ear.

Sir Thomas started.

"Good God!" he exclaimed, "surely, Miss Ismay is dying!"

Without further preliminaries the door of the lady's chamber was thrust open, and Sir Thomas, followed by Gervase Morden, and the female attendants, entered the apartment.

"Bring hither the light, Morden."

The lamp was uplifted, and its rays fell upon the bed. On that bed lay the apparently inanimate form of a young, and beautiful maiden. She had fallen backwards, as if from the sitting posture; her black and shining tresses, streaming over her neck, and a hand of the most exquisite sculpture, rested upon the coverlet, the fingers being expanded, as though still indicative of sudden fright.

"Constance! Constance Ismay!" cried the knight, as he took the hand of the maiden in his own and shook it gently.

The call was in vain. She, who should have answered to the name, neither heard nor replied.

"What is to be done?" exclaimed Sir Thomas, "I am fearful that she is dead already."

Gervase Morden advanced, and laid his finger on the wrist of the pallid girl.

"She is not dead," said he, "something has occurred to frighten her, and she has fainted. Let her receive attention immediately, and she will speedily recover

Sir Thomas directed the female servants to use their utmost endeavours in restoring the insensate maiden to consciousness. Then, turning to Morden, he drew him aside, and in a whisper, said,—

"What do these people mean? they seem to have had some knowledge that something was about to happen!"

"They have been troubled with foolish fears, Sir Thomas; and the least occurrence is sufficient to create alarm in their minds."

"But the time, Morden, what is the time?"

"It is just past midnight."

"Midnight! And you—these people—why do I see you up, and armed, as some of you are?"

"I will explain presently, Sir Thomas; but would it not be better that you should order more special assistance for Miss Ismay?"

"Right, Morden, right. I will go and let Lady Warrenton know of this matter, while, do you see that the physician be sent for with all speed."

Sir Thomas Warrenton sought the chamber of his lady, and quickly apprised her of the misfortune which had happened to Constance Ismay. In vain, however, did the lady desire to know for what reason the maiden had fainted, that being more than Sir Thomas himself knew. Lady Warrenton was a woman of very little sensibility. The natural emotions of her soul had been repressed in infancy, by the chilling forms of, what is falsely called, "good breeding." She had figured at court; and had, long ago, learnt the lessons which fashionable society inculcates, and demands that its votaries should know. To her it seemed strange, indeed, that a young lady should faint in her own bed-chamber, when no admirer was by to catch her in his arms, and be won by the winningness of beauty in distress.

"Gracious me! what is the girl fainting for, and at this hour of the night, too?" exclaimed the lady.

"That is more than we yet know, my dear," replied her husband, "I am afraid something fearful has happened while we have slept."

"Something happened, Sir Thomas?"

"Yes; the whole house seems awake, and every servant is armed with a weapon of some description."

"Armed, Sir Thomas—armed? Are they coming to kill us? Merciful heaven! what an act of Providence! Doubtless, the vile wretches meant to murder us in our sleep, and we have been saved by that cry from Constance."

"Tush, tush, my dear!" replied the worthy knight, "our serving-people seem as frightened as yourself, and by the looks, which they throw at one another, it seems to me that they have heard or seen more than we wot of this night."

"Gracious—Sir Thomas! What is there for them to see or hear? Where are my maids? Where is Lucy? Let her come to me immediately. I will sleep no more this night."

Lady Warrenton retreated hastily into her dressing-room, where she was quickly joined by her waiting-maids. Many and various were the questions which she put to the affrighted girls, but no explanatory reply could she obtain. Perceiving, at length, that Lucy, and her companion, were both fully attired, she demanded, in a voice of astonishment,—

"What is this I see! Why have you not been to bed?"

The maids trembled, their faces turned pallid, their answers died away upon their tongues.

"Lucy, is this how you should behave to your mistress? Tell me, instantly, why have you not retired to your bed this night as usual?"

"The ghost, my lady; we were afraid of the ghost."

"Ghost! Ghosts in Warrenton Hall! Whence this silly nonsense, hussies?"

"Indeed—indeed, my lady, it is no nonsense. Every one of us is certain that something is moving about the hall, and it was more than any of us could do, to go to sleep. Besides, my lady, Richard and Mr. Morden, have seen the prints of the ghost's feet."

"Mr. Morden, indeed! Is he, too, fostering this ridiculous nonsense in your minds?"

"Oh, my lady, he has ——"

Ere the maid could finish her sentence, Sir Thomas made his entry into the dressing-room of his lady, and inquired, in a hasty manner, if she were ready to accompany him to the chamber of Constance Ismay?

"Have you heard, Sir Thomas, who is at the bottom of all this hubbub?"

"Not I, my dear; I have, as yet, had no time to make inquiries."

"Lucy has just told me, Mr. Morden, it seems, has been playing his part in the creation of this disturbance."

"Mr. Morden, my dear, has doubtless been as much frightened as ourselves."

"Aye! but Sir Thomas, he has put the belief into these girls' heads, that the hall is haunted, and that ——"

"Pardon me, my lady," interposed the waiting-maid, "we all knew of the ghost before a word had been said to Mr. Morden about the matter."

"Ghosts," cried Sir Thomas, "ghosts, indeed! What are ye talking about, girls? Stuff and nonsense! Keep such things to yourselves in the kitchen. Come, Lady Isabel, let us to poor Constance, she is, probably, come to herself by this time."

Leading his lady by the hand, Sir Thomas passed out into the gallery, and directed his steps towards the chamber of the affrighted maiden. As he gained the short staircase, which led to the upper tier of sleeping-rooms, he was met by Gervase Morden.

"Tell me, Morden—how is she—is she better?"

"They say, she is fast recovering, Sir Thomas, but I have not had time to make constant inquiry, and I must now go to give more peremptory orders that they use despatch in fetching the physician."

"How, Morden! has not the physician been sent for yet?"

"In truth, Sir Thomas, I gave the order some ten minutes ago, and I have just heard that it has not been obeyed, through a reluctance in every member of the household, for stirring abroad till day-light."

"Pretty behaviour, in all conscience, for serving-men! Go, give my word to the varlets, that every one of them shall be discarded on the morrow, if the mission be not executed immediately. Let half-a dozen of the knaves go together, if they fear to stir out by themselves."

Morden departed to see this command was obeyed. Sir Thomas, accompanied by his lady, ascended the staircase, and entered the chamber of Constance Ismay.

Surrounded by numerous attendants, and attired in a robe—which, fitting as it did, loosely to the figure, gave the symmetry of the fair form which it enveloped, more visibly to the eyes of the spectators—sat Constance Ismay. She was seated in a chair by the bed-side; those who stood about her, being busily engaged in fanning her cheeks, and holding various scents to her nostrils. The Lady Isabel approached, and pushing aside the attendants, exclaimed,—

"Gracious me, child! what has happened to thee, that every one in the house is so alarmed?"

The maiden looked at her questioner with a vacant expression of countenance. Then, turning away her face, her eyes wandered round the room, and seemed to rest for a moment upon one particular portion of the opposite wall. Suddenly, her lips opened, the blood again retreated from her cheeks, and a tremor seemed to pass over her frame.

Sir Thomas took the place of his lady, and kneeling before the maiden, he clasped her hand gently in his own.

"Constance, good Constance, let us know what distresseth thee. Are you ill, or have you been frightened?"

The maiden, again uplifted her head, and looking at the knight for a single instant, shuddered, and then cast herself forward upon his neck.

"Make way there!" he cried. "There is something connected with this room, which prevents her from rallying. Lights, there! lights in the library, immediately! Lady Isabel, I beg you will accompany us thither."

Thus saying, Sir Thomas lifted his fair burthen in his arms, and preceded by the servants with their lamps, took his way of ou tthe chamber, along the gallery, and down the staircase, till he came to the library door. Here he was again met by Gervase Morden.

"Ha! have the rogues gone off on their errand? have they gone to fetch the leech?"

"They have, Sir Thomas; and a hard task it has been for me to compel them to obey. They have departed, saying each his prayer as he left the threshold."

"'Tis well, Morden; and now, we crave your skill in bringing my fair ward back to her wonted senses, until such time as the man of medicine arrives. Surely, a studious youth like yourself, should be acquainted with some remedies that may be speedily made use of in a case like this."

"It is no bodily affliction, Sir Thomas, else might recourse be had to the lancet."

"How say you? Nothing bodily! Why, look you, man, are not those eyes ready to start from their sockets? and have not those limbs been quivering for the last ten minutes, as if they were stricken by the ague? Talk you of using the lancet! Methinks those wan cheeks would be the better for more blood in them, than for any that might be taken out."

"It is as you say, Sir Thomas, she must not be bled. The air is close and sultry to-night. Let her be placed near the window, so that the breeze may blow upon her face."

"Aye, now talkest thou like a sensible man! Place her by the window, as thou sayest. When she hears the wind whisper in her ears, and feels the cool air play upon her cheeks, she will come too without a doubt. Look you, Morden, saw you ever cheeks whiter than those—cheeks that are wont to be so rosy?"

Gervase Morden did look; he gazed upon that beautiful face—that exquisite bust—that faultlessly symmetrical form—and never had he seen sight more enchanting—never had he beheld a figure of more perfect beauty. Constance had been placed in her chair; her female attendants knelt beside her, and behind stood Sir Thomas himself, patting the wan cheeks of the maiden, with the affectionate fondness of one who had a heart wherewith to feel, and a nature that could stoop to sympathize, as well, as stand firm to confront the stoutest danger. The gentlest feelings are often hid beneath the burliest form; and those, who are the roughest in outward appearance, not unoften prove the first to shed the tears of pity—to lend the hand of help. Especially is it the case, that among the stout-hearted sons of England, may be found men to whom fear is a thing unknown, but who have all a woman's weakness, when repentant error pleads in their ears—supplicating sorrow kneels at their feet—or, gentleness in adversity sues for commiseration and assistance. Goodness is ever brave; the coward is not only mean in his cowardice, but necessarily mean, also, in every other of the qualities pertaining to humanity. Those who then looked upon Sir Thomas Warrenton, and watched the tenderness which he displayed, might have fancied him to be the parent of the tender being before him, rather than her mere guardian and lawful protector.

All were silent in the gloomy, old apartment. The lamps gave but a flickering light, which served only to reveal the pallor of the countenances of those who stood around. Every eye was fixed upon the maiden—every mind was busily engaged in wondering what had been the occurrence of the night, and what strange story they had yet to hear, so soon as the maiden should be restored to consciousness.

And apart stood Gervase Morden. Like a person entranced, he gazed upon the beautiful, yet touching object before him. Statute-like he stood, though the existence of agonized feelings was depicted upon his countenance. There was a quick beating of his heart, a tremulous movement of his lips. Anxiety—deep anxiety was pictured in the expression of his eyes. His clenched hands told that he was striving to keep down powerful emotions, which involuntarily arose within.

"Mercy on us! man," cried Sir Thomas, "why stand you so stock-like? Can you not do so much as feel a pulse, or hold a smelling bottle?"

Gervase Morden stooped down, and surveyed the face of the maiden.

"She is recovering," said he; "her respiration is becoming better, and her lips are brightening in colour."

"Aye; but the pulse, boy—the pulse. Knowest not that the true leech always judges by the pulse?"

The student fell upon his knee, and took the wrist of the fair girl in his gentle clasp. His eyes were fixed upon hers; his heart beat almost as fitfully, as did the heart of the maiden. And there—before the open window—bathed in the silver moonlight, knelt Gervase Morden beside Constance Ismay. The student at the feet of the maiden—wisdom paying homage to beauty, as ever wisdom should.

Oh! there was something touching, yet beautiful, in the sight; touching was it, to behold the sad state of that fair girl: and beautiful was it, to look upon the solicitude of that young student. How lightly did his fingers press that delicately moulded wrist, yet how did his very frame seem to thrill at the gentle touch! How intently did he gaze upon that lovely face, fashioned as it was, in a beauty more exquisite than Grecian sculptor ever chiselled—than dreaming poet ever sung! And the bright moonlight passed in the window to fall upon both—to fall upon the cheek of her so wan, yet so beautiful: and upon the cheek of him so pale, yet so noble-looking. Perhaps, in that moment, the youth beheld the ideal of his former fancies realized, and, in that moment, loved the bright being before him. What but love could have made him regard her so tenderly? What but the adoration of the heart could have taught him to approach her with that gentle demeanour? Love hallows all its objects; love ever makes the loved one holy in the lover's sight.

And it may have been that at that precise moment, Sir Thomas Warrenton himself allowed a suspicion to cross his mind, of the conjecture which has just been stated; perhaps, a vision floated before his sight, revealing to him a story which has yet to be told. Certain is it, that he threw piercing glances at the student, as he demanded of him,—

"How now, Gervase, what does the pulse tell, and what does the physician predict?"

"See," said Morden, directing them to look upon the countenance of the maiden, "she will be well in a few minutes."

Scarcely was the last word well out of his lips, before the head of the maiden moved, and her own eyes sent forth a glance, which met another glance that issued from his. Volumes were told in that one—that single look.

"Where am I? Who are these people?"

"Do you not know me, Miss Ismay?"

"Ah! Gervase—Morden—yes, yes; is it you?"

"Gervase, she called me Gervase!" said the student exultingly to himself.

"My pretty Constance," cried Sir Thomas, "are you unwell? The physician will be here presently."

"I—I want no physician. Tell me where I am? Tell me why you are all around me?"

"You are in the library, child," replied Lady Warrenton, "you have been brought from your bed-chamber because the place seemed to frighten you."

"Right, right! I was frightened—I—"

"Why stare you so wildly upon us all, good Constance?" asked Sir Thomas, as he remarked the strange, apprehensive look, with which Miss Ismay regarded the various persons assembled in the room.

"I—l thought—but never mind. I am well now, quite well, and I know you all; that is you, Lady Isabel; that is you, Lucy; that is Martha, and that Susan; I am not dreaming now."

"Dreaming, my child! has it been nothing more than a dream that has disturbed you?" inquired Lady Warrenton.

"Yes, a dream; a—but tell me, which of you have been in my room to-night?"

"We all went there when we heard you shriek."

"My shriek—ah! you bring it to my recollection again. But which of you went there before?"

Sir Thomas started, and looked round upon the assembled group. Every one was silent.

"Answer me," he cried in an angry tone, "which of you has entered Miss Ismay's chamber this night, prior to the alarm which we all heard?"

An answer was returned by each in the negative.

"You are mistaken, Constance," said Sir Thomas, "no one has intruded into your bed-room from the time you sought repose, until I went there myself alarmed by your cry."

"Yes, yes, there was some one."

"Who should it be?"

"I know not; but some one was there."

"This is strange! exclaimed Sir Thomas. "Is it possible that one of you is telling me a lie?" then, turning to Morden, he said,—"Go you, Gervase, and give orders that the place be thoroughly searched. Perchance, we have robbers in the house."

"Your pardon, Sir Thomas," replied the student, "I have already given notice that every outlet be well watched and guarded. Meanwhile, would it not be as well to hear whatever Miss Ismay has to communicate, in order to direct our proceedings thereby."

"Rightly spoken, rightly spoken, lad. It may have been nothing but a dream after all. Ha! Where is my son! Where is Lambert? He sleeps near enough to Miss Ismay's chamber, and should have heard the alarm."

One of the domestics here stepped forward, and intimated that Lambert Warrenton had retired to his chamber in an early part of the evening, having stated himself to be very unwell.

"But go to him—go to him, some of you, and see if he be there now. Ask him if anything has disturbed him during the night."

This command was obeyed; and the domestic shortly after returned, bringing with him a message, to the effect, that his young master was awake, and wondering at the hubbub in the house, but that he had taken an opiate before retiring to his bed, and had slept so soundly as not to have heard the shriek of Miss Ismay.

"But why does he lie there—why does he not come down and render us assistance?" demanded Sir Thomas.

"Mr. Lambert says, that he feels himself so very unwell, that he cannot possibly leave his bed," replied the domestic.

"Plague on him! A pretty seaman, forsooth! who cannot quit his bed when the ship is in distress. But come, Miss Ismay, before we proceed further in this matter, let me be informed of the particulars of your fright."

"Stand nearer to me then, Sir Thomas; stand nearer, Lady Isabel; stand nearer, Mr. Morden. You must not ridicule me when you have heard my story."

"None will do that in my presence, Miss Ismay," returned Sir Thomas.

"Listen, then!"

CHAPTER XIII.

THE PHANTOM IN THE LADY'S CHAMBER.—AND THAT WHICH IT LEFT BEHIND
IT THERE.

THE listeners crowded round to hear that which Constance Ismay had to
tell.

"It was strange, Lady Isabel, but when I retired to my bedroom this evening
I felt no inclination to sleep. Even as I laid my hand upon the handle of the
door, something came over me, and I feared to enter my chamber. When I
bade Martha good night, and dismissed her, I felt a sort of shudder, and was
almost tempted to call her back again."

"Doubtless, you have taken cold, child," said Lady Warrenton, to whom presentiments were things unknown, and by whom omens were valued at their
lightest worth.

Constance Ismay turned away her face from the matter-of-fact lady, to take
the hand of Sir Thomas.

"It was as I have said," she continued, "I felt afraid that something was
about to happen. I had a consciousness that this night would not pass away as
other nights have passed."

"And what has happened, good Constance?"

"I will tell you. For more than an hour after I had gone to bed, I lay in a
dozing state, and thought over many things, and saw much, that passed, as if in
dream-work, before me. At length, the bright rays of the moon pierced into my
chamber, and fell upon my coverlet. I opened my eyes, and gazed upon the
beautiful lines of light. After amusing myself thus for some time, I felt a
desire to gaze upon the moon itself. The night being warm, I arose and
unfastened the casements. Delightful was the scene without—all was so calm
—all so placid—all so like to what I have read of fairy land, in the books of my
childhood. Far away in the distance, I saw the glitter of the out-spread ocean;
and by its side, the old, ruinous castle, upon the turrets of which I watched the
moonbeams play. Deep, in the woods beneath my window, the nightingale was
singing his song of love, and gently, hushingly, upon my ear, fell a soft hum,
like the breathings of a hundred sleeping things. While I was thus engaged,
and while I was thinking how happy, and how beautiful, all without seemed, I
suddenly heard a slight noise behind me. I started. I turned round; I looked
across the room. My eyes did not deceive me, for plainly as I saw it then, I
can figure it to myself now —"

"Figure what, good Constance? What was it you saw?"

"A form—a form in my bed-chamber. I saw it at the further end, in the
gloom where the moonbeams went not. For a minute it passed; then it
glided along. I heard the movement of its feet, I saw it pass across the room.
I followed it with my eyes. I shuddered; strength went away from me. I fell
upon my bed, and I know of nothing which has happened since, except that
which you have already told me."

"Gracious me! Sir Thomas," exclaimed Lady Warrenton, "there must be
robbers in the Hall. Here are arms in the library; why do not the servants take
some steps to secure them at once?"

"Hush, my dear!" replied her husband. "It is probable, that what you
suppose, is the real truth; but nothing must be done in a hurry. If we act not
carefully, instead of catching the house-breakers, we may only give them
warning to escape. Tell me, Constance, how did this man enter your apartment, and by what door went he out?"

"I know not, dear uncle; the figure was there when I turned round, yet the
door seemed to me to be closed. I know not how it departed, for I was too
much overcome to watch its actions."

"And you do not believe that you were only dreaming?"

"Am I dreaming now, uncle, as I look on you?"

"Well, Constance, I must credit your account, albeit there is much in it that is strange. A search must be at once set up, and if any have entered this house without license, they shall swing from the gibbet on next market-day."

Sir Thomas had risen from his seat, and was about to go forth, to head the search himself; Miss Ismay, however, laid her hand upon his arm and gently drew him back.

"Why, how now, Constance? The search must be conducted with care, but it must be immediate."

"Hear me, uncle; I have yet something to say."

"Well, child—well, Constance, I listen."

"Sit down, I pray you."

Sir Thomas resumed his seat.

"Do not scold me, uncle; do not be angry with me, and call me foolish."

"Tush, child; have I said one word that way? what is it thou hast more to tell?"

"I—I, but uncle, you will blame me?"

"Heaven's patience, child! Say what thou hast to say quickly."

Constance Ismay looked fixedly at the face of her relative, and in a serious, deep-toned voice, said—

"I do not believe, uncle, that it was a robber which I saw i my room."

"Well, child ; what then dost thou suppose it to have been ? "

"Nothing human, uncle—nothing mortal ! "

Sir Thomas started back in astonishment.

"Why, how now, Constance ; have the moon beams played freaks with thee, and hast thou gone mad ?   What think'st thou then the intruder was ? "

"Heaven knows that better than I do, uncle ; but it is my belief that it was something that is not earthly."

Sir Thomas Warrenton was on the point of falling into a serious passion with his niece, despite the promises which he had made.   At this moment, however, Gervase Morden drew him aside, and, taking him to a distant part of the library, briefly related the story which he had heard from Martha, as well as the various circumstances attendant upon the mysterious foot-marks in the cellar passage.   When he had finished, it seemed that some impression had been wrought upon the mind of his listener ; but Sir Thomas was not the man to place implicit credence in any such stories as the one which he had just heard related.

"Tell me, Constance," said he, "what was the man—the figure like, which you saw in your bed-chamber ? "

"The place was gloomy, dear uncle ; I was frightened and confused : the glance which I had was, as it were, momentary, yet I saw the figure distinctly—as distinctly as I now see you.   It wore the shape of an old man, it had grey hair, it was enveloped in a cloak."

"An old man, say you ?—and its movements—"

"Were quick and gliding-like."

"In good truth, a strange fancy ; old age and nimbleness associate not well together. But what, say you, is your opinion—what think you the figure to have been?"

"Nay, uncle ; I cannot say."

"But your guess ; think you not with us that it was a robber ? "

"No, uncle, no ; I cannot think that."

"Certainly, girl, robbers do not generally have grey hair, seeing that the gallows mostly lays claim to them before age has played its freaks.   But come, you have not yet said what you think."

"I know not, uncle—I know not ; it may have been a—a—"

"Well, Constance, what ? "

"A spirit, uncle ; a phantom."

"A phantom ! "

Was it really so ?—had the phantom paid a visit to Constance Ismay as well as to Amy Heyton ; to the lady in the guarded mansion as well as to the maiden in the humble cottage ?

Sir Thomas meditated for a few moments, and then said—

"It is my belief, good niece, that this object of your fright will turn out to be nothing after all.   Girls have wild fancies, and their imagination is apt to play tricks. If I am not mistaken, it was a dream which you had, and nothing but a dream."

"No, uncle, not so ; it was as a dream."

Gervase Morden stepped forward, and whispered in the knight's ear,—

"Have we all dreamt, then ?   Are the marks in the cellar-passage nothing but a dream, Sir Thomas ?"

"Right, Morden, right ! there must be something yet.   Let us at once, then, to the search.   Lady Isabel, I beg that you will deal kindly with my ward ; and, in the meantime, we will exert ourselves in obtaining an acquaintance with these robbers or ghosts.   Gervase Morden, I ask your aid."

Followed by a portion of the male domestics, Sir Thomas and the student set forth to make an examination of the old hall.   Their steps were first directed towards the bed-room of Constance Ismay, but they met with nothing to reward their search there.   After prying into a few of the adjacent apartments with equal unsuccess, they proceeded to inspect the foot-marks in the cellar-passage ; and, agreeably to a suggestion of Morden's, the cellars and vaults of the building were entered into and surveyed. Nothing, however, could they discover—no skulking intruder could be seen.

"We must not give up yet," said Sir Thomas; "the woman will not be satisfied, unless the house be ransacked thoroughly. Whither shall we next direct our steps, Morden?"

"Shall we to the great hall?"

"As you say. I think you said that you heard some one moving about there the other night?"

"That I certainly did, Sir Thomas, though it occasioned me no alarm at the time."

"Well, we will go thither, and see what is to be seen. Where is Thwaites with the keys?"

The old steward at once presented himself; and, preceding his master, hobbled up the oaken staircase which led to the great hall. The door was opened—they entered. The moonlight was streaming in through the coloured windows, lighting up the old pictures which hung upon the walls. Around were fastened the antlers of stags, which had once bounded over Warrenton Chace; and over the gallery at the farther end were suspended many dust-covered flags, which had been wrested from the infidel Moslems by one of Sir Thomas's ancestors in the chivalrous days of the Crusades. All, however, was silent in the vast apartment. The high-backed chairs looked as if they appertained to a generation that had passed, and disowned all alliance with the present. The carved ceiling had become dull and smoke-covered, the spider having chosen his home amid the arabesque work. Nothing moved— nothing living was to be seen.

"All seems quiet here, Morden," said Sir Thomas, as he passed from the hall into the servants' offices. "Whither shall we wend our way next?"

"Are there not many old closets in the gallery?"

"Old closets, forsooth! But he who could conceal himself in any one of them must have no fear of the rats, and such like animals."

"True, Sir Thomas; still, would it not be half-doing our work, if we left them unsearched?"

"Rightly spoken, lad! Lead forward. 'Twere best we met no burkers in these dark places, for their own sakes, seeing that we might be inclined to take summary vengeance, and leave their bodies to banquet the rats upon. On, Morden, on!"

The closets were searched, but nothing was found in them, except various articles of old lumber, and many half-decayed garments. Proceeding onward in their examination of the galleries, the bed-rooms of the domestics were thoroughly investigated, but no robbers were met with therein. Beds were looked under, curtains were drawn aside, and the lids of chests uplifted; but the result was, in every case, the same. No intruder could be found.

"Well, Morden," said Sir Thomas, "this is what I thought we should gain by our labours. From the first I could not believe that any predatory rascals had had the hardihood to enter my dwelling. They know Sir Thomas Warrenton too well, if I am not mistaken."

"Certainly, the fears of the household seem unfounded," rejoined Gervase; "but, were we to examine Miss Ismay's room once more, we might discover, perchance, some projecting bracket, or piece of carving, or some loose morsel of tapestry, which, thrown into shadow by the flickering moonlight, may have deceived the lady; and thus the whole circumstances will be explained at once."

"Spoken like one who has a learned noddle, lad. Such words are very death-blows to the existence of all ghosts. Let us once more, then, to the chamber of my niece."

Again was the apartment entered in which Constance had received her fright. The window out of which she had looked, was still open; the pillow upon which she had sunk in her fainting state was there upon the bed—the moonbeams playing with its fringed borders. There were portraits fastened against the walls and articles of female handiwork strewed about; but nothing was there which solved the riddle; nothing was there, which—Sir Thomas placing himself by the bed—could, by the exertion of all his imaginative power, transform into the representation of a ghost.

"Come, Morden," said he, "let us return to the women."

They were about to leave the room; the hand of the knight was already upon the door. Suddenly, he was drawn back by Gervase Morden, who uttered a slight exclamation, and pointed to one particular portion of the floor.

"Well, boy, what is't to see?"

"Look, Sir Thomas—look! How has that come there?"

Both fell upon their knees; both looked—first at the floor—and then at each other.

There—on the floor—revealed by the moonlight, were two spots of blood; blood which had recently fallen there—which was still moist, red, and shining.

"How is this?" asked Morden.

"Come," said Sir Thomas; "we will go and make inquiries."

They returned to the room, in which were Constance Ismay and the female attendants. Was Constance hurt?—No. Had any one of the domestics who entered the bed-chamber at the time of the alarm wounded himself?—Not one.

"This is of a truth strange!" ejaculated Sir Thomas.

"But why these inquiries, dear uncle?"

"Because, Constance Ismay, there are blood spots—fresh and moist, on the floor of my niece's bed-chamber."

"Blood-spots! blood-spots!" exclaimed the maiden. "Could a ghost—a phantom—have left blood-marks there?"

PART X.

CHAPTER XIV.

THE MYSTERY INCREASES.

MORE than an hour passed away in the consultation which was now held in the library. All attempts at elucidating the mystery of the night had proved complete failures. There was evidence, strong evidence that some one was moving about the hall, flitting before the eyes of one, and leaving his trail-mark for the beholding of others. Sights had been seen, sounds had been heard; yet none knew who was their originator, none could say whose blood that was which remained upon the floor in the lady's chamber, nor whose footsteps had been left imprinted on the sand in the cellar-passage. Every room and corner of the mansion had already been submitted to examination; yet no one had been discovered concealed, no place of hiding had been found to contain a habitant. Most unaccountable was it that nothing had been moved, nothing stolen, no act of injury inflicted on the premises. What could that be which was moving about? was it immaterial—a ghost, a shadow, a phantom? No; for it had left marks and blood-spots to indicate its corporeal existence. Was it some robber? If so, why had he been moving about the place for many nights past, yet without a single article of value being missed? If a murderer, who could be the object of his murderous intent; and why had not that intent been carried into execution before now? opportunities had surely not been wanting, time and place had been convenient for the committal of such a crime. These were difficult questions to answer, and puzzled the ingenuity of all who were there assembled in that library old and gloomy.

But the greatest mystery yet remained : why had the cause of all this disturbance penetrated into the chamber of Constance Ismay? Surely no ruffian was so ruthless as to wish to do harm to her ; and to whom had she done wrong, that they should wish to slay her in her gentle slumber? Or was it that the entrance to her bed-room had been made for the effecting of a yet unholier purpose ? What had been the dreadful intent of the intruder? had it been to violate sleeping innocence, to destroy the maiden's happiness and peace of mind, and, by consequence, to destroy her life? Certainly this could not have been the case ; for, had such been the intent of the intruder, he would have chosen a more fitting opportunity—he would have laid wait for the maiden in some lonely place, and not have attempted the committal of such a crime, when the cries of his victim would immediately summon her relatives to her aid, and when means of escape would be so few after the act of guilt had been accomplished. Besides, from the evidence of Constance herself, the interloper was an old man, one whose grey hairs had borne witness to his advanced years : what could be the motives of such a man, what his mysterious design ?

There was yet more that was inexplicable ; for how had the entrance to the chamber been gained ? Constance had not heard the door open, neither had she heard it shut ; the form had glided across the room, entering without noise and departing without a sound created by itself. Still more strange was the existence of the blood-spots on the floor. How had they come there ; whose blood was it that had flown ; why had the blood flown at all, or from what cause was the individual bleeding? Here was a chaos to defy conjecture, here were riddles for ingenuity to solve, and puzzles sufficient to create bewilderment in the minds of all ! The more that thought was given to the subject the more mysterious it appeared ; and the more they wondered, the more cause for wonderment arose.

"Sir Thomas," said Lady Warrenton, "I hope you perfectly understand that I will not abide another night in this place, unless this matter be explained?"

"Will Lady Isabel tell me how the explanation is to be gained ?"

"Not I, Sir Thomas, for how should I know ? But, gracious me ! it is perfectly dreadful to hear of such things, and not know how to account for them. Is there nothing more that can be done—is the search to be given up in despair ?"

"No, no, Isabel, we shall catch the villain yet. Mr. Morden, have you given directions that all the outlets be well guarded ?"

"Every one is at his post, Sir Thomas."

"And—ha ! suppose we take a look round the outside of the Hall ; the villain may have dropped from one of the windows, and if so, we may, with the help of a lantern, be able to track him."

"I have already caused such examination to be made, Sir Thomas," replied the student.

"Ha ! and the results—the results, man ?"

"None, Sir Thomas."

"How !—can nothing be made out ?"

"Not a trace. Sharp eyes have been employed in the search, and they have well scanned the gravel round the whole extent of the Hall. Not a footstep is visible, nothing can they find to show that any lurkers have been thereabouts."

"Then the ruffians must be in the house still—they must be in it now !" exclaimed Lady Warrenton.

"Heaven keep thee sane, woman !" cried the knight, in somewhat of an angry tone, "have we not searched every hole and corner ? Where would'st have us to look—in the thickness of the walls, or between the floors and ceiling ?"

"The closets, Sir Thomas—the closets and the chimneys !"

"Well,—come you here, Gervase. See that every press in the house be opened, and let a blunderbuss be fired up every flue. Go ! See that it be done instantly ; and—Gervase !——"

"Yes, Sir Thomas."

" To satisfy your mistress, my lady here, take you care that every bed be beaten with a sledge-hammer ; peradventure the robbers have hid themselves among the feathers."

The servant departed to obey the commands of his master ; and Sir Thomas— whom the perplexity of the subject had thrown into a passion—gave orders that the old porter should be sent to him immediately.

" Jeffereys," said he, addressing the porter as he entered, " knowest thou not, man, that thou art paid to keep watch and ward over the gates ? A pretty use thou makest of thy office, if thou allowest thieves and murderers to enter at their pleasure—a pretty use, forsooth !"

" Your pardon, Sir Thomas ; but I can give my word that I have not allowed any such characters to enter the court-yard. The keys have not been out of my hands, nor have mine eyes been off the gates for these two days past. I have not been missing from my post nor remiss in my duty, as my lady there and Miss Ismay well know."

" Well, go—keep watch ; and, if you value your office, see that none pass out this night, and that none depart to-morrow, without my permission has been given to that effect. See, too, that a watch be kept about the court-yard walls. If you see any one attempt to scale them, shoot him—shoot him, and then bring him to me. Don't forget, sirrah—don't let your dull head buy your office from you! Go !"

When Jeffereys had departed, Gervase Morden advanced, and, begging the favour of the knight's ear, said—

" I am afraid, Sir Thomas, that the circumspection of this poor porter will be of little avail. Those who could come in so stealthily have, in all probability, the power to escape as they came."

" 'Sdeath, murder !" cried Sir Thomas ; " are you as great a fool as the rest? If men come in—they must come in through doors or windows ; and, if they be stopped from coming that way, then can they no longer enter. There is nothing but plain sense in that."

Constance saw that her uncle was becoming very irate. Gently she laid her hand upon his arm ; and, looking him in the face, asked the question—

" Was it by door or window, dear uncle, that I saw the figure enter my apartment ?"

" Why, niece, girl, are you going mad with the rest? Didst see the villain come up through the flooring?"

" Not so, dear uncle ; yet my belief is that he ——, that it did not enter by the one door which alone opens into my chamber ; neither did it enter by the window, for I was stationed there myself."

" Cease, child !—cease, or we shall go mad together. The thing was no ghost, as your foolish servants prate of, for it has left blood behind it. What, then, could it have been ? You yourself say that it was a man, and describe what he was like to. Tell me, then, how mortal man could enter your bed-room otherwise than by the door ?"

" Indeed I know not. I—I—it was a dream, uncle : I will think it to have been a dream."

" But the blood, child ? How came that there ? "

" Ask me not—ask me not, for I do not know. I would wish to forget."

" Now, child, thou art more foolish still. Forget, indeed ! dost think Sir Thomas Warrenton will allow his house to be entered by any vile varlet, and forget the act ? In good truth, girl, if I had the rascal by the throat now, 'twould be seen how far I could forget !"

" But be gentle, uncle ; be not angry—there is none here with whom thou hast cause for anger."

" I know not that, child. Look you at Morden ; why does he listen to what these servants tell, and not report it to me ? Why does he do that ?"

" Mr. Morden is not willing to trouble you with an account of every foolish thing that is said and done, dear uncle."

" Foolish thing, girl—foolish thing, i'sooth, when robbers break into my house, and varlets roam about at night as they please—I shall deem thee foolish enough, child, if thou upholdest such opinions."

Gervase Morden again stepped forward to beg an explanation with the knight.

" Sir Thomas," said he, " not one word of these rumours reached my ear until I sat in this library some two or three hours ago. If I had been told them before, I should have submitted them to due inquiry."

" And what art thou doing now, man ? Methinks that one who has studied so much, and acquired so much learning, should turn his knowledge to account. Here is matter enough for the exercise of ingenuity, if thou hast it ; and here is a fit opportunity for proving what thou canst do with thy learning, if thou hast a mind to put it to the test."

Gervase Morden threw a glance at the various individuals in the room, then, drawing the knight aside, he whispered in his ear,—

" I have a few words to say to you, Sir Thomas, which it is my wish that you alone should hear."

" Speak on, man ; none will interrupt us. Say what thou hast to say."

" Not here, Sir Thomas ; it must be in the adjoining closet."

" Well, be it so—be it so. Take a lamp in your hand, and I will follow you."

There was a small room annexed to the library, which was used as a depository for sundry articles of lumber ; into this apartment Sir Thomas accompanied the student ; and, having entered, the door was closed by Morden.

" Well, Gervase—man ! what wilt thou have me to hear?"

" A few words, Sir Thomas, concerning the present cause of alarm. I think, from what you have both heard and seen, you must come to the conclusion that there is some real secret which has yet to be penetrated."

" If there were not, then ought every one to be whipped for disturbing the place at midnight. Proceed, Morden, proceed !"

" There is evidence, Sir Thomas, that the subject of our investigation is something more than a ghost, or any form of spiritual existence alone."

" Ghosts ! nonsense, man ! Wilt talk as the silly women talk? Knowledge has been, and is, of little use to thee, if it teaches thee to believe in that which was invented only to frighten children."

" Whether spiritual existences do or do not walk this earth, Sir Thomas, is not the subject of our present inquiry. But as to the prowlers about this place, I am convinced of their corporeality. Probably, they are robbers ; or, probably, they are those who have a worse intent than that of robbery."

" Murder us in our beds, I suppose ; eh, Morden?"

" Their intent may be that, Sir Thomas ; or, it may be worse."

" Worse ! Worse, man ?"

" Was it not to the sleeping-chamber of Miss Ismay that the entrance had been gained—a woman's sleeping-chamber, Sir Thomas ? Comprehend you not my meaning ?"

" Ha !" exclaimed the knight, springing from his seat ; " Gervase Morden, I thank you for that explanation. I will away at once, and scour every corner to come in contact with the villain."

" Stay, Sir Thomas ; the man may have escaped."

" Escaped ! No, no ; he is hidden somewhere, though we have missed him. Escaped ! Wilt tell me what possibility there is for him to have done so ?"

" And by what possibility, Sir Thomas, could he have gained entrance ?"

" Ha ! Tell me that, Morden—tell me that, and I will see that thou hast no mean reward."

" Listen, Sir Thomas, the court-yard is well protected !"

" Yes, if walls and watchmen may be accounted protection ; though the walls might be climbed ; and it is not impossible that the varlet watchmen may, at times, doze at their ease However, Morden, I believe that the old Hall is well protected, as you say."

" And the keepers say that they have observed no stranger to pass through the gates, and none to enter the porch —"

"Aye ; trust the rascals for saying that ! What is there they would not say to keep their service and their clothes ?"

"The night-prowler about this place, Sir Thomas, came not this night for the first time ; he has been heard before —"

"Death to the rascals ! Could they allow him to enter twice ?"

"And he has been heard in rooms and passages, Sir Thomas, where none could gain admittance but those possessed of a key."

"Have any servants lent their keys, Morden—have they lost them, and not told me of their loss ?"

"Why should such be the case, Sir Thomas ?"

"How could the prowling villains else have got hold of them ? How could the intruders have gained entrance else ?"

"What need of intruders at all, Sir Thomas ?"

"I don't understand, Morden. There is something which you are driving at, but which I do not, as yet, clearly comprehend."

"Why suppose an intruder, Sir Thomas ? Who could gain easier admittance to the places under key than those who hold the keys in possession ? Who could better obtain admission to all apartments, than those who were in the house already ? Who—"

"Why, Morden," exclaimed the knight, starting from h chair, "you would lead me to suspect my own servants ! "

"Your own servants, Sir Thomas ! you have guessed that which I was about to say."

Deep and dark grew the flush upon the countenance of the irritated knight. Clenching his hand and stamping his foot, he was about to rush from the room.

"Sir Thomas, may I ask what steps you are about to take ?"

"To dismiss the villains from my service to give them over to the constables, to—to—to gibbet them, Morden—to see them gibbeted in the court-yard ! "

"But for what crime, Sir Thomas ? "

"Crime ! why, for—for—for—but know you, Morden, why the villains hve played the knave's part."

"That is more than I either know or can guess, Sir Thomas. You must recollect, also, that we are not yet aware who out of so large a number is the guilty party."

"Right, Morden ; there is justness in what you say. Let me hear what you have to advise concerning the manner in which this inquiry should be proceeded with."

Gervase Morden perceived that Sir Thomas Warrenton was now growing more cool than he had been during the last few hours. The knight folded his arms, and, standing beside the small table on which the lamp was placed, listened with patience to the further suggestions of his companion.

"The probability being that some one belonging to the house is the cause of the present disturbance," resumed Morden, "renders it necessary that careful steps should be taken in endeavouring to detect the offender. Now, Sir Thomas, I have a plan in my head which I would submit to your consideration."

"Speak it out, man—speak it out !"

"It is this—the only clue which we at present have to this mystery is that furnished by the sand in the cellar passage. Some one has trodden upon that sand in the course of this night, and the mark of the footsteps remains there now. It is shown, also, by the same sand, that the individual has not returned by the way in which he came. How and why he gained entrance to the cellar is another matter. I would propose, Sir Thomas, that every male in the household be commanded to follow yourself to the cellar. Let the motive assigned be a further search in that direction ; but let no intimation be given of the ultimate design. When all are assembled there, let every foot be measured and compared with the marks in the sand. Let care be taken that there be no changing of shoes, but let every man's foot be measured over the shoe or boot which he then wears. What is your opinion of my plan, Sir Thomas ? "

"It is feasible, Morden, and it may lead to an important result. I think we shall catch the knave, if he be not more of the devil than I can well believe him to be."

"At least, Sir Thomas, such a proceeding will go far towards lessening or increasing our suspicion of the domestics."

"Let it be done, Morden—let it be carried out instantly! Go you, and bid Thwaites to wait upon me immediately."

In less than ten minutes every male member of the household had re-armed himself, and was ready to set out on the expedition. Sir Thomas, accompanied by Morden, placed himself at the head, and commanded the troop to follow him to the cellars. As the men were grouping together, Gervase Morden threw a glance from one to the other, in order to detect, if possible, any external symptoms of treachery amongst them. His endeavour, however, proved futile, for all of them seemed to be inspired with one common desire—that of meeting with and capturing the terrible object of their alarm and dread. On entering the cellar-passage, Sir Thomas gave orders that all his followers should arrange themselves in pairs. When they had done so, he turned to Morden, and desired that he would pass behind, close the doors, and keep a sharp watch upon every man.   The lamps were placed beside the sand.

"Now," said Sir Thomas, "I wish to assure myself that there is no mistake in this matter.   I wish to be certain that the foot-prints which I have seen are those of an intruder, and not those of one of my own servants, who may have entered the cellar on his own proper business."

"Please you, Sir Thomas," interposed Richard, the butler, "no one has any business in this passage, except your honour and myself."

"I know it, Richard; still, let it be as I say.   Every man of you take off his right shoe, and bring it to me in succession."

No sooner was the command given, than it was obeyed.   The boots and shoes of all present were taken off, and handed over one, by one, to Sir Thomas himself. Kneeling on the stone pavement, the knight compared each shoe with the foot-marks on the sand.   The shoes were larger than the foot-marks.   One by one the servants advanced, and submitted themselves to the test.   At last stepped forth a young man, who was the son of Sir Thomas's gardener.   Morden remarked that this young man took off his shoe with some hesitation, and that he looked wistfully at the marks in the sand, as he gave his shoe into the hand of his master.

"S'death ! young man, thy shoes seem wondrously near the size," exclaimed Sir Thomas, as he gazed at the shoe, preparatory to comparing it with the foot-mark.

The man returned no answer.

Sir Thomas applied the shoe to one of the foot-prints.   Somewhat to his surprise, he found it to be much smaller than the sand-mark.

"Has every one given his shoe ?"

An answer, in the affirmative, was returned by each.

Sir Thomas looked significantly at Morden; and the student expressed his disappointment, by the vexed appearance of his countenance.

Gervase here stepped forward, and observed—

"I don't think there is a shoe in this house that would make such a print as that, except, perhaps, my young master's—Mr. Lambert."

"Ha !" exclaimed Sir Thomas, whispering to Morden, "perchance some one of the rascals has tricked himself out in my son's shoes.   Go, fetch me one of Lambert's shoes, immediately."

This order was complied with ; and, on Sir Thomas taking the shoe in his hand, he remarked—

"This is nearer to the length than any one of the others.   Let me see how far it corresponds with the measurement in breadth."

On applying the shoe to the mark, it was found to be nearly correspondent in length, but the toe was pointed, while that of the mark was very broad."

"Are the toes of all my son's boots and shoes, made after this fashion ?" inquired the knight.

"All, Sir Thomas.   The narrow toe is the fashion now for young nobles ; those broad, roomy ones, are worn only by old persons."

"Ha !" cried the knight, addressing the student; "and the figure which Constance saw in her bed-room was that of an old man."

"It was," replied Morden, sententiously, apparently musing while he spoke.

At this juncture, a sudden exclamation escaped from the lips of one of the domestics; and the latter pointed out to the observation of Morden a dark spot upon the stone floor.

The student took the lamp, and examined that which had been pointed out to his notice.

"What is that, Morden ?" cried Sir Thomas.

"Blood !—blood, that has been recently spilt."

"Ha! blood here, too!"

"Here, Sir Thomas, as also in the chamber of Miss Ismay."

"Blood from one, and the same source, Gervase Morden?"

"Doubtless, such is the case."

"Then, these foot-marks——!"

"Prove, Sir Thomas, that the figure, which Miss Ismay saw, had a substantial form; for the same figure, which has this night visited her bed-room, has also trodden in this passage."

Sir Thomas was confounded. The mystery grew more and more perplexing—conjecture was defied—all guessing proved to be futile.

"I cannot leave this mystery unsolved," exclaimed the knight; "let the search be renewed. I will lay hands on the villain, yet, if he be hidden in the smallest corner."

Vain was the search; there was not a portion of the old hall that escaped the general ransacking; but, despite the thoroughness of the search, nothing of importance could be discovered—no hidden intruder was detected.—

"This matter is more than strange," observed Sir Thomas to the student; "can any one more innocent than the devil himself have played us such a trick?"

Morden shook his head.

"Time will develop the mystery, Sir Thomas; whatever there really is in it we shall know before long."

While Morden was yet speaking, a violent ringing of the bell at the court-yard entrance was heard.

The domestics started in affright.

Again the ringing was repeated.

"Why do you not attend, ye knaves?" cried the irritated knight; "why stand ye gaping there?"

"The ghosts—the ghosts!" ejaculated some of the cowards.

"Go you, Morden, with them," said Sir Thomas; "go, see who has the daring to alarm the Hall at this untimely hour."

Gervase Morden departed. He was some time absent; when he returned, Sir Thomas hastily demanded:—

"Who was the knave?—what did he want?"

"It was Mr. Heyton—Mr. Heyton from the cottage."

"Ha!" exclaimed the knight, seizing suddenly the arm of the student; "what did he want?—where is he?—why comes he here at this unseasonable hour?"

"I scarcely know, Sir Thomas; his appearance was very wild, and he appeared much agitated. He inquired of me whether his son had been here, and whether I had seen my brother Ernest this night."

"Your brother Ernest!"

"Yes; he returned from his voyage three days ago, and I have seen him but once since then."

"Where is Heyton?"

"He is gone."

"Gone!"

"Yes; no sooner had he obtained my answers, than he turned about, and made off with the utmost speed. The poor man seemed much excited, and I am afraid that some evil has happened to him; though whether my brother, or young Frank Heyton have to do with the cause of it, I know not."

"This is strange—very strange," ejaculated the knight; "I wish to see Heyton, I— said he anything about his daughters?"

"Not a word, Sir Thomas."

CHAPTER XV.

THE IDIOT'S SECRET.—HOW MADNESS HAS TO DO WITH THE STORY.

AGAIN the scene changes. Leaving the inmates of Warrenton Hall to wonder over the cause of their alarm, we return to the tower by the sea-side, and those who roamed amongst its ruins. When Frank Heyton saw some dark object glide behind the pillar, he at once stretched forth his hand to grasp it ; to his great joy, he found that he had something living in his clasp.

"Ha ! you have not escaped me. I have followed you far, but I have followed not in vain."

Frank Heyton thought that he had captured the phantom—that fearful object which he had pursued. Madly he dragged the captive towards where the faint light fell down the shaft : strength had returned ; he felt that he had power to wrestle with the strongest there : in that juncture, however, he regretted having left his cutlass behind him in the vaulted chamber. He yelled in triumph, as he drew his victim onward.

"I will kill thee, coward ; I will wrest thy secret from thee."

He was about to clutch the throat of his captive, to fling him with violence on the floor ; just then, a faint voice met his ear—he paused, he felt that it was no manly arm he grasped, that he had no strong opponent to contend with. The gloomy light fell faintly on the captive's face, and Frank Heyton started back in astonishment. Before him stood Archy, the idiot boy !

"Good God ! " he exclaimed ; " this is the second time to-night that I have nearly murdered thee, thou poor fool ! why didst thou not say, boy, who thou wast ?"

"Archy knew Frank wouldn't do him any harm."

"It is wondrous that I did not ; had my sword been in my hand, I might."

The idiot smiled, and saying, in a laughing voice, "No, no, Frank could not harm Archy," he rushed towards Heyton and seized his arm in playful fondness.

"It is God who has preserved thy life, boy ; to have twice escaped death in a few hours, as thou hast done, cannot have resulted from mere chance, when a madman had thee in his grasp."

"But who is the madman, Frank ? "

"I, boy—I."

"You tell me wrong, dear Frank ; do not people say that I am mad—that it is Archy who is mad ? "

"They say so, boy, but such is not the case now. Madness is more with me than with thyself."

"And why is Frank mad ?"

Heyton grasped the arm of his companion.

"Thou hast not told me, boy, how it is that I should find thee here. Where hast thou been ?"

"Archy has been wandering in the ruins."

"And heard you no call ?—heard you not me call you by your name ?"

"Archy heard nothing."

"Not a sound ?—not a cry ?"

"Nothing."

"That is strange ! But why have I found you here ? Why have you wandered in these dark places ?"

"Archy went in search of the Dark Man."

"Came you here at once, without ascending the tower ?"

"Archy has said what he came for. The dark to the dark."

"And you saw him, boy. He is here ; he is hidden in some of these ruins. We will not leave this place until we have sought him out."

"Frank had best go home," said the idiot.

"Home, boy ? No ; I will not return till I have seen that man again—until I have caught him, as I thought I had, some two minutes ago."

" Frank will not catch him."

" How sayest thou—wilt not catch him? What is thy meaning, boy?"

" The Dark Man is not here, now."

" Where then, boy? Where am I to seek him?"

" Archy must not say."

Frank Heyton could ill contain his anger, and could scarcely refrain from striking the poor fool who stood before him.

" Know you, Archy, who that man is?"

" Archy was afraid of the Dark Man, but Archy is not afraid of the Dark Man now."

" Answer me, boy; answer plainly, or I may do thee harm."

Archy folded his arms in a sullen manner, and replied in a low voice, " Frank may kill me in this place, but I dare not tell him that which I have seen and know."

" Is it so fearful, boy?"

" Archy cannot say. Let Frank leave this place. Ernest is lost. The Dark Man is not here, and Frank cannot find him. Let us go."

Heyton hesitated for some minutes. There was that in the words which the idiot-boy had uttered that convinced him of the truth of these assertions. Much as he desired to meet with the mysterious unknown—much as he wished for an explanation of the mystery enshrouding the fugitive—he felt that his further search that night was destined to be fruitless. He took the hand of Archy, and allowed the idiot boy to lead him onward. Greatly to his surprise, he found that Archy had a thorough acquaintance with all the turns and windings of the passages, progressing onwards in the dark as if every place was familiar to him, and as if he had roamed amidst those ruins from his childhood. Thus they went on. Not a syllable was spoken by the idiot. Many a time did Frank Heyton halt to look through the gloom, and endeavour, if possible, to obtain a glimpse of the mysterious one whom he had pursued; but nothing could he discern, no fleeting form met his view. They passed through large chambers, where the echo answered to the tread, and where, at times, Heyton fancied he heard the movements of some one in the distant gloom. When, however, he paused to listen, not a sound met his ear, save the low breathing of the one poor fool who stood by his side. Still onwards, till they trod in what had been the hall of the castle, where the shout of the soldier had once been heard, where the banner had waved, the coats of mail glittered to the torch-light—where the prayer for victory had ascended, and the song of triumph sounded high and strong. But all was silent, solemn, sombre now. The banners had rotted from their staves, the oaken table had fed some thousand worms, the walls had forgotten the strains they had echoed of old, the stone floor had ceased to sound to the mailed warriors' tread. And the warriors, the shouters—where were they? Sleeping upon some far off plain, or buried in one common grave in a lonely land, where no maidens have ever thrown flowers upon the sod which covers them; where no tears have ever wetted the grass above them, and where affection, in its lornness, has never sung the requiem of sadness over the lost one's tomb. The castle and its ancient owners had shared one common fate, save that the castle still told of its olden glory, while its former habitants had passed into utter and during forgetfulness.

Passing out through the hall, the man and the idiot-boy stood once more in the free and open air. How delightful seemed the transition from gloomy horror to the light of a starlit sky! Hitherto the intense excitement to which Frank Heyton had been subjected, had helped to support his strength; but now that the pursuit was given over, and the excitement was at an end, he found that his strength had departed also. The cool air of early morning, instead of invigorating his frame, produced the effects of drunkenness. He staggered on for a short distance, and would then have fallen, had not the idiot supported him with his feeble arm.

" I am weak, Archy; I cannot proceed farther yet. Come, boy, let us take seats upon this green turf."

Before them lay the deep, lazy-flowing moat, and beside that, the remains of the large bastions which had been designed to fortify the castle. On one of these bastions, upon which the moonbeams glittered, they took their seats. Frank Heyton fell, exhausted, and was desirous of some cool water to allay his intense thirst. No sooner had he expressed the wish, than Archy arose, and after being absent for a few minutes, returned, bringing with him a broken vessel containing a large draught of pure and delicious water. The cool fluid seemed to give new strength to him who drank it ; but Frank had experienced so much within the last few hours, that he felt no inclination to arise, being rather disposed to think quietly over the various and strange events which had that night happened. He rested his elbows on his knees, and covered his eyes within his hands. Time passed away. In the distant east the gloom had broken, and a long tract of greyish light, which was gradually widening, told that the coming dawn was fast approaching. And still the brother of Amy Heyton remained in meditation ; and more and more did his bewilderment increase as he thought over the mysterious occurrences which had concurred to place him in his present position. Suddenly he was aroused from his reverie by a low, rumbling sound, which seemed to proceed from some one near at hand. He uplifted his head, and looking round, saw the idiot-boy praying to the moon.

" Archy ! what are you doing ?"

" Archy is asking the bright lady to tell him what he does not know."

" Come hither, boy."

The idiot crept gently towards Heyton, and looked anxiously in his face.

" Tell me, Archy—did you see any other living person in those ruins besides myself ?"

" Archy saw the Dark Man."

" In the castle, boy—in the under-works ?"

The idiot nodded his head in an affirmative manner.

" And know you which way he went, boy ?—know you where he is ?"

" The Dark Man is not in the ruins now."

" Ha! how know you that ? Where is he ?—where may I now find him ?" and Frank Heyton partially arose as he said the words.

" Frank must not ask Archy those questions. Archy dare not answer him. Archy must never—never tell."

Frank Heyton saw that a shudder passed over the frame of the idiot boy, as he returned this reply. What did that shudder mean ?—whence did it proceed ?—What was its cause ? Had Archy really beheld that in the dark recesses of the castle ruins which his lips had not the power to disclose ? Had he looked upon some fearful form, and been an unwilling listener to some dreadful story ? Frank took the hand of his trembling companion, and in a compassionate tone of voice put the inquiry :—

" Have you been frightened, Archy ?—have you become acquainted with some secret too horrid to be told ?"

The idiot burst into tears.

" Frank must not ask, Archy," said he ; " Archy can never tell him."

" Good Heaven !" exclaimed Heyton, " what am I to understand from your words ? Listen to me, boy ! Know you not that my father is your protector, out of mere charity—that you were a foundling, and that you were taken in, clothed, and kept by my father, merely because you were destitute ; and, according to your own account, had neither father nor mother ?"

" Archy knows—Archy is very thankful."

" Well, boy ; you have grown up with us ; you have been treated by my father as if you were his own son. Every one of us have been kind to you—we have all protected and cared for you, from the moment you first came amongst us, until the present time."

" Do not tell Archy that, Archy owns it."

" And owning it, boy, what excuse have you for your conduct in this matter ? You know well that an injury has been done to my father, my sister, and myself ; you know well that I love my sister Amy with a brother's love. Common gratitude, boy, should teach you to aid me as much as you can in seeking the vengeance which it becomes me to seek, as I have sought it this night."

" Frank would do murder ?"

" It might be so, boy."

" Then would Archy be doing wrong to tell him anything. '

" But justice, boy. Are you so very moonstruck that you cannot understand the meaning of justice ? It is only that which I seek—only justice for the great wrong which Ernest Morden——"

The idiot suddenly interposed.

" Frank must know," said he, " that the Dark Man is not Ernest."

" But he is Ernest's friend, boy !"

The idiot was silent.

" And is this the extent of your gratitude, Archy ? will you give me no information ?"

Casting an imploring look at Heyton, the idiot threw himself upon the green sod, and laid his burning forehead upon the knees of his companion. Frank felt the tremblings of the agitated boy, whose loud sobbings sounded particularly sad in the cool, stilly air of the morning hour.

" Archy cannot—dare not tell."

Heyton experienced the rising of angry feelings in his breast, which he with difficulty kept down. " Archy," said he, " that which you will not tell to me you must make known to my father."

The idiot started back. His tearful eyes were fixed upon Heyton with a look of agony. The usual mindless expression of his countenance had disappeared ; and the traces of deep thoughts and feelings, which had their home in the idiot's breast and brain, were depicted upon his features. Wretchedness and woe seemed written on his pallid cheeks ; terror and fear were marked by the drawing back of his lips. For a minute he gazed at his friend with a wild, fearful stare. Then, suddenly throwing himself forward, he grasped Frank Heyton's hand, and in a voice, the tones of which were touchingly thrilling, said,—

" Frank must promise me—Frank will promise me to say nothing about Archy to his father or to his sisters. It would kill Archy to say to any one what he has seen and knows."

So imploring, so piteous were the accents in which these words were spoken, that Frank Heyton felt compelled, though reluctantly, to give that assurance which the idiot now required of him.

" Be it so, Archy ; God knows what you have seen, and what reasons you have for keeping your knowledge secret. I will say nothing. I give you my promise that not a word from me shall intimate to others that you have a tale to tell which, according to your own assertion, dare not be told. Yes, Archy ; keep your secret, boy—keep it, if it must be kept. That which I desire to know I will myself discover—I will gain the knowledge unaided and alone."

A smile of tearful joy glistened upon the idiot's countenance. He bent his head to kiss the hand of his companion ; and, in a manner indicative of his heart's inward happiness, exclaimed :—

" Now is Frank very good—very good indeed to poor Archy, who knows that he is acting cruelly to Frank. But Frank will forgive—Frank has forgiven."

" I have, boy. Now sit you by yourself for a time. I wish to think over this subject and devise my own plans."

Pressing the hand of Frank to his lips, Archy moved away, and laid himself upon the grass at some distance, to gaze upon the moon, and to watch the grey streaks of the advancing dawn shoot upwards and upwards into the sky.

And again Frank Heyton buried himself in thought. Every action of the night arose to his recollection, and every mystery was turned over and over in his mind. That Ernest Morden—Ernest who had professed his love for Amy so ardently and so long—should have treated her as he had done, and insulted the tender being to whom he had pledged his lasting affection, was an inexplicable riddle. And the change from love to hatred had been so sudden, so momentary ! how had it been brought about? Certainly the aged and unknown traveller had been the agent ; but what was the secret of his power, and how had he contrived to exercise such

influence over Morden ?   Were they friends or were they foes ?   Were they ——
and now Frank recalled to his mind the strange behaviour of Ernest in tearing
away the dress of Amy to gaze upon her naked neck ; what did he behold there?

Frank resolved to attempt at returning home immediately, and learning, if he
could, the cause of Morden's behaviour.   He was about to rise from his seat on
the bastion, when he observed that Archy had again crawled towards him, and was
now gazing wistfully at his face.

"What distresses you, Archy ; why do you appear so thoughtful and so
sorrowful ?"

The idiot-boy approached his companion, as if doubting whether or not he
should be kindly received.   Encouraged, however, by the faint smile of pity
which gleamed on Heyton's countenance, he at last summoned up sufficient
boldness to take the hand of his friend, and to seat himself near to where Heyton
sat.

"What is it, Archy—what have you to tell me ?"

No word of reply was given.   The idiot held down his head, and at the same
time kept the hand of Heyton in his clasp.   There was that which he wished to
say, but which he seemed not to possess the power of uttering.

"Take courage, Archy," said Frank, cheeringly.   "Whatever you may tell to
me in confidence, shall be kept a secret with me, I promise you."

Once again the idiot looked up at Heyton's face.   Apparently he was making a
powerful attempt to say something which it pained him to reveal.   There was an
intentness in his look, and a hesitating, half-formed resolution in his partially
open lips, which caused Heyton to believe that he was about to hear the story of
Archy's adventures in the ruins, and to be made acquainted with some new
mystery yet more mysterious than any which had preceded.

"Be not afraid to speak, Archy!"

The tongue of the idiot was loosened.   "Frank," said he, "tell me—why was
Amy so glad to see Ernest ?"

"Do you not know ?"

"I wish Frank to tell me."

"Because, boy, my sister loved him ; because her love for him was greater—
greater, I fear, than was the love of Ernest for her."

"And what is love, Frank ?"

"Why, thou poor fool! art thou so ignorant as to ask so simple a question?
It is love, boy, when man or maiden singles out one sole object amidst the wide
universe—on only whom to think, of only whom to dream, concerning whom to
manifest more regard than for aught else that inhabits the whole world."

"And did Ernest so love Amy ?"

"I doubt it, boy, I doubt it much.   If he have not played the hypocrite for
many years, I am much mistaken.   Love, boy, is lasting, and not to be overthrown
in a single moment."

"But did Amy love Ernest ?"

"Why ask me that, Archy ?   You yourself have had evidence of the fact.
Has she not spoken of him continually during his absence ; has she not been
delighted to receive his letters ; has she not ever appeared happy when even
his name was mentioned to her ; and has she not grown thin, and pale, and
melancholy because he delayed his coming so much beyond the appointed time ?
Yes ; Amy has loved Ernest—loved, if I mistake not, a villain.   I have been acquainted with Ernest Morden for years, and I have called him my friend—God
pardon me that I should now call him a foe !"

"I do not understand yet, Frank—I know I am foolish ; but tell me—why are
you sorry that Earnest has quarrelled with Amy and left her ; what would you
have had him to do?"

"Boy! you are more moonstruck than we have yet taken you to be.   You worry
me Archy, by asking questions which a schoolboy might answer."

"But I am no school-boy, dear Frank.   You know that they call me mad, and say that I can never learn. Do not be angry with me for asking you to explain this which I cannot comprehend."

"Well, boy, if Ernest were true—if he had but the feelings of a man, he would return, he would beg pardon of Amy, and of her father; he would make some recompence for the evil he has committed, and—and—"

"What else would Ernest do, Frank?"

"He should keep his promise, and make Amy his wife."

Even by the light of the moon, combined with the faint gleam emitted from the eastern sky, Heyton might then have discerned the pallor become one shade more pale upon the cheeks of the idiot-boy. Archy turned away his head, as if to muse unobserved, then again addressing his enquiries to his companion, he asked—

"If Ernest were to make Amy his wife, would he take her away from us?"

"He would take her to his own home, boy, and make her mistress there."

"But Ernest lifted the sharp knife againt Amy. He might kill Amy if she went away with him."

Frank Heyton clenched his hands in the fierceness of passsion. Presently, replying to the observation of his companion, he said—

"You, too, saw him lift that knife, Archy. If he had ever loved my sister he would not have done that; he would not have been so cruel. True love would not harm its object, even in thought."

"I am sure of that—I am sure I wouldn't harm Amy," said the idiot.

There was something so strange, so impressive in the manner in which Archy uttered these words, that Frank involuntarily turned upon him a look of amazement, which, however, speedily subsided into an expression of mingled pity and derision.

"Why, you moon-struck simpleton! You are speaking now of love yourself."

Still more firmly than before did the idiot clasp the hand of his companion. His lips opened, he made an effort to speak, but the syllables seemed to die away upon his tongue. Again he made the attempt, and in a low, husky voice articulated the enquiry—

"And why may I not love Amy, Frank?"

"In truth, boy, thou should'st, for she has been kind enough to thee; kind as a sister to a brother."

"As a sister to a brother," repeated the idiot to himself. Then, again interrogating Heyton, he asked—

"Does Amy love Ernest now!"

"She cannot—she cannot. If she did—if—"

"What then, Frank?"

"She would not be worthy of the name of Heyton, boy. I will not again call her sister if she does not consent to be at enmity with Ernest Morden for ever."

The eyes of the idiot-boy brightened—a slight flush came upon his cheek. He moved off to a short distance, and again falling on his knees, gave either his prayers or his thanksgiving to the moon.

In this scene between the idiot-boy and his foster-brother there may have been much that has proved uninteresting in the recital. Be that as it may, it was a scene which gradually faded from the recollection of one of the actors in it, until the memory of it again returned, and caused him, to whose remembrance it came, to shudder with horror. Days and weeks and years passed away, but still to the memory of one came the recollection of the conversation on the bastion of the old castle, and, looking through the retrospect of time gone by, his blood ran cold in his veins as he remembered to what misery, to what woe, to what deeds of unparalleled darkness that one conversation, apparently so simple in itself, had been the prelude, the fore-runner, the dim shadow which, in its hazy mist, contained all the looming horrors that at length broke forth into actual, substantial existence. In the days of the future, one of those—the idiot and the maiden's brother—one of them, and one alone, stood beside the same grass-covered bastion, lamenting and self-reproaching, because that on the night of the conversation he had refrained from shedding blood!

Frank Heyton arose.

"Come," said he to Archy, "let us retrace our way to the cottage; there are those who are waiting for our return, and there is that which I have yet to hear from the lips of my sister Amy."

Together they set forth on their journey homeward. Again they crossed the drawbridge, and passed over the level greensward, across which they had chased the phantom. Then having retrodden the path leading along beside the copsewood, they stood upon the summit of the hill, from which, on one side, they could command a view of the old castle, and on the other, a glance at the distant cottage which was the destination and home of both; below them, to the right, stood Warrenton Hall, while away to the left, the summit of the Eagle's Altar was kissed by the earliest ray of a midsummer's morning sun. The stars were lessening in their splendor; the moonlight had lost its silver radiancy; night had gathered up her sables, and the crow of the cock, the lowing of the herd, the bark of the cottage cur, the whirl of the partidge in its flight, and the carol of the lark in the distant heaven told that day was again returning to the earth—another day, bringing with it its assigned portion of sorrows and delights.

" Look you, Archy !" exclaimed Frank, " who is that man sitting upon yonder stile ?"

" Is it Ernest ?" asked the idiot.

" I know not. It may be as you say. Let us hasten forward and ascertain the truth."

As they approached the stile the man uplifted his head, and advanced towards them. An immediate recognition took place, and Frank Heyton exclaimed—

" Father, why have you left Amy, and why do I find you here ?"

Explanations were entered into. Mr. Heyton told his son the cause of his leaving the cottage, and informed him of the inquiries which he had made at Warrenton Hall. It appeared that he had roamed about in his frenzy until completely exhausted, and only stopped to rest against the stile because his strength had failed him, and support became necessary.

On the other hand, Frank briefly detailed to his father the outline of his own adventures, omitting, however, according to his promise, all reference to Archy's possessing a secret, which he could not, or would not divulge. Neither was he in the least able to explain the mysteries which perplexed the other; nor could either form any satisfactory conjecture upon the subjects which agitated his mind. Discoursing upon the occurrences which had happened to each, the father and son, accompanied by the idiot boy, took their way towards the cottage.

CHAPTER XVI.

THE SISTERS.—THE HEYTONS.—A TRAGEDY OF COMMON LIFE.—A LOVE TALE.

BEAUTIFUL is love. Was it found in any guise or existent under any condition ? Oh ! beautiful is the first love of the dreaming boy and the romantic girl—beautiful is the after love of the true-hearted man and the trustful maiden—beautiful the strong love of those who are wedded in soul as well as in body—beautiful the love of the mother for her child, or that of the child for the parent—baautiful, too, the love of the old man for his prattling grandchild—and beautiful—oh ! truly beautiful—the fond, the holy love of a sister for a sister, when sorrow has come upon either, and the heart of one has been pierced by the rambling arrows of disappointment, slight, or deadly wrong !

Thus beautiful was the tender affection with which Kate regarded Amy and Amy regarded Kate. The grief of one when communicated by speech to the other became her grief also. They had grown up together—

" Like to a double cherry, seeming parted;
    But yet a union in partition,
    Two lovely berries moulded on one stem."

They had ever been confiding to each other, and in that confidence was the strength of their love. All the little joys and sorrows of one became, in due course of time, the joys and sorrows of the other; and then, warbling one song in one key, the sisters had become sisters in affection—sisters in their wishes and their woes.

It was the same bed-chamber, from the window of which the struggle on the Eagle's Altar had been witnessed, that the picture which the pen now attempts to paint had its prototype and its reality.

On the bed lay Amy, and by her side was Kate. The arm of the latter supported the head of the former, and the hands of each were locked in the hands of the other—their pulses beating simultaneously, their eyes returning glance for glance.

Frail and fair and beautiful appeared the tender frame of Amy. Elegant, impressive, and womanly was the form of her younger sister. Both were lovely; but Kate was moulded after the form which sculptors carve; and Amy fashioned according to the ideal fancies which poets weave ; the beauty of the female in the one—the loveliness of the maiden in the other.

As Kate leant over her sister, the attitude which she assumed was at once striking and characteristic. Shielding Amy with her bosom, she pressed her hands in affection's fondness. Her head was bent aside to listen for the sound of footsteps, like the fawn, when hunters are in pursuit. Alternately her eyes were directed to the window and to the countenance of her guarded treasure ; and alternately she uttered the words of encouragement, and held apart her lips in the attitude of a listener, Each heard the beating of the other's heart ; each kept time in their breathings, and their chests moved with simultaneous movements. The rich dark hair of Kate intermingled with the golden tresses of Amy, like light and shade blended together, the one giving depth and beauty to the other.

" Are they coming, Kate ?"

" Hush, sister ! hush !"

" Do you hear footsteps ?"

" I think so."

" Is it father, or Frank, or—or Ernest ?"

" I know not. Hush—hark ! I—no ; it is nothing but the sound of the sea in the distance, or the falling of a leaf from one of the trees.

" But will none of them return, dear Kate ?"

" Yes, Amy—yes ; they are coming ; they must be very near. Be comforted, sister, they will bring good news."

Leaving the two sisters waiting for the return of those they loved, and delaying for a short time the revelation of the cause of Amy's fright, and the quarrel between her and Ernest, we proceed to discharge a debt which is owing to the reader, and to atone for our misbehaviour in introducing him to the company of certain persons without giving some prior intimation of the history and position of the individuals presented to his notice.

Who was the elder Heyton, and what had he been in his younger days? The furrows on his forehead gave evidence that he had known tribulation, and the sickly attenuation of his frame told that the sorrows of days gone by still prayed upon him, and were in memory, sorrows now:—

> " Joy's recollection is no longer joy,
> But sorrow's mem'ry is a sorrow still."

His was a strange story, one of those heart-rending tragic stories, which occasionally happen in real life, and which touch us more than the recountal of a monarch's woe, or the privations of ten thousand princesses.

Listen then, reader, while we narrate to you the main incidents of Mr. Heyton's life, thus making you acquainted with a tale which you will not readily forget, and which will cause you to take an interest in the future fate and fortunes of the family.

It was towards the eve of a summer's day, some forty years earlier than the period of our story, that a pale, dark-haired youth might have been seen wending his way along the Great Northern Road, in the direction of the metropolis. The youth was apparently not more than seventeen or eighteen years of age; his high forehead told of an open and imaginative mind, while his compressed, but finely-chiselled lips gave intimation of the existence of a brave and determined spirit. Toil-worn and weary he appeared. His dress was covered with dust ; and the staff and bundle which he carried in his hands proclaimed that he had travelled for some distance, and that he was proceeding upon a long journey.

The last rays of the sun were tinging the western sky ; and the workmen were returning to their homes. Seating himself on a bank by the roadside, the young man turned out the contents of his wallet, but found nothing wherewith to gratify his appetite, except a crust of bread which had become dry and hard. Seemingly disappointed at this discovery, the youth ransacked his pockets for a few coins, but none could he find, save one single halfpenny. Despair and misery were then portrayed upon his haggard and wayworn features. He felt that strength was failing him, that his limbs would not support him another mile. Starvation loomed upon him—starvation and death; for London was yet many leagues distant, and not a friend did he know on whom to depend when the end of his journey was attained.

"Good heaven!" exclaimed the poor youth, "am I to fall dead upon the stony road, or am I to stretch myself upon some ditch side, and there die as a dog would die?"

He clasped his hand to his burning brow; he buried his face in beween his knees, and wept as a child would weep.

Suddenly he sprang up. "No!" he exclaimed, "I will not die yet. I will not die, when manhood and the world is before me! So young as I am, and think of death? No, no. We were sent into the world to live—I was intended to live; and if that life must be sustained by begging, so let it be—the beggar may be an honest man still!"

Just then the poor youth lifted up his eyes, and saw a light chaise, containing two gentlemen, advancing along the road. Presently, an old man, bearin sickly-looking grandchild in his arms, arose from his seat under the hedg na going up to the chaise, implored its drivers to bestow their charity upon an old man and a starving granddaughter. His supplication was laughed at. He repeated his prayer. One of the two gentlemen flourished his whip and struck the beggar's child. At the same moment the old man started backward out of the way of the horse, and stumbling, fell heavily to the ground. The occupants of the chaise drove on, and their hoarse laugh was sent back upon the evening air.

"No!" cried the starving and wayworn youth as he witnessed this sad spectacle; "I will not beg—I will not beg now; but—" and he paused, and drew his breath with difficulty; "if I were to take that by violence, which is denied to supplicating poverty; if I were to turn robber instead of beggar, what then? Why, they would pursue me, they would hunt me as if I were a beast, they would speak my name as if I were some vile thing of which it was even profanity to think. Be it so. The God above me will not deal so harshly with me as they will. He will not regard me so sternly, nor punish me so heavily. Want is not wickedness; starvation is not the propensity to evil. Forgive me then, Heaven, if I wrong thy laws this night—forgive me if I take by force that which otherwise I may not be able to obtain!"

And so saying, the poor youth regaled himself with a draught of water from a neighbouring pool. Then, stepping aside to where a large black thorn flourished in the hedge, he selected and cut off with his knife a stout stick, stronger and more weighty than the staff with which he had hitherto journeyed.

"Ah!" he ejaculated, as he swung the massive weapon round his head, and then stopping to gaze upon it; "this will not break easily, nor fly to pieces at the first blow. "Ha! ha!" and his laugh was like that of a madman; "this will win bread when the honest hand and truth-telling tongue can earn it not; this will serve for a friend though every face wear a frown, and every lip be curled in scorn! In truth a good and trusty weapon!"

The youth grasped the stick in his hand, and thus armed, journeyed resolutely onward. He had, however, miscalculated his strength, and before he had proceeded three miles farther his eyes began to view objects indistinctly, and a dizziness came over his brain. He grasped the iron-bar of a gate by the road-side to keep himself from falling. This gate opened into a small garden, at the further end of which was a capacious and elegant mansion. Walking in this garden was a stout, elderly gentleman, and a young girl of surpassing beauty, whose age could not be more than seventeen.

"Charity, good sir! Give but a few pence to a poor traveller who has no money to buy him food," solicited the youth.

The gentleman hearing the voice, looked towards the gate, and seeing a beggar stationed there, gave orders to the gardener to send away "the strolling vagrant." Not waiting for the gardener's interference, the youth made an attempt to move from the gate, but his strength was unequal to the task, and after tottering onward a few steps, he fell exhausted and powerless again to the iron-bar. The lady saw the youth fall, and at once hastened towards the gate.

"Dear papa !" she exclaimed, "this poor young man is very ill. He will die if we do not render him some assistance."

"Pooh, pooh ! child," returned the gentleman, "such tricks are among the most common of those which the impostors practise."

"But this is no impostor, papa ; he is not—he cannot be !"

"Go to child ! Dost effect to know mrre than thy father in these matters ? Let Hughes give the boy into the care of the tip-staff."

"No, no, dear papa ; that must not be. Hughes, you must take this poor young man into the house, and give him some refreshment. Come, dear papa, you will oblige your own Kate in this one matter—will you not ?"

The fair questioner was really so beautiful, and she uttered her petition in so winning a manner, that when the father looked at the countenance of his daughter, and saw her bright black eyes beaming upon him, and gazed upon her beautiful lips, still open, as if still uttering the petition, and when he felt the touch of her soft hand upon his arm, and recollected that she was his only daughter, and that she had never wrought him pain in thought or deed, and that she had made his coffee that very morning at breakfast exactly to his liking, and buttered his toast for him with just the exact quantity of butter, his heart relented, and if Kate had asked him to bestow half his fortune upon her, instead of merely having petitioned him to bestow charity to a beggar, her request would have been granted even to the utmost extent of her desire.

"Go, Hughes, and do as Miss Catherine bids you. Let the poor youth be well attended to, give him a good draught of ale, and tell those in the kitchen not to be sparing in their bread and beef."

"Oh, that is a dear, good, kind papa !" exclaimed the laughing, bright-eyed girl, as she in a pretty and playful manner, bestowed a kiss upon her father's cheek.

"And, Hughes—"

"Yes sir."

"See if yoo cannot provide a bed-room of some kind for the young man's accommodation. Doubtless, he cares not to proceed farther on his journey to-night."

"Better still, dear papa ! better still ! Oh, now you are good indeed ! " cried the merry, kind-hearted girl.

And the toil-worn and travel-stained youth followed his conductor with a thankful, joyous heart. As he made his bow and returned his thanks to the maiden and her father, he thought that were the world to be conquered by one man he would be the conqueror at the desire of that bright girl.

Early the next morning he arose and was about to depart ; but a servant came to him with the message that Miss Catherine had given orders that he should have some breakfast before proceeding on his journey, and when the poor youth had finished breakfasting, a further command came that he should himself wait on Miss Catherine. And then when the bright, beautiful girl asked him whither he was going, and he told her that London was his destination, she slipped two golden guineas into his hand, and wished him a pleasant and prosperous journey ; oh, how happy was he ! and how happpy was the fair donor herself too ! for the feeling of happiness is over the reward that the heart receives when a good word has been said, or a kind action done.

The youth resumed his journey. It was a balmy and delightful morning; the birds sang sweetly around him ; the flowers bloomed in more than common beauty wherever he turned his eye. Happy and glad was his heart—happy and glad as the heart of blooming youth should ever be. The image of the bright girl who had acted so kindly towards him, haunted his path as he travelled onwards. He prayed Heaven to shower blessings upon her, to be benevolent to her as she had been benevolent to him. Then of a sudden he stopped, and gazed at the thorn-stick which he held in his hand. Back to his memory came the recollection of when, and why, and wherefore he had possessed himself of that stick. A minute he paused; then, lifting up the weapou he flung it far, far away from him, exclaiming as he did so—

"It is gone; I do not want it now. Last night when I cut it from the hedge, I believed that all the world was cold and cruel; that none had kind hearts or were ready to do a kind action; but I was wrong—I was very wrong! God forgive me for my wicked thoughts, and for my wicked intentions! No, no; all are not stony-hearted, all are not churlish, wicked, selfish and surly; there are some who are good and kind—some who deserve to have no ill-word spoken of them. If I did now but know what service I could render that young lady—if I did but know how I could reward her, I—I—but I cannot; I cannot! She is rich and great, and has friends and those who love her; but I am poor and lowly, with none to welcome me in the great place whither I am going—not one to whom I can appeal as to a friend."

And thus lamenting his forlorn condition the youth caused tears to gather in his eyes, but he quickly dashed them away, and tossing his small bundle across his shoulder, he accelerated his steps and tripped nimbly along.

The metropolis was reached, and immediately the young adventurer proceeded to seek employment. Fortunately for him he met with a young, though rich merchant, in the city, who consented to take him into his service. Here again had the poor youth met with a kind friend, and here again did he learn the lesson that the world is not in reality so cold, nor so cruel as it may at first sight appear. The generosity of the master was rewarded by the fidelity of the servant; and as day after day passed, so day after day did the industrious youth gain increased favour in the eyes of his kind benefactor.

Three years glided away and then, one morning, the youth, who was now just entering upon manhood, was summoned into the presence of his employer.

"Stephen Heyton," said Mr. Milbank," I have just been thinking that as the office of country-traveller to the establishment is vacant, you may as well fill it up—that is, if you have no objections."

Gladly was this proposal acceded to, and many were the thanks returned. And now again, on a bright summer's morning, did Stephen Heyton set off to journey along that same Northern-road which he had once before travelled when, as a poor adventurer, he sought the great metropolis.

How different, however, were the two journies! then, the youth had tramped along the road, bare-footed and half-clothed, now he was mounted on a horse and attired in comfortable garments. Three years ago he had nearly died with starvation upon that same road—now, he could take his ease at his inn, and avail himself at his pleasure of all the comforts which it is in the power of money to procure. Many had been the lessons which he had learned in those years, but the chiefest of all had been, that of trusting to the future while braving the present, and relying in the belief that patience and perseverance will ever bring fairer days; while merit will win friends, and faithfulness and integrity preserve them.

The shades of evening were descending as, mounted on his horse, the young man neared that very house at the gate of which he had, for the first and last time in his life, solicited alms. Already, at the distance of about three-quarters of a mile, he could discern the chimneys of the friendly mansion; his thoughts naturally reverted to the behaviour of the elderly gentleman and his beautiful daughter. Stephen Heyton was indulging in a reverie, and the fair girl, who had befriended him, stood before him in memory, bright, kind, and beautiful, as when she bid the adventurer farewell and wished him a prosperous journey. Thus meditating, the traveller rode along, when, of a sudden, the cry of some one in distress fell upon his ear.

He reined in his horse and listened—again he heard the cry—it seemed to proceed from a small shaded lane which turned in from the high-road, a few yards in advance. Stephen Heyton pressed forward and rode down the lane at full speed; he had not proceeded far before he saw a woman struggling with two men. The ruffians looked up when they heard the sound of the horses hoof, and seeing that a pair of holsters hung at the saddle of the horseman, they deemed it prudent to seek immediate flight. Heyton dismounted and ran to the rescue of the lady who had fainted by the side of the path. He uplifted her in his arms ; he conveyed her from the shade into the light; he looked upon her face; he started—could he—could he be deceived.

No, there was no mistake. She whom he held in his arms was the same beautiful girl, who had in years gone by, interposed between him and death.

Heyton scooped up some clear water from a neighbouring spring, and with it bathed the forehead of the beauteous being. In a few moments her eyes opened, and her first glance fell upon the countenance of her deliverer. She started.

" Fear not, lady," said Heyton, " those who would have harmed you, are far away from here. Be not distrustful. I will not do you hurt."

." You cannot—you cannot !" ejaculated the maiden, pressing at the same time the hand of her protector.

"[Let me accompany you to your home," said Heyton ; " I know that it is but a short distance. If you will lean on my arm, I will lead my horse with the other hand.

Once more Stephen Heyton passed through that gateway by which he had nearly fainted with exhaustion, in time that was past. Again he entered the large house, and again he stood before the elderly gentleman who had ordered food to be given to him, when starvation was looming in his face.

" Dear, dear papa !" exclaimed the lady, " how thankful you must be to this good gentleman. Had it not been for his timeiy arrival, I should have been robbed, if not murdered, by two ruffians who assaulted me in the lane. Thank him, dear papa !—you must thank him."

The gentleman advanced and held out his hand to Heyton ; as their eyes met, the recognition was mutual, and each started back, the gentleman apparently too astonished to utter a word.

" Do you not know him, dear papa ? Do you not know the young man to whom you rendered temporary assistance some two or three years ago ?"

" Yes, Kate—yes ; I see that it is him ; and amply as he recompensed us for the small service which we performed for him."

" Not small, sir—oh, not small," returned Heyton ; " it was you and your kind daughter who saved me from death—from the worst of deaths."

And you in return have saved my child from violence—perhaps from murder," rejoined the gentleman, as he grasped the hand of Heyton with firmness.

That evening Heyton stayed at the house of Mr. Leslie. And the story of his adventure and his success was told, and the gentleman and the bright-eyed girl were the listeners. The evening passed away too quckly ; for never in his life had Heyton felt so happy, because never before had he enjoyed the privilege of having a pair of such beauteous eyes smiling upon him. Catherine Leslie wept as she heard the narrative, and laughed and cried alternately as she heard how Stephen had cut the thorn-stick from the hedge, and had afterwards thrown it away, because of the kindness which he had met with. That night, the maiden on her couch, thought over the story of the starving traveller ; and that night, as he lay upon his bed, did Stephen Heyton dream of the beautiful, kind-hearted, dark-eyed Catherine Leslie.

The next morning Heyton arose to proceed onward about his master's business. Mr. Leslie made him a present in money at parting ; but Catherine gave to him a gift, which in his estimation was better than money—a squeeze from her own soft hand, accompanied with an intimation that she should be glad to see him when he returned by the same road. What better reward for his service could Stephen Heyton desire ?

And he did see her again on his return ; and twenty times after that he saw her again and again. Letters passed between them—letters written as only lovers write. Yes, the beggar-youth and the bright-eyed lady had pledged their vows to each other, and were lovers now.

Another year or two passed. Stephen Heyton had risen to be chief-clerk in his master's establishment. The world was going prosperously with him, when one morning he received the pleasant news from his employer that he had been chosen to fill the office of foreman, or superintendant of the business of Messrs. Milbank and Company.

How joyful was Heyton's heart when he heard this news; how gaily did his pulse bound, and how merrily did all things go with him! A letter was immediately posted to Catherine ; not addressed to her, however, at her father's house, but directed to Miss Leslie at Mrs. Barnes'. This same Mrs. Barnes being a milk-woman in the adjoining hamlet, who had been made use of by Stephen and Catherine, as a sort of go-between, or useful medium for the transaction of business.

A fortnight after his promotion, Stephen Heyton sought her whom he loved. They met—they wandered together down that same green lane in which he had rescued her from her assaulters.

"Kate," said he, "my sweet Kate! do you not believe that bright and happy days are in store for us both?"

"O yes, dear Stephen—indeed, yes!"

"But those days will never come to me, if you are not with me, Kate—if you are not with me to enjoy them."

"Well, but I—" Kate stopped suddenly, and turned away her blushing face. Heyton pressed her hand.

"Say it, dear Kate—say what you were about to say ; say that you will be with me ; that we shall be happy together! Oh, say that ; for is it not your wish—is it not your heart's-desire ?   Tell me—tell me, my sweetest Kate !"

A faintly murmured "yes," was all the reply which the maiden made."

"And you love me, Kate : you will confess to me now that you love me !"

Kate turned away her face, and looked at the pretty flowers, which were bending their heads over the small rivulet that flowed by her feet.

"Come, Kate, do not let me believe otherwise—do not give me cause to think that I am not loved by you. I have cherished the fond idea of your love as the treasure of my life. I have not cherished a dream—an unreality. Have I, Kate ?"

"No, no."

"Then you do love me—then you do own your love—then I am not mistaken—then I am reserved for blessedness!   You love me, Kate—you do love me ? "

The beautiful maiden threw herself into the arms of her wooer, and hiding her blushing face by laying it on his shoulder, exclaimed, in a low, sweet voice—

"Love you, Stephen ?"   Yes—better than aught else—better than any one in the whole world !"

Then am I happy now, Kate !—happy, sweet girl—happy, happy happy !"

Who shall tell the thrill of delight which each felt then ?   Who shall tell how much of happiness was felt by each Arm entwined round arm, and hand in hand, they retraced their way up the lane.

That evening Stephen Heyton sought Mr. Leslie, and obtained an interview with him in the library. It was a difficult task for Stephen to explain the object of the meeting ; but, making a strong effort, he overcame the difficulty, and told his story to the father of her whom he loved. Eloquently did Stephen Heyton relate the tale of young love's birth and growth ; eloquently did he describe how he first became enamoured of Kate, and how Kate had pledged herself to love him, and him only. With earnestness and fervour did the lover plead his cause, and solicit the grant of her whom he loved. Mr. Leslie listened without saying a word ; but, when Heyton had finished speaking, he arose from his chair, and, turning full upon the supplicant, said—

"Mr. Heyton, the confession which you have now made is to me most extraordinary. You have rendered me some small service, and, for that reason, I have been willing to account you as a friend. But, that you should presume to ask the hand of my daughter—and still more, that Miss Leslie should have acted so imprudently as you state that she has done, is matter of great astonishment to me. Do you forget, sir, your station—your rank in society ?"

"No, Mr. Leslie, no ! I am but a poor man ; yet have I health and youth in my favour. Were you to bestow your daughter upon me, I would use every exertion to promote her comfort. I would work—I would be assiduous—I would toil by night and by day."

"Cease !" exclaimed Mr. Leslie, somewhat wrathfully. "You have presumed too much, young man. This must not—cannot be."

"Cannot, Mr. Leslie !—must not ?"

"Shall not, sir. If Kate has really been so foolish as to give you any such promise as you assert that she has done, I must reprimand her for her folly, and desire that she will atone for it by immediate repentance."

"Oh, say not that, sir !   She loves me—your daughter loves me."

"No matter, sir. Have I not told you that she can never be yours."

Heyton seized the hand of Catherine's father ; and, in a deep, energetic tone of voice, said—

"Hear me, Mr. Leslie ! Words cannot express how much your daughter is beloved by me. Give her to me—say that you will consent to our union ; and there is nothing which man can do that I will not perform, to show you that you have not bestowed her upon one who deserved her not !"

" Cease, sir—cease ! I can hear no more. Catharine, I have told you, cannot be your wife."

" Not if I toil for her—not if I toil to win her, until I have heaped riches around me, and grown pale from excess of labour ?"

" Never, sir—never !"

" Then Heaven resign me to my fate !" ejaculated Heyton, as he left the library by one door as Mr. Leslie went out by another.

That night Stephen Heyton returned to London without bidding adieu to Catherine. He knew that he could not have endured such a meeting. Penning a letter therefore, he described to her the behaviour of her parent, and bid her not to mourn or weep for him. Assuring her that he still loved her fondly as ever, he could yet bear to resign her, if Heaven had so willed it to be.

But how great was Stephen Heyton's joy when the return of the post brought him a letter from Catherine ! In that letter she avowed that in spite of all the reprimands which she had received from her father, her love continued the same, though she could scarcely bear up against the sad turn which things had taken. Heyton pressed this much-loved epistle to his heart, and ejaculated as he did so—

" She shall be mine yet—she shall be mine. It is not in the power of man to separate those who love as we do !"

Again did Stephen write to Catherine, and again through the agency of Mrs. Barnes, did he receive a letter from his beloved. In this epistle he learned that Catherine was unwell. The news was agony to him, he trembled as he read the communication. What was he to do? Catherine might be dangerously ill—might be dying, and he not there to press her hand, to kiss away the death-sweat from her brow ! He raved, he thought, he meditated, he resolved !

" I will save her," he cried; " I will save her ! Even the authority of a parent is nothing when the life of the child is at stake !"

Heyton applied to his master, and obtained leave to be absent for a week. Hurriedly he packed up his small treasures, and taking the coach that very night, was set down the next morning at the door of good Mrs. Barnes, the milk-woman.

" How is she—how is Miss Leslie?" he exclaimed.

" Better, sir—much better. I expect her here to-day to inquire if a letter has arrived from you."

" Will she be here soon ?"

" That depends on whether she can leave the house without her father knowing it. However, she will not be long."

Anxiously did Heyton wait ; but the morning passed away, then came noon, and then the afternoon, and then the evening, and at last Miss Leslie herself,

" Catherine—dear Kate !"

" Stephen—dear Stephen !"

And the lovers embraced one another with fondness. They were together again; her hand was clasped by his, her waist encircled by his arm, her lips were pressed by his own ; and they were happy. Who shall doubt their momentary happiness? Again did they wander out together towards that same lane where they had so often wandered before. Again did they tell to each other the story of their love.

" Kate," cried Stephen, " I love you more than I did when I last parted from you; I love you with a love that will know no repulse—that will acknowledge no thrall. You too love me. Say then, my own Kate—say that you will be mine—that you will brave a father's anger—that you will prove your deep—deep love !"

" Prove it, Stephen !—do you need proof ?"

" Not proof, dearest, but assurance. Say that you will fly with me—say that you will venture all and become mine; say it, my own love—oh ! say so !"

"I cannot—I may not."

"And why, dearest—why?"

"I may not disobey my father's command. He would countenance me—he would curse me if I did."

"Be it so, Kate. Can you—will you not brave the curse of a father for the love of a husband, a husband who would dedicate his whole life to promote and ensure your happiness?"

"No, Stephen, it cannot be."

"But why not, Kate—Kate my own love? Surely you will not cast me off. I who have allowed all hopes and aims to be concentrated in you. No, sweet Kate, it is not in your power to do so; you will not doom me to despair—you who have been the object of my dreams—you, whom I have toiled, and striven, and exerted every energy to win; you will not, while the spring-time of my life is with me, turn me off, and bid me to pine in solitude, unloved, unpitied, and unblest. Oh, let your memory recall, sweet love, the pleasant days that have been, the pleasant dreams that have delighted us both: how we have painted the future, bright, beautiful, and glowing; how we made out of each other a world, and found in the society of one another every joy, every delight! Remember, sweet one, the vows we have made, the pledges we have given; remember how dreary the hours have passed to each other when distance has separated us; remember that our love has been to us a strong and holy passion! Will Heaven allow such love to be annihilated, to be destroyed, to be forgotten? Never, love, never! Believe me, Heaven itself has sanctioned it already—Heaven itself sanctions it now! No one dare curse us, love; not even your father dare curse us for having acted in accordance with the dictates of your soul! We are one, already, love—one now—one in the sight of yonder westering sun, and in the sight of Him to whom that great orb does homage! Come then, Kate, say not that such love as ours is wrong—say not that it is wickedness. You will be mine, love—you consent—you consent!"

"Oh, God, Stephen! that it were otherwise—that I might love you—that I might give you my hand!"

"And the God to whom you have appealed gives you that permission. Our vows are holy in His sight."

"Do not, Stephen—do not tept me; you will drive me to desperation!"

"Be not desperate, sweet Kate, but resolved. Why not in a week—in two days—by to-morrow—by to-night, be mine?"

"My father——"

"He wrongs you; he will forgive you afterwards."

"Never—he will never do so."

"Listen to me, Kate. Do you not remember how we first met—how the beggar and the benefactor saw each other for the first time? Was it not Heaven which brought about so strange a meeting? Do you not remember the scene which occurred in this lane—how the place was lonely—the hour silent and solemn as now? Was it not Heaven which sent me to your aid—which appointed that at that particular time I should be near you? Has not Heaven prospered me, sweet love—has not Heaven blessed me? And think you, then, that it has not to do with our love—that its wonder-working hand has not been employed in bringing us together, and wedding us in soul to each other? Yes, Kate, it is Heaven's doing, and you are mine—mine by an appointed destiny—by the decree of Him who made us both!"

Kate threw herself into Heyton's arm, and faintly ejaculated—

"Be it so—I cannot refuse—I will brave all—I am thine—thine for ever."

"Yes, for ever, beloved one, for ever."

On the evening of the next day Catherine Leslie left her father's house unattended, and without having given notice of her departure. Heyton waited ready to receive her, and kind Mrs. Barnes had made every preparation to aid the flight of the fugitives. Kate wept, but Stephen kissed the tears from her eyes; she desponded, but he pressed her to his side, and, encircled by his arm, she felt security and happiness.

A post-chaise was in readiness—the plan of proceeding had been arranged. Why describe how and by whom the lovers were united? Who is there that is ignorant of the ways and means for carrying out an elopement? How horses are spurred and beaten, how grooms halloo, and how bar-maids envy the happy pair, how finger-posts, signs, and mile-stones are passed as if the lovers fled on the lightning flash, yet how slow and creeping the pace of twelve or fifteen miles an hour seems to them! The destination is gained, the priest is waiting, the ring is ready, the words are spoken, the signatures are made, the ceremony is concluded, and the great central event of life is henceforth a thing of memory and of the past. Doubtless there is more of pleasure in such a marriage than in the common-place, dull, Methodistical manner of going to church in a hackney-coach, attended by your friends, having the bells clanging about your ears, and a dozen or two of relations staring yourself and your partner out of countenance. True love abhors all such display; for to the real lover the company of the loved one only is worth more than the society of a hundred friends.

But Stephen Heyton and Catherine Leslie were married; and on the day succeeding that of the ceremony a missive was sent to the lady's father, acquainting him with the true state of affairs. Then were all the fears and anxieties of the daughter realized; her father did curse her—curse her as having disgraced his name and family. By the return of post she received a letter from him, in which she was informed that he had discarded her, and excluded her from his house for ever. As much as he loved her once, he pledged himself to hate her now, and accompanied his promise with a warning that neither herself nor her husband should ever have the temerity to appear in his presence. Tears—flowing, burning tears—escaped from Catherine's eyes as the letter fell from her hand. Every thing that she had anticipated had come to pass; and although the epistle which she and her husband had penned and transmitted to Mr. Leslie had been written in the most touching manner; yet the reply was even more bitter than the transgressors had expected it would be. Catherine wept and mourned, and would have reproached herself for that which she had done; but Stephen sat by her side, smiled upon her face, and assured her that in the happy future there would be nothing to regret—nothing for self-reproach to exist upon. Thus assured the beautiful bride ceased to grieve, and resolved to wait that which her husband asserted would surely come to pass—the forgiveness of her parent, the reconciliation of her friends.

Heyton and his wife returned to town. The leave of absence had been duly taken, and the young husband now waited upon his employer to confess that which he had done, and to give his promise that his exertions in the future should be more unremitting than they had been in the past. Mr. Milbank smiled graciously upon the young and happy pair, assuring them that they should be kindly regarded by him, and comforting the bride with the intimation that he would take the first opportunity of advancing Mr. Heyton to a higher position than that which he at present occupied.

A year passed away, a child was born, the husband and the wife still loved each other with the fond affection of their happy courting time; but Mr. Leslie still continued to disown the daughter who had dared to act contrary to his commands.

Stephen Heyton had exerted his energies to the utmost, and his industry had been crowned with success. Already he had acquired a sum of money which was safely housed in the bank, and which, united to the small fortune which Catherine had brought him, being that which she enjoyed in her own right, made together a little capital more in amount than would suffice for the entrance of a young trader in a respectable business. The possession of this small treasure was the cause of much joy to the happy pair, and its gradual increase was watched with a constant thrill of delight. Great deeds were to be done with that money on some future day.

Catherine Heyton lived not now in the same style as when she resided beneath her father's roof. She had no carriage to take her airings in, nor any pony on which to ride at her pleasure. There were not so many changes of dress to be seen in her wardrobe, nor was her toilet-table set out with so many articles of fashionable luxury.   Ten or a dozen servants did not now wait her commands, and she had no beautiful flower-gardens, attached to her house, in which to wander at her will. But she had more than all these—she had happiness and a husband's love.   Often in the long winter's evenings would they sit before their parlour fire, Stephen with his arm entwined round her waist and Catherine with her head reposing upon his shoulder, their child sleeping in its cradle beside them, the wild storm raging without, and they so easy, so comfortable within.   At such times the wife regretted not that she had left her father's home to wed such a husband, and the husband in his fond adoration deemed that Heaven could not have given him a greater blessing than to confer on him such a wife.   They loved, they were prosperous, they were in the fullest meaning of the word, happy.

It was on one of those cold wintry evenings that Stephen returned home, looking even more smiling and happy than he was wont to look; when dinner was finished, Catherine called upon him to account for the cause of his merriment.

" Dear Stephen, what good news have you to tell me ?   Come, I am sure you have good news, for your eyes are brighter than ever, your cheeks are quite glowing with joy, and see—mercy me, Stephen! you are rubbing your hands as if you would rub them to pieces."

" Listen, Kate, listen, and don't go into hysterics if I tell you all.   Promise me that !"

" Nonsense, Stephen, don't be so ridiculous.   Oh! how I long to know what it is you have to disclose.   You have not heard from my father, have you?"

" No, Kate, no ; but listen :—This morning I received a message from Mr. Milbank, to this intent, that he wished to have an interview with me in his private room.   I waited upon him accordingly, he shook my hand in a friendly manner, and asked, my sweet Kate, after your health.   After talking with him for a few minutes I saw that he had something of importance to communicate.   He commenced by extolling my habits of industry, and then proceeded to detail to me some particulars concerning the present state of his affairs.   Presently he informed me that, owing to his constitutional ill-health, he found it necessary that he should relax in his attention to business and avail himself of the country air together with quietude and rest as far as he could possibly command them.   He had thought the matter over, and wished to know whether I had not saved up some money and whether you had not brought me a fortune.   I told him that by industry and economy I had contrived to keep a little money in the bank, but that the chief portion which my wife had brought me was her invaluable self.   Mr. Milbank smiled, and after a pause of some two or three minutes, asked me what I thought of my becoming his partner and adding my small sum of money to the trading capital of the house."

" Mr. Milbank's partner, Stephen." }

" Yes, my sweet Kate.   Do not be so astonisehd.   Do not look frightened at the proposition.   Mr. Milbank makes me the offer of becoming his partner, and proposes that one-third of the profits of the firm shall be mine."

" And what was your answer, Stephen."

" I could give him no answer, dear Kate, until I had consulted you.   Recollect that we are partners already ; and it would be highly wrong of me to take any such important step as that now proposed, unless you, my love, as the other member of the firm, were agreeable."

" But, dear Stephen, only to think—only consider that——"

" That the present prosperous business, my love, waits but your sanction to become conducted under the united names of Milbank and Heyton.   Think of that, Kate ! Think of the beggar boy becoming the merchant !   Think of Kate, the clerk's wife, becoming Mrs. Heyton, the merchant's bride !   What may not be the result?   Is it not probable that your father would relent—that he would own his child again ? Come, Kate—come, my sweet wife—am I to accept or decline the proposal?"

" Oh, no ! dear Stephen—not decline ; and Mr. Milbank so good—so generous !

Your becoming a city merchant will not make your love for me any the less : will it, dear Stephen?"

"Such a question from you, Kate! Were I made a king, would you not be my queen—queen of my heart then, as you are queen of it now?"

"Then, dear Stephen, I consent. Act according to your own judgment, and use the small, the very small sum which I brought you, in whatever way you may deem best. Only love me, as you have ever loved me, my dear husband, and I ask no more."

Stephen Heyton kissed the rosy cheek of his young and beautiful wife, giving her at the same time an assurance, that death alone should win him from his love. The evening passed away in happiness; and on the next morning preparations were commenced by Mr. Milbank for the future carrying on of the business in partnership with that individual whom, some years before, he had received into his house as a common errand-boy. Strange was the mutation! The errand-boy had, through the force of his own exertions, become the merchant now! " Give me a lever to do it with, and I will move the world!" said the sanguine mechanician of old. The nearest approach to such a lever is to be found in unremitting industry, for the limits of what it can accomplish have never yet been discovered or made out.

Two years were flown, and the Heytons had a son as well as a daughter. They had become people of some note in the city, though Mr. Leslie still continued to disown the child who had contemned his authority and had not consulted his desires. Two years were past, and Mr. Milbank had, during this long period, grown more and more remiss in his attention to the business of the firm. Nevertheless, owing to the untiring industry of the junior partner, the house prospered, and wealth seemed to pour in without check or cessation. Stephen Heyton would often contemplate his present position with a thrill of pleasure—not because he himself had become rich, but because his beloved wife would again enjoy those comforts and luxuries which had been hers while residing under her father's roof. During this period Stephen Heyton had become acquainted with a gentleman who paid occasional visits to his house. The name of this gentleman must not now be divulged, entering, as he does, so much into the mystery of our story. He was, in every respect, a singular individual. His manners were those of a perfect man of the world; yet his countenance wore an expression of deep gloom, and his demeanour was that of one who had some secret sorrow preying at his heart. Attired always in dark-coloured garments, he seldom laughed, and never was heard to utter a syllable in jest. Yet, who that looked upon his features saw not that he had laughed—that he had jested—that, at some period of his life, he had been as gay and as thoughtless as any one other of the poor butterflies who flutter and sparkle in the seducing flower-garden of the world? This individual had become Heyton's friend; and his fate is intimately connected with the fates of those who have figured, and who will yet figure, in this narrative of mystery.

Mrs. Heyton, the merchant's wife, was stepping into her carriage—for Heyton kept a carriage now—when the postman arrived at the door, and delivered two letters into the hand of the servant, "one of these is for you, ma'am," said the domestic, making his bow and handing the letter to his mistress. It was directed to " Catherine Heyton." The merchant's wife took it, and glanced at the superscription, her hand trembled; she turned it over and examined the seal—her cheeks turned pale. " Stop," said she to the coachman, and ordering the carriage to wait, she re-entered the house. Hastily the letter was broken open, " Where is Mr. Heyton?" she asked.

" In the counting-house, ma'am.

" Tell him that I wish to speak with him immediately."

The husband came; he saw the pallor which had overspread the cheeks of his wife; he saw the letter which shook in her trembling hand. " Good Heavens, Catherine!" he exclaimed, " what has happened, why have you sent for me, what is the cause of your agitation?"

" Read, Stephen—read! the letter is from my father, he is ill, he is relenting, he is about to forgive! See, he asks me to forget what has passed; he desires me to visit him immediately! and you too, Stephen—he is willing to see you. Oh! let us go, let us depart immediately, he will forgive me, he will call me his daughter again!"

"These are indeed joyful tidings, my Kate; there must be no delay; you must go to your father's immediately."

"And you, Stephen, he asks to see you."

"I will follow you, Kate, I cannot accompany you."

"Not accompany me!"

"No, sweetest. At the present moment I have some most important business to attend to; and I should be acting unjustly to Mr. Milbank were I to absent myself for a single day. Go, dearest, go; and in two days, or it may be three, I will rejoin you; your father does not seem to be dangerously ill."

Mrs. Heyton was, however, reluctantly obliged to comply with this arrangement. She parted affectionately from her husband, rejoicing in the anticipation of being clasped to the bosom of the parent who had once loved her most fondly and whom she still regarded with the love of a daughter, however much he had estranged himself from her.

"How is my dear father, Hughes?" said she, as she stepped out of the post-chaise, at the door of her childhood's home.

"Worse, miss—ma'am I mean—than he has been these two days; oh, how glad he ought to be to see you! for I am sure it does one's heart good to see your sweet face again."

"I thank you for your welcome; but my father, is he in the sitting-room, or the library?"

"Bless you, madam! he can't sit up. He's been a-bed these two days."

"A-bed!" exclaimed the daughter in surprise, as with a fearful presentiment of coming evil, she rushed up towards her father's bed-chamber.

"My father—my dear—dear—dearest, father!" she cried as she flung herself upon his neck.

"Catherine—Kate—I—I—forgive me—do not reproach me, my child."

"I have never done so, dear father—never."

The old man raised himself in his bed, and bade his daughter seat herself by his side.

"Come, tell me," said he, "is it as I have heard? you have not married a beggar, you are happy, you are comfortable, as the daughter of a Leslie should be?"

"Indeed, indeed yes, dear father! Heyton is rich now; he has wealth; he has good repute, and he loves me, dear father, he loves me, fondly, adoringly! I am happy in all but the want of your forgiveness."

"You have it now, child, you have it; I will forget the past, I will pardon you for your error; I am dying, my daughter; they may bribe the leech to tell me lies, but I feel that death is at its handiwork."

"Oh, say not that, father—believe not that!"

"The belief, child, is independent of my will."

That day and the next passed away. Mrs. Heyton heard nothing from her husband, and her father gradually grew worse. On the evening of the third day he sent for her in great haste.

"Catherine," said he, "come near me. See you this? it is my will, my will, in which everything is put down except the names of those whom my death wil benefit, mark you these blank places; they yet wait to be filled up. Tell me, child, what names shall I write?"

"Ask not me, dear father, give the matter your due consideration, and when you have formed your resolution write accordingly."

"Hear me, child! you speak as if I had years to live, while even the weeks, the days—ay—or it may be only hours are numbered. I have considered, child. When you married him who is now your husband, I disowned you—I disowned you because you had given your hand to a mere beggar; but they tell me Heyton is a merchant now—that he has got wealth—that he has won honour; therefore, child, I forgive you. Understand me well! not for your contumacy in wedding as you did, and now coming to beg my pardon do I forgive you—no, no, not for that, but because your husband has gained wealth, because he has won himself yellow gold and merchant's credit—that is why I forgive him and you. 'Tis well; I will be your friend now, I will do all that I can for you; death is on me, child—death is on me, and I shall never rise from this bed again; but the estate shall be yours child, I will make your husband the richer partner of the two. See, here is—"

The door of the chamber was suddenly opened, and a servant advancing, placed a letter in the hand of the dying man's daughter. Mrs. Heyton glanced at the superscription, which had the word "immediate" written in one corner; the seal was of black wax.

"Merciful Heaven!" she exclaimed, "what may this mean? My husband's handwriting!"

"What is it, Kate—what have you there, child?"

"Nothing, dear papa; a mere letter of business. Your pardon for a moment."

So saying, Catherine Heyton retired hastily into an adjoining apartment, and broke open the letter. A sudden exclamation escaped from her lips as she read the first words. The colour left her cheeks, her lips turned deadly pale, and her teeth chattered as she read the dreadful words.

The letter ran thus :—

"MY EVER DEAR KATE,—Be careful how you read this letter ; do not let any one be near you, do not read it unless you are by yourself. It would be wrong of me, dearest, if I wrote not to you immediately ; yet the task is a hard one, it being the first time since we have known each other that I have felt reluctance in writing to the dear idol of my heart. But, my sweet Kate, if it is a hard task for me to write, it will be harder still for you to read that which I have written. Dearest, I beseech you to be calm, and to peruse these lines with a bold heart and a trusting spirit. Believe that the great Disposer of events rules everything for the best ; believe that He will not forsake us, even in the sorrow into which we are now plunged.

"You will recollect, my own love, that prior to your departure, I said that I had some important business to attend to, which prevented my accompanying you in your journey. Little—little did I think how really important that business was !

"Dearest, we have nothing now ! You are startled, but be calm—be very calm. It came to my knowledge that the credit of the firm was reported to stand good no longer. Judge my astonishment when I heard such a report ! I conferred with Mr. Millbank ; he was confused, and gave me no explanation. I applied to our bankers, and, to my still greater surprise, was informed that the firm had overdrawn, and that our accounts were closed. I rushed home. I again sought Millbank. While I was asking for him, I heard a pistol-shot in one of the upper rooms. I flew up the stairs, I broke open a door, and, Millbank had shot himself— the red, warm blood was streaming on the floor.

"I have learnt it all, dearest. For what have I been toiling ? for what have I been saving money ? I will tell you. And your fortune, too—what has become of that ? Listen.—Millbank during these last two years has turned gambler ;—I have been toiling to win wealth, while he has been throwing away our gains—my gains—your gains, sweetest, at the gaming-table. He has deceived me by making false entries in the ledgers ; he has notified the payment of bills which have never yet been paid ; he has declared the disbursement of debts which yet wait to be disbursed ; and this is not all, he has committed forgery also—forgery, of which the decreed punishment is death by the hangman's hands.

"In one week, dearest—in a few days, as it were, the ruin has come upon us. Our pleasant dreams are dissipated ; we are dishonoured, and penniless now. Heaven knows how the investigation which has just commenced may terminate, and what further disclosures may be made ! One thing is certain, love, all that we had is gone—robbed from us by a villain.   .

"Do not grieve, my beloved ; do not despair. God in the high heaven will look upon us yet ! Stay at your father's, and I will send the children to you. I cannot write more. I cannot pen another line. Believe me, my sweet love, more than ever yours,   "STEPHEN HEYTON."

P.S.—"Millbank is just dead. He begged my pardon, and I forgave him. May God forgive him also !"

Uttering a shriek, Catherine let the letter fall from her hand, and she herself fell senseless upon the floor.

That shriek was heard by her father. He arose—the dying man crept out of his bed ; he stole across his chamber ; he approached the door ; he entered the room in which his daughter lay senseless ; darting forward he grasped the letter— his sunken, glassy eyes wandered over the lines. The contents were known to him. A wild laugh escaped from his lips.

"Beggars after all !" he cried, " beggars after all ! ha ! ha ! said I not so ? said I not she had married a beggar, and has not my curse worked well ?"

Then, suddenly recollecting himself, the dying man tottered back again to the table on which lay the open will. His hand still clasped the fatal letter; the exclamation which he had uttered still hung upon his lips; he rung the bell which stood upon the table, and then seated himself in the chair; a servant entered, who started in surprise to see her master risen from his bed.

"Send Hughes and Walters to me," said he, "send them directly."

The command was obeyed; in a few minutes the two domestics entered the apartment.

"Come near," said Mr. Leslie, "witness both of you that I fill up these blanks and sign this will."

He took the pen in his hand; he held it firmly; a minute he paused—only for a minute—the blanks were filled up; the property given way. "Put your names as witnesses to this, men," said he; the men trembled but they obeyed. "Now," said he, "see that I sign it myself."

Calmly, without trembling, without a shake of the hand, that might have been construed into an indication of weakness, he affixed his signature to the document.

"There!" he exclaimed feebly, "he was a beggar then, and they are beggars now!"

Catherine Heyton had, in the mean time, recovered from her swoon; her first thought was to look for the letter, but she saw it not. Hastily she opened the door to enter her father's apartment—the domestics started back—the parent faced his daughter.

"Curses—curses on thee!" he exclaimed.

He fell back in his chair—his eyes became fixed—his breathing suspended. With a quick, sharp sound, his lower jaw fell, still was his contenance turned upon his daughter, still in his right hand was the pen with which he had signed his name, and in his left hand, firmly, tightly clasped, the letter, which the husband had forwarded to the wife; still was the scorn upon his features—the hate upon his brow—the curse upon his lip—and he was dead!

Catherine rushed forward to clasp the inanimate form of the parent who had cursed her as he died, and at that moment her eyes caught sight of the name with which the blanks in the parchment had been filled up.

CHAPTER XVII.

THE STORY OF THE WRONGED ONE IS FINISHED.—THE RETURN TO THE COTTAGE.

FEARFUL had been the revenge of the relentless parent, and well had he carried out his curse. He had left his daughter penniless, and bequeathed his estates to a relative whom he had not seen for years, and who had no claims upon his kindness except that of the most distant relationship.

Mr. Heyton found, upon examination of his affairs, that after disposing of all the stock, the proceeds would only be sufficient to pay the debts of the firm. What to do he knew not. His wife had rejoined him, and it was only by looking at her and her innocent children, and thinking how desolate they would be in the world were he not with them, that he kept himself from committing suicide. It requires a bold heart to withstand such sorrow as Stephen Heyton then knew, without secretly contemplating that last and fearful resource—self-destruction.

Perhaps of the two, Catherine bore these calamities with more heroism than did her husband. Not a word of repining escaped her lips; never did she weep or sigh in the presence of him whom she so fondly loved; but the grief which sorrows in secret is the most severe; there is no woe comparable to that woe which gnaws the heart into a ruin, yet tells not to those around of the fearful work on which it is engaged. Not for the loss of her father's estate—not because he had transferred his property to another, and left his own daughter to starve, did

Catherine mourn : no, she could look starvation in the face—she had that daring which shakes hands with destruction and bids even death to do its worst; but, though she could forgive the cruelty, she could not forget the curse—that curse with which her own parent had cursed her, which escaped from his lips with the last breath he drew, and sate upon them when they were pale, and cold, and rigid—that curse which still rang in her ears, waking her from her sleep and haunting her in the darkness—that curse which sounded fearfully now as it sounded fearfully then, she could never, never, escape from. It was the curse of a father—a father who had once loved her, and whose memory she still loved : to be cursed by him—to have such a curse to haunt her through the world, was misery indeed. No wonder that she felt it, no wonder that canker, sorrow, preyed upon her spirit, causing her once bright eyes to become dim, her cheeks to pale, her countenance to become wan; no wonder that she grew attenuated, lean, and hollow-eyed ; the worm was within, ever gnawing, ever at its death-work there.

One morning, some eight or ten weeks after the sale of the property, Stephen observed his wife busily engaged in a domestic occupation. The establishment had, of course, been broken up and the servants dismissed. Mrs. Heyton had to do everything with her own hand; she did not observe that her husband was watching her, and in performing the little duty which occupied her attention she allowed a sigh to escape from her bosom. Presently afterwards her strength failed her, the utensil which she held in her hand fell from her grasp, and she herself sank back in a swoon upon a chair which happened to be within reach.

"Catherine—my Catherine!" exclaimed Heyton, rushing to her assistance. "God of mercy, what has happened to my sweet love?"

Mrs. Heyton heard her husband's voice, and by a strong exertion she contrived to rally, and to return an answer to his inquiry.

"It was nothing—nothing, dear Stephen. I—I—it is gone—quite gone ; I am free from it now."

"Free from what, dearest?"

"A pain—only a slight pain."

As the meek and enduring wife returned this answer, Heyton observed, in one glance, the effects which misery had wrought upon the countenance of his beloved. Not until that moment had the sad and terrible change been apparent to him, and until now Catherine had worn her mask well. But the illusion was now dissipated ; the reality—the dreadful reality understood. Heyton broke away from her as soon as he could, and locking himself in another apartment, he clasped his hand to his burning brow and ejaculated—

"It is I—I am her murderer! I stole her from her father's house, from happiness, from ease, from luxury ; I caused her father to curse her—to hate her whilst he lived, to contemn her as he died ; I too, have made her a beggar. Even now she is starving—even now the dart has pierced deep. 'Tis I have done it—I—I, her husband—her deceiver—her—oh, God, that it should be so,—her murderer—her murderer!"

Presently the ruined merchant attired himself in his walking dress and again seeking his wife, kissed her fondly and bade her farewell.

"Where are you going, dear Stephen?"

"On business, my sweet love, to some distance. I may be detained."

"For how long, when will you return?"

"Not till late, love—not till late."

Again he embraced his wife ; then kissing each of the children he left the house.

Throughout the whole of that day did Stephen Heyton wander up and down the streets of the metropolis. In vain did he endeavour to compose his thoughts, and to devise some plan for the future; all seemed dark and dreary, everything wore an aspect of gloom. In the course of three months he had become another man ; nothing of his former lightheartedness and sanguine nature now remained. He who had struggled so bravely against the most unpromising circumstances, felt no strength to struggle longer, even for a day; in his own thoughts, in his own estimation, he had committed an act of injustice by estranging his wife from her father and her friends, and it now preyed upon his mind, that the Catherine whom he loved was dying, and that he was accountable for her death. The very thought was madness. Evening had set in, and still the miserable man wandered the streets at random; at length his resolution seemed to be taken, and he directed his steps along the road leading towards Chelsea. On still he went—on without pausing, without looking at anyone whom he passed by the way. Having walked for some distance, he came in sight of the river Thames, and not far from him on his right was a large, lone house, which stood in a meadow beside the river. He started, he deliberated with himself, and then advanced towards the house.

That house was then a habitable mansion, it is now the desolate ruin—the " Haunted House " of the former chapters of our story.

Heyton approached the door, and laid his hand upon the bell-handle. He was about to ring, but a sudden thought seemed to paralyse his arm, and dropping rather than removing his fingers from the bell-handle, he turned about and left the house.

His eyes had caught sight of the gleaming river, and thitherward he went. Fire seemed to be consuming his brain. There was a demon by his side whispering fearful things in his ear.

On towards the bright, the shining river; all is stilly there, and the moon rides silently in the sky above.

Heyton thought he heard a footstep behind him; he turned hastily round, but seeing nobody, pursued his way as before.

And now he stood in the shade of a clump of trees by the river-side. Once, and once only, he looked towards heaven—then, turning away his eyes, he clasped his hands to his brow, and ejaculated in a low voice,—

" It must be so—it must be so ! I, who am a murderer, must live no longer."

He threw off his upper garments, and then fell upon his knees on the sod. Still was his head bent down, still were his hands clasped; the only words which he uttered audibly, were—

" Bless her ! God bless her as she should be blessed !"

Again he arose, again he gazed on the quiet, shining water.

" Be it so !" he said; " I cannot go to torture worse than that which I now endure."

He stepped forward—he stood upon the bank—his eyes were closed—he took that breath which he intended should be his last.

Suddenly a hand was laid upon his shoulder.

" Stephen Heyton, what are you about to do ?"

The would-be suicide started, and, lifting up his eyes, saw by his side a gentleman attired in black. It was the same individual who had visited him in his prosperity, and to whom, in the last chapter, we have taken occasion to refer.

The question was repeated—

" Stephen Heyton, why are you here ? What are you about to do ?"

" To atone," he replied, " to atone as I must atone."

" For what, man—for what ?"

" For injustice—for murder."

" What is it you speak of ? To what do you refer ?"

" To her—to my own wife. I took her from her home, I brought upon her her father's curse, I have led her to her present misery, and I can look upon her no longer."

" Then Mrs. Heyton is not dead ?"

" No, no; not dead ! But—yes—I have murdered her ! I have brought misery to her—I have deprived her of happiness for ever—is not that murder ?"

" And now you would kill yourself ?"

" Should not the murderer die ?"

" Leave that to the murderer's Maker. Tell me, has not your wife misery enough already ?"

" Enough—enough ? Aye, God knows that it is enough !"

" Yet you would increase it—you would increase it by depriving her of the only friend she has, and act yourself as only cowards act ! Hark you ! I watched you go up to the door of my house, I saw you raise your fingers to the bell-handle, I followed you to this spot, I have arrived in time to rescue you from destruction. Stephen Heyton, I bid you to follow me !"

" Follow you ?"

" Yes. This night you shall hear a story of horror, and when you have heard it, you will think no more of the imaginary greatness of your puny sorrows. Come, you will accompany me ?"

The gentleman took the arm of Heyton and led him away from the water-side. They walked on together for some distance, and at length entered the large and lonely house which stood in the meadow, and which is now a haunted ruin.

" We will proceed to business in this room," said the gentleman, as he closed the door of a large, dull apartment, in which there was no other light than that derived from the moonbeams flittering through the window.

The gentleman gave Heyton a seat, and placed beside it another for himself. When seated he addressed his companion, and in a solemn voice, said—

" You will listen, Stephen Heyton ; and if that which you hear told should cause your blood to chill and your flesh to creep, you must exert yourself to overcome the feeling of horror, and to deliberate calmly upon the proposal which I have to make."

" Proposal !—a proposal to me ?"

" Yes ; but the story must be heard first. This is the very night on which it should be told, for this is the anniversary of that fearful night on which it occurred—"

" On which it occurred !—What talk you of ? Why speak you in a voice so hollow—so husky ?"

" Listen, and you shall hear. It was on this night, I say, exactly two years ago—but you must draw nearer, Mr. Heyton. Such a tale must be told in a whisper only. Nearer still. Can you hear me distinctly ?"

" Louder—a little louder. That will do."

The tale was told.

What that tale was, will be divulged in the progress of the story. When the gentleman had finished its narration, Heyton sprang from his chair, and gazed wildly at his companion. Their eyes met ; the lips of each were fixed, yet apart ; the countenances of both indicated an inward feeling of horror existent in the mind of each. The face of Heyton was of a deadly pallor, and he seemed to shrink from his companion as from some frightful phantom, whose touch might be of deadly effect. Some minutes passed before he could command his power of utterance. When that power was regained his first exclamation was,—

" Is it—is it all true—all a dreadful reality ?"

" Every word, Mr. Heyton, has been truth. Would to Heaven I had not told you but a fiction !"

" And why—why have you confided it to me ?"

" Because I have a proposal to make to you ; one which, if you agree to it, will release you from all your present anxieties, and place you in a situation where the rest of your life may—"

The gentleman paused.

" You were speaking of my future life—of what it might be ; what were you about to say ?"

" That which it were not wise to utter. I will make no predictions, Mr. Heyton, but go at once to the proposal."

" Stay !" exclaimed Heyton—" is it—is it of the same nature as the story ?"

" How mean you ?"

" Is it one that I *may* hear—one that I might listen to in the open day, instead of hearing it in this gloomy room ?"

" You will know when you have heard it."

" May we not have a lamp, a light of any kind ?"

" Thought can be exercised more freely in darkness. You will have to think before you return your answer."

" And if I reject your proposal ?"

" You will be as you are now. But sit down and listen. Are you willing to hear ?"

" I am."

"The proposal then is this—." What followed was spoken in a whisper, and it was that which must not be related here. Stephen Heyton listened in breathless silence to every word, and when he heard all that his companion had to say, he again arose from his seat.

"Give me leave to think over that which I have heard," said he.

" The permission is granted," replied the gentleman.

" Heyton walked to and fro about the room for some minutes, and at length laid his hand upon the arm of his companion.

" Must I comply with each of your demands ?'" he asked.

" With all of them, Stephen Heyton."

" And I may not repeat that which you have told me to any one ?"

" To none but your wife—to her alone."

" All—all that I have heard ?"

" The proposal only. As for the narrative which I have confided to you, it must rest in your breast alone. None on earth must know it until—until—"

" Until when ?"

" Until the time has arrived when it becomes your duty to reveal it to that individual whom it will then alone concern.'"

" And she—"

" Must be told it under a solemn pledge that she will carry it with her to the grave. Do you understand ?"

" Yes."

" And you agree?"

"To-morrow morning I will give you my answer."

" Why delay—why not take your resolve this night, that I may know before it before we part ?"

" The proposal is strange—is unnatural."

" You may think so."

" To agree to it would be to incur many responsibilities."

" And therefore, Heyton, the greatness of the reward."

" But should she die before—"

" Hazard no such supposition. You, at least, would have discharged your duty."

" But the story—"

" Would be yours only ; its horrors known to you alone. Come, your answer of acceptance or rejection."

" I accept, I agree."

" 'Tis well. Here is money for you. Go home to your wife. Confide to her that only which you have permission to tell, and I will see you again to-morrow evening at your own home."

Heyton and the mysterious one parted. In less than a month from the date of this conversation, the ruined merchant, accompanied by his wife and children, retired to a cottage near the sea-side in a distant part of England. They lived in a comfortable, homely style, though the source whence their income was derived was a mystery to all. Strange reports were circulated concerning the subject, and surmises of all kinds were hazarded ; but no one could tell how the penniless merchant had suddenly become possessed of wealth sufficient to purchase a cottage ; and, despite all their conjectures, they could not unriddle the mystery of why Stephen Heyton had retired from the world of business to live upon an income which seemed sufficient for its possessor to commence the world with it again.

It may be as well to state, in this place, that all the wealth which Heyton possessed, with which he retired from the metropolis, and by which he supported his wife and family, was derived from his acceptance of the proposal made to him by the mysterious friend who had interposed between him and death, and whose fearful story had been so replete with horrors.

Often did this individual visit the cottage of the retired merchant. On every occasion he was attired in deep black—his countenance being overspread with one continual gloom. Of the three children of Stephen Heyton, Amy was the one towards whom the stranger appeared the most attached, and whose infantine prattle appeared to have the most music to his ear. He was in the habit of taking her on his knee and caressing her; and a careful observer might have noted that, when the stern and gloomy man played with the prattling child, his countenance relaxed from its usual austerity, and a tear sometimes escaped down his cheeks. Even upon the most hardened criminal the presence of a child has been observed to work an extraordinary effect. Guilt seems to shudder at its own guiltiness when it looks upon an infant form, fresh from its Maker's hands in all its holy purity.

It was late in the evening of a winter's day, when a message came to Heyton, hastily summoning him to visit this mysterious individual. He obeyed the command, and arrived in time to witness the gentleman's death. The room was cleared of every other visitant, and the two were alone together.

"Stephen Heyton," said the dying man, " I go to meet my God, and to Him every confession must be made ; but again I demand your promise to keep the story which you heard from me a secret—a secret till the time comes at which I have given you permission to reveal it."

" Your desire shall be obeyed ; my pledge shall be kept," replied Heyton.

"You will reveal it to none, except to — ?" The last word was spoken in a whisper.

" I will not, on my oath !"

" 'Tis well ! I die. Mine, Stephen Heyton, is a death which many would dread ; but I can meet it calmly. Tell me, man—tell me—those who have done as I have should not fear to look at death. Say you not so ?"

Stephen Heyton turned away his head, and was unable to make a reply. Suddenly he heard a gurgling sound behind him, and again he looked towards the bed. Awful was the sight which he beheld there ! The eyes of the dying man were fixed ; his face had turned of a dark purple hue. Convulsively he grasped the hand of Heyton, and made an effort to speak.

" Promise—keep—tell it not—the time will come—ha ! I see it—I see it—it is acted before me—I die—I—I—I—;" and vainly struggling to utter another syllable, he fell back upon his pillow never to rise again.

Heyton returned to his home, and told to his wife the particulars of the scene to which he had been a witness. He suppressed, however, everything which related to the dread secret which he was bound not to reveal until the arrival of the appointed time.

A twelvemonth passed away; and then Stephen Heyton was called to stand beside another death-bed—to hear the last words of another dying mortal. But how different was the scene ; for the dying one was his own wife—the wife whom he loved so well ! He shuddered not now ; he bore the trial with firmness. The event had been anticipated by him long, months before —knowing, as he did, that, however much his Catherine had tried to dissemble, and to put on an appearance of cheerfulness and resignation, she had still borne a sorrowing heart within, and had allowed the curse of her father to prey upon her spirits like a canker worm ever at its work.

She died. Encircled by the arms of him whom she had loved through life, she gave herself up to death. The struggle was but a short one ; for the frame of the poor victim had been worn away by the continual anguish of her mind. She called for her children, and they were brought to her. She pressed her lips to theirs—her lips that were so soon to become cold for ever—to theirs which glowed with the bright vermilion hue of young and bounding life. From her children she turned to her husband; and, repeating his name in that same soft melodious manner in which she had spoken it long years ago, she clasped his hand with her own pale, wan, skeleton fingers, and in that clasp shook hands with him for the last time.

Heyton wept bitterly, and well he might. Before him lay the form of that beautiful being who had won his heart in years gone by, and who had been the sole idol he had worshipped through life. Back to his mind came the recollection of the beggar boy pitied by the maiden, the wooing in the green lane, the avowal of love, the elopement, the bridal, the happy years, and the parent's curse. Everything that had been floated now in pictures before him. He had loved, and where was the loved one? There had been one to whom he could tell the tale of sorrow, and to whom he could apply for the pitying tear or the comforting word, and where was that one now? As he looked upon the attenuated form which lay in its lifelessness before him, he could scarcely bring his mind to believe that there

was the Catherine Leslie of his first and only love! Was that the bright, laughing, beautiful being whom he had worshipped in his courting time? was that the kind angel who had cheered him amidst all his sadness, whom he once toiled to win, whom having won he adored, and who had been more than the world to him when the world itself had frowned and lowered upon him?

Being now a widower, Mr. Heyton had to procure the assistance of a female domestic, to take charge of the household matters. As for his children, he was careful that they should receive an education suitable to their present condition and future prospects in life. Kate appeared to have more of natural talent than her sister Amy, and accordingly met with more success in the studies to which she applied herself. Drawing, painting, and music, were her delight, and notwithstanding that she had to attend to domestic duties, and to wait upon her father, whose declining health required every attention, yet she found sufficient time in which to acquire many accomplishments, and in which to avail herself of the gratification of those tastes, by which she had been endowed by nature.

Kate Heyton has been already described ; but as it is her sister Amy who forms the heroine of our story, we must be permitted to say a few words descriptive of her.

If beauty has ever yet visited this earth in female guise, it made itself known in Amy Heyton. Unlike her sister, she was possessed of few accomplishments, and presented no dazzling points of attraction. Kate seemed made to figure in the crowded ball-room, and to be the cynosure of every eye. Amy was more fitted for the silent dell, the woodland shade, or the seat beside the hearth-stone. Her gentle, loving soul spoke out through her soft blue eyes, while the tenderness and purity of her heart was made known by every word she uttered. Graceful as a wood-nymph in her movements, her form was fashioned according to that airy lightness of mould, in which painters depict the fairy beings of their fancies. The features of Kate were bold and expressive—those of her sister were delicately and softly chiselled. Amy had the most beautiful hair imaginable ; it was of a light colour, but of that particular hue which gives to the mind of the beholder the idea of sun-beams woven into tresses. Her complexion was clear and pearly, there being only a slight tinge of the rose upon her cheeks, varying, however, in its depth with each passing emotion of her soul. Be it distinctly understood, dear reader, that had you been introduced to the Heytons, and supposing you to be a young man, you would have sat and admired Kate for a full hour, without wishing to move from your position, but you would have given all the worldly wealth in your possession for the grant of ten minutes converse' with Amy, and leave to hold her soft hand in yours during that space of time.

Francis Heyton, or, as his sisters loved to call him, Frank, was a young man of apparently nineteen or twenty years of age. He was possessed of an open and commanding countenance, fine, dark, lustrous eyes, and auburn-coloured hair, which hung in rich bushy curls around a small but handsome-shaped head. His figure was manly, and the expression of his features such as was well calculated to make a favourable effect upon a beholder. Frank was the idol of his sisters, who seemed to take pleasure in calling him their own brother. He was especially fond of Amy, and had always manifested a desire to please her in the minutest particulars. His anxiety was always great whenever ill-health was felt by her, or when any secret trouble caused her cheek to pale, or her eyes to look downcast. Loving her then as he did, it was not wondrous that he felt acutely the wrong done to her by Ernest Morden. It had been his fond hope that he should have to regard Ernest as his brother-in-law, for already had they been friends together for many years. Now, however, that cup of happiness was dashed away from him ; it being his present belief, that Amy had been made the dupe of a villain, and that Ernest, however much he might have felt a liking for her in days gone by, now that he was advanced in station, wished to break off the connection in such way as he best could. Whether Frank Heyton was right or wrong in this conjecture, the course of the story will show.

Having thus sketched the main events in the history of Stephen Heyton, we return to the cottage, and to the two girls watching in the chamber.

" See, Kate, see !" exclaimed Amy ; " what is that bright light which I see yonder?"

" It is the first ray of the morning sun, dear sister."

" The morning !—and neither father nor Frank returned. Hark !"

They listened.

"Hush, Amy, hush! I hear footsteps. It is them—I know it is them."

Kate parted from her sister, and proceeded towards the door of the cottage. Amy meanwhile leant over the side of the bed and held her breath, that she might hear the slightest sound.

A few minutes passed, and then the father had pressed his daughters to his heart, and the brother had embraced his sisters.

"Where have you been, dear father? Why look you so haggard? Where is Ernest? Who were the men we saw on the Eagle's Altar?" asked Amy, not giving her parent time to answer one of her questions before she propounded another.

The maidens listened in breathless silence while Frank and his father narrated their midnight adventures. When the story was brought to a conclusion, Amy laid her hand on her father's arm, and in an impressive voice, asked,—

"But Ernest, father—where is he now?"

"I know not, child. Probably he has returned to his ship. I will accompany Frank this afternoon in rowing round the point, and endeavouring, if possible, to seek an interview with him in the vessel."

"Why take Frank with you, father? Why not get Jasper, the old fisherman, or Murray, or ——"

"And why do you object to my going with father?" asked Frank.

"Because—because, dear brother, you are so passionate—so hasty."

"You fear that I should do harm to Ernest Morden, were I to meet him?"

"You might, brother—you might."

And if I did, sister, how would that affect you? Surely you cannot love Ernest Morden now after the insult—the deep insult which he offered you last night?"

"Ernest did me no wrong, brother."

"No wrong, Amy—no wrong! By Heaven, sister, he shall never do such wrong again!"

"Be calm, brother—be calm, I implore you! It was not the fault of Ernest. Heard you not the words of the other—the traveller?"

"Well, sister, that which Ernest could not do without assistance, he employed his friend to perform, and excellently well they played their parts!"

"Hush, brother—hush. Whom do you mean by Ernest's friend?"

"Him, sister—the man who claiming the right of hospitable shelter, entered the dwelling of the charitable to do the work of a demon—he is Ernest's friend."

"No, not Ernest's friend, brother—Ernest's foe."

"You think so, Amy."

"I am certain."

Mr. Heyton here interposed.

"Peace, child," said he, "you know not the villany of the world. There is much that is plausible and probable also in your brother's conjecture. You, Amy, are but asserting that which you wish were in reality the case when you say that Ernest Morden and the traveller are strangers to each other."

"I said not that they were unacquainted, father."

"Did you not say they were foes?"

"The old man is a foe to Ernest."

"And how know you that?"

"Wait, father—wait till breakfast time, and I will give you the history of that portrait which sister Kate has in her possession."

CHAPTER XVIII.

THE MYSTERY OF THE MYSTERIOUS PORTRAIT.

THE Heytons were gathered round the breakfast-table; and the portrait of the old man was placed before them, carefully covered up, however, with a piece of black cloth.

"Let me again look at that picture, Amy," said her father.

The girl took the painting in her hand to give it to her parent. As she laid her fingers upon it, a sudden tremor passed over her frame, and her face became paler than it had been a few minutes before.

"You tremble, Amy?"

"I—I cannot help it, dear father. Take the portrait."

Mr. Heyton removed the black cloth from the picture, and having done so, surveyed intently the mysterious performance.

"It is wondrous like!" he ejaculated. "What say you, Frank, is not this the very image of the old traveller?"

"Every part is a perfect representation, father. But, say you that this is Kate's doing?"

"Your sister has confessed to it. The mystery, however, lies in this: Kate says that she drew this likeness from imagination only."

"Nay, dear father," interposed Kate, "you misconstrue my words. I said not that I drew it from my fancy."

"Then how, child—how? Did you not assure me that you had no copy?"

"Nor had I, dear father. Accurate, as by your own and Frank's admission, the picture is, I assure you that till last night I had never looked upon the individual whom that painting represents."

"But—Heaven's patience, child!—you must have had something to work from. What!—no copy—no sketch—no description—"

"Yes, father—a description."

"Well, come, there begins to be a gleam of sense in your words at last. They must have been clever in the use of words, though, who could describe by the tongue all that has been painted here. Quick then, Kate—who was the describer?"

"Sister Amy."

"Amy! then Amy had seen the original of this picture before?"

"Never, father, with these eyes," replied Amy, solemnly.

Mr. Heyton laid down the painting, and exclaimed somewhat hastily—

"Are ye all mad, children? Is this any time for teazing me with plaything riddles? Kate, you have said that your drawing was made from a description, and that the description was furnished you by Amy; I now turn to Amy, and hear from her that she gave you the description, but without having ever seen the individual she described. Are ye all as moonstruck as silly Archy yonder? In sooth, girls, 'tis my belief you are."

Amy arose, and moving gently towards her father, seated herself on a low stool, beside his chair, and placed her two hands upon his arm—

"Forgive me, father," she cried—"forgive me!"

Mr. Heyton assumed an angry look.

"This is a strange request from you, Amy! Can it be that you, whom I ever deemed ingenuous and open, have committed a sin which you tremble to confide to me? If Ernest Morden wantonly and cruelly did that which was done by him last night, he shall not go unpunished; but if you have wronged Ernest Morden, then child, must the reparation be sought from you. But, tell me—what have I to forgive?"

"Much, dear father—much!" ejaculated Amy, clinging yet more closely to her father's arm, and looking so piteously in his face, that the anguish of mind pourtrayed in the expression of her countenance was enough to awaken sympathy in the heart of the most callous beholder.

The angry look faded from the face of the parent, and its place was supplied by a pallor of the cheek and a trembling of the lips, which told that anger had subsided into apprehension and dread. Mr. Heyton smoothed, in a kindly manner, the beautiful, gleaming hair of the lovely girl who nestled by his side, and speaking in a compassionate voice, said—

"I will forgive you, Amy, be the pardon which you ask solicited for any offence. What have you done wrong?"

"I have not been the ingenuous child, dear father, which you have taken me to be; I have concealed things from you which I should have told you without reserve. This portrait—"

"Well, Amy, why pause? What means the riddle of your never having seen till last night the individual whom you avow having described to your sister some ten or twelve days ago?"

"You do not understand me, dear father. I said that I had never seen him as I now see you—never seen him with these eyes."

"What other eyes hast thou, child—what dost thou mean by seeing without thine eyes?"

"There is a sight of the mind, father, as well as a sight of the body. This flesh hath eyes; and how know we that the soul has not its eyes also?"

"Your words are mysterious, child; but such matters befit the investigation of people more learned than either you or I."

"Have you not heard, father, of persons who have had a foreknowledge of events which occurred in their after-life? Have you never visited some scene for the first time, and on viewing it, recognised it as a scene familiar to you—familiar as if you had witnessed it every day? I have heard, father, of people who have described all the circumstances of a transaction days, months, or years, before that transaction has taken place; and this not by magic, father, but by an involuntary power. It has been so with me, dear father, in the matter of this portrait."

"Indeed, child, I do not understand your strange sayings. Why not come to the facts of the story at once?"

"I will do so, father—listen! It is now ten mornings ago that I took a book in my hand, and wandered out by the sea-shore. It was a bright, beautiful, and sunshiny morning, and I felt more happy than I had felt for some weeks before. I thought that I had never seen the broad sea look more magnificent, gilded as it was by the glorious sun, and every ripple quivering in the golden glow. There was scarcely a breath of air to disturb my curls, or move the flowers which bloom upon the cliff-tops. A few birds were wheeling round and round overhead; and at some distance lay Sir Thomas Warrenton's yacht, sleeping, as it were, upon the beautiful waters. A feather had dropped from out of the wing of one of the sea-birds, and had fallen upon the cordage of the yacht; there it hung, for there was not wind enough to blow it away. The fishes with their glittering scales were disporting at their pleasure, or basking lazily in the sunshine. Never had I beheld a sight more grand, yet so passingly lovely. The blue sky seemed like the sapphire dome of some giant temple, and the flat sea like the golden floor, inlaid with mosaic work of diamonds, glittering in the dazzling sunlight. I could not read my book, dear father, for there was nothing in that which was half so beautiful as the magnificent scene around me."

"But what has this to do with the portrait, Amy?" interrupted Mr. Heyton.

"Everything, dear father; but you must be patient. You know that part of the cliffs which is just on this side of the Eagle's Altar, where the chalk is disposed like a staircase, and where, near the summit, there are so many beautiful flowers? I wished for a seat, and I climbed up the cliff-side to sit down in a small recess where I had the full view of the sea before me, and where the blooming flowers which clustered above and around my head sheltered me partially from the sun. The wide sea, and some ships which were just discernible in the distance, recalled to my mind the circumstance of my not having heard from Ernest for so many months. I thought over his long absence, and I endeavoured to form some conjecture to explain the cause of my not having received a letter from him. Thus occupied, the time passed quickly away, and the sun rose higher in the blue sky. Overcome by the warmth and sultriness, I fell into a sort of doze, and allowed my book to slip out of my hand. It was while so dozing, father, that I saw the figure represented in that picture."

"Then Amy, child, it was but a dream after all?"

"Something more than a mere dream, father. I saw, as plainly as I now see you and sister Kate, the inside of our cottage; I saw you, and Frank, and sister, all with smiling faces. Suddenly, I saw a man enter at the outer door; it was an old man—a man as you there see drawn—the man, father, whom you let in last night. I saw him coming towards me, and there was something so terrible in the expression of his eyes that I endeavoured to flee from him; but I could not, father—I could not. I felt frozen in every limb, and as if I were spell-bound to the chair in which I seemed to be seated. Onwards came the man towards me, and a voice behind me seemed to whisper in my ear—'Woe—woe—woe!' I endeavoured to cry out, but I could not, and I thought that you, and Frank, and sister, were looking at me, but could not help me. Presently, as the horrible figure came nearer, Ernest—for Ernest was among you—rushed forward to help me; but was immediately stricken to the earth. Then it was I exerted myself to move from my seat, and struggled to break the spell; but the fearful figure, putting forth its hand, grasped me by the neck and glared upon me with its frightful eyes. The gripe with which the figure seemed to hold my neck, caused me the most intense pain; it was as if a portion of my flesh was tearing away. Again I struggled, I forced apart my lips—I moved my arms—I drew a deep inspiration. 'Ernest!' I exclaimed—'Ernest!' but at that minute the figure flung me from him, and I awoke from my doze. Whether just before the close of my dream or immediately afterwards, I know not, but in my fright I sprung forward, and forgetting where I was seated, precipitated myself a distance of some feet, and should have fallen farther had I not clutched in my grasp one of the plants which grows upon the cliff. Thus suspended over the very verge of destruction, I cried aloud, and immediately I heard the footsteps of some one advancing along the top of the cliff. Presently my arm was seized by the hand of a man, and I was drawn up from my perilous position. Before me, as my deliverer, was Mr. Lambert Warrenton—"

" Lambert Warrenton!" exclaimed Mr. Heyton.

" Yes, father, it was he."

" And why, Amy, have you not told me of this before?"

" Because, father—because I was afraid that you would account it all as a silly dream."

" What else than a dream was it, Amy—what else, child, than a dream?"

" More than a dream, father; for in no dream have I seen figures so plainly as I saw them then. From the description which I gave to Kate, she drew the portrait which now lies before you. To her, in the hearing of Archy, I told the story, and the impression it made upon us both was such that we have thought about it ever since. When I heard last night the tap at the door, and heard you give orders that the applicant should be admitted, I was seized with an involuntary tremor. Something seemed to tell me who was about to enter. I felt—I knew it to be that man. It was not surprise that agitated me—it was not astonishment, for every event was no more than I had been taught to expect, and the scene to which you were witnesses last night seemed to me like the repetition of a scene which had once before been acted in my presence, and with every incident of which I was familiar. I knew that the terrible stranger would fix his eyes on me; 1 knew that he would address Ernest; I knew that something horrible was to happen, and I knew—but I cannot go on, father; the dread which overcame me then is overcoming me again now."

" Merciful God! child, this is a strange recountal! And say you, Kate, that this portrait was pourtrayed by you wholly from your sister's description?"

" From that alone, dear father. So graphically did sister Amy describe the person of the old man to me that I saw him as plainly as if I beheld his actual presence. I have dreamed about him every night since, and have been afraid to open my eyes in the darkness, lest I should behold him—lest I should see him standing by my side.'"

Mr. Heyton took the portrait in his hand, and examined it accurately. After some minutes he turned to his son and put to him the inquiry—

" Did you behold the countenance of the old man, Frank—did you observe his features?"

" You will recollect, father, that he wore his hat slouched over his eyes."

" He did so; but had you no glance—saw you not those eyes at all?"

" I did."

" And they were—"

" Bright, father—bright and piercing. Never before have I seen eyes appertaining to old age so bright and dark as those."

" Look well at this portrait, Frank. Tell me if what you observed of the expression of those eyes corresponds with that which is delineated there ?"

" The expression is the same, father."

" These, then, are the features of the man who entered this cottage last night ?"

" Yes, father, and they are those of him who looked upon me in the dungeon of the old fortress."

" I have forgotten, boy, which particular dungeon it was that you spoke of."

" That of the south tower, father."

" Ha ! the south tower—the south tower, where—"

Mr. Heyton suddenly paused ; bending down his head, so as to conceal the expression of his countenance from the view of his children, he mused for many minutes. Again he took the portrait in his hand, again he scanned it minutely ; then, handing it to his son, he demanded—

" Tell me, Frank—do you, in the lineaments of those features, in the expression of any one of them, recognise a likeness to any person whom you have seen or known ? "

"I do not. Heaven forfend that anyone of my acquaintances should, in the slightest degree, resemble the individual pourtrayed there ! Those eyes, father, tell of something which it is too fearful to muse upon. I shudder to look at them, even as they are represented there."

Taking the portrait with him, Mr. Heyton arose from his seat, and passed into an adjoining room. He was absent some five or ten minutes, during which time the two sisters remained gazing at each other in silence : when their father returned, he brought with him another portrait, which, with the mysterious one, he laid upon the table.

" Tell me, children," said he ; " see you any point of resemblance between those two pictures ? "

Each turned his glance towards the portraits. That which Mr. Heyton had fetched from the adjoining apartment was of a young and handsome man, whose hair and eyes were of a jetty blackness, and whose countenance was depicted as wearing an expression of deep melancholy.

" There is nothing in common between these two pictures," said Frank Heyton.

" There eyes, brother," observed Kate ; " it strikes me that there is a resemblance in the eyes."

" Kate is an artist," rejoined her father ; " and therefore best able to judge in this matter. Her opinion coincides with my own. I also perceive in the expression of the eyes of each a similarity."

" But of whom is this the portrait, father ? " asked Frank, laying his finger on the one which represented the younger man.

" Of a friend," answered Mr. Heyton.

" And is it possible that he could have any relation to—to the old man who came here last night? Now, as I look again, I fancy I can perceive the resemblance to which sister Kate alludes."

" There is no relation that I know of, Frank. The original of this picture," and he pointed to the one last produced, " has long since mouldered into dust. It was a fancy of mine to place the pictures side by side as I have there done ; the mystery is the mystery still."

" And you have no conjecture, dear father, as to who that old man was ? "

" None, dear Kate, none."

" There must have been a purport in his coming here last night," observed Frank, " to me there is but one explanation."

" Tell me what that is, brother ? " solicited Amy.

" Ernest Morden loves you no longer."

" No, Frank, no ; say not that. What have I done to estrange him from me?

how has poor Amy done him wrong? He cannot, brother, he is not so false as you would make him appear to be; he loves me still, brother, he loves me still!"

"What, sister, if he has owned that he does not?"

"He has not—he cannot have done so!"

"Hear me, sister Amy. Last night, I and Ernest Morden struggled for life or death on the summit of the Eagle's Altar. There, sister, upon that place, in my very ear, to me, as the brother of her whom he had professed to love, he said —he dared to say—curses on him for saying it—that—that—"

"Why do you not tell me, brother; why do you hesitate?"

"Will you hear me, sister, will you hear me bravely and boldly?"

"I will,"

"Ernest Morden, then, declared that he loved you no longer."

Amy turned deadly pale. With her beautiful tender eyes gleaming full upon her brother, she clung to his arm for support, and in a husky, breathless voice, articulated—

"Did he—did Ernest say that, brother?"

"In my very ear were the words spoken."

"Said he it seriously?"

"It was no moment for him to use playful words in; that which he said was spoken seriously as I speak it now."

Amy clasped her hands, sunk upon her knees, and lifting up her face, ejaculated—

"Then God forgive him—God forgive him for his unkindness! I have never done him wrong—I have never injured him in thought or deed! I loved him, and if he has deceived me—if he has played upon me with deceitful words—may Heaven forgive him as I forgive him now!"

So saying Amy laid her face upon the lap of her sister and wept bitterly. Mr. Heyton took the arm of his son and led him to the other side of the apartment. For some minutes they conversed together, and the expression of the brother's countenance was reflected in that of the father. Seated on a stool in the opposite corner was Archy, the idiot boy, his chin resting on his hands, his body bent forward, his eyes fixed upon the weeping Amy, and tears coursing down his own cheeks. Not a word—not a syllable did he utter—but there, mute in his idiotcy, he gazed upon the scene in silence.

All was still, all solemn in that narrow room. The sun which had shone brightly in the early morning had now withdrawn its beams and had ceased to peep in at the little window upon the breakfast party, as had been its wonted way.

Suddenly Amy started up, and rushing towards her brother caught his hand with a firm grasp.

"What have you to say, Amy? why look you at me with so fixed a gaze?"

"Listen, brother, list—I—" The words died away in her throat, and she found it to be almost impossible for her to command her power of utterance.

"Hark, father, there is something which Amy wishes to say."

"Brother," said the poor maiden, in a husky voice, "brother, did Ernest Morden say those words with no qualifications—without assigning any cause— any reasons?"

"No, Amy; he played the villain's part by resorting to the equivocation of saying that he was prevented from loving you longer; that events had occurred which interposed a barrier between him and you, and which would cause a lasting separation.

"Then, brother, he did not say that he had ceased to love me—that he had never loved me—that his affection was gone, and that I had become hateful in his eyes—he said not that?"

"The purport of his words, sister, was as I have already told you. The reason which he assigned for his behaviour was, that he *might* not love you any more."

"Thank Heaven, brother, that he said so!" ejaculated poor Amy, tears of joy trickling afresh down her cheeks. "Of his own free will I didn't believe that Ernest would forsake me, and his own words are assurance to me now!"

Frank Heyton laid his right hand on the arm of his sister, whilst in his left her own delicate fingers were clasped. An angry look reddened his countenance, and in a voice somewhat harsher than it should have been, he exclaimed—

"Is it possible, sister, you can be so foolish? Have you no clearer perceptions than the idiot, Archy?"

"What, brother—what have I said? Why are you angry with me?"

"You would excuse Ernest Morden."

"He loves me, brother ; he loves me still, whatever be the cause which forbids all future intercourse between us !"

"Where are your proofs, Amy ; where your grounds for such belief?"

"His words, brother."

"And nothing else?"

"My own feelings."

Frank led his sister to a chair.

"Hearken, Amy !" said he, "and father will judge what truth there may be in that which I am about to say. I have been friendly with Ernest Morden for years ;

it was my belief that he loved you—that he would at one day be the husband of my sister ; and I was happy in the belief. Last night that belief and that friendship came to an end. I am undeceived ; but you, Amy, because that you have, and may still really love Ernest, do not see that which is apparent to every other eye. Ernest Morden is a deceiver."

" Say not that, brother—do not be so cruel !" interposed Amy, tearfully.

" Do not interrupt me, sister. That I would not willingly wound your feelings, you well know ; but it is my duty to put this matter before you in its proper light. Ernest Morden, I say, has played a deceitful part. Recollect, sister, that in his long absence the letters which he sent were ' few and far between.' I know that he asserts having had no opportunity to send others, but what proof have we of the truth of that statement? He comes at last, sister, but he comes tardily. He pretends to be as loving towards you as before ; but when any approval is made towards the subject of your union, he finds an excuse for its being not carried into completion, by pleading the pressure of many duties. While he is here, a man enters, who is, doubtless, his accomplice. If not his friend, how came he to be acquainted with Ernest's name and history? If not his coadjutor, how did it happen that he arrived at the precise time, and took part with Ernest in the farce which was then carried on? A plan has been laid beforehand ; it is to be made seem that the stranger is able to interpose a barrier between the two lovers ; some juggling is used ; Ernest pretends to give a mark of his love for the object of his cruelty, by daring to press his lips to hers ; he then leaves the house without a word of explanation; is about to make off altogether; and does his best to kill the brother of her whom he had professed to love. What say you, Amy, to this summary ?"

" It is true, brother—it is all true ; but why should Ernest attempt to deceive me ? why, if he has ever loved me, should he wish now to treat me so cruelly ?"

" That, also, I will make evident to you, sister. Recollect, Amy, that the station which we occupy in the world is a very humble one ; recollect that we have neither wealth nor a great name. When Ernest Morden first wooed my poor sister, he was but a midshipman on board a small vessel. Time passes, and Ernest the midshipman becomes Ernest Morden, the lieutenant. How are all things altered now! During the years of absence, Ernest learns the lesson, that life resembles the cliffs on yonder beach, to climb them you must grasp every crag which presents itself, and disencumber yourself from every load. The boy-passion subsiding, principle gives way to the world's prudence, and the question suggests itself—Why wed myself to poverty when a prospect is before me of forming a union which may be conducive to my advance in life? What now more easy than to devise a plan for getting rid of the only obstacle, and obtaining the desired freedom? What says my sister Amy to this explanation, and will she forgive me for having spoken my thoughts without reserve ?"

" Yes, yes, dear brother ; I know that you would not say one word to hurt the feelings of your poor Amy ; but, brother, can it—can it be as you say ? "

" What is your opinion, father? " demanded Frank, turning towards Mr. Heyton.

" There can be but one opinion on the subject, ffom the summary which you have given, Frank. If Ernest Morden has not returned evil for good, in the service which I rendered his father some years ago, then God, in his mercy, pardon me for harbouring such thoughts concerning him, as now involuntarily present themselves to my mind ! "

" And you, Kate, what think you? " asked Frank of his sister.
Kate returned no answer.

Frank again addressed himself to Amy. " You hear that which father hath said, sister ; you have listened to the facts which I have laid before you ; and now, I would ask of you, cannot you form your own conclusions ? "

" Yes, brother. I—I cannot bear to think so cruelly of Ernest ; but I see that it is all plain, all possible. I forgive him, brother—I forgive him, and you and father must forgive him also."

"If he had not added insult to injury, I might have done so, sister; but to forgive him now were injustice to myself, to father, and to you."

"Not to me, dear Frank—not to me; from my heart's core he has my forgiveness, and my wish that he may be happy—very, very happy!"

Amy covered her face with her hands, and burst into tears. Mr. Heyton took the hand of his son.

"Had Ernest Morden," said he, "never visited us on his return—were it not that he spoke of his love for your sister under this very roof only last night—I would forgive his perfidy, but the means to which he has had resort are so despicable, that to recal them to memory only serves to waken up angry feelings. Here, in the home of his father's friend, to personate the play-actor, to act a rehearsed part, in order to bring about that which he has not the boldness to have performed in any other manner—argues little for his principles and less for his feelings as a man. But, Frank, remember you not how the part was played? what meant the jugglery of tearing her dress to look at the back of your sister's neck?"

"He spoke, father, of a mark which was there."

"A mark! and what mark is there to be seen on the fair white skin of my Amy?"

"None, father; see you it is as polished as ivory."

"Then why was the jugglery used?"

"I know not; perhaps—"

Mr. Heyton and his son were here startled by a sudden scream from Kate. They both looked around. Amy was seated on a stool, her head resting upon the lap of her sister, Kate had one hand resting on her sister's dress, the other stretched out towards her father and brother; her eyebrows were drawn up, her eyes wildly staring, her mouth was wide open, and terror and amazement—terror, as if she had suddenly beheld some hideous form—was depicted on her countenance.

"Kate! daughter! what frightens you? what is the meaning of that look—that cry?"

Unable to speak, she beckoned her father to approach.

"What is't, Kate—what hast thou to show me?"

"See, father, see! Draw close—look closely! *There is the mark upon my sister's neck!*"

CHAPTER XIX.

THE MALTESE CROSS.

As the parent cast a glance in the direction indicated by the fingers of his daughter, his eyes became over-clouded with a sudden mist, and he felt a dizziness of the brain which caused him to reel backwards and fall in the arms of his son.

"My daughter! God! what—what means this sight?"

Amy had fainted in the lap of her sister Kate, with the same fearful expression of countenance, still with her one hand held apart the upper portion of Amy's dress, while, with the fingers of the other, she still pointed in the same direction.

Frank stepped forward, and looked as his father had looked before him. On the instant, his cheeks turned pale, his lips became blanched. Turning his eyes towards the countenance of Kate, he articulated the one word—

"Sister!"

"What is it, Frank; what is it?"

"I know not. Cannot Amy tell?"

But Amy had swooned at her sister's first exclamation, and still lay in a half-senseless state. All were stricken with amazement and silence. Kate could not turn away her gaze from the object before her, neither could she move from where she sat. At her back, and with his usually stolid countenance, exhibiting the marks of terror and affright, peered over her shoulder Archy, the idiot-boy. Beside the two maidens was their brother—his finger pointing towards Amy—his face turned inquiringly towards Kate.   Behind him again, and clinging to his arm for support, was the parent himself—his features distorted by the sudden terror which had burst upon him—his lips apart—his eyes glaring wildly at the fearful thing to which the finger of his son pointed, on which the gaze of the idiot-boy was fixed.

Not a word was spoken ; not a breath was drawn !

Presently, as if awakening up out of a slumbrous state, Amy suddenly uplifted her head, and, throwing back the tresses from her face, beheld every eye fixed upon her own pallid, wondering, and terrified countenance.   She started like the dreamer starts, when, wakening from his dreams of horrors, he still sees around him the dim but fading outlines of the phantom-figures of his vision.

"Father!—God!—Heaven!—where am I?   What whisper was that in my ear?"

The parent shrunk back from his daughter, as if to touch her were contamination. Not a word of reply could he utter ; not a syllable would his tongue help him to articulate.

With a scream, Amy threw herself into that parent's arms—her arms clinging convulsively to his neck.

"Father! why look you at me thus?   Speak! tell me!   Did I not hear a whisper that I was a marked and hideous thing ?"

Mr. Heyton embraced her ; but, as he pressed her to his breast, his glance again lit upon the fearful object of his terror.   He again started, as if, in looking over his daughter's shoulder, his eyes had met the eyes of some demon lowering at him there.

" Why look you so frightened, father?—why do you avert your face ?—why turn you from me with a shudder ?"

Mr. Heyton rallied, and placing his daughter upon the chair which happened to be near to them, he demanded—

" Amy, child, how came that mark upon your neck ?"

The maiden started, again turned pale, and trembled so violently that had not her brother and sister supported her, she would have fallen from off the chair.

" The mark! my neck!" she exclaimed ; " Oh, tell me—tell me—my dear father, the meaning of those words ?"

Mr. Heyton turned on his daughter an incredulous and wondering look, as he replied—

" What! know you of nothing ?"

" Of the meaning of your allusions; nothing, on my soul, dear father !"

" Your neck—"

" What is there there ?"

" Do you not know ?"

" Indeed I do not.   I feel—I touch—but there is nothing which I can distinguish."

" And do you nothing suspect ?"

" Suspect! no—but—" she suddenly ceased from speaking, and turned her gaze upon her brother and sister with an expression in which terror, bewilderment, apprehension, and anguish, seemed to be intermingled.

" What have you to say, Amy ; why do you pause in replying to my question?"

Amy arose and taking her parent's hand, asked in a solemn and serious voice—

" Is there meaning in your words—was it a reality—is the mark of its touch to be seen ?"

" What touch, child ? to what do you allude ?"

" To the figure which I saw—the figure which Kate has drawn."

" Well, child, well !"

" I felt its touch upon my neck, father, when I was hurled forward.   It was as if it had taken my flesh in its grasp ; it was hot, burning, father, and it was here—here on my neck."

" Know you what is there, child ?"

" Indeed—indeed not! Tell me—tell me Frank? tell me, sister Kate? tell me,

Archy?'' and the frantic girl tore away her dress as if in its folds it contained some venomous thing.

" Fetch the other looking-glass, Frank !" said Mr. Heyton.

The glass was brought. Amy was directed by her father to stand with her back to the mirror above the mantel-shelf, and to look in the lesser glass which her brother held before her.

" Well, Amy, what is it that meets your view ?"

Amy snatched the mirror out of her brother's hand, gazed in it fixedly for one moment, then, uttering a shriek of horror, rushed forward, while the glass escaping from her paralysed fingers fell, and was shivered to pieces on the floor.

" Father ! what does it mean ?" she exclaimed.

" I cannot tell, Amy—can no one—cannot Kate give some explanation of the cause of this ?"

" Not I, dear father," replied Kate. " Do not ask me. I am frightened—terrified. There is deeper meaning in this, father, than we yet suppose."

Mr. Heyton led the trembling Amy towards the window, and, calling Frank to approach, pointed to his notice the cause of their terror.

" I see it, father—but how came it there ?"

What was that which Frank Heyton saw ?—what was that dread object, which alike caused fear and alarm to him and to the trembling beings around him, and who stood beneath the same roof with himself?

It was the mark which Kate had so suddenly descried upon the neck of her sister.

On the fair white neck of the gentle Amy was imprinted the representation of a Maltese cross. The stain was a deep black colour, and apparently incorporated with the very substance of the skin. It was apparently between the two shoulders, so that the dress, as usually worn, completely concealed it from observation. Around, the skin was of a pearly hue, but amidst its polish and its beauty, appeared the dusky mark. It did not shine, it did not glitter ; it was as if the skin in that particular spot had been scorched by the touch of a demon's finger, and had lost its vitality with that single touch.

" Kate," said Mr. Heyton, " know you of the existence of this mark upon your sister's neck ?"

" No, father. I never saw it there till now."

" And Amy—can you not explain its origin ?"

" I cannot, father—I—it is where, in my dream—in my vision, father, I felt the figure seize me in its clasp."

Mr. Heyton communed with his son in a whisper. After the lapse of a short interval, he again addressed his elder daughter—

" Amy," said he, " is it possible that by any means this stain could have been impressed on your neck at the time you speak of ? I have heard of imagination creating actual existence—I have heard of persons who have imagined that their hair was about to turn white, until the change itself was effected by that very imagination. Fear of a bodily deformity has before now caused that very deformity to ensue. Fright has induced in the person frightened the very object which gave rise to the terror when beheld in the person of another. Can it have been so with you ? Can the dream—the powerful impression which that dream wrought, have produced this ?"

Amy gazed with a wild stare at her parent, shuddered, and was silent.

Kate drew her father aside.

" Listen, father !" said she. " It cannot have been as you now suppose, for when Amy returned home after her fright, she recounted to me the fearful story which you have heard this morning ; during that recountal, she pointed out with her finger the place on her neck, where she had supposed the finger to have seized her, and desired me to see if anything was there visible——"

" And what saw you, Kate ?"

" Nothing, father—nothing."

" No mark—no stain ?"

" Nothing, but Amy's own white skin."

" And you looked at that particular spot ?"

" At the very place, father, where that hideous mark is now to be seen."

" This is indeed mysterious !" ejaculated Mr. Heyton. " There would seem to be some mystic connexion between that portrait now lying on the table, and this strange mark. There is nothing but what is unaccountable in each. Can no conjecture be made—can no explanation be devised ?"

Frank laid hand upon the arm of his parent.

" Do you not recollect," said he, " that the impostor of last night spoke of what we now see ?"

" He did, Frank, and——"

" Ernest Morden displaced my sister's dress, and gazed upon her neck as he lifted up the knife over her."

" Yes, boy—yes ; but what conclusion do you draw ?"

" That at that very moment, father, the mark which we now see was made by Ernest himeself."

Mr. Heyton started.

" Ha ! boy, I comprehend. This was one part of the jugglery—this was to found a plea upon for breaking the faith of years. Right, Frank ! it must have been made then, and by him. But how did it happen that we saw not to act—that neither Kate nor myself saw the mark last night ?"

" You must call to mind, father, that when sister Amy fainted she fell backwards, and that in removing her to the bed her face was kept upwards, so that her neck came not within the scope of observation."

" I see—I see, boy. But, look you, how was the mark made ; it is deeply imprinted—it will not rub off—it appears to be indelible ?"

" I know not, father. Let us send Archy to fetch Mr. Whittingham, the surgeon."

" Do so, Frank ; let him be sent for immediately."

The messenger was dispatched on his errand ; and during his absence the minds of each were busy in conjecturing how and by what means the skin of the fair girl had been so deeply stained. Indignation and anger were the prevalent passions in the breast of the father and son ; but Amy clung to her sister and paid little heed to the suggestions which were uttered in her presence. Kate endeavoured to console her, but her limbs trembled and her lips quivered as she continued to ejaculate,—

" I fear, sister—I fear !"

It was not long before Mr. Whittingham arrived. He was personally known to the Heytons, and was not received by them as a stranger. Amy's father invited him to a private conference in the adjacent room, where he briefly detailed to him the occurrence of the previous evening, withholding, however, as many of the particulars as he deemed it to be unnecessary to state. The surgeon listened in silence. When Mr. Heyton had related the circumstances attending the discovery of the mysterious mark, a look of astonishment displayed itself on the surgeon's countenance, and rising quickly from his seat, he exclaimed,—

" Good Heaven ! Mr. Heyton. Can any one have behaved so basely ? Let me see your daughter instantly."

" She is here," said the parent, as he conducted Mr. Whittingham into the room where Amy was.

Carefully did the astonished surgeon scrutinize the disfiguring mark. It was clearly impressed upon the fair white skin, and the outline of the cross was well defined. He felt the pulse of the poor trembling girl, and he gazed upon her pallid, dejected countenance. Again he submitted the mark to a more careful scrutiny, then turned round to Mr. Heyton with a look of amazement and consternation.

" What—what is it ?" inquired the anxious parent.

Mr. Whittingham led the father of Amy to a distant corner of the room, where their whispers could not be heard by the timorous and affrighted maiden.

" Good God ! Mr. Wittingham, why do you look so solemn—what have you to communicate ?"

" Does she—does your daughter say that she knew not of that mark being there till this morning ?" inquired the surgeon.

" She does."

" That is strange—very strange !"

" Why so, surgeon ? One night only has passed, and ——"

" Mr. Heyton, I beg your pardon. That mark has been where it now is for many days."

" How !—for many days !"

" For many days ; for a week at the least."

The father rushed towards his daughter and seized her arm.

" Have you told me the truth, Amy—have you spoken the whole truth in this matter ?"

" Indeed—indeed, dear father, I have !"

" You have not dissembled—you have not kept anything back ; you affirm that you knew not of this cross being where it now is, until the discovery was made by your sister an hour ago. Say you not so—and speak you the truth ?"

" I do say so, father, and I affirm it to be the truth—God's truth."

" You hear ?" said the parent, addressing the surgeon.

Mr. Wittingham nodded his head in assent, and, directing his question to Kate, said—

" And had you, my good young lady, never seen this mark before, till you saw it this morning ?"

" Never, Mr. Wittingham—never."

The surgeon appeared perplexed. Amy advanced towards him, and in an imploring voice said—

" Oh ! tell me, sir, what are your conjectures ? What explanation have you to offer ?"

" Simply this," replied the surgeon ; " the mark which I have just examined betrays, by its hue, the agent which has been used in effecting it."

" Then you know how it may have been produced—you know how a similar one may be made ? "

" I do."

" And what is there which would make a mark like this?" inquired Mr. Heyton.

" There is a substance known to chemists, which, if properly applied, will so affect the skin. I have little hesitation in saying that the stain which I have examined has resulted from the application of that substance."

" But you mentioned something about the length of time required for its production ? "

" I said not that. Under favourable circumstances such a stain might be quickly produced. That on Miss Heyton's neck must have been where it now is for at least a week past."

" Then," exclaimed Amy, " Ernest could not have placed it there last evening ; it was not made by him !"

" Peace, child ! "—and beckoning the surgeon and Frank to follow him, Mr. Heyton retired into the adjoining room. They conversed together for some time, and when they rejoined the maidens, the countenance of each wore a serious cast.

Amy crept to her father's side.

" What, father—what does it all mean ? What explanations can Mr. Wittingham give ?"

" None, child ; there is a mystery veiling the whole circumstance, which is evidently connected with other recent events, but which we cannot solve."

" Will the mark do me harm ?" inquired the trembling girl of the surgeon.

" It will produce no physical evil effect that I am aware of. Much injury would probably arise from an attempt to erase it. Let it be as it is ; with the lapse of time it will probably wear away and disappear.

"Aye, but before then—before then——"

"What may happen, dear Amy, I know not," interposed her father. "Situated as we at present are, conjecture only serves to make the mystery more mysterious and intricate still."

Mr. Wittingham having nothing further to say, took his departure. When he had gone, Mr. Heyton seated himself in a chair beside his daughter, and after meditating for a few minutes, said—

"I do not understand, Amy, why you thought proper to keep hidden from me the circumstances attending the production of that portrait which was first shown to me last night. Why did you not tell me, as well as your sister, of your dream —your vision?"

"I did not like to, dear father, I was afraid that you would think it silly of me, and reproach me for so doing."

"Am I used to reproach you then, Amy?"

"Oh no, no, no, dear father!" cried the fair girl, flinging her arms round her parent's neck." But Mr. Warrenton made me promise not to say a word."

"And why extort such a promise from you? I should have been informed of his kind interference, were it only that I might have duly returned him thanks."

"Yes, but, father; he has desired me not to say a word."

"Why, Amy—what reason did he assign for such a wish?"

"He said, father— he said—"

"What said he, Amy?"

"He said that as—but I was not to tell you, father; he made me promise not to tell you."

"No promise can be binding, Amy, which requires a child to withhold anything from the ear of a parent. There must have been some cause assigned by Mr. Lambert Warrenton, for wishing you to keep so slight a matter a secret."

"Perhaps, father, now that Ernest is not likely to return, I may break my promise and tell you."

"Why, what has Ernest to do with it, child?"

"Mr. Warrenton said, that as Ernest was my—my lover; he would perhaps be jealous if he heard that service was rendered me by another."

"Strange, child! very strange that Lambert Warrenton should have had such a thought, and that he should have imposed such an obligation!"

Mr. Heyton deliberated in silence for some ten or twenty minutes, then rising, he put on his hat and prepared to leave the cottage.

"Where are you about to go, father?" asked Amy.

"To Warrenton Hall. It is necessary that I tell Sir Thomas the occurrences of the past night. Frank will stay here to protect you both; and I shall soon return."

"But why not now to the ship, and inquire after Ernest, father?" interposed Frank. "If I understood rightly your words, it is not your intention to pass this matter over without calling Ernest Morden to account for his behaviour."

"That business shall be proceeded with afterwards, Frank. Stay you, and protect your sisters. I will away to Sir Thomas, and hold communion with the brother of Ernest. Probably he will accompany me to an examination of that south tower of the fortress, in which you met with your strange mishap. When that is completed, Gervase will, no doubt, take a part in the inquiry after his brother. The ship will not weigh anchor to-day, and therefore it is not imperative that we should follow Ernest thither immediately."

Frank Heyton demurred to any delay in the pursuit of his sister's insults. It was also his desire to accompany his father to the examination of the castle ruins; but he was forbidden so to do by his parent, who assigned as the cause of his denial, the necessity of Kate and Amy having some one left to protect them. He had passed without the door of the cottage, when Frank followed after, and detained him.

"Why go you, father, to Sir Thomas Warrenton?"

"Is he not my friend?"

"He is, but why seek him in this matter; why go to him whenever anything happens which concerns Amy?"

Mr. Heyton cast a sudden and piercing look at his son; then relaxing his face into a smile, he replied—

"Is not Sir Thomas the magistrate of the county, and should not every affair of importance be communicated to him?"

"Yes; but why go to him at times when the exercise of his duty as a magistrate is not required?"

"Go, mind your sisters, boy!" rejoined Mr. Heyton, angrily, as freeing himself from the detentive grasp of his son, he struck off along the path which led to Warrenton Hall.

An hour passed by, and Frank Heyton grew more and more restless. His hot and angry spirit ill-brooked the confinement to which his father had subjected him, when there was a chance of again meeting with Ernest, and of wresting from him the true secret of his behaviour. The two sisters remarked the growing restlessness of their brother, and, strange to say, they appeared to derive gratification from the sight.

"Kate," said the excited youth, "it is my wish to hear Sir Thomas Warrenton's opinion on these strange occurrences; there are suggestions which I could make, and which might turn to advantage if communicated to him."

"Then why not speed to him immediately, brother?"

"Because, Kate, father has imposed upon me the task of remaining to guard you."

"But will your assistance be required if a search be made in the old castle ?"

"Yes, sister, yes. There are particulars connected with last night—horrors with which father is unacquainted."

"And the knowledge of them would assist Sir Thomas in his investigation of the castle—would it not, brother?"

"It would, and—but Kate, now, in the broad and open daylight, it is my wish to ascend that tower again. It is possible that if I did so, I might now discover the means by which the fugitive escaped me in pursuit ; and I might gain some clue to the mystery concerning him."

"Then why stay, brother—why not go at once ?"

"And leave you and Amy alone, sister ?"

"Not alone, dear brother. There is Archy, he will stay with us and keep watch and ward, I warrant you. Go, then ; no harm will befal us."

"And you are not afraid ?"

"Neither I nor Amy, brother. What is there to fear now, in the broad day ? Trust me, we can be valiant in the sunshine, however much we may tremble in the darkness. Here is father's firelock—it is loaded—it shall be fired off if anything should occur to cause us alarm ; the report would certainly bring some one to our assistance if it should escape being heard by you."

"You have no objection then, sisters, to my leaving you for a short time and hastening to join father ?"

"None, dear brother. Why stay here to keep sentry over two poor girls, when there is a chance of distinguishing yourself in the making of some grand discovery ?"

Frank bade his sisters farewell—took a staff in his hand—hesitated for a single moment, and then left the cottage to join his father at Warrenton Hall.

Kate watched her brother as he sped on his journey. No sooner was he out of sight than turning to her sister, she exclaimed—

"All is as we could wish. Now, Amy—now !"

"Will you dare it, sister Kate?"

"Am I to be daunted by so little ? No, sister ; I should not be Kate Heyton, if I were."

"And you will do it ?"

"At once, sister Amy—at once. Hasten—hasten !"

Why had Kate and Amy done their best to rid themselves of the presence of their brothers ; and what was that which they were now about to do ?"

<hr>

CHAPTER XX.

THE FAIR MAIDEN AND THE DARK-EYED STUDENT.—SECRETS, SWORD-CUTS, AND SUGGESTIONS.

FOLLOWING up the course of events in the regular order of their succession we again change the scene; and leaving for awhile the cottage of the Heyton's return to the baronial hall of the good knight—Sir Thomas Warrenton.

It was in a small apartment, the window of which looked towards the front court-yard, that a breakfast party were assembled. At the head of the table sat the Lady Isabel Warrenton, Sir Thomas, her liege lord and husband, occupying a seat at her right hand, and Miss Ismay another on her left. There were present also the legal and medical advisers of Sir Thomas, together with Mr. Hilbourne, the resident chaplain, all of whom had been hastily summoned to hear the account of last night's mysteries, and to give, as far as they were able, their opinions thereupon. At the lower end of the table, and immediately opposite to the Lady Isabel, was seated Gervase Morden, the pale-faced, thoughtful secretary, whose assistance on the previous evening had been so readily rendered in carrying out the investigation which then took place.

The morning meal had been delayed to a later hour than was usual, in consequence of the confusion into which all parties had been thrown by the occurrences of the night. The domestics feared to move about singly; and even to fetch wood from the bin, or milk from the dairy, they went in pairs, and quarrelled as to who should enter the room first. So much had each to talk about that for an hour after the fire had been lit, the cook forgot to brown the toast, and the coffee-pot was placed on the hot coals, till the water within boiled, before it was discovered that the slight omission had been made of neglecting to put in any coffee.

Vainly had Sir Thomas, with the assistance of his physician, lawyer, and chaplain, endeavoured to unriddle the perplexing mystery which had caused so much tumult and affright, disturbing the peaceful serenity of Warrenton Hall, and turning, as it had, the brains of every one, by reason of the many conjectures which it had caused them to devise. Not a nook or corner that Sir Thomas knew of but what had been ransacked and minutely investigated—never had such violent proceedings taken place within the old hall—never before had the dust been so disturbed, and the sleek spiders sent so precipitately to the right-about. Even the rats and mice had taken their departure that very morning, under a decided impression that the walls of the hoary mansion were about to be levelled, and all the comfortable snuggeries therein contained, exposed to the light of day. But despite all these desperate proceedings, and notwithstanding the routing and rummaging, the perquisitions, the inquisitions, and the quizzings, nothing whatever to serve for a solution of the mystery, and as a reward for the search, had been discovered. Sir Thomas was half-disposed to adopt, from his own belief, the first suggestion of Constance Ismay, and satisfy his mind with the pleasant or unpleasant thought that a phantom, or ghost, or an evil spirit had been playing its pranks within the precincts of the quaint old mansion. But then, those blood spots—there was the difficulty. Sir Thomas could not bring his mind to believe that either ghosts or evil spirits have fine, rich, red-coloured blood, just the same as any living, breathing, kicking Christian. No; there are limits to every man's belief, and to credit this, was decidedly out of the limits of Sir Thomas Warrenton's articles of faith.

On the face of every one there seated at the breakfast-table wonderment and anxiety were depicted. Sir Thomas, however, was angry as well as puzzled; his lady seemed highly indignant; the clergyman, the doctor, and the attorney, were each disposed to quarrel with themselves, because their heads were not lengthy enough to dive to the bottom of the problem which had been propounded to them for explanation; Constance Ismay appeared terrified as well as bewildered; and lastly, Gervase Morden was, as every one else could perceive, intently studying the whole affair with the same coolness and depth of thought which he would have used had he been engaged in considering a particular philosophic dogma, or in unravelling a knotty point of old English law.

As, however, Gervase Morden plays an important part in the drama of our story, it may be as well just to sketch him off while he is there seated at the breakfast-table of his good master, the worthy knight of Warrenton Hall.

Gervase Morden was young in years, but thought and study had produced their usual effect in anticipating the advance of time, and writing on the foreheads of their victims the characters which usually indicate age. The high, pale brows of the thoughtful student, overhung as it was with dark clustering hair, told of the life to which he had dedicated himself—the mind-work to which he was used. Those black, large, and piercing eyes, gleaming, as they did, from the deep sockets into which they had sunk, spoke of secret, fierce, yet subdued passion, which would enable their owner to undertake any enterprise and succeed in any attempt. And the sallow, fleshless cheeks from which the roseate hue of youth had fled, of what told they, but of the midnight vigil, and of hours robbed from sleep to be dedicated to mental exercise and to the working out of the most ambitious aims? The previous history of the student is reserved for future narration; but his present capacity was that of secretary to Sir Thomas Warrenton, his industry, fidelity, and acquirements having long since won him respect from the good knight and from the various members of the household.

Already the name of Gervase Morden has been coupled with that of Constance Ismay. Even now, at the breakfast-table, a careful observer would have remarked that the dark eyes of the student were at oft-repeated intervals turned towards the dark eyes of the fair but pensive girl, and in the glances which the youth thus threw at the maiden might have been detected the secret of a story in which the heart of each was concerned, and which, by-the-by, is the most ancient sort of story that has ever existed on this earth—the story of the boy and the maiden—the story of the hand clasped in hand—the story of the blush and the confusion—the story of the only dream of real joy—the only true morsel of romance which brightens man's weary life. Who is there to whom that story is unknown—who knows not the oft-repeated, but never-tiring tale of man and woman's love?

Well might Gervase Morden love as he did the fair girl to whom as his polar star his eyes ever turned, telling, as they did, the secret which his lips spoke not. Trust us, ye wary ones; be you ever such adepts at disguising your own sentiments, and hoodwinking, as you think, the world, it is only necessary for us to watch the expression of your eyes during the events of one single day, to learn the most cherished secret which you possess. The cheeks may not blush at the affirmation of deceit; the tongue may speak out boldly when the heart is trembling within; the lips may utter the lie without quivering—without hesitation; but the eye never deceives—the eyes cannot lie; in their expression is the key to the most inward thoughts, and to him who studies them well, the thoughts of the most reserved present themselves for inspection. There is a magic influence in the eye which few are aware of. Go into company; fix your eyes steadily on any one person, and though his back may be turned towards you, he will experience a sensation of uneasiness, and involuntarily he will turn round and look inquiringly in your face. There may be a mystery in this; but the fact admits of easy proof.

It would be ungallant to proceed at once with our story without saying a word or two concerning Constance Ismay. Seldom is such beauty seen as was exhibited in her pensive countenance. You may walk from one end to the other of Regent-street on a fine afternoon in May and scarcely meet with one really lovely woman; but you might walk Regent-street a hundred times before you met with the equal of Constance Ismay. Lightness, elegance, and soft winning feminine grace constituted but a small portion of her charms. Her face was oval, the upper lip short, the chin delicately moulded. Not a tinge of colour was visible in her cheeks, except when that colour was worked by some emotion of the gentle heart which beat beneath that ivory-hued bosom. There was a constant pensiveness in the expression of her features which ill-accorded with a being so young, so beautiful. Long and finely pencilled eye-lashes canopied orbs of the deepest and darkest hue :—

    " Her eyes like dusky twilight were,
      Like twilight, too, her clust'ring hair ;"

but though those eyes were of the deepest jet, yet, when viewed in a side light, they sparkled like diamonds dipped in water and placed in the summer sunshine. Constance was pale; but her tresses were beautifully dark, and she wore them so looped up that they rested on her neck and shoulders, contrasting their gloomy blackness with the marble polish of the pearly and transparent skin. She was the reputed niece of Sir Thomas Warrenton, and had been left as a ward in his care, on the death of his sister some two years previous to the date of our story.

The materials for breakfast were arranged; the hot coffee was steaming away in the silver pot in which it was contained; the eggs were waiting to be cracked; the chicken, the ham, and all the other glorious *et ceteras* pertaining to the morning meal of a good and hearty knight, living some fifty years ago, were spread forth in due and proper order; everything was ready—why, then, was not the meal commenced, why did they wait?"

There was one chair beside that table on which no one was seated.

" Where is Lambert—why has he not taken his seat?" demanded Sir Thomas. There was no reply.

" I faith the boy shall not escape without a chiding! But where does he linger —why does he tarry?"

" You forget, Sir Thomas," observed the Lady Isabel, " that Lambert went to his bed unwell. Probably he has not yet risen."

" Not risen! why does the boy want the noon-sun to shine upon him before he wakes? Go, call him, Richard. Bid him use haste. Meanwhile, let not the good things lack partakers. Gervase—Mr. Morden, in the absence of Richard you must do duty to my lady by handing the brawn hitherward."

Without further delay the meal was commenced in good earnest. No small matter must that have been which could have caused Sir Thomas to lose his appetite; but there were those at the table who felt little inclination to eat, and it is scarcely necessary to state that their names were Constance Ismay and Gervase Morden.

Presently the servant returned with a look of astonishment on his countenance.

" Well, Richard, is my son coming—why does he delay?"

" I have been to Mr. Lambert's chamber, Sir Thomas, but he is not there. I have made inquiries also, but I cannot find that he is in the house."

" Lambert not in the house!—not to be found!—that is strange! Go; make further inquiries directly. He cannot be far distant."

The domestic departed to obey his master's commands. After the lapse of a few minutes he returned with the information, gathered from the porter, that Lambert Warrenton had passed out at the gate of the court-yard some three hours ago, mounted on his horse.

" Unwell, and out so early!" exclaimed Sir Thomas. " Who saddled his horse? Does no one know where he is gone?"

" Mr. Lambert saddled his horse himself, Sir Thomas, and he told Jeffries, who opened the gates for him, that having a head-ache he believed a ride through the wood in the early morning air would be of benefit. He said, too, that he should return within an hour."

" Within an hour! and yet, according to Jeffries, three hours have passed already. Lambert knows the hour of breakfast, and that, too, is past. Where is he—why has he not returned?"

" That is more than I know, Sir Thomas," replied the domestic, " I should not have known so much had I not learnt it from Jeffries."

"This is strange!" ejaculated Sir Thomas. " It is not usual for Lambert to absent himself in this fashion; when you have finished breakfast, Mr. Morden, you will oblige me by taking two or three of the servants with you, and making a circuit round the wood. The boy may have become worse and not able to return, or some accident may have happened to him."

Morden promised to comply with this request, and immediately arose from the table, to act accordingly; he had made his bow to the breakfast-party, and was about to leave the room, when a sudden outcry was heard in the lower part of the house.

" What, are the varlets conjuring up another ghost?" exclaimed Sir Thomas. "Why is there this disturbance?" he asked, as a servant advanced, breathlessly, along the passage.

" Oh, Sir Thomas!—Sir Thomas!" ejaculated the man.

"Speak!—You are pale, fellow. Wherein is your fright?"

"Mr. Lambert, Sir Thomas—" want of breath prevented the man from finishing the sentence.

"What of my son?—where is he?—what—"

"Mr. Lambert is—oh, Sir Thomas!——"

The worthy knight not having at any time a superabundance of patience, was particularly in need of an additional quantity at the present moment. Pushing aside the domestic, he made towards the staircase, accompanied by Morden, and followed by the other members of the breakfast-party ; at the bottom of the steps he was met by another of his servants.

"Oh, Sir Thomas! Mr. Lambert has been brought home wounded."

"Wounded!—my son wounded?"

"Nearly killed, Sir Thomas."

"Where is Dr. Cosgreave?—send for Mr. Wittingham at once—where is my son—where is Lambert?"

In one of the lower apartments, the knight found his son surrounded by a group of servants. The arm of Lambert Warrenton was bare, and immersed in a tub of warm water; the water being tinged with blood.

"Lambert! What is the meaning of this?"

"It is nothing, father ; a mere nothing. These good people are making a great disturbance about that which is really of very small importance. The cut, father, is but trifling."

"The cut!—what cut?"

"A mere scratch on the arm, father, gained in making a few passes with one of the interloping gentry, who make free to avail themselves of the good things in your woods."

"What, have the rascals been felling my trees, or snaring my hares again?"

"They have. One of them I happily chanced to fall in with. He proved a somewhat desperate rogue ; but although he has drawn blood from my arm, he has not escaped without carrying with him a warranty of the goodness of my own trusty steel. Fortunately I met with this lad, who lent me assistance in reaching home, and to whom some sort of a present must be given."

"Go, Morden," said Sir Thomas, "let the men be gathered, and the wood be well surrounded. I, myself, will be with you soon, and it will be strange if we do not manage to lay hands on one or two of these marauders."

Morden bowed and took his way accordingly. Sir Thomas turned towards his son and perceiving that his arm still lay immersed in the warm water, exclaimed—

"Why, Lambert, are you mad, boy? keep a cut wound in hot water! mercy me! know you so little surgery as that?"

"The scratch smarted, father, and the warmth gives relief from the slight pain."

"But the blood, boy, the blood! blood and life go together, and see, you are mixing up the one with the water. But what says Doctor Cosgreave?"

The physician advanced, and gently lifting the arm out of the water, exclaimed—

"Mr. Warrenton could not have done a worse thing. Why not have bound the wound up tightly and merely washed it a coming home? This soaking of the flesh will materially prevent its adherence."

"Please you, Sir Thomas," said the gardener, bowing, "that was just what I told Mr. Lambert, but he would not go by what I said."

"Peace, man, go you after Mr. Morden, he will want as many of you in the wood as be can muster."

At this moment a domestic announced that Mr. Heyton had come to the Hall, wishing to speak with Sir Thomas, immediately.

"Is he waiting?"

"He is, Sir Thomas."

"Ask him to walk into the library, if he pleases, and tell him that I will be with him in a few minutes."

Sir Thomas lingered only a few minutes to watch the binding-up of his son's arm, then, leaving the patient and the physician together, he wended his way towards the library. As he ascended the staircase he suddenly paused, and placing his hand on his forehead, as a man is apt to do when struck by a sudden thought, he ejaculated—

"Heyton here ! let me consider—he called last night, and now—here again this morning ! Surely, Amy—"

It was curious that Sir Thomas Warrenton should then and there mention the name of Amy. However, he said no more, but hastened towards the library.

Sir Thomas took Mr. Heyton's hand in a friendly manner and the latter uttered a few words in an under-tone. Had they been words of cabalistic power and of magic import they could not have caused Sir Thomas to start more than they did. Hastily he closed the library-door and took a seat beside his visitor. They conversed together for nearly an hour, and during that time the countenance of the knight changed repeatedly in its expression. To some it might have been a matter of mysterious conjecture had they obtained a glimpse of those two conversationists, that the lord of Warrenton Hall and the humble inhabitant of the sea-side cottage should have manifested such familiarity the one to the other, seeming rather as friends and equals, than as the knight and his poor neighbour, for such, compared with Sir Thomas Warrenton, Stephen Heyton really was.

At length each arose. The countenances of both were pale and there was a meaningness in their looks. Sir Thomas laid his finger impressively on the arm of his companion, and in a serious voice, said—

"Remember, Heyton, this must be kept a secret, it must be told to none."

"Perfectly secret, Sir Thomas."

"Ay, man ; as secret as *our secret* has been kept hitherto. You promise?"

"I do."

"That is well. And now for Ernest Morden ; he must be laid hands on as soon as possible."

"He has, in all probability, returned to his ship."

"That is the most likely supposition. I will accompany you, Heyton, to the vessel ; for, either there or here, we must submit the young man to an examination. If I am not mistaken, there is more at the bottom of this affair than either you or I can now guess."

"But will Ernest Morden disclose."

"We shall see ; we shall see. There must be no time lost in seeking after him."

"The castle, Sir Thomas. Would it not be better to examine that first ?"

"Right, right, Heyton. We can take that in our way. It is very extraordinary this account which your son gives ! There must of a certainty be some connection between the figure which he followed and that which Miss Ismay saw in her bed-chamber."

"And the man who accompanied Ernest, Sir Thomas."

"Exactly. We must do our best in unravelling this perplexity, and doubtlessly we shall derive some assistance by a visit to the castle. Come, Heyton, we will go forthwith."

"To the castle, Sir Thomas."

"Ay, to the castle."

CHAPTER XXI.

MYSTERIES ACCUMULATE.—THE BRIGHT THING AT THE BOTTOM OF THE WELL.

ACCOMPANIED by Mr. Heyton only, Sir Thomas left the hall to institute a search in the ruins of the old castle, and more particularly in that part where Frank Heyton had had his rencontre with the phantom-figure on the previous evening. Each had taken the precaution to arm himself, and a lantern, rope, and crowbar had been provided, as requisite articles for the full carrying out of the exploration.

It was their intention to proceed to the ship which Ernest belonged, after completing the examination of the ruins.

Sir Thomas and his companion had not proceeded far before they were met by the party who had gone out to scour the wood, and at the head of which was the student, Gervase Morden.

"Have you not found any of the rascals ?" inquired Sir Thomas, addressing Morden, and perceiving that the countenance of the man wore the look of chagrin and disappointment.

"Not one, Sir Thomas," replied the student.

"But have you searched closely ?"

"With all care, Sir Thomas. The wood is as quiet as it could possibly be ; there does not appear to be a single human being moving about in any part of it."

"They have escaped, the rascals ! they have escaped. You should have spread out your men, Morden, so as to have commanded the wood at all points, and in such a manner that no one could enter or leave it without being seen."

"We did so, Sir Thomas. My first plan of proceeding was to inclose the wood with men, each so far apart as to be in sight of the others on his left and right, and, having thus completed a circle, I gave orders for each to march towards the centre, still keeping his eyes directed to the spaces on each side of him."

"Well planned, Morden—very well planned ; and you have not caught nor seen any one?"

"Not a trespasser could we lay hands on, Sir Thomas; not one could we see."

"The rascals have been nimble in getting off. But send home the men, Morden, and fall in with us. The expedition on which we are going is, doubtless, one that is suited to your taste."

Gervase Morden joined Sir Thomas and Mr. Heyton, and was immediately informed of the intended exploration of the castle ruins. The student manifested a ready inclination to join in the search, listening with deep attention to Mr. Heyton's recountal of the adventures which had befallen his son in the very place to which they were now going.

Sir Thomas and his companions were just about emerging from the wood into the open fields, when the figure of a man at a short distance off, but apparently advancing swiftly towards them, attracted their attention.

"Why, Frank !" exclaimed Mr. Heyton in astonishment, as he discovered the individual to be his own son, "why are you here—why have you left your sisters ?"

"Both Kate and Amy assured me that they did not wish me to stay with them, so long as they had Archy in the cottage," replied Frank. "I heard you say that you should examine the castle, and there are certain parts of it connected with my last night's adventure which I wish to survey again myself. Sir Thomas, I hope, will not object to my forming one of the party."

After some demurring on the part of Mr. Heyton, caused by his disinclination to leave his two daughters unprotected, Frank was allowed to join them and to give his assistance in carrying out the forthcoming search. Sir Thomas called the young man aside, and questioned him minutely concerning the occurrences of the previous evening. Frank detailed every particular connected with his pursuit of Ernest, and his chase after the fugitive who had alluded him at the summit of the old tower. He told also of the finding of his own cutlass, and of the pool of warm blood which he had suddenly lit on in the grove near the brow of the hill. This last communication caused Sir Thomas to start with surprise, and pointing with his sword towards an adjacent group of trees, he asked,—

"Is that the place where you discovered the blood-pool ?"

"It is."

"Let us go thither, then ; haply we may meet with something which may form a clue to guide us in our search."

Sir Thomas at once led the way towards the grove. The sun was now shining brightly in the broad heavens ; and as the party entered the embowered shade they looked up and saw the golde beams flickering amongst the green leaves above their heads.

There, on the green sod, was the clotted blood, and around were numerous stains of a similar character.   From the appearance presented by the trampled grass, it was evident that a severe contest had taken place on that spot the previous night ; who the combatants had been, remained a mystery, and equally as great a mystery

was contained in the circumstance that it was at that place that Frank Heyton again met with that weapon which he had cast from him preparatory to the struggle on the Eagle's Altar.

"Ernest Morden must have fought here," observed Frank ; "the sword which he here threw down bears testimony against him."

"But with whom should my brother have fought?" asked Gervase, puzzled to account for the appearances which he beheld, and unwilling to admit the suppositions which had been made to explain them.

No. 21.

"I know not," returned Frank Heyton ; "but my belief is that your brother and the figure which I chased to yonder castle, were the two who fought in this place."

"And who's the blood—my brother's ?"

"Probably so ; the fact of my finding the weapon, which I believe him to have used, argues that he was wounded, and that, unable to carry it with him, he cast it away."

"But where is he now ?"

"That remains to be discovered."

While the two young men were thus engaged in conversation, Sir Thomas Warrenton was employing himself in minutely scrutinizing the place, with a view to detect, if possible, some vestige that would afford a clue to future discovery. Presently he took the arm of Mr. Heyton, and drawing him towards one particular spot, pointed to where many foot-marks were visible on the green sod.

"See !" said he, "they struggled there—those are the prints of their feet. If now we could be certain that those are the foot-marks of Ernest Morden ?"

"Or that the others, in the longer grass, correspond to those of the cellar-passage ?" observed the secretary.

Sir Thomas started.

"Ha, Morden ! It would be strange if such were the case. Gadzooks ! methinks there is a wondrous resemblance !"

"Can it not be tested ?" asked Heyton.

"Easily—easily, man—if we had the measures of the others here. Look you, Gervase, are they not wondrously alike ? Shall we return to the hall at once and make the comparison ?"

The secretary knelt on the green turf and examined the marks—not a syllable escaped his lips for some minutes ; then, beckoning Sir Thomas and his companions to stoop likewise, he pointed out that which had till now escaped their notice.

"Do you recollect, Sir Thomas, the peculiarity of those foot-marks which are in the passage at the hall ?"

"Mean you the breadth of the toe ?"

"I do ; examine now these marks, and you will at once perceive that the impressions in each place have been made by the same feet."

"Gadzooks ! it is as you say. I see it, man—I see it."

"And what conclusion do you draw, Sir Thomas ?"

"Why—Heaven preserve us, Morden ! the same villain who fought in this grove afterwards entered my own house."

"More than that, Sir Thomas ; he it was who was present in Miss Ismay's chamber."

"It must have been so, man—it must have been so : and this blood is from the same veins as the drops which we espied on the flooring of the room."

"There can be little doubt of that, Sir Thomas. It is useless to stay here. Let us away to the castle yonder, where, if I mistake not greatly, more important discoveries await us."

Adopting this suggestion, the party started immediately in the direction of the old fortress. Frank Heyton pointed out the small copse, in the shade of which he had from a distance discovered the flitting form of the phantom figure. Passing over the level green sward, they came to the drawbridge, and there, upon the dust and sand with which it was covered, the marks of the mysterious feet were also dimly discernible. Frank saw the broad sunlight swooping down in its golden spendour upon the grass-covered bastion, where, on the last evening, he had sat along with the idiot boy. The moat was crossed ; the ruins were gained.

Fronting the open sea, and exposed to the stormy wind and weather, stood the proud old fortress. Time had crumbled its battlements, and rounded the angles of its stonework. It had been reared by Roman hands and adorned by Norman craftsmen. The *thelemii*, or rows of bricks disposed according to the fashion of herring-bone, betrayed that, although erected on an English shore, its builders ha^a

once trodden the banks of the Tiber. At the loopholes, through which the arrow had once sped its way, the dauntless, impudent ivy now crept in, fearless of being grappled by martial hand. Birds had built their nests in the castle-keep; ants had upheaved their sandy palaces in the open footpath of the court-yard. Where the iron-cased foot had trodden in the olden time upsprung the daisy now; and on the stone coping, against which with battle-axe in hand, the chatelain had once been wont to lean, the moss now spread its velvet covering. Decay's "effacing finger" had touched the whole, and with the touch the walls had mouldered, the battlements had fallen, the warrior had laid him down to his lasting sleep, the battle-axe had rusted to a relic, and the ivy—the reckless, roistering ivy, had cast its arms around, clasping stone and tile, buttress and moulding, carved arch and chiselled column, like a beautiful but heartless wanton, exulting over the victim caught in her enchanting toils.

Frank Heyton led the way towards the tower at the southern part of the ruins, in which was the staircase that had been ascended by him on the previous night. He looked up, and saw the fearful gap where the steps had fallen away, and above which was the small opening leading into into the vaulted chamber. To venture across this gap in its present state and without some help, was a task too difficult and daring for any one to attempt; yet Frank and Gervase Morden had fully made up their minds to ascend to the highest step. How to accomplish this object they knew not; but after a slight search they discovered two old oaken planks which they placed across the breach in the staircase, and over which they were bold enough to scramble.

"Surely," said Gervase Morden, " he must have been a hazardous adventurer who had the temerity to lead the way up such a place as this in the darkness of the night-time."

" Yet it was here I followed him," rejoined Heyton, " for on this step he stood when I touched his garments with my hand."

Emerging upon the battlements, Frank Heyton and the student commenced a minute examination of the various parts, but no way by which the figure of the preceding night could have made its descent could they discover. Retracing their path, they descended the upper steps and entered the gloomy chamber where hung the remaining portion of the broken well-rope. Here they were joined by Sir Thomas and Mr. Heyton, who had ventured to scramble over the planks which had been placed across the gap. Both shuddered when they gazed down the dark abyss, into which, by means of the now broken rope, Frank Heyton had ventured to descend but a few hours ago. They handled the dangling cord, and endeavoured to fathom the depth of the hole, but they found it deeper than they had calculated it to be, and could scarcely bring themselves to believe that a descent into it had really been made under the circumstances which they had heard narrated.

Following up their original intent in seeking to discover the track of the mysterious fugitive, every nook was pryed into, and every corner of the chamber scanned. In vain were there examinations; no place of concealment could they descry, and there were evidently no other means of effecting a descent than by going down the staircase, dropping into the well, or springing from the outer battlements; no other way could they discover, and yet Frank Heyton felt certain that by none of these means had the fugitive which he had followed contrived to elude him.

" I fear, my young friend," observed Sir Thomas, " that there must have been some mistake here. In your eagerness to capture the object of your pursuit, you were, in all probability, deluded by the darkness of the place and time, and followed nothing more substantial than your own shadow."

" Sir Thomas, it was the form of an old man which I saw ascend this staircase. I heard the rustling of his dress; I heard distinctly the sound of his footfall on the stone steps down yonder in the gloom."

" You may have been deceived, Frank," observed his father. " Excited as you were, nothing was more easy than for fancy to have created a score of seeming realities. In the echo of your own steps you might have been led to believe that you heard the foot-fall of a second person; and your own breath might, at every respiration, have sounded in your ears like the rustling of garments. Fancy can delude the senses strangely when the mind is before-hand duly prepared."

" It is only of the vision and the hearing that you speak, father," rejoined the youth. How say you when I assert that with my own hands—with these hands I touched the soft garments of another person on the stairs above me ?"

" Even there imagination may have played its part, Frank. Touch is but a sense ; and is liable to the fallibilities of other senses, though, perhaps, not in the same degree."

" Will you account all to fancy, father ? Will you solve every riddle by such a solution? Was it fancy alone which wrought last night's perplexities ? Saw you only in fancy the behaviour of Ernest Morden ? Did we only fancy that we perceived blood in yonder grove ? and do the foot-prints there and on the draw-bridge exist but in our fancy only? In truth, good father, if that be the case, I think we may as well relinquish our search, and deem the whole affair neither more nor less than a strange and bewildering dream."

Sir Thomas Warrenton took the hand of Mr. Heyton.

" There is some argument in the observations of your son," said he. " It will not do for us to be too sceptical in this matter; recollecting that, according to all appearance, it must have been no less difficult for mortal man to have entered the sleeping-room of my ward without passing through open door or window, than for this figure to have escaped from the tower top without passing down by the staircase or clambering over the battlements. Gadzooks! I am ready to believe anything now !"

" But what are we likely to gain by staying here ?" asked Mr. Heyton.

" I fear nothing," replied Sir Thomas. " Allowing the subject of this mystery to have ascended to this most unpleasant place, it seems pretty certain that he is here no longer. By what means he took himself off, though that is precisely that which we wish to know, happens to be precisely that which it is not yet given to us to comprehend."

Mr. Heyton shook his head, as an expression of his scepticism on the point.

" Mortal men," he observed, " of a certainty fought in the grove yonder, for they have left the evidence of their being such behind them ; and when I see foot-marks, as on the drawbridge below, I know that feet must have been there to cause them ; but what have we here to assure us that one of us, at least, has not been merely illuded by his own fancy ?"

" This, Stephen Heyton, this !" exclaimed Gervase Morden, as he seized the arm of the sceptic and drew him towards the step which immediately adjoined the entrance to the vaulted chamber. " Do you see that ?" he asked.

" I perceive a spot—a single spot."

" And what is it ? Bend down and look."

Immediately every eye was busied in examining this new discovery. A single close inspection sufficed to make evident the nature of the object."

" It is blood," said Mr. Heyton seriously—" blood that has not been long spilt."

" Gadzooks, Master Morden ! " exclaimed Sir Thomas, " you have a sharp eye for such business as this. Of a truth, I believe that not one of us would have seen that spot if you had not been here to point it out."

Frank Heyton laid his head upon his father's shoulder.

" Speak you of fancy now ?" he demanded. " Is it but in fancy that you see that spot ?"

" No, Frank ; this is evidence—this is something which cannot be gainsayed."

" And what does it tell, father ? What but that one of those who fought in the brow of yonder hill fled to this tower—that he was followed here by me—that he passed up this very staircase on which you now stand—that he ascended to this height—and that he concealed himself or descended by a way of which we know nothing ?"

" The youth is right," observed Sir Thomas. " These blood-marks are serving for an excellent trail, and they will lead to something at last."

" Recollect, Sir Thomas, this discovery does but increase the mystery," observed Heyton. " We are certain now that the fugitive fled hither ; but whence went he ? how did he conceal himself afterwards ?"

" That is, indeed, a puzzle. Let us examine things again."

Agreeably to this proposition, the battlements and the vaulted chamber were again submitted to a scrutiny, but nothing satisfactory could be elicited. Indeed, to such an extent was every one mystified, that none could form even a conjecture to account for that which at once called forth their wonder and tasked their ingenuity.

Making their way down the tower staircase, they lit the lantern, and proceeded to explore the deeper parts of the building, more especially the dungeon into which Frank Heyton had fallen, when the rope to which he had clung snapped asunder, and precipitated him into the depth and the darkness.

The under-works of the castle were of great extent, and of most ingenious construction. Steps cut in the solid chalk led down into a spacious chamber, excavated in the bowels of the cliff. Leading out from this were two long passages, each of which was of great length but exceedingly narrow. Choosing out that which appeared the larger of the two, Sir Thomas marshalled the way down it. At the other extremity was another large subterranean chamber in which a rusty chain was suspended. This chain when let free from the hook to which it was attached, allowed two iron-doors, one at each end of the long passage, to fall down and close up the entries ; such having been the contrivance adopted by some of the late inhabitants of the castle to protect them in the event of a siege, when, supposing the castle to be taken, they could flee to this chamber, and if the besiegers following them entered the passage nothing could be more easy than to pull the chain, let the two iron doors fall, and then having made captives of the enemy suffocate them by pouring down burning sulphur from above. Contrivances of this kind are still to be observed in many of our island fortresses and the dreadful use which has been made of them in times gone by is to be found recorded in the pages of the commonest history.

Nothing of that which they sought, however, could Sir Thomas and his companions discover in these chambers, or in the communicating passages. Keeping up the scrutiny as they proceeded onwards, they at length reached the door of that dungeon which, some twelve or fourteen hours ago, Frank Heyton had deemed would be his chamber of death ; the door was still open as he had left it, and its shattered wood-work and deranged fastenings bore witness to the desperation of him whom it had nearly shut out from the world for ever.

They entered the dungeon, and as he did so, Frank Heyton felt his blood run cold, and his flesh creep beneath his skin. A single glance sufficed to recal to his mind all the torture which he had suffered during the hour or more in which he had been there imprisoned. It was as if he had arisen from his tomb, and now come back again to take a look at the gloomy receptacle in which he had been immured. So foetid was the atmosphere of the place that the lamp burnt dimly, and with a lurid, dull flame. Each one by turns gazed up the high, perpendicular shaft at the faint daylight, which was discernible at the top, and then turned round to shudder at the gloomy horrors of the dungeon in which they stood.

On the floor, at their fleet, lay the one-half of the broken rope, and above them dangled the other portion, hanging where it had hung for years.

Frank Heyton recounted again how as he lay expecting momentarily to die, the door of the dungeon had opened, and for one single moment he had beheld the countenance of that mysterious individual, in pursuit of whom he had narrowly escaped being lured to destruction. Sir Thomas examined the dungeon, in order to find out if possible why and with what intent the door had been unbarred, and then, on the old man perceiving the prisoner, so suddenly barred up again, but the search seemed likely to terminate most unsatisfactorily. The walls of the place were firm and unyielding, and the rust on the bolts of the door told plainly that they were not often thrust back.

"What does that rubbish conceal?" asked Gervase Morden, pointing to the place upon which Frank Heyton had fallen, and where, if it had not been for the rubbish and dust which chanced to be heaped together there, he would have broken some one or more of his limbs.

"It is, in all probability, the continuation of the well," replied Sir Thomas; "see you not that this rope must have once descended lower than where we now stand?"

"Let us determine if such be the case," rejoined Heyton, as assisted by the secretary, he applied himself to the removal of the rubbish.

After some exertion a quantity of dry brushwood, pounded mortar, and loose stones were removed from the mouth of the well. They were about to relinquish further working in that direction, under the belief that their labour would prove fruitless, when the crowbar with which they worked, struck a large slab that returned a hollow sound.

"Ha!" cried Sir Thomas, "there is something beneath. Lift it up, Heyton—lift it up, and let us know what it conceals."

By the united efforts of the various members of the party the slab was raised, and removed from its position. A deep, dark hole was disclosed, from which the pent-up vapours at length escaping, nearly overpowered those who endeavoured to look into the abyss.

"What see you, Heyton—what see you?"

"There is nothing to be seen, Sir Thomas. The hole is merely the old well of castle, and it is not unlikely that there is water at the bottom still."

"But why has it been covered up so carefully?"

"Probably, Sir Thomas, to prevent any one from falling in."

"And who, Heyton, would be likely to run the risk of that danger, by entering this place, or by daring such a feat as that performed by your son, in clinging to yonder dangling rope?"

"I cannot answer you, Sir Thomas. But what other cause could have induced any person to adjust this stone so nicely, and to gather together this mass of rubbish?"

"There must be something concealed, man—there must be something concealed. Cannot you throw a light into the place?"

Gervase Morden advanced, and tying the lantern to the rope with which he was provided, endeavoured to lower into the well. Gradually, however, the noxious vapours acted on the light; and, as the lantern descended, the flame flickered, grew redder and duller, till at length it became like to a faint blue star twinkling down in the darkness.

"Pull it up, man—pull it up!" exclaimed Sir Thomas. "Heaven keep us man! do not let the light go out."

"Hold!" cried Morden. "What is that which shines at the bottom of the well?"

"Shines!—shines! why, the water, man. What should it be but the water?"

At that moment the light in the lantern became extinguished.

"Where is the firebox?" inquired Sir Thomas. "Quick! let us have flint and steel, for it is not pleasant to be in a place like this without a light. Give me the lantern, Morden. Deftly there, Heyton, or you will not get the match to burn. This air is by no means favourable to the best of tinder."

After some trouble, the lantern was relighted, and a proposal was made, that the search should be proceeded with in another part of the ruins. Morden, however, seized the hand of his master, and drawing him towards the margin of the well, said—

"Listen, Sir Thomas! I am about to throw this stone into the hole. If that be the water which glimmers at the bottom, we shall hear the splash."

Every one bent his head to listen.

The stone was dropped from the hand. A second—two seconds—three seconds passed, and a sharp quick sound announced that the bottom of the well was reached.

"Heard you, Sir Thomas?" exclaimed the secretary. "Was there any splash? Has that stone fallen into water."

"Gadzooks man! I cannot say. It was not exactly the kind of sound which should have been given forth, had it struck water in its way."

"To my thinking," observed Mr. Heyton, "the stone struck some hard substance. Let us repeat the experiment."

Another stone was thrown, and the like sound was heard.

"Of a certainty that was not water which was struck then," remarked Sir Thomas. "Doubtless the old well has become dried up and empty."

"Then, if there be no water, Sir Thomas, what is that which I saw sparkle and shine at the bottom?" asked Morden.

"It is not for me to tell you. Perchance the chalk is white, and can be seen through the darkness."

"Chalk would not glitter, Sir Thomas. See, I will light this piece of paper, and throw it down. As it falls, look again at the bottom of the well."

Sir Thomas complied with the desire of his secretary. The two Heytons also gazed in the same direction. Down through the gloom fell the burning paper.

"Look you, Sir Thomas! See you not the bright thing now? It gleams—it glitters! Heaven befriend us! how brightly it shines."

"I see it, man—I see it; but what can it be?"

"See again. Here is another piece of paper. Watch!—there!—there! Look you how it glitters like the eyes of some wild beast. It sparkles as if a star were at the bottom of the well."

Each member of the party had caught sight of the glittering object, and each was now anxious to ascertain its real nature. Various were the surmisings concerning what it probably was. A shudder crept over the elder Heyton, and he involuntarily became fearful that that he was about to learn some hideous secret to which he had as yet been a stranger.

"Can no means be devised for fetching up whatever may be at the bottom of the well?" asked Sir Thomas. "We have a strong rope with us now. Who will venture to imitate the adventure of last night?"

"Your pardon, Sir Thomas," said Morden, "but you must bear in mind that the effluvium of that pit would speedily overpower any one who ventured to descend into it."

"Then what is to be done? Are we to depart without having our curiosity gratified?"

Frank Heyton now stepped forward, and produced from out of his pocket two large eel-hooks, which, being used to angling, he was accustomed to carry about with him.

"Let us attach these to the end of the rope," he said. "Probably we may fish up something to satisfy us for our trouble."

The suggestion was at once carried out. Having fastened on the two hooks, the rope was lowered into the well.

"Throw in another piece of paper," said Sir Thomas; "let us see if the bright object be there still."

The paper was lit and thrown down.

"See!—it is there—it glitters more brightly than before!"

"Then try the hooks, Heyton. Drag them gently. Do they catch, boy—do they catch"

"Not yet."

Every one was silent, and the noise made by the rope as it knocked against the sides of the wall, was distinctly heard. Presently, a smile of triumph gleamed on the countenance of the younger Heyton as he exclaimed,—

"They have caught—the hooks have grappled something."

"Up with it, boy—up with it!"

"I—I cannot; it is heavy—very heavy."

"Heavy! Hold you the light, Morden, whilst I give assistance. Softly now, or you may lose your grapple. It comes—it comes!"

"Gervase Morden, hold the light over the mouth of the well. This is good angling," said he, "for the bright thing is coming upwards with every haul of the rope."

"Pull, Heyton—pull! Gadz ooks! there's weight enough in it, be it what it may!"

Another pull, and then another, and the object was drawn out of the well. At that moment the hand of Gervase Morden trembled, and the lantern fell from his grasp; while Sir Thomas Warrington, fixing his eyes on the fearful object which he had uphauled, started back, let fall the rope, and in a voice of terror exclaimed,—

"Merciful God! what have we here?"

Heyton and his son simultaneously uttered a cry of horror, and clung to the wall of the dungeon to support themselves from falling.

CHAPTER XXII.

THE TOMB-MAKER AND HIS TROUBLER—THE INJUNCTION.

Not far from Warrington Hall, by the side of the high road leading to the neighbouring town, was a small village, containing not more then ten or a dozen habitations. It was dignified by the high-sounding title of St. Gillot's cross; but this had been corrupted and vulgarised into the more plebeian name of Gill-cross. A quiet unassuming little place it was, possessing but one humble ale-house, and one single-legged cobbler; the cobbler and the ale-house keeper being the only tradesmen of the village: the one retailing ale; the other stale jokes.

In the rear of the village stood an ancient church well adorned with ivy; its sun-dial posted over the porch, and its gilded vane glittering on the top of the moss-covered tower. Within its precincts many of those who had once been the residents of the adjacent town, lay buried. Here, amidst the blooming buttercups and pink-eyed daisies, they slept their last, long, peaceful sleep, without knowing anxiety—without a consciousness of the hubbub and turmoil existent in the noisy world around. Over them waved the green grass—above them the merry birds sung masses all the day;—

"Oh! 'twere sweet to the grave to go,
If one were sure to be buried so."

Very near to the grave-yard, and not more than a stone-throw from the village itself, stood an isolated cottage, or rather hovel, of most humble aspect, and having nothing connected with it which was likely to attract the eyes of a passer-by, except, perhaps, the various stones which, carved in various forms, ornamented the adjoining yard and garden. This cottage was the dwelling place of Sampson Summers, usually called Sandy Summers, on account of the light colour of his hair. He was stone-mason of the village, and tomb-maker for the church-yard. Altogether he was a most singular and eccentric individual, presenting, in his whole appearance, the look of a man whose brain had become turned from the assiduity with which he had followed up some favourite study.

Sandy Summers was an adept in his art; few men could handle a chisel and mallet better than he, and the grotesque shapes into which he was in the habit of carving the pieces of stone, excited the admiration as well as the merriment of all who beheld them. In early life he had been nothing more than a mason's labourer, but watching one day the process of chiselling out a medallion on a tomb-stone, he took it into his head that he too could carve tomb-stones, if he were but to set about it. Now there is no better plan of gaining success in any art than being beforehand, thoroughly impressed with an idea of your own abilities. Men must have a little self-conceit, or they never achieve anything worthy of notice. Sandy Summers feeling satisfied in his own mind that he could cut out a coat of arms as well as carry a basket, threw down the basket, and began the coat of arms. To the surprise of every one, he used his chisel as if he had been apprenticed to the art. From carving coats of arms, he proceeded to cut out weeping angels and chubby cherubs, from doing which again, he tried his hand on death's heads and

skeleleton dart-throwers. Thus he went on, caring not to be recompensed for his labour, but chiselling away with right good will, and then leaving off to rub his hands together, and to admire, with a chuckle of satisfaction, the work which he had just executed.

Sandy Summers was a small and lean man, looking, however, more like an exaggerated boy than an individual who had really attained the age of fifty. He had a large head, which was covered with a profusion of light-coloured frizzy hair ; his eyes were small and deeply sunken in his head, but they twinkled and sparkled beneath his large, overhanging brows as if they enjoyed continual happiness in their snug retreat. Undoubtedly the eyes of Sandy Summers were merry eyes, for who could tell a merrier tale than he ? Alas ! tale telling and joking were his two weak points, for every one concurred in saying, that if Sandy Summers would but tell less tales and use his chisel more, he might soon become a rich man ; but Sandy cared not a straw for riches, and if he could but get the making of all the tombs and tablets required by the inhabitants of the neighbouring town, and had but tobacco in his pipe and ale in the brown jug which invariably stood by his side, Sandy Summers was a contented and happy man. In the evening time he would wander into the adjacent churchyard, and there meeting the cobbler, would sit down on down on one of the tombs together, enjoying their pipes and chatting familiarly over the passing events, and on matters connected with Warrenton Hall, and its worthy and respected owner.

It was now the the afternoon of a hot summer's day, and Sandy had laid aside his chisel to regale himself as usual with his brown October, as well as to hold converse with a dark-visaged, unprepossessing-looking visitor who called in for half an hour's chat. Sandy was seated on one block of stone and his companion upon another similar block. The latter person was habited in a cloak and slouched hat ; his age was apparently about forty ; he had dark, bright eyes, and a roguish expression of countenance. Sandy Summers seemed little desirous of his company, but the visitor seemed one of those agreeable persons who never wait for an invitation and never take a hint to go. The stone-cutter at last took up his chisel and recommenced his work.

" But Sandy——" said the visitor.

Sandy brought down his mallet with such thwacks that the words drowned the words of his companion.

" But Sandy, what I mean is——"

Sandy did not seem to care about the meaning, for he now knocked away harder than before. The visitor arose, and put his hand on the stonecutter's thoulder.

" Do you think, Sandy, that——"

If Sandy was not thinking, he was working, for the chips of stone now flew about with more force than ever. Down, down, came the wooden malllet ; chip, chip went the chisel, and away flew the little pieces around and about the head of Sandy and that of his troublesome visitor. Never before had Sandy seemed so provokingly deaf. Not a word that was uttered by the stranger did he appear to hear.

" Sandy Summers !"

" Yes," replied Sandy.

" King Death and the mason are partners old,
   And traders old are they ;
They entered on trade when the world was made,
   And their union will last for aye.
With his dart so keen, the jolly king,
   Strikes the lord and his serving men ;
Then they dig up the ground, and they throw up the mound,
   And the mason is wanted then !"

" Sandy Summers, man !"

" And the mason is wanted then !"

" But I beg your pardon, Luke Masters, I thought I heard you speak?"

" Your ears must be no better than the stone ones on the figure yonder if you didn't, Sandy. Hark you Sandy Summers !"

" King Death and the mason are partners old,
   And tra——"

" Well, I'm listening."

" Sandy, are you mad ; or have you not lived long enough in the world to learn your manners yet?"

The stone-mason turned round and threw a look of withering scorn upon his visitor.

" Ask the best of them at Warrenton Hall," said he, " if Sampson Summers don't know his manners better than Luke Masters knows his? Ay, ay, they'll tell you that Sampson Summers, the tomb-maker, and Humphrey Whiffin, the cobbler, are about the two best bred men in this village. Look you, Luke Masters, could you carve out a cherub's face to look anything like that one?"

" Every man to his trade, Sandy. But I was about to say——"

" You were not about to say that you'd ever seen a better bit of workmanship than that headstone, were you?"

" No, Sandy. I— But suppose we take another sip from the jug a-piece?"

" With all my heart, Luke Masters. It's a strange thing, a very strange thing ; but do you know that I think one-half of those beautiful stone babies and watching angels in our church come out of neighbour Seymour's ale?"

" Out of the ale, Sandy? I—I was quite ignorant of the fact."

" You are ignorant of a great deal which you've yet to learn, Luke Masters. You see now I can never work without a draught of ale now and then ; and yet, to look at me, it don't seem to do me any good, does it? I can't work without, as I was saying ; and it's after I've had a pint or two that all my ideas come, and something like ideas they are, too. Just step back now for a few feet—there!— look now!—look at that cherub's cheeks!—look at its lips and forehead! They say there's some good works of this kind in London, but they've nothing to come up to that, I should say."

" Nothing, Sandy Summers. But just listen to me for a moment. I wished to ask you—"

" That's certainly as good a nose as ever I've cut in stone—don't you say so, now?"

" Very good indeed, Sandy ; and if you will have the goodness to tell me—"

" How it's made? No—I couldn't do that. Besides, if I did, it would be of no use to you, seeing that you must be born to it. A man must be born to every-thing, Luke ; some are born to be kings, and some are born to cut out cherub's faces."

" And some to be leaden-eared dolts, Sandy."

" And some to be hanged, Luke Masters."

The dark eyes of the visitor flashed upon the stonemason a glance of anger. Sandy took up his chisel and reseated himself before the work on which he was engaged. He had no sooner recommenced his work that he broke out again in his favourite song, and the chips of stone flew merrily about to the tune of—

" King Death and the mason are partners old."

" Sandy Summers, now don't be a fool. I've got a word to say to you."

" And traders old are they.
They entered on trade when the world was made,
There union will——"

" Luke Masters, what do you want at that part of my shop?" exclaimed the stone-cutter, as he observed that his visitor was stealing his way towards a small door which communicated between the workshop and the room behind.

" I was looking at one of your carvings here."

" You'll please to step back, then," said Sandy, placing himself against the door. " I don't allow any intrusion amongst my models."

" Tush, tush, man! Come, here's the money for another jug of ale, if you will step out and fetch it."

" And leave you here by yourself—eh? No, no; that's out of my line of conduct. How do I know but what you would steal some of my ideas from these models, and turn them into tombstones yourself?"

" It's extraordinary, I take it, Sandy Summers, that you should be so jealous about your bits of clay and stone."

" Bits of clay and stone, indeed! That's quite enough to show me what your taste is, Luke Masters ; so you'll greatly oblige me by stepping to the other part of the shop. I never allow visitors to have anything to do with the models, if so be they don't want to look out a pattern for their own stone."

" And how should you know, Sandy, but what I am about to give you an order myself?"

" Humph! Luke Masters, I'm fearsome they'll never let a stone stand at your head, except it be—"

" Except it be what, Sandy?"

" One of the flags in the town gaol."

The mason's visitor broke out in a loud, hoarse laugh. Slapping his companion on the shoulder in a careless manner, he said—

" Why, Sandy Summers, you don't seem to have a very good opinion of your old friends. Is it that you are getting pride as well as money—eh, Sandy?"

" I am not proud, and you know it, Luke; but there's a sort of pride which one must have in this world, and which keeps us from having anything to do with —with those who can't do any good to us."

" Amongst which number you class your old acquaintance, Luke Masters. Is it not so, Sandy?"

" If I make caps," replied the tomb-cutter, " I don't take the trouble of fitting them on myself."

" Sandy, you're a sad rogue to treat old friends in this way. Any one would think that we are strangers."

The tomb-cutter drew back with an air of scorn, Folding his arms, he replied,—

" And we are strangers, Luke Masters. You have said the right word. Let us be strangers from this time."

" Fine words, Sandy! fine words to one who was your playmate in past years; one who used to pluck the buttercups along with you in the churchyard which is close at hand."

" Luke Masters, you speak not the truth. I never was your playmate; I did as you own to having done—plucked the pretty, blooming buttercups from off the graves of children, and from around the tombs of gentle women. No, Luke Masters, I saw *you* do so, and I chid you for it; but your's was a cold heart, and you cared not for my words. I disliked you, Luke, then—God forgive me for disliking any one of his creatures!—but I could not like you, Luke; I did not like you: and I may as well out with the truth at once, and say—I like you not now."

" In sooth, Sandy, a very kind and friendly confession! And all this hatred because, if I recollect rightly, I used to switch down the flowers with my whip while you would loll on the grass and hang over the yellow blossom as if they were the children, and not those who were buried beneath."

" You say rightly, Luke, and you have spoken well; except in using the word 'hatred.' I have no hatred for you—none. And if I dislike you, it is because I cannot help it, and because there is that in your nature which always has kept me, and I am afraid ever will keep me, from accounting you my friend."

" Because of my switching the buttercups, Sandy?"

" No, not for doing that, but because your doing so told me what you were in heart, Luke. Remember, man—as I do—the day when we met in this very churchyard—it was long ago, Luke, for we were both boys then. There was a grave—a small grave in the yard—where, a few days before, poor Patsy Phillips had been buried. You recollect Patsy Phillips; you recollect that she lived with her poor widowed mother at the little cottage, on the left of the high road. Even now I see her as she was when I and her were children. I see her with her blue eyes and her bright golden-coloured hair. She was the only child of that widowed mother, Luke. She died—she played with me on neighbour Seymour's green one day, and three days after she was dead. In a corner of the churchyard I saw her buried. Her mother dug up the plants out of her cottage garden and planted them over the little grave. I saw her plant them there—I saw her water them with her tears. There was a white rose over the head of the grave, and there were primroses round the border. That rose and those primroses I saw planted, and I heard Patsy's mother say, as she planted them, that the rose was Patsy herself, and the primroses were Patsy's playmates. Luke Masters, it was a summer's afternoon— a bright summer's afternoon—when you and I entered the churchyard together.

You left me to wander about. In a few minutes I looked towards you; by Patsy's grave you stood, and with the whip which you held in your hand, you were cutting down the primroses around that grave. I rushed to the place—I bade you to desist. You laughed. I asked you why you did so? You again lifted the whip. I tried to seize your arm. At that moment Patsy's mother entered the churchyard—tears burst from her eyes when she saw what you had done. She reproached you for your wantonness. She asked you what poor little Patsy had ever done to harm you? Again you lifted your arm, and with a stroke, a single stroke, you cut off the one white rose which a mother's love had planted—which a mother's tears had watered. I struck you to the ground, Luke Master's, and I did hate you then. Hark you, man! the opinion I formed of you then has never changed—has never altered. The deed I speak off was done in days gone by; it may have been forgotten by you; but that which I have forgiven, Luke, I cannot forget. I do not hate you now—I do not scorn you as I did then. We are acquaintances, Luke—old acquaintances; but go, man, go; we can never, shall never, be friends!"

"As you please about that, Sandy. But it is odd that you should dislike me because you are womanish, and I have a little more of the man in me."

"The man, Luke Masters—the man, do you say?"

"Ay, the man, Sandy; for, if I judge rightly, there is very little of the man in one who would go wheedling about a few flowers, and who would whimper to see a rose cut down."

"You are wrong, Luke Masters; you are much in the wrong! If to play the bully, or the fighter, or the marauder were all that man was made for, he would not have been better than the beasts. He is no man, I tell you, Luke, who would not do a kind action when he had opportunity for doing it; who would not heal a wound in another if he had the means at hand: who would not say a word of comfort to the wretched, and give them his own right hand. No man is he, Luke, who can look at a widowed mother weeping over the grave of her only child without weeping himself; who can deal lightly with any object which affection has made holy; or who can take delight in adding one drop of sorrow to the heart which is overflowing with it already. Say what you like to it, Luke Masters, but I'd not give the value of a button for a man who can make the boast that no one ever saw a tear in his eye. That's what I say, Luke, and that's my opinion in the matter."

"Well, Sandy, and what does it all come to—what is your opinion of myself?"

"I judge no one, Luke. It is my belief that there is a sprinkle of good in all. Let Him with whom we both shall have to do, decide who is in the right and who in the wrong."

"That is all well enough, Sandy, and I'm to understand, I suppose, that as my acquaintance is not good enough for you, I'm not to speak to you again."

"I neither know what you are doing or whether you are worse or better than you used to be, Luke; if I said that I wished for your company, I should be telling an untruth."

"Then I am to keep away, Sandy Summers?"

"I've told you, Luke, that you and I can never be friends."

"There's nothing like a man having a good opinion of himself, Sandy, as for myself I don't profess to be the right thing which you choose to call yourself."

"You've not heard me say so, Luke."

"If you've not said the words, you've said as much."

"I've not said that I'm better than the rest of the world, Luke Masters."

"Are you any better than you should be, Sandy Summers?" demanded his companion in a grave voice and with a piercing look.

"What mean you, Luke?"

"I ask you the question. It isn't unlikely that you think me blind and deaf as well as bad; but I've been listening to your talk for some time, Sandy Summers, and I now ask you if you are a better man than you would have the world to believe you be?"

" The world may say of me as it pleases ; but it has never reached my ears that it has spoken badly of me."

" But wouldn't it, Sandy—wouldn't it if it knew all ?"

" Knew all, Luke Masters ?"

" Aye, knew all.   You are not a smuggler, are you ?"

" There is no one who can say that I am, Luke Masters."

" You are not a thief ?"

" Ask any one in the village, Luke, and I warrant you they'll give a good character to Sandy Summers."

" And you are not a murderer ?"

" I a murderer, Luke Masters !   What right have you to put such a question ?"

" Never mind about the right.   I'm only asking you for argument's sake.   You are not one, you say ?"

" God forbid there should be the stain of blood on my head !"

" That's a touch of the parson, Sandy, and sounds none the better for being such.   Now then, tell me—are you not a friend to the French ?"

" I !—to the French ?"

" Aye, to the French, who are the enemies of this land.   I ask you,—are you not their friend ?"

" If the land and the King have no worse enemies than I am to them they have no cause for fear."

" And you have not robbed, murdered, cheated his Majesty, or favoured the French, Sandy ?"

" I have not."

" Then, Sandy Summers," exclaimed Luke Masters, rising from his seat and stepping forwards, " what have you in this room ?"

The tomb-cutter turned pale and answered with some hesitation,—

" There is nothing, Luke—nothing but my models."

" Will you swear to that ?"

Sandy Summers turned yet paler.

" I will swear nothing—nothing to you, Luke Masters."

" But you assert that you have nothing hidden in that room—nothing which you dread should see the light."

" Nothing, Luke Masters."

" Then you will give me permission to look inside.   If there be nothing which you fear that I should see, you can have no objection to granting me that privilege."

Masters had laid his hand upon the handle of the door ; but the tomb-cutter hastily interposed.

" You have no right to make any such demand, Luke Masters; and you may take my word for it you shall not enter this room unless I please."

Masters tried the door, but found it to be locked.

" Hark you, Sandy Summers," said he in a low whisper, " it is my belief that there's more villany about you than most people suspect.   Will you tell me what it was which you took into your house this morning before day-break ?   What sort of goods are those which people take in out in the dark ?"

" Mayhap you know more about those matters than myself, Luke Masters ; and if I were asked for some one who could answer such a question, I should make answer by saying, that the likeliest person to apply to would be yourself."

" But it is of you that I speak, Sandy Summers ; and it is to you I put the question—what sort of goods took you in at daybreak this morning ?"

" Better that what I took in some two hours ago when Luke Masters entered this workshop."

Fearful was the expression which the countenance of Masters suddenly assumed.

" You play your game well, Sandy Summers," said he ; " Listen man ! the lock upon this door is a new one—it used not to be here ; the shutters of the room are shut—they have always been kept open.   This very forenoon when your daughter Fan tried to look in at the door, you drew her away, and threatened to punish her if she repeated the act."

" Ha ! " exclaimed Summers. " Did Fanny tell you that ? '

" Never mind what Fan told me. I ask you, what have you in this room ? "

" Nothing—nothing but a model, which—which I do not wish any child to see."

" Then let me see it ? "

" I shall do no such thing, Luke Masters."

" And your reasons——"

" Are my own."

" Then, by the God of Heaven, I will both see and know ! " cried Masters, as he again laid his hand upon the lock, and endeavoured to force open the door."

" Back, Luke Masters—back ! there is nothing which you shall touch here without my leave."

" Do you say so, man ! you little know Luke Masters, if you think he would ask your permission for aught. Stand away, I say ! for I will open the door."

Masters seized a clump of wood, with which he was about to break open the door, Sandy caught up the mallet which he had just been using, and boldly faced his opponent.

" I have said it, Luke Masters, and you go not into that room unless I please."

" And do you think, Sandy Summers, I would ask your leave for the doing of anything which I could do without? Know you not which of us is the stronger man ? "

" It may be you, Luke, or it may be me, that's a question which can only be settled by putting it to a trial. I am not afraid of you, Masters—I do not fear your words."

" Stand away, man ! " cried Luke, putting forth his hand, to seize the tomb-cutter by the shoulder.

" You'd best not provoke me to do you harm, Luke," continued Sandy, most valourously flourishing his mallet as he spoke.

" Away, I say ! and let me enter the room."

" Stand back, Luke—stand back ! "

Luke Masters made an attempt to push the tomb-cutter aside, in order that he might break open the door. No sooner, however, did his hand touch Sandy, than with a quick and powerful blow, the mallet of Sandy Summers descended on his arm, and the limb fell paralysed by his side.

It was now a fearful moment—the countenance of Masters changed from a deep crimson to a dusky black, the great veins in his forehead and temples swelled up, and his features amply expressed the hellish rage which had suddenly taken possession of his soul. Flinging down the clump of wood, he grasped one of the stonemason's chisels, and in a voice, rendered thick and gutteral by his extreme passion, said—

" I'll have your life, Sandy Summers !—I'll have your life ! "

" Not yet, Luke ; you've wanted it a long time, but not yet."

Throwing himself forward that his whole weight might fall upon the tomb-cutter, Luke Masters endeavoured to plunge the chisel into the neck of his opponent. Sandy glided aside, and again swinging his mallet aloft, brought it down with his full force on the head of Masters. The blow was a powerful one, and its effect was proportionate. Masters staggered, the chisel dropped from his grasp, and he, himself fell powerless upon the floor.

Sandy Summers examined his fallen foe, and finding him to be devoid of sensation, left him for a moment, to unlock the door of the adjoining room, and enter for some purpose best known to himself. After being absent four or five minutes, he returned to the workshop and locked the door after him, fastening it up carefully as before. In his hand he held an old blunderbuss, which he submitted to scrutiny, with a view to discover whether it was duly charged and primed. Having found such to be the case, he laid it upon the bench by his side, and stooped down to make another examination of the fallen and now powerless Masters.

"There's life enough in him yet," soliloquized Sandy; "but what shall I do with him? I don't like to give him over to Bayliss, the tip-staff; and it's not improbable that when his senses return, he'll think better of what he's done. However, he's got no arms about him it seems, and in the present state of affairs the strongest party is myself; so, having nothing to fear I may as well let him lie there and watch him."

Sandy stepped aside and procured some water, which he sprinkled over the face of his prostrate enemy, remarking as he did so—

"Well, as I haven't made any crack in the skull, and not having drawn any blood, he can't say, when he comes to, that I've done him any unnecessary damage. Only to think now of his impudence, in fancying that he was any match for Sandy Summers, when Sandy had his mallet in his hand! I should think I know how to use a mallet by this time, and it will be wondrous to me, if, when he comes too, he ain't about the same opinion."

Having satisfied himself of the present impotence of his late opponent, Sandy re-seated himself before his work, and proceeded to chisel out the angel's head on the tomb-stone which he was engaged in decorating.

"That's a splendid nose!" ejaculated Sandy, pausing in his work to contemplate the labour of his hands—"I don't know when I've cut so good a nose to a cherub as that one; it's quite a Roman nose. Now, I wonder whether the cherubs are Romans? Humph! that's a curious point of nat'ral history, and one I should say which it must be difficult to decide. But certainly that is a nose! I never made another like it; and it shows that Sandy Summers is improving. There's no gainsaying such a nose as that!"

And feeling satisfied with what he had done, as well as elated to think that Sampson Summers had surpassed himself, Sandy placed the old blunderbuss across his knees, and again taking up his chisel resumed his work in a merry mood, accompanying the labour of his hands with that of his voice. Bravely from within the tomb-cutter's workshop, sounded the merry song.

> "King death and the mason are partners old,
>   And traders old are they.
> They entered on trade when the world was made
>   Their union will last for aye—

And I'm of opinion that such work as this ought to last,'" observed Sandy breaking off in his song to contemplate his work again. "There's not much chiselling of this kind to be seen, I warrant! All the cherubs that I've seen looked more like alderman's babies than cherubs, and they might have done for one or the other; but there's no mistaking such a face as that—there's no doubting about what it is, and what it's meant for! Look, there's a beautiful effect! I've even made a stone tear falling out of its eye; and that's quite enough to show that it's no alderman's baby; for whoever saw them cry I should like to know? Such a bit of work as this ought to last, and it will too—that it will!"

Thus comfortably assured in his own mind, once more the tomb-cutter plied his mallet and chisel merrily. But the manner in which he continued his song was curious, inasmuch that he made for every note a stroke of the mallet, and kept time to the tune by rolling his bushy head from side to side. Omitting the remainder of the first verse he passed on to the second verse of his ditty, as being more fitted to express his feelings at the moment.

> "Together they worked, like right good friends
>   Through the earliest days of yore,
> In the ancient lands they plied their hands
>   And piled up their goodly store.
> 'Ha! ha!' laughed the King, as with dexterous art
>   He the dooming death-blow gave,—
> 'Friend, the task is your own to carve out the broad stone,
>   Which shall rest on the rich man's grave!'
> 'Which shall rest on——"

"Sandy!" cried a voice at the mason's left hand.

"Well, Luke, you're coming to your senses again I see. You'd better take care of yourself for the future."

"Help me, Sandy—help me to rise!"

"It's unfair, Luke, to want me to do so much. I helped you to fall, and that was quite work enough for me to do for nothing, without helping you again at the same price. However, as you're an old friend, I don't mind it so much this time. The sooner you get upon your legs the better."

Luke Masters had only been stunned by the blow of the mallet, and the return of consciousness was all that was wanted to restore him to strength. Sandy lifted him up, placed him in a chair, and then, taking a bottle from out one of the small cupboards in his workshop, he said, in a good humoured manner—

"Take a draught of this, man; and it'll soon set you all to rights."

Masters took the bottle, and smelt its contents with a suspicious expression of countenance.

"Why do you do that, Luke?" asked Sandy.

" It isn't poison—is it ?"

A look of scorn gleamed upon the features of Sampson Summers.

" Poison !" he replied, " do you think that I am the same mean, dirty sort of fellow as yourself ? Hark you, Luke Masters ! As you lay upon that floor, I could have left you, and sought the assistance of those who would at once have taken you to the town jail ; or I could have shot you with this gun, and who would have blamed me for doing so when they heard that I had done it in self-defence ? Why have I not given you up, Luke—why have I done what I could to bring you to again ? Because, Luke, we were children together—because I knew your father and mother, and have seen them weep when you had done wrong. They are dead now, Luke, but if I did harm to you I should expect to hear them speaking in my ear and telling me that I was a playmate with their child. Go, Luke Masters ; leave this cottage as quickly as you can, and do not return to it, or worse things may happen."

" You think I fear you, Sandy ?"

" I know you do."

" Luke Masters fear Sandy Summers the tomb-cutter !"

" Aye, Luke. It is the kind of life which a man leads that gives to him either boldness or fear. If you had lived differently you would have had no cause to fear your old schoolfellow."

" Nor do I !" cried Masters, springing from off his seat. " By Heavens, if you say another word, weak as I am through your cursed blow, I'll show you that there is little fear in Luke Masters !"

The angry man made a spring towards his companion to clutch him by the throat, but not having fully recovered his strength, he again staggered and fell back in the chair.

" Beware of me, Sampson Summers—beware ! I will go now and lay information against you. There will soon be those here who will make you unlock your door, I warrant !"

" Let them come !" replied Sandy boldly.

" But mind what I shall tell them, Summers ; beware, I say, of me—beware !"

" You can do me no harm, Luke Masters, but the case is different as to what I have the power to do for you."

" And what is your power, Sandy Summers ?"

" Will you know it ?"

" Aye, and dare it !"

" Listen, then——"

Sandy approximated his lips to the ear of his guest, and said a few words in a low whisper. Masters startled and turned pale in the face, losing on a sudden the air of bold defiance which he had hitherto assumed, and trembling beneath the touch of Sampson Summers, as the hand of the latter rested on his shoulder.

" That is what I could do, Luke !" exclaimed Sandy, exulting as he perceived the powerful effect which his whisper had wrought—" that, Luke Masters, is what I could do !"

" And will you ?"

" What is there to keep me from doing it ?"

" If you were to, Sandy—if you were to !——"

" No threats, Luke. So long as you behave yourself properly I shall do nothing of the kind."

" And you would bring your old playfellow to the gallows, would you, Sandy ?"

" I will never harm you, Luke, if you will keep away from me. I don't want to be harsh with you, because I very well know that when the world turns against a man it's not likely that he'll ever become better than he is. Go ; we were distant when children—let us be as distant now."

" Your cursed knock, Sandy, has pretty well sent the strength out of me ; you will let me sit here till I begin to feel myself a little right again ?"

" I don't wish to drive you away, Luke. Sit there, if you choose ; but I shall be the better pleased with you the sooner you are gone."

Luke Masters made no reply, but folded his arms and hung down his head, Sandy took up his mallet and chisel and resumed his work.

Delightful is the dreaming thought of that man—be he poet, painter, architect, or sculptor—who while engaged in working out the ideas of his brain can comfort himself with the pleasant delusion that those ideas as thus eliminated—as he is now working them out—are to become existent for ever! What happiness can equal that of the poet who while weaving his plaintive love-song indulges in the pleasant thought that in a thousand years to come, when those who live around him now will be no more, and he himself will have rotted into dust, that very song shall be sung by youths like himself but with whom he is destined to have no acquaintance, and will be warbled by lovely maidens who will wonder as they sing, by whom those sweet words were written? What joy, too, must have been that of the sculptor who carved the Memnon statue on the plains of Egypt, when, as he looked upon his finished work, he knew that when thousands of years would have passed away, still from the east, and from the west, from the south and from the north, admirers would come to gaze upon that statue, and to celebrate the beauty of the work after the workman had slept in the tomb for ages! Something of this description of pleasure was felt by the tomb-cutter as he carved out the figures upon the stone tablets.

Never before had Sandy Summers achieved such a triumph in his art as that which he had now won, in having made out of the rough stone the resemblance of a tear on the cheek of a weeping angel. There was the tear, true enough, and very prettily and correctly was it carven. So perfectly had it been wrought that it appeared in the very act of falling; and although Sandy was aware that it was as perfect as a stone tear could be, yet he could not refrain from touching it up with his chisel, and endeavouring to give it a polish greater than it at present possessed. He was thus engaged, and his attention was diverted from every other object, when his eye caught a side view of Luke Masters creeping forwards and stretching forth his hand to grasp the gun, which Sandy had placed on the adjoining table. In an instant the mallet and chisel were out of his hands, and he himself had seized the fire-lock. Catching it up hastily he twirled it round, and, in so doing—oh! misery of miseries!—struck off with the muzzle that tear—that beautiful tear, which he had wrought with so much labour, and which, by the exertion of all his ingenuity, he could not replace. Up sprang he from his seat, and swung the weapon aloft.

" Away, Luke Masters, away, or I shall commit murder !"

For a minute Masters paused and hesitated whether he should offer any resistance. He had laid his hand on a block of wood, when, casting his glance upwards, he beheld the fire-lock levelled at his brain, and the finger of Summers on the trigger.

The expression of the tomb-cutter's countenance was fierce enough even to inspire Luke Masters with fear. He relaxed his grasp of the block of wood, and attempted to move forwards to wrest the weapon from the hands of the desperate man by whom it was held.

" Move not, but towards the door, Luke Masters ! Move instantly, or I shall fire before I know it !"

It was in vain to think of resistance under such fearful odds. Masters gathered his cloak around him and stole towards the cottage-door.

" Do not linger—do not tarry, Luke ! Man cannot easily forgive under circumstances such as these. Go !"

" I will be even with you yet, Sandy Summers. Beware of me, I say—beware !"

" Stay not to threaten. Go, go, I implore you, before you urge me to what I would not do. Begone, Luke—begone !"

With a scowl on his dark countenance, and with his clenched fist uplifted in a threatening manner, Luke Masters departed from the cottage, and took his way down the narrow lane, which led along beside the churchyard. When he was out of sight, the tomb-cutter, who had watched his departure, turned about, and, flinging down the gun, exclaimed in a deep voice,—

" Thank God I did no murder !"

All was now silent in the cottage. Luke Masters had taken himself away, and Summers alone remained, with his hands clasped, and his eyes directed upwards.

Suddenly the tomb-cutter glanced downwards at the floor ; he started as a man would do on making some great discovery.

" Ha !" he exclaimed, " Luke must have seen these, and this accounts for his being led to suspect ; he must have seen them when he first entered !"

That which Sandy Summers alluded to was visible on the floor of the cottage. There—on that floor were several stains of blood, which apparently were of recent origin, though, from their dried state, they must have been where they now were for the last ten or twelve hours. Some of the spots were very small, and others of the size of a shilling. They were so disposed as to form a trail which extended from the door of the cottage to the door of that into which Masters had manifested so great a desire to obtain entrance.

" I did not know of these ; I thought I had removed every mark of this kind," said Summers to himself, as he rubbed out each mark with the sole of his shoe. " There's no doubt but what that Luke has a quick eye."

Having thus effaced the blood-stains, Sandy Summers threw a glance round the work-shop, and, in so doing, his eyes lit upon the stone which he had been engaged in carving. He rushed towards it ; he gazed upon that sweet face, which he had wrought out with so much labour. It was no longer the same ; it was disfigured, destroyed, and dismantled of all its beauty. The tear—that one exquisitely-carved tear which had lent such a sweetness—such an expression of pity—to the countenance of the angel, was no longer there. The face was now as any other face, and that which had been the object of the artist's love, as well as of his labour, was now looked upon by him with a feeling of disgust.

" It is gone !" he cried, " that which I can never restore I have destroyed, and wherefore should I labour again ?"

He had taken his chisel in his hand to endeavour to repair the loss ; but he flung the implement from him in vexation, and then, after a pause of a few minutes, threw himself on his knees before the tablet, and burst into tears.

He was still in this position, when there stepped into the room a beautiful girl, whose age did not appear to be more than twelve years ; she was in herself the very perfection of girlhood's beauty. Her hair, which was of a rich chestnut colour, was braided neatly, and hung in profusion down her well-turned neck ; she had hazel eyes—those beautiful hazel eyes which seem so warm, so full of love, so full of tenderness and gentle feeling. She wore a small straw hat which was set jauntily on her head, as if to expose the redundancy of her tresses. In her hand she held one end of a piece of red ribbon, the other end o which was attached to the collar of a small spaniel dog, that, in merry mood, toyed with the dress of its young mistress. The very lightness of the step with which the girl entered the cottage told of the lightness of her heart, and the free, unconstrained outline of her figure spoke of the merriment of her pure young soul. When she opened the door of the workshop and crossed the threshold, she did so in a gaysome mood, pulling her little spaniel after her, and playfully beating him with the stem of a white lily, which he himself had in his naughtiness broken off from one of the plants in the cottage garden. As, however, the young girl glanced around the workshop and discerned Sandy on his knees before the disfigured tablet, her countenance became a shade more serious, and taking up her spaniel in her arms, she advanced on tip-toe and without noise, till she stood by the side of the sorrowing workman.

The tomb-cutter was too much absorbed in his grief to notice the approach of the young girl ; she stood by his side and he knew not of her proximity.

Strange to the light-hearted girl appeared the silence and solemnity of the place : pressing the mouth of the little spaniel against her bosom, so that he should not bark, she glided on tip-toe towards the door of that room which Luke Masters had endeavoured to enter. Applying her eye to the key-hole, she peeped into the apartment, and then stepped back again to where, with his face hidden by his hands, Sandy Summers yet remained. The colour on the cheeks of the maiden became a shade more pallid as she bent down and tried to look at the man's countenance. He did not speak,—she could not hear him breathe —what did it all mean?—tremblingly she laid her small white hand upon his shoulder, and in the prattling voice of childhood said—

"Father!"

The tomb-cutter started. Looking up, he saw the young girl standing by his side, and catching her by the arm, exclaimed—

"Why, Fan, child, where have you been since dinner?—what have you been doing?"

"I have only been playing with Pompey in the churchyard, father. Pompey has been so naughty, he ran away from me, and when I went to look after him I found him in the garden, breaking down the lilies and rolling in the mignionette. Doesn't he deserve a beating, father?"

"Remember, Fan, Pompey is only a dog, and though he may do mischief at times, there are people in this world who, with ten times more understanding than Pompey has, do twenty times as badly."

"Are there such people, father? Where can they be?—I never saw any of them."

"Pray God, child, that you may meet with few!"

"They must be very wicked people indeed, then, father, but—" and the girl left off speaking to turn her eyes towards the door of the mysterious room.

"Tell me, Fan," said her parent, "have you seen Luke Masters to-day—you know Luke Masters?"

"Oh, yes, father; I saw him pass along the churchyard lane about half-an-hour ago. Hasn't he been to see you?"

"Yes, child; but had you not seen him before?—had you not seen him earlier in the day!"

"Two or three hours before, father. I saw him when I went out, just after dinner. He met me on Seymour's Green, and he took Pompey up to play with him, but naughty Pompey never likes Mr. Masters, and to-day he tried, as much as he could, to bite his finger."

"Did Luke Masters ask you any questions, Fan?"

"Yes; he asked me why I didn't teach Pompey better manners? but I told him that Pompey was wicked and wouldn't learn."

"Did he ask nothing more, Fanny—didn't he ask any questions about me and the cottage?"

"Yes, that he did. He gave me a sixpence; look at it, father, isn't it a bright new sixpence?"

Sandy Summers took the piece of money from the child and flung it indignantly upon the floor.

"Why do you do that, father? what is the matter with the money?" and the child stooped down to pick up the coin.

"Touch it not, Fan! leave it—throw it from you!" commanded the father, as he checked her while she was in the act of picking it up.

"But why, father—but why?"

"Because it is Luke Masters's money, and you know not whence it was obtained. It might turn to a serpent in your hand, child."

"Oh! I'm sure then that I'll never take any more money from Mr. Masters. But you look angry, father—you look very angry."

The tomb-cutter took the hand of his child and drew her towards him.

"You must tell me, Fanny," said he, "what it was which Luke Masters asked you when he met you on Seymour's Green."

"He asked me, father, if I knew what new things we had in the cottage."

"Well, Fanny?"

" I told him that I didn't know ; and he then asked me what you had taken so many new stones into your workshop for so very early in the morning."

" He is an artful villain, child ! But you have not told me, Fan, what answer you gave him ?"

" I told him that I didn't know you had taken in any new stones, father. I have been looking about for them, but I don't see them. Have you taken in any ?"

" Go on, Fan ; you have not told me yet all that Luke Masters said to you."

" No, not yet, father. He asked me if everything was the same in the cottage as usual, and if I hadn't seen some alteration this morning. So I thought for a minute, and then I told him about that door, father, and the window-shutter, which you told me I was not to try to open."

" Ha ! you told him that, Fan ?"

" Yes, father, I did so because he asked me."

" And what else, Fan—what else did you tell him ?"

" Nothing else, father, because I didn't know anything else which I could tell. He asked me if I knew what was in the room, but I didn't know, and so I could not say."

" You must not know, Fanny, and you must not answer any more questions on the subject."

The child smiled.

" Why do you laugh, Fan ? You must mind what I have now said to you."

" And mustn't I know why you lock that door, and why you have fastened up the window-shutters ?"

" You must not, Fan."

" Ah ! but I do, father—I do know !" rejoined the girl, bursting into a merry laugh.

" You know, Fan ?"

" Yes, that I do, father !"

Sandy Summers rose suddenly from his seat, and drew his daughter to a distant corner of the workshop.

" What do you mean—what do you know, Fan ?"

" I am afraid you'll scold me if I tell you, father."

" You must tell me."

" Well, but promise then that you won't scold me."

" I—I will not, child. I promise."

" Then you must know, father, that when Pompey ran away and I followed him into the garden, after I had caught him I happened to look up at the window with the closed shutter. I did so want to know what there was inside the room !"

" Well, Fan ?"

" I—but you are not to scold me you know, father—I tied Pompey to the cherry tree while I got the wheel-barrow and placed it under the window. Then I mounted up and tried to peep in under the shutter; but the crack wasn't wide enough, so I got down again ; and there was one of your chisels upon the seat in the summer-house. I took that, and worked away a little of the wood in the shutters, and that made the hole larger. When I had done that I peeped through again, and I saw—"

" Hush ! Fan—what was it you saw ?"

The child inclined her head and whispered in her father's ear.

" You did wrong, child—you did wrong ; you had no business to look when I told you that you were not to do so."

" Come, dear father, you promised now not to scold ; you—"

" Nor will I, Fanny ! but listen, child ! What you have seen you must keep secret—you must tell it to no one."

" But may I not know, father, why—"

" Hush ! say not a word. Ask no more questions. You must be very particular, child, not to speak a word about this matter to any one. You know not what mischief you might do. Above all, be careful not to answer any more questions."

" Not if Mr. Seymour should ask me, or—"

"Not if any one should, Fan. Especially say not a word to any of the Heytons if you see them."

" Not to Miss Amy, father, or—"

", Neither a syllable nor a hint, child. Serious consequences might ensue were you to do so. Do you understand ?"

" Yes, father."

" And, remember, Fan! you must keep the secret; you must do as I bid you."

" Fanny will try to be good."

" Not one word to the Heytons, mind !"

" Yes, father—yes."

There are two classes of people in the world to whose keeping it is absolute foolishness to commit a secret—we refer to pretty women and young children. Let us see whether Fanny Summers kept the important secret which was committed to her care.

CHAPTER XXIII.

THE CONTENTS OF THE WELL.—THE DIAMOND RING.—THE PLEDGE OF SECRECY.

IT was the one glimpse which Gervase Morden had of the object that Frank Heyton had uphauled out of the well, which caused his arm to tremble, and the lantern to fall out of his hand. He and those who had accompanied him, were now in perfect darkness, while a strange, unearthly kind of odour had become diffused throughout the entire place.

" Let us leave this dungeon," said the younger Heyton, endeavouring as he spoke to feel out the door by which he had entered.

" Stay !" exclaimed Sir Thomas; " why should we leave before we fully understand this matter ? "

" But the light ?"

" Where is the lantern ?"

" I have let it fall, Sir Thomas," replied Morden. " I will try to find it again if you think that we can procure a light."

" And why not, boy,—why should we not ? We have still a plenitude of tinder and matches, and we are not all such cowards as not to have one amongst us who has enough strength left for the knocking together of flint and steel. Search for the lantern ; but take care that you fall not into the well."

The lantern was found, and Sir Thomas himself undertook the task of procuring a light. When he had accomplished the object he turned round to address his companions, and found them ranged against the wall of the dungeon, clinging to it for support, and doing their best to discover the whereabouts of the door.

" Why, Heyton !—Morden ! are you frightened at a mere nothing ?"

" A nothing ! Sir Thomas ?"

" Well, if you can tell me what it is, Morden, I'll not gainsay your words. Take the light again, and be a little less the woman. None of us leave this vault till we have made a full examination of our discovery."

Encouraged by the boldness which Sir Thomas exhibited, and doing their best to shake off the feeling of fear which had taken possession of them, Morden and the two Heytons advanced to assist the knight in the examination of the mysterious and dreaded object which had been drawn out of the well.

" Hold down the light, Morden. Closer, man—closer !"

" Good God, Sir Thomas, this is an awful sight !" ejaculated the elder Heyton.

" Patience, man—patience ! and let us do what we can to understand how we are placed, and what it is which we have before us. Give a pull to the rope there, Morden, that we may make our scrutiny without a chance of tumbling headlong into the well."

" See !" cried Heyton, "it glitters still."

" And the smell," observed Morden.

" Bad enough, indeed," replied Frank. " We might as well be shut up in a tomb at once, as to stay in this place."

The object which had given rise to this alarm and dread, and which had been hauled up out of the well by the dexterity of the younger Heyton, was in truth of such a nature as might well call up fear and amazement in the beholders. They would have been bold men indeed had they looked upon it without a shudder.

On the stone flooring of the dungeon lay that which appeared to be the decayed remains of two human bodies. The fish-hooks, by which they had been brought up, had caught in the eye-hole of one of the skulls, and in the open mouth of the other. Scarcely a vestige of clothing remained, but the little that there was indicated the wearers to have been vain and wealthy in their day. How long each had lain at the bottom of the well, it was impossible at the first glance to say. Years —long years, must have passed since their assignment to that unhallowed resting-place. The flesh had partly decayed, and partly shrivelled. No traces of the features were discernible and, although there was evidence to show that one had belonged to the female sex, and the other to the male, there was nothing from which the beholder could now learn whether they had been beautiful in their life —whether they were peaceable at their death. That they had joyed, and wept, and sorrowed, was to be inferred from the mere fact of their having been members of the human race ; but, beyond this, who could say what particular joys they had known—what more than common allowance of sorrow had fallen to their share?

Had they died in their youth, or had they tasted to the full of life's weariness, and this world's cares and pains? Who was to answer this question ? Their limbs, if soft and rounded once, were hard and angular enough now; their forms, if light and graceful then, had become less in weight, but grace had given place to ghastliness, and elegance had merged into repulsive loathsomeness. If the fingers of the lady had been taper fingers, if, as perhaps had been the case, she had once held them playfully before the candle, that she might display the thinness of the skin, and the transparency of their structure ; if they had once awakened the strains of sweet music, worked the embroidered handkerchief, or depicted forms of beauty, they were altered—fearfully altered now. Perchance, a time had been when for leave to press those very fingers to his lips a gallant youth would have given half his fortune away ; yet, could he have looked upon them now he would have turned away with loathing, and shrunk from defiling himself with their touch. And what if the male form—if that very male form, which had also passed into decay had been the very youth, who, by day and night, by morning and by even-tide, had sought to win the heart of her who now slept with him the last, long, dreamless sleep ? His, perhaps, was the manly shape, the athletic build, the Adonis-like figure, the winning voice, the curled lip—that mark of birth and breeding, the rosy cheek, the bold, bright eye, and the various other excellencies which win a woman's heart, and ofttimes entrap her into deep and lasting misery. And such this shrivelled form might have been ; as such he might have wooed the lady with the taper fingers, and, loving and beloved, they might both have gone down to the grave together ; never to win hearts again, never to fascinate, bewitch, allure, as one of them, perchance, had done of yore.

Oh ! how foolish—how simply foolish are they who assert, in the depth of their ignorance, that there is nothing in man or woman more than the mere bone, muscle, sinew, and nerve ; who daringly say, that there is nothing within us which shall outlive the tomb—which shall be existent when this shape of earth shall exist no longer ! Let such bold dunces stand beside the dead form of some beautiful being whom they once loved, and then and there ask themselves wherein is the great difference between that loved one and this loathed one ? The lips that it were worth a world to press, it were now hideous to think of touching ; the eyes that spoke of pity, love, and gentleness, now have a ghastly glare, or seem like leaden things which have never sparkled, never moved. Wherein consists the repulsiveness? What accident must that have been which could have caused a change so sudden, so startling, so stern? But we assert, and it is our faith, that no man or woman on this earth, who has ever watched beside the death-bed of the being whom he or she loved the best, and seen the change come, and seen the strife between life and the grisly king—who has felt the agony of parting, and watched the last breath pass, and held the pale hand in their own, until it has become

marble cold—that no one who has experienced those awful feelings, which the suddenness of such an event awaken, and who has watched at midnight beside the lonely bier, marking the gradual progress of decay, the gliding away of beauty after beauty, of excellence after excellence, the fading of the rose from the cheeks, the withering of the lily from the garden where it grew, the ashen mist gradually upspreading and obscuring all—no one, we confidently affirm, who has witnessed and experienced as much as this, has ever at any time afterwards believed for a single moment in the dull doctrine of those who tell us that we are no better than the beasts—that there is no world afar, to which the spirit of man may fly, again to taste of happiness, again to find a home !

And were these two shrivelled forms those of youth? or had age come upon them before they had met with death ?

They had died young, for there was evidence of the fact. It is a curious circumstance that, of all the parts of animal bodies, the hair is that which for the longest time resists decay. And on the heads of the two bodies thus so strangely discovered, the hair still remained in all its pristine redundancy; its glossiness had departed, but the tresses still hung in ringlets over the shoulders of her who had once tended them with all a woman's care—with all a woman's vanity. On the head also of the male figure the short, crisp, auburn-coloured curls attested to young and healthful manhood. Everything else had faded, but the hair told the answer to the question of youth or age.

They had died young. How, then, had it happened that they had died as they had died—that they had been buried in so strange a place ?—buried, too, in the garments which they had worn in the streets and the assemblies; buried, adorned with jewels and decorations—buried with their arms entwined around each other, as if death had overtaken them in the midst of happiness ! It was a strange and fearful mystery—for who was there to tell their names, or make known the story of their life and death ?

That which had attracted the attention of Gervase Morden—the bright thing which had sparkled at the bottom of the well—was nothing else but a large and resplendent diamond, of the purest and clearest water ; it was set in a ring, and the ring was on one of the lady's fingers ; the finger had shrivelled and dried up ; the ring rattled as it slid loosely up and down the finger which it once had fitted.

"Hold the light nearer still, Morden," said Sir Thomas ; and as the student did so, the eyes of the beholders saw that on the other hand of the lady there was a ring also ; but in this no diamond was set, no jewel glittered. It was a wedding-ring—that little circle of gold by which so much is meant—in which so great a mystery is encircled.

The lady, then, had not died a maiden, and he who had been buried with her must have been something more than a mere wooer. What was the mystery ? How had they both died ? Why had each been buried there ?

Was it probable that they had fallen from the vaulted chamber above into the well below ? No ; for what business could have led them to that vaulted room ? And if they had fallen thence, why had no inquiries been made after them ? Why had not their remains been sought?

They could not by accident of their own have met such a death. For, in that case, who would have closed up the mouth of the well afterwards, and placed the stone over it as it had been found by Sir Thomas Warrenton and his companions? This fact alone was sufficient to testify that some one had been privy to their death, and that some one knew, or had known, the why and wherefore of their strange burial.

Was it likely that they had been the prey of the robber or the murderer? Certainly not of the former, for not a jewel had been taken away—nothing had been stolen.

They must have been murdered, and afterwards thrown into the well," observed Sir Thomas ; but the secretary pointed out the manner in which they had been found, with their arms entwined round each other, as if they had voluntarily and together sought the same dreadful death.

"This is indeed a fearful discovery !" observed the elder Heyton. "It is wondrous that persons of wealth and station as these evidently were, we should never have heard about them—never have heard that such individuals were missing."

Sir Thomas Warrenton shook his head.

"It must be inquired into," said he, " and that speedily. Doubtless we shall easily obtain a clue."

"And what is to be done with these remains ?" asked Gervase Morden.

"They must be taken hence and exposed for identification. There must also be a lock and seal affixed to this place, that nothing may be disturbed until the inquiry has been fully carried out."

"And the jewels ?"

" We will take them with us."

" Have they no marks, Sir Thomas ? Do they bear no initials, no motto, no crest ?"

" Nothing of the kind," replied the knight. Then, after a pause, he added— " Unless this ring ——"

" Is there a mark on the diamond ring ?" asked Morden.

Sir Thomas made no reply; but, after feeling the ring with his finger, he started, and commanded the secretary to give the lantern into his hand.

"There is a crest or mark of some kind, no doubt," observed Morden to the younger Heyton. " Jewels of such worth have generally — ; but, good Heavens ! look at Sir Thomas ! What can be the matter with him ?"

The countenance of the lusty knight had become ashy pale ; his fingers trembled ; his features wore the expression of sudden alarm.

" Heyton !" he cried, in a faint voice, " Heyton !"

Mr. Heyton stepped forward in obedience to the call. He was struck with fear and amazement when Sir Thomas caught him by the arm, and gazed at him with eyes which were fearfully wild in their expression. The knight drew him aside, and, holding up for his inspection the diamond ring, pointed out that portion of its inner surface which was immediately behind the jewel with which it was set.

" Look, man, look !" he exclaimed.

Morden and the younger Heyton pressed forward to satisfy their curiosity by obtaining a glimpse at the object, the sight of which seemed to have affected the knight so strongly; but Sir Thomas turned round upon them, and in a furious voice exclaimed—

" Stand back ! stand back !"

" I see nothing, Sir Thomas," said Heyton. " What is there which you would show me ?"

" Now, man, now !" and the knight held the jewel nearer to the light. " Discern you nothing there ?"

A sudden exclamation burst from the lips of Mr. Heyton, and his countenance experienced a like change to that which was observable in his companion.

" Do you understand ?" whispered Sir Thomas in a deep voice, speaking in the ear of Heyton.

" I do."

" You have no doubts ?"

" None."

" And what is to be done ?"

" The secret will be—"

" Never !" interrupted the knight wrathfully and with emphasis, "never, Stephen Heyton, never !"

" But the bodies ?"

" Come hither, man !" said Sir Thomas ; and, forcing Mr. Heyton to follow him, he passed out of the dungeon and conferred privately with his friend. During this conference, Morden and the younger Heyton remained in the dark, clinging with apprehensive dread to each other, and wondering within themselves as to what the suddenly strange behaviour of the knight might portend.

Sir Thomas and Mr. Heyton re-entered the dungeon. The countenance of each was pale—the lips of each quivered—they looked meaningly at each other—and both seemed to have no power of saying a word.

Again they advanced towards the bodies—again they submitted them to an examination. As they did so, their companions observed that tears flowed from the eyes of each.

A mystery, indeed, it was. The fearless and stalwart knight was there on his knees beside the mouldered remains of one who had doubtless been fair and beauteous in her day. He had taken the emaciated fingers in his clasp, and, as he bent over the loathsome object, tears flowed down his cheeks and fell upon the shrivelled parchment-like skin of the half-dried, half-rotten corpse, with the history of which he seemed to have suddenly become acquainted.

Their eyes wandered. Sir Thomas looked at Heyton, and Heyton tremblingly returned the glance; but not a word was spoken by either.

The vapours from the well continued to rise, and the air of the apartment had gradually grown more vitiated. Once again the light in the lantern burned dull and flickeringly.

And still beside the skeleton remains knelt the lord of Warrenton Hall and the care-stricken father of Amy. Different as were the stations of each in life, yet was it evident that they had long been friends together, and that there were secrets common to each of which the rest of the world knew nothing.

Yes, there were secrets—secrets which belonged to them, and which they were desirous of keeping hidden. And what man or woman amongst us is there who has not his or her secret? All who have ever loved—all who have ever felt the excitement of one strong passion or obeyed one resistless impulse—have secrets concealed in their breasts which must and will be buried with them in their graves. If at any past time we have had cause for joy or sorrow, reason to laugh or mourn, something to exult over or regret, we have that which cannot be told to all. We cannot have ever loved sincerely if we have not stored within our heart a story which it is fit for only one ear to listen to, and which will never be communicated to more than that one. There are secrets which we would not for the worth of empires tell aloud to the whole world—secrets which must sleep within us as reserved and holy things. Many are there who loll in their carriages and smile haughtily as they pass along who have bitter secrets in their bosoms, which are unknown to those who look upon them, and who envy their apparent happiness. Go forth into the streets, and mark well those whom you encounter there. Every fifth person shall be one who has—known to himself alone—a dark and terrible secret which is ever apt to gnaw the heart, and which too oft has the power of banishing sleep from the pillow. To the novelist, therefore, and to him who makes human nature his study, the streets of the crowded town are like a magnificent museum, containing a million objects of curiosity, and innumerable subjects for inquiry, speculation, and research.

Sir Thomas and the elder Heyton knelt beside the mouldering things which had been updrawn from the well. They knelt beside all that remained of the lady who had died in her youth, and the gallant, or the husband, whom, in all probability, she had deeply loved. Wherefore was it that the knight and the cottager knelt? Why did they regard with such interest the corpses of those who had so strangely died? Why did they each allow the tears to trickle down their cheeks, wetting, as they fell, the dust and the corruption?

They knelt. Not a word was spoken—not a syllable was uttered.

"Sir Thomas," asked the secretary, respectfully, "what have you discovered—what do you know?"

The knight sprung to his feet.

"Hark you, Gervase Morden," he cried; "I took notice of you when you were a mere boy. I have protected you. I have befriended you since then. You cannot say that I have dealt more harshly towards you than I have towards my own son—you cannot say that I have treated you otherwise than kindly, friendly, fatherly; if you can say so, Gervase Morden, speak!"

"I cannot, Sir Thomas," replied the young man, fervently. "You have ever been kind to me—you have done for me more than I have deserved. The debt of gratitude which I owe you is large indeed!"

"Let that debt be paid, Gervase Morden."

" Paid !"

" Aye ! paid."

" But how ? I cannot. God knows, that if I had the power——"

" You have the power. Listen—that which you have witnessed within the last hour you must keep a secret from every one. Not one word must escape from your lips bearing any reference to what you have seen or heard in this place to-day. I have reasons for imposing this obligation on you; and I must desire rather than request your silence. Come, you must give me the promise."

" You have it, Sir Thomas. I will not speak or hint the slightest information on the subject to any one."

" And you, Francis Heyton; I suppose that your father has asked and obtained from you a similar pledge of secrecy?"

" I have made him the promise, Sir Thomas."

" That is well," replied the knight. " The time may arrive when this matter will be fully explained to you; for the present it is not only desirable but necessary that you maintain the silence which both I and Mr. Heyton think it right to enjoin upon you both."

" Are we not to know the true nature of the secret which we are to keep ?" asked Frank.

" That which you are required to be silent upon is simply that to which you have this day been witnesses. The why and the wherefore of such an injunction you must be content to remain in ignorance of for the present. All that I or Mr. Heyton dare yet to tell we have already told you. Wait, and you may know more."

" Must no mention of this be made at home, father ?" asked Frank. " Not a word to Amy or to Kate ?"

" To neither," responded Sir Thomas ; " and especially not to Amy Heyton."

" Does it, then, concern her ?"

" You are making inquiries which cannot now be answered. I have explained how you are to act; and you, Morden, must be particular that you say not a word about it at the Hall."

" Will it help to explain the mysterious occurrences which have happened there ?" inquired the student.

" Possibly it may," was the reply.

" And the bodies—these skeletons ?"

" We will leave them where they are. Taking care, however, to shut out intruders by duly securing the door, and closing up that hole which is above our heads."

" But the jewels, Sir Thomas ? "

" I will take them with me to the Hall."

The party now prepared to leave the vaulted chamber, and to return to those dark passages which stretched out in every direction of the underworks. Sir Thomas was the last to quit the dungeon, and a sigh was heard to escape from his bosom, as he closed and made fast the door by which the entrance had been gained.

" Look you, Morden," said he, " I entrust the charge to you ; and before this day is past, I expect that you will see this door well nailed up, and so fastened that no intruder within these ruins may enter the place which we have just quitted."

Gervase Morden promised to act according to Sir Thomas's desire, and afterwards, with much hesitation, put the question,—

" Shall we pursue our search further ? "

" What have we to search for now?" replied Sir Thomas, who appeared to be so absorbed in thought as to be unable to recollect for the minute the business which had brought him to the castle ruins.

" I do not know," observed the secretary, " whether we have fully made out the cause of the mysterious occurrences at the Hall. |Besides, my friend Mr. Francis

Heyton has not satisfied himself. Now, the individual whom he followed into this place contrived to elude him at last."

"Right—right!" rejoined Sir Thomas, "I had forgotten—let the search be continued."

Morden and the younger Heyton at once proceeded with the investigation, but Sir Thomas and his friend lingered behind, deeply engaged in conversation, and apparently uninterested in the explorations which their companions were so industriously carrying out.

Passage after passage, chamber after chamber, was wandered through and examined, but nothing could be found explanatory of the mystery. The footsteps of the wanderers sounded hollow in the dull and dreary places, the least noise being echoed and re-echoed again.

"What say you, Frank," asked Morden; "will you now acknowledge yourself to have been fairly outdone by the old man who was fleeter on foot, than a young gallant like yourself?"

"That he eluded me, I acknowledge," replied Frank, "but that he did it with merely the assistance derived from swiftness of movement, I am not disposed to allow."

"Then what explanation have you to offer?"

"I cannot frame any."

"You will not persist in saying that he was nothing but a phantom?"

"I say not what he was, nor attempt for a while to solve the mystery of his disappearance. That I should have followed him to this ruin, and that within but a few minutes afterwards, it seems that a similar figure was seen at Warrenton Hall affords matter for wonder and astonishment, but does nothing in the way of affording a single conjecture."

Gervase Morden was of the same opinion as his friend; and as it seemed perfectly useless to remain longer in the ruins, Sir Thomas proposed that the search should be given up in that direction, in favour of a different method of proceeding. This proposition was at once agreed to.

Leaving the castle, and pausing as they crossed over the drawbridge to take a look at the foot-mark which had before attracted their attention, they proceeded along the sea-coast towards the residence of Stephen Heyton. Their present intention was to put out to the ship in which they believed Ernest Morden at present to be concealed.

Some hours had passed since Heyton had quitted the cottage, and the sun had now journeyed towards the western sky. The atmosphere was sultry, and a hazy mist hung over the meadows wrapping them in an intense heat. The sea was glistening and calm, a few small vessels were visible in the offing, and a fisherman in his boat was plying his net at a short distance from the shore. Over head a bevy of sea-birds were wheeling round and round, while from inland field and hedge came the hum of a hundred happy things disporting in their glee.

"Before we proceed further in quest of Ernest Morden," observed Sir Thomas, "I should like to have an interview with Amy Heyton. How say you, my friend, will your daughter object to seeing company in her present distress, think you?"

"Amy would feel honoured by a visit from you, Sir Thomas; she is not one of those girls who affect more than they really feel, and the act of kindness, which you contemplate, would doubtless meet with her thanks."

"Then let us thither at once."

"But Ernest, Sir Thomas?" observed Frank.

"Well, man, there is time enough yet for that business. What are your feelings so vengeful towards your old friend that you cannot brook a delay of some thirty or forty minutes?"

"Suppose the ship should stand out to sea again before we start in pursuit?"

"Let it do so; we will give her chase in my own nimble and handsome skiff, which, I warrant you, can dance through the waters to a merrier tune than can any man-of-war in his majesty's service. Come, Heyton, let's to the cottage."

Bending their steps in an upward direction they approached the summit of the high ground on which the cottage stood. A thrill of mingled sorrow and delight passed through the breast of Stephen Heyton as he gazed at the habitation in which he had passed some of his happiest days. There was a charm to him in glancing at the trellised porch, the clambering flowers, and the pretty casements through which, for many past years, he had watched the sun sink to its repose, and had looked upwards at the starry host of evening. Presently he halted for a moment, and observed,—

" It is strange that Kate has not thrown open the windows on so warm a day. See, they are all closed as if it were the depth of winter."

" From what I understood, Heyton," observed Sir Thomas, " your daughters are left with no one to protect them. Doubtless, then, they have kept the windows close to prevent unwelcome intrusion by that way of entry."

" But the girls—why do they not welcome our approach ? Call to them, Frank, and let them know that we are coming."

Frank Heyton obeyed the command, but his call was either unheard or disregarded, for neither of the two girls made their appearance.

" Can they have gone to sleep ?" said Mr. Heyton in astonishment; " or can they ——?" and he threw a glance at his son, which was full of anticipative dread.

Frank Heyton understood that look, and without lingering to say another word, set off at full speed towards the cottage. His father, Sir Thomas, and Morden followed. Alarm and consternation seized upon each, when they found both the doors and windows of the cottage to be firmly fastened, and no one within to answer to their calls.

" Where are my children ?" cried Heyton, in a voice of anguish ; " where is Kate and her sister ?"

No one had a reply to give.

" And Archy, too ?" added Frank. " He also is not here."

" They have been carried away ; they are lost—lost to me for ever," cried the sorrowful and phrenzied parent, covering his eyes with his hands, and bursting into tears."

" Lost !" exclaimed Sir Thomas. " Lost ! say you ?"

" Where are they ? Where is my Kate ? Where is Amy ? Hark ! Kate's poor bird is singing a mournful song, as if bewailing the loss of its mistress."

CHAPTER XXIV.

THE SEARCH FOR THE LOST ONES.—HOW FAR FANNY SUMMERS KEPT HER SECRET.

THE reader need scarcely to be informed that Frank Heyton fell in for his full share of blame, consequent upon his having left his sisters unprotected, in direct disobedience to his father's express desire. Frank endeavoured to exculpate himself in the best manner possible, but could not do otherwise than avow that his past act had been an infringement of duty on his part.

" Do not blame me now, father !" he implored. " I acknowledge having done wrong, but I will pay the penalty by not sitting or resting again until I have discovered and brought back my sisters."

" And where, boy, will you seek for them ?" demanded Sir Thomas.

" Everywhere—throughout the length and breadth of the land."

" That is a bold promise ; but would it not be better to act with more calmness ? Cannot you conjecture, Heyton, the cause of this mishap—cannot you form a guess as to how it has been brought about ?"

" I cannot, Sir Thomas. See ; the windows are fastened on the inside, and the door is locked—locked, and the key gone."

" That augurs well," replied the knight.

" How so, Sir Thomas ?"

" Does it not seem to say that your daughters have of their own free will abandoned the cottage ?"

" What ! without leaving a notice ? And Archy too—where is he ?"

" Gone with them, you may be sure. Ladies are wont to have their cavalier in attendance upon them, go where they may."

Mr. Heyton turned towards the knight, and with an agonized expression of countenance, said,—

" Do not jest, Sir Thomas, I implore you—do not treat this matter lightly." Then, suddenly altering his tone, he seized the hand of the knight, and whispered in his ear, " You cannot—dare not jest. It is Amy who is among the lost !"

" Hush !—I know it—she shall be found," was the reply.

The secretary now stepped forward and made the observation,—

" Would it not be more wise of us, Sir Thomas, to search round about after the Miss Heytons ?" It is not improbable that, disliking to stay in the cottage, they have taken a ramble about the cliffs."

" Nothing more likely, Morden. Gadzooks, man ! you are as good as a dozen lawyers when advice is wanted on any subject. Come, Heyton, we will make an examination of the cliffs and look along the beach below. Depend upon it, the girls have gone shell-gathering, or shrimp-fishing, or in search after the young fulmars. They wanted amusement, and have gone to seek it in the open air."

" God grant it may be nothing worse !" ejaculated the parent, clasping his hands together in his anguish.

" Worse, man—worse ! How should it be worse ?"

Mr. Heyton looked earnestly at the knight.

Sir Thomas whispered in his ear,—

" I am as much interested in this search as you are ; but, as you well know, it will not do for me to seem so before these men. Come, let us to the cliffs !"

Frank Heyton led the way, knowing well the favourite walks of his sisters. There were certain portions of the cliff where Kate and Amy were wont to seek out a projecting crag, and seating themselves thereon, spend hours in watching the wide ocean, and contemplating the many beauties and sublimities which were around them. All of these places were submitted to scrutiny, but no trace of the two sisters could be discovered. Frank called out their names at the highest pitch of his voice, but no answer was returned, no handkerchief or scarf was waved in the distance.

" Let us descend to the beach," said Sir Thomas. " They may have rambled to some distance, and I should not wonder if we were to descry them on the sands some mile or so away."

The beach was gained, and the search continued ; but the sultriness of the day seemed to have affected every living thing. A drowsy, sleepy appearance was presented by every object. There were some boats out at sea, but the boatmen seemed resting on their oars ; there was a small vessel riding at anchor, her sails unfurled, but hanging loosely, and without the least motion. The surge rolled lazy-like upon the shore ; the fish floated, as if asleep, on the surface of the water.

Suddenly Gervase Morden, who had lingered behind the others, called Sir Thomas and the Heytons back.

" What is it, man—what can you see ?" inquired Sir Thomas, who was ill-disposed to more exertions than was necessary, his burly frame having already suffered much by the extreme heat of the atmosphere, and by the agitation of mind, caused by the course of late events.

" Look !" exclaimed the secretary, pointing to the sand on the beach. " Here is evidence of a boat having put off from here within the last few hours. See ! here is the groove made by the keel !"

" Ha !" cried the elder Heyton, " the very boat in which Ernest Morden accompanied me from the ship hither. There is meaning in this !"

"What is your supposition now?" inquired Sir Thomas.

"That ——" and the feelings of the father almost overpowered his voice, "that Kate and Amy have been carried hence in the boat, which has put off from here."

"Carried hence, Mr. Heyton?—carried where?"

"I know not, Sir Thomas—I know not!"

"But by whom, man?"

" cannot say."

Frank Heyton looked gravely at the knight, and in a deep voice said—

"It is my impression, Sir Thomas, that Ernest Morden has been concerned in this matter; that he it is who has taken away my sisters."

"He!" cried Sir Thomas; "why? bethink you, man! the idiot, you say, is also missing. Ernest Morden could not, let him use what force he might, make off with three people in the manner you speak of."

"But are there none, Sir Thomas, who would assist him—who have assisted him?"

"If they have they shall suffer for it," exclaimed the knight, "insults, robberies, and abductions! G.dzooks! the world has come to a pretty pass—a very pretty pass!"

The secretary took the hand of Frank Heyton, and placing his other hand on the hilt of the weapon that hung by his side, said—

"Hear me, Heyton. Ernest Morden is my brother—my own brother—my father's youngest son. From childhood unto boyhood we grew up together, and I have loved him as ever brothers should love; but—and God be my witness—if Ernest has done that which you now accuse him of, if it be proved against him, and I meet with him face to face, he shall not go unpunished, even by the brother who was his playmate in his earliest infancy. No man can lay a criminal charge against the memory of him who was the common father of us both; and by this right hand and this good weapon, I swear that the father shall not be disgraced in his sons!"

"That is a brave declaration, Gervase Morden," observed Sir Thomas; "but happily, as yet, we have no certain knowledge that your brother is as culpable as you may imagine him to be."

"Not as I imagine him to be, Sir Thomas. We were educated under the same roof; we were taught the like lessons; and Ernest was ever the high-souled, brave-spirited boy, which I could wish a brother of mine to be. He must be fearfully altered, if he be the guilty person who has done such a deed as that now laid to his charge."

"Ernest Morden is fearfully altered," rejoined Frank Heyton. "There was a time when we were friends together, but deep is our hatred now."

"Gadzooks!" cried Sir Thomas, "if he be but one-half so bad as you represent him, he is a very villain indeed, and there is a long account for him to settle. But we must not be too hasty, though, to say truth, this weather is apt to warm the blood a few degrees—we must not be hasty; for already have we allowed one or two circumstances to escape us in our calculations."

"What, Sir Thomas? what are they?" inquired Mr. Heyton, eagerly.

"You have supposed the two girls to have been carried off in this boat. Now it is, in the first place, hard to reconcile the supposition of their having been taken by force from the cottage, with the facts of the door being locked, and the windows fastened on the inside; while in the second place, from the mark which this boat has left upon the sand, it seems to be that its dimensions admit only of its carrying four persons."

"Three, Sir Thomas," interposed Mr. Heyton; "it will not carry in safety more than three."

"Well, then, according to your calculations, there must have been the two girls, the idiot, and Ernest Morden, which together make four in number; while, if you think over the matter, Morden alone could not have made three captives unaided, and therefore there must have been a fifth or a sixth."

"Yes, yes," cried Mr. Heyton; "it is not Ernest who has done this; my children—"

A sudden exclamation from the younger Heyton caused every eye to be directed towards him. The young man dashed forward into the water, and seizing upon something which floated on the surge, held it up, and cried—

"See, father! What is this?"

The countenance of the parent became pale, he trembled as he replied—

"I know it—I know it! It is Amy's riband, it is that which I have seen her wear!"

Consternation now seized upon each member of the party, for this last discovery forced upon all a terrible and unwelcome conviction; that which had until now been supposition only, had suddenly become certainty—that which every one had feared might be the case was now known to each as a reality. Stephen Heyton clutched the piece of riband in his hand, and gazed at it with a wild maniacal stare. The father's heart was full, even to bursting—it suddenly became exertion to him merely to draw his breath. He endeavoured to articulate the names of his lost daughter, but his voice would not obey his bidding, and the sounds died away in his throat. Before his eyes was the mark which had been formed by the keel of the boat, and the story which that mark told was one that it was torture to listen to. Grasping nervously the arm of his son, he with much difficulty, and in a hoarse-muttered tone, said—

" We will follow him, Frank. Quick, quick, boy ; we will follow him !"

" At once, father, at once," replied the younger Heyton, speaking in a similar voice, and in a fearfully resolute manner.

The Heytons had pledged themselves to track Ernest Morden to the ship, and that instantly, but the means by which they were to redeem their pledge were not apparent at the moment.

" A boat, Frank ! we must have a boat," cried the distracted parent.

" Where shall we obtain one ? There is none at hand."

" Hail you yon drowsy fisherman, Frank ; beckon him hither with all speed."

" He is more than a mile distant, father."

" Hail him, boy, hail him ; your voice is strong, and if he be not in a dead sleep he will hear you call."

Frank Heyton was about to obey his father's command; he had lifted his two hands to his mouth with that intention, and had just inhaled a sufficiency of air prior to his testing the strength and capacity of his vocal powers, when he suddenly paused, and, still holding his hands to his mouth, stood fixed and motionless as a statue.

" Heaven's patience, boy, what has come to thee ? Why dost thou not hail ?"

Frank hastily seized the hand of his father, and drawing him forward, pointed with his outstretched finger across the ocean."

" What see you, boy ? what point you at ?"

" Look, father, look !"

" At what ?"

" There ! See you not ?"

" Where would you have me look ?"

" On the water, just where the white crag juts out upon the ocean."

" Well, I cannot perceive anything more than the shadow of the crag upon the waves."

" Do you see nothing else ? Do you not see a dark body ?"

Mr. Heyton threw a hasty glance at his son, his pale countenance betraying the anxiety of his mind. Once more he strained his sight in endeavouring to discern that which he feared to behold. The last words of his son had inspired him with a terrible presentiment, and had it not have been for the support he derived from the arms of Sir Thomas and Morden, he would have fallen overpowered on the beach. For a brief space of time he continued to gaze fixedly upon the distant waters, until, at length, his eyes caught sight of the object to which his notice had been directed. He started, making a movement as if his intention was to rush into the water, and in his temporary madness endeavour to reach that which his eyes now beheld. He was detained, however, by the firm grasp of Sir Thomas, who had also, together with the secretary, descried the distant object, and remarked its onward motion.

" Hold me not, Sir Thomas," cried the distracted parent ; " do not keep me back."

" Where would you go, father?" asked Frank.

" Where, boy, where ? What is that which floats upon yon wave ? What is it, boy ?"

" It is——"

" Quick ! It is the body of one of your sisters ; is it not so ?"

" Heaven forfend that it should be, dear father ! Oh no, it is not that."

" Not that, Frank ! what say you then it is ?"

" I— Look ! it moves ; it comes onward ! See, it will soon be out of the shadow cast by the crag. Ha! it dances in the sunshine, now. Do you not see it? Ha! it is a boat, father, a boat!"

Frank Heyton said the truth. It was a boat—a boat with rowers in it, which was now from a distance gradually approaching the shore. Every time that the wet oars were lifted out of the water, they glistened brightly in the sunlight that fell upon the sea. Swiftly over the sparkling wave the little vessel sped onward, although the rowers appeared to keep but bad time with their oars, and to be somewhat deficient in skill. The boat seemed to be shaping its course towards the little party on the beach.

"They are pulling this way, Heyton," observed Sir Thomas. "Perchance they may be able to yield us some information concerning your daughters."

"Miss Catherine and Miss Amy may be themselves in the boat," suggested the secretary; "those who have taken them away may be now about to restore them."

"That cannot be the case," replied Frank Heyton. "My sisters are not in the boat, for it contains but three persons, and two of them are making use of the oars."

"And the third, Frank?"

"Is acting as cockswain. Doubtless they are from Ernest's ship, and perhaps they have some message from him."

Sir Thomas Warrenton smiled, and shook his head.

"No seamen in his Majesty's service are they who ply yonder oars," said he. "Why, look you, man, saw you ever such vile pulling? The jackanapes ought to have the oars beaten about their ears for not knowing better how to use them."

"See!" cried Morden, "they are making a signal to us. I saw one of the oars held up, as if in token of their desiring some assistance. See again! they are waving a handkerchief—they——but, by my faith, I am right in my supposition, I swear! Look you, there is a woman in the boat; it is a female who sits at the stern."

"Gadzooks, boy!" cried Sir Thomas, "you seem determined to forestall us to-day in every discovery. Now, if I had but my long glass, which lies on the shelf in the hall library, I——"

"It is not wanted!" exclaimed Frank Heyton. "Yes, yes, Morden, it is so; my sisters are in the boat; that is Amy at the stern, for I know her red shawl. Ha! and it is Kate who has the oar in her hand. Watch them, father! It is Amy who is waving her handkerchief to us now."

"Yes, it is her!" cried the parent joyfully. "I know it to be her now; and that is Kate, too, who is using the oar. But—but there is some one else."

"A man," observed Sir Thomas.

"Do you not know who it is, father?" cried Frank; "do you not know Archy?"

Many minutes had not elapsed before the boat had drawn sufficiently near to the shore for Mr. Heyton to call to his daughters, and they to hear the call. Kate and Archy exerted themselves lustily to make the vessel skim over the tide, while Amy managed the rudder with due nautical skill. The countenance of the parent wore an anxious expression, very different from that displayed on the features of his daughters. The exercise of rowing had called up the colour into the face of Kate, darkening and making more brilliant the usual rich, deep hue of her complexion. Her glossy ringlets were tossed back over her shoulders, gleaming in the sunshiny glow, and dancing to every stroke of the oar which the hands of the maiden plied.

Frank Heyton hauled the boat up the beach, and the two sisters, throwing down their oars, stepped nimbly out upon the wet pebbles.

"My children—Kate—Amy, where have you been?" cried Mr. Heyton, flinging his arms around the necks of his daughters, and embracing them most affectionately.

"We have been to the ship, dear father."

"To what ship, Kate?"

"To Ernest's ship; the one to which you thought he had returned."

"How!" exclaimed Sir Thomas Warrenton; "has not Lieutenant Morden returned to his ship?"

"He has not, Sir Thomas. It was to ascertain whether he had or had not done so that I, and sister, and Archy, visited his ship."

"But you, Kate—why did you make such an attempt, and for what purpose? Before I left you this morning, you heard me say that I should visit the ship as soon as I returned from Warrenton Hall. What could lead you to dare so rash an act, and to endanger not only your own, but your sister's life?" asked Mr. Heyton.

"Do not blame Kate, dear father!" interposed Amy. "It was my wish, as much as it was hers, that we should make the attempt; and on so calm, so beautiful a sea, what danger was there to daunt us?"

"But the reason, children, of such mad behaviour; you must have had some design in acting as you have done; and it is but proper that you should give some explanation, as a recompense to Sir Thomas and myself for the trouble and anxiety which you have occasioned."

"No other design, dear father, than that of seeking Ernest Morden, in order to ask of him certain questions, which Amy thought he would be more likely to answer to her than to you or Frank."

"And Ernest, what explanations has he given you?"

"None, dear father."

"How! has he openly refused to do so? has he refused to beg pardon of her whom he has injured so deeply?"

"No, father; he has not done so."

"Then what answers did he give you?"

"He could give us none, for we have not seen him."

"Then he denied you an interview?"

"Not so, father; Ernest Morden is not in the ship, nor has he returned to it since he last left it to accompany you."

"Have you not been deceived, child? Have they not told you an untruth?"

"They cannot have done so, father: the captain is ill, but the mate of the vessel informed us that Ernest had been sent to London to transact business there; most probably he is already far on the road."

Mr. Heyton mused for a few seconds, and then, addressing his daughter in a serious voice, said,—

"Are you sure that no deception has been played on you, and that Ernest Morden has not given his instructions to his messmates as to how much and what they should say?"

"Stephen Heyton," said Sir Thomas's secretary, "Ernest Mordon is my brother, and he is not base enough for the performance of actions which would be unworthy of him as a man."

"Already has he proved his baseness in an action which no man would have performed," replied Mr. Heyton; "he is your brother, Gervase Morden, and it pains me to have to speak of him in your presence using such terms as I now reluctantly use. It was my wish that you should not become a partner with us in this search. I would have spared the feelings of a brother, albeit Ernest Morden cared little for the feelings of either a parent or his child."

"Say no more, Heyton," rejoined the secretary, "I will not abet Ernest in this matter, for even his near relationship imposes upon me the task of watching that he sully not the name which was borne so well by the common father of us both. I will follow him to London, and there call him to account for the evil which he has wrought you."

"Gadzooks, young man!" exclaimed Sir Thomas, "you speak as if you yourself were my Lord Chief Justice or the *custos rotulorum* of the district. You must please to remember that the offence was committed within the limits of my jurisdiction, and that the offender, whenever caught, must be duly conducted to Warrenton Hall, where, if you will, you may act as clerk, and record the confessions of the prisoner. Go to London, indeed! You forget that I might be in want of a secretary in your absence, and that I might then be disposed to elect another in your place.''

" Pardon me, Sir Thomas," supplicated Morden, " I am your servant, although I had forgotten it for the moment. Ever have I been ready to do your bidding, and ever have I esteemed it an honour to be intrusted with the execution of your commands. Permit me to claim the privilege of a few days' absence—a week at the utmost, that I may pursue my journey to London ?"

" To London, gadzooks ! Why, what wouldst thou be doing there ?"

" I would seek my brother Ernest."

" Well, and having found him, what then ?"

" I would demand explanations from him to account for his past behaviour, and I would ask from him a recompense to those whom he has so deeply insulted."

" And what if he refused thee ? What if he gave thee no better answer than he gave to Frank Heyton here when they last met on yonder cliffs ?"

A red flush gathered upon the countenance of Gervase Morden, and his hand involuntarily played with the hilt of his sword, as he replied,—

" Ernest is my brother—my younger brother ; he bears the same name with myself, and is the son of a man who went to his grave without one stain upon his character ; Ernest will not dare disgrace, further than he has done, the fair fame which the Mordens have hitherto borne."

" You talk of what he will dare. Now, judging from that which he has done, it seems unfair to suppose that the gallant lieutenant will pause at the performance of any lighter freak,'' observed Sir Thomas, in a satirical manner. " What if your brother were to disappoint your expectations, and forfeit your good opinion of him, how would you then proceed ?"

The red flush deepened on the young man's face.

" I would—"

He was interrupted by Kate Heyton, who laid her hand lightly upon his arm, and in a tone of rebuke said,—

" Remember, Ernest Morden is your brother—your own brother."

Gervase bowed as he made answer,—

" It is because he is my brother, Miss Heyton, that I speak as I do. Were it not that we have slept in the same cradle, and sat beside the same hearth, I should feel less interest in his good repute than I at present feel. Sir Thomas Warrenton will not deny my request ; and at our meeting, Ernest will doubtless give me cause to rejoice in our relationship again.''

" If he do not, boy, he is a greater knave than I have met with for many a year ; aye, and as great a fool, also, '' rejoined Sir Thomas. " Go—go to London by all means ; there are good horses in the stable, and there are servants to take with you. Speed you then, in haste, and give good warning to your brother, that, if he do not repent him of his doings, they shall be made known to the king."

" I will set off to-night, Sir Thomas."

" Do so, boy ; for the matter is not to be trifled with. But stay ; we have made no inquiries as to where in the metropolis your brother may be found, or on what errand he is gone ; perchance these fair boat-women can afford us the information?"

Kate Heyton explained the manner in which she had become possessed of the knowledge that Ernest Morden was on his way to London, at the same time giving Sir Thomas Warrenton to understand that the business on which he had departed thither was entirely unknown to her, further than that she had learned from Ernest's shipmates that he had received instructions for his journey from the captain, who was now unwell in his cabin.

" Hark you, then, Morden," said Sir Thomas: " we will proceed to the dwelling of our friend, and after partaking of some refreshment, pay a visit to the ship and make further inquiries ourselves. It may be, after all, the wiser plan for us to wait your brother's return."

" I had rather there should be no delay, Sir Thomas. It is my desire to see Ernest as speedily as possible, for his past behaviour seems but the prelude to some worse proceedings in which he is about to engage; or otherwise his actions have been very mysterious."

" We must use coolness and caution in our inquiry, Morden. If it seem best that you should follow your brother at once, you may rely upon receiving every assistance from me."

" I shall not fail to avail myself of your offer, Sir Thomas. I will follow Ernest at once."

" And you will bring him back with you, if he refuse to give explanations."

" Ernest will not refuse me," answered the young man, again grasping his sword-hilt as he spoke.

Amy Heyton now approached the secretary, and gently took his hand.

" You will not be harsh or angry with your brother, Mr. Morden—you will not forget how close is the relationship between you and him?"

" I will forget nothing, but will call much to his remembrance."

" Oh, be careful—be very careful! I fear lest you should be tempted to the doing of some rash act. Ernest has not done harm to me. I can and do forgive him for all that is now past."

" But I cannot forgive him, Miss Amy, unless—as I hope will be the case—he fully explain his motives for his conduct, and make that recompense which honour and duty alike demand from him."

" He will explain; he will ask pardon, I am sure he will," ejaculated Amy.

" I trust that he will not fail to do so," returned Gervase; " I shall be sorry for his own sake if he refuses to act in the only way which is left open to him as a just and honourable man."

" Ah ! but if he should refuse?" suggested Amy.

" Then I would force him into compliance, or——"

" Yes, yes, you would be hasty with Ernest ; you—but you must not seek him alone; Sir Thomas, perhaps, will be kind enough to accompany you ?"

" And why do you desire to trouble Mr. Morden with so bad a travelling companion?" demanded the lord of Warrenton Hall. " It is merely to be a meeting of brothers, and a third person would probably be regarded as an intruder."

" Yes ; but Mr. Gervase might——"

Amy hesitated. Sir Thomas Warrenton took her hand in a kindly manner.

" Do you doubt the prudence of my well-tried and trusty secretary ?" said he.

" No, Sir Thomas ; oh no, indeed not !"

" Then why are you desirous, my pretty maid, that he should not go alone in search of his brother?"

" Because Ernest may refuse to confide everything, and Mr. Morden may forget in a hasty moment that Ernest is his brother."

" Humph ! I understand your meaning. I think, however, that you take more interest in the welfare of this same ungallant lieutenant than he deserves. Gadzooks ! a better man than he would have reason to be proud of being the favourite of so fair a maid."

Amy blushed, and, hanging down her head, rejoined in a faint voice,—

" Ernest Morden has long been my father's friend."

" And the friend of a certain pretty maiden also in times gone by," added Sir Thomas, jocularly. " Well, fear not, your wish shall be complied with, and Mr. Morden shall have a companion on his journey."

" And that companion, Sir Thomas——"

" Shall be myself."

Amy attempted to fall on her knees, in order to express to the worthy knight her deep feeling of gratitude for his kindness ; but Sir Thomas prevented her so doing, and after having gallantly bestowed a kiss upon her blooming cheek, permitted her sister to lead her to the cottage.

Sir Thomas Warrenton and his friends stayed to partake of some refreshment, and afterwards departed to visit the ship to which Ernest Morden belonged. From the rank of the chief visitor an audience was readily gained with the valetudinary captain, who detailed the nature of the business on which his lieutenant had been despatched to London, and gave every information that Sir Thomas or his party expected to obtain. The worthy knight took occasion to rally the sailors upon their want of gallantry in allowing the two maidens who had visited their ship in the morning to row back again without receiving assistance from them ; but the seamen exonerated themselves from the charge by stating, that although they had offered to take back the two sisters in the large boat belonging to the ship, both Kate and Amy had resolutely refused to accept their proffered kindness.

On the evening of the same day Sir Thomas and his secretary started for the metropolis. Travelling was performed in a very different manner then to what it is now ; and where you can now be whisked by a steam-carriage in half-a-dozen hours, it was then a journey of two days and three nights. People talk of the good old times ; but the coaches were slow enough then, and they must be confoundedly " slow coaches " who extol their goodness now. Thank Heaven, that in our day they sell sheep in Smithfield instead of burning men ; and the only fires to be seen there are those of the drovers' pipes by day and the gas-lamps which twinkle by night.

Our story has progressed somewhat slowly owing to the number of the incidents which it has been necessary to relate. We must now, however, leave Sir Thomas and Gervase Morden to pursue their journey, while we proceed to the narration of other events.

It was the day after the departure of the knight and his secretary for London, and a bright, beamy, beautiful day it was ; but it so happens that we have now to do with a certain somebody who was as bright and as beautiful as the day itself ; therefore, ceasing to eulogize the day, we will endeavour to say what we can in favour of the certain somebody.

The lovely, laughing, light-footed, merry-eyed, rosy-lipped little Fanny Summers is the " somebody" of whom we speak. Fanny Summers, the tomb-cutter's daughter, has been already introduced to the reader ; and may it often fall to your lot, good reader, say we, to be introduced in real life to similar beings as happy and as beautiful ! A good man may be distinguished from a bad man with perfect ease by this one simple rule—he who is good loves the society of beautiful children, because, like himself, they are pure and innocent : but to a bad man there is no music in the prattle of a child ; and a laughing, light-hearted infant, fresh from the hands of its Maker, is no object of interest to him. The reason is obvious—those who are vile in themselves cannot bear to look on purity, for the purer that purity is, the more it reminds them of their own vileness.

Fanny Summers and the two daughters of Stephen Heyton were friends ; their intimacy had been of long standing, for when Fanny was a child Kate Heyton had oft-times been her nurse, and, together with Amy, had watched her in her cradle and played with her in the green fields. All the schooling which Fanny had hitherto received she had to thank Kate and her sister for ; nor could she have had better tutors, nor the tutors a more apt pupil.

It was to pay a visit of friendship to Kate that Fanny now approached the cottage of the Heytons with her usual light and tripping step. She lifted up the latch of the small gate which gave admittance to the front garden, and after calling her favourite Pompey to follow her, she proceeded to smell the beautiful roses which bloomed around and against the cottage palings. Beautiful children always love beautiful flowers, and to Fanny the roses and the pinks were playmates. Charming was the sight to behold her bending down amidst the blossoms ; her polished neck putting to shame the white bindweed and the spotless lily, while her cheeks so matched the blushing roses, that as the two intermingled it was hard to tell which were the rose-blossoms and which the cheeks. There were many great bees buzzing about amongst the flowers, but Fanny did not fear the bees, for she knew that she had never done them harm, and therefore why should they attempt to sting her ? There is remorse to sting the guilty, but to the innocent the world is without a sting.

Fanny Summers scarcely could summon up sufficient resolution to leave the roses and to tap at the cottage-door. She had watched those roses put forth their first leaves, she had seen their earliest buds, and she now experienced delight in being able to smell one and then the other, and thus collect perfume from all. When, at length, she turned about to seek entrance at the cottage, she missed her favourite spaniel from her side.

"Pompey! Pompey! Where can that mad, wicked Pompey be?"

The spaniel did not answer to the call, and Fanny glanced around the garden in order to see what had become of him. At some little distance she saw some flowers agitated in an unusual manner, and on going towards them discovered the dog busily engaged in rolling over and over in a bed of pinks.

"Oh, dear me, Pompey! Come here, you wicked Pompey, do!" cried poor Fanny.

But Pompey, to his infinite delight, took another roll in the bed of pinks, snapping and barking as he did so, apparently thinking it to be the best piece of fun he had enjoyed for many a day : in vain did his mistress call to him, in vain did she burst into tears when she beheld the mischief he had done. The dog seemed to have an especial enmity to the pinks, for the blossoms of some he bit off with his teeth, and the stems of the others he broke to pieces by the wildness of his capers. While Fanny was doing her best to entice the dog away, and while at the same time she was bemoaning the damage he had wrought, the door of the cottage opened, and the idiot-boy, rushing out, made towards the dog, seized him ruthlessly by the neck, and was about to make an end of him altogether, when Kate Heyton and little Fanny both caught hold of his arms to restrain his anger.

"Do not—do not, dear Kate, let him harm Pompey ; I will plant you more pinks—I will tie these up for you, and come to water them every day !"

"The naughty dog deserves a beating," returned Kate.

Archy took the hint, and forthwith proceeded to twist Pompey's neck, just as a poulterer would serve a fowl.

"Oh, do not—do not let him harm my poor dog?" cried Fanny, the tears flowing down her cheeks in aidance of her petition. "Let him go, dear Kate— pardon him this once, and I will tell you something—I will tell you a secret, which I know you will like to hear."

Kate Heyton playfully demurred to letting the dog escape without his due punishment, but she could not resist the intercession of her weeping supplicant, and accordingly desired Archy to let the offender go free. This was a command which the idiot-boy seemed but ill-disposed to obey, for he was fonder of the pinks than he was of Pompey, and his inclination to twist the neck of the latter was almost too strong for him to conquer. The command was, however, repeated, and the criminal was duly transferred from the rude hands of Archy to the arms of its fair mistress. Kate Heyton now led Fanny aside.

"Come," said she, "what is the secret which you have to tell me?"

Fanny hesitated and hung down her head.

"I—I did not mean to say so," she replied.

"But you promised me, Fan, and you must learn to keep your word."

"Must I keep my word?" she asked ingenuously.

"That, indeed, you must, Fan. I have released your dog, and you must perform your promise."

Fanny took a pencil and a piece of paper out of a little bag which she held in her hand, and after writing some words on the latter, handed it to Kate Heyton.

"There," said she, "I promised my father that I would not tell you, and I promised you that I would let you know a secret. I have not broken my promise to either, for writing cannot be telling—can it, Kate?"

Hastily did Kate Heyton read over the words which Fanny Summers had written, and as she read them, her face became pale, and the paper trembled in her hands. Surprised and agitated, she drew Fanny towards her, and asked—

"Tell me more, Fan: are you sure of the truth of what you say? Are you sure that in your father's cottage ——?"

Fanny placed her finger on her lips, and removing it said—

"I am not to tell you anything, Kate."

"Was that your father's command to you?"

"It was."

"Did he expressly say that you were not to tell this to me?"

"He did."

"This is most strange !" ejaculated Kate, with a look of astonishment; "but you must tell me——"

"No, dear Kate, I must not tell anything. Writing is not telling."

"Then write, Fanny; write all that you know."

Fanny again took the piece of paper, and wrote a few lines at the back of those which she had already written. Kate Heyton read them eagerly, and when she had thus read them, she started up and exclaimed—

"Merciful Heaven, Fan ! I must go to your father's at once."

"No, Kate—no ; you must not do that. He will scold—he will beat me."

" He shall not do so, Fan. But come, you must show me the window, through which you saw what you here describe."

" Yes, Kate, I will do that ; for I did not promise father that I would not do so."

" Then come—come with me directly."

Kate Heyton only stayed to put on her bonnet and shawl, then taking the hand of Fanny in her own she set out with hasty steps towards the habitation of the tomb-maker.

And the secret of Sandy Summers was known. He had extorted from his daughter a promise that she would not say a word to anyone of what she had seen, but to communicate secrets to children, and tell them that they must be kept, is acting as wisely as if you were to put water into a sieve and wish it not to run through. That which had not been told, the pencil had written, and cunning had accomplished its object. Woman's wit will, at any time, prove more than a match for man's wisdom ; both have been tested, and the strength of each is by this time well known.

CHAPTER XXV.

THE DEBT OF HONOUR.—A SCENE AND A SEQUEL.

HITHERTO the scenes of our story have been laid in the country ; we must now take the reader to the metropolis, in order to make him acquainted with certain incidents which happened there, and which have much to do with the plot of our most veracious narrative.

It was drawing towards evening, and the sun was fast sinking below the horizon, as two men, the one some score of years older than the other, walked slowly, arm-in-arm, down Pall Mall, towards the western end ; each was attired in strict accordance with the fashion of the time, the younger having his wrists bedecked with elegantly-worked ruffles, and the elder carrying a black cane, and wearing his hair powdered and arranged after the pattern of a beau, who aspired to be the ruler of the world of fashion and of foppery.

The two gentlemen were evidently well acquainted with each other, for they conversed familiarly, and used that license in their speech which can only be used by a friend to a friend. There was an elegance in the dress, and a gracefulness in the movements of the younger of the two, which caused him to be an object of admiration to many a fair maiden whom he passed by the way.

The two friends had nearly reached the corner of St. James's-street, when they suddenly came to a pause, before the entrance to a large house.

" What say you to our seeking amusement here for a few hours ?" asked the senior of the two, addressing his companion. " There is nothing more bracing to the nerves and more strengthening to the spirit than a frisk now and then with Dame Fortune. Shall we enter ?"

" It is too early in the evening."

" We shall have all the more time to spend in our amusements."

The younger gentleman reluctantly, as it seemed, consented to the solicitation of his friend.

A porter arose from his seat in the hall, as the two visitors entered, made his bow to them, and then reseated himself, with a smile upon his countenance.

On the first landing-place of the staircase stood the marble representation of a Grecian nymph, bearing in her hand a magnificent or-molu lamp, the light from which diffused itself with a mellow radiancy upon the various objects around.

Ascending this staircase, the two gentlemen were ushered by a domestic into a large room, which was filled with company. This apartment was profusely decorated : golden cornices, costly pictures in costly frames, vases filled with flowers, trays of polished silver on which stood wines of various hues, composed the chief of the adornments.   Although there was so much company a profound silence reigned, and the entrance of the two visitors was only noticed by a nod of the head from one or two of the gentlemen who happened to be seated near the door.

The house was one of those places of assembly which have been so aptly termed "Hells!" Thanks to the age we live in, such places are lessening their numbers every day, and becoming things of the past—things for the novelist and romancer to write about, as the dark stains which civilization once bore, but bears no longer, as of old.

Onwards passed the two visitors towards the upper end of the room.   There were busy domestics, who noiselessly tripped over the carpeted floor and attended to the wants and wishes of the various individuals who were seated at the tables. The silence was broken only by the noise made in shuffling a pack of cards, or in the moving of the counters.   Some young men, gaily dressed, but with pale and haggard countenances, that gave evidence of habitual dissipation, were lolling over the chairs of the the players, watching the progress of the various games : some held small books in their hands in which they recorded the several bets they made, and others eyed the progress of the games with envious looks, merely because they themselves had not the wherewith to take part in the play.

"Warrenton," said the elder of the two gentlemen who had last entered, addressing his companion, "here is an empty table, let us call for wine and the cards."

"Not to-night, Dourville—not to-night."

"Pooh, man ! why not to-night ?"

"I have no inclination—no desire.   I would rather be a looker-on this evening."

"Come, come, my dear Warrenton, you are low-spirited.   Wine will cure your ailment ; and the excitement of a single game will be sufficient to dissipate your *ennui*."

Dourville beckoned to one of the attendants, and, the gesture being understood, wine and a pack of cards were immediately placed on the table between them.

"To the health and good fortune of my friend Lambert Warrenton !" said Dourville, as he lifted a glass, filled with sparkling claret, to his lips.

Warrenton merely nodded in return, and taking up his own glass, emptied it without saying a word.

"Why, Lambert—Lambert Warrenton, what has happened to you ?   One would think from your behaviour that you had just finished playing instead of having yet to begin, and that you had found yourself the loser to some large amount."

"I tell you I have no inclination for play.   I am wearied ; I have the headache."

"Want of stimulus, man.   I once contracted a low fever—a pyrexia, I believe those rascally doctors call it—which I fell under, merely through giving way to such feelings as those you speak of.   Stimuli, my boy, are required in this dull world of ours, and a stimulus is all you want to set you to rights this evening. Another glass of wine, and then what shall it be—faro ?"

"I am not disposed to join the company."

"Cassino, then ? we can manage that by ourselves !"

"I do not like it."

"Horror !" cried Dourville, lifting up his hands as if astonished, "not like cassino?   What say you then to picquet ?   Come, you can have no objection to a game or two at picquet?"

"As you please—as you please."

Readily, and, as it seemed with great pleasure to himself, Dourville took up the pack of cards and removed the threes, fours, fives, and sixes of each suit, preparatory to playing the game which he had proposed. Having done so, he remarked that the weather was very sultry, and instead of commissioning one of the domestics to throw open the window, arose from his seat to do it himself.   He had not placed the thirty-two cards out of his hands, but took them to the window with him, and as his back was turned to the company, he held up the pack to the moonlight, and with much adroitness contrived to run his finger-nail along the back of some five or six cards which he had apparently selected from the rest.   As he replaced these in the pack he looked round to see if he was observed, but Lambert Warrenton was idly tapping his glass with the handle of his cane, and paying no attention to anything which was passing around.

" Now," said Dourville to himself, as he glanced at his friend, " this night I shall accomplish my aim.   He will be mine now—mine – mine !"

Picquet is a game which, though seldom played now, was formerly in great repute.   Like most of the games at cards it was introduced from France, and, like everything else which comes over from that land of knicknackeries and follies, it was at once and for some years a fashion with John Bull.   In the drawing-rooms of the wealthy and the *salons* of the gaming-house it was studied and played with an industry worthy of a better pursuit.   The game is a difficult one, and he who attempts to play it must shake off all drowsiness, betaking himself to the business with energy and wary precaution.   In one respect it bears an analogy to cribbage, since the player must be a good and ready accountant.

It fell to Dourville to have the first deal ; this was to his disadvantage, as it constituted his opponent's elder-hand.   Twelve cards were dealt out to each, and the remaining eight cards placed upon the table.

Warrenton had now to take from his hand the five cards which seemed of the least use to him, and select as many from the top of those which had been laid aside.   Then Dourville having picked out in like manner three cards from his hand, substituted in their place the three which remained of the pack from which his opponent had already taken five.

It is not our purpose to describe the game throughout, nor to follow the two players in their play.   One hundred and one points constitute the game, and these are won by tricks ; there are no trumps, and the trick is won by the highest card of the suit which happens to be led.

Lambert Warrenton was no novice in the game which he was now playing with his friend.   He had been a visitant to Paris, and had there been duly initiated into the art and mystery of card-playing; his knowledge, however, was not sufficient to make him a match for Dourville, who was himself a Frenchman by birth, and who had handled cards until their use had become familiar to him, and every combination of which they are susceptible was as well known to him by heart as the multiplication table which he had learnt in his early childhood.

Warrenton was the winner for the first three games.   The excitement of success and the quantity of wine which he had drank flushed his spirits, and caused him now to play with more eagerness than he had yet displayed ; and still his companion plied him with wine, and still he shuffled his cards and counted his points with increasing celerity and increasing zest for the game.   But now the bird was caught, the victory was achieved ; too intent on the play, he saw not the grin, the smile, the exultation which was seated on the countenance of his companion. Every time that the eyes of Lambert Warrenton sparkled with delight as he perceived four, five, or six successive cards of the same suit in his hand, just so often were the brows of his companion drawn inward and his lip curled upward ; just so often did he smile upon his victim with the same inward chuckle of satisfaction, with the same look of mingled triumph and scorn with which the angler views the giddy fish disporting in the water, knowing full well that it will ere long take the bait, and that the end of its merriment will be certain death.

Whenever we divest Reason of her sway, and allow the cool judgment to be thrust from its throne, we at once become the most powerless and pitiable of created things.   It has been well said, that he who gives himself up to passion, submits himself to be seen through a microscope. The man who gives himself up to revenge, envy, or " vaulting ambition" becomes mean at once in the eyes of all who look upon him.   Passion makes man weak ; even the lover becomes a madman when he yields himself up to the strong passion which agitates his breast. The passion for place, the passion for wealth, a passion for drink, or a passion for play, alike renders the subject of that passion a mere plaything in the hands of those who look on coolly and act with deliberation.   Just so was it at the present moment with Lambert Warrenton.   Success had awakened the gambler's spirit within him, and the passion for play had reduced him to a state of helplessness till he had become caught in the toil which had been laid for his ensnarement. The gamester was no longer a man—for liberty, freedom of mind and thought, the power of controlling self, the faculty of reflection, had left him—and deprived of these, not one of us is any longer a man. But "many a time and oft" have lessons been read against gaming, therefore it will be best to abstain from repeating the dose, lest, by our so doing, nausea should ensue.

It has been already said that at the game of picquet it is necessary that you should pay great attention to the enumeration of your points. Excited as Lambert Warrenton had now become, to do this was impossible, consequently he now became the loser: game after game was played, and still he lost—to win is exciting, to lose is maddening : it is the triumph of victory which carries you on when winning—it is the madness of desperation which will not allow you to pause in defeat. Many of the company had now gathered round the table at which the two players were seated, but in accordance with the gamblers' code, they gave no word of warning to the loser.

"What! every trick to me—capot again?" exclaimed Dourville, in a tone of seeming wonderment. "Seventy-five points already, and forty for the capot makes ahundred and ten—the game is won. Come, take some more wine ; you will retrieve this before long. Oblige me by cutting for another deal."

" I cannot," replied Lambert Warrenton.

"Cannot! Surely you will not let Fortune serve you so scurvily without trying to revenge yourself on the saucy jade. Come, you will not rise from your chair while there is wine in the bottle and cards on the table—that would not be brave nor man-like."

"You have won all. I have nothing more to stake."

' Pooh! is that all ? We are friends, are we not ? Your note-of-hand by-and-by will suffice, if indeed, before then, I have not to solicit a similar favour from you."

Lambert Warrenton endeavoured to rise and take his departure ; but the attempt was vain ; too strongly over and around him had the spell of enchantment been woven ; it was as if the pips on the cards had changed into the eyes of living syrens, gleaming at him with soft glances, and bewitching him with their gleam. Fascination was in every thing which he looked upon, and in vain was the wish to flee. Mechanically his fingers grasped the cards, and he played them as if not himself, but some malicious demon at his elbow guided the movement of his hand.

" I will be more cautious," said Lambert Warrenton to himself. " The devil must be in the cards if I am beaten again as I have been beaten hitherto.'

In vain was all the caution. Dourville had ace—king and queen of diamonds; king, queen, and knave of clubs ; queen, knave, and ten of spades ; knave, ten, and nine of hearts. Here were four *tierce-majors*, each of which reckoning for three, made twelve points. The game went on—*quatorze, quart, sixieme*, and *capot*. Again were the hundred-and-one points made, again was the fortunate Dourville winner of the game.

Lambert Warrenton ground his teeth.

" D—n!" ejaculated he, inwardly. " How came it that he had quatorze and so many tierce-majors again ? He must have taken up most fortunately when I showed *carte blanche ;* but such luck will not last—it will be mine ere long !"

Foolish Lambert Warrenton! What true gamester ever trusts to luck alone ? Did Dourville do so? Not he. It was not mere luck which caused him to have four aces in his hand, it was not mere luck which brought him the four *tierce-majors*. What did he when he took the cards in his hand as he went to open the window ? What had the moon seen him do then ? Was it wondrous that he won ? Was it wondrous that game after game was his? No; it was not wondrous—it was a mere matter of course—it was no chance, no luck, no favour of fortune ; it was the effect of a cause, the certain issue of the certain plan. There was that which rendered it impossible for Lambert Warrenton to win, despite all his care, all his dextrous play, all his acknowledged skill.

The cards were marked; roguery had pitted itself against fair play.

It were useless to detail the particulars of each game. The dial showed that the hours of night were fled, while through the half-open window came peeping in the first faint rays of the early dawn. Lambert Warrenton had continued to play, although fortune had not befriended him once since the first part of the evening. His features were terribly expressive of the fierce, wild passions which had taken possession of his breast—phrenzy, despair, rage, desperation and revenge were all depicted there. The excitement and the wine had flushed his countenance with a deep crimson flush, his hair hung loose and disorderly about his temples, his eyes appeared as if about to dart from their sockets, his teeth were closely set, his lips compressed against his gums, causing the latter to become pale and bloodless. Not a word had he spoken during the whole of the last game, and now the stake was larger than any former one had been, while fortune appeared to be as froward as ever. No longer slowly and with caution did he play his cards, but with the wild, reckless manner of one who cared not whether he lost or won; yet it was easy to perceive that he risked much upon that game, and that his anxiety of mind was great. Cool and calm was the play of his antagonist. No flush was visible upon his cheek, no sparkle of the eye betrayed to him there was excitement in the game. The cards were thrown down, were counted, were played, were counted again; the tricks were reckoned for the points, the points calculated for the game: the contest was decided.

"You have lost again, Warrenton," said Dourville, in his cool, calm manner. "Come, what shall be our stakes for the next game?"

Lambert Warrenton arose, and rising, flung down the chair on which he had been seated. Then, clasping one hand to his brow, and sweeping the cards from off the table with the other, he exclaimed,—

"I will play no more. I am a beggar—a penniless beggar!"

"Mr. Warrenton!" ejaculated Dourville, in a tone of well-feigned astonishment.

For a few moments the maddened man meditated over his position, gnashing and grinding his teeth as he mused. Then lifting up his eyes, and fancying that he beheld a grin upon the countenance of Dourville, he rushed forward, and grasped him by the collar.

"Look you!" he thundered—"we have played from evening to morning, and never once within the last six hours have I won a single game. How is it, man, that I have lost all to you?"

"If fortune, Lam——"

Warrenton tightened his hold on the throat of his late antagonist.

"Fortune! No, Dourville, you have ruined me—you have robbed me of all—everything. Rascal! you have played falsely—you have used no fair means to be the winner which you have been."

At last the flush of apparent anger gathered on the cheek of Dourville.

"Do you accuse me of cheating, Mr. Warrenton?"

"I—I—yes. I tell you there has been robbery—foul robbery; thievery—not play."

"This is most excellent behaviour of you, Lambert Warrenton, and it is more than I expected. A gentleman would bear his losses in a manly way."

"But I tell you, rascal, I have not lost. I have been cheated—robbed—robbed by a villain!"

"I shall not limit you in the use of your terms, Mr. Warrenton. Suit yourself in the choice of epithets, I beg of you."

The imperturbable, cool manner in which Dourville received and replied to the charges of his accuser, only awoke the ire of the latter in a greater degree. All that was now taking place had been expected by the experienced gamester, who was by no means unaccustomed to such a scene. A faint smile of triumph was all that was expressed on Dourville's countenance, and that smile told of the success of a well-planned scheme and the fearlessness with which the accused treated the accusation made by the desperate man.

"I have been cheated—vilely cheated!" cried Lambert Warrenton.

By a violent effort, Dourville detached himself from his victim's grasp.

"Hold off, Warrenton!   I can listen to your words ; but you had best not touch me with your hands."

Warrenton threw himself upon a chair, and clutched his hair with the demeanour of a maniac.   The nervous agitation of his whole body was visible in the play of his foot upon the floor.   He spoke not, he said not a word ; but his wild-looking, bloodshot eyes glared upon Dourville, as if their owner was meditating some revengeful act, and gloating over the destined victim prior to the accomplishment of the deed.

Heavily, heavily, did the chest of the desperate man heave to his short, deep inspirations, so tightly were his lips compressed against his gums, that the blood oozed forth, and trickled out of his mouth.   His fingers twined and intertwined about and around one another with that peculiar motion which indicates the strongest mental agitation—the deadliest resolves of the human breast.   Suddenly a change came ; the flash faded from the cheeks of the tortured man, his fingers ceased from their contortuplicative movements, his chest worked with more freedom.   Up sprang he from his seat, and laid his hand upon his hat.

"Where are you going, Lambert Warrenton?" asked Dourville, detaining him by the arm.

"Away.   Stay me not !   Let me pass, I say—let me pass !"

"You forget, my friend, there is a little account which you have to settle. Before you leave this room, I must have your signature for the sum which is now owing to me by you."

"Owe !" cried Warrenton, turning round upon his detainer, with a look of fury. "Owe !—owe to you?   Hark you, Dourville—do not provoke me more—do not make me more desperate than I am.   All the money which I had when I entered this room, you have stolen from me ; you have beggared me already, and what would you have more ?"

"By the Virgin, a cool question.   Why, in the first place, my good friend, you have treated me rather scurvily, I am inclined to think, and your treatment has impugned my honour; therefore, I am entitled to cross swords with you, or give you view of a pistol-muzzle at twenty paces distant."

"Be it so, Eugene Dourville, I am at your service, and care not what weapons we use, nor how early we have our meeting."

"That is kind and obliging, certainly ; but I also will show my generosity by waiving my right to call you out, provided that you at once sign your name to a piece of paper, and then part in a friendly manner."

Warrenton grinned savagely at the last speaker, and replied,—

"We meet, Dourville, whether you or I act the part of challenger."

"As you like about that.   Meanwhile, that all things may be done orderly, I must beg you to sign your name, as I have before requested."

"To what—sign to what, Eugene Dourville?"

"To a paper which will make you my acknowledged debtor in the trifling sum of one thousand three-hundred pounds."

"Owing to you! when, and how?"

"The debt incurred this night, Lambert Warrenton ; the money lost by yourself at yonder table."

"Ha, ha, ha!   Lost, say you, Dourville?   You speak the truth, when you say that you have played the robber and the cheat—that I have lost—that I have been robbed—that I have been cozened by a rogue."

"It becomes you not, Warrenton, to use such terms.   To these gentlemen around, methinks you are striving vastly to make yourself appear the rogue, by endeavouring to shirk the payment of a debt of honour."

"A debt of honour !"

"Aye ! a debt of honour ; for I had your word that you would give me an acknowledgment for any sum that I might chance to win from you in the course of our play."

"In the course of fair play, Eugene Dourville, but not when cheating entered into the game."

Dourville turned towards two or three gentlemen who had listened to the quarrel, and who were now standing beside the disputants. Before addressing them, he took up the cards with which he had been playing, shuffled them in an apparently careless manner, and, after having passed the ball of his thumb over the backs of some half-dozen, threw the whole pack again upon the table.

"May I request, gentlemen," said he, "that you will act as umpires in this controversy? Fortune has dealt badly with my friend this evening, and he has become the loser of a few hundreds; most strangely, he now charges me with having played unfairly, and with having won by dishonourable means. You have partly witnessed our play, and know, perhaps, what ground there is for the charge now brought; there are the cards with which we have played, and, as far as I am ware, they constitute a perfectly legitimate pack. Whether my friend will or will not abide by your decision I cannot prophesy, but, as your opinion will have weight, I trust, with each of us, you will, doubtless, not refuse to confer the favour?"

The persons addressed by Dourville took up the cards from the table, and submitted them to examination. On replacing them, one of the party said deliberately, "There is nothing wrong in the cards; ill-luck, alone, must have caused the unsuccess of Mr. Warrenton."

"It is a combination!" exclaimed the young man. "You are one and all——"

He was interrupted by one of the bystanders.

"Be careful what you say, Mr. Warrenton; there are those present who would not bear patiently such an accusation as you have now cast upon your friend. Be advised. Did you, or did you not, during your play, promise that, in the event of your losing, you would give your note of hand for the sum lost?"

"I did; but——"

"It is enough. You gave the promise, and, as a gentleman, you will fulfil it. No conditions were annexed to the promise; none, therefore, can have any influence on its fulfilment."

Lambert Warrenton hung down his head, and in a musing attitude paced across the room.

"My friend need not be so desirous of escaping the performance of his pledge," observed Dourville; "the probability being, that by this time to-morrow he will be riddled through by a pistol-bullet, and unable to pay; or, that I shall be the unfortunate recipient of the leaden dose, and, therefore, most incontestibly incompetent to make any demand. Here is paper, and I may as well amuse myself by drawing out the form of acknowledgment; the signature, no doubt, will follow in proper order."

Warrenton paid little or no heed to the flippant raillery of Dourville. After pacing the room two or three times, he came to a pause before the individual who had played the part of umpire.

"Say you," he asked, "that this is a debt of honour?"

"The word of a gentleman is always accounted as the word of honour," was the reply. "Your word has been given to your friend, and it matters not how you have been treated by him; the pledge must be redeemed *coute qui coute.*"

"Then be it so," cried Lambert Warrenton. "Give me the pen. Where am I to sign?"

"The paper is especially smooth just where the honour of your signature is required," answered Dourville, placing the form which he had drawn out upon the table.

Lambert Warrenton hesitated for a moment, and seemed irresolute whether to sign as desired or to rend the paper in half and fling it upon the floor. Desperate and excited as he was, however, he still had sufficient self-command left to consider the position in which he was placed; he perceived that there was no going back, and accordingly, dipping the pen in the ink with a savage gesture, he wrote his name to the bond, and then flung it at Dourville before the marks were dry."

"Take it," he cried, "and let us be friends no longer."

"Why so, my good Warrenton?"

"You require no answer from me. Let these be the last words spoken by either of us to the other; they are my last to you."

"You are mistaken, Lambert Warrenton, much mistaken. But go home, man, and go to bed. Trust me, we shall be good friends yet."

"Never, Eugene Dourville; never!"

Warrenton stayed not to bid adieu to any one in the room, but, placing on his hat, hastily took his departure, his eyes still glowing fiercely, his lips muttering indistinct sounds as he went."

"Let him go," cried Dourville, "let him go. I warrant ye, before two days are past, he will tell a different tale."

Eugene Dourville was right; he knew well the character and nature of his late opponent—he understood the predicament in which he was placed, and could well prognosticate the means by which Warrenton would attempt to free himself from the toils that had been cast around him. The experienced man of the world knew well enough how a man's actions and words are influenced by the time of the day— how hot and hasty sayings uttered at night are recalled in the morning—how vows are made when the brain is heated which are entirely forgotten by the time that same brain has become cool. It was not his purpose to quarrel with Lambert Warrenton—otherwise ample opportunity had been provided him, there being much in his remembrance which he could not easily blot out, and which it was almost impossible to let pass into oblivion without some notice being taken of the same.

Yes ; on the afternoon of that very day, Eugene Dourville was seated before his writing-desk in a private chamber of one of the west-end hotels, when a knock was heard at the outer door, and presently afterwards Lambert Warrenton entered the apartment.

"Good morning to you, my dear Warrenton," exclaimed the ever polite Dourville, rising from his seat and taking the hand of his visitor. "I have expected your call these two hours past."

"Expected me ?"

"Ay. Why do you look astonished; are we not old friends? Besides, after the conversation at our last meeting, I had a right to expect a visit from you, or you one from me, had I not?"

"I am not come to quarrel but to offer apologies," replied Warrenton. "I knew not what I said last evening, when I took in earnest that which, with you, was but a jest."

"But a jest, Lambert Warrenton? Pardon me, I do not comprehend your meaning."

"The sum which I gave you a bond for."

"Well?"

"It was but a joke of yours, and I had the silliness to suppose that I really had lost so large an amount, and that you demanded payment."

Eugene Dourville started from his seat, and surveyed his visitor with a look of astonishment.

"Mr. Warrenton," he exclaimed, "may I be pardoned for desiring to know the true object of your visit?"

"The paper, Dourville—that paper which I gave you ; were you to die, or any accident to happen, it might fall into the hands of those who would consider it as a real bond."

"Consider it as a real bond, Lambert Warrenton ! Why, what in the name of Heaven, do you consider it yourself?"

Warrenton attempted to laugh.

"From your words and behaviour, Dourville," said he, "a stranger might suppose that you were in real earnest, and intended to make use of the piece of paper yourself."

"And what other intention should I have, Mr. Warrenton? You owe me a sum of money, and I have your written bond for the payment of that amount. As a matter of course, till the debt be paid——"

"Paid, Dourville ? You—you don't mean—you do not suppose—you are not going to demand money from me?"

"Humph! a singular question. I have your promise for a certain payment, and till that payment be made I shall, of course, consider you my debtor."

"But Dourville, my dear Dourville! you are carrying the joke too far. We are friends, we—we are old friends. I had no other intention than that of playing for amusement, and I thought that you were aware that such was my real intention."

"Most excellent, my friend! a most excellent idea of yours! Indeed I had no such thoughts, not being addicted myself to joking after such a fashion."

"Then you intend to keep the paper, to—to——"

"To expect payment from you."

Warrenton seized the hand of Dourville, and with a pale countenance exclaimed,—

"You cannot—will not do as you say, Dourville? You surely will not take advantage of my imprudence last evening!"

"You will pardon me, sir, if I say that I do not understaad your words. I am not conscious or having taken advantage of you as you say; nor do I comprehend the full meaning of your insinuations. You lost to me a sum of money, and, not having the means of payment at hand, you tendered me your note of hand for that amount—of course I expect that you will duly honour your bond."

"Dourville! you must be in jest. What money I had is already in your possession; and the sum which you now demand is more than I could pay, were I to give you every penny to which at present I have a just claim."

"That is strange information, Lambert Warrenton: a man of honour would not act as you have done. Knowing, as you must have done, that you had not the means to pay, why did you give me the promise?"

"Because—because—but I was maddened—insane; I knew not what I did. I did not suppose! Come, Dourville! say, I beg of you, that you are not in earnest!"

"Do you deem me to be mad as well as yourself, Lambert Warrenton? Had it happened otherwise, and had you won the like sum of me, instead of I winning it of you, should I have attempted such trickery as this? And if I had, in what manner would you have treated me?"

"But we played for amusement, Dourville. We are friends."

"No more of this, man! Friends, forsooth! a pretty plea! Hark you, Lambert Warrenton! I will tell you that which as yet you seem not to know. The gamester, sir, has but two friends—the stake for which he plays, and the pack of cards which he holds in his hand. I thought that you had learned better lessons in the world than not to know that friendship ceases at the edge of the card-table, when men sit down to play for gold."

Warrenton mused for a short time, and then, again seizing the hand of his companion, said,—

"Do I understand you rightly, Dourville? You are in earnest, and deem me to be really your debtor?"

"There is nothing difficult to understand in that, Mr. Warrenton."

"And you will not acknowledge our friendship? You will not restore me that paper?"

"Certainly not the latter request—I cannot oblige you in that."

Warrenton flung the hand of Dourville from his grasp. A smile of triumph gleamed upon his countenance: he gave vent to a burst of loud and derisive laughter, rocking himself backwards and forwards in a chair as he laughed.

"You are pleased, Mr. Warrenton; I am happy to perceive that you have regained your usual merriment."

Again Lambert Warrenton laughed, and in that laugh scorn and exultation seemed to be combined. He once more grasped the arm of his companion, and, scarcely able to speak for his merriment, said,—

"Look you, Eugene Dourville; I am young, and have not, therefore, had that experience in the world which has fallen to your share. Knowing this, you thought to impose on me—to play upon me as a mere boy; but you are mistaken, man; you have reckoned without your host. The greenhorn is a match for the gamester; the biter has himself been bit."

"How so, good Master Warrenton?" asked Dourville, smiling placidly.

"I will tell you, Eugene Dourville—I will show you how clever you have been. What if you have a piece of paper in your possession? what if it be a bond for hundreds of pounds? what if to it my signature be affixed? Think you I knew not what I was doing when I signed it? Think you I was an idiot, or asleep? No, Eugene Dourville, you have the paper, and to it you have my name; but what of that? I am under age; my signature is of no account; the bond itself is not worth one pin! Ha! ha! my friend, you may put your paper in the fire now; you may do with it as you please!"

Dourville had folded his arms and listened to the exultation of Lambert War renton without uttering a word or changing the expression of a single feature. When, however, Warrenton had finished speaking, Dourville threw himself upon a lounge, and allowed a dark smile of contempt to gather upon his countenance.

"This very good acting of yours, Lambert Warrenton," said he, "and it is just that which I expected to see. Allow me to set you right, however, in one point. Your signature is, as you have been pleased to inform me, of no legal value whatever; but your signature to this bond has a peculiar value—a value *sui generis*, to use an expression which, as a scholar, you, of course, understand. I give you due praise for having acted as judiciously as you have, but the common fault of youth is to jump too hastily to its conclusions, and from that fault, I am sorry to say, you are not, as yet, exempt."

"You will not acknowledge that you are outwitted, Dourville?" remarked Warrenton.

"Not until I am certain that such is the case, Lambert Warrenton. At present, however, our affairs seem to me to stand thus:—You owe me a sum of money; I, because of your minority, have no legal hold upon you; but your name is to the acknowledgment of the debt, and it becomes me at once to enter into communication with your father——"

"With my father, Dourville! Oh no! not with him!"

"Why not?"

"He—he—he will——"

"Listen to me, Lambert Warrenton. Your father detests gambling; you know that he has expressly said if he detects you losing or winning money at the card-table, he will at once disinherit you of that property to which otherwise you are the heir. See you not the position in which you are placed? See you not the situation which you occupy?"

Lambert Warrenton fell on his kees, and clasped the hand of Dourville in his own.

"You will not," he implored, "oh, say that you will not let this affair come to my father's ears!"

Eugene Dourville smiled, and in a mocking tone of voice replied,—

"Why, look you, man, how powerless you are; you that were but five minutes ago vaunting your own good skill—your own sagacity and sharp wit. Lambert Warrenton, you are on your knees! Up, man, and to business in proper fashion! You can see now who has played the game best."

Warrenton's countenance had again become of a pallid hue, while anxiety was traced upon his features. In a voice of agony he again petitioned the gambler, in whose toils he had been caught.

"Oh, promise me, Dourville—promise me that you will keep this hidden from my father! He would cast me out—he would take all from me—he would discountenance me for ever. Promise me that he shall not know this, and I will accede to any terms."

"Well, come now, that is pleasant to hear you talk of terms; it has a business-like sound. You are strongly desirous that this little affair should not reach Warrenton—say you not so?"

"Yes, Dourville, yes. I will agree to anything, if you promise to keep this a secret."

"To anything, say you?"

"Yes, yes—to any terms."

A fiendish smile gathered upon the features of Dourville, as taking the hand of his companion he led him into an inner room.

"Let us be sure that there are no eaves-droppers," said he, as he closed the doors of both apartments.

"Why do you take such precautions, Dourville?" asked Warrenton, somewhat terrified.

"Because, my good friend, it would not do for us to be overheard in that which we have now to talk about."

"And what is that?"

" You shall hear. Take a seat. I will restore to you this paper—I will refund you the money which last night I won from you—I will add to that sum, as a gift, ten times the amount, if you but consent to the proposition which I am about to make."

" And what is that ?"

" It is——" The words which followed were spoken in a whisper, and were addressed to the ear of Lambert Warrenton only. They were listened to in silence.

" What say you to the proposal ?" demanded Dourville in a louder tone, as he finished the statement of his terms.

Whatever the proposition had been, its nature had been such as to have caused the cheeks of the listener to have become blanched, and his lips white and trembling. He staggered as he rose from his seat, and sought the support offered by the adjacent mantel-shelf."

" Are there no other terms ?" he asked.

" None."

" Will you take no other ?"

" I will not."

" If it be discovered, Dourville——"

" You will run the same chance that I shall, that is all."

" And that chance——"

" Is death—death on the scaffold."

Lambert Warrenton could not utter a word. So pale were his cheeks, so white his lips, so wild and ghastly the expression of his eyes, that his companion stepped forward and caught him by the arm, under the impression that he was about to fall.

" What—what would you have me become ?" ejaculated the young man.

" I have told you, Lambert Warrenton, that which I require you to perform. I am willing to make you——"

" A traitor, Dourville—a traitor to my country and my king !"

" As you please about the title which you desire to have ; but that which I will make you, if you agree to my terms, is—a wealthy man."

Warrenton hesitated for a few minutes, then, turning round, he laid his hands upon the shoulders of Dourville, and in a hoarse voice asked,—

" What is your reward—what is to be the price of my perfidy ?"

" I have told you, Lambert Warrenton. For the small service which I require from you, I, in return, restore you your money, give you back your bond, promise you good payment, and more than that——"

" What can you give me more, Dourville ?"

" Hearken, and I will you."

Again did the two men sit down beside each other ; while the elder disclosed to the younger further plans of villany. But the effect which these disclosures produced upon the listener was different to that which had resulted from the proposal made some quarter of an hour before. The eyes of Lambert Warrenton now sparkled with delight, his cheeks glowed, his tremour ceased, courage had returned to him, and in a bold voice he demanded,—

" Have you told me truth, Dourville? am I to believe your statement ?"

" You shall have proof, Lambert Warrenton—you shall have good proof."

" Then I consent."

" You would be a fool if you refused to do so. But, hark ! I thought I heard a footstep outside the door."

" Open it and see if any one be there," said Warrenton.

Dourville turned the key and thrust open the door. Suddenly he started back, on perceiving the body of a man standing in the doorway.

" Luke Masters !" he exclaimed, " you here !"

" Ay, Dourville, it is Luke Masters ; and he is happy in being enabled to say that he has been where he now is for the last half-hour."

" Then you have heard——"

"Nearly all that you have said, Eugene Dourville. But this is fine work of yours—very fine, indeed! However, nothing will come of it unless you enlist your friend into the service, I can promise you that."

"But, Masters—"

"It is no use, Eugene Dourville; you cannot play the fool with me. Either I must make one in this little business, or the affair shall go no further."

"Be it so, Luke. You are aware what hold I have on you, therefore be careful how you act."

"Luke Masters knows how to take care of himself," was the reply.

"Dourville," said Lambert Warrenton, "I have agreed to your terms; now then I demand the restoration of my bond."

Dourville unlocked his writing-desk, and, taking out two papers, placed them on the table.

"There is your bond," said he. It shall be yours when you have affixed your signature to the other paper."

"And what is that other paper?"

"Read and know."

Lambert Warrenton did read; and, as he read, his face once more became pale, his limbs once again trembled.

"Must I sign this?" he asked.

"You must. What objection can you have to so doing; it is but the acknowledgment in writing of that which you have already agreed to in words."

"And if I refuse?"

"I retain possession of your bond; and it would be ten chances to one, seeing that I have pistols at command, that you left this room without being carried hence."

"Then I must sign?"

"Do so at once, Mr. Warrenton," said Masters. "There's nothing like a little boldness when a man's pushed to it and don't know what to do."

Lambert Warrenton signed his name to the paper.

"That will do," said Dourville, with a smile, as he rolled up the paper and replaced it in his desk. "Take up your bond, Lambert Warrenton. We are friends now if we never were before; we are friends, I say, for we have a common interest in a common cause."

"But the cause, Dourville, the cause?"

"Tush, man! there is nothing to fear. It is enough that you play your game well, and everything will go smoothly."

Whether everything did or did not go smoothly with Lambert Warrenton remains yet to be seen. On the following day he returned to Warrenton Hall, and this chapter is somewhat out of its place in our story, since the events just related occurred nearly a fortnight previous to the return of Ernest Morden from his voyage.

The progress of the narrative will explain what the nature of the contract was which had now been entered into by Eugene Dourville and Lambert Warrenton; while the character of Luke Masters will also be duly developed.

Lambert Warrenton had entered upon a course from which there was no turning back. He had done that which admitted not of being undone.

Eugene Dourville laughed to himself when he on that night parted from Lambert Warrenton.

"So far all works well!" he exclaimed. "I have played the cards to perfection, and the game is mine!"

CHAPTER XXVI.

THE DOOR THAT MUST NOT BE OPENED.

KATE HEYTON accompanied Fanny Summers to the tomb-cutter's cottage. On arriving there, she was led by the child to the window, which had been closed up, and through which Fanny had been forbidden to look. Kate was much taller than Fanny, and, therefore, she found no difficulty in peering in through the crack above the shutters, having first elevated herself upon a stool which Fanny had provided for the purpose. She grasped a projecting portion of the shutter in order to facilitate her attempt at clambering, and to steady herself by while she peeped into the apartment, but the rotten wood-work creaked and yielded to the strain. Kate trembled, for she was afraid that the noise would awaken the attention of those who she wished should not know of her proximity. So much did her agitation of mind and body increase, that it became no easy matter for her to retain her footing and to keep herself from falling. Luckily there were some iron staples fastened in the wall just above the window, and to these Kate Heyton managed to cling. Her position was a perilous one, her right foot standing on the garden stool, and her left being planted on the sill of the window, so that, had any one within, alarmed by the creaking of the wood-work, suddenly thrown open the shutters, Kate would have been dashed to the ground, despite the feeble hold which she had of the iron staples.

Sandy Summers was busy in his little workshop. Diligently had he been labouring during the whole night to restore the stone tear to its proper place on the face of the weeping cherub. His efforts had been unavailing to reproduce the beauty of expression which he had once gained ; but perseverance and ingenuity had effected much ; and, although the new tear did not seem so tear-like as the former one, and did not appear to roll out from the corner of the eye so naturally, and had not the pear-shaded, dropping, translucent semblance which its predecessor had possessed, yet it was an unmistakable and most respectable tear, which would have satisfied the eyes and done good to the heart of its sculptor, had it not been that poor Sandy had been compelled to resort to the sad expedient of lessening the chubby fulness of his cherub's cheeks, in order to give the tear its requisite convexity. Sandy Summers, however, was not the man to repine at any untoward freak of fortune ; nor was he at all disposed to follow the example of some people who make it a rule to rail at their ills and accidents in " good set terms," instead of exerting themselves to repair the damage done, or to win back the treasure lost. Trust me, if Sandy Summers had, in his youth-time, been jilted by his lady-love, he was not the sort of man to have thrown himself into the village pond in consequence ; nor to have done as some foolish people do under such circumstances— condemn the whole race of womankind, because one individual of the species has happened to prove an unsatisfactory specimen. There is not the least doubt that if one woman had played the jilt with Sandy, he would quickly have sought out another more constant and sincere ; and had he, in the present instance, but had another piece of stone in his workshop which would have served his purpose, he would at once have set about carving his cherub afresh, and would, in all probability, have produced a second tear which in symmetry, expressiveness, and beauty, would have completely eclipsed the remembrance of its precursor's glory.

It was a summer evening—warm, sunny, and still. Sandy felt the oppressiveness of the warm atmosphere, and accordingly plied his mallet and chisel less vigorously than was his wont. Gradually the feeling of sleepiness overpowered him ; he rested his mallet on his knee, and held his chisel with a loose grasp. It must be confessed that he had pretty freely investigated the nature of the liquid contained in a certain can which stood by his side, and the laboriousness of this investigation, coupled with the warmth of the atmosphere, had induced that feeling of drowsiness which he could not conquer. Sandy found his head to be perversely inclined to fall forwards, and his eye-lids had taken up with a strange whim of their own—those of one eye amusing themselves by winking at those of the other ; and so on alternately. In the course of a few minutes Sandy became completely bewildered. Surrounding things assumed appearances which he had never before witnessed : as he winked, the stone eye-lids of the cherub which he had carven on the tablet appeared to wink at him ; and as he leered at them, so did every one of the weeping angels, crying cherubs, and bemoaning babies appear to leer also in return.

Strange to say, there was a representation of the angel Gabriel on one of the tomb-stones, which had suddenly taken to displaying the most ridiculous capers. Sandy thought he had never beheld anything so extraordinary ; the carven figures were all in motion around him ; and what was more unaccountable, the very tombstones themselves had commenced dancing, and were promenading, pirouetting, gallopading, turning partners, and chassezing right and left, apparently to their own most infinite enjoyment. The chubby children began to turn head ove

heels; the company of cherubs set up a game of rolly-polly; and the death's
head which had been carven on the tomb-stone of an old man, was industriously
at work, snapping its jaws, and turning round and round as if it had suddenly
found a spine upon which to turn.   But to crown the whole, the angel Gabriel
flapped its wings, spread them out, made a jump, and soared away towards the
roof of the workshop.   Sandy could not stand so much as this : he had no notion
of one of his own angels serving him any such shabby trick.   " Hilloa there ! "
he cried ; but the angel seemed to put its fingers to its nose, and irreverently
laugh at him.   " Stop! stop, you Gab—Gab—Gabriel ! "   cried poor Sandy,
flinging his mallet across the workshop.   This last action of Sandy's produced a
wondrous effect; he was startled by the noise, he woke up, he gazed around
him, and, to his utter astonishment, discovered that all his old companions were
behaving themselves properly in their proper places ; the cherubs were weeping
as was their wont; the children were crying after the most legitimate fashion ;
the angels were looking as prim and demure as creatures so pure as angels ought
to look.   Sandy arose and staggered towards the stone on which the Gabriel was
carved ; but Gabriel was there just as tightly fixed as when Sandy had last touched
him up with the chisel : he had not altered his position in any manner, nor did he
seem to evince the least disposition for flight.

" This is very extraordinary ! " ejaculated Sandy to himself ; " bless my soul,
it's the most remarkable occurrence which ever I knew to take place in this
workshop ! "

Picking up his mallet, which, by-the-by, he was surprised to find upon the
floor, and making towards the can which stood on an adjoining bench, he lifted it
to his mouth, and, with some degree of wonderment expressed on his countenance,
exclaimed,—

" And all the beer gone too! why, what has become of it ?   I can't have drunk
it all myself ; and who has been here to do it ?   Those angels have not played me
a trick surely—they couldn't have been so mischievous.   It's very warm this
evening.   I—I wish there was about half-a-pint of the beer left.   But I suppose
I drank it ; I suppose I must have done so.   How very strange ! Everything
to-day is, I declare, quite a mystery !"

Leaving Sandy Summers to recover from his mystified state in the best manner
he could, we return to Kate Heyton at the window.

" Can you see, Kate—can you see ? " asked Fanny.

Kate held up her finger and replied in a low and whispering tone,—

" Hush, Fanny—hush!"

But Fanny Summers' stock of patience was about as extensive as the quantity
usually assigned to children. She could not wait, and, therefore, desired immediate
information.

" Do you see him, Kate—is there light enough for you to see him ?"

Kate Heyton started ; her hands trembled as she clung to the iron staples, the
colour fled from her face, she pressed her eyes to the crack above the window-shutter.

" Do you see, Kate—do you see?"

The maiden neither heard the question, nor returned an answer ; that which she
saw engrossed her whole attention.

Fanny Summers would not be put off; she caught hold of Kate's dress, and,
shaking it pettishly, exclaimed—

" I will never tell you anything again, Kate, if you will not speak to me, nor say
a word when I ask you a question."

Just at that moment Kate Heyton was alarmed by a sudden noise within the
cottage. She knew not that it was occasioned by Sandy Summers flinging his
mallet out of his hand on awakening from his drowsy fit, but, fearful lest she
should be discovered prying in at the moment, she made a backward movement,
and would have fallen to the ground had she not received timely assistance from
the feeble arms of little Fanny.

Some minutes passed before Kate could subdue her agitation sufficiently to enable
her to support herself without assistance, and to utter a few short words.

" Let us go, Fan," said she, " let us go."

" Where would you go, dear Kate?—tell me where."

" To the cottage."

" The cottage ? "

" To your father, Fan."

" A pallor overspread the countenance of the child, and her lips quivered, as she seized the hand of Kate and said—

" No, dear Kate, you must not—you will not do that?"

" I must see and speak to your father, Fanny," returned Kate.

Tears burst from the eyes of the child, and flowed down her cheeks, as in a tender and imploring voice she besought Kate Heyton not to carry out the intention which she had avowed.

" You know, Kate, you promised me not to let my father know that I had brought you here; he would beat me if he knew I had disobeyed him, though I can't see how I could be doing wrong in telling you what I did, seeing that I have always told you everything, and no harm has come of my so doing."

" Stay here, Fanny, or go into the churchyard and play with Pompey. I will go to your father as if I paid him a mere accidental visit, and will not say a word that will cause him to be angry with you."

" You will promise poor Fanny that, Kate ? "

" I have promised you. Go, take Pompey with you, and I will come to you by-and-by in the churchyard."

The child lingered as if unwilling to obey the command.

" Why do you not go, Fan?—do you wish your father to come out and find us talking together ? "

Fanny Summers hesitated in her reply. Again taking the hand of Kate Heyton, she asked—

" Do you understand, dear Kate, what it means ? " and as she spoke she pointed with her out-stretched finger towards the closed window-shutter.

" No, Fan; I do not comprehend all. But go, and I will talk to you again by-and-by."

" Did you see, Kate, the ——

" Stay not to ask questions, Fan. If you wish your father not to be angry with you, go at once, and let him not see you here."

Fanny Summers reluctantly did as she was desired. Pausing as she passed out at the garden-gate, she watched Kate Heyton make her way round to the cottage-entrance, then, calling Pompey to accompany her, Fanny bounded across the lane, and passed through the little wicket into the grassy old churchyard.

Kate Heyton went to seek Sandy Summers, in order to obtain from him the explanation of what she had seen through the crack above the window-shutter.

The door of the cottage was open, but there was a small half-door, which was closed with the intention of keeping the children of the village from trespassing within the tomb-cutter's workshop. On the top edge of this half-door was perched an old starling, that had been the protege of Sandy for many past years. So used to the cottage had the bird become, that it never thought of flying away, but hopped about from tomb-stone to tomb-stone, from Sandy's shoulder to the door, and from the door to Sandy's shoulder, as if it desired no other paradise, nor longed for any happier scene. There, from grey morning to dusky eve, would the starling watch the sculptor at his work, looking on with the air of a sagacious critic, and flapping its wings and uttering a shrilly cry of delight whenever Sandy, by one felicitous touch of his chisel, completed some difficult piece of carven work, finished off in one of his happiest moods. It may be as well to state that Sandy had certain theories concerning the bird, which he had built up from facts of his own observation. Most pertinaciously did he believe that the starling had learnt to read the inscriptions engraven on the stones, and could duly appreciate the beauty of a four-lined metrical epitaph. Certainly it was a strange bird, whether Sandy was right in his conjectures concerning it or not, for, though it never left the cottage on any one of the six working-days, it had a habit of its own, which consisted in hopping across the lane into the adjoining churchyard on Sunday afternoons, then and there to mount some moss-covered, age-rotten, head-stone, on which to plume its wing and muse for hour after hour, like another Hamlet philosophising over the remains of the "poor Yoricks" who had passed away.

The starling uttered a shrill cry as Kate Heyton approached the door. Sandy Summers was at that moment engaged in looking into the beer-can, in a vain search after that which was no longer there. Alarmed by the cry of the bird, he hastily put down the can and glanced towards the door: his glance encountered that of his visitor.

"Miss Heyton!" he exclaimed, apparently little pleased at the visit, and adding in a lower tone, "if you want Fan, she's not at home, but out at play in the fields somewhere."

"I do not want your daughter, Mr. Summers; but I would fain speak a word or two to yourself," replied Kate.

"With me! I—I beg pardon, but I have some work—I—you will excuse me. It's very warm—warmer than it's been these last ten days; don't you think so?"

Kate merely nodded assent, and then, unfastening the door, despite the impediments which Sandy Summers offered to her progress, entered the workshop.

"If you've come to see my new tombs," said Sandy, "I've some to show you which are better than any I've yet had in the shop. Here, for example, there is one that I've just sculptured for Lady Margery Mackworth's grave; and here's one for Tomkins the old butcher, who used to live in the market-place; and here——"

Sandy Summers observed that Kate was making her way towards the small door which opened from the workshop into the lesser room; he at once placed himself between his visitor and the door, just as he had done on a former occasion when troubled by the impertinent behaviour of Luke Masters.

"There's nothing worth seeing at this end of the shop, Miss Heyton. Go you and look at that stone yonder with the verses on it. Chidlins, the parish clerk, made those verses; and, I should like to know, who could make any to match them?"

Kate did not evince any willingness to comply with this request. On the contrary, she edged towards the closed door, and in a low-toned voice said,—

"I wish to know, Mr. Summers, if——"

She was interrupted by Sandy, who perceived that her glance was directed to the door, and that she cared not to examine any of his handiwork.

"Miss Heyton," he cried, "if you want to talk to me you must come to the other end of the shop: I've a job there which I must finish this week; and if I talk at all, it must be with the chisel in my hand."

"But, Mr. Summers——"

"I can't talk here; I—But Miss Heyton what do you want with that door? what——"

"I wish to know, Mr. Summers, who it is you have in that room?"

"I— in that room—I—I— it is my room."

"I know it to be so; but——"

"You cannot go in, Miss Heyton. There is nothing for you to see."

"There is, Sandy Summers," replied Kate.

"Say as you like, Miss Kate; but I tell you there is not. If you want Fan, you will find her in the fields, as I have told you before."

"I do not want Fanny."

"Then who or what are you looking after?"

"After——" and Kate Heyton whispered in the tomb-cutter's ear the remainder of the sentence.

Sandy Summers started, and in a confused manner hastily made answer,—

"Not here, Miss Kate;—why seek you here?"

"Because I know that I shall find."

"Find!—find where?"

"In that room."

"No; not in that room : there is some mistake, Miss Heyton ; you have been——"

" Do not deny the fact, Sandy Summers. I know that I am not mistaken."

" Mistaken or not, you must not open that door."

" Will you assure me, Sandy, that you speak the truth in saying that I am searching in the wrong direction ?"

Sandy endeavoured to stammer forth a reply.

" I have told you, Miss Heyton," said he, " that I can't allow you to search about my cottage. If I choose to keep that door shut, I don't see any reason why you or anybody else should want to meddle in the matter. As for what you say about——"

" Ah !" cried Kate, " will you swear that it is not as I say ?"

" To what do you allude ?"

" The room, Sandy, the——"

" Keep back, Miss Heyton," cried the tomb-cutter somewhat roughly, as Kate made an attempt to reach the door; " there is nothing but my—my——"

" Your what, Sandy Summers?"

" My models."

" And not——"

" Not there, Miss Heyton, as I have told you already."

Ha !" exclaimed Kate suddenly, without seeming to pay attention to the tomb-cutter's last asseveration.

The eyes of the maiden and her outstretched finger were directed towards the door. To her surprise it slowly opened, and stricken with astonishment she beheld——.

CHAPTER XXVII.

THE SECRET OF THE TOMB-CUTTER'S COTTAGE.

What Kate Heyton beheld when the door of the room slowly opened will shortly become apparent :—

Some two hours after the occurrence of the events last related, the following scene took place.

Kate had returned to her own home; she had led Amy into a room apart from the rest of the family, and was diligently engaged in persuading her to do that which Amy was reluctant to perform.

" I cannot think, dear sister, why you are so pressing."

" That you shall know presently, Amy. Come, place on your bonnet, and let me put your shawl around your neck. It is a warm evening, but the air may be chilly as we return."

" Chilly as we return!" echoed Amy. " Where, then, are you about to take me to, that we are likely to be out so late,?"

" Not far, Amy—not far; only to the tomb-cutter's cottage."

" To Sandy Summers'?"

" Yes. Quick ! I promised him that you should be there soon."

" Whom did you promise, Kate ? you said you promised 'him' ?"

" Sandy, Amy ; I meant Sandy."

" And why did you do so? What can Sandy want with me ? What has he to show me, or what has he to say ?"

" Much, sister Amy—very much."

" But why now ?—why so quickly ?"

" At once, Amy ; there must be no delay ; we must go at once."

" But you have not told me why, Kate; you have not told me for what purpose."

" That I have promised you that you shall know presently. But, mercy me, Amy ! I never before knew you to be so long in dressing."

" Why are you so impatient, Kate ?"

" Because—because; but come—hasten !"

" I am ready, Kate—quite ready."

" That is well, sister.   We must not tell father or brother where we are going, but——"

" Sister," cried Amy, " what means this?   Why must not father nor brother be told where we are going ?"

" They must not, Amy."

" Must not, Kate?   Why, what harm can there be in saying that we are going to pay a visit to Fanny Summers ?   Fanny's father has been our friend these many years, and we have never been ashamed of visiting him."

" Certainly not, Kate.   However, my poor, dear sister, if you will be guided by me for once, you will only say as you go out that you intend to take a ramble along the beach, and I will say likewise, if father or Frank chance to question me."

" But would it not be telling a lie, Kate ?"

" You may so construe it, Amy.   Say then, instead, that we are about to take a walk in the fields.   There will be truth in that statement, for we must cross the two clover-fields before we reach Summers's cottage."

" I cannot see, sister, why we should disguise the truth."

Kate Heyton did not reply to this remark ; but, after musing for a moment, took the hand of her sister, and urged her to leave the cottage.

Passing through the front garden they met their father, who was employed in tying up some branches of the clustering woodbine which trailed over the trellis of the door.

" Where are you going, children ?"

" Into the fields, father.   Amy and myself are going for a ramble through the hay-fields."

Mr. Heyton made some few objections ; but, yielding to the persuasions and solicitations of Kate, finally gave them his permission to take the ramble as they desired.

And onwards they went ; over fields of scented clover, over meadows where the grass was fresh, green, and wavy.   It was the beautiful evening time.   The sun was sinking to his western home, gilding as he sank the tree-tops of the distant forest, and flooding the hill-sides with a golden, fiery gleam.   Some two or three clouds floated above in the translucent ether , but they seemed more like to the bedizened equipages attendant on some great carnival than mere collections of vapour.   A dreamy stillness pervaded all, broken only by the hum of the honeyed bee as it swept hastily by, or stopped to suck sweets from some of the blooming hedge-flowers, and by the shrill chirp of the grasshopper, disporting at his pleasure in the waving grass.   The two girls passed over a stile and entered a corn-field.   There happened to be a cool, shady spot, carpeted with flowering tares, garnished with crimson poppies, and encircled by the stems of the ripening corn.

" Let us rest here for a few minutes, dear Kate," said Amy.   " I am too warm to walk farther without resting for a few minutes."

It was with great reluctance that Kate Heyton consented to seat herself beside her sister in the green and pleasant shade; but Amy was persuasive, and the spot was inviting, for a little rill of clear, sparkling water trickled by at the distance of a few feet, affording music in its flow, and thus luring the passer-by to linger on his way.   Kate took off her bonnet, and allowed the soft breeze to wanton with her shining tresses, and to kiss her beautiful cheek.   Amy saw, however, that her sister was unwilling to prolong the stay.

" Dear Kate," said she, " tell me why you are in such haste to reach Summers's cottage.   What is the purpose for which you are taking me thither ?"

" You shall know it, Amy, as soon as you reach there."

" But why not tell me now ?"

" I cannot—I may not."

" Cannot ! May not ! Kate, sister Kate, what can be your meaning ?"

" Were I to tell you now, Amy, you might——"

Kate Heyton checked herself, and refrained from finishing the sentence.

" I might do what, sister ?"

" Pardon me, dear Amy ; you might, I am afraid, act foolishly, were I to do as you wish me. Rather come with me at once."

Amy threw a distrustful glance at her sister, and then, looking earnestly in her face, said—

" There is something hidden in your words, Kate, which I do not understand."

" But which you will understand soon, dear Amy."

" Soon !—understand soon ! Kate, you make me fearful. I—I dread to go with you. I am afraid that something terrible is about to happen—that what you have to show me is connected with the recent sorrows which have afflicted us both ; is it so, dear sister—is it so ?"

" It is connected with your own present and future happiness, Amy."

" My happiness ! Dear Kate, your very words forebode something horrible."

" Not so, sister Amy ; they have no such import."

" They have, Kate, they have, or you would not look so grave ; your very countenance almost dissuades me from accompanying you."

" My countenance, Amy ?" returned Kate, endeavouring to laugh.

" Yes ; it is not the beaming, joyaunt, happy countenance which belongs to my sister. There is a cloud upon it ; it is overcast—it is indicative of troublous events and of coming sadness."

Whether voluntarily or not, Kate burst into a loud fit of laughter.

" Gracious me, Amy !" she exclaimed. " You would make me to appear some dark-visaged, repulsive villain, with a scowling brow, a grim aspect, a gruff demeanour, with a brace of pistols stuck in my belt and a blunderbuss over my shoulder. A truce to such silly fancies. Come, sister, a cool breeze has just sprung up, and our walk is now more shaded. Let us hasten on our journey."

" I know not, Kate, whether I do right in accompanying you."

" Do not be so silly, Amy," returned Kate, seizing her sister's hand, and drawing her onward. " Think you that I would willingly lead you into harm ?"

" Oh, not ; not you, dear Kate. I do not think that ; I know that you love me too well."

" Then trust me, sister—trust me this once."

" Be it so, Kate," said Amy, resigning herself to her sister's guidance, and following accordingly as she was led.

They reached the cottage of the tomb-cutter. Sandy Summers was standing at his door, apparently waiting their arrival. His favourite starling was perched upon his shoulder ; and Fanny was amusing herself by offering an ear of green corn to the bird, and then, when it attempted to seize it, snatching it away.

" Is he asleep ?" asked Kate, whispering in the ear of the tomb-cutter.

" Not he," was the reply ; " he has been expecting your coming with great impatience."

" Then he will see my sister—he will see Amy ?"

" Yes ; quick—quick ! I will lead you to him directly."

" Do so, Mr. Summers—do so."

Amy pressed the arm of her sister and looked inquiringly in her face.

" What does this mean, Kate ? Whom is it you speak of ? To whom does Mr. Summers refer ?"

" Peace, sister ! you will soon see."

Sandy Summers had left the two maidens in his workshop to go into the inner room. He was absent for only a few minutes. When he returned he did not close the door after him.

" Is he ready ?" asked Kate.

" Quite so," was the reply.

" Will he see her ?"

" Yes."

"Come then, Amy—come."

"Where, sister—to see what?"

"To see—"

But Kate took the hand of Amy, and following in the rear of Sandy Summer passed into the room from which she had been excluded only a few hours before.

"She has come," said Kate.

Amy started ; she doubted the truthfulness of what she saw ; she could not believe the evidence furnished by her own eyes.

"Ernest!" she exclaimed, "Ernest Mor—"

Put before she could finish the word, a pallor came over her countenance, her s turned white, her eyes were fixed, and she fell back into the arms of her sister.

On a bed in one corner of the room lay a young man, whose countenance was as pale as that of the poor maiden who had fainted on beholding him ; whose arm was bandaged up and stained with blood ; whose eyes glistened wildly when the maidens entered ; whose lips vainly endeavoured to articulate the word which he wished to speak ; whose whole appearance was that of blooming health suddenly transformed into debility and helplessness. He was weak ; he was powerless ; he was overcome by the event of the moment.

That young man was Ernest Morden.

CHAPTER XXVIII.

THE INSULTED AND THE INSULTER FACE TO FACE.

Through the intervention of Fanny the secret of Sandy Summers had become known.

On the night when he was pursued by Frank Heyton Ernest had fought hand to hand with the stranger who had before gained entrance to the cottage of the Heytons in the guise of a wearied traveller. The issue of the contest had been that Ernest was severely wounded. It was his blood which Frank and Archy had discovered in the moonlit grove. That blood was still warm when the pursuers discovered it ; and, though they knew it not, Ernest himself was not far distant from where they stood.

It was a warm evening, and the loss of so large a quantity of blood caused the young man to become faint, and scarcely able to move. He managed, however, to crawl into the recesses of the wood, and there to hide himself for a while, until Frank and his companion had passed by in their pursuit after the dark-looking stranger. Ernest had received the wound in his shoulder, the point of his adversary's weapon having pierced to a considerable depth. An hour passed away ; and gradually recovering from the faintness which had first siezed upon him, he contrived to stanch the flow of blood by the application of water from an adjoining rivulet, and by tightly bandaging the wound with some of the long grass which grew in abundance within the shadow of the wood. Having done this, and being aware that his pursuers were now at some distance, he arose in order to seek a place of shelter and to obtain the assistance which he needed. Suddenly, the cottage of the tomb-cutter caught his glance. Years ago he and Sandy Summers had been friends ; many a time and oft had he conversed with the carver of the churchyard monuments, and many a time had he and Sandy taken walks together in the neighbourhood of where he now was. Ernest gazed at the little cottage as it stood boldly outlined in the clear moonlight, knowing well that, could he but reach it, he should not fail to meet with a kind reception. Summoning up the little strength which he still possessed, he attempted to gratify his desire and accomplish the object which he had in view. So long as his path lay through the wood, and so long as he had trees near him, the labour was not so difficult, he being able to support himself as he progressed onward ; but when the boundary of the wood was gained—when the line of trees lay only on his right hand and his left, and he had to emerge upon the open green sward, he felt the extent of his weakness, and staggered as if he were drunk.　The exertion caused the flow of blood from the wound to break out afresh.　He endeavoured to stay it by means of pressure, but still the welling stream bubbled up, despite his efforts, and trickled over his fingers.　There chanced to be a pond in the middle of the meadow, and near it grew some large water plants.　Ernest plucked two or three

of the largest leaves, and, wetting them in the pond, placed them over the wound binding them on with his handkerchief.　It was not the first time in his life that he had been wounded, for he had known engagements at sea, and had used his own good sword, with his feet planted upon the decks of an enemy's vessel ; he was also hale, young, and had a good reputation for bravery ; but the present accident affected him much more from the concomitant circumstances than from the mere nature of the wound itself. It is when both mind and body are wounded that the man is truly overpowered; and the occurrences of the preceding evening were distracting the thoughts of Ernest Morden, while the weapon of his antagonist was rankling in his flesh. The pain of the mere wound was not the whole of what he had to endure—there was the torture of both body and mind—the torture of remembrance and of present agony. No wonder, then, that he was overpowered—no wonder that he staggered and fainted by the way.

Again had he succeeded in stanching the flow of blood. He looked up; the perspiration stood in huge drops upon his brow; the cottage of the tomb-cutter was still the third of a mile distant from the spot where he stood.

He swallowed a draught of water, and again set forward on his journey. At that moment a light breeze sprang up, and oh, how balmily did the cool air seem to kiss the brow of the fainting man!

Joy! joy! the cottage of the tomb-cutter was nearly reached—was, at most, but some twenty yards distant. Just then a fearful question suggested itself to the mind of Ernest Morden :—what, if in that cottage Sandy Summers had ceased to make his abode?

There was agony in the thought, but still the chance was great; and when the extremity is terrific, the slightest chance becomes a cable to which Hope attaches her anchor.

" Sandy—Sandy Summers!" cried the fainting man, in a low, weak-toned voice.

It was night-time; there were no lights in the cottage-window, and no sound of footsteps within could be heard. Peace and repose were within, while without were strife, bloodshed, and agony.

Ernest Morden stretched forth his hand; a sensation of floating in the air came over him—a dizziness of the eyes—a reeling of the brain, and with a dull, heavy shock, he fell against the cottage door.

The noise awoke the tomb-cutter from his sleep. Starting up in his bed, Sandy Summers listened, and fancied that he could hear the groan of some one in distress. He arose, felt his way through the workshop, opened the door, and the head of a man fell against his legs, and rested upon the threshold.

Sandy Summers was too much alarmed to cry out. Besides, to all appearance, the man was dead. Sandy was about to seek a lamp; when the moonlight fell upon the countenance of the senseless one, and the dark hair having fallen back, Sandy recognised the features of his old acquaintance.

" Ernest! Ernest Morden!" he exclaimed.

Being thus called by his own name caused the swooning man to return for a moment to consciousness. His eyes rolled, he looked up, his lips opened.

" Take me in ; hide—hide me !" he ejaculated.

" God have mercy!" cried Sandy, " what does this mean? Blood too! Why, Mr. Morden, I—I haven't seen you for years; I—but wait till I put on my things, and I will step up to the Hall and fetch your brother.'

The wounded man grasped the hand of the tomb-cutter, and with a hasty gesture, and in a low, husky voice, said,—

" You must not, Summers. Go not to Gervase, let him not know. Hide me—hide me !"

" Mercy on me !" cried Sandy, " what have you been doing? what has been the matter ?"

" Hide me—take me in—hide me !" repeated the wounded man.

Sandy paused only to light his lamp. Then assisting his almost helpless applicant into the cottage, he barred the door, and proceeded to render all the assistance in his power.

The tomb-cutter was an adept in surgery; having, by-the-by, acquired his knowledge of the art by cultivating the acquaintance of the village barber. After furnishing himself with some rags and a basin of water, he proceeded to remove the patient's coat, and to make an examination of the wound.

" This is a most awful slash, Mr. Morden," said he, " where can you have been, and what have you been doing to get such a wound ?"

Ernest shook his head, and offered no explanation.

In vain were all the tomb-cutter's inquiries. His curiosity was great, but for reasons of his own, Ernest refused to satisfy him; entreating to be concealed in some part of the cottage, and to be denied to all who might chance to inquire after him.

Sandy Summers was naturally kind-hearted, and therefore could not well refuse the request of one who was his old acquaintance. He found that it was utterly useless to interrogate his patient, and accordingly settled the matter in his own mind, by supposing that Ernest Morden had been engaged in some disreputable fray, or had done that for which justice would punish him in the event of his being detected. If this was not the case, why did he so particularly desire conceal-ment; and why had he expressed a wish to be denied to all who might come in search of him? Sandy was fearful lest he should inculpate himself by assisting his friend; but benevolence conquered caution, and he resolved to give him all the aid that was in his power, contenting himself with the belief that in the course of the ensuing day something would meet his ear, which would explain the mystery and make that plain, which at present he could not understand.

Ernest Morden was accordingly located in the inner room of the tomb-cutter's cottage. In compliance with his own request, the window-shutter was closely fastened, and, in order to gratify his wish, Sandy placed a lock upon the door, and assured his patient that no one should enter to disturb him.

During the remainder of the night, or rather the early morning, Sandy watched beside the bed of the wounded man. The warmth of the weather, the depth of the wound, and, more than all, the agitation of his mind, caused Ernest Morden to endure intense agony, and induced his injury to assume the most threatening aspect. Sandy Summers applied such anodynes as he had in his possession, and exerted himself to alleviate his patient's agony, and to procure him sleep; but a state of feverishness ensued, and the fever was heightened to an alarming extent by reason of the mental anxiety.

Sandy grew distrustful of his own ability, and suggested to his patient that it would be most proper to seek the assistance of a surgeon from the adjoining town; but Ernest resolutely demurred to this proposition, on the plea that to do so would be only to publish that which he wished should have concealment. Sandy, therefore, was compelled to exert himself to the best of his power, and use such treatment as seemed to him most fitting for the emergency.

In imposing the injunction of secrecy, Ernest Morden had expressly commanded that no intimation of his place of hiding should be communicated to any of the Heytons. Sandy, therefore, was but repeating this injunction, when he gave the caution to his daughter Fanny.

Ernest grew worse—the fever increased—delirium ensued. The tomb-cutter bent over him while in his delirious state. Muttered words escaped his lips; but so incoherent were those mutterings, that from them the surgeon could not learn his patient's secret.

Thus it was that Sandy had denied Luke Masters entrance to the room.

In the state of prostration which succeeded the fever, the patient mused upon the past occurrences of the last few days. The image of the Amy whom he had loved haunted him in his dreams, and stood before him when delirium fevered his brow, and freaked with his senses. At times he muttered her name, at times he spoke of her to himself; but whether he blessed her or cursed her, could not be understood from the indistinctness of the terms which he used. He was awake, and was musing upon the subject of his plighted love and broken promise when Kate Heyton peeped in through the chink above the window-shutter, and when she afterwards entered the cottage.

Ernest Morden heard the voice of Amy's sister; he heard her conversation with the tomb-cutter; he heard her mention his own name. Suddenly he was seized with a wish to speak with her, to ask her certain questions, to explain a portion of his own seemingly unaccountable conduct. Whether he accomplished so much remains yet to be seen.

Sandy Summers denied her admission to the room; but while he was persisting in the refusal, Ernest Morden had contrived to rise from his bed, to crawl across the room, and to pull open the door. Kate Heyton looked upon the pale, haggard features of her sister's injurer.

Ernest beckoned Kate to him; it was with a feeling of dread that she approached—it was with trembling, with faltering voice, and feeble limbs, that she had sustained the interview.

The result of the interview had been, that Ernest had desired to see Amy, and that Kate had promised that Amy should visit him. As it it was thought, however, by the tender-hearted girl, that her sister might object to such a visit, Kate had so planned it, that Amy should not know the object of her journey until she had arrived at the cottage of the tomb-cutter.

And now the wish was gratified—Amy Heyton and Ernest Morden were together —the insulted stood before the insulter.

" Amy! " exclaimed the wounded man.

" Ernest—Ernest Morden! " cried the maiden, shuddering as she spoke.

Minutes passed, and there was a deep silence. Amy was supported in the arms of her sister; the tomb-cutter was a spectator of the scene. It was Morden who commenced the conversation.

" Amy," he cried, with a choking, gutteral voice—" Amy, will you not speak— will you not speak to me for once—for the last time ? "

Amy unclosed her eyes to look upon him, but quickly closed them again, while a tremor passed over her frame, and she shuddered in her sister's arms.

Morden stretched forth his hand, in an endeavour to take that of Amy, but the maiden recoiled from his touch.

Kate whispered in her sister's ear.

" Hear him, dear Amy—hear what he has to say," said she.

Amy heaved a deep sigh, but did not speak a word in answer to her sister.

" It is well, I expected this," observed Ernest; " I had no right to hope that this meeting would be other than it is."

" What—what meeting? " said Amy, rubbing her eyes, and speaking in an incoherent manner.

" The meeting between ——" Ernest paused, faltered, and forbore to finish the sentence.

Amy gazed round the room with a wild, vacant kind of gaze, like a person who had been suddenly transported to some strange land, stricken with wonderment at his or her new position, and confused by the appearances of surrounding things. Presently, however, her glance alighted upon Ernest Morden. She started, and passed her hands over her eyes, as if to dispel some mist which clouded her sight, and gave indistinctness to the objects of her vision. For the space of a single minute her gaze was fixed upon the wounded man; eye met eye; the wronged one, and he who had done the wrong, looked upon each other. Thronging thoughts arose in the maiden's mind, her heart swelled, and her memory brought back other days to imagination's view. Like some wild phantasy of a dream, swept through her brain the recollection of days that were no more. That one look—that one gaze upon the figure of him whom she had loved, caused pictures to arise before her of what that love had been—of what the days of other years had been composed; re-opened to her view the long-closed mine; woke memory from her sleep; showed the thousand gilded things which had seemed lovely to the lover's eye; placed before her him whom she had loved as when first he clasped her burning hand in his—as when first she felt his warm breath upon her blushing cheek, and found his lips pressed unto her own. Alas! how different now! Could she believe that the occurrences of the last few days had had actual existences, and were not her mere dreams ? Could she believe that the days of love had gone, when the loved one was before her now—when she now looked upon those eyes which had then beamed so fondly upon her—when she now beheld that countenance which, to her enchanted sight, had seemed the most beautiful among all the sons of earth—when in her very presence was that one form which had been worshipped by her—which had been the idol of her waking thoughts, the ever-recurring object of girlhood's midnight dream;—could she believe with this—with these before her, that the days of love were gone? And yet it was Ernest Morden whom she looked upon; he who had taken up a knife against her, who had pressed her to his bosom one moment, and the next had cast her ' like a worthless thing away.' But this was forgotten; this became nought; this existed in her mind only as the shadow of a fearful idea, when suddenly as she gazed, she observed, for the first time, that the lips of he whom she looked upon were pale; that his cheeks were colourless; that his shoulder was bandaged—the bandages stained with blood; that sickness had swept over him, and left its trail-mark there. She was no longer the slighted maiden, indignant in her scorn. God pardon him! her scorn was all forgot. When they who love deceive, too often in the breast of the deceived does hatred find a home. But with Amy where was hatred now? No more the injured and indignant one, she felt as gentle woman ever feels towards suffering man; she saw that he who had done her wrong was weak and helpless now; could she then deal in wrath; could she turn aside, forsake, and pity not? Oh no! within her then—within that soft and winning form, beat woman's gentle heart; upsprang a woman's sympathy; and woman's kindliness awoke. More beauteous did she appear then than she had ever before seemed, more beauteous than when she first confessed her love, did she appear, when throwing herself on her knees beside him who had wronged her, and clasping the hand which had been uplifted against her, in her own, she exclaimed,—

"Ernest—dear Ernest, what means this—these bandages—this blood? Your face is pale—your lips are white—your eyes. Tell me, Ernest, what is this I see—why do I find you thus? You are ill—you—you—. Hold me, sister—hold me, sister Kate, I—I ——"

Still pressing the hand of the wounded man—still bending over him with fondness, she found herself unable to gaze longer on his face. Terror, not for herself, but for him; the dread of his being about to die; the fears that he was suffering, overcame her, and her head fell forward on her sister's arm.

Ernest turned away his face.

The man returned no answer; the maiden drew her breath with fitful sobs.

And, save the maiden's sobs, there was silence—a deep, a thrilling silence.

And the hand of Ernest Morden was held by Amy Heyton.

Still the silence continued.

Amy looked up; the face that she would have looked upon was turned from her, and he to whom she had appealed regarded her not.

"Oh, God!" she ejaculated in her agony; "this is fearful! You do not answer me, Ernest; you do not say one word!"

Ernest Morden turned towards her.

"Be seated, Amy," said he, "and I will answer you."

"No, dear Ernest, I will remain as I am—on my knees—on my knees by your side."

"Be seated, or I will tell you nothing."

Amy clasped his hand the tighter.

"Bid your sister take a chair," said he, turning to Kate Heyton.

Kate complied; and with much trouble persuaded Amy to rise and to accept the proffered seat.

"And now," said Ernest, "you wonder to see me as I am; you wonder at meeting with me here. If you would know why I am as you find me I must go back to that night——"

"That night!" repeated Amy, with a shudder.

"Would to Heaven that had never been!" ejaculated Morden; and yet——"

He paused abruptly.

"Why did you say ' And yet?" demanded Amy, in a trembling voice.

"And yet," continued Morden, " if it had not been for that night. But—but—

no matter. On that night, Amy, I knew more agony than I had known for nearly four years——"

" What knew you then, Ernest?"

" Do not ask me—do not interrupt me. Let me speak as I would speak."

" I listen, Ernest—I listen."

" On that night, Amy, I was made miserable, and that misery will probably continue with my life. The individual who addressed me in your father's cottage I have reason both to bless and to curse——"

" You knew him then, Ernest—you knew him?"

" I knew him not."

" Not—not know him?" ejaculated Amy.

" I speak the truth," returned Ernest.

Kate here interposed.

" Do you assert, Ernest Morden," said she, "that the stranger who held converse with you at my fathers, who—who spoke to you of sister was unknown to you?"

" As unknown to me then, Miss Heyton, as he is now."

" What! do you say that even now you know not who he was?"

" I do say so."

" But he spoke to you; he told you of—of—of my sister—of something—something——"

Kate could not finish the sentence. Morden assisted her to do so.

" Of something, Kate Heyton, which it was the worst of misery for me to know; and yet that which, had I not known, I should have been ten thousand times more miserable for life."

" You speak in riddles, Ernest Morden."

" Because, Kate Heyton, if I would I could not—might not speak more plainly."

" Could not! might not!" repeated Amy.

" Yes, Amy; that I could not—might not speak. On that night I followed the man you allude to when he fled from under your roof. I met him, I grappled with him, and asked him questions. I received answers which I could not brook. The wound which has thus unmanned me, which has thus paled my lip, and blanched my cheek, was inflicted by him. The contest was a desperate one—a bloody one; and this is the result."

He laid his hand upon his wounded shoulder.

Amy bent forward, and wept upon his arm. He removed her somewhat rudely.

" Do not so, Amy;" said he; " this blood was not shed in your cause—it was not shed for you."

" This is ungenerous of you, Mr. Morden," cried Kate, as Ernest repulsed Amy.

" It is not ungenerous, but just," returned he. " I would not that your sister—that Amy should deceive herself."

" It is well that there should not be more deception," rejoined Kate—" she has been deceived enough already."

" You say 'deceived' Miss Heyton."

" I said so; and had I no cause for what I said?"

" Not so much, Miss Heyton as others have—others who have been cruelly deceived.

" And who are they? Mr. Morden."

" I am among that number," replied the young man, speaking in a husky voice, and using much exertion to give utterance to the words."

Amy again cast herself on her knees and clasped the hand of the wounded man.

" Deceived, Ernest!—You speak of having been deceived. How mean you—have I deceived you?"

" Nay, Amy; I said not that."

" But your words—your terrible words!"

Again did Ernest Morden turn away his face from Amy Heyton; and again was there silence in the apartment.

Silence—silence; unbroken except by the sobs of the gentlest being there, and by the heavy heart-beatings of him whose hand she clasped.

Kate had retired to a distant part of the room, and stood in a musing position with her arms resting on a chair-back. Thoughts—thoughts which we may not mention here—were passing through her mind. She was gifted by nature with a quick apprehension, and was not dull in observation, nor slow in conception. Not a single sentence—not one half-word which had fallen from the lips of Morden had passed unnoticed by her. She had weighed every sentence, she had sought for a meaning to every syllable. By those thoughts she acted ; and we leave her future actions to reveal her thoughts, instead of stating them, and thereby anticipating her actions.

After musing for awhile, Kate approached Ernest Morden, and addressing him said,—

" I understood, Mr. Morden, that you wished me to gain you this interview with my sister in order that you might have an opportunity of entering into an explanation with her ; understood I rightly ?"

" You did, Miss Heyton, and your kindness demands my utmost thanks."

" More than that, Mr. Morden, the presence of my sister calls upon you for an act of justice."

" Be it so," replied Morden ; " will Amy see me alone ?"

Amy started and clung to her sister.

" What—what is it he asks ?" she inquired.

" He would speak with you only, sister Amy."

" With me ! What does he want with me ?" rejoined the poor girl, speaking like a person in a state of bewilderment.

" He would——"

Ernest Morden interposed.

" Pardon me, Miss Heyton," said he, " I must beg that you will not presuppose anything of that which I have to say. I have made bold to solicit from Amy a private conference for a few minutes, and I await her answer."

" You hear, sister ?" said Kate.

Amy answered with a nod of affirmation.

" My sister doubts if it be safe for her to comply with your request," said Kate.

" What has she to be afraid of ?" rejoined Ernest ; " does she fear the company of a weak and helpless man—one who is at the present moment more powerless than herself ?"

" I am not fearful, Kate," said Amy ; " I am not afraid of trusting Ernest—of being left alone with him."

" You hear her ? she consents," observed Morden, addressing Kate.

" If my sister is willing," returned Miss Heyton, " I have no objection to make, other than to doubt the propriety of the proceeding."

" You will recollect, Miss Heyton, that your sister has been brought here by you with the intent that she should hear certain explanations from me. Does not the thought suggest itself to you that there may be that which I have to say which it is fitting should meet her ear alone ?"

Kate ventured some words in reply ; but hesitated and faltered as she spoke.

" Dear Kate," said Amy interposing, " the request which Ernest makes is just—is natural. Do not wish me to refuse him, I beg of you."

" Then you agree, Amy ?"

" Yes ; but—but——"

" But what, sister ?"

" You will keep this a secret, Kate—you will not tell it—you will not prate of it ?"

" Have I ever done you harm, Amy ?"

" No, dear sister ; not you—indeed not ! You could not if you would."

" Then be it as you wish. If Ernest desires this conference with you, and if you are willing to assent to the request, then by all means let the conference take place. I will not baulk you in your wish, Amy ; be it as you desire."

" It is not my wish, Kate, but Ernest's; that which he may have to say is doubtless that which could not be told, except under the conditions named. I should reproach myself in after life, perhaps, if now I refused to accede to those conditions."

" As you will, sister—as you will. Then, if I understand you rightly, you wish me to withdraw."

" Again, sister, I must remind you that it is Ernest's wish, not mine."

" But you agree—you consent ?"

" I must do so, sister."

" And the conference——"

" Will last but for a short time," interposed Ernest.

" Well then, sister, I will leave you. Mr. Morden dare not do you harm, neither am I afraid that he will make an attempt to do so. I was fearful that you would doubt his good faith ; I was fearful that you would not give your consent so readily as you have done. I leave you, sister, and before I see you again, I trust that you and Ernest Morden will be the friends which I knew you to be only a few short years ago."

Amy hung down her head, and hid her blushing face at her sister's remark. Kate kissed that gentle sister's cheek, pressed her hand in an affectionate manner, and then left her with the wounded man.

" You will not go far, Kate ?"

" I will make friends with Fanny, in her father's workshop."

Kate Heyton departed. Amy and Ernest Morden were left together. In the one room—the one dusky, confined apartment were the man and the maiden, shut up together and alone—beneath the same roof, and surrounded by the same walls ; were looking upon one another's face, and hearing the pulsations of each other's heart, the two who had once loved fondly, but who had so suddenly and so mysteriously become estranged. He, on whom Amy had often looked with the fond gaze of admiring love, was before her there ; he who had whispered in her ears so often vows which she had listened to with pleasure, yet blushed as she heard ! he, who had clasped her hand and pressed her lips a thousand times, was before her there, and yet she felt not happy—yet she knew not delight. Nay, she rather shuddered than felt the thrill of pleasure ; she felt lonely and desolate in the presence of him who had once been to her the most plenteous company. Wherefore was this change? What was that which had wrought it, and how had it been brought about ?

They were together—the one who had vowed love, and the one who believed the vow—the one who had, apparently, acted as a deceiver, and the poor being who had seemed the object of his deceit. In one room—beneath one roof—within a few feet of each other ; yes, within a few feet only, and yet how great was the gulf which really yawned between !

They were alone—they were together; yet they spoke not, for each was too much the coward to break the fearful silence.

What were the explanations which Ernest had to give? and would he give them as he had promised ? Amy trembled ; for that which she desired to hear was that which filled her with dread.

Their faces had been turned from each other, but in the same instant they met ; glance answered to glance ; both felt that it was folly to keep so long a silence.

Ernest spoke.

CHAPTER XXIX.

LOVE AND MADNESS.—SOME OF EACH.

" AMY !" cried the wounded man, beckoning the maiden to approach him.

The summons was obeyed. Amy took the proffered hand, and held it with a gentle clasp.

" I have a few words to say to you, Amy."

" I listen, Ernest, say on."

" They may be hard words—harsh words, Amy, but you will promise to hear them ?"

" I will hear all—anything."

So said poor weak Amy, and yet she recoiled and shrank back as she made the affirmation. What was that to which she had consented? what was that to which she was destined to hear? She had given her word that she would listen to those disclosures whatever they might prove to be, and yet she knew not but that they might be more terrible than she would have strength to listen to. Ernest Morden had acted strangely, mysteriously; there must have been a cause for his so acting, and that cause must be as horrible as the effects to which it had given rise. Amy could not say with certainty that it was in her power to listen to the explanation of that cause; but yet she had resolved to summon up her strength, and use that presence of mind, which women more especially have at their command, and which they have at times the power of using to so great an extent. She knew not if in that disclosure she was fated to hear her doom; she knew not whether by it her future happiness or misery should or should not be decided; of all this she was ignorant, and yet she pledged herself to listen.

"Come nearer to me, Amy, come quite near; for I have lost much blood, and my voice has not its wonted power."

Amy obeyed, and drew closer, in compliance with the request. She crouched beside him. Suddenly he uplifted himself on the bed on which he had been lying.

"Amy," said he, in a deep impressive voice, "we are old friends; we have met each other many a time before; we have sought each other's company; we have joyed in each other's presence; but how fearfully have we been deceived!"

"Deceived, Ernest?"

"Ay, deceived. Dost thou not understand me? dost thou not know what deception means?"

"Yes, Ernest—yes," replied poor Amy, in a vacant manner.

"Then you understand me when I say that we have been deceived. Both, Amy, both. It has been a fearful and cruel deception."

Amy neither understood nor replied to the words, which had just been spoken in her hearing. Bewilderment had seized upon her senses, and for the time her understanding seemed to be reft away.

Morden perceived the vacancy of the look with which she regarded him.

"Do you hear me, Amy? do you hear my words?"

"Yes, Ernest, I am listening."

"That is well, Amy. A sad, a very sad meeting is this; it is one which I can scarcely bear, and yet one which must be."

Amy wept; her deep choking sobs were audible to her sister in the adjoining room.

Ernest continued.

"Listen to me, Amy. It is years now—long years since we first became acquaintances. We have known each other for years; and more than mere knowing, we have been foolish enough to let our acquaintanceship ripen into love."

"Foolish, Ernest, did you say foolish?"

"Ay, foolish; for this is the result."

"And this—!"

"Listen! We became lovers. And never Amy—never do I solemnly avow has man on this earth loved maiden more than I have loved you. In you—in you alone have my young years delighted; in you have I painted all my future happiness; in you have been concentred all my hopes, my wishes, my joys, my aims. You have been the one pole-star of my youth, that star, which I have believed to shine so brightly around my path, and by which I have steered my course. In the duties of my calling—in performing those duties, in pacing the deck at midnight, in standing by the helm as the ship sped on her way in the dark and silent night, my thoughts have been of you; and they were not thoughts of misery, but thoughts of the purest and most enraptured joy. When storms have arisen, when the sea has boiled and foamed around us, when all on board except myself had resigned themselves to what they believed to be their coming destruction. I alone have been without fear, I alone have spoken up cheerily, and said, 'We are not to perish,' because, Amy, I had within me the faith, the strong conviction that you and I were destined to see each other again—that we were destined to become united ; that the happiness in reserve for me was that one day I was to have the great, the truly great pleasure of calling you my own ; and thus, Amy, I believed no winds could destroy me, no sea could drown me. In the battle—in the contest, when I and the enemy had grappled hand in hand, when I saw fierce eyes looking into my own, and saw the bright keen blade flashing in the air above me, I feared not, I knew it could not do me harm. Mine was then—even then, the stout faith that we were to meet again—that I was to delight in your presence—that you were to give me the hand, which had long been mine by promise ; that we should be as one ; that you would be really and fully my own. Yes, Amy, I had that belief. Nor could the allurements of glittering honours, preferments, or rewards, drive it from my mind ; there was but one honour which I truly sought, one preferment, one reward. Yourself, Amy, was to me all that I have named. To win you was the one great reward which I coveted ; the being blessed with your hand was the preferment I sought ; your love was in my estimation the brightest honour I could gain. I tell you, Amy, that the happiest days of my past life have been those when I enjoyed the p leasure of your company, when, hand in hand, we have roamed the fields together, or when in close converse we have strayed on the beach at eventide. My happiest moments have been those when you have occupied my thoughts ; when in the happy day, or in the dreaming night-time, your image has risen like an actual presence before me. Do you believe me, Amy ? do you believe that I speak the truth—that I am not lying to you now ?"

" I do—I do !" sobbed Amy, in tones of deepest passion.

" You do not doubt me—you do not believe that I am inventing a romance ?"

" No—oh, no !"

" And yet, Amy, it is a romance, it bears all the colours of a romance. Like some impressive dream of gaudiness and grandeur—some dream of fairy lands and fairy beings—some dream of a life in paradise—some dream of tumultuous pleasure, walling up for ever around—some dream of most exquisite music, of footsteps wearying the merry dance—of laughing, gladsome faces—of flowers and festal wreaths : so passes before me now that dream of joy. All the happiness which I have known seems rather to have been the happiness of another, than my own. Oh, indeed, it was a romance—that one—that only romance which earth-born mortals ever know ;—the unequalled romance of rapturous, trustful first-love ; when to woman's glance the pulse of manhood thrills ; when the heart beats like a glad, gay, sportive thing, because it knows that it beats not for itself alone. I have loved you, Amy ; you cannot doubt that I have done so. My actions have proved it ; my words have proved it ; the emotion which I exhibit—which I cannot restrain, prove it now. I have loved you not less than woman ever yet was loved. Would to God that I had never done so !"

Amy started, and withdrew her hands from her eyes.

" Ernest !" she exclaimed.

" Why do you start, Amy ? You heard my words ; it is needless that I should repeat them."

" But you meant them not, Ernest—you meant them not ?"

" I meant them."

" Not so, Ernest ; it cannot be ! Have you not just told me of the depth—the fervency of your—your love ?"

" I have, Amy ; and I have told the truth."

" That you have loved me truly—deeply ; that you have not given me false promises ; that you have not wilfully or cruelly deluded me ; that you have not played upon me, and made me the toy with which you have gambolled and sported ; that you have not sought to make me wretched, to bring me to misery, to wrest away from me all my little joys, and leave me only a dull and barren world ; that you have not maliciously nor sinfully sought to wound this poor heart, and cause it to break, and throw a blight upon it, and give it occasion to moulder in its wretchedness away ; that——"

" By Him whose eyes now look upon us both, I swear, Amy, that I have had no such thoughts."

" Nor any like them ?"

" None, Amy—none ! Such thoughts, nor any like to them, have never influenced my conduct—have never made me the vile, the worthless being which they would have made me, had they had existence. I have sworn, and do swear before my Maker, Amy, that such thoughts, such intentions, have never been mine !"

" And yet —— "

Amy paused ; her lips faltered ; she could not finish the sentence.

" What was it you were about to say, Amy ?"

" You said, Ernest, that ' would to God we ——' "

Her voice became choked. In vain was her exertion. The words which she dreaded to hear her own lips reveal, were those which her tongue refused to utter.

Ernest Morden saw the anguish of the poor maiden.

" Amy," said he, " I did say those words—I did say that ' would to God that I had never loved as I have loved !' "

" But why, Ernest, why ?—tell me—tell me !" gasped Amy, only half articulating her words.

" You wish, Amy, for an explanation ?"

" I do, Ernest—I do."

" Come nearer, then."

" I—I— do not frighten me !"

" I will not, Amy. Let me ask of you a question. I have declared to you what my love has been ; tell me now—has yours been love like that ?"

It was a hard, a trying question, that which Ernest Morden now addressed to Amy Heyton. A trying question was it for one who had spoken and acted as he had done, to put to the poor, weak, trembling girl by his side. Well might the blush rise upon her cheek ; well might her eyes grow dizzy, her pulse bound with unequal beatings. Faint and low, and sweet was the tremorous voice in which she replied,——

" It has, Ernest—it has !"

" You have loved me only and wholly ?"

" I have."

" With your full heart, Amy ?"

" With my full heart."

" With your soul too—your deep—your inmost soul ?"

" With and from my soul."

" You have encouraged similar hopes ; you have revelled in similar joys ; you have indulged in a similar belief ; you have built up a similar faith—the faith that our love would be ever-enduring ?"

" I have—indeed I have !"

" Then as I have loved you—deeply, fondly, madly, fervently, as I have loved you, so have you loved me ?"

" Have loved you, Ernest !" exclaimed Amy.

" Ay ; so have you loved me—has it not been so ? I ask the question ?"

" It has."

" Your love has been wholly, entirely given to me ?"

" Do you doubt it, Ernest, that you repeat the question ?"

" I do not doubt it, Amy ; but it is your own admission which I seek in explanation of the ejaculation which I just now used. To me have you not given, wholly and entirely, your young love ; have you not loved me with the depth of love ?"

" Have I not loved you, Ernest ?"

" Ay, Amy."

" Why ; oh why such a question ?" cried Amy, giving vent to a sudden burst of tears, and throwing herself upon the breast of Ernest. " I love you, now, dear Ernest—I love you now ! Deeply, fondly as ever—fondly as when I promised

you my hand, I love you now. It is cruel of you, Ernest, to doubt my love
—cruel to ask such questions as you have this day asked me—cruel to put me to
such pain—such anguish—such torture of heart and brain. You have known me
for years, Ernest—for long years; you have had proofs of my love; you have
heard the confession from my tongue. There is nothing that I am not willing to
do to prove to you my love—nothing that I am afraid to attempt—no sacrifice
that I am unwilling to make."

"Do you say so, Amy?"

"Prove me, Ernest—prove me. If it be to dare the greatest danger, I will
dare it, to show you how great is my love. I am willing to do as you bid me—to
venture much for you!"

Tears of joy or sorrow—from their appearance it were hard to tell which—
coursed adown the cheeks of Ernest Morden. Amy looked up at his countenance;
she saw those tears; she felt them trickle upon her hand.

"Amy," cried Ernest, "this is madness! fearful madness!"

"What is madness, Ernest? Not the assertions which I have made; for I will
stand the test."

"Desist, Amy—desist! My blood burns! my brain reels! my senses swim!
It is madness—perfect madness!"

Amy gazed in awe-struck amazement upon the terrible expression of Ernest
Morden's features. The convulsive quivering of her muscles indicated the fearful
agitation of her mind.

She again took the hand of Morden.

"I understand you not," said she. "Wherein is the madness you speak of?"

"In this, Amy—in this! Oh, God! the words refuse to be pronounced! In
this—that between us there is a gulf which separates us, and which cannot be
passed."

"Cannot be passed?" cried Amy, in a wild scream of terror; "cannot be passed,
Ernest?"

"What cannot be passed?"

"And that gulf—"

"Is ——. But ask not to know it, Amy. Enough. I have told you that it is
madness for us to love."

"Madness! madness!" repeated Amy to herself. "What can be the meaning
of those words?"

Ernest overheard the words which Amy uttered.

"Yes, madness, Amy—madness! You ask the meaning of my words? I will
answer you. I will tell you why it is madness. That is madness, Amy, which
leads those to love each other when that love is for ever and irrevocably prohibited.

"Prohibited, Ernest?"

"Such a prohibition, Amy, as I have named."

"But—but I do not understand you—I—I—you say, Ernest, that you love
me. I thought I heard you say so?"

"That I have loved you, Amy."

"And not now, Ernest?"

"Not now, Amy, because I may not."

Amy gazed at Morden with a look expressive of mingled amazement and
inquiry. The answer which had been returned to her last question was one which
she knew not how to understand, and which she was willing to believe she had
dreamed, and not heard. What could it mean? What could its import be? The
fear which seized on the poor girl, and the fit of trembling which accompanied it, in-
capacitated her from speaking during the space of some minutes. When she was
able to articulate, she turned her swollen eyes towards Ernest, and faintly said,—

"Did you say, may not—may not?"

"I did, Amy."

"May not love!" ejaculated the poor girl.

"I may not love you, Amy."

It is impossible for words to describe the wild look of sudden amazement, the fixed stare of agonized bewilderment, which Amy's countenance expressed when the last words of Morden fell upon ear. To say that the assertion came like a death-blow were to use a feeble expression. It was as if in those few syllables some deadly and benumbing poison was contained, which had the power to affect soul or body at one time; the spell of life was broken, and happiness and hope faded like a morning mist. The agony of years is concentrated in such moments; the whole of misery is felt in the space of a single minute. What is life if love be unknown? What is there in the world left to charm us if we know that the fiat has been passed, declaring that we shall never love—never be loved? Let us be once assured that we are never destined to feel, know, and enjoy the delights of that most holy passion, then farewell to life; for to live afterwards would be but a protracted death. To Amy the pang must necessarily have been great, considering that it was from the lips of the only being whom she had loved, whom she felt that she ever could love; the words of separation had fallen; a blight passed over her soul, and happiness became but a dreadful remembrance to her.

"You may not love me, Ernest—you will not?"

Ernest Morden turned away his face, having no power to reply. In the turning away of that face Amy felt as if light itself had vanished from the earth, and that there was evermore destined to be darkness—evermore gloom.

There were sobs and there were sighs; there were two hearts which swelled with the emotion under which they suffered, and which knew then to the full the meaning of such words as agony and anguish; but whether Amy Heyton or Ernest Morden endured the most painful feelings—whether the trial was more severe to the maiden than it was to the man—whether the grief of each was sincere and without hypocrisy, was, at that moment, best known to the God who had made them both, and to whom the springs of their several actions were known.

"Go, Amy—go!" said Morden, endeavouring to induce Amy to take her leave.

Amy once more sank upon her knees.

"I will not go, Ernest—I will not leave this room until I know the meaning of your dreadful words. What have I done, Ernest—wherein have I wronged you, that you should declare that our love may continue no longer?"

"Ask me not, Amy—ask me not!"

"I must ask you, Ernest; I cannot help doing so; and you must answer me. Have I ever proved unfaithful to you?"

"Never, Amy—never!"

"Can you accuse me of having done you wrong in thought, word, or deed?"

"I cannot; I do not."

"Have I ever deceived you—ever told you an untruth of any kind?"

"Not to my knowledge, Amy."

"To your knowledge, Ernest! Do you suspect me of having done so?"

"I do not, Amy; I never have. To suspect were worse than to be assured!"

"Then why, Ernest—why have you spoken as you have? Tell me—if you would keep this poor heart from breaking—wherein I have erred, and why it is that I have forfeited your love."

Ernest Morden looked kindly on the maiden, as with some difficulty he replied,—

"You have not forfeited my love, Amy. It is not you, Amy, who have done wrong; no sin of yours demands that we should be separated for ever."

"Demands, Ernest?" exclaimed Amy, in a husky tone which seemed to indicate that her heart-strings were about to snap asunder, unable longer to bear the tension to which they were subjected. "Demand, Ernest!"

"Do not wish me to repeat the word, Amy."

A choking sensation in her throat almost overpowered the maiden's power of utterance. Those words which it was her wish to speak were those which it was torture for her to articulate. With a violent effort she drew herself nearer to Ernest Morden, and, clasping his hand with fervour, spoke in a low-toned voice, and with deep sobs which formed pauses between her words.

"Hear me, Ernest!" said she; "a terrible thought has occurred to me; a supposition has flashed across my brain, which I almost fear to hint to you!"

"What Amy,—tell me what?"

"I—pardon me, Ernest!—have you done wrong—have you done some deed which has caused this unhappiness?"

Ernest was silent.

"Tell me—oh! tell me, Ernest," continued Amy, "if you have done so, if you have committed some folly—some crime. Why should that cause us to love no more,—why should that separate us for ever?

Morden looked seriously at the supplicating maiden by his side, as in a serious voice he asked the question,—

"If I had done so, Amy—if I had committed a crime, and were to confess it, would not that change your feelings towards me?"

"Change, Ernest, change! Nay, you know not what the heart of woman is—how deeply and how fondly it can love—if you believe that so small a matter could cause that love to change!"

"So small a matter, you say, Amy; but what if the crime were great, were monstrous, were such as I dare not name?"

Amy started up, and gazing at Morden with a look of wild horror, exclaimed,—"Ernest!"

"Answer me, Amy. What if the supposed crime were of so fearful a character?"

The maiden had placed her hands before her eyes, and had concealed her countenance. Deep was the agony she felt, and torturing were the suggestions which arose one after the other in her mind. Only for a single minute she hesitated, then, bursting into tears, she threw herself upon the bosom of her young love's first fond object, and cried,—

"Tell me—oh! tell me, Ernest, I conjure you, can that which you have said be true?"

"I have made no assertions, Amy; I have but asked you if, supposing that I had committed a crime of such a character as I have described, could you still love me,—would you not spurn me from you for ever?"

"Do not be so cruel, Ernest. You know that I would not spurn you—that I would still love you as I have loved you hitherto; that I would share your misery; that I would dare the world's contempt; that I would go with you to prison; that I would suffer any indignity, undergo any scorn, if still the assurance of your live were mine."

"Yes, Amy, you might pity me,—you do not mean that you could love."

"Oh! Ernest, how cruel is this torture! Pity you! would pity lead me to share your woe; would mere pity make your sorrow mine and give me strength to dare all for your dear sake? No, Ernest; I shall not pity you when I cease to love you."

"But if my crimes be so great?"

"Would they were greater, my Ernest! that I might show to you how much greater still is the deep love which I have given to you."

"Remember, Amy, I may be the criminal which I have supposed; there may be reality in my words; there may be contamination in my touch!"

"Not so, Ernest—not so! If you have done wrong it is not for me to punish—it is not for me to wrest from you, for ever, the hope of better days. There is nothing which you can have done that I have not pardoned you already for doing; there is nothing which you can do which will ever estrange you from my love."

"Say you so, Amy?   But what if I were to tell you that I loved you not—that in my sight you are no longer lovely ?"

Amy recoiled suddenly, and for a few seconds remained like a motionless statue ; then, again throwing herself upon the breast of Morden, she replied,—

"I should still love you ; I would love you even then !"

Involuntarily Ernest pressed Amy to his heart.

"Ernest," she murmured, "it is not as you say,—you are not so wicked ?"

"I am not."

The embrace was repeated.   Amy laid her head upon the breast of Ernest, and Ernest enfolded her gentle form with his arms.   In the rapture of the moment everything was forgotten ; the past became as a dream ; there seemed to have been no intermission to their love—no cold words—no moments of anxiety and despair ; they stood together in the bright and open sunshine of happiness ; there was nothing around them to cast a shadow ; though they, themselves, projected one dark shade, which lay before them, but which they did not see.

And Amy was happy—happy, with an overflowing heart.   She had no longer a doubt ; the realisation of her girlhood's visioning was with her now ; the dreams of her youth had merged into the reality which she now enjoyed.   Her head reclined on the breast of him to whom all her young vows had been given ; on whom all her fond hopes had been fixed ; with whom she had ventured to believe that she was destined to journey through the wide and weary earth.   There is this peculiar characteristic in love, that while in the enjoyment of happiness of any other description, we know that it must be brief—we feel that it is fleeting ; but when we love and know that we are beloved, we hold the stout faith that the bliss we now enjoy shall be ours for ever.   Lovers make it their creed that time will not deteriorate their love, that the flight of years will not filch from them one particle of their bliss, that the roll of the seasons will not dull the flame, nor cause the torch to burn less brightly ; it is not for to-day, to-morrow, or the next year only, that they promise to love, but for countless years, and through unending ages.   The lover places his arm around the neck of her whom his soul loveth, and fondly, trustingly believes that the bright eyes which smile upon him now shall smile as brightly when the days of youth are fled ; and the warm heart beat as warmly when it has withstood the weary wasting of years.   Pressing his idol to his side, he whispers,—not for life only, my love—not in this life merely shall we love, but hand in hand, and heart to heart, and eyes beaming upon eyes, so shall we pass through earth together ; so shall we spend the day here, and in a like manner enjoy together the long and cloudless day of eternity.   Alas ! alas ! how many are they who, in after life, have laughed with scorn at the recollection of these phantasmata of their courting-time !   Rely upon it that of the similes to which love has been likened, that one is the best which compares it to a Highland plaid—all stuff, and very full of crosses.

Yet, let us speak reverently of love, using that reverence which we should pay to some great master ; for where is there a greater master than love, and where is there one whose sway is more unlimited?   All earth acknowledges its sovereign, the whole human race have at one time bowed to the mighty despot.   When the world was young, and our first parents walked in Paradise, they owned the sway of love ; the shepherd on the plains of Egypt, the Athenian in the temple of his gods, the Roman in the pomp of his martial triumph, all felt the bliss of loving—each knew what it was to have the head of a dear one reclining on his breast, a heart beating to his heart, bright eyes looking upon him in the twilight, and gentle lips murmuring soft syllables in his ear.   The story of love is the oldest story which this old earth can tell ; it is the story which has been told most often, which has been repeated a million times, and will be repeated a million times more ; it is the story which never tire s—which we are always pleased to listen to ; for it is the story of our own feelings, our own wild hopes and joys.

But Amy was happy ; and so sudden had been the change, so quick the transition from the depth of despair to the height of bliss, that it was a matter of wonder the heart-strings of the poor girl did not break, and the rush of happiness overwhelm her in its flow. Artlessly, yet most affectionately, she took the dear hand of him she loved, and, holding it with the grasp of fondness, said,—

"You have been doing your best to make me afraid, Ernest; you have attempted to make me believe you to be wicked and criminal; but you did it only to try me—only to test my love. Bnt were it so, dear Ernest—were it that you had spoken the truth, it would not cause me to alter in my love towards you—it would not cause me to love you less fondly than I do now. Yet tell me, Ernest,—confess it—let me know for certain that no deed such as you have named preys upon your mind—that you are guiltless—quite guiltless!"

"I am, Amy—I am."

"Thank Heaven for that! And now, Ernest—and now, there is another question, one which you will perhaps think me a bold girl for asking, but one which you must answer before I can be happy. I have told you, Ernest, how much I could dare—how much I could venture for your sake; I have confessed my inmost soul to you; there is no pain, no trial which I would not endure for you;—answer me, then—satisfy me—tell me that you love me —that you love me as you have ever professed to love me! as you told me that you did long years ago?"

Ernest Morden clasped Amy to his heart.

"God knows, sweet girl, I love you."

"As you did, Ernest?"

"As——"

Amy's head rested against Morden's breast; he had held it there with feelings of rapturous delight As, however, Amy looked up to question him as she had, her neck became exposed to his view, and the mark—that fearful, mysterious mark—was presented to his sight. Starting back as if an adder had stung him, he detached htmself from the fond embrace of the poor girl, and holding her at arm's length, gazed upon her with an expression similar to that with which a person is wont to regard some accursed and loathsome thing.

Face looked upon face; the eyes of the one gazed upon those of the other; but the eyes of both stared wildly; and the face of each was of a marble pallor. The very stillness was awful, and the scene was terribly altered from what it had been only some short five minutes before.

"Dear Ernest!" ejaculated Amy, articulating the words with great effort.

Ernest Morden pushed her yet further from him, and exclaimed,—

"Do not use that word !"

"What word, dear Ernest?"

"Withhold, I say! there is eontamination—there is crime; withhold, I say!"

Was Amy still living; or, had the sudden change in the behaviour of Ernest transformed her into a mere statue? Her chest did not rise and fall; her lips did not move; her eye-balls did roll; her muscles did not contract. Pale, startled, motionless, mute and terror-stricken, she appeared like some fair form which had been changed by an enchanters's touch, or by the power of some avengeful god. There are emotions which wring the soul in silence, and which are too deep for the tongue to express; there is a grief which cannot be painted on the features—a woe which no external signs will indicate. If mania appeared to have seized Ernest, idiocy seemed to have become realized in Amy; there was the maniacs look of wildness in the one—the idiots vacant stare in the other.

Ernest Morden pushed Amy away from him; she made some resistance; she attempted to cling to his arm, but he repulsed her harshly, and shrunk from her touch as if she were some pestilent thing.

"Ernest! what have I said—what have I done?"

"Away—away from me! I—I—come not near me, I say! I might be tempted —tempted to——"

"To what, dear Ernest?"

"For your life use not that word! it is unholy; it is worse than poison from your lips!"

"Ernest!"

"Stand still, Amy—move not from that place! I have said words which I meant not to say; I have been lured onward until I have nearly fallen a victim to my folly. I have been mad, Amy; I have uttered words in my delirium which you should not have listened to. Trust not these words, girl—trust them not! You have not believed them—you have not given them faith?"

Amy muttered an answer indistinctly.

"Speak up—speak boldly!" cried Ernest. "You assure me that you have not believed these words?"

Still gazing at Ernest with fixed and staring eye-balls, Amy repid by saying,—

"They were sweet words, Ernest. Why should I not believe them?"

"You must not; you will not dare to. They were words which had no meaning —words which should never have been heard by you—unholy words!"

"Nay, Ernest," interposed Amy; "the words were not unholy, for they spoke of love—of your love."

"Of my love?" returned Morden, with the laugh of a madman; "of my love, say you?"

"Yes, Ernest, of the love which you vowed to me long years ago."

" Love, love," repeated Ernest Morden, " it is false. I—but you did not believe me, Amy, you did not think me to be sane when I said such words ?"

" Not sane, not sane, Ernest?"

" Was it like sanity, girl ? Answer me ! was there in it even the semblance of sanity ? Madness, Amy, madness has prompted me to speak as I have spoken. Leave me, leave me at once ! let us not look on each other again."

Mechanically Amy arose. No sigh, no sob escaped her. She hung down her head, and turned her face from Morden. She stood upright ; she attempted to move forward. Vain was the attempt ; all power had left her ; she stood statue-like, as stand the marble figures of the sculptor. Suddenly she struck her forehead with her hands ; her chest heaved visibly ; her whole frame was agitated with convulsive throes ; the fountains opened allowing the tears to gush forth, and without the power of supporting herself, she fell forward on the small bed which occupied one side of the apartment.

Whatever cause Ernest Morden had for treating so cruelly the gentle being who had given him her love, it would have been inhuman of him had he not in the present instance stepped forward to her assistance.

" Amy," said he, taking her gently by the hand, " not for my happiness only but for you own also, I entreat you to be calm and to remain no longer in this room.

The maiden fell upon her knees at his feet. With a voice that was nearly choked by tears, she addressed him to whom she had given her love, and in piteous accents asked,—

" How—how have I become so hateful in your sight ?"

" No more, Amy, no more. Leave me, leave me !"

" Then I am hateful to you, Ernest ; then you do not love me. I have listened to lies ; and yet—yet no—I will not believe it ; you do not entirely hate me, do you, Ernest ?"

" So simple, so touching were the tones in which this question was put, that had Ernest Morden been the most strong-hearted of men, he could not have dealt harshly with the gentle questioner. Apparently perplexed for one moment, the next he squeezed tenderly the soft hand which he held and replied,—

" I have not said, Amy, that I hate you."

" But you tell me to leave you, that you cannot bear my presence. If so, Ernest, all tha you have said of your love for me has been untruth—cruel untruth. You have been sporting with me, and have never loved."

" Hush, Amy ! say not that. I, to my deep, deep sorrow, have love you ; and it is that which works my torture now."

" Your torture, your———"

" Nay more than torture, Amy."

" And you love me no longer ; you will love me no more—never any more ?"

A sob—a deep, heartrending sob, followed by a burst of tears accompanied the words which Amy last spoke. Ernest Morden moved aside, clapsed his hands and uplifted his eyes towards Heaven. In that hour he had sustained much, and there was torture and torment yet. His lips muttered inaudibly a prayer to the Omnipotent. His chest heaved with those quick, deep inspirations which indictate the tumult of excessive mental anxiety. Presently he turned toward Amy, caused her to be seated, and then taking both her hands in his own, addressed her in a serious tone.

" Attend to my words, dear Amy," said he—" I have owned already to loving you, and I do but reiterate the truth when I again assure that to you, and to you only has my love been given, and that love is yours now. There has been a strange fatality in our love ; for, instead of having added to our happiness, it has entailed upon us both unavoidable misery."

" Misery, Ernest ?"

" The misery of blighted hope, of irrevocable woe, Amy. I am not mad, Amy, when I tell you that there is a bar to our love, an obstacle which will and must for ever prevent our union. No indiscretion on my part or on yours has caused the existence of this insuperable bar. We must shun each other henceforth, dear Amy.—we must avoid converse with each other for ever. I cannot, dare not tell you why it is that we have thus cause to be separated ; there are stories which must not be told—there are words which cannot be spoken. It is well for us both, Amy, that the discovery has been made as it has. A few weeks later you would have been my wife, and both I and yourself would have to mourn over an act, the performance of which would have destroyed our peace of mind, caused us to execrate ourselves, and might have led to even worse results. Repine not, Amy, that we must part ; rather rejoice that this parting has been so opportunely brought about—that it has saved us from being precipitated into a gulf where we should both have perished in our fall ; it has saved us, Amy, from that which would have been worse to us than death."

" Ernest, dear Ernest, your words are frightful ! What can this mystery be ?"

" I dare not tell it, Amy."

" You must, Ernest—indeed, indeed you must. Has it any reference to this mark upon my neck ?"

" It has."

" Ha ! and do you know how the mark came ?"

Amy saw that the question was a disagreeable one to Ernest ; for, as she uttered the words, his countenance assumed a graver aspect ; his lips became compressed ; his eyebrows were drawn down ; his hands became convulsively clenched. Bending forward, he spoke in a tone very different to that in which his last words had been uttered.

" Peace, Amy ! Not one word on that subject. If you have the least regard for me, say not a single word."

" Then, do you know how the mark——"

Ernest Morden suddenly arose from his seat.

" Is this your love for me !" he exclaimed. " Amounts it, girl, to nothing better than this ?"

" Why, what have I said, Ernest ?"

" I have charged you not to utter another syllable on the subject. There are those who may tell you ; but, God knows, that I dare not do so. Desist from your inquiries—believe that which I have told you ; and, if you require proof that I am not deceiving you—that I have told you the truth, you shall find it in this :— listen, Amy ! I have said that I love you, and to prove to you that I lie not, I make you this promise—this solemn promise——"

Amy interposed.

" Do not, Ernest—do not say anything which you may hereafter wish to retract."

" There shall be no retracting—no going back, Amy. It shall be a vow and an oath. Hear it."

" No, Ernest, no ; I cannot—will not."

Morden took Amy's hand and held it firmly.

" Nay, you must grant me this one favour," said he. " Months may pass, Amy—years may roll by, yet still I can never be yours ; never shall I be able to call you my bride—my wife. This is truth, Amy ; and, as a proof that it results not from any wish of mine to deceive you, I pledge myself never to marry—never to seek the hand of any woman so long as you still live. We may not join hands before the altar, Amy ; but there is nothing to prohibit us from testifying our love to each other by one at least keeping the love of his youth sacred. Amy, I have made the promise."

" Oh! Ernest—dear Ernest ! must it be so—must we never be kind to each other—never know the pleasure of each other's company ; must I never call you my Ernest ?"

" You may do so, Amy. Think of me as a brother—a brother who loved his sister with more than fraternal love ; but whose love was given most unwisely. We must part, Amy, and it will be to the happiness of each that we meet not again."

" Not meet, Ernest !"

" Why should we bring back the memory of a frightful past, Amy? Why should we cause the wound, which [may become partially healed, to become a wound again ?"

" But not to meet—never to see each other," said Amy, in an under tone, as she reflected on the words which had been addressed to her by Ernest Morden.

" Nothing requires that such a meeting should occur, Amy. Through the future of long years we can and must journey apart ; and there is nothing to prevent you, if you feel so inclined, from seeking the love of some worthier object, and becoming the bride of another who will never cause you the torture which has arisen from the love which I pledged to you. There is nothing to restrain you from making such a union, Amy, except——"

Morden paused ; his brow contracted.

" What agitates you, dear Ernest ?"

" A thought, Amy—a thought."

" Is it a sad one that you look so distressed ?"

Ernest mumbled some words to himself, but made no reply to Amy's question. At length, grasping more firmly the delicate hand which was pressed in his own, he asked,—

" Are you willing, Amy, to make such a promise to me as I have already made to you ?"

" A promise of what, dear Ernest ?"

" Have you forgotten so soon ? To you I have pledged eternal love—to you I have given the promise of unending faithfulness. That pledge shall be fulfilled ; that promise shall never be broken. I will court the love of no other ; I will never make those vows to another which I have once already made to you. There is no selfishness in the act ; there is but a fervent desire for your happiness, when I advise you that it will be to your future comfort to do as I have done—to make a similar compact; but you are free—quite free."

" Not so, dearest Ernest," cried Amy, throwing herself into the arms of him she loved , " I am yours—wholly yours—yours for ever !"

" Consider your words, Amy. Make no rash promise."

" It is a promise, Ernest, which has stood for years."

" It has, sweet one !" replied Ernest, in a passionate tone. " And will you ratify it now—will you ratify it by making a pledge similar to that which I have made to you ?"

" What is that pledge to be, Ernest ?"

" Never to break the holy bond which bound us in our youth ; never to give that hand to another which cannot be given where it has been already promised."

" It never shall, dear Ernest ! My poor hand is yours; and if you will not accept it, you have my promise that to none other shall it be given."

" Are you sincere in that promise, Amy ?"

" What guarantee of my sincerity do you desire ?"

" This," and stepping aside, he took a small Bible from the pocket of his coat,—" this, Amy : that kissing this book, you will call Heaven to witness the vow which you have consented to make."

" I will do so, Ernest."

" And I will bind myself in a like manner. Listen Amy, I will set you the example."

And falling on his knees, Ernest Morden took the hand of Amy, and holding the book to his lips, pledged himself never to seek another for his bride, never to break that sacred promise which in his youth-time he had made. Seriously, and with solemnity he called upon Heaven to attest his vow ; and having done so, tendered the book to Amy.

" If it is not of your own free-will that you do this, it will be unholy. Tell me, Amy, is it with willingness that you make this pledge ?"

" It is my duty," replied Amy.

Using nearly the same words which Ernest had used, the generous girl vowed as she had promised, and gave the pledge that had been required of her.

"It is well, Amy; there is no retracting now. In the sight of Heaven you are mine, by an indissoluble bond, though it is fitting that we part now, and shun each other's company for all time to come."

"If it be necessary, Ernest ——"

"It is necessary—it is required of us both, Amy."

"Then be it so, Ernest. I will still love you—I will still think of you often—very often."

Ernest Morden kissed the white hand which he held in his own; then, pointing towards the door, he desired Amy to call her sister Kate.

Amy was about to obey. Ernest replaced the book in the pocket whence it had been taken. He was so engaged, when on a sudden a cry of terror escaped from his lips; he staggered, reeled forward, and would have fallen to the ground, had it not been that he was supported by the framing of the bedstead.

Alarmed by the cry, Amy turned her face towards Ernest, and perceived that his countenance was pale, that his arm had fallen by his side, and that he had become powerless, like a person struck with paralysis.

"Ernest!" she cried, hastening to render him assistance.

Morden pointed to a sealed parcel which lay at his feet, and which had apparently fallen from the pocket of his garment.

Amy picked up the parcel.

"What is this?" she asked.

"Death!"

CHAPTER XXX.

THE DESPATCHES.

"Death!" answered Ernest; replying to Amy's question.

The sealed packet fell from her hand. Amy uttered a shriek, and clung to Ernest for support.

Alarmed by the shriek, Sandy Summers and Kate Heyton hastened towards the apartment.

Ernest heard them approaching.

"Hide it—hide it," he cried, pointing to the parcel, which lay upon the floor.

With that presence of mind peculiar to women, Amy at once understood the request of Ernest, and despite her feeble state, rallied sufficiently to pick up the parcel and to thrust it under the mattress of the bed.

Summers and Kate entered.

"Sister, what has happened?—has Mr. Morden——"

"Nothing, Kate, nothing. I am quite well."

"And Mr. Morden——"

"He has promised."

"Promised what, Amy?"

"To---to---your arm, sister. I am faint. The heat overpowers me."

In obedience to Amy's request, Kate led her from the small apartment into the more open workshop.

No sooner had the two girls left the room, than Sandy Summers hastily barred the door, and then as hastily laid his hand upon the shoulder of Ernest Morden.

"Mr. Morden!" he cried.

"Leave me, leave me to myself," returned Ernest.

"For God's sake, Mr. Morden, hear me!"

"I cannot---I---leave me, I beseech you!"

"Are you mad, Ernest Morden?"

"I am, I am."

"Do you know what danger awaits you?"

"Danger!"

"Yes; listen to me. I did not know of this---I---for the love of Heaven, M Morden, hear me, that you may save yourself while you can."

"Save myself!" cried Ernest, starting up.

To his surprise, Ernest Morden perceived that the countenance of Sandy Summers was as pale as his own. Large drops of perspiration hung upon the tombcutter's forehead.

"What---what does this mean, Sandy?"

"You must fly: I must hide you. They may be here searching for you before the morning."

"They! Who?" cried Ernest, trembling as he spoke.

"The king's officer's---the men of the ship---the——"

Ernest Morden seized the arm of the tombcutter with a firm grasp.

"Tell me, Sandy," said he, "what does this mean!"

"'They are after you, Ernest Morden."

"Who?"

"The officers."

"And for what?"

"I---I---they say you have deserted; they say you have stolen some papers——"

"Papers! stolen!" exclaimed Ernest.

"Yes; they were given you to take to London, and they have found out—so they say—that you have never done so."

"Well." '

"It is the talk of the whole village. I did but step out just now for a cannikin of neighbour Seymour's ale, and there were ever so many talking about it in the tap-house."

"And—and what said they?"

"I—I didn't hear all; but I heard them say, that the papers were very valuable; that they had been given into your care by your captain, and that you had ran off with them, instead of carrying them to London as you were told. They said too——"

Sandy Summers pause abruptly.

"What more, man—what more?"

"They said when you were caught, you would be hung for it; that you would be sure to be hung."

"And what said you to them, Sandy?"

"Nothing. It was as much as I could do to keep my feet, and to make off towards home as quick as I could. I hope it's all a lie; I hope there's no truth in it after all."

Ernest Morden drew Sandy Summers towards him.

"Is the door fastened?" said he.

"Yes, yes."

"And there is no one listening?"

"No one."

Morden took the sealed packet from the place of concealment into which Amy had thrust it. Then placing it in the hand of Summers, —

"There," said he, "is that which they accuse me of having stolen."

"This!"

"That which you now hold in your hand."

With a look of horror Sandy Summers threw a glance at the packet, and then let it fall out of his hand.

"Then it is true?" he cried, gasping for breath as he spoke. "They wil hang you for that."

"Not so, I hope, Sandy; listen—stop! Can any one see or hear us at that window?"

"No one."

"I thought I saw a shade pass before that lower crevice."

Sandy Summers arose, and placed a board against the window, on the inside.

"That will do, Sandy. Now listen. Those papers are of great importance : they were intrusted to my care, and were to be delivered by me to the Admiralty Office, in London. If it were once proved that I had disposed of them otherwise, I should certaintly be deemed a traitor, as well as a deserter, and my punishment would be accordingly. Now it is for you to witness that my wound has prevented me from doing my duty, and delirious as I have been, the circumstance of this trust had entirely passed from my memory."

"I am afraid, Mr. Morden——"

"Of what are you afraid, Sandy ?"

"That anything that I may say will be of no use ; for I hear that your orders were to go to London directly, and they have found out that you went to Mr. Heyton's cottage first."

"Ha ! have they discovered that ?" exclaimed Morden.

"They have, and they say it is likely that Heyton will be called to give evidence against you ; your orders, they say, having been to proceed to London without delay."

"They speak truth, Summers, it is as they say ; and I shall suffer for having disobeyed orders. I cannot—dare not—go back to the ship."

"But the papers ?"

"Heaven alone knows what I am to do about them. It is useless my sending them on to London now—that should have been done before. Even were I well and able to do so, I could not dare take them myself."

"Then what must be done ?"

"I know not. I would I had some friend—some powerful friend who could and would intercede in my behalf."

"And have you none ?"

"Not one."

"Your captain ; he knows you well, and I'm sure, Mr. Morden, that he can know nothing bad of you. When you tell him, or send a message to him, saying how you have been prevented from performing your duty, he will be sure to do all he can for you, and, most likely, get you clear of the charge which I hear they are making against you."

"What charge, Summers—what charge ?"

"They call you a traitor."

Ernest Morden clasped his hands to his brow, and hung down his head in anguish.

"Don't be down-spirited Mr. Ernest," said the tombcutter, cheeringly. "There's nothing so bad about the case. Let me go to your captain at once."

"Not so, Summers—you must not do that ! Captain Charnock is a strict man —one who will not sanction any dereliction of duty ; there must be no going to him."

"Then how am I to help you ?"

"Listen ! Am I safe here for this night—for this night only ?"

"Quite safe."

"They will not seek me out—they are not likely to search the cottage ?"

"There's no chance of their doing so to-night, Mr. Morden ; but I must find a better place to hide you in by the morning."

Ernest grasped the arm of the tomb-cutter, and, bending forward, said,—

"To-morrow morning, Summers, I set out for London."

"To-morrow, Mr. Morden ! Why don't you know it would be death to you to do so ; it would bring on the fever again, and perhaps make a mortification in your arm. You must do no such thing."

"Hear me, Sandy Summers ! Be it at what risk to myself it may, I take the coach for London in the morning—in the early morning. Stay me not for it is my resolve."

"But your life, Mr. Morden."

"Is worthless if I bear a traitor's name."

"You know not what may happen—you may die on the road."

"My life I cannot preserve at my pleasure—my honour is in my own keeping."

"But what will you do there—what will you do in London ?"

"Carry these papers to their proper destination, and tell the truth concerning them."

"And if they don't believe you ?"

"Then must they do with me as they please."

Sandy Summers hung down his head, and rubbed his fingers on his chin, after he had heard this last declaration of his friend.   In his own mind he was disposed to consider the plan proposed and decided on by Ernest as imprudent in the highest degree, and involving very much hazard ; but he likewise was well assured that his guest meant to do as he had said, and that if not either by force or artifice prevented, he would risk his life in order to preserve his honour. Sandy having hitherto acted as surgeon to his friend, believed himself to be entitled to impose any restraint, or to tender any advice. Considering, therefore, the condition of his patient, he secretly determined to do his best towards preventing his executing the rash design which he had framed on the spur of the moment.

"Are you sure," asked Sandy, "that you have no friend in great London who could speak a good word for you in this affair?"

"I know no one in the metropolis," he replied.

"Well, and what sort of a person must he be who could do you any good?"

"He must have power, Summers—he must have power and influence."

"What, with the king?"

"It is not necessary that he should have so high an acquaintance. There are those who hold power under the king to whom I am amenable, and by whom my actions will be judged. Knew I any one who could make interest for me with them, I should have no fear; but as it is—"

Ernest Morden paused.

"What do you think they will say to you?"

"I know not."

"They—they will not punish you?"

"The probabilities are that they will."

"What!—imprison you?"

"They may do that; aye, and worse."

"Worse! Why Mr. Morden—worse!—what could they do worse?"

"That which they will do—dishonour me; and dishonour, to those who have been educated as I have, is worse than a thousand deaths."

Some further conversation ensued between Sandy and his guest, the result of which was that Sandy advised Ernest to seek immediate repose, in order to fit himself for the journey which he had designed to take. We will not attempt to describe the leave-taking between Amy and Ernest, more than to say that it passed almost in silence. Amy retired with the tomb-cutter, and the wounded man was left to seek repose.

No sooner had Sandy got out of his patient's apartment, than he drew Amy aside, and talked to her without being overheard by Kate. As may be supposed, the conversation was concerning Ernest Morden and the perilous position in which he was placed. Sandy knew well that Amy and Ernest had been close friends for many years, and therefore he did not hesitate to speak what he had to say freely, and without reserve. Amy listened attentively, trembling occasionally as the words of the tomb-cutter happened to be of fearful interest to her.

"You see, Miss Amy," said he, "something must be done. There's no telling what they may do to him. I heard them say to-day that he was nothing better than a traitor, and you know they cut traitors' heads off always, just as easily as I would chop a bit of stone. I shouldn't at all wonder but what they'll serve him as they did the great king Charles I've heard them tell of, whose head they cut off one holiday time a long while ago, when they wanted a show for the people. Then, you see, they say that he's got to do with the French, and that these papers are just what the Frenchers want to get into their hands. I'm sure if we let him go to London, they'll have no mercy on him, for London's a most terrible place. He'll be shot, or have his head cut off, depend upon it."

Sandy Summers shook his head sagely as he pronounced this opinion. Amy had listened to him with quivering lip and trembling limb; she now seized his hand involuntarily, and exclaimed,—

"It must not be—oh, indeed it must not be!"

"He musn't go to London, you mean, Miss Amy?"

"Not for a thousand worlds! There would be danger—there would be death."

"That's just what I say, and what I've said to him already," rejoined Sandy; "but he's very obstinate like, and I don't know how we shall be able to keep him where he's safe."

"Something must be done, Mr. Summers—something must be done directly."

"By all means, Miss Amy; but what is it that is to be done—what is it that can be done? It won't do, as you say, to let him go there to have his head cut off."

Amy mused for a few seconds. Then, again seizing the hand of the tomb-cutter, she said, eagerly,—

"I have thought of something, Mr. Summers; it has just come into my head."

"What is it?" asked Sandy.

"Listen. Do not let sister hear. I—" Amy whispered what she had to say in the tomb-cutter's ear.

Whatever the suggestion may have been which Amy made to Sandy Summers, it was one that caused his eye to brighten, and one which evidently met with his approval.

"That will do, Miss Amy," said he; "that is an excellent idea. But how will you contrive to carry it out?"

Amy again spoke in a low whisper, while the tomb-cutter bent down his head to listen.

"What! at night?" he exclaimed, as Amy ceased speaking.

"This night, Mr. Summers—as soon as it is dark."

"But how are we to—to——"

"While he sleeps. Hush! do not let him overhear us; that would ruin all. Be careful, too, not to let him have any suspicion about it."

"Leave Sandy Summers alone for wariness," rejoined the tomb-cutter, a grin of delight beaming on his countenance. "But, Miss Amy, will you dare to do this, or ——"

"Alone, Sandy Summers—alone. Amy Heyton is no coward, let sister Kate say what she please."

Just at this moment a newcomer sauntered into the workshop. Amy started on perceiving Archy, the idiot-boy.

"Why, Archy, what has brought you here?" she cried. "I thought you were at home with father."

"Archy wanted a walk," replied the idiot; "and Archy came to see sissy Amy home,"

"But how did you know where to find me, Archy—who told you that Kate and I were gone to see—to see Fanny Summers?"

The idiot hung down his head and was silent. Amy repeated her question.

"Archy guessed it," was the reply.

There was something peculiar in the tone of the boy's voice, and in the manner of his behaviour as he gave his answer· This peculiarity was remarked by Amy; but as the boy had many strange tricks, and was accustomed at times to deport himself somewhat oddly, his present mode of behaviour was passed over without further notice.

Why had the idiot-boy used deception? Neither Kate nor Amy were aware of it; but Archy had been a witness to the whole scene in the inner room, which he had surveyed through the chink in the window-shutter.

Sandy Summers again beckoned Amy to him.

"The boy—Archy," said he, "would it not be as well for you to——"

"Not so, Mr. Summers; I will do it alone."

"And to-night?"

"As soon as the moon is up."

They parted.

CHAPTER XXXI.

FIDDLER'S POND.

MR. HEYTON and his children were accustomed to retire to rest at an early hour. So soon as the sun had sunk to rest in the western wave, and so soon as the lesser convolvulus closed its cups, and the yellow lupins drooped their leaves, it was the practice of the family to seek their several couches. Perhaps it was this habit which had done the most towards causing the roses to bloom so deeply on the cheeks of the handsome Kate. Unlike the belles of the metropolis in our own day, the two sisters arose each morning in time to view the first rays of the eastern sun, and had half finished their day's labour and amusements before the hour of breakfast. They had cultivated this habit from their childhood, and those who have thus cultivated it in their youth, ever after adhere to it in their age. Sweet it is to feel the balmy breath of morning kiss your cheek; magnificent is the spectacle of the sun in its rising, chasing onwards the white mists which roll from before its pathway, and paving for itself a golden track through the wide-spread field of heaven. The dawn which brings light, and life, and beauty to another day must necessarily be in itself majestic and sublime; it is so, and, more than that, it is lovely. No sight on earth is comparable to the break of morning over the blue hills of the eastern world, when streaks of gold shoot forth, and intermingle with the bluest of all blue skies, and when the bright orb itself mounts to the mountain top, like a monarch regally adorned, ascending to his gorgeous throne.

But it was night; and the sun had passed to his ocean home, the stars had made their appearance, and were twinkling in their radiant splendour. There was a general hush and stillness; for man, and beast, and little timid bird had all sought, or were then seeking their places of rest; the man to dream, the beast to forget its weariness, the little bird to hide its head beneath its wing, and for awhile to cease its song. It was night.

Quiet and secluded stood the cottage of the Heytons. The moonbeams falling on it from behind, causing the front to be hidden in masses of dark shade. Two hours were yet wanting to midnight, but the inmates of the cottage seemed retired to their rest; and darkness had commenced its reign.

All was still, no lights were moving to and fro in the cottage windows, no smoke curled upwards from the chimney. The bird had ceased to chirrup; the gnat had ceased its wheel.

Presently there was the noise caused by the opening of a door—it was the door of the cottage slowly, slowly opening.

Who was it that was stealing forth at that quiet hour? who was it that was venturing forth in the chill night air so stealthily—so very stealthily?

It was Amy; she was dressed in her usual attire, and had very evidently not retired on that evening to her bed. Her bonnet was on her head; her shawl loosely thrown over her shoulders. She opened the cottage-door with caution, and when she had stepped out, closed it again with equal care.

The maiden listened; there were no sounds other than those of the plashing waters on the shore below, and the baying of a dog on the deck of a vessel some distance out at sea. Amy drew her shawl closer about her, and left the cottage.

Fleeting by, and with caution, the girl pursued her way. The same corn-fields which, in company with her sister, she had passed through a few hours before, she passed through again now. But the rustle of her garments, as they brushed against the waving corn-stalks, caused her to start; and the little field-mouse, as it crossed her path, caused her to shrink back. Nevertheless she had a task to perform requiring her full energies, and she taxed those energies to their full amount.

Some more corn-fields; then a clover-field, and then a field of flowering vetch; over a stile, down a narrow lane, and then Amy had reached again the cottage of the tomb-cutter.

Sandy Summers was waiting at his door to receive her. Ere she had gained the end of the lane he had descried her, and a wave of the hand told her that she was recognized by him.

" Have you succeeded ?" she asked.

" I have ; he knows nothing—suspects nothing."

" And it is here ?" said Amy, as the tomb-cutter placed a small basket in her hand.

"It is. Look you first, and see that it is safe."

Amy uplifted the lid, gave one peep into the basket, and with a smile upon her countenance, said—

"Oh ! I am so glad! I was afraid that he would wake; I was afraid that you would not succeed. But I must begone; I must be on my way quickly."

" I think I had best go with you, Miss Amy. I can lock the workshop door."

"You must not, Mr. Summers. You must stay to take care of him—of Mr. Morden. Some ill might befal him if you were to be absent, even for an hour,"

" Then God keep you from meeting with harm! You are sure you have no fear, Miss Amy !"

"None, good Sandy—none. I know the way well, and am not afraid to go through the wood by moonlight."

" Go then go at once. Remember to keep to your right when you get to the two tall elms."

" I will—I will !" replied the courageous girl ; and waving her hand to the tomb-cutter she sped onwards with the basket tightly clasped to her bosom.

Sandy Summers watched her on her way so long as she kept in sight. Just as he turned about to re-enter his dwelling, he fancied that he saw the dark form of a man glide out of the enclosures immediately behind the cottage, and pass off into the road, taking the same direction which had been already taken by Amy. Scarcely able to give credence to the evidence of his senses, Sandy watched the gliding form until as it passed away from his sight he became confident of its being that of a man. Somewhat astonished at the circumstance, and half-suspecting that some mischief was on foot, the tomb-cutter crept round to the back part of the cottage, in order to investigate affairs in that direction, it being the very one from which he had observed the dark form to issue. The moon was at its full, and high in the starlit heaven, albeit every now and then large fleecy clouds intervened between it and the earth, thereby causing particular spots to be overshadowed and illuminated alternately. Sandy had turned his eyes towards the closed window in the rear of the cottage, when, at that very moment a cloud passed away and the moonbeams fell brightly in that part of the ground which was immediately beneath the window. To Sandy's great surprise he suddenly discerned foot-marks—recent foot-marks on the soft earth ; he stooped down and examined them narrowly—they were the foot-marks of a man ; could he doubt their being those of the man whom he had watched pass off into the road, following in the same direction as that which Amy had taken? Sandy was perplexed, and anxious about the safety of the adventurous girl, who had so recently parted from him. A presentiment of danger near at hand came over him, a chilliness of the limbs followed ; he was irresolute as to what course he should take, and as he turned back to regain the door of the cottage he was compelled to place his hand against the wall for support.

Leaving Sandy Summers standing in a musing attitude at the entrance to his dwelling, we return to Amy and follow her as she proceeds on her adventurous journey, in order to chronicle the particulars of the exploit : which it is necessary to do as the events of that evening ultimately became of some importance.

So long as Sandy was able to keep his eyes fixed on Amy, just so long did she turn around her head at every ten yards to see if he were still looking. It was when the poor girl came to the two elm trees of which the tomb-cutter had spoken, that being the place where she was to turn off from the high road, and that being where she lost all view of Sandy Summers's cottage, that she first felt a sensation of loneliness and dread. There were more clouds in the sky than there had been ten minutes ago. The moon did not seem to shine so brightly, and its beams were intercepted by the thick foliage which over-arched the path along which Amy now proceeded witd a quick, yet stealth-like pace. The very solemnity and silence of the sheltered grove made it more fearful to the poor girl. Had the nightingale been singing in the bushes, or the glow-fly buzzing in the hedge, it would have been a relief to the monotony, and would have caused the poor girl to think that she was not altogether without company. But the dreadful, awful silence, was by far too solemnly impressive ; the loudest sound being the girl's foot-fall and the pit-a-pat of her own heart, as it beat with strong pulsations. Not even a leaf rustled in the breeze, not a bough moved to the impulse of the wind. The path was narrow, but of considerable length, presenting a perspective view of an extensive berceau, with meadows and woods in the distance, seen through the opening at the further extremity.

There were times when Amy's heart failed her for the moment, and she felt more inclined to turn back than to proceed onward ; but the task was of her own appointing, and it was one which she was determined clearly and fully to perform. Now and then a bat flew by her face, fanning her by the motion of its leathery wings as it flew. Then again large beetles knocked against her in their flight, while the sudden outcry of an owl, which had esconced itself in an adjacent barn, caused poor Amy to start with alarm, and caused the cold clammy perspiration to burst out upon her brow. Still forward—forward with the little basket clasped to her bosom. The middle of the avenue was gained ; at a short distance was the stile over which she was to pass.

And forward—forward again, regardless of the horrors of the way, regardless of every threatening danger. Pleasant enough was such a path to travel in on a summer's noon, pleasant enough to the wanderer by the broad daylight ; but to a maiden, young and unprotected, journeying there by the light of a clouded moon, it was far from pleasant ; fancy, of its own accord, investing it with a thousand objects of terror. Each quaint and ancient bough became as if it were some living, hideous form ; each gnarled oak, some crouching group of ill-doers ; each moss-covered sturdy pollard in giant form, gaunt, and grim, and frightful. Not knowing how else to dissipate or keep down her rapidly increasing terror, Amy closed her eyes so as to shut out the view of surrounding objects, and hurried on without glancing to her right hand or her left. In such cases, however, the more terror is attempted to be kept down, the more intense it grows : so it was with Amy ; her very efforts at bravery caused her fear to become greater, and the more she kept her eyes from looking round her, the more frightful things did she fancy were besetting her path. As she was about to turn off to the stile a sound as of a distant foot-fall fell upon her ear and arrested her attention. Pausing for a moment, she listened attentively, and again was she convinced that some one was coming up the avenue, that she was not, as she had supposed, entirely alone. Her agitation increased to a fearful pitch, nearly paralysing her limbs, and in that way divesting her of all power, either to advance or retreat. It was with an effort of desperation that she clambered over the stile, and entered a thickly-wooded plantation. Through this plantation her course lay, and still, as she moved forward, she again and again fancied that she heard footsteps in the rear. A series of questions was instinctively presented to her mind. Whose footsteps were they? was it the footsteps of a man, or of some straying animal ?—of friend, or of foe ?—or of one who would not offer insult to an unprotected maiden, or of one who would use the opportunity for the committal of a deed of sin? Each and all of these were questions which Amy could not answer—were questions, which were actual terror in themselves. In vain all pausing to conjecture ; in vain all halting to look behind. To stand still, were to die ; to turn back, were to make the danger doubled. What, though the path was long and dreary? Amy knew that she must not—dare not pause ; she knew that all her courage was required, and that it was no time or place in which to play the woman. Still onward she sped—onward—

———" along the lonesome road
She walked in fear and dread,

> Not daring to look back, but on,
> And turned no more her head,
> Because she knew a frightful friend
> Did close behind her tread."

Having traversed the plantation, Amy emerged into an open road, which led by a somewhat circuitous route to the back of Warranton Hall. As this road was only used by people passing to or from the Hall, it was at the present hour very lonely, being apparently untrodden by any other feet than those of Amy. Rejoiced that she was well out of the plantation, the poor girl pursued her way along the road with increased speed. There were but few trees on either side of her for the space of some sixty yards, while above, the silver moon shone with its wonted brilliancy. In the intention, however, of making her journey as short as possible, Amy determined to turn off into a small wood on her left hand, and by taking her course through that, avoid a considerable bend of the road. She hesitated but for a single minute, than dashing boldly into the wood, ran as fast as her feeble strength would allow her to.

If night be solemn and impressive on an open plain, how much more so is it in an antique wood ; the trees tell of another age—of an age, when they had their birth in the world's younger day. Fancy peoples, and ever has peopled the massy gloom with gliding forms of fairy things, of gnomes, of satyrs, and of elfin tribes. Strange faces seem to peep from between the entangled boughs, dark beings seem to tread in the yet darker shade ; the rustle of the leaves is startling to the ear of the lonely wanderer, the low moaning of the wind comes like the death-wail of a spirit. All is gloom, and impressiveness, and deep—still deep solemnity.

Bold and adventurous as Amy was, she could not help a shiver of fear passing through her, as she took her away between the trunks of the tall and thickly-leaved trees. She had often, in company with her sister, with Frank, ay, and more than once with Ernest Morden, traversed that same path when seeking shelter from the heat of a noon-day sun. Every step of the way was well-known to her, but the darkness and her own excited fancy, caused strange forms to gather around her, and caused her to discern appearances, which she could not recollect having before observed. Suddenly, she came to a pause, and her fear became doubled.

Why did poor Amy listen so breathlessly? why did she bend forward, and clinging to a projecting stump for support, gaze so intently through the shadowed gloom ?

She looked, she listened. All seemed still and quiet; yet was she confident that she had seen a human form glide between the trees at some short distance before her. Whose could that form be, and was it any one who was following her to do her harm ? Was it the same individual whom she believed had been behind her in the avenue, where she had on that evening first felt fear ? For the moment, her courage failed her, and she was irresolute whether to go or not ; but again the recollection of the important nature of her enterprise came to her mind, and she determined to dare all at every hazard.

Once more she proceeded onwards, keeping her gaze directed to that part of the path along which she had yet to take her way. The figure whose movements had caused her such sudden dread, was no longer to be seen ; but something seemed to whisper in Amy's ear that it was hiding behind a tree. Still she could not, dared not pause. Once she halted as she imagined that she heard a footstep ; but the recollection of Ernest Morden's position came into her mind, and she involuntarily ejaculated,—

" He will die, or be dishonoured, if I do not save him ! Poor Ernest would once have done as much for me."

This thought inspired bravery—the woman's love conquered the girl's fear. Amy increased her speed and fortified her resolution.

The maiden now approached a part of the wood, where, not many feet from the path which she had to traverse was a large and deep pond, the water of which was covered with floating duck-weed, with the delicate flowered zanichellia, and with the white and greenly water-lilies ; that part of the pond, however, which was nearest to the footpath was not so covered, owing to the water there being continually disturbed by the children who were wont to dibble in it on returning home from school. The pond itself was of large extent, and was fed by a bubbling spring. Thickly over-canopied as it was with green boughs, there was yet space enough for a single ray of moonlight to break in, and kiss the water-lilies, and make shadows here and there. So secluded, so still, so flower-decked as the old pond was, one would have thought that it was the most pleasant object in the whole neighbourhood—that lovers there delighted to roam together, hand in hand, unobserved by the common world : that there meditative men chose to wander and to muse in the shade of evening; and that there by its side maidens loved to saunter. Not so; the place was in the gloomy hours shunned by all who knew it; no one would pass that way after nightfall ; no one would venture along the path which led by its side after the evening shadows had descended, unless they had company with them on the way, and unless they had good reason for not taking the road.

Why was it that the old pond was so much dreaded—and why was it that Amy shuddered when she first caught sight of the single moonbeam glittering on the motionless water ?

It was called " Fiddler's-pond." The story connected with its name being this : —Some years ago an old, half-blind fiddler had attended at a scene of revelry which had been enacted at the adjacent Hall. The old musician had long been an especial favourite with all who knew him; he having been without a doubt the merriest, best-natured, light-heartedest old man that the village had ever produced. It so happened that on the particular night in question, the fiddler had used his bow even more vigorously than was his wont, and it also so happened that to keep up the vigour of his movements, he had imbibed a more than ordinary quantity of good October ale. At the breaking up of the revel, he had departed for his home bearing with him his fiddle and a bottle of wine, wherewith he was to make his heart merry at his pleasure. Many and urgent had been the pleas of his acquaintance, to dissuade him from venturing home at so late an hour of the night. Old Thomas paid no regard to their pleas and representations, but determined to go to his home. At that home he never arrived. Day after day passed, and no one had seen the fiddler, or could give any account of his whereabouts. Week after week went by, and still his fate was a mystery to all. At length, on one fine autumn evening, some children chanced to be playing beside the shaded pond on the confines of the small wood ; while they were thus playing, their attention was arrested by something which they saw floating on the surface of the pond. As they perceived it to be something extraordinary, and were desirous of knowing what it really was, they collected stones and threw them into the water, so as to cause the floating object to approach the water's edge. Their consternation was naturally great when they ascertained this object to be the form of a human being. The whole village was at once alarmed, and the dead body being drawn out, there was proof positive in the clothes of its being the body of old Thomas the fiddler. Although, however, the pond was dragged, and a diligent search made, no vestige of his fiddle, his bow, or the bottle of wine with which he had been furnished could be brought to light. The unanimous conclusion therefore was, that he had been robbed and murdered while passing through the wood—that the wine and the fiddle had been stolen, and that he himself had been thrown into the pond. The circumstance constituted the whole talk of the village for many months, and ever afterwards was the pond in which the drowned fiddler had been found avoided by timorous maiden and by village youth ; they liked not to pass by it alone even in the daytime, and at evening they were not bold enough to venture near.

Amy knew the story; she knew that the pond was reported to be haunted, and that there were those who affirmed having seen at evening the form of the old fiddler dancing, capering, and playing around the bank. Some said that his ghost howled nightly in concert with the howling wind ; and others declared that the strains of the plaintive fiddle had lured travellers into the recesses of the wood, and that they had been never more heard of. The recollection of all these reports rushed upon Amy's mind so soon as she approached the spot. What to do she knew not; her fear was involuntary and could not be suppressed, while duty urged her forward. She turned away her eyes from looking in the pond, for her shadow in the deep water seemed to her like a grim companion walking by her side. On she went, but having her eyes partially closed, and her mind being too much agitated for her to attend to her footsteps, she suddenly found herself treading on

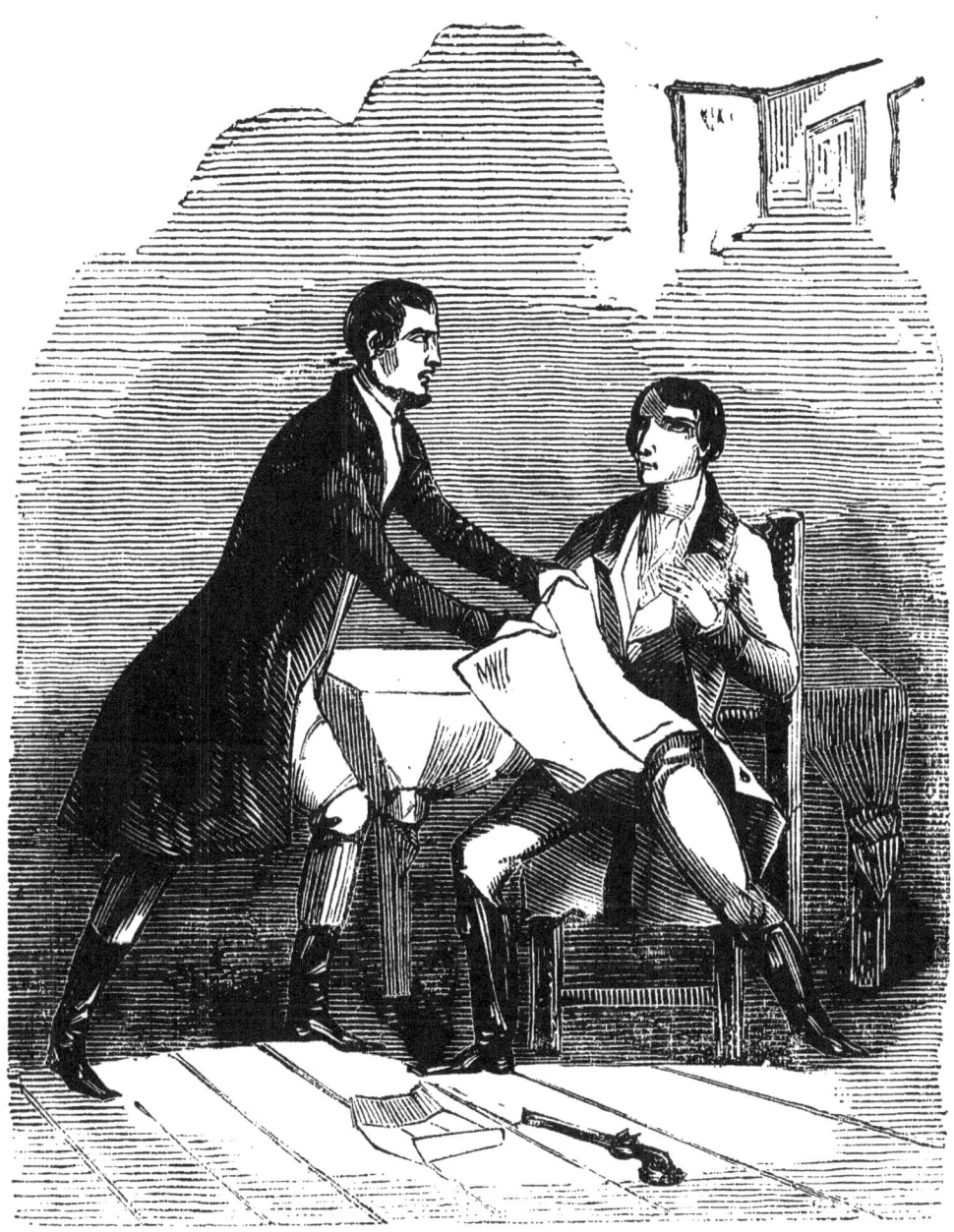

the very brink of the pond. Feeling that she trod in water, she opened her eyes with a start. As she did so her glance fell on the water, and she saw that there which struck her with terror, so that she with difficulty kept herself from falling.

She could not move; she had not the power to speak; fixedly and wildly her eyes glared upon the sleeping water.

There were two shadows on that water—two shadows of two persons; one was the shadow of herself, and the other the shadow of a man—of——

CHAPTER XXXII.

THE SHADOW BY FIDDLER'S POND.

Amy saw the two shadows; her strength fled from her; she glanced round and beheld the face of one whom she dreaded, and who, in her sight, was as dark as the shadow which his form cast in the water of the pond.

With a faint shriek which reverberated through the depths of the else-silent wood, poor Amy stumbled, and fell senseless upon the ground.

A man stepped forward and endeavoured to save the maiden from falling, by catching her hand. Failing, however, in the attempt, he bent down beside her, and gazed on her face. There was prostrate beauty and triumphant darkness; for the countenance of the man wore a smile of triumph, though that of the maiden who, characterised by features wearing the air of pale fear and settled aversion, her lips were open, and drawn to one side; her eyes were fixed, and rolled outwards; her eye-lids retracted, and every muscle of her countenance so disposed as to represent the passion of fear; yet all so motionless, so fixed, so rigid, that for the while the face of the maiden appeared like that of one who had been suddenly transformed to stone by the power of some fell enchanter, just as the characters are represented to become in the opera of Oberon, when the magic trumpet is blown by Sir Huon.

Silently, and with an expression of mingled triumph and scorn, the man regarded the countenance of the maiden. Presently he crept towards the edge of the pond, and procuring some water, sprinkled with it the face and the neck of the senseless girl. Minutes passed, and Amy regained her consciousness. Looking up, she saw that she was supported by the arms of the man who had caused her fear, and that his eyes were attentively watching her own, sparkling as if in fiendish triumph. Amy shuddered, turned away her face, and attempted to regain her feet.

As the poor girl turned aside her head, she caught sight of the gloomy wood, and of the dark, weed-covered pond beside which she lay. Instantly her true position was revealed to her, she saw clearly in what circumstances she was placed. Her limbs trembled, and her lips quivered as she beheld the water by her side, and felt the pressure of the man's hand upon her arm. In vain she endeavoured to cry out; her tongue was paralysed, as much so as if its nerves had been severed; in vain she endeavoured to rise, fright had divested her of nearly all muscular power, while over her crept a cold, chilly sensation, causing the blood to recede towards her head.

Aware of the maiden's helplessness, the man took her hand, pressed it, and raised it midway to his lips. As she felt the pressure upon her fingers, a shudder passed through poor Amy, as if some deadly reptile had crawled across her hand. The man paused in his intent, and, carrying the prostrate girl to a bank at a short distance, placed her on the green sward in a half-sitting posture.

"Luke—Luke," muttered plaintively the poor girl—"you will not harm me, Luke Masters?"

"Why do you ask me that, Amy Heyton?"

"Because I am afraid—I——"

"Afraid of me! And havn't I been doing all I could to serve you—havn't I followed you to——?"

"Followed me!" ejaculated Amy in terror.

"Ay, of course I have."

Amy contrived to raise herself up, so as to grasp the arm of Luke Masters. Regarding him with a fixed gaze, she asked,—

"Do you say you have followed me, Luke Masters?"

"If I hadn't, how would it have happened that I should have been here to have helped you now;"

"But why—why have you done so?"

"Why did I follow you, Amy? Come, that's a strange question for you to ask of me. Do you suppose if I saw you going along a lone road, I could let you go by yourself? Do you think that when I caught sight of you entering this wood, I could let you go through it alone ? No, Amy Heyton, you ought to know Luke Masters too well for that. I shouldn't have believed that you'd have harboured any such hard thoughts."

" I have not, Luke, I only wondered how you came to know that—that——"

" How I knew that you were out to-night, I suppose, Amy. Well, never mind how that came to be. You see I did know it, and of course as I did know it, I couldn't do anything less than take upon myself to watch you, and to see that no harm came to you on your way. I didn't offer myself to be your companion, and I didn't let you know that I was following behind, because I was pretty well aware that you have a dislike for me, and cared more for my being away than for my being near you. Of course I knew you hated me——"

" Oh!—Luke—Luke, do not say such frightful words. I never hated you ; I have never—never said so !"

" But you don't like me, Amy ?"

" I have told you often that it is not in my power to regard you as you would wish me to."

" Well, it comes to the same thing after all, Amy. I'm no friend of yours, and I know it ; but I can't help that. I don't know exactly what I've done to make you have such a spite against me, Any one would think I was something very bad—something worse than any mortal thing that ever breathed."

" Indeed—indeed, Luke, you wrong me. I have never had such hard thoughts of you. Never, in word or act, have I given you occasion to think that I hate you. If I cannot be so friendly with you as you wish, it is because there are numerous circumstances which compel me to treat you as I do."

" Humph, Amy ! and one of the circumstances is, I suppose, because I have got a bad name in the village, for which it seems I have to thank my enemies."

Amy was silent.

" Well, I've got a bad name I know," resumed the man. " Perhaps it's not all lies they say of me either. But there's some who like to shew their spite, in saying things behind a man's back, which they wouldn't have the courage to say in his face. There's some who call over Black Luke Masters, and there's some who wouldn't mind making me out to be a thief, or a murderer, or something worse than either of those. Of course I don't know which you give in your word for ; nor whether as how you think me to be quite the sort of character they make me out."

" I do not, Luke—I do not indeed ! Not one half of the common reports of the village do I give any credence to."

" One half, eh ? Well, I suppose you take your share in thinking with most of them. Let that be as it may. Black Luke Masters, as they call him, may pay them back in their own coin one of these days ; that's all to come, however. But to go back to what I was saying. It wasn't likely when I saw you taking this dreary walk that I should let you go all alone. Luke Masters may be Black Luke Masters perhaps, but he's not hard-hearted for all that. No, no, I followed after you to see that no harm should happen ; and it was well I did, for if I hadn't, you'd have had no one to have picked you up when you fell down, and you'd have had no one to take such pains to get you well again as I have taken. I don't know for certain, but I dare say you've no thanks to give me for it. I don't want any however, I haven't expected any. I should be a fool if I expected any thanks from you, Amy Heyton."

" Oh, say not so—say not so, Luke ! Indeed—indeed you are mistaken. Heaven witnesses that I have no ill-will towards you !"

" Ill-will—and what should you have ill-will towards me for, or why should any one else ? I am a man, like the best of them ; but because my parents were not quite so well off in the world as the rest of those who lived in the village, they looked down with their scornful eyes upon me. And then, when my poor mother sent me to the village school, and spent every penny of her earnings to keep me there, they turned up their lips at me, and the schoolmaster made me his whipping post to practice on, because I was the poorest child there. Many a time did I vow to have my revenge for it, many a time had I vowed that in the hearing of all. So at length when the old school-house caught fire, and when the bright flames rose up and licked the sky, they looked on and said—"It is Luke Masters's doing—it's the son of old mother Masters who has set fire to the school-house." Luke Masters was there, he stood up on the high bank, and saw the flames flash upwards, and watched the play of the fire, and laughed as he heard the crackling of the beams, and the crash of the falling timbers. There was a child there—a niece of the old schoolmaster; the old man loved that child, I have seen him seat her on his knees, press her head against his breast, play with her flaxen hair, and bend his wrinkled face down to kiss her rosy cheeks. Well, the child was in the burning house, and the old man stood without; he heard her scream, he tried to rush forward into the flames. "Save her—save the poor child, save my Nelly!" he cried. "And I heard him cry, and I stole up to him, no one noticed me in the noise and the confusion, and I whispered in the old man's ear 'Luke Masters sees you now, Luke Masters remembers how you treated him, and he laughs.' Yes, and the old man remembered them, for bitter was the look he turned upon me. At that moment little Nelly cried out. 'Save her—save her!' shrieked the old man in his agony. Ha! ha! ha! I laughed. But at that minute a man rushed into the burning house, risked his life, caught the child in his arms, and bore her through the flames. And Luke Masters heard the old man contínue to moan and weep; he heard him continue to shriek for some one to save the child. Many minutes passed before the old man found that child safe on the green sward at the back of the house. He asked her how she came there; she said that she had been rescued by a man, but who that man was her fright had prevented her from knowing. Then fell the old man on his knees upon the grass, and with his hands uplifted to heaven, he blessed the man who had saved that gentle child, albeit the name of the man was to him unknown. And the fire burned brighter, and the walls toppled down, crash went the old chimney, up—up into the night air capered the dancing sparks. Presently the back wall fell in upon the burning ruins. There was one crash, one fountain of sparks, and all was dark and desolate. The old man shrieked as he saw the last brick fall; yet at the same time he pressed the child to his breast. Luke Masters stood upon the high bank and laughed; a loud laugh was his, and many eyes were at once turned towards him. Then the old man arose, and creeping towards his friends, whispered—'Luke Masters has done this; it is he who has set my house on fire.' There was a screech, and there was a cry. Luke Masters fled; and as he outstripped those who pursued him, he heard their curses far, far behind. Still to this day, do they say that Luke Masters burnt the old school-house; but they cannot prove it; and Luke Masters does not trouble himself to tell them they are liars. He has heard that old schoolmaster curse him; he has seen the flaxen-haired child—who is now a woman pass by him with a shudder; and yet, Luke Masters it was—Black Luke Masters, who saved that child from the fire, and who wept with joy himself, when he saw the old man press her again to his breast."

"Oh Luke, Luke, was it so, did you save Nelly?"

"Luke Masters doesn't brag of his good deeds, Amy. He can hate, and he can revenge; he would have loved too, if—if—"

"You will let me go on my way, Luke. I am afraid to stay longer here in the wood."

"Is it the dark wood, or Black Luke Masters you are afraid of? Like the rest of them, you believe me to be some fiend, some devil, I suppose."

"Not so, Luke. I never had such hard thoughts of you. And now—now that I know it was you who saved little Nelly——"

"Silence, Amy Heyton! not a word of that to any one. Hark you! that is a secret which I have told to you only, and never must it pass your lips."

"Why not, Luke! If it be known, people will think better of you."

"What cares Luke Masters how they think of him? Let them call him 'Black Luke Masters' if they will. There is only one man who dares not do so to Luke Masters's face?"

" And he——"

" Is Ernest Morden; the hard-hearted, iron-souled, unfeeling Ernest Morden."

"Luke—Luke Masters ! I beseech you do not use such words ; do not speak so harshly—so cruelly of Ernest Morden !"

" Harshly, cruelly—eh ? You plead for him then ? Hark you! I would as soon trample on that man as I would upon this stone on which I now put my foot. Think you if he were in such a fire as that of the school house I would stir one step to his rescue ? No, no, Luke Masters remembers too well."

" For Heaven's sake I implore you not to speak so horribly !" cried Amy, in affright. " Your words chill me; they make me tremble ; and as I hear them my blood seems to run back to my heart in ice-cold streams."

" And how must I feel then, I——I, Luke Masters—the man to whom Ernest Morden never spoke but once, and then to put a blight upon one for ever ? I curse him, girl ; I curse him as being a strong-hearted villain !"

" You mistake, Luke. Ernest Morden is not that which you——"

" Silence, Amy Heyton ! Plead not for him. There are wrongs that I can forget, and injuries that I can forgive ; but the ill which Ernest Morden has done me lives— do you understand me ?—lives here, in my brain—my burning brain ; it lives, and rankles there. Were I bidden by Heaven to do so, I could not forgive him !"

" But why, Luke——"

" Hark you ! It was the night before that of my poor mother's death ;—and let them say what they please of Black Luke Masters, they cannot say but what he was always kind to his poor old mother—it was on that night, and the snow lay thick on the ground, and there had been a hard frost for three weeks past. My poor mother lay on her straw bed, and she had been so ill for the month before, that she hadn't earned a penny. I, too, because of the frost, couldn't get a job of any kind to do. The cheeks of my mother were wan and sunken, her eyes were hollow and lead-like in their look ; nothing had she eaten for days before ; and as I stooped over her bed she muttered feebly to me that she thought she could eat a small piece of fowl if she could but get it. To hear her say that, and not to know how to procure for her what she wanted was worse than madness. I thought for a few minutes, and I determined, that come what might, if Luke could prevent it, his mother should not die. I stole out of the cottage as my mother fell into a doze. It was, as I have said, a bitter cold night, aad the snow was coming down in flakes. I hesitated what I should do ; and I recol ected that Lawyer Grabble, who lived in the large white house on the right as you go towards Darlingham, had a stock of young fowls. I knew very well he was not the sort of man who was likely to give me one if I asked him, besides, who would have given anything to Luke Masters, except a horsewhipping, or a place in the stocks ? It was near midnight too, and that again made it useless for me to think of begging anything from the lawyer. Well, I thought and I thought, and at last I determined to go and see if I couldn't lay hands on one of the young chickens, come what would of it. There's no one can tell the exact sort of feelings I had at that moment ; and if there is any one who thinks that Luke Masters went about his job with a bold heart and an untouched conscience, Luke Masters tells him he lies ; for never had Luke before then taken anything to which he had no lawful right. To cut my story short, Amy Heyton, I crept into lawyer Grabble's hen-roost and stole the fowl—it was a young pullet, and I took the poor thing off its perch while it was asleep. Few know, or can guess how I felt while I was about the act. That, however, is gone by. Well, I had got the fowl under my coat, and was going along home with it as quickly as I could ;—somehow or other I hadn't been bold enough to wring its neck, as I should have done, I hadn't strength enough in my trembling hands —on the way I met this Ernest Morden ; he knew me—every one knew Luke Masters. A sort of feeling that I had wouldn't let me touch my hat to him, as I otherwise should have done ; but I crept along in the shadow of the edge. Just as I was about to pass him the poor fowl cried out, and endeavoured to get loose. Ernest Morden stopped, and seeing that it was me, caught me by the arm, and said—' Luke Masters, whose fowl have you there?' Well, I trembled so that I could not think of an answer to give him.   He pulled open my coat, and seeing the pullet, said—'you have stolen that fowl, Luke.'   'I have,' I stammered. ' Where from?' he asked.   I told him where ; and then, looking at me sternly, he asked me if I knew what the punishment for such a crime was.   I fell upon my knees, told him why I had stolen the fowl, told him how badly my poor mother was, and begged he'd not say a word about meeting one.   'You had better carry it back to the hen-roost,' said he ; then, without giving me a promise as to whether or not he would keep silence, he walked on.   I hesitated what I should do. Examining it, I saw that the poor fowl was dead, having died because of the tight grasp witn which I had held it.   I thought it would be doing no good to lawyer Grabble to take him back his dead bird : and I remembered the state of my poor mother.   With that I went home, plucked the pullet, prepared it, and placed it on the fire.   After I had cooked it, my poor mother was too ill to make any inquiries as to where I had got it from ; and she could only drink a few spoonfuls of the broth—litttle did she think the pain I had gone through to procure those few spoonfuls for her."

Luke Masters paused to wipe with the sleeve of his coat the tears from off his cheeks.   Still, with a firm grasp, he retained his hold of Amy's hand: she, poor girl, terrified and anxious, besought that she might be allowed to go on her way.

" Not yet, wait!" replied her detainer, " you have not heard me out, Amy."

" Forgive me ! I—I do not call up old grievances."

" Old grievances, Amy Heyton ; that which keeps fresh in my memory will never grow old.   Lawyer Grabble missed his fowl and made inquiries about it. Ernest Morden told him who the thief was.   That day—that very day I was taken off to prison, never to see my mother more—she died that night.   When I heard of my mother's death—while I underwent the long imprisonment which I had, my heart grew steeled ; the fire burnt steadily in my brain ; I swore to have my revenge on Ernest Morden ; I cursed him with the bitterest of curses.   Before then I was but a wild and wayward boy—now, they call me Black Luke Masters—Black Luke—Black, ha! ha!   Well, perhaps the name is a good one, perhaps it suits better than another, would, Black Luke I may be ; but how did the blackness come ?   It came in the prison ; it came when I heard the clank of the chains which bound my legs to the stone floor ; it came when I felt that I was an outcast—a reprobate—a something that everybody would hate and shun.   They might have done what they pleased with me before, but I became what I was to be then.   In the prison, with his fierce thoughts for his friends, Luke became, Black Luke Masters; and for that, he has to thank none other than Ernest Morden."

" No, no—not him.   He did, but as duty compelled him to."

" Hush, Amy Heyton, it is well for you to say that ; but I tell you it is cant—cant, girl—the cant of the heartless world, that will not take the trouble which it can pass over by the use of such lying words.   God help those who have made it out to be their duty, to send a poor starving youth to prison ; many have been the hearts they have hardened—many the villains they have made !   Had Ernest Morden given me a shilling on that night, and have gone back with me to my poor old mother's cottage, I should have placed the fowl back in the roost, have bought another one ; never have been called a thief; never gone to prison ; never been a villain now.   But this is foolish talking ; they would call me ' Mad Luke' if I preached it to them ; forgetting that money and kindness are as much duties as justice is. Ernest Morden has made me what I am, and for that he has to answer."

" You would not do him harm, Luke—you would not——"

'Ha ! you plead for him again. Yes, yes, I had forgotten.   You are his sweetheart—his wife that is to be."

Amy shuddered as she replied, " Ernest is my friend, Luke."

" Your friend—your lover you would have him to be, Amy Heyton, but he has deceived you just as much as he was cruel to me."

Amy rose to her feet.   " This of Ernest!" she exclaimed.

" Yes—of Ernest Morden. And you know it, Amy Heyton, you know that he has been duping you, and that at this moment he does not love you."

" Not Ernest—not Ernest !" ejaculated Amy, turning very pale, and struggling to free herself from the grasp by which she was held.

" Yes, of Ernest—of Ernest Morden. You like not to believe it, Amy Heyton, and yet you know that he loves you no longer, if ever he really loved you at all. Has he not tried to break his plighted word, has he not relinquished all claim to your hand ? You cannot deny that, Amy Heyton."

" I can ; it is not true."

" It is as true as Heaven !"

" Ernest is not false."

" He is ; you know it. And he is cruel too in wishing you to give your word, never to wed except with him."

" Ha ! cried Amy starting. " Then you know——"

" I knew you were going to take this walk to-night. From what I have said, it is easy for you to see what I know. Tell me truly, Amy Heyton, if on this very night, Ernest Morden has not declared that he will cease to love you ?"

" No, he has not," stammered the poor girl.

" But has he not assured you, that he will never be wedded to you ?"

Amy was silent.

" He has, and you heard him say it with his own lips, Amy Heyton. Well then, you have heard him ; it is now time that you should hear me."

" I cannot, Luke—I——"

" Why such haste ? See, there is a lamp still burning in yonder window of the Hall. You must—you shall hear me, Amy Heyton. There was a time when you used to talk to Luke Masters—a time when you used to look kindly on him. When all curled their lips at me, and snapped their fingers as they past me by, you alone was kind to me ; you took pity on the outcast : you made me feel that it was well to live, and well to have some one in the wide world to call one's friend. Oh ! there have been times and seasons, Amy, when horrible thoughts have risen up within me, when I have cursed my enemies, and wished to put an end to my own misery—they may well call me Black Luke. It was then, Amy, that a word— a smile from you saved me from doing that, which my dark thoughts urged me to commit. Pardon me—pardon me, Amy, that I loved you then—that your own kindness caused me to dare so much as loving you ! There was nothing—nothing in the wide world that I would not have done to serve you then ; there is nothing that would prevent me from serving you now. I ceased to speak to you ; I ceased to trouble you, because I heard that you had given your love to Ernest Morden, and because I saw that day you put more belief in the reports of Black Luke's villany. Now, however, Amy, you know Ernest Morden for what he is—you know him to be selfish, cruel, hard-hearted, deceitful ; it is now then, that I ask you to look on Black Luke again as kindly as you once did, and he will avenge you for the injury that Ernest Morden has wrought."

" No, Luke, no—no vengeance."

" Be it so. I have my own account to settle with him, But you, Amy, you— what is there that Black Luke shall do to make you treat him as kindly as you once did ?"

" I will—I will."

" And more, Amy—Black Luke loves you ; he will be an honest man to win your love. Say that it shall be his."

" Leave me, Luke—leave me, I beseech you ?"

" Not without one word, Amy."

" I—I cannot say it."

" You must. Until you do we may not separate this night,"

" Spare me—spare me !"

" One word, Amy."

" I cannot—I—"

Luke Masters tightened his grasp of Amy's hand, and in a deep, stern voice, exclaimed,—

"Nay, Amy Heyton! there is no time for trifling. Answer me at once. There are dangers around you now which you know not of—dangers which may bring more woe to you than even your fears at this moment imagine."

"Dangers!" ejaculated Amy, trembling as she spoke.

"Ay, dangers, as I have warned you, Amy. But they must not harm you. Give me your word; say that you can love me."

"Do not—do not torture me!"

"That is a hard word, Amy Heyton, but it matters not. Hear me! By fair means or by force you must become the wife of Luke Masters,—you must go with him, and that shortly."

"Mercy! mercy!"

"Be calm, be womanly! You have heard my words, Amy. Luke Masters is not like Ernest Morden—he tells no lies. Give him your promise that you will at some day consent to be his wife, if he becomes an honest man."

"I may not—I dare not."

"Then Amy——"

"Help! help!" shrieked the poor girl.

At that moment footsteps sounded as if some one was approaching in great haste. Luke Masters partially relinquished his hold of the maiden, and turned round to reconnoitre. In another moment a dark shadow glided between the trees; there was the sound of a voice, and Sandy Summers appeared, holding in his hand an old blunderbuss which he had brought with him from the cottage.

"Stand back—keep your distance, Sandy!"

"Not so, Luke. Sandy Summers is no coward, if you are."

"Coward in your teeth!" cried Luke, upraising a large stick which he held in his hand, and making a move as if to spring upon the tomb-cutter.

Amy rushed forward and threw herself between the two men. Sandy fired his blunderbuss. When the smoke cleared away, Amy was there, but Luke Masters was not to be seen.

"Something of this I feared," said the tomb-cutter. "I watched that serpent follow you, and I was afraid there would be mischief on foot. If you had not taken the wrong footpath, Amy, I should have come to your help sooner. As for that villain, if I were sure he had done you any harm, I would follow him and hunt him to the death,"

"Ha! ha! ha!" laughed some one in the depth of the wood. "Black Luke and the tomb-cutter have accounts to settle now."

Sandy Summers made a movement as if about to rush into the wood in pursuit of his foe. Amy caught his arm and held him back.

"Do not follow him—do not leave me here alone!"

"I will not. But we must hasten. That serpent will make his way to the cottage, and ferret out our secret."

'Back then, Sandy—back quickly."

"Yes, so soon as I have seen you out of the wood."

Amy lifted up the lid of her little basket to see that the parcel was still there. Having assured herself of that, she hastened forward with the tomb-cutter, until they had passed out of the wood and were within a stone's throw of Warrenton Hall.

"Now, Amy, make all the haste you can. Mr. Lambert starts for town very early in the morning; so you see he is busy enough to-night packing up his traps. There is a light, too, in the windows of Jeffery's lodge; the old man will let you in, and you must get him to promise that he will keep your visit a secret. You are not afraid, Miss Amy?"

"No, good Sandy, no. I am fearful that something will happen to Ernest. Go back to him at once—go!"

"I will; and when you have seen Mr. Lambert, wait there in Jeffrey's lodge.

After I have seen that all's safe, and that Black Luke is nowhere prowling about, I'll come back to meet you."

"Do not—do not harm Luke Masters, Sandy."

"No child, no. But you have got the papers?"

"Yes, they are here."

"Go then, and call up old Jeffrey at once. Heaven bless you, child!—Heaven bless you!"

So saying, the tomb-cutter took his leave of the maiden, and with all speed retraced his way to the cottage.

CHAPTER XXXIII.

THE FAIR GIRL AND THE DARK-BROWED MAN TOGETHER AT MIDNIGHT.—THE ONE SEAL WHERE THERE SHOULD HAVE BEEN THREE.

ALARMED as he had been at the strange occurrences of the last few nights, it were but natural that poor grey-haired Jeffery, the porter at Warrenton Hall, should have been startled by the gate bell ringing at so late an hour. Whether to answer the summons or not was a matter of hesitation with him. As, however, it was repeated, he determined upon mustering up all the small stock of courage which his heart yet owned—a quantity, by-the-by, almost too trivial to be recorded here. The first thing the poor man did was to take his large horse-pistol off the shelf, lest he had to encounter any mortal enemy ; his second act was to catch up his small pocket bible, and place that within his waistcoat, so that he might have a protecting charm in the event of his having to stand face to face with the evil one. Finally, taking up his lamp, the old man, tottering and trembling, proceeded to open the gate.

If the phantom which had created so much disturbance at Warrenton Hall had appeared in proper person at the gate, it could scarcely have occasioned more astonishment to the porter than did the presence there of Amy Heyton. On seeing who the applicant for admission was, Jeffery perceived that he had no use for his pistol, and still less for his bible ; all that he could use were his eyes, for he was too much surprised to be able to find words for the employment of his mouth.

" Can I see and speak to Mr. Lambert Warrenton ?" inquired Amy.

" Mr. Lambert !" ejaculated the porter, opening his mouth as if he were showing his bad back teeth to a dentist.

" I wish to see him very particularly—at once."

" But, Miss Heyton—you—bless my soul ! I don't know whether Mr. Lambert is gone to bed yet. I left him, half an hour ago, busily at work getting ready to go to London in the morning with Monsieur Dourville, the Frenchman. I don't know—yes, there is a light in the library window, so I suppose he is still there."

" Then I can see him ?"

" Yes, that is—but see Mr. Lambert now, Miss Heyton ! What can be the matter ?"

" It is of importance," replied Amy.

" And you really do want to see Mr. Lambert alone—did you say alone ?"

" I wish you to conduct me to him, Mr. Jeffery ; but quickly—very quickly."

Poor Jeffery was in a state of the utmost consternation. Hastily, and scarcely knowing what he was about, he closed the gate after admitting Amy, and in so doing, jammed his finger. Then he went into his lodge to hang up his bunch of keys, but let the bunch fall out of his hand and drop upon his corns. It was not long, however, before he had trimmed his lamp, and was ready to accompany the maiden to the apartment of Lambert Warrenton.

" Stop, Mr. Jeffery !" said Amy—" you are good—you are kind ; you will promise me not to say a word about this visit to any one ; you will let me into the Hall, without noise, and without being seen ?"

The porter was confused : he was well acquainted with Amy ; and from what he knew of her and of her family, it was a puzzle to him why she had come to the Hall in such a manner ; more especially as her visit was to the son of Sir Thomas, with whom Jeffery was unaware that Amy was upon any terms of intimacy.

" Does your father or your sister know about your coming here ?" asked the old man ; his prudence causing him to hesitate.

" Neither, good Mr. Jeffery ; and you must promise me not to say a word to either of them. I am sure you will do so when I tell you that my errand is to save the life of one of my friends."

" To save the live ! Why—why it can't be one of the poachers you mean, surely ; because if you do, I can tell you Sir Thomas has sworn that he will shoot every one of them."

" Be quick, Mr. Jeffery—be quick, or I shall be too late !"

" And you do say that somebody's life is in danger ?"

" Yes, yes !"

" Well," muttered the old man, as he led the maiden onwards towards one of the back entrances to the Hall, " it is a strange time of night for a gentle young lady like you to come here to see our young master ; but if, as you do say, there be somebody's life in danger, and if as how the man's a true man, and no poacher nor smuggler, why it aint to be wondered at that you've been a little bold. Still, at this time of night, and to see our young master, too———"

"Quick, good Mr. Jeffery—quick!"

The porter drew a key from his pocket, and unlocking a small door, let himself and his companion into a stone passage within the eastern extremity of the Hall. Stepping noiselessly onward, the old man and the maiden took their way up a stair-case which led to the great gallery; passing along which they came to the door of the library, where, through the crevices, the light of a lamp was streaming forth, and shining upon the opposite wall.

"Is Mr. Lambert alone?" asked Amy of the porter.

"Shall I knock and see?"

"Yes—yes; and while I'm—while I'm speaking to him you'll wait without—wait here—just here, in the gallery, I mean?"

Jeffery promised Amy that he would do as she wished. Then tapping at the door, he found that Lambert Warrenton and Eugene Dourville were engaged together in the library. On the porter making his statement, Mr. Warrenton sprung up from his seat in surprise, and going himself to the street-door, took Amy by the hand.

"You, Miss Amy! Good Heaven! What can have brought you here?"

"Pardon me, Mr. Warrenton," said Amy, blushing as she reflected on the peculiarity of her situation. "May I speak with you for one moment—one moment only?"

"Command me in anything that I can do to serve you. But you are pale and wearied-looking, Miss Heyton. What can be the object of this visit?"

"It is important, Mr. Lambert. Forgive my imprudence. Let me speak to you alone but five minutes only."

Lambert Warrenton led Amy into the library. At the table near the eastern end was seated Eugene Dourville; the table was covered with papers, while various half-packed trunks, and letters ready for sealing, told that the two gentle-men had been busily engaged.

"You will excuse me, my dear Dourville?" said Warrenton, offering at the same time a seat to Amy:

Dourville arose, and making a polite bow to the fair girl, took up a taper, lit it, and then quitted the apartment.

Seated there, in silent night-time, companions in that lone and gloomy library, were Lambert Warrenton and Amy Heyton. They occupied the same chairs on which Gervase Morden and Constance Ismay were seated, when, on a former occasion, a scene in that old library was described.

Amy bent down her head, trembled, and clasped tightly the small basket which she had now placed in her lap.

Lambert Warrenton was a young man of a dark complexion, with massy locks of black hair, which hung down in such a manner as nearly to conceal his face. His complexion was of a brownish hue, void of any tinge of red. Beneath his dark overhanging eye-brows peered out a pair of small but sparkling eyes. His forehead was of a moderate height, and was calculated at first sight to inspire a beholder with a good opinion of the individual. This feature, however, ill-accorded with the small but sensual mouth, and the expression which the whole countenance wore of weakness of character, and a proneness to deceit. He carried his arm in a sling, being compelled to do so on account of the wound which he had received a few mornings previous.

Drawing the lamp nearer, Lambert Warrenton threw a scrutinising glance at Amy, and then said,—

"On a former occasion, Miss Heyton, I assured you that you might at any time command my services; and it would give me extreme pleasure to render you assistance of any description. Possibly you have now availed yourself of my offer, and if such be the case, I am willing to prove that I am as ready to perform as I was to promise."

Amy had not as yet uplifted her head. No reply did she make to the words of

Lambert Warrenton. Her bosom heaved ; deep sobs broke the stillness of that old apartment. Suddenly she burst into tears, threw herself at the feet of the young man, seized his hands, and in a wild, frantic manner, exclaimed,—

" Save him !—oh, save him !—save him !"

" Save who, Amy Heyton ?" asked Warrenton, in astonishment.

" Do not let them know of it—do not let them punish him !"

" Punish who? Calm yourself, Miss Amy, and for God's sake let me know what this strange excitement means."

" It—it means," said Amy, uttering the words with much difficulty, " that Ernest Morden will die."

" Ernest Morden !"

" Yes, listen !" And rising up, wiping the tears from her eyes, and exerting her strength to go through with the relation, Amy detailed the circumstances which had given rise to her present visit, and which had concurred to place Ernest Morden in his present fearful position. In so doing the poor girl took especial care to make no reference to the proceedings at her own home, nor did she say one word relative to the strange behaviour of Ernest towards herself. In explaining the causes which had prevented Ernest from delivering as he should have done the despatches with which he had been entrusted by Captain Charnock, Amy represented Lieutenant Morden's illness to be of a sufficiently serious character to form an excuse for the non-performance of his duty.

" And where is Lieutenant Morden now ?"

Amy hesitated before she returned an answer to this question. Determined, however, not to betray Ernest if she could not serve him, she replied,—

" Mr. Warrenton must pardon me for declining to give him an answer."

" I compliment you on your prudence, Miss Heyton. And what is the request which you have to make—what little act of kindness am I to perform ?"

Amy explained to Mr. Warrenton that knowing him to hold office at the Admiralty in London, being aware that from his own and his father's position his influence was great, and relying upon his own offer to befriend her whenever she chose to apply to him, she had ventured to bring the despatches with her, in the hope that Mr. Warrenton would carry them to their destination, and that he would intercede in the proper place for Ernest Morden. Poor Amy made this request with weeping eyes, and in a voice which was half choked by the violent emotions which agitated her bosom. Mr. Warrenton listened in silence ; when Amy had finished, he inquired—

" Were you sent on this errand by Lieutenant Morden himself ?"

Amy blushed, hung down her head, and was almost too much confused to enable her to find a reply.

" Ernest Morden knows not that I have come here," she answered.

" Indeed ! Then he did not entrust you with the despatches?"

" He did not."

" Am I to understand that he requested you to make any intercession of this sort in his favour ?"

" After a pause of a few seconds," Amy replied, " He did not; he has not done so."

" Then it is wholly a plan of your own to save him from punishment, Miss Heyton ?"

" It is."

" This is strange !" said Lambert Warrenton, in a musing manner. " I thought, Miss Amy, that I had heard something about a slight quarrel between you and Lieutenant Morden. I heard no particulars, certainly ; but judging from what little did meet my ears, I was led to suppose that the meditated union between you and him was no longer to be anticipated. Pardon me for presuming to ask such a question ; but—have I heard rightly ?"

Amy started, looked fixedly at the inquirer, and in an anxious-toned voice exclaimed,—

" Was it my father who told you this ?"

" It was not, Miss Heyton. Indeed I cannot say from whom I got the knowledge. I received it more as a rumour than as a piece of positive information. As yet I have given very little credence to it, because I understood that you had accepted Lieutenant Morden as your suitor, and because I believed him to be an honourable man. Have I been mistaken in my estimate of the character of the brother of my father's secretary ?"

" No—no, indeed not, Mr. Warrenton!" replied Amy with some warmth— "Ernest Morden is honourable—very honourable!"

" I am glad to hear you express such an opinion concerning him, Miss Amy. Then of course I am to conclude that the attachment between you is not in the least degree lessened ?"

" It is not."

"And your union, I suppose, is contemplated to take place at an early period?" Amy was silent.

" Excuse me, Miss Amy, for presuming to be so impertinent. I have no desire to trouble you with rude questions, I assure you. As however you require me to plead in Lieutenant Morden's behalf, it is as well that I should have some information relative to his position in regard to yourself, in order that, if possible I may make a successful representation of the case to the authorities, and urge his position in exoneration of his misdemeanour, and a plea for obtaining pardon for him. If I say that he is just about to be wedded to—"

" No, Mr. Warrenton no,—you must not say that!" interrupted Amy, her bosom heaving convulsively as he uttered the words.—"There is to be no wedding, no marriage !"

" How, Miss Heyton! do I hear rightly ; said you that Morden has broken his engagement ? " asked Warrenton in a voice of peculiar intonation.

" No, not broken, not broken. He cannot, may not marry me."

" And will not Amy Heyton ?"

" Will not now, not now."

" There is a mystery in this, Miss Amy. The very interest which you take in Lieutenant Morden's concern is sufficient to show that he has not entirely lost his place in your heart, and also to show that the quarrel is on his side, not on yours."

" There is no quarrel, none," said Amy pensively.

"No quarrel, and yet a separation, Miss Heyton! Of a truth you puzzle young heads like mine. Nothing seems more evident than that Morden has used you ill, and yet you have undergone the trouble and risk of coming hither to do him an act of service. It strikes me that this ungallant lieutenant is not aware how well and how deeply he is beloved."

" I do love him, love him deeply," muttered Amy in a low voice.

"And that has prompted you to this adventure, Amy. Well, the case is a serious one, being one which deeply involves Lieutenant Morden's honour, as well as his loyalty. I have heard something about certain despatches which Captain Charnock was expected to bear, and I have also heard that those despatches have to do with the existent quarrel between this nation and France. Perhaps, Miss Heyton, you are not aware that many of his majesty's servants have been acting disloyally, insomuch that abandoning the interests of their own country they have aided those of the enemy ; assistance has been given, information afforded, secrets betrayed. The consequence of this is that at the present moment there is a more than ordinary degree of severity displayed towards those who are detected acting unfaithfully, or who in any way fail to fulfil their duties as servants of the state. It is not my place, neither is it my wish to lay any blame to Lieutenant Morden for any misdeeds which he may have committed, or any duties which he may have neglected ; nevertheless I cannot refrain from thinking that as a true and trustworthy officer he might have found some means of transmitting to their destination those papers you speak of, at a period much earlier than the present."

" He might, he ought to have done so," ejaculated Amy. "But do not censure him ; do not condemn him too harshly ! "

" With neither censure nor condemnation have I aught to do, Miss Heyton. I speak but as I think ; I speak as a friend. Lieutenant Morden's explanations I will make known in the proper quarter ; what the effect of my so doing will be, I cannot say. Without wishing to pain you, let me ask if you are aware what the punishment for such a misdemeanour as that which I have supposed Lieutenant Morden to commit, really is ?

" Yes,—yes ;—disgrace—terrible disgrace !"

" Disgrace in the first instance, Miss Heyton ; but a worse punishment is liable to ensue. For such a breach of trust, especially in these war-like times, the penalty may even amount to death.

"Death !" shrieked Amy, starting forwards and regarding Warrenton with a wild gaze, and with eye-balls that seemed starting from their sockets.

" Yes, death, Miss Heyton ; the death which the law records."

Amy clasped her hands to her bewildered brain, she pressed them upon her bursting eye-balls ; she clutched with them the stray locks of her unbound hair. "Death !" she cried, " you did not say death ? " Then tottering backwards, if it had not been for the support which Lambert Warrenton afforded her, she would have fallen upon the floor.

"Calm yourself, Amy ; endeavour to be calm," said Warrenton, at the same time filling up a glass with wine. "Drink this ; you require it after having passed through the cold night air. Take courage! I will do my best for Morden ; I will obtain pardon for him if it be possible to do so."

" Pardon !" cried Amy ; " Ha ! said you he will be pardoned. Ernest pardoned ? "

" You mistake me, Miss Heyton. It is not for me to say that absolute pardon will be granted to Lieutenant Morden. All that I can promise is to interest myself as much as possible in his behalf and that without any delay."

" You will, you will do that ?"

" I have given you my word."

" And Ernest——"

" I may not advise him what to do in the meantime. Perhaps, however, his remaining secret till the answer be known may be the safer plan ; especially so as from what you say I glean that his illness incapacitates him from visiting London himself."

"He would do it, but he would die," responded Amy.

" Very well, Miss Heyton. Already I have told you that I dare not to advise him, except to say that he might possibly meet with more leniency if he presented himself in person and explained away the causes which have occasioned this unfortunate breach of trust."

"No, no,—do not advise him that. He is ill—too ill ; the journey would kill him."

" He must act upon his own responsibility in that matter, Miss Heyton.— The despatches I will place at once in my portmanteau, if you will give them to me."

" They are here," said Amy, opening her basket, taking out the paper parcel, and placing it in the hands of Warrenton.

There was a pause of a minute's duration. Lambert Warrenton drew the lamp nearer to him, and examined the outside of the parcel.

" This is very extraordinary, Miss Heyton," he exclaimed, " Captain Charnock, I believe, usually secures his despatches more completely than in the present instance."

" What is wrong, Mr. Warrenton ?" asked Amy, wondering at the cause which had given rise to the observation she had just heard.

" Nothing is wrong, so far as I know," replied Warrenton. " Still, it strikes me as singular and strange that, with a despatch of so much importance as I believe this to be, no better means of securing it should have been adopted."

" How ?" asked Amy, simply.

" Look you, Miss Heyton, it is sealed with *one seal only—there should at least have been three.*"

" And does that matter ?"

" I know not that it does. However, let me call my friend, and inquire of him if it be Captain Charnock's custom to use such carelessness."

CHAPTER XXXIV.

THE PROMISE THAT BROUGHT MISERY TO THE PROMISER.

LAMBERT WARRENTON recalled Eugene Dourville to the apartment, submitting to his notice the sealed paper which he had just received from Amy. Many whispered words passed between the two friends, not one of which was heard by the trembling girl. After consulting together for some minutes, Warrenton, turning towards Amy, observed,—

"My friend agrees with me, that, from what is known to us both of the usual care which is taken of such documents, it is very extraordinary that Captain Charnock should not have secured these papers more strongly than he has done. Simple as the circumstance is, it argues well, however, for Lieutenant Morden's misdemeanour being looked over and forgiven."

"Oh! are you sure of that—quite sure of that?" cried Amy, a faint smile of joy beaming on her wan countenance.

"My grounds for holding such a supposition are that from the outward appearance of the packet I conclude that the contents are not so important as at first I believed them to be."

"Then you think they will excuse him?"

"I cannot satisfy you on that point. The case will no doubt meet with the due consideration of the authorities who have jurisdiction in the matter. Whether they will think as lightly of Lieutenant Morden's venial misdemeanour as I would have them to, I cannot predict."

"But you will plead for him; you will tell them how ill he is—how very ill?"

"I will exert myself to the utmost."

Amy looked round, and saw that Eugene Dourville had moved off to a distant part of the library. Hesitatingly, and with a countenance expressive of the emotions which were agitating her breast, she grasped the arm of Lambert Warrenton, and, in a supplicative voice, petitioned,—

"Do not tell of my coming here to my father; do not let Sir Thomas know of it!"

"Is such your wish, Amy!"

"It is, it is; do not let it be known."

"I will not, unless called upon to do so."

"I thank you—thank you from my heart, Mr. Warrenton. There is nothing which I would not do to express my gratitude to you for such kindness."

"Nothing, Miss Heyton," said Lambert Warrenton, fixing his gaze on the countenance of the maiden, as he put the question.

"I shall ever be grateful—ever ready to render you any service in return!"

Lambert Warrenton turned aside his head, and mused in silence. Presently, taking Amy's hand in his own, he drew her towards the large bay window, through which fell the moonlight in rays of silvery beauty.

There was silence—deep silence.

"Amy Heyton," said Warrenton, in a low voice, "I am afraid—nay, I am certain that the intimacy which has so long subsisted between you and Lieutenant Morden has lately been disturbed by the occurrence of no common events. There has been, if I mistake not, an unhappy rupture between you, though I am ignorant of its precise nature. Feeling the interest which I do in all that concerns your welfare, pardon me if I do wrong in offering myself as a mediator between Ernest Morden and yourself."

"I thank you, Mr. Warrenton—heartily thank you; but—but ——"

Amy had not power to finish the sentence. Abruptly she burst into tears.

"Indeed—indeed I beg your forgiveness if I have said anything that has wounded your feelings, or called up anything unpleasant to your memory, Amy," said Lambert Warrenton, in a sympathising manner. "All that I wished to say was, that if it be in my power to effect a reconciliation between you, and to restore the happiness of both, you are perfectly at liberty to command me in whatever way you please."

"Yes, yes; you are kind—very kind, Mr. Warrenton; but it cannot—cannot be!" replied Amy, her tears bursting forth afresh.

"There must be some serious cause for this agitation of mind, Miss Heyton," said Warrenton, in a tone of the tenderest solicitude. "Morden has done you wrong. Let me know where he may be found, that I may go to him at once, and persuade him to make amends for his misbehaviour. Possibly my mediation may not be without effect."

"It would be useless—quite useless," answered Amy.

"Useless, Amy Heyton! It cannot be that the quarrel is so serious as your words incline me to imagine it to be. Morden has not openly insulted you?"

"Oh, no! he has not—he could not!"

"You have avowed that you love him, Amy. Am I to understand that he has disowned that love—that he has cast it off—that he has declared never to wed you?"

No other answer than deep-drawn sobs and flowing tears did Amy return to this inquiry.

"There is yet a question I would put to you Amy," said Lambert Warrenton gravely—"were Ernest Morden at any time openly to disown all love for you—openly reject, despise, curse you, would you, or would you not, then cease to love him?"

"Reject—despise—curse!" repeated Amy, uttering the words mechanically.

"Ay, if such should be the case; if he should spurn you from him; if he should openly avow that he held no other sentiment or regard for you than that of contempt; if he should thrust you from him with curses?"

"Ernest do that;" said Amy, in an idiotic manner.

"Ay, if he were to do so, would you love him then?"

For a minute Amy looked at Lambert Warrenton; for a minute she stood silent, tearless, statue-like. Suddenly her countenance assumed an expression that approached to boldness; her chest heaved, her bright eyes, usually so mildly beautiful, flashed forth rays of fire. There was a convulsive movement at her throat, a swelling of the muscles of the shoulder, an upward expansion of the brows. Drawing herself up, as if to concentrate her energies for the declaration which she was about to make, she heroically replied,—

"When Ernest Morden does so, I will cease to love him more—not till then!"

A grim smile gathered upon the face of Lambert Warrenton as Amy made this declaration.

"That is well," said he. "Fully do I understand the meaning implied in the provision. You have promised, Amy Heyton, if that I exert myself in your cause on this occasion, to render me any testimony of your gratitude that I may desire."

"I have."

"And I accept your promise. Listen to me, however. In the event of Ernest Morden ever behaving as I have supposed, there would be one small act of kindness which I should require from you. Do you promise me that in the event of Ernest Morden so contemning you and rejecting your love, you would then grant me any favour which I might in honour ask, and which you might, consistently with your honour, accede?"

"I will do so, whether Ernest Morden continue to love me or not," replied Amy.

"But my question is, Amy, whether you would do so should Ernest Morden ever prove so villanous as to treat you as I have supposed; would you then, I ask, accord me any favour consistent with your own honour and with mine?"

"I would."

"Mind, I ask you in all seriousness. Take my hand, Amy Heyton, and while the moon is shining on us both, pledge yourself to abide by that promise."

"I do so."

Amy made the promise—the fearful, dreadful promise. And at that moment dark clouds passed over the moon; there was the cry of a raven, which had perched itself up high in one of the embrasures above ; the night wind moaned a lonely wail ; the screech-owl responded to the cry of the raven ; the old hall itself groaned as the blast swept round it.   A ring, which on a bygone day Ernest had given to Amy, slipped from off her finger and fell upon the floor ; the lamp flickered and then went out ; all, all was perfect darkness.

"You will never forget your promise, Amy ?"

"Never—never."

Amy quitted the old, gloomy library ; and no sooner had she done so than Eugene Dourville laid his hand upon the shoulder of Lambert Warrenton and asked, "How works it ?   What success ?"

"All, all—reject—despise—curse her, he will do it all; and she must redeem her promise."

At that moment there was a tap at one of the panels in the library. Eugene Dourville removed a vase from before the panel; the panel itself slid aside, and a man stepped into the apartment. Lambert Warrenton rose up to greet his new visitor.

"So soon!" he exclaimed in a whisper; "so soon and so safely, Black Luke!"

"Why am I Black Luke to you?" retorted the new comer. "Let those call me so who know me less; with you I am Luke Masters."

"Well, Luke Masters, then—bold, fearless Luke Masters. Be it so."

CHAPTER XXXV.

THE SUSPICION OF TREACHERY.—THE QUARREL.—FRIEND AGAINST FRIEND.

AWAKING at an early hour on the morning following that of Amy's adventure, Ernest Morden proceeded to attire himself preparatory to making an effort to reach London by the stage-coach, which passed through the village at eight o'clock. He was still busily engaged in making his preparations when he was disturbed by the unannounced appearance of his good host, Sandy Summers.

"Perhaps you won't mind telling one, sir, what you're doing of there, if a body like me may know," said Sandy, addressing Morden, and, at the same time, throwing an inquisitive glance round the room.

"I must away to London, my friend, and that immediately," replied Ernest.

"Perhaps you don't mind telling me how you mean to get there," observed the tomb-cutter.

"By the stage, Sandy; you must stop it so soon as you see it coming through the village."

"It wouldn't be much good if I did, Mr. Morden. It'll be too full to take you in it; you may be sure of that."

"Nonsense, good Sandy. Go I must; and some means must be contrived for my reaching London without delay. You will assist me, my good friend—you will promise to assist me?"

"I shall assist you to stay here," replied the tomb-cutter, quaintly; ' and as for thinking of Lunnun, it will be better for you to think of going to bed again as quickly as you can."

"Your advice, Sandy, is doubtless well meant; but I am compelled to neglect it on the present occasion. Were I even worse in health than I am, duty would still dictate to me the expediency of this journey."

"That's what you think, Mr. Morden; but begging your pardon, I know King George too well to believe that he wants any one in his service to kill himself in his service. No, no; that's not King George."

"Duty, my station, my honour, all command me to go immediately," said Morden, still making preparation for his intended journey.

"I don't know much what you mean about honour, Mr. Morden; 'tisn't any honour to kill one's self for the sake of keeping in King George's favour. That honour is a fine sounding word in gentlemen's mouths, perhaps, but it's a sort of thing which a poor man like me can't understand. Some time ago there were two gentlemen who lived up in Darlingham, they had a quarrel about something or another, and they came out here, in the fields behind the church, to fight with their long swords, as they said, for their honour. Well, the upshot of it was, one of them got stuck through the chest, the wound turned all mortified-like, and he died; as for the other, he's gone about with one arm ever since. Now I can't see there's any honour in having one arm only; but may be, there is some honour in being like the other one is, seeing as how he's got the finest stone in the whole church-yard, and seeing as how I had the job of making it."

During the time in which Sandy Summers was occupied in telling this little anecdote, Ernest Morden was busily engaged in completing his preparations. No sooner did the tomb-cutter perceive that his guest was really intent upon the journey, and would not be dissuaded from attempting it, than Sandy determined to use less gentle means in order to prevent the carrying out of his plan.

"My arm is still very bad, Sandy," said Morden; "you must assist me in getting on my coat, for I am not able to do it by myself."

"It's well you can't, Mr. Morden, seeing as how you don't make this wild-goose chase so long as Sandy Summers has got two arms, and you've got but only one."

"Fool!" ejaculated Morden, in wrathful passion; his temper getting the upper hand of his good manners.

"Fool I may be," returned Sandy; "at any rate, I'm not such a fool as to be thinking of doing things that only a madman would want to do. You see, Mr. Morden, you've made me your doctor, as I may say; and you being the patient and I the doctor, I don't mean to let you have your own way in everything just now. A pretty concern you'd make of it, by going and riding in a coach in that sort of plight. You'd get a fever to begin with; then the 'liriums would come again; then there 'd be the mortyfaction; then your arm would have to come off; then you'd die; and then I should have to go cutting out a cherub on a stone to put over your body. Very pretty it would be, too; for if you did any such mad-cap trick, I can tell you what—I'd make the cherub on your stone with only one arm, and I'd write on it as how you'd murdered yourself out of a whim of your own. No, no, you don't go to London nor anywhere else just yet awhile, I can tell you. I happen to have too many jobs in hand just now to waste any time in making your head-stone. You'll stay here, Mr. Morden, or I aren't Sandy Summers."

"It is useless—quite useless—for you to attempt to stay me," rejoined Morden. "Go to London I must, and go to London I will."

"That's if you can get there, I should say; but that won't be while you are under the keeping of Sandy Summers."

"Am I a prisoner?" exclaimd Morden.

"Well, you aren't just that, though I should say you are something of the sort," answered the tomb-cutter. "It mayn't seem so to you, Mr. Morden, but it strikes me you've got another touch of them 'liriums; there's something wery wild-like about you this morning, I must say."

"I am determined—fixedly determined," said Morden, as he proceeded in his work of preparation.

"To do what?" asked the tomb-cutter.

"My duty—the duty which I have pledged myself to perform. If it be possible I will save my honour also. I have fought for my king already—I can die if he will it now."

"Well, that would be doing a great deal of good for King George, and a remarkable deal for yourself, I suppose," returned Sandy. "Hows'ever, though, I'm not a going to humour you in this particular; and as for King George, if he wants to get hold of you, he'd better come and fetch you, and then he'll have a bit of a job to find you out, I can tell him. But perhaps you'll tell me what you think of doing in Lunnum when you get there, if so be you ever do, which aren't altogether likely."

"The despatches—the papers!"

"Well, you needn't trouble yourself about them."

"I must present them myself."

"That wouldn't be the easiest job in the world, Mr. Morden," said the tomb-cutter, a grin forming on his countenance. "King George will have the papers long enough afore he sees anything of you."

"How!" exclaimed Morden, turning round and staring in the face of the tomb-cutter.

"What I say is," exclaimed Sandy, "that dokkyments have gone to Lunnun in a post-chaise and four, full three hours ago, can't easily be catched by a stage-coach, which won't be on the road for another half hour."

Ernest Morden listened with open mouth and quickly-heaving chest to the words of the tomb-cutter; then, darting to the hiding-place in which, on the previous evening, he had hidden the despatches, he discovered that they were no longer there.

"What—what does this mean?" exclaimed the pale and terrified man, as he seized with nervous grasp the arm of the tomb-cutter.

"It means just about what I said, neither more nor less,'" returned Sandy, chuckling.

"But the papers—you have not stolen them?"

"Well, I suppose I have."

"Answer me, Sandy Summers!" cried Morden, his terror giving place to rage, and his countenance becoming of a deep red hue. "Answer me, where are those papers, which I brought into this hut with me?"

"That's more than I can exactly say," replied Sandy, with a coolness of manner which heightened the rage of Ernest Morden.

"Traitor!" cried the infuriated man, "your life shall answer for this act of treachery."

"That would be a pity, Mr. Morden, seeing as how I've got a good many orders for headstones that I haven't begun yet."

"But the papers—the—the despatches?"

"Don't you bother your head about them. They'll get to Lunnun by themselves, I warrant you."

"To London!"

"Ay, to Lunnun to be sure, and they are half way there already. Though to say exactly whereabout they be is a thing unpossible; seeing as how horses arn't like headstones, if you know the ground you may tell how many inches a stone will sink in ten years, but if you know the road ever so well, there's no saying to a dead certainty how far a horse will do in ten hours."

"Again I ask you, Summers, where are those papers? This is no matter to trifle about; the loss of that parcel would be death—death to us both."

"And that wouldn't be agreeable. Well, mind what I say to you. Never trouble your head about me, there's no fear of death coming to a poor body like me. Perhaps you don't know why it is tomb-cutters don't die as soon as other men?"

"Fool! madman! why talk this childish nonsense now? Where are the papers?"

"Ah, the papers," returned Sandy with the most imperturbable coolness. "'Well, but as I was saying it's a cur'ous fact in nat'ral history how tomb-cutters don't die as soon as other people, and the reason of it, I suppose is, that if they make good gravestones it is a sort of temptation for folks to die; and so death takes them like a kind of partners, you see, into the business. It may be, though—"

Ernest Morden had possessed himself of an old rusty cutlass, belonging to the tomb-cutter, and which had hitherto been suspended from the wall, over the head of the bed. Unsheathing the weapon, he flashed it in the eyes of Sandy Summers, and in a paroxysm of fury exclaimed—

"Your life shall answer for this treachery, villain! Confess to me what you have done with those papers; or, by Heaven, I will deal with you as you deserve."

"Well now, I didn't think, Mr. Morden, you could put yourself into such a passion with an old friend, especially as he's your doctor too," said Sandy, at the same moment rushing forward, and grappling the two arms of the incensed Morden, "Sit ye down, man, and listen to reason. Sandy Summers isn't frightened at the glisten of a piece of steel."

Weak as Ernest Morden had become through the illness to which he had been subjected, his remaining strength formed no match to that of the sturdy tomb-cutter. The limbs of the latter were closely set, while his broad expansive shoulders indicated the animal power of which he was possessed. Almost without effort he forced his opponent back upon the seat behind him, and having done so, wrested the cutlass from his grasp, and flung it to the opposite end of the room.

"Ye'd fight, would ye ? There must be no fighting here between friends. If you want to show you've got the tiger in you, wait—wait, man, wait, and perhaps you will have cause to do it by-and-by. I thought Ernest Morden knew his old friend Sandy too well to draw a sword upon him. "That's a pretty return for all the kindness I've done you, and all the doctoring I've given you—isn't it ?"

Ernest was completely overpowered. Exhausted by the short struggle in which he had been engaged, he could barely articulate in a faint voice :—

"The papers—the papers, Sandy. You have not let any one steal them, have you ?"

"What do you talk of stealing and all that nonsense for, man?" retorted Sandy. "The papers I've told you are on their way to Lunnun, in safe hands; and, what's more, they are in the hands of those, who'll make the best of your case to King George, that they can. You've got friends, man; don't I tell you you've got friends ?"

"Friends—friends !" ejaculated Ernest; "and who are they ?"

"Don't you trouble yourself about that. They are friends, who'll do you all the good they can, and that's no little either."

"Are you sure of that ?"

"I shouldn't tell you so, if I wasn't. To say the truth, I'm ashamed of you, Ernest Morden; you don't deserve to have friends, seeing as how, if they're ever so good, you don't know how to treat them."

"Pardon me, Sandy ! But assure me that the papers are safe as you say."

"Well, if you won't be satisfied, what's the use of my telling you ? The dokkyments are half up to Lunnun at this time ; and mighty thankful you ought to be to those who've had a hand in getting them there ; but you are the most ungratefulsome dog that ever I came near—that you are !"

"But who am I to be grateful to, good Sandy—who are these friends you speak of, and who have done me this service ? "

"You'll hear all about that, by-and-by. Meantime, there's a bit of serious business for you to attend to. The papers are gone to Lunnun, and if so be you get the king's pardon there, all will be well enough. In case, however, that shouldn't happen—and there's no telling what may happen in this lottery-box of a world—in case, I say, you shouldn't be so lucky, it will be as well that you should be quite ready to make off as soon as possible, seeing as how an ounce of lead in a man's head is apt to make him feel a kind of all-overishness. So, just to arrange that matter, I mean to go down to the beach, and try if I can't fall in with the French smuggler, who, I hear, is somewhere about there just now. We are somewhat of friends together, and I dare say I can make up a plan with him to take you off in his boat to-morrow night, if so be I hear that King George has been obstinate."

"You forget, Sandy, that I am a servant of his majesty, and that I have pledged myself to behave loyally towards him. I would rather let this matter take its course, and stand the chances, whatever they may be."

"That would be all very well, if the world was a better sort of world than it is, Mr. Morden. But as it so happens that it isn't always them who have the best intentions that get the best served, we must all look out for ourselves. I shall go down and make all right with the Frenchman ; while you must hide yourself away somewhere to keep clear of the mischieful people that are stirring about. There's a place down under my shop, where I keep some of my models. We must put your bed down there, and you must make a hiding-place of it. Fanny will keep watch while I'm gone to see about the boat."

Somewhat reluctantly Ernest Morden acceded to this arrangement. No sooner had he safely ensconced himself in his hiding-place, than Sandy Summers departed to seek the smuggler.

CHAPTER XXXVI.

SOME PARTICULARS RELATIVE TO A REMARKABLE TONGUE.—DANGER AND
DARK CELLARS.

IT was late in the afternoon of the day succeeding that on which the events
detailed in the forgoing chapter occurred, and Sandy Summers was busy in his
workshop, when he was interrupted in his labour by the entrance of an individual,
who must now be introduced as a new character in our story.

Gilbert Griffiths, or Glib Griffiths, as he was popularly denominated,—they
called him Glib because he was a free-trader in words—was a little, round-headed,
florid complexioned man, who performed the double duties of barber and postman
to the good people of the village. Glib was a curiosity in his way, whether considered physically or mentally. In his parlour, where he was accustomed to perform
the operation of shaving, he had collected and arranged various odd birds, odd
insects, odd reptiles, and odd plants; people said, however—and people are apt to
say provoking things—people said that when Glib was out of his parlour, the
oddest curiosity of all was wanting there. Certainly Glib was no common man;
he was something to look at, albeit he was only four feet eleven; he was worthy
of being barber, postman, and carrier to the village of St. Gillott's-Cross, notwithstanding he was the shortest specimen of a dull humanity which that village
possessed. Indeed, so short was Glib, that when he attempted to shave any of his
tallest customers, he invariably had to mount up on a stool in order to do so.
Then Glib was so squat, and nature had taken such pains to make him as
much like a sugar-tub as possible, that when he had to undertake the onerous duty
of polishing the chin of the village innkeeper, who was himself most respectably
stout, he found some difficulty in getting his razor to operate, from the fact that
from the rotundity of both operator and operated, it was the most troublesome
affair in the world for one to try to touch the other's chin. Glib's head was a
miniature resemblance of his whole corporation, it being perfectly round, and bearing
every similitude to a monster cherry placed on the top of a dropsical mammoth
orange. The eyes of Glib were small and twinkling; the hair of Glib's head was
short and curly. As for Glib's tongue, there were the most unaccountable reports
abroad respecting it; some people had averred that its length exceeded two feet;
there were others who protested that it was as long as Glib's whole body; and there
were others again who maintained, with a degree of pertinacious assurance which
gave an air of probability to their assertion, that Glib's tongue was without end, and
that even if any one was to set up an inquiry on the subject, they would find it
utterly impossible to determine how long Glib's tongue really was. Such being
the case, it is a curious matter for speculation to account for the where and the how
Glib manged to keep this monstrous tongue of his. Perhaps he kept it coiled up
like a harpoon-rope in a whale-tub; or perhaps, like the lingual organ of the chame-
leon, it had the power of elongation, and of being darted forward to an indefinite
extent, and afterwards could be contracted again for the convenience of stowing
away. Leaving alone these conjectures, however, and discrediting many of the
strange reports, there is still not the least cause for doubt that Glib Griffiths possessed a most extraordinary tongue; for it was a tongue that knew what a tongue
should be, and was steadfastly resolved to perform its functions faithfully; it was
never still, never asleep, never quiescent; it was always wagging, always talking,
always telling either truth or lies; from the first thing at morning to the last thing
at night Glib's tongue was constantly at its work. People said too, that when Glib
was asleep, his tongue kept awake, and that it chattered while he snored—but
people do say such invidious things. Unfortunately for society Glib's tongue,
though a very serviceable one, was far from being proportionately good; it was a
naughty tongue, inasmuch as that it was never very particular whether it told
truth or lies. Glib had got into many scrapes on account of his tongue's volubility,
but gradually people had learned to consider Glib as not responsible for anything

that his perverse and wicked tongue might say ; though whether Glib's mental constitution was not as much to blame as his vocal organ, is a question for dispute. Phrenologically speaking, Glib had a large development of the bump of " Gammonativeness," for Glib took especial delight in deluding his acquaintances by stories of the most incredible description. Then Glib's brain was a microscope in itself, for the smallest fact which came to his knowledge was sure to be magnified by him into something very extraordinary. On a moderate computation, about the one-hundreth part of what Glib said was solid truth, the other ninety-nine parts might always be set down for fiction. This characteristic of Glib fitted him especially for the situation of barber to the village, inasmuch as some dozens of people came to him to be shaved merely to hear the relation of some of his wonderful accounts ; it being always, they said, a treat to hear Glib tell them such news as they could not hear anywhere else,—which, by-the-by, was very likely, since Glib's news was peculiarly his own, and he had a private manufactory for making it, situated somewhere in the recesses of his head-piece.

It was Glib Griffiths who now came to disturb the tomb-cutter at his work.

"So you are at it as usual, Summers," said Glib, as he entered. "That's an uncommon fine piece of stone-work you are doing there. It's a cherub, holding a wreath, isn't it ? Well, it's a fine one—a very fine one. I never saw a better, to my thinking, except it was one which I saw once in Westminster Abbey. Now, that was a wonder. Talk about stone-cutting, there never was before, and there never has been since, any stone-cutting to come up to that. They say it was done by a Frenchman—it took him nine months to cut, and I've heard say he never left off from the time he began to the time when he gave the last touch——"

" What, didn't the man eat, Glib ?" interrupted Sandy.

" Eat, bless you, no ; he hadn't no time for it. One penny roll, they say, was all he had ; and he was kept alive by the interest he took in his work. It's a fact, you know, Mr. Summers, that these great sculptors, and painters, and poets, scarcely ever eat ; while they are at work they don't want any food ; it's the work that keeps them alive ; though what they want to do the work for if they don't want the money to buy food with, I can't tell."

" You can't ?" said the tomb-cutter, laying aside his chisel and mallet, and turning round to eye Mr. Griffiths.

" I can't," said Glib.

" Well, I don't know how you should," said Sandy. " But I'll tell you, Mr. Griffiths—I'll tell you, if you can understand me, though 1 doubt if you can, seeing as how you are no artist, but only a barber——"

" And postman, too, if you please, Mr. Summers."

" Very well ; and how's a postman or a barber to know anything about art ? I'll tell you why such men work, and why they don't care about the money, Mr. Griffiths. It's fame they care about—fame that comes to them and makes them live when all barbers and postmen are dead and gone !" So saying, Sandy took up his mallet and knocked it upon the stone to give strength to his assertion.

" And is fame any good to them while they are alive, may I beg to know, Mr. Summers ?"

" Good—any good?" returned Sandy, his eyes glittering, and a smile as of triumph beaming on his countenance. " Yes, it cheers them through want, starvation, and illness ; the hope of having their name talked about a thousand years to come, makes them toil and fag through every difficulty ; it warms their hearts when the world is cold without ; it makes summer to them when winter is with other men. Their works, are not mere works, but parts of themselves, that live for ever and ever, and tell other people, in long days to come, of the men who starved to make them: Look you there, Glib Griffiths, that stone with the sleeping babby on it, and the two seraphs, with their wings folded, watching over the babby, is for Mrs. Redmond's child. She came to me and said she wanted a plain stone ; I told her she'd better have some cherubs on it ; but she said the expense would be too much. ' Never mind,' said I, ' you let me put the cherubs on, and I'll only want you to pay me the same for it as if it was a plain stone.' And there it is, Mr. Griffiths—there it is, the very best bit of carving in my whole shop. I shan't have one penny for all the work I've had on it, but I don't care for that—not I."

"Well, that's very strange of you, Mr. Summers."

—"Strange ; no, it isn't strange at all.   There's the stone, and there's the seraphs and the baby, and there's my name written underneath : so by-and-by, perhaps it may be a hundred years to come—people will stop in our churchyard, and read that stone, and say to themselves ' S. Summers'—*S. Summers* you see is what I've written on it—' was a good stone-carver.   He must have been somewhere about the best tomb-cutter of his time.'   That'll be better than having money for one's work now, Mr. Griffiths, and that's what we artists call fame ; fame it is, too. But of course you can't comprehend the feeling.   I don't know how you should, considering you only scrape chins."

"And delivers letters, please Mr. Summers, as well as as parcels and packages every Tuesday, Thursday, and Saturday," observed Griffiths.

"You do, do you? and who'll know anything about your having done so fifty years to come ?" asked Sandy, with a look of ineffable disdain.

"That's true, Mr. Summers—that's very true.   And now I come to think of what you say, I don't know but what I should like to be talked about when I'm dead myself.   I must go home and see if I cannot make a   figure to stand on my mantel-shelf, or something of that sort ; so that I may write my name upon it, and that people may read it when I'm dead and gone."

Sandy jumped off his seat, threw down his mallet, gave a leap for joy, and then grasped the hand of his friend.

"That's the sort of feeling, Glib Griffiths ; there's hope for ye, man, if ye stick to that.   Gads me ! if I don't think you'd make a good tomb-cutter, and I wouldn't mind taking you myself."

"You wouldn't, Sandy ?"

"I—but no, no, it wouldn't do ; you talk too much, Glib Griffiths, and—"

"Talk !" exclaimed Griffiths, starting—"talk ; yes, and I've talked till I've forgotten the news I had to tell you."

Sandy saw that an extraordinary change had suddenly come over the countenance of his friend, and he also imagined that he perceived an expression of fear displayed on his features.   The tomb-cutter began to be alarmed.   Seizing Griffiths's hand, he demanded of him,—

"What news, Glib ?   Didn't you say news ?"

"I did say news, Mr. Summers, and most extraordinary and astonishing news it is too.   There hasn't been anything like it ever since the battle of Bunker's Hill."

"Why—why, what can it be ?" stammered Sandy.   "It isn't anything about Ameriky, is it ?   They haven't eat up all King George's men out there, have they ? I've heard they are all a set of cannibals."

"No, Sandy, it's something more wonderful than even that would be ; it's something that's quite amazed me, and made me feel so astonished that I don't think I shall recover the shock for some time to come."

"Well, has it anything to do with the Frenchers ?   They haven't set fire to all King George's ships, have they ?" asked Sandy, in a breathless voice.   Then suddenly remembering Mr. Griffiths's propensity to speak in high-flown language on common subjects, he relapsed into a smile, and letting go his friend's hand, said,—

"You are at it again, Glib ; it's mortal odd that a decent man like you can't keep your tongue to the sober truth."

"You may say as you like about my tongue," returned Griffiths, bridling ; "but what I very well know is, that I have news to tell, and very wondersome and strange news too, though you may choose to laugh.   It isn't about Ameriky, nor is it about the frog-eating Frenchers."

"Well, what is it about, Glib ?"

"It's about yourself, Sandy."

"Me—about me !" ejaculated Summers, turning very pale. Then seizing again the arm of his companion, he asked in a low, breathless tone, " Did you say it was about me?"

" Yes, it's about you and it would be well for you to know it too. What it all means is not for me to say ; but that you, of course, know yourself."

" What—what ! tell me what is it ?"

" Why, as you say I don't tell truth, perhaps it's no good my telling it you at all. However, as I shouldn't like to see any harm come to you, I'll let you into the secret as far as I can. So to begin : haven't you some sea faring man hidden somewhere in your house ?"

Sandy's agitation increased ; he trembled violently, and turned paler than even he had yet turned.

"I, Mr. Griffiths?"

"Yes; you needn't tell any lies about it. They say you have, and they say he's a dreadful wicked fellow, who's played up some awful prank. I don't know whether he's exactly a pirate or a smuggler, or some seaman that's murdered his captain. Perhaps, however, he's a privateer, that's put to death a dozen men and half-a-dozen young shivering women and babies."

"Mr. Griffiths, you—you know not what you are talking about; you cannot mean what you say!"

"I'm only telling you what I hear, and I don't want to go further from the truth than I can help. 'Tisn't for me to say what the man is; he's one who's done something wrong, that's very clear, or they wouldn't make such a rumpus about him."

"What—what are they saying, Mr. Griffiths?" asked Sandy, with scarcely breath sufficient to give utterance to the words.

"Why, I'll tell you how it came to my ears. You must know that Sir Thomas, at the Hall, went up to London three or four days ago; he went all in a hurry, and there was no one could tell exactly what he'd gone for. Well, just afore I came here I was up at the Hall myself to take a letter, and there was Sir Thomas come back again. They do say the post-horses flew all the way, at sixty or seventy miles an hour. As for Sir Thomas, he's all in a terrible flurry; and he's in such a way, that they say he's broken all the things at the Hall in his passion; whether he's quite killed my lady or not I can't be certain. There's a rare uproar, and the servants are flying to the rightabout, and there's messengers gone off for the constables at Darlington; and old Ruggles, the tipstaff, has been sent for up to the Hall; and they've got a messenger off to fetch the ministry—military, I mean. I hear there's two whole regiments of the king's body-guards a coming, and they're taking down all the great pistols and guns that hang up in the Hall entry, and they're looking up all the swords they can find, and—"

"But—but what is it all for, Mr. Griffiths?" interrupted the tomb-cutter.

"It's for you—for you and the strange seamen, who murdered the dozen men, and the half-dozen young women, and the bab.—But I think you said he hadn't been as bad as that. Well, it's for him they are coming, they are going to gibbet him, and cut him up in quarters and hang him in irons; and they are going to try you too, and perhaps shoot you, or hang you, or make a traitor of you, and cut your head off!"

"But Mr. Griffiths—good Mr. Griffiths!"

"Oh! it's all truth—all solemn truth."

"You—you are certain, Mr. Griffiths—you—you saw them getting ready? You—you heard they—they were coming down?" stammered Sandy, his very teeth chattering as he spoke.

"I saw, and I know all as I've said," responded Griffiths. "May be, however, the two regiments of body-guard won't be down here for some hours to come; they are awful fellows—they ministry, or millery, or miltaires, or what terrible name you call them by."

"Tell me, Mr. Griffiths—tell me, did you hear how soon they'd be here?"

"Why, they've got to load the guns first, and to take aim, and see their cutlasess are loaded—sharpened I mean. There was something said, too, about having to twist two or three ropes together to make a strong one to bind this great, terrible fellow with. But, perhaps, you won't mind letting me know whether he's as big, and as awful, and as terrible-like as they say he is? you know, Sandy, I can keep a secret about as well as any one in the village, and if he hasn't been too murdersome a villain, I didn't know but what—"

The tomb-cutter drew Griffiths towards the back part of the shop.

"You won't betray me, Mr. Griffiths, will you? I think I can trust you; and

I think that though they do say you've a way of talking a great deal, they've never said that you've betrayed a friend."

"That's not Glib Griffiths to do anything of the kind, Sandy Summers. I am as I am; but the man isn't born yet who has ever said that he knew me to get him into trouble, or say a word against him, if he was any friend of mine."

"And you won't say a word about—about—."

"About this awful murderer, do you mean? Well, if you wish it, Sandy, I—.'

"He's my friend; he relies upon me for safety; you—you will not say half a word?"

"If he's any friend of your'n, Sandy Summers, I wouldn't speak a syllable to harm him if he'd killed twenty thousand men, and a million of the prettiest women, all with black shiny eyes, and red lips, and white teeth, and with beautiful curly ringlets, and—no, Sandy, I won't say a syllable, even if he's Paul Jones, or the great slaughtering, rampaging, man-eating pirate that they say makes such awful work out in them 'Lantic Oceans. But where is he, Sandy? Has he got a great black, bushy beard? And has he a death's-head and cross-bones painted in black on his forehead? And are his hands covered with blood? And—."

"Hush! he is here," said Sandy, moving towards the door of the inner room. "What they say of him is all false. He's one of His Majesty's officers, aboard ship."

"His Majesty's officer! and isn't he no pirate?"

"Nothing of the sort. He's done wrong, and he's going to have the king's pardon for it, only you see they want to lay hands on him at once."

"I see," observed Mr. Griffiths, "they want to hang him, and get him out of the way before the pardon comes, but we mustn't let them do anything of that sort—eh, Sandy?"

"Not if we can help it, Mr. Griffiths."

"Help it! of course we can. I'm one to take part with you, Sandy, and what should I care for the two regiments or body-guards, or all the ministry, militarmens, or what you call them, put all together? Where is he, Sandy? let me see him."

"He is here," said Sandy, tapping at the door against which he stood.

Bolts were withdrawn, a key turned in a lock, the door opened, and Ernest Morden looked out upon the two men.

"Back—back, man!" cried Sandy. "Don't let your face be seen. Here's a terrible outcry about you; though how they came to know I had you in hiding here, I can't tell, unless that villanous Black Luke has—"

"I have heard all that this good man has said," interposed Ernest, nodding at Griffiths as he spoke. "What is best to be done I know not."

"You mustn't let the militarums get at you, sir," said Griffiths, "they are dreadful, awful fellows, and don't mind any more shooting a dozen men, one after another, than they do buckling on their belts. I couldn't shave one of those fellows like I could any other man—I know I couldn't."

"I think all had better be conducted peaceably," said Morden, in a musing manner; "and I give myself up to those whom they may send to fetch me."

"I beg pardon, sir," observed Griffiths, "but did you say—give yourself up?"

"I think I had best do so to insure peace," answered Morden.

"Indeed sir, but it mustn't be. There's a sort of wickedness in such a thought. Our lives are given us to take care of, and if we turn them over to the militarums, there's no knowing what may become of our souls for such sinfulness."

"Peace, Griffiths!" interposed Sandy; "Mr. Morden won't do anything of the kind."

Griffiths drew the tomb-cutter aside.

"Morden, did you say!" whispered he; "he's not the brother of Mr. Morden up at the Hall, is he?"

"He is."

Griffiths now turned to Ernest.

"If so be as Mr. Summers says, sir, you are the brother of Mr. Morden at Sir

Thomas's, I shall be proud to help you; for I must say there's not a better, more gentlemanly, and more right sort of person in the neighbourhood than Mr. Morden at the Hall. Though, whichis very strange, I heard him giving very strict orders to the men about finding you, and I heard him say there was no punishment too bad for you."

"Did he—did my brother say that?" asked Morden, eagerly.

"I won't say that those were his exact words, sir; what I mean is, they were somewhat of that kind."

"You must excuse Mr. Griffiths," observed Sandy, who perceived the agitation of mind which the words last spoken had wrought in Ernest Morden. "Mr. Griffiths is a very well-meaning man, though he is apt at times to talk more freely than is quite right, seeing as how truth is truth."

"I know my brother's character," said Morden, clasping his hands to his brow in an agonised manner. "Gervase is high-minded, noble, and brave-spirited; he will not forgive me for having been remiss in my duty, neither will he be lenient to me for having acted as I have. I would give worlds not to see my brother—not to have him reproach me, as he will do."

"Mr. Gervase shall know nothing about your being here if you wish him not to —that is, no more than he knows at present," said Griffiths.

"But he must—he will—it cannot be prevented!" said Morden, despairingly.

"Yes, yes, Mr. Morden," interposed the tomb-cutter, "you must hide yourself at once, and if they do come after you, they may just look till they are tired."

"Leave me to talk to them," volunteered Griffiths.

"I am afraid it will be useless," said Ernest, drooping his head upon his hands.

"Trust me and Mr. Griffiths to see you safe through it," said Sandy. "There's the hole under the workshop, which you must go down into as you can. Take all your traps, and that old cutlass with you. Keep yourself snug there; and I'll put a stone or two over the trap. If any of them smell you out there, they must have keener noses than any of Sir Thomas's hounds have got."

"But you, Mr. Summers?"

"Never mind for me. Griffiths and I will take our standing together: there won't be any harm happen to us."

"We haven't any fear of the militarums ourselves, sir," chimed in Griffiths, throwing back, with an air of defiance, his little round head as he spoke.

Just at that moment Fanny Summers came running into the room with an alarmed expression of countenance, and almost out of breath, owing to the haste which she had made.

"What is it, Fan—what is it?" asked her uncle.

"The men—the constables!"

"Where, girl—where?"

"Coming down the village. They say, Uncle Sandy, they are coming to your cottage; and one of them got hold of me, and wanted me to tell all about tis gentleman; but I slipped away from him without telling him anything, and run home the shortest way as fast as I could."

Griffiths moved towards the window of the workshop, and immediately exclaimed,—

"I can see them—here they come; but I don't know whether they've got the militarums with them yet."

"To the cellar, to the cellar—quick, quick!" cried Sandy, pressing the old cutlass into Morden's hand, and hurrying him towards the trap-door in the workshop.

"You'll let all pass off as peaceably as you can, Summers," said Ernest.

"Yes, yes, it's all their own doing; and if they come here, they must fare in the best way they can."

Sandy and Griffiths accompanied Morden into the workshop. Moving away a large stone, and lifting up a trap in the floor, the tomb-cutter disclosed a large dark hole, into which descent was gained by means of a short ladder. No sooner had Ernest reached the bottom, than Sandy closed down the trap, and, assisted by Griffiths, placed over it a large slab of stone, on which Sandy deposited some tools and a few chips of marble to give the appearance of his having just used it as a workbench.

"Quick, Griffiths, quick!" he cried. "Lend a hand to move this clay model into the next room. We must put it in there, and cover it over with a cloth, as if it was something secret, in order to make them believe that's why the shutters have been kept closed."

"Ay, ay, Sandy," responded Griffiths; "we'll be a match for the militarums."

The model was moved into the inner room, the door locked as it had been before.

"Uncle," cried little Fan, "the crowd is just here."

"Go, Fan—go and play in the churchyard," bade Sandy. "Griffiths, man, here's a horse-pistol for you, which you can button up under your coat, in case you should want it. My old blunderbuss is loaded and ready; I'll just clap it under this stone, where I can pull it out when the time comes. Now, then, for my mallet and chisel, and I should like to see the man who'd dare to insult Sandy Summers."

"Let them come as fast as they like, militarums and all, we're ready for them," echoed Griffiths.

"Hush, Glib, hush!—they are here!"

CHAPTER XXXVII.

THE USE OF A TONGUE, AND THE UTILITY OF MALLETS.—THE CONFLICT.—BROTHER MEETS BROTHER.

THERE was not a man in the village of a merrier heart than Sandy Summers. It mattered not much how circumstances were with Sandy, nothing could prevent him from singing and whistling. If at work or not it was all the same with him; and those who chose to listen could hear him singing a merry strain, or humming one of those rich old English airs with which the peasantry are so familiar. There was method and art in all that Sandy did; even in his whistling he was perfect, and he had, by dint of extreme practice, contrived to use his mallet and chisel as an accompaniment to the tunes which he loved best to hum. Pleasant enough it is to witness the artificer so disposed, telling as it does that, despite of his toil, his tired limbs, and sweating brow, he has a living, bounding spirit within,—a spirit which days of toil and nights of weariness have not entirely crushed—a heart into which the iron has not completely entered—a soul which still retains a portion of its early buoyancy and gladness. The man who, while at his labour, can trill some merry carol reminiscent of his boyhood's time, or whistle some lively melody, which gives the imagination ideas of dancing groups and woodland glades—can be no bad man at heart; neither, without doubt, is he the worst of workmen. Sour souls are they, and somewhat frost-bitten too, who cannot endure the whistle of merriment, or the musical hum of the joyous heart. The bee sings while at his honey-making, the lark trills his glad song as he rises in high air, the sparrow twitters in the eaves, the cricket chirrups on the hearth—all these are merry in their labours, and why should man be sad?

Sandy Summers plied his mallet, and carrolled his song with an appearance of the utmost industry, while Glib Griffiths seated himself on a tombstone, and folding his arms on his chest, waited the moment when he should be aroused to action.

The moment came—there was a knock at the door of the workshop.

"Let me talk to them first, and if that won't do, we'll try the fire-arms, eh ?" said Griffiths, whispering in the ear of his friend.

"Yes, yes ; we'll let them see what we are."

The knock was repeated.

"Who's there?" cried Sandy.

"Open," replied a voice from the other side.

"Glib," said Sandy, "open the door, if you please. I'm too busy to leave off work just now."

Griffiths obeyed ; he threw open the door, and beheld the faces of Gervase Morden, old Jeffery, the porter at the Hall, Ruggles the tipstaff, two constables from the adjoining town, together with a concourse of villagers, all of whom appeared much excited, and all of whom set up a shout so soon as the opening of the door disclosed Sandy perched up on his seat diligently employed in chiselling a death's head and hour-glass upon the top of a tombstone.

"What's all this hubbub about?" demanded Griffiths, putting on a well-assumed look of astonishment.

"Can I speak with Mr. Summers for a few minutes?" inquired Gervase Morden in a polite manner.

"No; you can't, Mr. Morden, though I'm sorry to say it. Mr. Summers has in hand a job of the utmost importance, which must be finished at precisely five minutes to eight o'clock this evening. He's got now just two hundred and ten strokes of the mallet to give; each stroke takes a minute, and he's only got one hundred and ninety minutes altogether."

"Don't mind, Glib Griffiths ; he's a liar !" shouted some one from the midst of the crowd.

"I should like to know who it was dared to say those words," exclaimed Glib, bristling up and looking very fierce.

Sandy increased the force of his mallet strokes, and forbearing to look round, attempted to lead his neighbours into the belief of his being unaware of their proximity.

"Mr. Summers must pardon me for the interruption," said Morden ; "but it is necessary that I have a few minutes converse with him, and that immediately."

"If you'll be kind enough to come in and wait, sir, for the hundred and ninety minutes, my friend Sandy will have done his job, and won't mind chatting to you."

"Mr. Summers !" cried Morden.

Sandy continued to ply his mallet as if every thought was concentrated in his work, and no one near to disturb him.

"Let me in to speak to him," said the secretary.

"It's absolutely a thing impossible, sir," responded Glib, holding the wicket close as he spoke.

"Just let me come and talk to him, Mr. Morden," said Ruggles, the tipstaff edging his way through the crowd, "I warrant ye I'll make him hear."

The tipstaff approached, and uplifting his baton of office banged it against the wicket. Sandy, alarmed for the safety of his domicile, thought proper to turn round and fall upon the besiegers.

"What are you banging away at my door for, you Tom Ruggles?" he wrathful exclaimed. "Do you want to smash it into splinters? 'cause if you do, you'd better put down the money to buy a new one with first."

"I don't want to harm your door, Mr. Summers. But here's Mr. Morden, from the Hall, has business with you, and you won't pay any attention to him."

"Well, if Mr. Marden wants me, he can ask for me—can't he?" said Sandy, somewhat abruptly.

"So he has, and he's called you once or twice ; but you make so much noise with that wooden hammer of your'n, that you can't hear him."

"Well, who's fault's that?" demanded Sandy, in a bold manner.

"Mr. Summers, I have a few words to say to you. Can I speak to you for five minutes ?" asked Morden, stepping forward.

"Certainly, Mr. Morden—certainly, by all means," replied Sandy, very obsequiously. "Will you mind coming into my poor workshop?"

Gervase Morden entered, and Griffiths quickly re-closed the wicket. The secretary drew the tomb-cutter to the back part of the shop, and then said,—

"Sir Thomas has commissioned me to pay you a visit, with the view of inquiring of you whether you have not a —a person concealed in your house, whose presence at the Hall he requires immediately."

"Do you mean Mr. Griffiths?" said Sandy, pointing to the man of razors.

"I mean one who is a stranger to the village," replied Morden, "and who has been in the village but a few days; he —"

"Glib," cried Sandy, "have you seen any stranger about the village lately?"

"Can't say as I have, Mr. Summers. There hasn't been one in for the last twelve months and twelve days."

"If I am rightly informed," resumed Morden, "the person I speak of is concealed somewhere in your house, and —"

"My house—did you say my house, Mr. Morden? Why—why, Glib, here's a pretty affair! Mr. Morden thinks that robbers have hid themselves somewhere in my cottage."

"Have you looked under the beds, lately, Sandy?" returned Griffiths, speaking as if seriously alarmed.

"Did you say they were robbers, Mr. Morden?"

"I said that the person to whom I allude is in hiding, and that he is secreting himself from justice. It is imperative that he be found."

"Oh, lor! lor!" ejaculated Sandy,—"hiding from the justices, did you say? Then he's a murderer, I suppose. Glib—I say, Glib, take one of my mallets in your hand; there's a murderer somewhere about who'll be out upon us all in a minute, perhaps."

A severe expression gathered on the countenance of the secretary. Grasping the arm of the tomb-cutter he said in a strong voice,—

"This trifling is useless, Summers. Certain am I that a person answering the description I have given is secreted in your cottage. How far it becomes you to harbour those who are defying justice, I leave you to consider."

"I—I harbour murderers, Mr. Morden!" stammered Sandy; "did you accuse me?"

"I have every reason to believe that you are guilty of so doing," replied the secretary.

"Glib—Mr. Griffiths, you hear—you hear what Mr. Morden is charging me with?"

The round-faced barber advanced towards the secretary, and putting on a bold look, demanded—

"Is it robbers, or murderers, or some pirate who has slaughtered a dozen men, and half-a-dozen young shivering women, and a lot of babies all in long clothes— is it my friend Mr. Summers you are accusing of having anything to do with such ruffians as that?"

"The individual I seek is neither a robber nor a murderer, so far as I know," replied Morden, "his crime is that of acting disloyally to his king, I believe."

"Then you won't find any such kind of man as that here," said Sandy, "there's my friend Mr. Griffiths, who will tell you the same too."

"Did you say disloyally—acted disloyally, Mr. Morden?" asked Griffiths.

"He is accused of having done so," answered the secretary.

"Now look you here, Mr. Morden," said Griffiths, waxing warm as he spoke— "disloyal means traitorously, and a man acting traitorously—begging your pardon for speaking so to a fine scholar—is a traitor. Now what I want to know is—do you, or Sir Thomas, or Lady Warrenton, or anybody suspect my friend—Mr. Sampson Summers here, the best tomb-maker in all England—do you suspect him— have you the least bit of suspicion, I ask, that he could have anything to do with a man who was an enemy to his glorious majesty King George? No, Mr. Morden;" and here Glib mounted up on a stone, and threw the door more open that he might be heard by those on the outside—"Mr. Summers and myself are both loyal, honest men—men who wouldn't mind going forth any day of our lives to fight King George's enemies, be they Frenchers, or be they 'Mericans. I'm sure I express my friend Sandy's feelings as well as my own, when I say there's nothing we hate more than traitors, and—and Frenchers, eh, Sandy? Yes, Mr. Morden, when King George does want men, and when he does want honest men, and true men, and men that will stand up for him, and men that won't mind shedding their last drop of blood for him, and for old England; let him come down to St. Gillett's Cross, and he'll find plenty of them—dozens of them—scores of them—every one of them will turn out, won't we, boys?"

" Ay, ay, Mr. Griffiths, that's the bare truth, that's just our own words. Hurrah! for Glib Griffiths! he's the man to stick up for his king!"

The little barber bent down his head and whispered in the ear of the tomb-cutter.

" I'm doing it, Sandy—beant I? they are coming round. Only leave them to me."

" Three cheers for Glib Griffiths!" was the general cry.

" What's it, my boys?" cried Glib enthusiastically. " I'm surprised and downright astonished that Mr. Morden should mention such a thing, as there being any traitors in the village of St. Gillott's-cross. I should like to know who ever saw one; I should like to know where one's to be found; I should like one to be pointed out. Traitors, indeed! What I say is, give us each a sword, or a pike, or a poker, or a broomstick, or anything 'fencible at all, and put a Frencher, or two Frenchers, or three Frenchers afore each of us, and then see what we'd do —then see whether we are traitors or not—then see if we didn't know how to fight, and a right heart for it too. I can judge how every one of you'd behave in such a case, because I know what I'd do myself. Give us the tools, say I, and set us to work, and let the standard of old England with the golden lions on it, stream from the tower of the Hall yonder; and if we wouldn't beat all the Frenchers and 'Merikins that ever lived and breathed, then I'm not Glib Griffiths. I'll tell you what we'd do, boys: we'd do jist like a great auncester of mine as they call him, who lived some two hundred years ago, did.—He was out in battle and was left by himself in the field, and had to fight all alone by himself against a whole hundred of red-haired, rampaging Scotchmen; all come down from the hills with great swords in their hands that weighed about forty stone each, and great targets on their arms all covered with sharp iron spikes. Well, what did he do? Why, he had only one long lance in his hand, and when he saw how it went with him, and how the one hundred—one hundred and one I think there were—when he saw how the one hundred and one rampaging Scots were on him—I say when he saw them, he buttoned up his coat, tossed up his hat, grappled hold of his lance, cried out—" Hurrah for King George! and——"

" King George two hundred years ago, Glib Griffiths," cried one of the villagers in a sneering manner,—" how's that?"

" Well, couldn't there have been King Georges then as well as now, fool?" retorted Glib.

" Ay, ay, of course there could, and who knows that there wasn't?" exclaimed the little village tailor, who had left his shop-board to join the crowd. " Let Glib Griffiths have out his story."

" Ay, ay, let Glib Griffiths go on!" shouted a score of voices.

" I don't know that I shall tell ye any more, ye are such a set of unbelievers," said Glib indignantly. " As I was saying, however, my auncester fastened on his cap, threw off his coat, took up his sword——"

" I thought ye said it was a lance, Glib," observed the innkeeper.

" Well, what's the difference between a lance and a sword, I should like to know—can anybody tell me?" returned Glib. However, it was a lance he took up ; and then he looked fierce at them, and rushed forward and cried—"Hurrah for King George or King Harry !" and dared the two hundred and twenty red-faced Amerikins——"

"Scots, Glib—keep to the Scots—one hundred and one Scots," cried the inn-keeper again.

"I tell you what it is, I'll not go in at all to such an uproarious lot," threatened Glib. "What's the use of stopping a man to know whether they were Scots or Amerikins ? Haven't the Scotch people gone over to 'Meriky, and

haven't the 'Merikins come over to Scotland ? and didn't all the lot of them spring from one tribe, which lived in the high latitudes of Mesopotamia, in Northern Ireland—haven't any of you read that ?"

"Ay, ay, that's right enough, that's just as it is in the book," cried the tailor. "Leave Glib Griffiths alone to know about these things. He can tell you where the 'Merikins came from."

"Well, of course I can; and what's the use of talking such nonsense then?" continued Glib, apparently very vexed. "My ancestor, I say, rushed in with his long lance upon the three hundred and fifty Scots and 'Merikins, and when he'd run the first through the body, he kept him on, and ran 'another through, and then a third, and then a fourth, and so on, till he'd got a whole dozen on his lance—just for all the world like a lot of sausages on a skewer—and then he shook them off, and began again, and so went on, doing a dozen at a time, till he'd cleared the whole five hundred and seventy. It was rather toughish work, I've heard him say, but he was a strong man, and he kept on crying out—'Hurrah for King James!' and fighting away, until he hadn't left one of the nine hundred and eighty alive on the field. That's what a Griffiths did, boys. And what I say is—let King George but order us to the field, and we'd show ourselves all Griffithses in that way."

"Ay, that we would—that we would, Glib! and you should be captain over us," cried a dozen voices.

"Well, of course I should; and yet you come here looking for traitors. What's the use of making yourselves such fools?"

Gervase Morden had listened to the words of the orator with interest, nor could he help being amused by them. Now, however, he again applied to Sandy, and, in a voice which testified to the earnestness of his purpose, said,—

"I would not willingly put you to any inconvenience, Mr. Summers, but the orders of Sir Thomas are strict, and I cannot quit this house until I am certain that the person whom I seek is not here."

"Well, Mr. Morden, you are at liberty to look for him where you please. It's hard, certainly, that I should be put to such disgrace, as to have my poor cottage turned upside down on a suspicion of traitors to King George being in it. How's-ever, here's the workshop; there's the stairs which lead to my room, and you'll find Fan's room on the opposite side. You can look where you like; only I do hope you'll be careful and not do more harm than you can help to what few poor things I've got."

Morden beckoned one of the constables to accompany him, and followed by Sandy himself, the party proceeded to make an examination of the upper apart-ments of the cottage. While they were thus engaged, Griffiths took occasion to remonstrate with the crowd without on the unlawfulness of the act.

"I don't know what you think about it," said he, "but this is what I think—that, considering my friend Summers is one of the gentlest, harmliest men in all the village—one who wouldn't do wrong to any one, but is always ready and glad to help any one of us, if we were in difficulties,—I say, considering this; and considering too that the law of England says, "every man's house is his castle," mind that! "every man's house is his castle"—considering that much, it does seem cruel that poor Summers is to have his cottage ransacked for just nothing at all. Right is right; and what I say is—never mind whether it's Summers or any other man who does wrong, let them suffer for it; but if a poor, honest, hard-working man is to be treated as a knave and a rogue, I do say it's a crying shame; and I do say it oughtn't to be; and I do say it is inconsistent with English law; and I do say that if anybody says it is, he knows nothing about the matter. There! I've given you my opinions, and now I'll take yours."

"You really don't think, Glib Griffiths," said the tailor, coming forward, "that Sandy Summers has been hiding away any traitors in his cottage?"

"Think it, Mr. Snipkins—think it! I could swear to it he hasn't. Bless you! where could he hide such a one even if he had the heart to do it—where could he, that's what I want to know? there's nothing of that kind about Sandy; he's open and downright honest like myself."

"Well, there's no gainsaying that," remarked one of the villagers to some of the others, "Glib bean't the man to tell a story, unless it's a true one; and as for Sandy, we've known him long enough to trust him; I should think."

" Yes, yes," rejoined the innkeeper " I'll wager a cask of my best October ale that Sandy Summers is a true man, let the world say what it will against him. I can't think what can have led Sir Thomas to think of sending out Ruggles and the constables to worry poor Sandy for ; 'tisn't quite the right thing of Sir Thomas."

" No more it isn't," echoed half a dozen voices; " poor Sandy oughtn't to be treated in this way."

Just as the group of villagers were thinking about returning to their homes, Morden, Sandy, and the constable came down from their examination of the up-stairs rooms. Sandy's apparent frankness had won upon Morden ; so much so indeed, as to have induced him to suppose that Sir Thomas had been misinformed, and that his brother Ernest was not beneath the same roof as that under which he now stood. He was debating with the constables as to whether or not they should relinquish their secret, when a man passed forward from amongst the crowd at the door-way, and exclaimed in a loud voice—

" The inner room—let the inner room with the closed shutters be looked into."

" That's Black Luke who spoke," cried one of the crowd ; " there's no mistaking Black Luke's voice.—Black Luke who set fire to the school-house."

" Where is he ?" cried many voices.

This was a question more easily asked than answered. Many a pair of eyes were immediately turned in search of the man whose presence had been thus announced ; but Black Luke could not be seen. One or two persons certainly averred that but a few minutes before they had observed a man standing on the outside of the throng, whose hat was slouched over his eyes, and whose dress was gathered up round the chin. Whether or not it was Black Luke, no one could confidently say, though all had their conjectures, while each was certain that they had heard Black Luke speak.

The constable turned towards the door, opening it into the inner room, and found it to be locked.

" We must have the key of this," said he, addressing the tomb-cutter.

Sandy objected.

" You promised that you would afford us every facility in carrying out our search," said Morden. " That search, Mr. Summers, would be far from complete if we gained not entrance to this apartment."

" I am sorry to disoblige you, Mr. Morden, but that apartment is——is——"

Sandy hesitated, and placed himself between Morden and the door.

" Do you see that ?" said one of the villagers to his companion. " Ha ! that looks suspicious, don't it ?"

" That's the room that Black Luke spoke about," said another.

" Ah ! and Black Luke knows a mortal load of secrets," remarked a third.

" Well, I've wondered myself why the shutters of that room have been kept closed up for the last day or two," observed the innkeeper.

During the time occupied by the passing of these colloquies amongst the throng without, Sandy remained with his back planted against the locked door, his arms crossed on his chest, and his right hand firmly grasping a ponderous mallet. Griffiths still continued to act as porter, standing inside the wicket, with another mallet, similar to that held by Sandy, firmly clenched in his hand.

" May I beg to know on what grounds you object to my entering this room ?" demanded Morden, in an authoratative manner.

" I suppose, Mr. Morden, begging your pardon,—I suppose I can have my own reasons about my own places.

" But those reasons did not apply to the rooms which we have already visited."

" Perhaps they didn't," returned the tomb-cutter, doggedly. " But I've my reasons about this room ; and no one enters it either, unless I give them permission."

" I can answer for my friend Sandy, that there's nothing there as can be of any consequence to you," chimed in Griffiths. " Mr. Summers may surely have some place to himself, if he wants to lay out his poor dead sister, and keep her till the coffin's made."

"Oh! did you ever hear the like of that?" exclaimed one of the crowd. "Sandy Summers has been pulling up the people out of the church-yard; he's got some of the bodies in his room."

"Open the door—break open the door!" sounded from a score of throats.

Incited by the new apprehensions which had taken possession of their minds, the crowd made a rush to enter the cottage, and assist the officers in forcing the inner door. They were driven back from the wicket, however, by Griffiths, who flourished his mallet most heroically, exclaiming as he did so,—

"Back—back, every one of you! If you put a foot inside, I'll rap you over the brains!"

"There is a mystery in this, Mr. Summers," said Morden, angrily; "it becomes my duty to see what you have hidden in this room. Am I to understand that it is a dead body, as Griffiths states?"

"Glib says what he pleases," returned Sandy, "there's nobody in here that ever had much life in it."

"Hark—hark! he owns there's a body there," cried the tailor to the crowd.

"I don't own anything of the sort," proclaimed Sandy, at the top of his voice. "If there is a body in here, it's one which none has a right to meddle with, and it's one which never did any harm. Besides, I've got some little models and inventions of my own in there, which it wouldn't do for every one to see, and which I'm not going to have pulled about and broken to pieces."

"I'm sure that's all plain and fair enough," added Griffiths, who was sure to outdo every statement. "Mr. Summers has got some inventions and models there that will fetch him a mint of money, when he gets the patent, and how will he ever be able to get the patents, if he lets everybody see them first, I should like to know? 'Tisn't reasonable, and it isn't common sense!"

"If the truth be as Griffiths states," said Morden, "you cannot have any objection to my entering the room alone, Summers."

"Don't do that, Mr. Morden, he'll murder you!" roared out one of the crowd.

"What can you want to see my models for?" asked Sandy, addressing the secretary.

"Will you assure me, Mr. Summers, that you have nothing there which you wish to conceal, except your models?"

"What else should there be?" returned Sandy.

Gervase Morden was indecisive how to act, when just at that moment one of the constables, in moving about the stores in the workshop, descried something glittering on the floor. Picking this object up, the constable glanced at it for a moment, and then handed it to the secretary.

"Ha!" exclaimed Morden; "what is this?"

"Hark—hark!" said those on the outside, "something's found out at last!"

"This is indeed corroborative of our suspicions," said Morden, in a tremulous manner; "here is a button belonging to a naval officer's uniform, together with a portion of the cloth torn off with it. Mr. Summers, any excuse of yours is useless —that door must be opened immediately."

"The window—the shutters!—round to the window!" bellowed a dozen voices at once.

"You'll not let anybody go into that room without you choose they shall, Sandy Summers, if you take my advice!" said Griffiths, speaking out in a bold manner.

At that moment there was the sound of a crash in the inner room, a shout was heard without, pieces of glass rattled as they fell upon the ground, and a wild cry of triumph which thrilled on the tomb-cutter's ear, told that the unruly throng had broken into the apartment which he had attempted to guard.

"Out, and after them, Glib—after them with your mallet! they've forced my window, and they are— ha!"—then hear the sound of something falling heavily on the floor—"they've broken my model—my best model!"

One blow from his mallet broke the lock, the door flew open, and Sandy rushed into the room to drive back the marauders.

On the floor, broken into two halves, was the model which Sandy had covered over with the cloth.

"Keep back!—keep back every one of you. My model— my beautiful model!"

"Where's the dead body?—where's the traitor?" cried the voices of the rude villagers, as they forced themselves through the window into the apartment.

"Keep back! do you hear? or not one of you is safe!" exclaimed Sandy, brandishing his mallet aloft, and bringing it down with all the force of his fury on the shoulders of the nearest intruder.

"Pay 'em out, Sandy! don't spare 'em! don't give 'em any quarters at all!" cried Griffiths from the outside of the window—"Give it 'em with your mallet, and don't be particular. Give it 'em, they deserve all they catch!"

"The traitor! where's the traitor?" continued to be the cry.

"My model!—you've broken my model, and I'll do murder to every one of you!" threatened Sandy.

Fierce and terrible grew the fray: the enraged Sandy wielded his mallet with fearful fury ; not caring where the blows fell, nor on whom they lighted. There were yells, and screams, and execrations, and cries of anger and maddened ferocity. Growls and curses escaped from the lips of the tomb-cutter. Whoops and maledictions found their utterer in Glib Griffiths. "Ye shall pay for it with your lives!" vociferated Sandy. "Down with 'em! don't hit too gently, and don't be afraid of the lot of 'em!" responded Griffiths. Heavy and thick fell the blows of the stone-cutter. Down, down they rattled like iron-hail. The very impersonation of universal fury, the very spirit of vengeance itself appeared the infuriated artist. Unheeding friends or foes, caring not where he hit, who he hit, or how hard he hit, down fell the massy weapon over heads and shoulders—over breasts, backs, and arms. From end to end of the room, from corner to corner—phrenzied, mad-like—the tomb-cutter chased his assailants and drove them howling away. Neither Morden nor the constables had dared to enter the apartment. In vain did the secretary uplift his voice to put an end to the fray; no one heard him, no one regarded him. "Ye'll break my models—will ye? ye'll force my window—will ye?" cried Sandy, accompanying every question with a thwack with his mallet. There was a rush to the door, but it was too narrow to give egress to so many; there was a retreat to the window, but as each one tumbled through he received a blow from the mallet of Griffiths, accompanied by a salutation. "Drive 'em out, Sandy—break their backs and drive 'em out. I'll give 'em a finishing, knock a piece out with 'em!" And lustily, valiantly, desperately, did Glib Griffiths keep up to his engagement. They were hard knocks those, which the barber dealt, and they told well, wherever they chanced to fall.

The greater portion of the marauders were now driven out of the apartment ; and the officers, alarmed at the thoughts of what might be the probable issue of the fray, summoned up their courage and determined to interfere. Rushing in upon Sandy, they contrived to wrest the weapon from his grasp, while Ruggles, the tipstaff, exerted himself to effect the complete clearance of the room. As for Griffiths, no sooner did he perceive that he and his friend had come off conquerors than he gave a shout of victory ; leaped up and spun round for joy ; flung his mallet back through the window, and then made his way round to the assistance of Sandy Summers.

"We've done 'em, Sandy! I told you we'd be a match for 'em, if they brought the body-guards and militarums as well. There's a few of 'em, I warrant, who'll feel the thwacks I gave 'em for a long week or two ; and as for coming to be shaved, there's a dozen or two who'll have chins too tender for me to scrape these many mornings."

"Summers," said Gervase Morden, approaching the stone-cutter, "do you know what you have done? Are you aware what injury you have inflicted?"

"Injury—injury, did you say?" groaned the aggrieved man. "Look you there Mr. Morden! See you what the ruffians have done? See you the damage the have wrought? This—this, which they have broken into pieces cost me lon

g

nights and days of toil; it was finished—it was perfect; there was not its like in the whole wide world. And they have destroyed it—destroyed it, see you! Injury—ay, they know not—you know not the injury they've wrought!"

And stooping down, the sorrowing artist picked up the separate pieces of his work, and arranged them so as in some measure to restore the broken object of his love. It was the representation of a child, carved in pure white marble; beautiful in the delicate chiselling of the features, and the exquisite finish of the rounded limbs. The countenance was placid, and calm, and heaven-like. There was that in the expression of the face which told of purity—of sinless, spotless purity. A smile sat on the lips of the child—it was no smile of earth—no smile which expressed joy for delights experienced here; but joy in the anticipation of the delights soon to be realised in another world. The sculptor had fashioned a pair of wings to his handiwork; and the wings appeared folded over the child's smooth breast, as if they waited only the breeze of heaven to separate them, and to waft the child away. No angel-form, wrought by the most cunning of earthly hands, ever approached the angelical beauty displayed in that object of exquisite art. No fond mother, dreaming by the death-bed of her first-born, and picturing to herself how bright and beautiful the child of her love would appear in the starry halls of heaven, ever fashioned in her fancy form more beauteous—more divine, than had the sculpturer carved in that cold, inanimate marble. Inanimate! no, not inanimate; for the better part of life was there. All that wins, and charms, and softens—all that appeals to the heart, and purifies the imagination, that carven image had. Even Gervase Morden—stern disciplinarian though he was—hung entranced over that object of high art, albeit rude hands had spoiled it of much of its former beauty. Yes, the pale, but strong-souled secretary—he, whose close-set lips testified to the unflinching firmness of his nature, stooped over that broken image, and, touched by its exquisite beauty, allowed his tears to trickle down upon the shattered fragments.

The tomb-cutter saw that the student wept. He approached him, and folding his arms resignedly, said,—

"Ay, sir, you do well to weep. I had one child—one only child—born to me in my early days. It was beautiful as was its mother; it was lovely as some heavenly thing which had just quitted paradise to flit for awhile on earth. I loved that child, as never yet fond parent loved his offspring. My own life I would have given—freely given to have saved the life of that bright child. But disease came —disease with the burning breath, and the poisonous touch; it touched my child— my only, lovely child. I sat by its cradle, and saw the skeleton fingers press upon its cheeks, and could not keep them off. I saw the cloud come over the smiling, beamy eyes; and saw my beauty wither—shrivel—shrivel as does the bloom of this flower as I press it in my warm hand. My child died, sir— God grant you may never have a child to love, and then to die—never have a thing of beauty but a thing of air to set your heart upon, and see it dissolve and pass away like a dream. I saw my child so pass; I saw it fade from me as if it were too holy a thing for any vile eyes to look upon. It was a dream—a dream; but a dream that will not—cannot be forgotten. There is that child, sir. It was the first human form I ever chiselled; and I worked without food or drink, to carve it in its beauty. For years I have wept over it; many a time have I pressed my lips to those, and thought them the lips of my child—they, the cold marble lips which you see there. And as I've looked at that image I have thought, to be like my child, it must perish like my child—it must perish, as my child did, in its beauty. And it has; you see it! There—there—fragments—broken stone—nothing but bits of broken stone—that is my child! Ha! ha!—ha! ha! ha!—that is my child!"

Gervase Morden laid his hand upon the arm of the sculptor, and pointing to the scattered image, said,—

"Can you not put those pieces together again? Can you not mend them?"

"Mend!" exclaimed the sorrowful artist—"mend what? mend a heart that is broken like that marble? No, sir—no—no—no; it is not to be mended—it is broken—both are broken ; and they will be broke for ever !''

" Come hither, Sandy !" cried Griffiths from the workshop. " There's Ruggles and a dozen others, playing up pretty pranks with your works.   Come hither, man."

" What are they doing ?—what dare they do ?" exclaimed the tomb-cutter, as he broke from the grasp with which the secretary endeavoured to detin him and rushed into the workshop.

" What more do you want to break ! what else do you want to destroy ?", demanded the infuriated man, as he pushed aside one of the constables, who was about to lay hands upon a small tablet, partially carven, which was intended, when finished, to be affixed to one of the walls of the church.

" That's it, Sandy !" chimed in Griffiths. " Say the word, man—only say the word, and I'll bundle Ruggles and these officers all out together."

Gervase Morden again interfered.

" This behaviour is both useless and unbecoming, Summers.'' said he. " These men have received authority from Sir Thomas Warrenton .o. .ke a full examination of your cottage; to impede them in the performance of their duty is, to say the least, very foolish on your part, as it not only strengthens suspicions, but leads to unpleasant measures, which it were well should be avoided."

" But my carvings—the work of my own hands—''

" Only suffer all the more injury, Summers, from your occasioning a fray."

Whilst Gervase Morden was speaking, a constable placed his hand against th e stone slab which covered the entrance to the cellar, and had so far move it aside, as to have revealed to view a portion of the trapdoor.

" Lend a hand here, mate," said the constable, addressing the tipstaff, who was none other than the redoubted Mr. Ruggles.

" If you move a step that way, you do it at your peril, Ruggles !" cried Sandy, darting forward to place himself between the constable and the tipstaff, as well as to guard the cellar entrance.

" Is the stone to be removed, Mr. Morden ?" asked Ruggles.

" Who says that it is not to be ?"

" Sandy says so !"

" Move it, and show Mr. Summers that with the warrant, which you possess, your right to make such investigation is not to be disputed."

" Ye may tell that to them as will believe it," resumed Sandy.   " As for your warrants and bits of paper, keep them to yourselves ; I'll have nothing to do with them ; I want none of them here—not I."

" Here's a door underneath this stone, Mr. Morden," cried the man who had succeeded in detecting the entrance to the cellar.

" Let it be opened,'' replied the secretary.

" I should like to see the man who'd dare to break another thing of mine,'' growled Sandy. " Back there—back, I tell you ! What are ye after with that stone ?"

" The mallet, Sandy—where's your mallet ?" asked Griffiths. " We'll beat 'em back somehow, the rampaging rioters !   One would think they had done enough damage for one while, without their wanting to pull up a man's floor."

" Will Mr. Summers inform us where that door leads to ?" demanded the secretary.

" There's no door there," returned Sandy ; " what do ye want to get pulling a man's place to pieces for ? There's no door there except the flooring, and they must be fools who fancy they can see one."

" That's right enough," added Griffiths ; " I never saw any door there myself, and can't see one now. All that's underneath there is the ground the cottage stands on ; and you don't want to go sapping and mining at the foundations— do you ?"

" There's a door plain enough," said the constable, " and it only wants this table to be moved to allow me to get at it, though where it goes to, or what place is underneath, I can't exactly say."

"You can't, can't you?" said Griffiths, stepping up beside the officer, and placing his hand upon the stone-slab. "It's to be wondered if you could, as there's nothing to be seen that's very like one."

"Don't you call a square crack in the floor and a couple of hinges very like one?" asked the officer.

"No, I don't," returned Sandy. "I don't think there's any likeness between a door and a crack in the floor, which was made by one of Sandy's big stones happening to fall plump on the place, and smashing it through; so Sandy, you see, had to let in a square piece, which is just the one which you are making this fuss about."

"But the hinges?" observed the officer.

"Well," replied G   'they are only half hinges after all, and Sandy nailed them on just to keep h.s b :s of board together.'

"Don't believe a word Glib Griffiths says!" cried one of the villagers, a group of whom had again gathered round the door of the cottage.

"You don't believe Glib, don't you?" returned the barber, "and yet Glib told you all you'd get a sound hiding if you meddled too much in other people's affairs, and you've had it, you know—you've had it, though you beant satisfied enough."

"Mind not the threats of those men. Let the door be forced open!" commanded Gervase Morden.

Sandy Summers seized the blunderbuss which he had hidden before the commencement of the fray. Presenting its muzzle towards the constable, and placing his fingers on the trigger, he exclaimed—

"Back—back every one of you! Who dares to move another step in this shop, shall have this fired at him, I warrant ye!"

"That's the way to deal with 'em, Sandy," cried Glib, drawing the large horse pistol with which the tomb-cutter had furnished him, from underneath his coat. "Now then, I should like to see the man who'd touch either of us with his little finger. They is beant fond of cold lead in their stomachs at supper time, had better keep their distance. Sandy and I won't spare any one of ye, not even Sir Thomas's seckkittary there. Ye're sure you put bullets enough in that gun of yours, Sandy? As for this pistol, it's as ugly to deal with as it looks. It's one I've had by me for many years, and it's one that has killed its share in its time. The best thing about it is, it never misses neither; for it's what Julius Cæsar shot Alexander the Great with, when the Greeks wanted to come into this country. It's the very identical pistol, and here's Julius Cæsar's mark on the handle. So keep back; don't let it have to do with any of you; for ye'll repent it if you do —ye'll repent it, as sure as Glib Griffiths swears to it, ye will; and Glib never tells lies, as ye all know."

"Disarm these fools, and break open the door!" thundered Gervase Morden.

"That's easier said than done, boys," returned Griffiths, undauntedly. "Sandy and I say what we mean, and we are both ready to pull triggers on ye."

Ruggles the tipstaff seized a crowbar, which stood in the corner of the workshop, and advancing quickly dashed the blunderbuss out of the hand of the tomb-cutter. Infuriated to a pitch of madness, Sandy caught up one of his carving chisels, and rushed in upon the tipstaff. Desperate and deadly was the struggle. The tipstaff was a sturdy villager, but rage and revenge lent strength to the arms of the stone-cutter. In vain the constables endeavoured to interfere. Sandy had entwined his limbs round those of his foe, and held him with an iron grasp. They struggled, as struggle men who have been mortal enemies for years, and who have at last met to wreak their enmity upon each. From side to side, backward and forward, twisting, twining, wrenching, writhing, and glaring at each other with eyeballs bursting from their sockets, the two men continued to struggle. At times the stone-cutter would free one of his arms, and uplift the chisel, as if about to dash it in to the brains of his foe; then bearing up against some stout effort of the tipstaff, to cast him upon the ground, he grasped the throat of his antagonist, until the

blue blood gathered in the countenance of the half-strangled man.   Muttere^d
curses continued to escape from the lips of the stone-cutter, though his teeth wer^e
closely set, and his breath was drawn in quick, deep inspirations.   A moment
they loosed their grasp of each other, then grappling arm to arm again, they renewed their struggle with increased ferocity.   Now, however, Sandy was obtaining the mastery over his foe, having contrived to get both his arms above those of

the tipstaff, and having managed to place his right leg between the legs of his opponent.   He nerved himself for the effort.   Then, with one tight grasp, with one
strong wrench, with one deep-drawn inspiration, he threw his whole strength forward, and with a growl of triumph, hurled his adversary upon the floor.   Both,
however, fell together, but the tomb-cutter was uppermost, grasping in his fury
the throat of the prostrate tipstaff.

No. 38.

"Hold him, there, Sandy, and move away your own arm that I mayn't hurt ye," cried Griffiths. "I'll put lead into his brain if ye but hold him still."

Glib Griffiths approached, and planted the muzzle of his horse-pistol against the head of the tipstaff.

"Shall I fire, Sandy?"

The tomb-cutter nodded his head.

The finger of Glib was on the trigger of his pistol; his eyes were glistening with excitement—furious excitement.

"God forgive ye your sins, Ned Ruggles," said he.

The tipstaff endeavoured to turn his head, but a strong hand was on his throat; the muzzle of a loaded weapon was pressed against his ear, he heard the fingers of Glib Griffiths playing with the trigger of the pistol. Another moment, and—

It was then that the trap in the floor was suddenly thrown up, and a man emerging from the cellar beneath, rushed upon Griffiths—wrested the pistol from his grasp—flung it into the open road, and exclaimed,—

"Away! do no murder here!"

Then turning to Gervase Morden; Ernest said,—

"Brother, your prisoner is here—take him."

CHAPTER XXXVIII.

THE BROTHERS HAVE MET.

IN wresting the pistol from the grasp of Glib Griffiths, it had gone off, fortunately, without any accident resulting therefrom, the bullet having lodged in the ceiling.

Although Griffiths was disarmed, the hand of the stone-cutter was still upon the throat of the prostrate tipstaff; vainly did those around endeavour to separate the strugglers, and remove the hand of the enraged man from the throat of his helpless adversary. With a firm, unyielding gripe, Sandy continued to press upon the neck of Ruggles, notwithstanding the eyes of the tipstaff were almost starting from their sockets, his countenance of a livid hue, and his respiration so impeded, as nearly to induce suffocation.

The gripe of the stone-cutter grew firmer; the prostrate man was convulsed. A deep stertorous breathing announced that the struggle was hastening to a termination.

"Separate them! There will be murder else," cried the secretary.

In vain the attempt. Sandy Summers had fastened upon his foe as firmly as the boa of the Eastern Indies twines itself about the poor animal which it is about to crush to death.

Ernest Morden seized the crowbar, tore it from the grasp of the man by whom it was held, and uplifted it to strike and disable the hand of the stone-cutter. Ere he could do so, however, that hand was no longer pressed against the throat of the prostrate man.

Terrified at beholding the concourse of people which had gathered round the cottage of her uncle, little Fanny had hitherto refrained from taking part in the confusion. Alarmed, however, at the report of the pistol, and fearful lest some accident had befallen her uncle, she now rushed into the cottage, and fell upon her knees before the face of the stone-cutter, just as Ernest Morden lifted up the crowbar to strike the old man's hand.

"Sandy—Uncle Sandy!" she exclaimed, uplifting her arm to stay the impending stroke. "Do they want to kill you, uncle?"

The old man looked up, his glance met the eyes of his child—his glance, which was compounded of ferocity and madness, met that of hers, which was so tender, so expressive of kindness. For a moment he gazed as if in idiotic amazement. Then, just as though paralysed by the sight of what he beheld, his hand relaxed its savage grasp, the fury faded from his countenance, the hate fled from his brow. He started up, caught the small hand of the delicate being before him, and, laying his face upon her shoulder, ejaculated,—

"No—not with thou here—not with thou who art so like the one I loved, looking at me, can I do murder. No—no—no. Thou hast saved me, child—ay, and him too, for murder I should have done. Pardon me, Fan—pardon me !"

"Why do you talk of murder, uncle, and why are these men looking so fiercely at you ?"

"Why—why ?" returned the tomb-cutter distractedly,—" Why look they, Fan, say you ?—why look—why—Ha ! my model—my model ! that is why they look ; but I have not forgotten it—not forgotten it. No, Fan, no—I cannot forget it."

"Mr. Morden has given himself up, Sandy," said Griffiths, "so it's no use making any more to do. Though I must say that if he hadn't taken that pistol from me, I'd have shown him that I could stand my ground 'gainst all the constables and militarians in the world if I chose. Ruggles knows that, and he knows, too, I'd as soon have done what I was about to do, as I am to shake hands with them now. Constables are good, and militarians are good ; but dang it, say I, let 'em keep in their proper places. Do they think nobody knows nothing of Maggy Carter, which King John gave to the people above a thousand years ago ? Do they think we don't know that it says in Maggy Carter, that everybody's house is his castle, and that he has a right to defend it against thieves, robbers, and vagabonds ? It's all very well for Mr. Morden, or Sir Thomas himself, to bring his constables here, to Sandy's house, but let me catch one of them coming into my cottage to play up such pranks, and if I don't take the laws which I know is the law, and cut the throat of the first man who dares to do it, then I'm not Glib Griffiths."

Gervase Morden tapped one of the constables on the shoulder, and in a stern voice said,—

"Take Mr Summers and Mr. Griffiths into your custody, and bring them to the Hall. They must answer there for that which they have done here."

"That's all very fine and bold of you, Mr. Morden," returned Griffiths ; "but may be you'll let Sandy and myself know what you have got to say against us afore you take us."

"There are witnesses sufficient to support any charge, which I may think proper to make against you," returned the secretary.

"And what say you to this, Sandy—do you mean to let 'em haul us off in this uncivil manner, or do yon mean to stay where you are ?"

"Let them take me where they please," answered the dejected artist whose thoughts were occupied on the subject of his broken model.

"Very well, Sandy," said Glib ; " if ye'll go, of course I'll go with you. Only I just wish to let these constables know, that it is because I choose, I go—it is because I want to have some talk to Sir Thomas, myself. I've got to let him know that I read my books as well as he, and knows what Maggy Carter is, too. What I want to do is just to tell him what the laws are, and how they were made, and when they were made, and why they were made. There's one or two points of law in which I don't think he's quite clear,—though he's the magistrate of the county. That's what I want to argue with him ; and as I don't doubt but what a little argument will make us both agree at last, and I shall be doing him a service in setting him right on the points, why, I'll go with ye, Sandy ; I'll go and talk the matter over to Sir Thomas."

"Where are you going, uncle ?" asked little Fan, clinging to the stone-cutter's arm. "Why are they taking you away ?"

"They may take me, Fan—they may take me—but—Ha ! they must not separate us,—they must not take me and leave that ! Where is it, Fan ? Go, fetch the old violin-case from your little room—fetch it quickly."

The child obeyed the order ; the old man, accompanied by the officers, passed into the inner room. Piece by piece he picked up the fragments of his broken model—that model of the tender being he had loved—and placing them in proper order in the violin-case, kissed them, wept over them, shut down the lid, and said,—

"Take me—take me now. We go together. Come, Fan, why should we stay here?"

"But where are you going, Uncle Sandy?" asked Fanny, in a tremulous tone.

"Anywhere, Fan, my pretty one—anywhere."

"And leave home, uncle?"

"But where are you going, Uncle Sandy?" asked Fanny, in a tremulous tone.

"Anywhere, Fan, my pretty one—anywhere."

"And leave home, uncle?"

"Home!" returned the tomb cutter, in a vacant manner, "home, Fan—where is that?"

"This is home, uncle."

The tomb-cutter shook his head, clasped his broken model to his heart, took the hand of his weeping niece, and joined the party, in obedience to the orders of Gervase Morden.

Not for many years had the peaceful village of St. Gillott's Cross been the scene of such a tumult as it exhibited on the present occasion. Every one of the villagers had quitted his or her cottage, to take part in the fray at the dwelling of Sandy Summers. The farrier had left his horseshoe heating in the fire, and worthy Job Seymour, the publican, had neglected to fill Mrs. Grimstone's tankard, Mrs. Grimstone herself having hastened out of the ale-house, to make inquiries into the cause of the uproar.

"Take 'em up to the Hall, Mr. Morden," bawled forth one of the spectators, "we've guessed as much as this about Summers, and now it's all come out."

"Perhaps you'll oblige me and these gentlemen, by telling us what has come out, and what you did guess, Giles Hutchins," returned Griffiths.

"Why, if it comes to that, Glib Griffiths," continued Hutchins, "there isn't many of us in this village as has had a good opinion of Sandy Summers, or of yourself either."

"Come, come, Hutchins," interposed the landlord of the ale-house. "Speak for yourself, my lad; there's nothing that I have to say against Mr. Summers or Mr. Griffiths; they've both been very proper sort of men ever since I knew them, and I don't know who can say to the contrary, if they say the truth."

"Bean't they traitors, Master Seymour?" asked Roger Dugson, the village well-digger. "Bean't they be going up to the Hall because they've been playing tricks with King George?"

"That has to be proved against them yet," replied the landlord.

"Ay, faith! and pretty strong proofs there'll be too," exclaimed Hutchins, "It isn't all to be wondered at, that its all come about as it has; and I should'nt feel very much surprised if it turned out that theyv'e a plot in hand to kill King George himself. It hasn't been very wise of us to let Glib Griffiths carry our letters, seeing as how them who bean't true to their country be as likely as not to open other people's letters."

"Giles Hutchins!" cried Griffiths, as he darted aside and grasped the arm of the last speaker. "You are a liar! and you know that you are telling lies,—only say out boldly what you have to say, and may be you'll find that you've got more than your match in Glib Griffiths!"

As it was evident that a serious quarrel was brewing, Gervase Morden thought proper to interfere; while the tipstaff suggested the propriety of securing the hands of Glib Griffiths by means of a pair of handcuffs. After some little dispute, and a fair show of resistance on the part of Griffiths he submitted to the indignity. Then, lifting up his hands, and shaking them at Hutchins, he cried in a tone of bravado,—

"Never mind, Giles Hutchins; you and I shall meet again some day; and if you do come to me to have your chin scraped, and if I do happen to have the razor in my hand—I won't say what would be likely to happen, Giles; but you and I haven't been the best of friends for some time past."

"Don't be down-hearted, Glib, my lad," advised Seymour, the landlord of the village inn. "You'll come back again, Glib, and have the chance of paying off all your debts. Don't be afeard, lad."

"Afeard of whom?" returned Glib, heroically. "I'm going up to the Hall just to have a chat with Sir Thomas. It's odd he has sent Sandy an invitation as well as myself; but I'll speak up for Sandy, and let Sir Thomas know the rights of the matter. Let 'em tie up Glib Griffith's hands, if they like, I warrant ye they can't tie up his tongue—they aint clever enough for that !"

The procession moved onward towards the Hall. In the front, and on horseback, went Gervase Morden, followed by his brother in the custody of the constables. Next to Ernest went the tomb-cutter, leading little Fanny, and immediately behind them, with a bold front, a swaggering step, and a look of self-confident pomposity, marched Glib Griffiths, with his letter-case at his side.

No conversation passed between the two Mordens. Whether it was that Gervase felt too overpowered by the sadness of the duty which he had to perform, or whether it was that he felt too deeply incensed against Ernest to permit of his holding converse with him, could not be told from his manner. Ernest was his brother's prisoner; they were the sons of the same parent, and yet one was now a captor and the other his captive. Gervase rode on without even looking round, or for once glancing at his brother. Ernest followed behind, his head bent downwards, and his arms folded on his chest, apparently deeply absorbed in thought.

Then came Sandy Summers and Fanny. The tomb-cutter carried with him the remains of his broken model, over which he bent with affectionate fondness. His niece accompanied him ; but tears were in Fanny's eyes, nor did she care to notice Pompey, who gambolled playfully by her side. Weeping Fanny and sportive Pompey !

It was not easy to tell, from the expression of his countenance, whether Glib Griffiths disliked his situation, or whether it was to him a source of joy. Certainly there was not the least semblance of either in his eye, nor did he in anywise appear downcast and sorrowful. On the contrary, there was a twinkling radiance in those grey eyes of his, combined with an impudent pout of his lips, which seemed to indicate, that Glib Griffiths thought himself to be a very important personage, at that particular moment, and was, moreover, fully resolved to attempt bringing Sir Thomas Warrenton to the same opinion, by the delivery of an eloquent oration upon loyalty, King George, the provisions of Magna Charta, and other such tempting subjects, on all of which Glib Griffiths believed himself to be thoroughly well-informed.

As the party was passing through the gate leading into the courtyard of Warrenton Hall, Ernest Morden halted for a moment, and gently tapping the arm of the tomb-cutter, said in a low voice,—

"Those papers, Summers—where are they ?"

"Safe—quite safe," replied Sandy.

"But where? My character—my life hangs upon them. Tell me quickly where they are."

"Hush! Mr. Gervase is watching us. You shall know all presently."

CHAPTER XXXIX.

THE CHARGE AGAINST THE PRISONER.

SIR THOMAS WARRENTON was a magistrate and one of the justices of the peace for that division of the county ; it was his province, therefore, to take cognisance of the dereliction of duty with which Ernest Morden was charged, as well as to inquire into the truth or falsity of the other accusations which had been made against him.

Leaving his brother in the care of the constables, Gervase Morden passed on to confer with Sir Thomas, previous to the examination which was about to take place. Glib Griffiths availed himself of the opportunity to make some general reflections upon magisterial law, as well as to apply those reflections to his own particular case.

" I know," observed Glib, " that Sir Thomas is a magistrate, and that he's what they call a justice. Now, I've got nothing to say against Sir Thomas as a gentleman ; and as far as I know, he is not a worse magistrate than any other ; but what I have got to say is, that neither Sir Thomas, nor Mr. Morden know anything of the law of England as laid down in Magnay Carter,—leastwise I should say they don't, from what they've taken upon themselves   do this day. Sandy," continued Glib, addressing the tomb-cutter, " you'll lend me the key of your cottage for a short time. I've left that little book of mine, with Magnay Carter in it, underneath a marble slab on one of the shelves of your workshop, where I put it the other day after argying a point with you. Mr. Jefferies won't mind going and fetching it for me. I must bring Magnay Carter and Sir Thomas face to face—that's what I must do. I must show him that he's wrong in everything he's done——"

" Do you mean Magnay Carter, Mr. Griffiths ?" inquired the village cobbler.

Glib threw a glance of mingled scorn and contempt upon the questioner and replied,

" If people don't know what Magnay Carter is, they should keep silent. I meant Sir Thomas—I meant that I must show him how he's breaking the laws of Magnay Carter, as laid down by King John in the Parlyment house——"

" I beg your pardon," interrupted the cobbler again, " but wasn't it at Runnymede, Mr. Griffiths ?"

" Well, and where's Runnymede ?" demanded Glib, indignantly. " You don't know what a parlyment-house was like in those days, I suppose ? As I was saying, however, it's one of our glorious privileges, given to us by the laws of the realm, that no man has a right to assault another man in his own house—no man dare enter another man's house without leave—no man can legally put his foot over my threshold without my first giving him permission. Why, don't Magnay Carter itself say, 'that every man's house is his castle'— don't it say that, I ask ?"

" Ay, Ay, Master Griffiths, that's right enough—that's about it, lad," responded Mr. Seymour.

" Well, I know it is," responded Glib, " and that being the case, I want to speak to Sir Thomas ; I want to see him at once, and ask him if he knew what he was doing, when he sent down Mr. Morden to break into the dwelling-place of my friend Sandy Summers. That'll puzzle him—that'll be a question which he won't easily get over, nor Mr. Morden either. I tell you what, friends—Sandy Summers ought to be a merry man to-day—I should be if I were in his place. He's got nothing to do but to bring an action against Sir Thomas, and lay his damages at what amount he may think fit, to get the whole affair set in the right light, and make Sir Thomas pay down pretty handsomely."

" Yes, but he won't do that," suggested Mr. Seymour. " Sir Thomas is a good sort of a landlord to us, and I don't think Sandy would like to put him to any trouble."

" I don't advise him to do so," returned Glib ; " I'm only showing him what he could do if he chose—there's nothing for him to look downhearted about. Let him leave it all to me, and I'll make it square enough with Sir Thomas, and get him to pay for the breaking of that model into the bargain. I'm sure, too, if Mr. Ernest Morden would be kind enough to trust me with all the points of his case, I'd engage to get him out of his hobble, and,—"

At this moment the door of the room opened, and Mr. Thwaites, the steward, making his appearance, announced that Sir Thomas was ready, and that he had desired the immediate attendance of Lieutenant Morden.

Ernest followed the deliverer of the message into one of the longest apartments of Warrenton Hall. Occupying a chair near the centre of this apartment, was Sir Thomas himself, while seated at a table before him was his secretary, Garvase Morden. On a seat at his right, and attired in the height of the then prevalent fashion, reclined the friend of Lambert Warrenton, the accomplished and gentlemanlike Eugene Dourville.

" Sir Thomas Warrenton, I believe," said Ernest, bowing to the knight, as he approached the table.

" It is Sir Thomas Warrenton to whom you speak, Lieutenant Morden," was the reply, delivered in a somewhat embaarassed manner. " You are aware, I presume, that I hold the office of magistrate, and that it is my duty to investigate into the particulars of any offence committed within this division of the county.

" I have been so informed," replied Ernest. " There is no one whom, under the present circumstances, I should prefer to select as my judge, in the place of Sir Thomas Warrenton."

" Not so, Lieutenant Morden. If the charge already made against you be substantiated—which God forbid!—judgment will have to be passed upon you by those who hold higher authority than is intrusted to me."

" Still, Sir Thomas, it gives me pleasure that the confession which I have to make should be made to you. Equally convinced of your impartiality, and your power of discrimination. I entertain no fear of being treated harshly or with injustice ; while at the same time, I am confident that you will listen to that which I have to say, and form your own opinion of me accordingly. It is truth which I have to tell."

Sir Thomas paused for a few moments, and then made answer,—

" Be assured, Lieutenant Morden, that from me you will receive that patient hearing, and that impartiality which you desire. There is a chair beside the table. May I beg you to be seated !"

Ernest complied. Again there was a pause. It was evident that each individual present—Eugene Dourville excepted—felt the embarrassment of his situation.

" Lieutenant Morden," said Sir Thomas, " it painfully grieves me, that you should be brought into my presence on such a charge as that which is now laid against you, and that it should fall to my lot to investigate into an affair in which, I am afraid, you stand in a very unfavourable position. I knew your father—we were friends together, to his honour be it said, that I never knew a man more honest, more loyal, or more worthy. I trust Lieutenant Morden, that you have not disgraced that father's name—that you have not done aught which he would have been ashamed to do. There is much that you have to answer to. I hope that you will be able to reply in such a manner as may exonerate you from the present charge, and free us from what would otherwise be the performance of very unpleasant duties."

" I am prepared to speak the truth, Sir Thomas."

" It is that only which I wish to hear," replied the knight.] Then addressing his secretary, Sir Thomas inquired whether Captain Chaddock had arrived.

" Not yet," was the reply.

" He should have been here by now," rejoined Sir Thomas, who after a minute's pause, drew his chair nearer to the table, fixed his eyes upon the prisoner, and in a tone of voice which betrayed the discomposure of his mind, said,—

" Captain Charnock not having arrived, I may as well detail to you, Lieutenant Morden, the nature of the charge to answer which you have been summoned hither. You must know, then, that from my acquaintance with Mr. Heyton and his family, I became apprised of some very extraordinary circumstances which took place in their cottage a few nights since. You, Lieutenant Morden, are fully acquainted with the particulars of the event to which I allude, and it is to you that I shall subsequently apply for an explanation——"

" Your pardon, Sir Thomas," said Ernest, rising from his seat, and interrupting the speaker, " but, if I am not mistaken, the occurrences of that evening have nothing to do with the charge which I have to answer here."

" Resume your seat, young man," angrily commanded the knight. " Whatever your opinions may be on that subject, it is mine that you should be called to a count for your behaviour; so utterly unworthy as it was of a gentleman, a man of honour, and a servant of his majesty.   In faith, I can tell you that I took some trouble in looking after you on Mr. Heyton's behalf; and it was in so doing that I heard from Captain Charnock of your being despatched to London.   To London I went ; but on arriving there, found that you had not presented yourself as it was your duty to have done, neither had you delivered the papers entrusted to your care.   Forthwith I returned, and again seeking Captain Charnock detailed to him the result of my adventure.   He was struck with astonishment that one whom he had put such trust in, should have acted so faithlessly.   We waited ;—nothing was heard either of you, or of the despatches with which you had been entrusted.   In fact ——"

Sir Thomas was interrupted in his speech by the door opening, and Mr. Thwaite's announcing the arrival of Captain Charnock.

Ernest Morden bowed to the captain, but the salute was not returned.   That the captain was a stern disciplinarian was evident, even in the very cast of his features. With an aspect of command dark, deeply-seated eyes, a contraction of the eyebrows, an habitual compression of the lips, short, grey, and grizzly hair, a portly figure, and a firm step ; his very appearance afforded sufficient indication of the character of the man.   Glancing at his lieutenant, he contracted his brow, drew up his chest, and in a cold haughty voice, said,—

" You are here, Lieutenant Morden."

" Here, to explain everything, Captain Charnock," replied Ernest.

The captain took a seat.

" I have been informed, Lieutenant Morden, of the position in which he is placed," said Sir Thomas, addressing the captain, " and was proceeding to detail to him the nature of the charge.   Now that you have arrived, Captain Charnock, we will resume the inquiry according to the usual form."

" You must permit me to observe, Sir Thomas Warrenton," said the captain, " that the crime with which Lieutenant Morden stands charged is one which ought to be investigated by a court-martial."

" True, Captain Charnock.   Yet it will be as well, if possible, to spare the young man the indignity of appearing before such a tribunal, by allowing him an opportunity of clearing himself from the charge at once, if it be in his power so to do."

" I will not object to that arrangement, Sir Thomas.   Let the inquiry proceed.

It was notified to Captain Charnock that as he was the principal accuser of Ernest, it was necessary for him to take the oath, preparatory to making his depositions.   Complying accordingly, he proceeded to state the accusation which he had to make against Lieutenant Morden.

Gervase Morden acted as clerk.

" You will state the circumstances which led to Lieutenant Morden being entrusted with the despatches," said Sir Thomas.

" That I must necessarily do," replied the captain, " for in dishonouring his trust, Mr. Morden has placed me in an unpleasant position as well as himself."

" You, Captain Charnock !"

" Yes.   The papers, which I gave into his care, should have been conveyed to London by myself.   Unfortunately, however, a sudden attack of illness prevented me from undertaking the journey. The documents being of the utmost importance, I felt it to be my duty to lose no time in transmitting them to their destination. Lieutenant Morden I believed to be a gentleman in whom I could put trust.   To him I committed them, giving at the same time instructions that he was to make no delay in proceeding with them to the metropolis.   He left the ship.   I believed that he had obeyed my instructions.   On the morning of this day, I received notice that no such despatches have been delivered by him in London."

" And you are wholly unaware of where those papers are at present, Captain Charnock ?"

" Entirely so."

" Do you know of any motive which was likely to have led Lieutenant Morden to the commission of this breach of trust ?"

"I do not."

"Nor have you any suspicion of such motive?"

"None whatever."

"From what you knew of Lieutenant 'Morden, had you any reason to doubt that he would prove unfaithful to his trust?"

"Certainly not. On the contrary, I believed him to be a man of honour. Had I not entertained that opinion of him, I should not have confided the papers to his care."

"And you say that those papers were of value?"

"You, Sir Thomas Warrenton, can judge of their value, when I tell you that they contained information relative to one of the nations with which we are at war —I mean France."

"Ha!" cried Sir Thomas, "and supposing them to be lost—what then?"

"The result would be according to the hands into which they happened to fall.'

"Hey, man! and what if monsieur himself were to get hold of them?"

"He would use them to his own advantage; while those to whose care they had been committed would have to answer to a serious charge."

"Treachery man—downright treachery! King George would hang them for traitors.'

If Captain Charnock, or Sir Thomas Warrenton, had observed the countenance of Eugene Dourville during the latter part of the preceeding conversation, either would have seen that which would have attracted his attention, and perhaps excited his curiosity.

"Lieutenant Morden," said Sir Thomas, "you have heard the charge which Captain Charnock has made against you, nor can you be otherwise than aware of its serious nature. It is a grave charge—a very grave charge. I do hope for your own sake that you may be able to answer it satisfactorily, although I am at a loss to guess what explanation you can give that will be likely to exonerate you. Proceed."

Ernest arose from his seat, and, after some little hesitation, proceeded to relate how he had paid a visit to the cottage of the Heytons, on the night of his leaving the ship, endeavouring to excuse himself for that act of delay, on the plea of the unfavourable state of the weather, and the impossibility of procuring a conveyance at the time. He then narrated in a brief and unsatisfactory manner the incident of his meeting with the stranger at the cottage, who, he affirmed offered him a deep insult, and with whom he was subsequently compelled to cross swords. Next he desired that Sandy Summers should be produced to corroborate his account of having sought the tomb-cutter's cottage in a wounded state. Then, after displaying his still unhealed arm, he offered a plea for his remissness in failing to forward the despatches to their destination; inasmuch as that in the agony of his wound, and the delirium which had supervened, he had forgotten having them in his possession, and was unconscious of the serious error which he was committing. This explanation was attentively listened to by Sir Thomas and Captain Charnock, the latter making the remark,—

"It is strange to me, Mr. Morden, that an officer of such reputed discretion as yourself, should have allowed the love of pleasure to have become paramount to a sense of duty."

"Yes, yes, Captain Charnock," interposed Sir Thomas, "that was wrong— very wrong indeed; nor must Mr. Morden escape without punishment for so doing. Yet the young man has offered a good plea; for we know what youth is, captain, when the fascination of a pretty face is in the way. Gad's me! I think I should have done as badly myself, if sent on such an errand, and had a chance of stepping aside to sip the dew off a pair of rosy lips. Young blood, captain— young blood. It's the failing of us all when the fever's in the veins."

"You surely do not mean to defend Mr. Morden, on this charge of breach of duty to his sovereign, Sir Thomas Warrenton?" said the captain in a somewhat wrathful voice.

"Not I, man,—not I. The youth has committed a very grave offence, and he must stand his punishment. Nevertheless, captain, his plea is good—very good; nor have I a doubt of its truth. I know the girl myself, and I must say that I envy the young dog in possessing the favour of a pair of such bright eyes. It's not to be wondered at, captain—not at all to be wondered at. Mr. Morden will deliver up the papers, and we must see that they are forwarded immediately; he himself must answer to the Admiralty for the fault which he has committed."

Ernest Morden turned pale, faltered, and addressing Sir Thomas, said,—

"As to the despatches, I——"

"Well, man, you must hand them over to Captain Charnock, at once, that he may atone for their delay in the best manner he can."

"But, Sir Thomas—I—the despatches——"

"Gadzooks man! what do you mean? Give them up, I say, at once!"

" I cannot—they——"

" Hey! What now? Where are the papers?"

" Pardon me, Sir Thomas. I do not know."

" Not know!" ejaculated the worthy knight, turning red in the face as he spoke, " not know, man?"

" I—I——"

" Why, is the man mad? Can you tell me, captain, if I heard rightly?"

" Indeed, Sir Thomas Warrenton," replied Captain Charnock, " it is nothing more than I expected to hear. They who can place pleasure before duty, can as easily play the traitor, as the man of honour."

" But—but," stammered Sir Thomas, rising from his seat, and looking fiercely at Ernest, " what does this mean, sir? what am I to understand? I ask you, sir, what does it mean?"

" It means," replied Ernest, in a firm voice, " that the despatches that were in my possession twenty-four hours ago are not so now; neither do I know where they are."

" Not know!"

" They have been taken from me, and I am ignorant into whose hands they have passed. Sampson Summers, the tomb-cutter can afford you that information which it is not in my power to give."

" This is a strange piece of news, Mr. Morden! Let Sampson Summers be called immediately."

A few minutes passed, and then the tomb-cutter entered the room, leading Fanny by the hand, and attended by Glib Griffiths, who, regardless of the assertions which the messenger had made to the contrary, had persisted in affirming that his presence was required as well as that of Sandy.

" Come this way, Mr. Summers," commanded Sir Thomas. " Who is that man behind you?"

" It is Mr. Griffiths, Sir Thomas; he—"

" Well, what does he want here?"

Glib Griffiths stepped forward.

" Begging your pardon, Sir Thomas," said Glib, " as my friend Sandy isn't the best hand at making a speech, I thought I'd better—"

" Tush, tush, man! Leave the room. Send him away, Thwaites."

" Please you, Sir Thomas, Mr. Griffiths is a prisoner," observed the steward.

" What, Griffiths!" exclaimed the knight in surprise. " Why, what has he done?—what charge have you against him?"

" He has been apprehended for assisting Mr. Summers, and the gentleman who——"

" Ha!" cried Sir Thomas, " a conspiracy—a whole nest of villains! Stand back, Griffiths, that I may hear what you have to say presently." Then addressing the tomb-cutter, Sir Thomas exclaimed, " Gadzooks, Summers, man! have you brought your tombs as well as yourself? What does all the stone mean?"

Sandy Summers placed his shattered model on the ground by his side, and was too much overcome by his feelings to reply to the question which he had been desired to answer.

" It's Uncle Sandy's pretty angel!" said little Fanny in a timid manner, " Mr. Morden was very naughty to break Uncle Sandy's angel, because it was what Uncle Sandy loved."

" What does it all mean, and what is that stone brought here for?" inquired Sir Thomas of those around him. " Summers, man, do you know that you have a serious charge to answer?"

" Yes, Sir Thomas; they broke it—they dashed it to pieces, though I had taken so much care of it for years."

" Is the man mad? What does he mean?" demanded Sir Thomas in a voice of passion.

Glib Griffiths advanced towards the table.

" It means," said he, " that Mr. Morden, under your direction I believe, Sir

Thomas, has acted wrongly; and has illegally broken the laws of England in forcing his way into the house, tenement, or earth inhabited by my friend, Sandy Summers, and demolishing by destroying the goods and chattels therein contained. I haven't my little book with me; but if you've got Maggy Carter in any one of those big books by your side, Sir Thomas, I'd thank you to—"

"Mr. Morden," exclaimed Sir Thomas, addressing his secretary, "will you explain to me what is the meaning of this man's nonsense?"

"I think, Sir Thomas," replied the secretary, "that as the case of Mr. Griffiths is a matter for after inquiry, and does not concern the business in hand, he had better be excluded from the room until his presence is required.

"Give me leave to put Mr. Morden to rights, Sir Thomas?" interposed Glib, "Maggy Carter gives every Englishman the privilege of saying what he has to say. Now, I go by Maggy Carter; and—"

"Turn him out!" cried Sir Thomas, "take the fellow out."

Glib Griffiths was forcibly removed from the room.

Sir Thomas fixed his eyes upon the tomb-cutter.

"Sampson Summers," said he, "you are accused by Leiutenant Morden of stealing certain papers from him, which charge, if it be proved against you, will be like to help you to the gibbet. What have you to say, man?"

Sandy Summers hesitated for a few minutes; then, looking up he asked the question,—

"Must I tell you all I know about them, Sir Thomas?"

"If you do not, man, it may be the worse for you."

"Well, then," commenced Sandy, "as I haven't told Mr. Ernest Morden where the papers are, perhaps he'll be as glad to hear about them as you will, Sir Thomas. But where is Mr. Lambert Warrenton?"

"Mr. Lambert—my son? he is gone to London. What do you want of him, man?"

"I'll tell you, Sir Thomas. You must know that Mr. Ernest only remembered about these papers yesterday, and a sad way he was in about them, sure enough! What he wanted to do, was to take the coach, and set off with them himself; but I wouldn't let him do that, because it would have just brought on his fever again, and made his wound mortify. So I talked over the matter with Miss Amy Heyton——"

"Amy Heyton!" exclaimed the knight.

"Yes, Sir Thomas, Miss Amy is a sort of sweetheart of Mr. Ernest's; and came to see him at my cottage."

"Hey, man! and so you've dragged a petticoat into the plot too, have ye? Let Miss Amy Heyton be called."

Sir Thomas paused for a minute, when presently the door opened and Mr. Heyton entered, accompanied by his son and his two daughters.

"Give them chairs, Thwaites—place chairs," commanded Sir Thomas.

"Amy here!" ejaculated Ernest, as his glance lighted on the slender graceful form of the fair and delicate girl.

"Miss Amy Heyton," said Sir Thomas, after the completion of some few preliminary matters, "it has just been stated by Mr. Summers, that you knew of yonder prisoner's concealment in the tomb-cutter's cottage, and that you visited him there,—is that the truth?"

"It is," replied Amy faintly, blushing as her glance wandered in the direction of Ernest.

Frank Heyton turned towards his father, and with a look of astonishment depicted in his countenance, said,—

"Do you hear father? Can Amy have done so—can she so have debased herself?"

Sir Thomas continued:—

"And you knew, Miss Heyton of certain papers being in the possession of Lieutenant Morden, which he had illegally detained in his own keeping?"

"I did," again replied Amy.

" He confided the secret to you, I suppose ?"

" No," answered Amy, " Mr. Ernest did not tell me that he had done wrong in neglecting to forward the papers.'"

" Nor did you know such to be the case ?"

Amy hesitated and faltered in endeavouring to reply.

" I told her," said Sandy Summers. " Mr. Ernest let me know all about it, and I told it to Miss Amy. But it was Miss Amy herself who planned what to do with the papers."

" Amy planned !" ejaculated Ernest in amazement.

" Speak, man—speak plainer !" commanded Sir Thomas. " Do you mean to accuse Miss Heyton of having anything to do in this affair ?"

" Yes, Sir Thomas. Miss Amy is a sweet girl, and I am sure that she is very fond of Mr. Ernest, whatever he may think of her. It would have made you cry to have seen the distress she was in—poor girl! when she heard of Mr. Ernest's trouble. It was some time before she knew what to do. At last, however, it came to her mind that Mr. Lambert—your son, Sir Thomas, was just about to start for London, and knowing that he holds a situation in the Admiralty Office, she thought that if I'd let her have the papers, she would carry them to him, and ask him to do what he could on Mr. Ernest's behalf. So you see, Sir Thomas, I let her have them ; and she carried them to Mr. Lambert last night, and he promised to take them to town with him this morning, That's what Miss Amy has done, and Mr. Ernest ought to love her doubly more than he has ever done before."

" A pretty kettle of fish—a pretty kettle of fish, upon my honour !" exclaimed Sir Thomas, " so this is all true, girl ; and I'm to understand that my son has the despatches in his possession ?"

" He has," answered Amy in a faint voice.

Consternation, wonderment, and surprise were depicted upon the countenances of most of those present. Amy bent down her head to hide her blushing face ; Ernest Morden sprang forward, caught the hand of the fair girl in his own, and pressing it to his lips, ejaculated,—

" How shall I thank you, dear Amy ? This has been kind, noble, generous, of you indeed."

Frank Heyton laid his hand upon the arm of the young man.

" Ernest Morden," said he, " you have to give an explanation of your past conduct to the brother of Amy Heyton, before he can permit you to take his sister's hand."

Sir Thomas Warrenton observed the action of Frank Heyton, and saw the angry expression which darkened the brother's countenance. Addressing Mr. Heyton, he pointed towards the group, and said,—

" He must not interfere. Have you forgotten the compact, Stephen Heyton?"

The father of Amy immediately interposed.

" There must be no quarrelling Frank," said he. " Let Ernest Morden talk to Amy if he wishes to do so."

" What father ! Before he has explained his conduct—before he has asked forgiveness for the insult ?"

" Yes. Come away."

After the lapse of a few minutes, Sir Thomas Warrenton desired silence, then, addressing Captain Charnock, he said,—

" From what we have just now head, Captain Charnock, I think we may look leniently upon the case of Lieutenant Morden. The despatches are by this time within a short distance of London, for Lambert departed at an early hour. You will forgive me for have kept the secret, but this gallant deed to which Miss Heyton pleads guilty, was known to me previous to the commencement of this inquiry, such knowledge having been communicated to me by my son's friend, Mr. Eugene Dourville. It will of course be necessary to keep Lieutenant Morden a prisoner, until we have heard the pleasure of the authorities respecting him. He shall remain here, for I have something further to say to him, which must be said in private. I think, captain, that you and I must do what we can to get the young scaramouch excused, eh, captain ?"

"In whatever light you may choose to view Lieutenant Morden's conduct, Sir Thomas," replied Charnock. "I cannot regard it otherwise than as a breach of trust, as well as a neglect of duty."

"Well, well, man, we know that. But he is young, you know, and if I am not mistaken, he is about to wed the girl. Consider circumstances, captain. Men are apt to be a little mad, and to do foolish things, when the fire is in the blood. Is it not so, captain ?"

After demurring for a while to the plea of excuse which Sir Thomas had set up on behalf of Ernest Morden, Captain Charnock at last consented to look at the transaction in the most favourable light, and at the same time, promised to exert his own influence in averting the disgrace which threatened the culprit. Having shaken hands with the captain, and invited him to stay to dinner, Sir Thomas proceeded to inquire into the nature of the charges which had been brought against the other prisoner. Sandy Summers entered into a brief explanation of the part he had taken in resisting the attack which had been made upon his cottage, and offered his broken model as a plea for his having injured the heads of some half dozen turbulent villagers. He was dismissed with a caution, warning him against hiding any more fugitives within his dwelling. This warning he promised to observe, and departed, taking with him his shattered model.

"What has the other varlet been guilty of ?" inquired Sir Thomas, as the constables brought forward Mr. Griffiths.

"Please you, your worship," said Ruggles, the tipstaff, "we found Glib Griffiths at Sandy Summer's cottage, and he has nearly cut my head open with a mallet-stroke."

"Hey ! what now ? Cutting heads open, indeed! a pretty game that ! Let the rascal be taken to the market-place, and kept there for twelve hours in the stocks. His inpudence deserves that punishment."

"I object, Sir Thomas, I offer legal objection," stammered Glib. "There's nothing about the stocks in Maggy Car——"

"Take him away, d'ye hear ?" repeated Sir Thomas, in a louder voice.

Glib was removed by main force.

There remained in the apartment only Sir Thomas Warrengton, the Heytons, Gervase Morden, and his brother Ernest. Amy was engaged in conversation with the last mentioned individual, and Frank Heyton was listening and replying to the remarks made by his father, and his sister, Kate.

One individual there was, who stood apart from the rest ; it was Gervase Morden, the student. His head was bent downward and resting on his hands; his elbows were supported by a chair-back. Never once, since the commencement of the inquiry, had he spoken a single word to his brother, nor in any way acted as if there was the slightest relationship existing between him and the accused. Neither did he now venture to approach that brother, albeit, Ernest at times turned his face towards him, as if anxious that the strange silence should be broken. The cold manner of the elder brother was observed by Sir Thomas Warrenton.

"What, Gervase, man," said he, "hast thou no word of rejoicing to offer Master Ernest, inasmuch as he has so narrowly escaped a visit to the town-gaol?"

Gervase Morden was about to reply, when an interruption occurred, from the entrance of a domestic, who seemed to be the bearer of important tidings.

At the same moment, Sandy Summers returned, in quest of a portion of his broken model.

"What is the matter now, Jefferies ?" inquired Sir Thomas of his servant.

"The smugglers, Sir Thomas—the smugglers who wounded Mr. Lambert in the wood !"

"Well, what of them ?"

"They were in the woods again last night; there's the marks of where they killed one of your deer."

" Are you sure of that Jefferies ? "

" Quite sure, Sir Thomas. Old Grayson, the fisherman, tells me that he has seen Red Martin prowling about to-day, and Grayson thinks there'll be some brandies come on shore, below the cliffs, this evening."

" Brandies, eh, and Red Martin too ? Gadzooks ! I've longed to lay hands on that fellow these many months past. What say you, Gervase Morden—shall we get the yacht in trim for to-night, and have a boat or two out ? "

" Red Martin is not easily to be caught," replied the secretary.

" So much the better, man ; there will be the more sport. Egad, I should like a bit of a tussel by moonlight, and here is an opportunity. We'll have at him, man. Tell Hilson to get the yacht ready, Jefferies ; and don't forget to remind him that he provides us with a few stout hands, and a good chest of arms. Well thought of too ; here is a fair opening for Master Ernest. He can go with us, and prove his loyalty to King George by making prisoners of two or three of these rascally sea-thieves."

" You forget, Sir Thomas, that my brother is wounded," remarked the secretary.

" Ay, the wound—the wound, as you say. That is a bad business. Otherwise he might have done something for himself to-night."

Strange to say, Sandy Summers had listened to this conversation with a pallid countenance, and with lips that were wide apart. At the first mention of Red Martin's name, he had let fall the piece of stone from his hand, and had fixed his eyes upon the speaker with a look of terror. Advancing, he laid his fingers upon the arm of Sir Thomas Warrenton, and in a voice which seemed to indicate extreme agitation of mind, said—

" You will not pursue, Red Martin ?—you will not attempt to fight him to night ?"

" Why not, man ?"

" He is strong—very strong ; and he is well armed."

" We will be the same, Mr. Summers. Red Martin may be assured that we shall not go forth to meet him without being prepared to give him the reception he deserves."

" You would not kill him—you—"

" Why, what do you mean, Master Sandy ? You surely haven't a wish that Darlingham gibbit should be cheated of its legitimate heir ? Let Red Martin be caught, and, dead or alive, he shall have his deserts, and furnish food for the crows, if they choose to pick him. He shall hang, man—he shall hang !"

" Hang !" repeated the tomb-cutter, his face turning yet paler, and his eyeballs rolling to and fro, as if he were labouring under some perplexing fear.

Sir Thomas Warrenton turned towards his secretary.

" Your brother and I have a few things to talk over together," said he ; " Mr. Heyton and his children will keep us company. In the meantime, you can go down to Hilson, and instruct him about to-night's adventure."

" And my brother——"

" He will be here when you return."

Gervase Morden departed. In the courtyard he overtook the tomb-cutter.

" Sandy Summers," said he, as he laid his hand upon the arm of the person to whom he spoke, " know you of any better reasons than those which you have stated, why Sir Thomas should not attempt the capture of Red Martin ?"

" Better reasons, Mr. Morden ?"

" Ay. Setting aside the risk of the adventure, are there any other grounds on which you would advise Sir Thomas not to pursue his present intention with rela-lation to the smugglers ?"

" Not I, Mr. Morden—not I, I assure you," stammered Sandy.

" That will do, Mr. Summers. I am glad that you know no other reasons," said the secretary, as he parted from the tomb-cutter.

Gervase Morden proceeded in search of the steward.

" Thwaites," said he, " see that some one is sent into the village immediately, to keep watch on the cottage of Sandy Summers. Let the tomb-cutter be followed, go where he may."

About an hour afterwards, Sandy Summers placed a paper in the hand of little Fanny, and telling her to take up Pompey, sa id,—

"Go into the churchyard, Fan, and play with your dog for about a quarter of an hour ; then, slip out by the wicket at the other side ; make your way down to the cliffs, at the further end of the bay, and give this letter to any one whom you may happen to find at Michael Warner's cottage."

"Who is the letterfor, Uncle Sandy ?"

"They will know, to whom you give it, Fan. Hide it in your bosom, and be careful not to let it drop out."

Fanny left the cottage. The tomb-cutter went to the window, and kept watch till he saw the child make her way through the churchyard. No sooner was she out of sight, than falling on his knees, he clasped his hands, and ejaculated,—

"God grant that it may reach him ! God grant that he may take my warning !"

Was it Red Martin whom Sandy Summers meant ? and if so, why did he pray for him ?

CHATER XL.

THE PRESENTMENT OF EVIL.

The interview between Sir Thomas Warrenton and Ernest Morden had been brought to a conclusion. Mr. Heyton and his daughters had departed. Conversing together in the drawing-room of the mansion, was the Lady Isabel and Eugene Dourville.

Gervase Morden having executed his commission, returned to the Hall, and was met in the lower gallery by Sir Thomas Warrenton.

"Morden, man, I have been seeking you for the last half-hour," said the knight. "Accompany me to the library, for I have that to say which must be said in private. Have you arranged matters for this evening ?"

"I have. Hilson says, that if we really mean to give chase to Red Martin, it will be better for us to take the cutter. His men are all in readiness ; and there is a plenitude of arms on board."

"That is well. Now, for this matter of your brother Ernest. I have had an hour's converse with the youth, but there seems to be no penetrating into the secret of his conduct with regard to Miss Heyton."

"What !" exclaimed Gervase—" will not my brother explain—"

"He will explain nothing ; neither does he seem inclined to furnish us with any clue to the mystery."

"Ny brother refuse, Sir Thomas !—Ernest Morden refuse to account for offering an insult to Frank Heyton's sister !"

"Do you know of what nature that insult was, Mr. Morden ?"

"I do not, Sir Thomas. But Frank tells me that Ernest had promised marriage to Miss Amy, and that he has now recalled that promise, without assigning his reasons for so doing, either to Amy or to her friends."

"To Mr. Heyton and his other children your father certainly refuses to make any such explanation. The girl, however, affirms, that Lieutenant Morden has confided to her the cause of his strange behaviour, that he has offered an apology, and that, moreover, she has accepted the apology, and is now perfectly satisfied. But I suspect the jade—I suspect her strongly."

"Of what, Sir Thomas ?"

"Of story-telling, fibbing, prevarication, and all the other wickednesses which this sweethearting leads to."

"Do you think that my brother has not explained his conduct to Miss Heyton ?"

"I do—I am sure that such is the case. Girls—bah !—they will say anything, or do any foolishness to shield from reproof a young spark, for whom they have an inkling. What the cause of this quarrel has been, I cannot unriddle; though I have exerted myself to effect the discovery in every way which I could devise. Your brother is now alone. Go you to him, and see what you can do. Gadzooks! the lad must be a simpleton! The girl is fair, nor will she want for dowry. Nevertheless, Master Ernest has just had the impudence to assure me that he never will wed her, even were she to become a queen."

"And did he give you no reason whatever, Sir Thomas, for coming to that resolution ?"

"Reason, indeed! Zounds! I doubt if the lad has any reason left. He pleads obstacles, impediments, hindrances, and I know not what ; yet defines nothing, nor utters a word of common sense. Go to him, Mr. Morden. Talk with him. Get him to speak out plainly, if you can."

"I will make the attempt, Sir Thomas.   There is Hilson waiting outside.   He wishes to know how the affair with the smugglers is to be conducted."

"Ay, ay, I'll speak with him directly.   I'll show him that I have not been off the sea so long as to have forgotten my nauticalities.   Go you to your brother. You will find him in the bay-parlour.   And Morden, man, hark ye!—say nothing about the smugglers to Lady Warrenton, or to that French spark who came here with Lambert.   Red Martin, you see, is a friend to the frog-eater's ; and this Dourville as they call him might object to our little plan for a night's sport.   Now go, man—go to your brother, and get him to talk reason, if you can.   Go, go!"

It was an antique room, with oaken walls, hung round with crimson drapery. The panelling was painted ; each compartment being decorated with arabesque work, surrounded by a carven frame.   There was an embayed window, on the panes of which shone forth in stained glass the heraldic bearings of the Warrentons, of Warrenton Hall.   Curtains of dark velvet fell in massy folds from the cornice to the floor, enclosing a recess, well-fitted for the resort of a quiet muser, or for the pleasantries of a flirtation with some gentle maiden, possessing a heart warm as her own fair hand and her own ruby lips.

In this apartment, seated on a quaint, old, high-backed chair, with his head bent down, one arm resting upon the window-ledge, and his forehead supported by his hand, sat Ernest Morden.   He was alone and musing, when the door opened, and the secretary of Sir Thomas Warrenton apologised for his intrusion.

"Ernest," said the elder brother, "shall I disturb you by taking a seat, and spending the next half-hour with you?   Nearly two years have passed from the day on which we last conversed together."

"It has been a long time, Gervase—a very long time," said Ernest, rising and offering his hand to his brother. "Such length of absence puts friendship severely to the test."

Gervase Morden winced. "Brother," said he, "you have remarked the apparent cold and distant manner in which I have behaved towards you this day ; doubtless you have thought it strange—perhaps it has been the cause of painful feelings to you.   I regret that it should so have been.   You, however, brother Ernest, must consider that you have looked upon a servant of Sir Thomas Warrenton—upon one who had a duty to perform, and who, stern and sorrowful though the duty was, felt the painful necessity of performing it to the best of his abilities. God knows, Ernest, I have experienced enough of inward torture through the part which I have had to take in this day's proceedings!   I would have given my right hand rather than that you should have appeared on the charge which you have had to answer to.   I would have made a greater sacrifice, rather than it should have gone forth to the world that a son of Reginald Morden had been accused of neglecting his duty to his sovereign."

"I believe you, Gervase—indeed, indeed I believe you!" exclaimed Ernest, clasping his brother's hand, while tears trickled from his eyes.

"Yes, brother," continued Gervase, "the lessons of our father have never been forgotten by his eldest son.   You remember, Ernest, that no man was more just, more upright, more true to his duty, or more proud of the honourable name and fair reputation which he bore, than was the common father of us both.   It cannot have passed from your mind that the chief labours of his later years were directed to the one sole object of instilling into the minds of his sons a love of the virtues which he himself practised ; and a sense of the invaluable importance of those qualities so eminently possessed by him.   Nor can you have forgotten, dear Ernest, that our father's dying words were, that he hoped the labours of his later years would prove productive, and that the sons whom he so dearly loved would uphold themselves honourably in the world.   Those death-words, that dying wish, became to me, dear Ernest, a sacred charge ; I have ever considered them as such.   It is my pride—my delight—my joy, to know that I have never done anything since our father's death that he would have blamed me for doing in his life-time.   You too, dear brother, have hitherto acted nobly, bravely, honourably ; your integrity has procured you friends—your assiduity has won you promotion.   I have dropped tears of delight when I have heard your name mentioned by approving tongues. I have felt a thrill of joy on hearing that you had distinguished yourself by a noble action; I have exulted in your success, as much as if it had been my own. Guess, then, what my feelings were when I heard this accusation against you? Brother, I have told you how much I have loved and honoured you—how much I have rejoiced that Ernest Morden was my brother, my own brother; but bear with me when I also tell you that, if you were ever to disgrace the name you bear—the name of my father as well as of your own—if you were ever to bring dishonour upon that name by a deed of crime, I should no longer love you as a brother, no longer hold you in my esteem, or regard you as my father's son. God pardon me, Ernest! but I should wish you dead!"

Gervase Morden clenched his brother's hand in his own, and heaved a deep sigh as he made the fearful assertion.

And then, even then, while the hand of the younger brother was clasped in the hand of the elder one, while the olden remembrances were being recalled, and while the strong words were being spoken, demons unseen were at their work, and the stern student knew not in how short a time he would have to put his sternness to the test.

"I never will disgrace, never dishonour the name I bear—never, brother, so long as I live."

"That is your promise, Ernest?"

"Wish you that it should be my oath?"

"No, brother. I can believe you—I can trust you; for I know that you are truly noble, truly worthy of all my admiration and esteem."

"I should not be Ernest Morden if it were otherwise."

"You would not, brother. Indeed, indeed, you cannot imagine the joy which it affords me to know and to feel that in Ernest Morden the wishes of my father have been granted, his hopes so completely fulfilled. Our father died in a strange land, Ernest, and I was not by his bedside. You, however, stood there: you heard the last syllables he uttered; his dying prayer was communicated to me by you. Oh, brother—dear brother! let us never cease to remember that prayer—let us never give occasion for the shade of our father to come back to reproach us. Let us maintain through life our honour unstained—the fair name unsullied which our good father left us, as the only heritage he had to leave. Let there be no blot on the 'scutcheon, brother Ernest—no blot on the 'scutcheon."

"Brother, I will never place one there."

"You will not, I know you will not. And yet —"

Gervase Morden paused abruptly. A cloud seemed to pass across his countenance.

"You were about to allude to my present position, dear brother?" suggested Ernest.

"Yes, brother—yes, Ernest. There is much that I cannot understand, much that—that—"

"An explanation of past occurrences is what you desire, dear Gervase. Will you listen, if I confide to you all that it is in my power to say?"

"Willingly, Ernest—most willingly."

Gervase Morden drew his chair nearer to that of his brother, and leant his arm upon the window-ledge.

How strange was the contrast! They were the sons of one father, and yet the younger was light-complexioned, open-faced, and noble-looking; while the elder was of a darker aspect, with a thoughtful, meditative cast of features, and deep, overhanging brows, both, however, had flashing eyes, both had noble foreheads; both possessed those distinctive marks by which the man of elevated sentiments and gentle bearing may be distinguished from the common herd. It was the stern brother and the weak one—the student and the sailor—the man of thought and the man of action. They had played upon the same hearth in their infancy; they had sported together in their school-days; each had received the benedictions of th same parent; each had entered life at the same time. Their journey, however, had been along separate paths. Seldom did they meet together. And now two years had nearly elapsed since the date of their last interview.

Two years, and now they met as of old—met to clasp each other's hand, and listen to each other's words. They had met.

Alas! how little did either of those brothers suspect that the last of such meetngs was at hand!

His love of Amy—his love of the fair, fond, beauteous girl, who had so well proved her love for him, was confessed by Ernest to his listening brother. The tale was told of the early wooing, the plighted vows, and the protracted correspondence. Ernest omitted not to tell of the bright dreams he had formed, when returning on his homeward-bound voyage, of a future life of happiness with his beloved, of pleasures innumerable that were to arise out of that blissful union. He told how he had longed with impatience for the good ship to touch the shores of England. He told how he had hastened to press Amy to his heart, and listen to her love-words murmured in his ear. He told all this. Lastly, he told of that scene at the cottage—of the sudden overthrow of his cup of bliss, of love that was turned into loathing, of words uttered that wrought madness in the brain of the hearer, of memories recalled, which came back to work desolation. And to his brother Gervase, Ernest Morden declared that he would never become the husband of Amy Heyton.

"Ernest!" exclaimed the student, "what means this madness? What foolish whim possesses you, that you retract your most sacred vows, and make so strange a declaration? Is it—is it that you suspect Amy Heyton of—of—"

"No, Gervase—not her. Amy is pure, and good, and lovely."

"Then why despise her?—why reject her in such scorn?"

"Hush, brother! Far be it from me to scorn her of whom you speak. Have I not told you that she is good, pure, and stainless? Have I not told you that I have never loved any but her, and that my love shall never be given to another? Hear me, Gervase; I cannot marry Amy—I cannot do that; but I would die for her—I would die for her, even now!"

"Die for her, and yet not wed her! Why talk so paradoxically?"

"I have spoken truth. Brother, were I to tell you that which I could, but dare not, you would kill me—kill me, Gervase, rather than you would allow me to wed with Amy."

"Ha!" exclaimed the student, astounded at this strange avowal—"Tell me—tell me—what have you heard? Was the wife of Stephen Heyton false—did she—"

"Hush, brother Gervase! I have our father's word for it, that Catherine Heyton was one of the best of God's fair creatures. Stephen Heyton himself will assure you that she died a true and honoured wife."

"Then, what is this riddle? Why must Amy Heyton —"

The student was interrupted by Ernest Morden.

"Your pardon, brother. From the conversation which has already passed between us, I have been led to believe that you respect all solemn engagements, and would look in contempt upon the man, who, regardless of his honour, broke the most sacred vow. If, then, I have understood you rightly, you will not press me to dishonour, by requesting further information on this most painful subject.

"Not press you to dishonour! Why, already—to the maiden whom you promised to love—you have broken your most solemn vow!"

"Not so, good brother. Amy I shall ever love, more fondly, perhaps, than in times that have past. I break no vow made to her. But were I to make the confession which you wish me to make, you would no longer call me your brother. Peace, Gervase; let this subject rest."

In vain were all the attempts of the student to pierce that strange and fearful mystery; in vain were his guessings; in vain his cogitations. Ernest went on to relate the particulars connected with his seeking a retreat at the tomb-cutter's cottage, and to explain more fully than he had yet done the circumstances connected with the charge, on which he was now a prisoner. When he had concluded, the student observed,—

"Still, Ernest, it was wrong—very wrong of you not to have forwarded the despatches at an earlier hour. You might have sent them yesterday instead of to-day. I am glad, however, that you have explained the affair so satisfactorily. There were strange rumours abroad; and I had the pain to hear the name of Morden connected with the word *traitor*. I treated them but as rumours, dear Ernest, for full well was I assured of your fidelity and loyalty. I know that Reginald Morden's son could not be guilty of treachery; and though I listened, when they accused you of misconduct, I smiled when they charged you with crime."

"That was kind—that was noble of you, brother! Gervase Morden judged rightly then of his father's son."

"How could I think otherwise, dear brother? Come, be happy! Miss Ismay is in the drawing-room—shall we go there? Come, come, I doubt not this first error will be forgiven; Captain Charnock and Sir Thomas will intercede in your favour; there will be no notice taken of your breach of duty, and Lieutenant Morden will go back to his ship happy and light-hearted. Do not be downcast, Ernest."

"I do not wish to be, Gervase; and yet—this is strange—this is more than strange!"

"What is strange?"

"These feelings—this depression—these presentiments."

"What presentiments, brother?"

"I—I know not. There seems to be a leaden weight at my heart; there is a strange cold sensation in my brain. I shiver, brother,—I shiver."

"Shall I close the casement, Ernest?"

"No, brother—no. It is not cool air. This is—Ha! see you there? What does it mean?—what—what—"

Ernest Morden fixed his eyes upon the centre of the room, and sank for support upon his brother's arm.

Gervase Morden moved towards the bell-pull.

"You are ill, Ernest. Shall I ring for assistance?"

"No—no. It is gone—it is all gone!"

"What is it? and what has gone?"

"The feeling. I—brother, I believe in presentiments. I believe there is evil about to happen—evil which I cannot avert."

"Why such belief?"

"Because—because, as I looked across the room there seemed to arise a figure before me—a fair figure with a fair face that changed into the countenance of a demon. It looked at me; it laughed; and then it went its way."

"You are ill, brother. This is illness."

Ernest Morden started, grasped his brother's arm, gazed fixedly on the student with his wild, flashing eyes, and said—

"It is not illness, brother! Mark me! there is evil coming, and it is near at hand. I feel it—I felt its cool breath blow upon my brain!"

CHAPTER XLI.

THE EVIL COMES.—THE CHASE AFTER THE SMUGGLER.

On consulting with Hilson, who was the revenue-officer stationed on that part of the coast, Sir Thomas Warrenton saw reason for deferring his intended chase of Red Martin. What those reasons were can be readily explained.

At the period of our story, France and England were on unfriendly terms, if not at actual war. Red Martin the smuggler, was believed to be a Frenchman; though rumour had at times hinted that England was the real birth-place of the daring outlaw, and that his French accent and foreign manners had been acquired through

a prolonged intercourse with the rival nation.   At any rate, Red Martin was known
to be more friendly to the country whence he brought his brandies than to the
land which he occasionally visited, but which had long since denounced him as an
outlaw.   Besides having a reputation for great daring, and very much skill in the
illegal traffic which he carried on, he was also suspected of doing worse things than
smuggling brandies, and trading in Brussels lace.   In fact, Red Martin was believed to be as great an enemy to England as England was to him ; inasmuch as
reports had gone abroad of his being engaged in playing the part of a spy, and in
transmitting intelligence to the enemy of such facts as he could glean in his repeated visits to the British coast.   Many had been the times that the officers of
the coast blockade had used their endeavour to capture this formidable foe, but each
attempt had proved unsuccessful.   A strong arm and a heavy sword had Red
Martin ; nor were witnesses wanting who could testify to the strength of the one
and the weight of the other.   Repeatedly had Red Martin fought his enemies in
desperate contests : some had fallen beneath his blow ; others yet lived, bearing
about with them the marks of their engagement.   The lugger which Red Martin
commanded was called the " Daredevil ;" and well did the vessel merit her name.
Well built, and admirably adapted for the service in which she was used, the
Daredevil was the terror of that part of the coast which her owner best loved to
frequent, while at the same time she had hitherto defied the many attempts which
had been made to effect her capture.   Red Martin gloried in the possession of
such a vessel, believing, with all the superstition of a sailor, that so long as the
Daredevil was able to ride on the billows—so long as the good vessel which he
loved more than aught else he ever had loved in this world, could still baffle with
the waters, and dare, as for years past she had dared, to run a race with her enemies—
just so long would Red Martin remain to be the haunter of the sea.

From the conversation which took place between Sir Thomas Warrenton and
Hilson, it appeared that although the latter was quite as ready and as eager to
make an attempt at capturing the Daredevil as was the gallant, spirited owner of
Warrenton Hall, still there were certain circumstances, which in his opinion rendered it advisable that the attempt should be delayed for a short time.

" You see, Sir Thomas," said Hilson, " the craft was in sight this morning, and
was riding at anchor just down under the cliffs.   We were about to pay her a visit
ourselves ; but looking more narrowly into her, we saw that she wouldn't do for a
prize, inasmuch as she rode high in the water, and couldn't have anything of a
cargo on board.   However, I crept round to the beacon to take a better look at her
with the glass, and while I was looking she spread out her canvass to stand to sea.
At first I thought we'd give her chase in the cutter, if it was only to make another
trial at laying hands on Red Martin himself; but I soon saw that I was out in my
reckoning, and that it wouldn't do to act in a hurry.   I've known the Daredevil
long enough not to know her tricks.   I know something of Red Martin too, and
though he is a long-headed sort of a chap, and is up to as many tricks as a ring-
tailed monkey is, he can't play the artful with old Dick Hilson.   I tell you what,
Sir Thomas ; there's something more than usual in this present visit of Red Martin.
He hasn't come to bring us brandies this time, and may be he has come to take
away instead of bring——"

" Take away what, man ?" demanded the knight.

" That's more than either you or I know, Sir Thomas ; but this much is certain
—Red Martin is walking the deck of the Daredevil at this present moment."

" Hey, man !   Gadzooks ! he isn't in my wood, is he ?"

" There's no telling where he is, Sir Thomas.   He's on shore ; and as for his
craft, she's only stood out to sea, to keep herself from harm's way, till he is ready
to go on board her again."

" And when will that be ? "

" Can't say, Sir Thomas.   Might as well ask when the next whale will be caught.
Red Martin don't leave his card behind him, to say where he's gone to, or when
he will be back."

"Well, but Hilson, we must ferret him out—we must after him at once, and see that he never sets foot on that craft of his again."

"So please you, Sir Thomas," replied the officer, "I think we'd better not do that. I think we'd better try and circumvent him in another way."

"In what way, Hilson?"

"Why, you see, Sir Thomas, they who are on board the Daredevil, know the time when their skipper will be waiting for them, and will make in for the shore. Now, it strikes me that we couldn't do better than lay in wait for her till then, and be all ready to be down upon her, just before Red Martin steps on board. It will be a sort of guide, you see, to tell us where to look out for the gentleman; and then if we had two or three good hands in readiness amongst the cliffs, I don't see but what Red Martin might go to Darlingham gaol this time, after all."

"I see, Hilson. Your proposition is a good one. Go, get the cutter in readiness, and as soon as the saucy Daredevil makes her appearance, send up word at once."

This arrangement being concluded, Hilson departed. Two days passed away without the smuggler making his appearance; when on the evening of the second day a messenger arrived at the Hall, to apprise Sir Thomas that the Daredevil was in sight, and making in towards the land.

No time was lost. Sir Thomas, accompanied by Gervase Morden, was quickly on board the cutter; and the master of Warrenton Hall rubbed his hands with delight, at the thought of once again combating the enemies of his king, on the broad water; as he had done so often before, in his gay, yet well-spent youth-time.

All the arrangements for the chase and for the contest were carried out orderly and in silence. The plan was that the crew of the cutter should work their way round the headland, and, if possible, bear down upon the Daredevil just as her commander was getting on board. With this design, they had stationed men in such a position on the beach, hidden by the cliffs, that it would be in their power to intercept any retreat towards the shore. Unfortunately, the night was foggy, and the moon had not yet risen.

Half an hour passed away, and the cutter by this time had doubled the headland. The Daredevil was in the neighbouring bay, and could not be more than two miles a-head.

"What say you Morden, man?" asked Sir Thomas of his secretary; "will the moon be up soon, think you?"

"You had better apply to Mr. Hilson," answered the student; "he is more acquainted with these matters, and will give you his opinion as to whether or not there is any chance of our having moonlight with us in our sport."

"I don't know what to think," observed Hilson, whose ear had caught the observation made by Morden. "The moon must be up now, though hidden from us by the clouds. Then, as to this fog, unless the breeze starts up off the land, I'm afraid we shall have no chance of coming to close quarters with Red Martin and his saucy craft that must be lying there away at the other side of the bay."

"Hark!" exclaimed Gervase Morden, "was not that the report of a gun?"

"The youngster's ears are sharp," observed the old officer. "True enough, there was the report of a small piece. There again is the talk of another of the same dimensions."

"What does it mean Hilson, man?" inquired Sir Thomas.

"I cannot say, Sir Thomas; unless—unless—yes, it must be that Red Martin has stolen away from the shore under the cover of the fog, and our men are sending a few bullets after him to fetch him back again."

"Ha! Hilson; think you so, man? Why, at that rate the varlets will take the alarm, and be getting ready to receive us."

"Isn't it more likely that she will make off in the fog, and we lose her altogether?" observed Morden.

"How is she to do that, man?" returned Sir Thomas. "How can she play us such a trick as that, when there isn't breeze enough in the bay to puff a feather off a sail?"

" Yes, yes, Sir Thomas," said Hilson ; " the breeze is coming. Hark you how the sails are beginning to rattle ! We shall have it directly."

And even as these words were being uttered the fog separated, moving away in large masses of misty vapour, which rolled over one another like billows of smoke ; then scudded off in the distance, like troops of evil spirits, hieing to some other meeting place far, far away.

Out broke the moon, the queenly silver moon, in all the majesty of her beauty. Out broke she through the snowy clouds to shine upon the glittering sea—to spangle it with diamonds—to paint on every ripple a portrait of herself—herself all regal in her majesty, all lovely in her beauty.

Moonlight upon the sea !

And as the moon broke forth, and as the mist-clouds rolled away, the white sails of the smuggler's vessel burst upon the view of those who were eager for her capture. Tall and light and proud-like she sat upon the waters—the home of the outlaw—the one loved thing of him who was never known to have loved one human being. Her sails were set, she had caught the breeze, her long sweeps were run out, she was gliding through the waters, and Red Martin, the smuggler, walked her deck.

" Gadzooks, Hilson, we shall lose her !" exclaimed Sir Thomas. " See ! she is making headway already."

" Ay, ay, Sir Thomas. Now's the time. Pipe the crew away for both boats, Mr. Manning, and let there be two extra hands in each."

" Will it be a fight, think you ?" asked Sir Thomas, exultingly.

" No fear of it—no fear of it in the least, Sir Thomas. We are not going to let her play tricks on us this time, Daredevil as she is. Take you charge of the cutter, Watson. Sir Thomas, will you take your place in the gig ?"

" Ay, ay," replied the knight. " Come, Morden, man, keep a tight hold of your cutlass, and see whether you can do a service to your king by a swoop of that young arm. Away, Hilson ! let us away ; for the varlets are crowding sail, and the Daredevil is doing her best."

" Let her do it, Sir Thomas, let her do it. The wind is veering round, and she will have to go on the other tack directly. Give way, my lads, give way ! We shall soon have a look at Red Martin. Give way—give way !"

And through the dark water, beneath the beamy moonshine, sped the boats with their stout rowers. Strong arms were they which plied the ashen oars ; swiftly dipped they their wands in the dancing tide, and onwards flitted the light galley, like a spirit over the wave. Oh, it is a beauteous sight, that moonlight on the ocean ! Beauteous is it to gaze upon the ripples, as they sport in the silver sheen. Beauteous is it to cast the eyes across the wide expanse, and watch where fall the moonbeams on the distant brine ! But still more beauteous, still more glorious, still more grand is it, to bend to the stout oar at that moonlight time, to cut your way through the gleaming water, and laugh as the spray springs up around, and gambols beside your skiff !

" Give way, my boys !" shouted Hilson. " Pull stoutly, for the Daredevil is pressing on all her canvass."

Down dipped the strong oars into the gleaming water ; merrily sped the chasers on their way. The moonlight grew still more beauteous, and the silver beams glittered upon the dancing spray and on the naked weapons which each man had brought with him to use in desperate fight.

On sped the boats. Yet, though they cut gallantly through the water, it was evident that they were gaining very little upon the Daredevil. Every minute the breeze grew stronger, and helped to fill the sails of the smuggler's lugger. The men in the boats perceived how much the odds were against them, and bent still more to their oars. On, on through the dark-green water—on, on ! On, on through the seething wave, and the dashing spray—on, on ! On, while the light foam hisses and boils ! On while the ripples sing their song of madness as they dance around the bows of the arrowy boat ! On, chasers, on ! The chase is a merry one—the fight will be a bloody one. Bend to your oars, then, and onward hie. Ha! ha! the distance diminishes ; the white track of the wave spreads far,

far behind. No pause—no relaxation! Down with the oar into the water; let it spring thence elastically. Away over the tide! Away to conquest—to bloodshed —to victory! No pause, no drooping. Still on! Away, away!

"Hurrah, boys, hurrah!" shouted Hilson. "Another half mile, and we are up with her."

Just then something dark was seen to drop from the deck of the lugger, and rest upon the surface of the water.

"'Tis the skiff, Sir Thomas," exclaimed Hilson. "That wily rascal will make to the shore again. Ha! see, he springs into it, he and another. There they go! After them, boys! bear down upon them quickly."

"I'm afraid that he'll touch the shore first," observed Sir Thomas.

"If he accomplish that, we shall have had all our work for nothing, Sir Thomas. There'll be no taking him if he once gets on land."

"Tush, Hilson. Red Martin is nothing more than Red Martin, and is no match for half-a-dozen stout fellows like these."

" We shall see, Sir Thomas, we shall see," answered Hilson. "Give way, boys —give way, my lads, give way !"

But the sound of dipping oars was audible in the distance—a dark moving something was seen gliding over the surface of the moonlit waters, and speeding towards the shore. All knew that the glancing skiff contained the object of their pursuit— all knew that one of the two persons in that frail boat was Red Martin, the smuggler.

Presently the skiff ceased to glide over the water ; it flew—actually flew. Strong arms were those of Red Martin, and well did he know that he had occasion for exerting his strength. Away over dancing ripple and crest of foam ; away through the splashing spray, and the hissing, seething sea, fled the boat of the daring outlaw. And behind, in hot pursuit, followed the galley of the pursuers. It was a chase of life and death ; a sport where the destined prey was a human being, possessing flesh, blood, and brain, like his pursuers. No timid hare, no paltry fox, no regal stag, was the object of the fierce pursuit. It was man—man in the daring of his dark strength—man in the helplessness of him who has broken the law, and who has been given over as a prey to the hunters of men.

The boats neared the shore. Suddenly, the smuggler ceased from rowing, took off his hat, and waved it derisively at his pursuers.

" Gadzooks !" cried Sir Thomas, " we shall lose the fellow now. Pull away, boys—pull for the shore !"

" He's done us, Sir Thomas," exclaimed Hilson in a voice which betrayed his extreme vexation ; " the villain's done us. See !"

At that moment the prow of the skiff grated on the sand. Out sprung Red Martin and again waved his hat in a mocking manner at his followers.

" Shall I give him some lead, sir ?" asked a sailor, who held a musket in his hand ready to fire.

" Yes. Fire, man—fire quickly. Wing him, but don't kill him !" exclaimed Sir Thomas.

The seaman fired ; the bullet passed through the smuggler's hat. One second he paused ; then, whirling his hat in triumph, he flung it from him upon the sand, and plunged into the wood which formed a portion of Warrenton Park.

" Quick, Hilson, quick !" vociferated Sir Thomas. " Another pull, boys. There ! After him, and twenty guineas to the one who first draws his blood."

The sailors sprang out of the boat, seized their cutlasses and pistols, paused for one second to look around, and then plunged into the wood on the track of the outlaw.

" Take care of the boats, Christie," said Hilson, addressing an old seaman who was left in charge of the galleys belonging to the revenue cutter.

" Ay, ay, skipper. But hadn't some of us better make after the lugger ?"

" No. It is Red Martin we want to catch. We will make friends with the Daredevil afterwards."

Away into the woods plunged Sir Thomas, Gervase Morden, and Hilson. They could hear in the distance the shouts of the seamen who were on the track of the fugitive. Sir Thomas having lost some of the nimbleness of his youth, could not keep up with his friends in the chase. Panting, breathless, and fatigued with the violence of the exertion, he called out to Morden, ordering him that when Red Martin should be caught he was to be detained until Sir Thomas's arrival. Afar sounded the derisive shout of the bold outlaw, while from every part of the wood arose the wild whoops of the seamen. Onward through bush, and brake, and brier, up rugged acclivities, and down into deep dells, sped the hunters on their way. Now they caught a glance of the object of their pursuit, as he stood in daring defiance upon some moonlit knoll, and sent his mocking laugh back upon the night-breeze. The next minute he plunged into some shady portion of the wood, whither the sharp eyes of his hunters could not follow him. His yell of triumph was heard in the deep ravine. The next minute his dark form was seen upon some distant hill. Fleet was the hunted one ; untiring were the hunters. Whoops and halloos broke the stillness of the ancient wood. Wild cries rose upwards on the midnight air. Now the pursuers were on the track of their destined prey. In another second they found themselves at a loss, and knew not which course to take. "Follow him, my boys ! Run him down !" shouted Hilson. "Ha, ha, ha !" laughed Red Martin in return. Like the wily hare, the outlaw doubled through the wood. His laugh was heard far, far ahead in the gloom of the dark old forest. The hunters plunged on after him ; and anon the same mocking laugh was heard pealing from behind them, where they could catch no glimpse of any moving form, and where the boughs shut out the moonlight. At length the wild laugh ceased, the track of the fugitive was lost, the pursuers were baffled.

"Silence, lads !" commanded their leader. "Keep still, and listen."

A minute had not elapsed before they heard the snapping of boughs at the distance of a few yards behind them.

"Back, lads—back on the other tack !" shouted Hilson.

Away through the wood dashed the infuriated men—onwards with fleet steps, and fiercely-flashing eyes. Still before them, they heard the snapping of boughs, and thought they could descry a dark figure flitting through the gloom. On, on, through the forest ! On, on, over brushwood, brier, and moss ! On, on, to the death !—on on !"

Hilson and Sir Thomas again met.

" Which way, man—which way for the varlet ?" demanded the burly knight.

" Ahead, Sir Thomas,—straight ahead !"

The hunt continued, the hunters sped onwards. Every minute one or the other of them thought that he descried the form of the fugitive. They knew not which way they were speeding ; they knew not the direction of their flight. Their whoops had ceased, their yells were silenced. There were no sounds in the dark old forest, save those occasioned by the trampling feet of the hunters, as they sped in their fleetness on.

"After him, Morden, man !—after him shouted Sir Thomas !

The party rushed onwards, emerged from the wood, and to their surprise found that they had retraced their way back to that very part of the shore from which they had started. Bewildered they looked around, but the open ocean was before them, and Red Martin had vanished, they knew not how or whither.

"Hey, man !" exclaimed the knight, grasping the arm of Hilson, " have we lost the varlet ? Where has he skulked to ?"

"That is a question, Sir Thomas, which I cannot answer. We have lost the scent, and I think may as well give up the pursuit."

At that moment a cry was raised by one of the seamen ; the whole party looked round, and to their amazement and dismay beheld the two boats out in the middle of the bay drifting towards the distant headland.

"How is this ?" exclaimed Sir Thomas ; " has the tide been up ?"

" See you not that it has been ebb-tide for the last two hours, Sir Thomas ?" replied the skipper of the revenue vessel.

" But where is Christie ?" asked one of the men.

" He must have left the boats, and followed us into the wood," suggested Hilson.

Just then Gervase Morden chanced to descry some dark object lying upon the shore a few yards distant. Hastening towards it, he recoiled in sudden terror, on discovering it to be the dead body of poor Christie.

A cry from Morden brought the whole party to the spot.

Hilson stooped down, and drew a small poniard out of the bosom of the murdered man. The moonlight fell upon the haft of the weapon, and one of the sailors immediately exclaimed—,

" 'Tis Red Martin's dagger ! I've seen him carry it in his belt."

It was evident that the poor fellow, to whose care the boats had been committed, had been cruelly murdered, and thrown into the sea. His hair was tangled amongst the sea-weed ; his fingers were cut in half, demonstrating that he had struggled with his murderer ; and as the student assisted by some others of the party uplifted his inanimate body, the blood gushed out anew from his death-wound, and trickled upon the sand.

"Hilson, man, are you sure that this is Red Martin's work?" demanded Sir Thomas, in a voice expressive of vexatious rage.

"It must be," replied the skipper.

"Then," cried the old knight, suddenly unsheathing his sword, "the blood-thirsty varlet shall meet with his deserts before the setting of another sun. The chase must not be given up, until payment has been made for this crime."

"It shall not be, Sir Thomas," replied Hilson, in a determined tone.

"Ha! ha! ha! ha!" laughed some one in the distance.

Every one turned his glance in the direction whence the sound came. On a small eminence, which formed a portion of the distant cliff, stood Red Martin, the smuggler.

"After him, boys! Hunt him to the death," shouted Sir Thomas.

The command was promptly and readily obeyed. Again sped the hunters after their prey. No longer, however, were they chasers for the sake of blood-thirsty pleasure; no longer was it the excitement of the terrible sport which led them on: it was the spirit of revenge which nerved them to the race; it was vengeance which lent swiftness to their feet. Poor murdered Christie had been their shipmate and companion for years. He had sailed with them over many a dark sea; with them he had weathered many a heavy storm. He and they had stood together on the same deck, and clung to the same mast, when the ocean was boiling and heaving around them; and when each cast his eyes to heaven, believing that he was never to voyage more, save across that one gloomy gulf, which separates life from eternity. Poor Christie had watched with them at midnight on the ocean lone; he had sported with them in their freaks of merriment. Often had he sung to them most touching ballads. Still more often had he joined in chorus with them, at the weighing of the anchor. And now he was slain—slain by a vile desperado, who had hitherto defied the laws of God and man with impunity, and who had dared to triumph over this last act of atrocity, and send back his taunting laugh to those who were the murdered one's friends.

"Hunt him down, men—hunt him down! Give him no quarter!" shouted Sir Thomas.

Far different was the manner in which the pursuers now followed the track of the outlaw, to the way in which they had first given him chase. There were no hallooings, no outcries; each man sped on his way in silence, with his cutlass tightly clenched in his hand, and his lips firmly compressed. In the depth of the forest was heard the mocking shouts of the outlaw, his scoffs of reckless daring were hurled back upon his pursuers, from the gloom into which he had penetrated. Again, however, all became silent. No trace of Red Martin was to be seen; his voice was not heard. The hunters became perplexed; they were fearful lest their prey should at length finally escape them. Onwards they hastened, taking care to plunge their cutlasses into every thicket, and every apparent hiding-place, which they chanced to pass. Still they were not sure that Red Martin was before them, they were not certain but that he had glided by them in the gloom, and was again retracing his steps towards the beach. These fears were duly communicated to their leader.

"No, no, lads," replied Hilson; "Red Martin is still ahead of you, though he may be lying in ambush. Divide into two parties. Mr. Morden will take half of you, and skirt the shore-side of the wood; while the other half follows me towards the cliffs."

This manner of proceeding was at once agreed unto, and the party forthwith divided; each division hastening onwards in separate directions.

"Hist!" exclaimed Hilson, grasping the arm of one of his followers, and pointing towards a rise in the ground at some distance, where the moon light, unobstructed by spreading boughs, illuminated the grassy sod,—"Hist! Did you see a figure make its way over yonder slope?"

"I thought I seed a bit of a shadow, thereaway," replied the seaman.

"It was Red Martin. On, men, on! He shall not escape us this time."

" Ay, ay, skipper, We'll be down upon the blood thirsty shark directly."

Hilson, who was well acquainted with Red Martin by sight, had discriminated rightly, when he believed that it was the form of the outlaw which he had seen pass over the moon-lit slope. Despite his bravado and his daringness, Red Martin now found that it was no easy matter to elude those by whom he was pursued, stimulated as they were by the desire for vengeance, and led on by men who proved indefatigable in keeping up the chase. It was the aim of the outlaw to reach that portion of the shore which was immediately opposite to where the Dare-devil was riding at her ease, awaiting a signal from her commander; but before he could accomplish that object, there was still a considerable tract of land to traverse.

The smuggler had gained the summit of a small eminence; before him was another ascent which led to the edge of the cliff, but between that ascent and the place whereon he stood was a hollow of some thirty or forty yards across.

Red Martin glanced round; he saw that his pursuers were upon his heels—that they had gained upon him—that they were still vigorous in the chase. Swiftly he plunged into the hollow; but hardly had he gained the bottom, before his feet stumbled, and he fell forwards, his left temple striking against a stone.

For a minute Red Martin remained motionless, stunned, and prostrate. It was, however, but for a minute. He heard the footsteps of his pursuers; his ear caught their wild shout of triumph as they beheld the condition of the outlaw. With one bound he sprang to his feet, and unsheathed his rapier, which was stained in many places with the dark stains of blood.

At the distance of a few yards was an old wall, forming part of the ruins of a cottage which had stood there in days gone by. Red Martin perceived that he was almost within the grasp of his foes; while, to his vexation, he discovered that he had so severely sprained his left foot by the fall, that further flight was impossible. Driven to desperation by the fearful position in which he found himself, he made his way towards the old wall, placed his back against it, and throwing a look of bold defiance at those who rushed forward to seize him, flourished his rapier as he exclaimed—

" Hold back ! the first man who dares to lay his finger on Red Martin, will meet death for his pains !"

A loud laugh of scorn was returned by Hilson and his companions, all of whom regarded Red Martin's threat as mere idle words; inasmuch as that he had to contend with six stout seamen, who had before then boarded the decks of a pirate's vessel, and fought hand to hand with the boldest and bloodiest of human kind.

" Have at him, men ! strike away his weapon ! Make him your prisoner, and there shall be a prize to each of you," cried Hilson.

The seamen needed no incentive to the attack. At one and the same moment six cutlasses were opposed to the single rapier of the smuggler. Hilson himself pressed forward the first, being followed by his companions.

" Ha, ha !" cried Red Martin, as he struck the cutlass from the hand of the old officer, and sent him reeling backwards down the slope. " Ha, ha !" he repeated, as he dashed aside the weapons of his aggressors, as if they were toy-swords, and their wielders but puny children. The seamen pressed forwards fighting like demons, though he whom they opposed was more of the demon than any one with whom he fought. Maddened and excited, the assailants made a rush, intending to throw themselves on the smuggler, and wrest his weapon from his grasp. Red Martin was prepared for the attack, and two of the men met their death-wounds in the attempt. The ire of the rest now became still more aroused ; they would have used fire-arms if any had been in their possession. They howled, they sprung forward, they opposed steel to steel. Still, however, the dark form of Red Martin towered above them, while the long rapier which he held glittered in the moonlight, as it swept round and round, cutting down and dashing aside every thing which came in its way. There were no pauses, no halting; steel sent back the stroke of steel ; and every repulse was but the signal for a renewed attack.

" At him, lads, at him !" shouted Hilson ; and the seamen, making a sudden rush, beat down the smuggler upon his knees. Not a second had passed, however, before Red Martin was on his feet again, his rapier whirling round with increased velocity—his dark eyes flashing fire at his assailants, and a scowl of triumphant daring gleaming upon his countenance. Two of the seamen were already disabled, owing to the severe sword-cuts which they had received; Hilson himself was wounded, and the remaining men began to quail before the ferocious countenance and well-wielded weapon of the outlaw. At this juncture, Gervase Morden and his party appeared at the top of the slope, the ring of the clashing steel having fallen upon their ears, and attracted them to the spot.

"Quick!—quick! we have him now!" exclaimed Hilson, as he beheld the approach of Gervase Morden and his companions.

Instinctively as it were, Red Martin perceived that he had no longer any chance of saving himself by combating his foes, especially as some of the advancing party were provided with muskets. Exasperated, maddened, and furious, the outlaw saw the desperate situation in which he was placed, without at the same time seeing any way by which to escape. Pausing for a single instant, he cast a glance around him ; then drawing out a small pistol from his belt, he fired it at the man who stood nearest to him, drove aside the others with his rapier, and, quitting the shelter of the old wall, scampered onwards across the cliffs.

"After him, lads!—run him down!" exclaimed Hilson, faintly; his wound not permitting him to join in the pursuit.

The upper surface of the cliffs was exposed and nearly barren ; there were no places in which the outlaw could hide, and no tree or shrub behind which he might seek shelter. Thus situated he knew not which way to turn nor what course to take ; his enemies were gaining upon him every minute ; his great exertions had almost exhausted his strength ; the beach was many scores of feet below him, and the crew of the Dardevil were too far off to be able to render him assistance. Bold and dauntless though the smuggler was, his heart failed him in this terrible dilemma. Visions of death, and of a long life of crime, expiated in an ignominious manner, flitted before his eyes. Still he fled onwards,—still he kept up the chase with his pursuers. But the hunt was nearly at an end, the hunters were closing on their prey, and the hunted one felt that the struggle was near its termination. Just then, however, a figure was seen to appear upon the summit of the high cliff which adjoined the one whereupon Red Martin then stood.

"Martin!" cried a loud and rough voice.

The smuggler heard the call, and at once turned his gaze towards the cliff, on which stood the man who had so strangely made his appearance. The man pointed with his outstretched hand over the edge of the cliff. Red Martin understood the gesture. Not a moment did he pause. The unknown disappeared immediately, but the smuggler hastened onwards towards the eminence, and gained it, while his pursuers were many yards behind him.

"Be ready, men. There is no way by which he can escape us now," said Gervase Morden.

But while these words were being spoken, and while they were on the very lips of the speaker, Red Martin was seen to make his way towards the edge of the cliff, to stand upon its very verge, and for one single instant to pause.

"We shall lose him now!" exclaimed one of the seamen ; "he intends to make a jump and shiver himself upon the rocks."

"Not so," replied Morden in a breathless voice. Then, laying his hand upon the arm of one of the party who carried a musket, he commanded in a quick voice,—

"Fire—fire at once before he makes the plunge!"

The seaman had not time to raise his musket to his shoulder before the smuggler was seen to throw out his arms, spring forward, and disappear over the edge of the cliff. Just as he was taking the leap, a small paper parcel was observed by one of the seamen to escape from the pocket of the smuggler's coat and fall upon the ground.

"Quick, quick !" cried Morden, as he hurried his companions to the edge of the cliff. "Have your firearms ready."

The verge of the precipice was gained, Gervase Morden and his men looked down, and beheld the broad sea beneath them, with a boat making its way across the waves, and in which boat were seen seated two persons, one of whom was Red Martin.

"Fire !" commanded Morden.

The command was obeyed ; but the bullets fell harmlessly upon the glistening waters, while Red Martin flourished his oar in triumphant derision.

"He's out of musket reach now," observed one of the men, as he watched the light skiff spring nimbly over the tide, bearing the adventurous and daring smuggler towards the vessel which formed his floating home.

"Curses on him !" ejaculated Hilson. "None but Red Martin would have been daring enough to have taken such a leap."

Gervase Morden had remained in moody silence gazing from the elevation upon which he stood at the boat of the smuggler, as, propelled by lusty arms, it sped over the waves towards the invincible Daredevil : the musings of the student were now, however, interrupted by a man stepping up to him, and producing the paper parcel which had fallen from out the pocket of Red Martin.

"Beg pardon, sir." said the seaman, doffing his cap in a respectful manner, "but may be this packet may turn out a something.'"

"What packet is it, my good fellow ?" inquired Morden.

The seaman told how it had come into his possession ; and expressed his hope that it might in some measure serve as an equivalent for the body of the smuggler himself.

Gervase Morden took the parcel, and eager to ascertain its contents, tore off the outer envelope. He was proceeding to unfold the inner cover when suddenly his fingers became paralysed ; he gazed upon the parcel with the wild stare of a maniac ; his countenance turned of a deadly paleness, while he raised the mysterious parcel nearer to his eyes, as if attracted by its fearful fascination.

At this moment Sir Thomas Warrenton, who had not been able to keep up with the rest of the party in the chase, arrived at the summit of the cliff ; his attention was at once arrested by the attitude of his secretary.

"Hey, Morden, man !" exclaimed the old knight, "what have you there? Gadzooks !—why, man, have you got anything to frighten you, that you look so white-blooded in the face ?"

"I—I—. Pardon me, Sir Thomas ; I must return to the Hall. I am unwell —very unwell."

"But the papers, man—what are they ?"

"Nothing, Sir Thomas ; you will know by-and-by. Do not stay me. I must hasten home immediately."

So saying, and without casting a glance at any one of the wondering group that stood around him, Gervase Morden thrust the mysterious packet into an inner pocket, and started off with wild speed in the direction of Warrenton Hall.

"Is the man mad ?" cried the old knight, when he had sufficiently recovered from his astonishment to be able to speak. "What wildness has entered his head now ?"

"It's something he's made out about this Red Martin, I suppose," observed the man who had picked up the parcel.

"Ha ! do you think so ? But where is the villain—where is Red Martin ; you haven't let him make clean off, have you ?"

The particulars of the last daring deed of Red Martin were detailed to Sir Thomas, who listened to the narration with various emotions of wonderment and vexation depicted on his countenance. The desperate manner in which the smuggler had defended himself, the courage he had exhibited in the short but severe conflict, his flight to the summit of the cliff, the leap which he had taken into the waters below, and the gesture of defiance and triumph with which he had afterwards saluted his pursuers, were facts which were all duly dilated upon by the garrulous seamen as they replied to Sir Thomas Warrenton's inquiries on the subject. Every circumstance was duly weighed by the old knight, and as duly placed by him to the account of Red Martin. Some of the occurrences, however, puzzled the good knight's sagacity and ingenuity to explain : that a boat should have been in waiting at the bottom of the cliff at the very moment that Red Martin took the leap was in itself a singular circumstance; then, again, it was very strange that the outlaw should have determined with his confederate upon this particular mode of escape, inasmuch as he might have reached the sea-shore by a far less dangerous path. Sir Thomas was perplexed—the whole affair was to him a mystery; and so many mysteries had bewildered him of late that his brain was now unable to grapple with the matter in hand or to sustain any very severe shock in the shape of another mystery. One particular of the narration had, however, forcibly impressed upon his mind.

"The varlet must have some of his friends lurking about in the woods," observed Sir Thomas to Hilson. "Did none of you perceive where the man went who made his appearance on the top of this cliff, and directed Red Martin to the boat?"

The answer was in the negative.

"Bad management, Hilson, man," growled Sir Thomas. "You should have secured the accomplice when you found there was no chance of making fast hold of the criminal."

It was explained to Sir Thomas, that in the first instance the eagerness of the seamen to captive Red Martin himself had deterred them from pursuing his confederate, and that, after the escape of the outlaw, they were astounded to think of what course it was prudent for them next to take.

"Then, for all you know, the man may be hidden in the wood at this moment?" said Sir Thomas.

"You'll excuse me, your honour," said one of the seamen; "but somehow or other it strikes me there's a likelier place to look for that man in, than the wood or the cliffs."

"And where is that, my honest fellow?"

"In the village, I should say."

"How!—in the village—in Gillcross?"

"Ay, Sir Thomas; may-be there are some queer customers in the village—some who sail in a queer way, and whose papers wouldn't bear over-hauling—this Sandy Summers, for instance—"

"How! Mr. Summers!" exclaimed Sir Thomas, interrupting the speaker, "do you know anything wrong of him?"

"Well, I may say that I know the cut of Sandy pretty well; and I may say too, that it was none else than Sandy Summers who was seen a-top of this hill just now. I——"

Sir Thomas darted forward and grasped the arm of the speaker.

"What mean you, man,—what is this you say,—do you accuse Sampson Summers, the tomb-cutter, of being a confederate with Red Martin?"

"Seeing as how I don't know much about their concerns, it's impossible for me to say whether they sail under the same colours or not, your honour," replied the seaman; "however, Sir Thomas, that's a matter as can be made out by-and-by."

"You are sure that the man you saw upon this hill was Sampson Summers?"

"I can't say that I have many doubts about it, your honour."

Sir Thomas Warrenton was silent for a few minutes; then breaking into a soliloquy, he clutched his sword-hilt firmly, as he observed—

"There is something at the bottom of all this. Sampson Summers in league with the smugglers, indeed! A pretty nest of traitors we must have round about us And, now I think of it, that packet of papers which Master Morden was looking at, may be the clue to the whole mystery. Gadzooks! I should not have let him gone so soon if I had thought of that. Get ready, men. We must away to the Hall at once."

"But what is to be done with these poor men, Sir Thomas?" inquired Hilson, as he pointed out to the notice of the good knight the unfortunate seamen who had been wounded by the rapier of the smuggler. " Red Martin has given them some smartish cuts; and as for poor Miller there, I scarcely think he'll get over it, having, it appears, about an ounce of cold lead in his chest."

" It has been scurvy work—scurvy work indeed," replied Sir Thomas; " and Red Martin shall account for it before long. As for the wounded, let them be carried carefully up to the Hall, and we will find a surgeon to attend to them. Come, Hilson, man ; let us to the Hall. There are strange things for us to hear, without a doubt."

Sir Thomas was right—there was strange news indeed for him to hear; nor did he guess what that news was destined to be, although he made many attempts at guessing on the road, and more than once fancied that he had succeeded most cleverly in unravelling the whole mystery.

What was that strange news?

———

CHAPTER XLII.

THE CONFERENCE.——THE AGONY.——THE DECEIVER DENOUNCED.

LEAVING for a while Sir Thomas Warrenton and his party, we follow Gervase Morden to the Hall, in order to become acquainted with the contents of the mysterious parcel.

On entering the court-yard of Warrenton Hall, the surprise of the student was great at perceiving a post-chaise covered with dust, from which the heated and tired horses were in process of being removed. This post-chaise Morden knew to be the one in which Lambert Warrenton usually travelled. The excitement of the student was too great to allow of his pausing for the purpose of making inquiries, notwithstanding that he had many questions which he wished to ask. That there was an unusual stir among the domestics was very evident; and that something of importance had occurred during his own absence and that of Sir Thomas was visible in the perturbed state of the household, and the confusion which reigned around. Without stopping to reply to the questions addressed to him by some of the domestics, Gervase Morden passed onwards, and entered the library.

Near the window, at the eastern end of the library, a party of three individuals were conversing together. No sooner did the secretary make his entrance than one of the party turned round, and exclaimed,——

"This is most opportune. Mr. Morden, we have just sent a messenger in search of you."

A pallor overspread the countenance of the student, as he observed,——

"Your sudden return from town is very extraordinary, Mr. Lambert. Captain Charnock too is here. Surely there must be business of importance in hand."

"There is," was the reply of Lambert Warrenton. "Where is my father?"

"I know not. He will be here presently."

"You wonder at my sudden return, Mr. Morden. I have a communication to make to you which will afford an explanation of the cause of my being here."

Lambert Warrenton drew the student aside, and conversed with him for a few minutes in a low tone. Whatever was the nature of the conversation, the magic of the words was powerful indeed. Stern, and reserved, and passionless as the student generally seemed, the effect of the communication was such as caused his eyes to flash forth fire, his cheeks to burn, and his lips to become compressed. Then again, as he heard further, other emotions seemed to steal over him; the flush subsided from his cheek, and gave place to a deadly paleness; his eyes rolled wildly from side to side; a nervous tremor seemed to pervade his whole frame, so as almost to deprive him of the power of standing erect. After listening for a while, he laid his hand upon the arm of Lambert Warrenton, and said,——

"Sir Thomas will be here soon. Excuse me; I cannot hear more now. I must see him, I must speak to him at once."

"To whom?" inquired Lambert Warrington.

Gervase Morden did not reply; but passing out of the library, took his way towards the staircase which led to the gallery. Meeting a domestic, the student stopped to ask the question,——

"Do you know where Lieutenant Morden is?"

"He is in the drawing-room, I believe

"Is he alone?"

"Lady Warrenton and Miss Ismay are with him," was the reply.

Gervase Morden passed onwards. As he neared the room in which his brother was, he paused to arrange his dress. A few minutes passed, and every trace of his late emotion was removed from his countenance; his eye no longer rolled wildly, the pallor had left his cheeks, and his lips had resumed their usual expression.

The student tapped lightly at the door.

At that moment a merry burst of laughter escaped from the inmates of the apartment, while a soft and sweet voice desired the applicant to enter.

"Mr. Gervase!" exclaimed Lady Warrenton, "gracious me, where is Sir Thomas? Is he returned? They tell me that he and you have been in the wood to hunt the smugglers."

"They have told you truly, Lady Warrenton. Sir Thomas will be here presently."

"Have you had any startling adventures in the green wood?" inquired Constance Ismay, in a playful manner. "Ah! I fear that you have no such enchanting stories to tell us as those which we have just heard from Lieutenant Morden."

"My brother seems in a merry mood," observed Gervase, bitterly.

"And why should he not be?" demanded Constance. "You are looking grave, Mr. Gervase. Surely you are not about to preach a homily against our harmless merriment?"

"Pardon me, Miss Ismay, and you also, Lady Warrenton. I have a communication to make to my brother which requires that I speak with him alone for a few minutes. You will excuse his absence. Ernest will accompany me to another room."

"You look serious, brother," observed Ernest, as he arose to comply with his brother's request. "Has any news arrived from London?"

"You will know presently. Here is my own private room—enter with me here, and we shall be alone."

It was a small, gloomy chamber, strewed with books and mathematical instruments. The rays of the morning sun stole in through the quaint, old window, and fell upon the weird things around, as well as upon the countenances of the two brothers.

Gervase Morden fastened the door on the inside; then pointing to a chair near the window, he desired his brother to be seated.

"Brother," said Ernest, in an anxious manner, "what have you to tell me? You look sad, brother—very sad."

"Think you so?" returned Gervase, as his lips gave expression to a bitter smile.

"I do. Something has happened; some bad news must have met your ear."

"Indeed, brother Ernest, do you think so? Whence should such bad news come?" asked the student, seating himself, and regarding the countenance of his brother with a piercing glance.

"Is it from London? Does it concern myself?" inquired Ernest.

The student fixed his glance upon the countenance of his companion, so as to observe attentively every change of expression. After a pause of a few seconds, he said, in a grave voice,—

"It is strange that you should expect bad news from London, brother Ernest, having been assured by those who have power to make interest in your favour, that your misdeeds would be looked over and forgiven."

"They are kind, brother—very kind!"

"And you have not deceived them?"

"Deceived!" exclaimed Ernest. "Pardon me, brother, for expressing my belief that you have used an ill-chosen word; or, it may be, I have mistaken your meaning."

"My meaning was plain. I simply ask of you, whether, in the explanation of your misdemeanors, you have not attempted to deceive your own brother, or your friend Sir Thomas Warrenton?"

"God witnesses that I have not!" replied Ernest, fervently.

"I would willingly believe you, brother; and yet——"

The student paused abruptly.

"Gervase," cried Ernest, seizing his brother's hand, "what meaning is there in this? Why these doubts—these suspicions?"

"Brother Ernest, you have assured me that you have spoken truth."

"Do you disbelieve me, Gervase?"

Without replying to this question, the student continued,—

"And you have given your word that you have not dealt treacherously either with your king or with your country?"

"I have not."

"You are willing to swear to that?"

"I am!"

The elder brother arose from his seat, and paced to and fro across the room in evident agitation of mind: his chest heaved; his lips writhed; his hand fumbled nervously in his bosom; more than once he grasped, as it seemed involuntarily, his sword-hilt; then moving onward, he struck his brow with his open hand, and muttered some few words in an indistinct manner. Intently did poor Ernest regard the movements of his brother; intently did he watch every action, and mark every symptom of mental agitation which the behaviour of Gervase Morden betrayed. At length, unable longer to restrain his feelings, he arose from his seat, passed across the room, and grasped the hand of the agitated man.

"Gervase, dear Gervase! Do not keep me in suspense. Tell me, I implore you, the news which you have to communicate."

"How know you that I have news? whence your guess, brother Ernest?" asked Gervase, in a bitter tone.

"You have—you must have," replied Ernest; "your manner—your agitation tells me that you must have tidings for my ear. I am afraid that they are sad tidings."

"Why do you think that, brother?" demanded Gervase, quickly.

"I know not! It is my fear."

Gervase Morden suddenly lifted up his head, and seizing with his two hands the shoulders of his brother, gazed fixedly upon the face of the latter.

"Ernest," said he, "you have assured me in solemn terms that you have acted uprightly, notwithstanding the whispered accusations which some have made against you; seriously, and in serious words, have you given me such assurance—an assurance, brother, that you have acted loyally to your king, faithfully to your country, honourably to yourself; that you have not in any way acted deceitfully, and that you are guilty of no offence which might tend to sully the good name our father left us. Brother, I have listened to your affirmation with joy—with great joy. I——"

"And you believe them, dear brother?" interrupted Ernest.

A dark, fearful expression gathered upon the countenance of the student, as he replied,—

"I do—I must believe them, Ernest. If I did not, I——"

"What, brother?" stammered Ernest.

"I would shoot you where you now stand;" answered the student, sternly, and at the same moment he drew a small pistol out of the folds of his vest.

"Brother! you cannot mean this; you do but speak in jest."

"There are no jesters here, I trust," replied the student, gravely. "I have told you before, brother Ernest, that you are my brother only so long as I feel honoured by the relationship. The good name our father left us was the only heritage we possessed—that good name I have sworn to keep unsullied. To do so is my ambition—my strong and resolute determination. So long then, brother Ernest, as you bear that name without dishonouring it, you are my brother, and I rejoice in your being such. But mark me! Once let that name—the name of Morden, become disgraced through an act of yours; once let the sneering world have cause to throw their sneers at a Morden—have cause to speak slightingly of one who owns that name; once, I say, let that come to pass; and—hear me, Ernest—I, Gervase Morden, your own brother, will be your deadliest enemy. Understand me clearly and plainly,—I have all a brother's love for you, Ernest. There is no sacrifice that I would hesitate to make in your behalf, so long as you are worthy of my love. But the spirit of my father has descended to his elder son, brother Ernest, having become a portion of his being, controlling, inspiring, and directing him in all his thoughts and actions. Need I tell you what that spirit was and is—you, who are the son of that same parent ? Ernest Morden knows that it was the spirit of honour which guided his parent; and, thanks be to Heaven ! the same spirit, descended to his sons, has raised them to what they now are—to the positions which they now hold—to the favours which they now enjoy. Yes, brother Ernest, in our youths we were poor and almost friendless ; we had the wide world before us to work in ; we had to engage in life's contest, and win our way by our own good valour. The high principles our father had taught us, the ennobling sentiments which he had inculcated in our minds, constituted our sole treasure. We have worked upon those principles ; we have attended to those precepts; and the result is, the good report and honourable stations which we now possess and enjoy. Be careful then, brother, to preserve that which we have gained ; be vigilant that by no act of folly or of crime you darken that which is at present bright, or sully that which is at present pure. You hear my words, let them not be forgotten or disregarded ; on your hopes of happiness, I charge you not to do so. It is a charge which I have long wished to deliver to you ; it was a duty which I have now performed. You hear me, brother, and you have understood my words ?"

Ernest Morden had listened attentively to every syllable which the student had uttered : not a word had escaped his hearing. At first the stern tones of the speaker had the effect of striking terror into the soul of the listener ; but, as the student proceeded, and as his exhortation assumed more the form of a command, the haughty spirit of the younger brother was aroused—a blush of anger glowed upon his cheeks, the feeling of insult was in his soul. The stern glance of the speaker was answered by a sparkle in the eyes of his hearer, which indicated that passion was generating within the brain, and that the hot blood was beginning to bubble up, as it coursed through its sinuous channels.

" Gervase !" cried Ernest, in an excited manner, as he detached himself from his brother's grasp, " I know not by what right, or on what authority you take upon yourself to address me in the manner you have done. Am I your ward, and are you my guardian ?"

" Not so, Ernest. I am the guardian of the good name borne in common by us both."

" You have taken upon yourself the holding of a very pretty office, good brother, and I trust that you are equal to the task," returned Ernest, sneeringly. " It is unfair, however, that you should load me with all these pretty cautions, and reserve none of them for yourself. The charge being in common, methinks there is an equal chance on both sides of cautions being requisite ; and for aught I know to the contrary, the ward himself may, at some future day, have to play the part of guardian towards the very individual who has so kindly taken him under his care. I would have you to beware that your own feet do not slip, good brother ; and that the immaculate guardian may not be caught tripping. Advice for advice—favour in return for favour, good brother !"

These taunts were listened to in silence by the student, who, with head bent down, and arms folded across his chest, had concealed from the observation of his brother the various emotions awakened by the address of the speaker. No sooner, however, had Ernest uttered his last taunt, than the elder brother lifted up his head, and disclosed to view a pair of dark eyes in which an intense fire seemed to burn, and lips that were of a deadly whiteness, by reason of the compression to which they had been subjected. Again the student seized the arm of his kinsman, but this time the gripe was like that of an iron vice—firm and unyielding ; while the voice which sounded in the ear of the taunter was deep-toned, hoarse, and guttural, like that of a man when struggling to keep down some strong passion, that pants to express itself in words of storm, and fire, and frenzy.

"Brother," said the student, and Ernest quailed as the stern voice of the speaker fell upon his ear—"brother, you have mistaken me; you treat my words lightly and with derision. God knows that I have spoken the feelings of my heart—that I have given utterance to the determinations of my soul! You listen, Ernest, to a brother who never told a lie—to a man who has never wilfully or knowingly uttered a falsity. I arrogate to myself no authority beyond that which I have a right to assume, nor do I lay claim to any jurisdiction over you whatever, save and except in the one matter of the common honour of both. This, however, I declare to you, that if you fail to keep sacred the trust committed to your care—that good name which your father bore before you—I, your own brother, who bears no malignity towards you, who desires, more than any one else, your prosperity and happiness—I, mind me, would track you to the earth's end, i order to punish you for that breach of faith. You would cease to be my brother, and I might be your murderer."

"This from you Gervase!" exclaimed Ernest, clapping his hand to his side, as if in search of his sword which usually depended there,—"and to me too—your own brother!"

"To you, Ernest; and may the words be never forgotten!"

An ancient and half-rusty spear-head lay upon a table near to where the two brothers stood. Ernest Morden stepped aside, and in the excitement of his anger suffered his fingers to close upon the weapon. In another moment his arms were in the firm grasp of the student, and he was powerless.

"There must be no quarrelling here, or on this matter, brother Ernest," said Gervase. "Be patient, and I will make plain to you the causes which have occasioned my addressing you as I have done. You are aware that Sir Thomas and myself have been engaged during the past night in the pursuit of certain smugglers who have made themselves obnoxious on this coast. Chief amongst them is a man, who though said to be a Frenchman, has yet many of the characteristics of our countrymen, and who, under the name of Red Martin, has for years past committed sundry outrages, which have stamped him with the reputation of being a blood thirsty and reckless villain. Latterly, suspicions have arisen that this man has been serving our enemies, the French, by carrying communications from traitors here to foes across the Channel. This night we gave Red Martin chase; though, by an act of more than common daring, he contrived to elude us at last. However, brother, from the pocket of that man—of that known traitor and rebel, from the pocket of Red Martin the smuggler—was seen to fall a certain paper parcel. That parcel is now in my possession, I alone know its contents. I alone, of all that serve truly their king, know what papers are contained in that parcel. I too—but your cheeks have become blanched, brother; your lips are pale; you tremble! Whence this strange agitation?"

"The parcel—the papers—"

"Well, what of them?"

"Are they nothing, brother? Do they not concern me?"

"Concern you, Ernest! Why ask that question?"

"I fear, I——"

Gervase Morden tightened his grasp of his brother's arms; and looking steadstly in his face, demanded,—

"Fear, Ernest! Why, what cause have you to fear? Why should anything that I have said make you afraid?"

"I know not; but my presentiment—my feeling that evil was coming, haunted me again last night, brother, and terrifies me now."

"And does your terror arise from that sole cause, Ernest? Does no accusing conscience induce that pallor of your lips?"

"No, brother. It is strange; it is unaccountable. I dread danger; yet know not whence to expect it?"

"Remember, Ernest Morden, you have given me your solemn assurance of having acted with honesty and good faith towards all with whom you have had dealings. Do you wish to retract one word of what you have said? Have you any confession to make?"

" Confession of what, dear Gervase ?"

" Of lack of fealty to your sovereign—of dishonourable deeds—of acting the traitor's part?"

" Nay, brother Gervase, I am not that guilty man—on my honour and m hopes of heaven I am not !"

" And yet, Ernest—Ernest, my brother—my playfellow in childhood, my partner in the struggles of youth, and my dearly-loved brother now, this parcel of which I have spoken—this parcel which was in the possession of a traitor, has been sealed with three seals—bears the superscription in the handwriting of a true and loyal man—is addressed to those who are interested in the welfare of the nation, and must be——"

" Not my despatches, brother—not Captain Charnock's despatches," exclaimed the terrified man.

" Yes, Ernest Morden, the despatches with which you were entrusted, found in the possession of your country's foe—the seal broken—the secre m k wn —the trust betrayed. They are here brother—this is the packet—these the papers—this the broken trust !' '

Ernest Morden staggered forward, gazed wildly at the papers which his brother displayed, sank upon that brother's arm for support, and clasping his hand madly to his brow, ejaculated,—

" My God—my God ! this is fearful—this is incredible—this is mysterious !"

" Come, brother," said Gervase. taking the hand of Ernest, " there is no time for trifling. Sir Thomas and Captain Charnock wait for us in the room below."

" But Amy—Lambert Warrenton—the despatches—London!" exclaimed Ernest in a bewildered and incoherent manner.

" All must be explained, brother, and your explanation is waited for. There are footsteps approaching. We have no time for delay."

Ernest suffered the student to lead him towards the door. They were about to emerge from the apartment, when falling upon his knees at the feet of his elder brother, Ernest Morden clasped the hand of Gervase, and in a heart-broken, agitated voice, exclaimed,—

" Be gentle with me, dear Gervase ! I have not the stern, noble nature which you possess—I am weaker—much weaker. But here, upon my knees, and in the sight of my God, I swear to you, brother, that I am innocent of this heinous crime ; I swear it, dear brother, I swear it !"

For once a glistening tear stole down the cheek of the austere student. It was hastily brushed away, and helping his brother to rise, Gervase Morden answered,—   I

",I believe you, Ernest—I believe you since you have heard the words which g have spoken. May He whose testimony you have appealed to, assist you inp rcn your innocence ! But come, we must away."

At that moment the door of the room opened, and Lambert Warrenton, accompanied by the Lady Isabel and Constance Ismay, came to give notice to the brothers that their presence was required in another part of the Hall.

CHAPTER XLIII.

THE MESSAGE.—THE WINDOW TOWARDS THE SEA.—THE MAD BOY IN HIS MADNESS.

WHEN Gervase Morden left the library to seek his brother in the drawwing room, he did not perceive that his departure was intently watched by Eugene 'Dourville.

" Warrenton," exclaimed Dourville, hurriedly, " know you the nature of the expedition in whichyour father has been engaged this night ?"

" I have not hear.d"

"I will tell you, then, for I have gained the knowledge within the last ten minutes. Listen!"

Eugene Dourville and Lambert Warrenton conferred together in whispers. The interest taken by each in the conversation appeared to be intense. Their countenances suffered several changes of expression; and a certain nervous anxiety perceivable in the manner of the listener, indicated that the nature of the communication was far from being agreeable. After a short deliberation with his companion, Lambert Warrenton summoned a domestic to the apartment, and gave him instructions that he should speed forthwith to the cottage of the Heytons, with a message that Amy should at once repair to the Hall, in order to be present there by the time Sir Thomas and his party arrived.

The servant bowed and departed.

It was early morning, and Amy Heyton sat at the window of the same room where we found her seated at the opening of the story. Alas, how changed since then! It was a lovely morning; the air pure, clear, and balmy; the weather giving promise of a delightful day; and the blue ocean, across which the eyes of poor Amy gazed, was as sparkling and as bright as ever; its myriad of ripples dancing in the golden sunshine; its waters glittering in showy splendour, and smiling as it were in return to the smiles of the rosy morning. Ships, with their canvas glowing in the sunlight, were gliding on their way in the distance; while lesser vessels with their sails set, and their keels glancing through the bright waves, speckled the surface of the bay. Amy looked upon the fair scene spread out before her, and called to mind that evening on which the scene had been still more glorious, when with impatient expectancy she had waited the coming of her heart's love, and longed for the arrival of that hour, which afterwards proved to be the hour of bitterest sorrow that even in her young life she had known.

And at the same window, gazing not upon the gleaming ocean, but upon the gentle sister seated by her side, reclined Kate—laughing, blooming Kate, as in years gone by she had been christened. Not laughing Kate now; for never wore the face of maiden beauty a more serious expression than did that of Catherine Heyton, as she regarded in silence the pensive countenance of her much-beloved sister. Amy was dear to Kate—dear because of her gentleness, her warm affection, her sufferings, and her sorrows. So Kate bent down her head to look upon her sister's face; and in that face she saw so sad a change, in that pale face she beheld such traces of grief, and discerned such marks of inward woe, that involuntarily the sympathising girl clasped her arms round the neck of the gentle mourner, and ejaculated,—

"Sister—dearest sister, you know not how much it grieves me to see you look so sorrowful. Cannot this bright scene charm you—this beauteous, delightful morning?"

"I am not sad, dear Kate; indeed I am not sad," returned Amy, looking up, and speaking in a sweet, but pensive voice.

"Ah! dear Amy, you deceive yourself, and would also deceive me. But your countenance belies your words, my poor sister; so pale have grown your cheeks, so dull have become your eyes, and so dejected—so wanting in spirits do you seem. Courage, Amy, courage, my sister! You own that you still love Ernest, and he will not—he cannot do otherwise than love you, now, after the noble service which you have rendered him."

"He does love me, dear Kate."

"Then why this sorrow—this melancholy? Ernest Morden will soon cease to be a prisoner at the Hall. He will remember the kind act achieved in his behalf by you. The mystery of his past behaviour will be explained. There will be a few secret meetings, many words of repentance and prayer, a little hesitation, some fair share of blushing, and then—why, sister, what can possibly occur then but the realisation of all my poor Amy's anticipations of happiness, when she becomes the bride of Lieutenant Morden, and goes to the altar with a wreath of orange-blossoms on her brow?"

"Orange-blossoms for me, dear Kate? No, sister, no. They will never be worn on this poor, pale, aching brow."

"You deceive yourself, good sister, or are trying to deceive me. Come now, I must not have my poor Amy so melancholy and so sorrowful; she must not weep and sob on such a bright day as this. Why, look, sister—you have made the pretty bird moody; he has ceased to sing; his head is bent down; the little fellow seems inclined to be as sadsome as yourself. This must not be, sweet sister,

indeed it must not be; ! I shall be very, very angry with you, if you continue in this gloomy manner; for what cause have you to be so? Surely Ernest will not hesitate to wed you now—he cannot do so."

"And do you wish me to become Ernest's wife, dear sister?" asked Amy, king seriously at the face of her companion.

"My wishes are all for your happiness, dear Amy. If to wed Ernest Morden would be to bring again the brightness to my sister's eye, I could wish that wedding to take place immediately."

" Would it give you pleasure too, dear Kate ?"

" I have assured you, Amy, how great that pleasure would be."

" Yes ; but it is your wish, sister, that—that Ernest should be my husband—should you be pleased at having to call him brother ?"

Kate Heyton hung down her head, and was silent.

" Tell me, sister ; tell me for I much wish to know !"

" It is a needless question, Amy—why ask it ?"

" Nay, sister, it is an important one. I have watched your countenance when Ernest has been the subject of our conversation, and from what I have seen, I believe that you, as well as father and brother Frank, think Ernest unworthy of being the husband of your sister."

" Unworthy, Amy ?"

" Yes ; you do not consider him to be so honourable, so sincere, so deserving of your poor sister's love as you once thought him to be. Is it not so, sweet Kate ? Do not deceive me. Tell me, Kate—tell me."

Miss Heyton hesitated for a few moments, and then replied,—

" You ask me to speak my thoughts, dear sister, and I will comply with your request. First, however, I must have your promise that you will not be offended with me for speaking frankly."

" Indeed—indeed I will not, dear Kate !"

" Well, then, sister Amy, I must inform you that the merits and demerits of Ernest Morden have lately been much canvassed by your father, and by Frank ; neither have I, sweet sister, been a silent listener. That there is something strange, reserved, ungenerous, and inexplicable, in the character and behaviour of Lieutenant Morden we cannot but agree in thinking. It is doubtful, Amy, whether it would be to your future happiness to become the wife of such a man—of one who could so far allow whim or passion to get such command over him, as to take up a weapon against his affianced bride. Yet, Amy, your father has imposed certain restrictions upon both Frank and myself, forbidding either of us to interfere in this matter, or in any way to oppose you in your wishes. Therefore, sweet sister—my own good Amy—if you can forgive Ernest Morden his past conduct, if you still retain a particle of your old affection for him, if he be willing to explain and to atone, if he ask your hand in honourable marriage and you can dream of happiness in becoming his wife, accept him, my sweet sister, endow him with your hand and heart."

" And you will not be offended with me, dear Kate ?"

" I promise you that I will not, sister. Let Ernest but explain his past behaviour in a satisfactory manner, let him ask pardon for the insult he has offered to us all, let him act in an honourable, open way, and none will be more kindly disposed towards him, none will value his friendship more highly than will our father, Frank, and myself. Even while I speak, however, I feel assured that Ernest will do this—that he will redeem his honour. Then, 'Amy—then, my sweet sister, there will be a season of happiness. The bloom will come again on those pale cheeks ; the lustre to those blue eyes. Oh ! for that happy day, that it may come quickly—quickly as my desire for your felicity wills that it should arrive !"

" Stop ! dear Kate," exclaimed Amy. " What if Ernest do not choose—if he be unable to do that which you think it requisite for him to perform—if he refuse to explain the mystery ; and if he should—"

" Why these suppositions, dear Amy ?" interrupted Kate. " Assuredly, if Ernest Morden refuse to act with candour, he will never win the hand of my gentle sister ?"

Amy turned very pale, drooped her head, and made no reply. After a short pause, Kate took her sister's hand, and in a faltering, tremulous voice, said,—

" You surely would not be so imprudent, dear Amy, as to give your hand to Ernest without his first affording such explanations ?"

Amy lifted up her pale countenance, and looking with her mild blue eyes at her sister, said,—

"I love him, sister; you know not how much I love him!"

"And think you that love to be so great that it would conquer your prudence?"

"It is great enough to conquer all."

"Nay, Amy, you wrong yourself; you would not be so unwise. Know you not, sister, that the past conduct of Ernest amounts to a tacit denial of all love —of all true affection for you?"

"I know it, sister, and yet I love him—love him, sister, deeply as ever."

"But if he reject that love? If he contemn you? If he reject you with disdain?"

"Contemn—reject—disdain!" murmured Amy, remembering at that moment the words which Lambert Warrenton had addressed to her at the time of their midnight meeting. "Sister, why do you ask me these questions? When Ernest tells me in plain words that I am hateful to his sight, I will cease to love him then."

"Ernest Morden will never, I trust, utter such words, or any of like import," returned Kate. "I did not mean to make you angry, dear Amy—I am sorry if I have done so. Far be it from me to think harshly of Ernest. On the contrary, I believe that he will act as becomes a man of honour; that he will show himself to be worthy of your love; and that I, sister, shall one day have the pleasure of saluting him as brother. It would be a pleasure to me for your sake, sister; but whether it would otherwise be so, I know not. I do not think that I could endure parting with you, dear Amy."

The sisters had not perceived that for some minutes previous Archy, the idiot boy, had been a listener to their conversation; he had stolen gently into the room, had taken a seat at some distance from where the sisters sat, and had listened to every word which had fallen from their lips, with a degree of interest not easily to be accounted for in one who was at most times remarkable for his indifference and stolidity.

When Kate Heyton said that it would cause her pain to part with her sister, the idiot boy crept forward, fell upon his knees beside the sisters, and asked with much earnestness,—

"Where is sissy Amy going? Archy cannot part from sissy Amy."

"Tush! Master Archy," answered Kate, smilingly. "Amy will be married to Mr. Morden, and Mr. Morden, you know, is a sailor; the consequence of course will be, that Amy will no longer waste her time in this lonely cottage but will go forth to see the world, and will go away in a great ship, like one of those which you see upon the water, with tall masts and large white sails."

"Go from home?" asked the idiot, in a tremulous voice.

"Home, you silly fellow! Why, the great ship will be Amy's home then."

"And will she go—will sissy Amy go?"

"Why should she not, good Master Archy?"

The idiot boy turned towards Amy, and looking in her face, said, with tears in his eyes, and in a faltering voice,—

"Sissy Amy will not go away? Sissy Amy will not leave poor Archy?"

Amy was touched by the earnestness of the manner in which these words were uttered. Passing her hand over the fair hair of the suppliant boy, she inquired,—

"Is it not your wish, Archy, that I should go away? Would you rather have me remain here?"

"Sissy Amy is kind to Archy, and Archy loves sissy Amy," was the answer. "If sissy Amy go away, then Archy will die."

"Come, come, Master Archy," cried Kate, playfully attempting to push aside the idiot; "there must be nothing of this. Amy has given all her love to Ernest, and she must keep true to her word."

"All her love," echoed the idiot, trembling as he spoke.

"All, my poor Archy," replied Amy, amused by the earnestness of the idiot's inquiries. "You must prepare to part with me, Archy, if the prophesies of sister Kate are to be relied upon."

The idiot tightened his clasp of the fair girl's hand, and ejaculated,—

"Sissy Amy must not kill Archy. Sissy Amy must promise poor Archy not to go."

"No, Archy," answered Amy, shaking her head with much gravity, "I cannot give you that promise."

The idiot turned aside his head, and rising from his kneeling posture, betook himself to the door. As he passed out, a dark expression gathered on his countenance—a strange, wild light glistened in his eyes; he clenched his hands and teeth as he ejaculated,—

"She shall not go. Archy will keep her here."

Such were the words of the idiot boy; they were words of strange meaning—strange even as the character of the individual by whom they were uttered.

The messenger from the Hall made his appearance at this juncture, and apprised Amy and her sister that Sir Thornton Warrenton had bidden them to his presence. The command was obeyed, and with them went Archy, the idiot boy.

And now for Love and Madness—Love at its severest trial, and Madness at its wildest work.

CHAPTER XLIV.

THE TRIAL OF LOVE, AND THE TRIUMPH OF MADNESS.

It was the same large, quaint old room in Warrenton Hall, as that described in a former chapter. There were present, Sir Thomas Warrenton, the Lady Isabel, Mr. Lambert, and his friend, Eugene Dourville; together with Captain Charnock, Gervase Morden, and some of the seamen who had assisted in the expedition of the previous night. Ernest was also there as a prisoner; and as he walked up towards the table at which his brother had taken a seat, the door opened, and the two Miss Heytons, accompanied by their father and brother, with Archy, the idiot boy, crouching behind them, entered the room.

One single glance did Amy cast towards the place where Ernest Morden stood; then, taking the seat which was offered to her, she turned aside her head, and waited, trembling and anxious, to know the cause for which she had been summoned thither.

Some few preliminary matters were disposed of; and then Sir Thomas turned towards Ernest, and in a grave, yet sympathising manner, said,—

"Lieutenant Morden, I know not what charge is about to be made against you. That circumstances materially affecting yourself, and having to do with the question of your guilt or innocence, have transpired, I have been recently informed, but with the particulars I am as yet unacquainted. The disclosures made in this room a few days since acquitted you in my opinion of any unloyal or unpatriotic conduct; and it was under that impression that I gave you my promise of exerting myself in your behalf. Your term of confinement here has, I trust, come to an end. Mr. Lambert brings me certain instructions from the authorities in London; he has travelled post-haste to reach the Hall; and it is now time that whatever he may have to communicate should be made public to all who are here present."

As Sir Thomas finished speaking, Lambert Warrenton arose. From the agitation of the young man's manners, and the downcast expression of his countenance, it was evident that he was ill-prepared for the duty which he had to perform.

"Lieutenant Morden," said he, addressing the prisoner, "it gives me great pain to be called upon to afford information concerning a transaction in which the honour of an officer in his majesty's service—and that officer the brother of one of my most valued friends—is so deeply implicated.   Let me trust that it will be in your power to throw light on that which is at present dark ; and that a few words of explanation from yourself will be sufficient to resolve into a simple mistake that which now wears the appearance of a very serious affair."

"Does this preamble relate to the papers which, at Miss Heyton's request, you conveyed to London?" inquired Sir Thomas.

"It does."

"Well, come to the matter itself, Master Lambert.   Have you obtained pardon for Lieutenant Morden, or have you brought down a special warrant for his arrest ? What said they to the despatches, boy?"

"Nothing, Sir Thomas."

"What !—they were taken then, and no remark made ?"

"No, Sir Thomas ; they have never seen them.   The despatches to which you allude have never reached the Admiralty."

Gervase Morden glanced meaningly towards his brother.   On the countenances of every other auditor, not excepting the prisoner himself, an expression of sudden astonishment told in what manner this announcement was received.

"Gadzooks, boy !" exclaimed Sir Thomas, starting from his seat, "did you not take the packet to London yourself?"

"What I did was this," replied Lambert Warrenton :—" At the request of Miss Amy Heyton, by whom I was informed of the unfortunate position in which Lieutenant Morden was placed, I undertook to carry with me to London a certain parcel which she committed to my care ; and which, she informed me, consisted of certain despatches that had been entrusted by Captain Charnock to his lieutenant, under orders to convey them at once to the Admiralty office in London. At the time of receiving this parcel from the hands of Miss Heyton, I particularly remarked the careless manner in which it was sealed, and noted the same to my friend, Mr. Dourville, who was then with me in the room, and to whom I spoke in the hearing of Miss Heyton herself.   It was this comparatively unimportant appearance of the parcel which induced me to believe that I should be successful in obtaining pardon for Lieutenant Morden ; and by so doing, not only gratify myself, but serve Lieutenant Morden, and be the means of administering comfort to the heart of the fair girl at whose request I had undertaken the task.   That morning found me on the road to London, having the parcel in my portmanteau. On my arrival in the metropolis, I lost no time in presenting that parcel at the proper quarters.   It was received ; and I proceeded to state the cause of its transmission having been delayed, whilst at the same time I so framed my speech as to place Lieutenant Morden's faults in the most favourable position.   Before I could finish what I had to say, I was interrupted by the person to whom I spoke opening the parcel, and in a voice expressive of surprise and wrathfulness, demanded what I meant by bringing him a mere bundle of blank paper."

"Blank paper !" echoed Ernest.

"Such indeed were the only contents of the packet," continued Lambert Warrenton. " Certain despatches, it seemed, had for some past days been expected from Captain Charnock, and that I was the bearer of them I fully believed. When, however, the contents of the packet were shown me, my astonishment was so great as for some minutes to prevent me from having a word to say. That there was some mistake became evident.   Accordingly, I received orders to take post immediately, return here, seek Captain Charnock, apprise him of the circumstances of the case, and obtain an explanation from his own lips. Captain Charnock is here, and will give further evidence upon the subject."

"Hey ! but this is a strange story !" exclaimed Sir Thomas Warrenton, as the last speaker resumed his seat.   "A pretty story, forsooth! And now, Captain Charnock, what have you to say before we make further inquiries of the prisoner himself?"

"All the evidence that I have to offer is simply this :—Certain despatches of more than common importance were written by me in my own hand, sealed by me with my own seal, and intrusted by me to the care of Lieutenant Morden, to be by him conveyed to their proper destination. The strange affair which has arisen out of this simple transaction is as mysterious to me as to any one else here present. I again assure you, Sir Thomas Warrenton, that I placed the most entire confidence in the integrity and honour of Lieutenant Morden. That such confidence was misplaced appears unfortunately to be too evident. With our present amount of information the whole affair wears an air of mystery ; the most unaccountable stories are related ; strange disclosures are made ; the papers themselves seem to be entirely lost. It is Lieutenant Morden alone who can make the mystery clear ; and I, for one, will think the better of him if he does so without further delay."

"No, Captain Charnock, I cannot agree with you there," observed Sir Thomas, magisterially. "The laws of England do not require an accused person to inculpate himself by his own confession. If there be any one else here present who can offer further evidence upon this matter, let him speak at once."

There was a profound silence—a silence broken only at intervals by the quick, hysterical breathings of poor, agonised Amy.

"Is the evidence concluded? Can no one disclose what has become of these despatches?" demanded Sir Thomas after a short pause.

"I can," answered a clear, cold voice, from the upper end of the apartment.

Every eye was at once turned in the direction of the speaker. Gervase Morden —the high-principled and austere student—had risen to give evidence against his brother.

"You, Mr. Gervase? you, Morden, man ?" exclaimed Sir Thomas, in a tone of surprise.

Not a trace of inward emotion was betrayed upon the countenance of the student as he made reply,—

"Yes, Sir Thomas, it was I who spoke. You asked if any one present could inform you what had become of the despatches intrusted by Captain Charnock to Lieutenant Morden. It is in my power to do so. Those despatches are here."

And as the student spoke, he placed the papers, which had fallen from the pocket of Red Martin, the smuggler, upon the table. At that moment, of all who stood in the apartment, Kate Heyton alone remarked that the countenances of Lambert Warrenton and Eugene Dourville assumed a sudden paleness.

"These are the papers !" exclaimed Sir Thomas Warrenton, as he leant over the table to gaze at them, whilst others pressed forward to gratify their curiosity with a glance at the important documents.

"Those I believe are the despatches of which you speak," returned the student. "Let Captain Charnock look at them, and say whether they are such or not."

"These are the very papers," cried Captain Charnock, as he cast his eyes upon the opened sheets. "This is the envelope, and with the seals broken."

"Do you hear, Kate—do you hear what he says ?" asked poor trembling Amy of her sister. But the question was unregarded, for the eyes of Kate Heyton still continued to be intently fixed upon the forms of Lambert Warrenton and Eugene Dourville, watching every change in the expression of their countenances, every movement of their lips, every shade of meaning in their eyes. Nor knew the two men that there was one individual in that room who was watching them with the closest scrutiny ; neither guessed they what strange thoughts had entered into that silent watcher's mind.

"At what are you looking, dear Kate—what is it that engages your attention ?" inquired poor Amy, wondering at the silence of her sister.

"Hush, Amy ! Do not disturb me."

"Disturb you in what, dear sister ?"

There was no reply.

Eugene Dourville and Lambert Warrenton were seated near each other. Though remote from the rest of the company, and occupying seats in a distant part of the room, no individuals, of all who were there present, appeared to regard the proceedings with deeper interest than did the son of Sir Thomas Warrenton, and the courtly Frenchman whom he treated as his friend.

Amy turned her eyes towards Ernest; her glance did not meet his. With his arms folded on his chest, his head proudly erect, and his dark eyes fixed upon the documents which had been thus strangely brought forward, he appeared to be unconscious of the presence of those around, and wholly absorbed in contemplating the critical nature of his position.

"Yes, Sir Thomas," said Captain Charnock, after looking over the contents of the packet, "these papers are my despatches. The question is, how came they to be here?"

"Ay, and a very just question truly, captain!" returned Sir Thomas. "Gadzooks! there is a pretty bit of mystery here! Why, Morden, man, how is this—what business had you with these papers?"

The student paused for a moment, looked towards his brother, turned again to Sir Thomas, and while every eye was directed towards him, said,—

"My honour, my loyalty, duty, justice and truth bid me to disclose all. Even if my brother's life rest upon that which I have to say, I will still neither withhold nor falsify—I cannot do it; and Ernest will forgive me, knowing as he does the character of the brother who loves him with all a brother's love, however much he may be called upon by duty to act towards him in a part which he unwillingly assumes."

"Humph!" observed Sir Thomas. "That is all true and very well, Morden, man, but how about the papers? Let us hear about them."

Calmly, clearly, and succinctly, Gervase Morden detailed the manner in which he had become possessed of the documents in question. He was listened to in breathless attention, and when he had finished speaking, Sir Thomas hastily observed,—

"Ay, ay, a pretty affair, forsooth. So this was the affair which caused your sudden illness, when you sped off so quickly? You of course went to confer with your brother; and if he made any confession, duty, you know, man—duty requires you to make it public. There must be no hiding secrets—no mystifications."

"All that my brother told me, Sir Thomas, it is my intention to disclose."

"Not so, Mr. Morden! Indeed—indeed you must not!" exclaimed the sweet voice of Constance Ismay, as Constance herself, with tears in her eyes, rushed forward, and laid her white hands upon the arm of the student—"you will not say anything to harm your poor brother!"

"I have promised to declare all, Miss Ismay."

"But you will not. Oh! do not act so unkindly—an act which you will repent hereafter."

"Nay, Miss Ismay, I must."

"Come, Morden, man, we are waiting," observed Sir Thomas. "What has the prisoner confessed?"

"He has declared, and that solemnly, his entire ignorance of how Red Martin came to have these papers in his possession. My brother has given me his word, his most solemn assurance, that he is guiltless of having played the traitor to his king or to his country."

"And do you believe him?" inquired Captain Charnock.

"He is my brother; and he dares not to lie."

"Do you hear him, sister Kate—do you hear what Mr. Gervase says?" asked Amy of her sister, in a joyful voice.

Still Kate Heyton was silent; and still were her eyes directed towards the forms of Lambert Warrenton and the Frenchman. The countenances of these two men had resumed their usual expression; though the attention with which Eugene Dourville listened to the whisperings of his companion betrayed the importance of the subject upon which they were conversing.

Had Gervase Morden turned his eyes to where, supported by Lady Warrenton, stood the fair form of Constance Ismay, he would have seen a face radiant with gratitude, and discerned certain tokens of a warm heart then beating to deeper emotions than any that he suspected that bosom to contain.

"He would not—I knew he would not act cruelly towards his brother!" ejaculated Constance.

A consultation respecting the course next to be pursued had for some minutes been carried on between Captain Charnock and Sir Thomas Warrenton. The son of the latter now approached the table, and placing upon it a small paper, said,—

" I have as yet but partially executed my mission. The orders that I received were, that if Lieutenant Morden failed in giving a perfect explanation of this affair, he should immediately be conveyed to London, there to answer for his misdeeds. In this paper, Sir Thomas, are instructions to that effect; and it is for you to act upon them according to your discretion."

" To London, dear father! take Ernest to London!" exclaimed Amy, in a voice of terror, as she clung for support to the arm of Mr. Heyton.

" He must go, Amy. His fate will be a sad one if this mystery be not better explained."

" But he is not guilty, dear father—you hear that he is not guilty."

" We have but his own word for it, child."

" And do you not believe him, father? Do you think that Ernest would tell a lie ?"

" It may not be the first which he has told," answered Heyton, gravely.

" Oh, father, dear father, it is cruel of you to say such words. I will go to Ernest, and ask him what it all means."

" Stay, sister !" cried Frank, seizing the arm of Amy, as she moved forward towards the prisoner. " Stay, I bid you!"

" Why is this, brother? Why may I not speak to Ernest—to Ernest Morden ?"

" Amy Heyton hold converse with a traitor! No, sister, it shall not be."

" But you wrong him, Frank—you accuse poor Ernest wrongfully. He is no traitor; none here have proved him to be such."

" Wait, then, sister; wait till he be pronounced an honest man."

While this scene was passing, occurrences of another description were taking place at another part of the room.

Sir Thomas Warrenton, Captain Charnook, and Gervase Morden were seated at the table; near them sat Lambert Warrenton and his friend. The attention of each was directed to a small note which the student had found attached to the packet containing the despatches, of the origin of which note Captain Charnock averred his entire ignorance.

The note was written in a cypher, being, therefore, perfectly unreadable to any person not possessed of the key. By whom it had been written, what its import was, or for whose reading it was intended, there were no means of ascertaining.

" As black a case of treachery, Sir Thomas, as any that have been heard of for many years past," observed Captain Charnock. " The papers found in the possession of a well-known traitor, outlaw, and spy ; the seals broken ; a writing attached which cannot be either more or less than a communication from traitors here to enemies elsewhere."

" But are the traitors here, captain ?"

" It is not easy to answer that question, Sir Thomas. I am loath to make any such charge against Lieutenant Morden, yet I cannot do otherwise than accuse him of being the traitor."

Sir Thomas arose from his seat, and, looking towards the prisoner, said in a serious voice,—

" Lieutenant Morden, you are accused by your superior officer of a betrayal of trust, and of acting as a traitor towards your country, nor does the charge appear to be without foundation. Papers intrusted to your care are kept back by you, and are now found in the possession of one who is a known rebel and foe. A parcel is manufactured and transmitted to London, that parcel being nothing else than a mere deception, made up and forwarded with an intent known only to those concerned in the villany. I assure you, Lieutenant Morden, that this is a most serious affair—it affects your honour, your reputation, ay, your very life. I do not wish to press you into saying anything that may criminate yourself, neither have I any legal right to do so ; but if you can offer one word in explanation of these mysterious circumstances—an explanation that may save me the pain of a more formal investigation—I trust that you will do so. There are many in this room who are deeply concerned in your welfare—many who are afflicted at beholding you in your present position, and who long to see you acquitted of this charge. For their sakes I ask you to be candid, and advise you to be so, not in my character as a magistrate, but as your friend—your sincere friend."

"Sir Thomas Warrenton," returned Ernest, "I thank you for your kindness and for your advice : both are duly valued by me. You have asked me to speak the truth, and I will speak it ; you have asked me to explain a mystery, and I cannot explain it. Of the man to whom you allude—Red Martin, as you call him—I know nothing, nor of how those despatches came into his possession, can I tell you anything. Heaven witness to the truth of what I say ! The papers were committed to my care ; I know that they were in my keeping five days since.

They were removed at night-time from beneath my pillow, and missed by me on the following morning. I need not recapitulate that which you have already heard, inasmuch as Miss Amy Heyton has already related her own adventure, and the circumstance of her delivering a sealed packet to Mr. Warrenton has been owned to by himself, and has also received the testimony of Mr. Dourville. During the past four days I have rested in the belief that Captain Charnock's despatches were on their way to their proper destination. The imposition which was practised upon Mr. Warrenton as much excited my surprise in the relation, as it no doubt did the surprise of those who were present at the opening of the fictitious parcel. That the genuine documents should have been found upon the person of a French smuggler is to me a greater mystery than all. I beseech that this investigation be proceeded with; and I trust that no pains will be spared to bring the really guilty person to light. Once more, Sir Thomas, I assure you of my ignorance and my innocence."

The expression of the prisoner's countenance during the delivery of this speech had been most intently watched by Gervase Morden. So fixed and searching was the penetrative glance of the student, that it was as if he desired to read the most hidden secrets of that brother's heart. But Ernest stood well the scrutiny; for his tongue did not falter, his eyes were not downcast; the words which he spoke were uttered with an emphasis, which seemed to bear witness to their truth.

The inquiry was now commenced in due form; Sir Thomas being determined to bring home the guilt to the real offender, by means of a most searching investigation.

It was deemed proper in the first place to examine the seaman who had picked up the parcel when it fell from out the pocket of Red Martin. The evidence given by this man was clear and conclusive; there remained no doubt of the smuggler having been in possession of the papers.

"Mr. Morden," said Sir Thomas, addressing his secretary, "you have the notes of Lieutenant Morden's examination before you, let them be gone over carefully; and let every individual therein mentioned be called upon to give evidence in due succession."

This was done. The first name called was that of Sampson Summers.

In obedience to previous orders which had been issued by Sir Thomas, the tombcutter had made his appearance at the Hall, in company with his friend Glib Griffiths.

"Don't be downhearted, Sandy," recommended Glib; "if they put any questions to you that it wouldn't be easy for you to answer, just turn your eyes towards me, and I'll be spokesman for you in a trice. I'll witness to anything."

"You must tell no lies, Glib."

"A pretty caution, indeed, to come from you, Sandy Summers! Whoever heard of Glib Griffiths being caught out in a lie? Dunna you be afeard on that head."

"Sampson Summers! Where is Sampson Summers?" demanded Sir Thomas.

"Here, your honour," replied Sandy, advancing towards the table, and closely followed by Glib Griffiths.

"Mr. Summers, it appears from statements which have already been made in this room, that on the night of the 14th instant, you took a certain sealed parcel from underneath the pillow of Lieutenant Morden, then a resident in your cottage, and delivered that sealed parcel into the hands of Miss Amy Heyton, who had arranged with you to receive it—was such the case?"

"I did so, Sir Thomas. I gave it to Miss Amy Heyton."

"Let Amy Heyton step forward."

Amy advanced towards the table, supported by her father and her sister.

"You have heard the confession of Mr. Summers. Do you, Amy Heyton, acknowledge having received such parcel from his hands?"

"I do; and it was at my own request."

"Your object in making that request was—what?"

"That I might convey the packet to Mr. Lambert Warrenton."

"And you carried out your intention?"

"I did."

"At the time of receiving the packet from Mr. Summers, did you observe its shape and form—did you observe whether it was secured with one seal, or with more?"

"Sandy Summers gave me the packet in a basket. I merely opened the lid, and saw it there. I did not touch it with my hands."

"Well, you brought the basket to this house, and sought the presence of my son; what happened then?"

"I gave Mr. Lambert the packet; he took it, and remarked at the time that it was but carelessly secured."

"Let Lambert Warrenton stand forward, and take his oath to give true evidence in this matter."

The command was obeyed.

"Miss Amy Heyton has stated that, five nights since, she delivered a certain packet into your hands. Do you remember accurately the appearance of that packet, and how it was sealed?"

"I have a distinct remembrance of Miss Heyton's visit. The packet which she delivered to me, and which I carried to London at her request, was sealed with one seal only. Mr. Dourville was present at the time, and witnessed also to the fact."

Eugene Dourville was called upon to give his evidence. He was about to do so, unmindful of the usual preliminary.

"Let Mr. Dourville take the oath," exclaimed Kate Heyton, and as the Frenchman raised the holy book to his lips, the eyes of Kate Heyton were fixed upon his countenance with a gaze which seemed fearful as that of the dreaded basilisk.

Sir Thomas applied for further evidence to the tomb-cutter.

"Mr. Summers," said he, "do you remember at the time of your placing the packet in the basket, whether you observed the manner in which it was secured?"

Sandy stammered forth an answer in the negative.

"Then," continued Sir Thomas, "you are not aware, Mr. Summers, whether the packet which you took from beneath the pillow of Lieutenant Morden, and which he had told you were certain despatches intrusted to his care, was sealed with one seal, or whether it had more than that number?"

"No, Sir Thomas. I—I did not look—I do not know."

Glib Griffiths perceived the awkward position in which Sandy's evidence was likely to place all parties, and seeing that Sandy himself was too much confused to return a coherent answer, the prattling barber determined, even at the risk of committing perjury, to have a word to say in the matter.

"So please you, your honour," observed Glib, making at the same time a bow to Sir Thomas, "my friend, Sandy, here, is not a man who is particularly sharp-witted, and it is isn't always that he has his eyes open either. Now it may be that I have a few things to say in this affair which will save you the trouble of asking Sandy again."

"Let the oath be tendered to Mr. Griffiths," commanded Sir Thomas.

Glib mumbled over the words which he was directed to say; then having made a feint of kissing the book, he proceeded to make his statement.

"First and foremost, Sir Thomas," said Glib, "I must be allowed to say, that there isn't a man who can give more important evidence upon this affair than I can. I don't wonder that you're all staring at me so, ladies and gentlemen. When Glib Griffiths says anything, it's sure to be something to the purpose. Now, as I was in Sandy Summer's shop, when he put the packet into the basket, it was easy enough for me to see what sort of a packet it was. Well, I did see it, and I can't say about the exact number of the seals; I can't say whether there were four or five, or what they were, but talking about one seal is all nonsense. You don't suppose that Lieutenant Morden, who is a perfect gentleman, would carry a packet with only one shabby seal to it for the best captain in the world ; there's nobody thinks that, I should say."

"Then, Mr. Griffiths, if I understand you rightly," said Sir Thomas, "you were present when Mr. Summers put the packet in the basket, and chanced to observe what that packet was like ?"

"Well, I think I may say yes to that, your honour. It's as near the truth as you could possibly put it."

"And the seals upon the packet—you saw them—were there as many as three?"

"Quite as many, your honour : three and a half, as one might say, considering they were rather large."

Sir Thomas and Captain Charnock took occasion to make a few remarks upon the importance of the evidence just adduced. While they were speaking to one another, Sandy Summers availed himself of the opportunity to grasp tremblingly the arm of Griffiths, and with pallid lips to whisper in the ear of the latter,—

"You are not speaking truth, Glib. You know that you were not in my shop that night."

"Dunna be a fool, Sandy," returned Glib. "Ben't I getting you out of a hobble, and can't you be quiet ?"

"Will Mr. Griffiths give some information as to what time of the day it was when he saw Mr. Summers put the sealed packet in the basket?" inquired Sir Thomas.

"Begging your honour's pardon," replied Glib, "it wasn't in the day at all, but at night, just at eleven o'clock."

"Glib Griffiths ben't a telling the truth, your honour," cried Roger Dugson, the well-digger of the village, who had contrived to obtain admission to the court-room ; "he knows he ben't a telling the truth."

"What has that man to say?" inquired Sir Thomas.

Dugson stepped forward, and, pulling at his hair, by way of making a bow, said,—

"I've stood here, Sir Thomas, and I've heard Mr. Griffiths tell you what he has. He's told you a lie, and I will say as how my blood boiled to hear him tell it. I don't believe he was in Sandy's house at all last Monday night ; leastways, I can say this, that as to his having been there at eleven o'clock, I can as much as swear that I met him in Blackthorn-lane, just as the old church clock was striking that very hour. So if that ben't one of his lies, I don't know what is."

"Softly now, Dugson, softly, man," rejoined Glib. "You've got a strong memory, but yours isn't the head for taking in all the points of a case. Somehow or other, you've managed to forget the old church clock being twenty minutes too fast the week before the last one, and as how it wasn't put right till last Tuesday. Now there's Mr. Purchiss down in the village, who put the old clock right, and who, if you'll go and fetch him, will put you right in what you don't seem to have clear ideas about, Roger Dugson."

"Well, Mr. Griffiths, and what has this quarrel about the village clock got to do with the business in hand ?" inquired Sir Thomas.

"Just this, your honour · if Roger Dugson saw me in Blackthorn-lane, at eleven of the night by the church clock, and that was twenty minutes too fast, there was plenty of time for me to reach Sandy's cottage by eleven o'clock of the right time. Now, it so happened that I was at Sandy's then ; and it so happened that I looked at my watch and saw what the real time was. Look at my watch, your honour. I'll just hand it over to you, and you'll see that it keeps good time."

While Glib Griffiths was fumbling with his watch, Sandy Summers again whispered in his ear.

"Glib," said he, "Glib, man, you're telling a mortal lie."

"Well, I know it, don't I? But let me finish it, Sandy," was the answer returned in a whisper also.

Sir Thomas, after a pause of a few minutes, said,—

' Then you persist, Mr. Griffiths, in affirming that, at eleven o'clock on the night of the 14th instant, you were present in Mr. Summers's cottage, and saw him place a sealed paper packet in a basket, observing at the same time that the packet was sealed with three seals ?"

"That's just it, your honour. The time was eleven o'clock to a minute—I like to be particular about facts—eleven o'clock, Sir Thomas, by that very watch; and all I can say is, that if Roger Dugson was worth a good watch of his own, he wouldn't have made such a fool of himself to-day."

The evidence which Glib Griffiths had offered was of very serious importance. Sir Thomas and his secretary perceived such to be the case, and entered into consultation accordingly. While they were conversing, other scenes were being enacted by individuals in the same apartment.

"What are you saying, dear Amy ?" inquired Kate Heyton of her sister, having remarked that, for the last five minutes, Amy's lips had been in constant motion, and that she had spoken many muttered words.

"I am praying, sister, praying to God that he will help poor Ernest, and bring this trial to a happy end."

"Then you still believe Ernest to be innocent, Amy ?" asked Kate.

"Sister, why that question? Ernest cannot be guilty of the wicked crimes they lay to his charge. His innocence will be proved, sister—it will be made plain presently; and then, oh, how happy I shall be !"

At that moment, then, when the fair girl was expressing her hope, and picturing her happiness—when she was gilding the future, and dwelling delightedly in the fairy palace which she had herself reared—the idiot, who had hitherto crouched by her side, arose to his feet; his eyes glistened with a wild, unearthly light; his countenance was dark as that of a fallen spirit. Once, and once only, he paused to look upon fair Amy's face; then, stealing gently across the room, the idiot-boy sought the side of the accused man. He went as goes the murderer to the chamber of his victim; he crept as creeps the wily animal towards his prey. It was madness going to its triumph—its triumph, so fearful and so fell !

"What want you with me, Archy ?" demanded Lieutenant Morden.

"Hush ! Archy has something to say. Archy must whisper."

And Ernest Morden bent down his head to listen. As he did so, Sir Thomas Warrenton resumed the inquiry.

"Amy Heyton," said he, "from what has already transpired in your hearing, it would seem that the packet which Mr. Summers placed in the basket was not the same which you delivered to Mr. Warrenton. Is it possible that you could have made a mistake ?"

"Oh, no, Sir Thomas! It was the same parcel—the very same."

"It is difficult, my good girl, to reconcile that assertion with the preceding evidence. Are you sure that on your journey from the cottage to this place that the basket never passed out of your hand ?"

"It never did."

"On the way, did you meet or speak to any one ?"

Amy hesitated for a moment, and then replied,—

"I met Mr. Masters—Luke Masters."

"Ha! and that man bears a disreputable character. Did he stop you? Did he speak to you ?"

"He did. I knew Luke Masters some years ago; and he stopped me to speak of things that have been—to ask me about his friends in the village."

"And did you tell him the errand on which you were going? Did you show him the packet of despatches ?"

"I did neither. Luke Masters did not know what I had in the basket."

"But did he touch the basket—did it pass into his hands ?"

"No, Sir Thomas ; I am sure it did not."

"Well, you finished your interview with Mr. Masters, and you went on till you arrived at the Hall gate? Did you meet any one else by the way ?"

"No one, Sir Thomas."

"You sought the presence of Mr. Warrenton, and you gave the packet into his care. I believe you said that it was then your attention was first directed to the manner in which that packet was secured, and you saw that it had but one seal?"

"I did, Sir Thomas. Mr. Warrenton pointed it out to my notice."

Sir Thomas knew not what further question to ask. He deliberated for a few moments, and then addressing those who stood near him, said,—

"This is all very extraordinary! We have evidence to the effect that a packet sealed with three seals was put into the basket by Mr. Summers, and we have also evidence to prove that a different packet was delivered by Amy Heyton to Mr. Warrenton. How the transformation took place on the way is the mystery which we want cleared up. There is something very strange, very inexplicable in such a story." ·

"It is strange, but not inexplicable, Sir Thomas Warrenton," exclaimed Ernest Morden, in a loud voice, as he advanced nearer to the table. "There was a mystery; but that mystery is dispelled now."

"Hey, Lieutenant Morden! but I am glad to hear you say so. Explain it, man—explain it quickly!"

Gervase Morden directed his gaze towards his brother.

"Hark! Sister Kate," cried Amy, a ray of pleasure beaming on her countenance. "Did I not say so—did I not say that Ernest would prove his innocence? God has heard your poor sister's prayer!"

Ernest Morden glanced towards Amy Heyton before he spoke.

"Sir Thomas Warrenton," said he, "I must beg you to listen calmly to the accusation which I have to make. That there had been treachery used towards me, I well knew; that some one in this room had spoken lies, I was certain some half-hour since. It is a painful task which I have to execute—I would to Heaven it were not my task! I have suffered much; I have been wronged much; I have been dealt with perfidiously. There was one individual whom I trusted, and that one has wrought me evil—one whom I believed my friend, but who has done me the work of an enemy. That person is here—is in this room—is listening to my words. Sir Thomas Warrenton, I accuse Amy Heyton of having stolen the despatches intrusted to my care by Captain Charnock, and of having placed those papers in the hands of Red Martin, the smuggler."

"Kate—dear Kate, what does Ernest say?" asked Amy, in a faint voice, as she clung to the arm of her sister, pale, quivering, and affrighted.

The words which Ernest had uttered—the accusation he had made—produced but one effect upon each individual present. There was an involuntary start as if an electric shock had passed through the whole. Every one rose to a standing position; every eye was directed towards the bold accuser; the lips of all were sealed. There was silence, wonderment, horror, and surprise.

Minutes passed; and then Sir Thomas Warrenton, addressing the prisoner, said,—

"Will Lieutenant Morden repeat his accusation—repeat it plainly?"

"Of the crime of stealing those papers which now lie upon the table before you, and of the further crime of transferring them to Red Martin, the smuggler, I accuse, openly and declaredly, Miss Amy Heyton!"

One look—one wild look, expressive of consternation, horror, and shuddering affright, did Amy cast at Ernest. A mist rose before her eyes; she felt her mind to wander—her brain to reel. Her consciousness departed; her respiration became heavy; she raised her hand to her forehead, and found it to be cold—icy cold.

One look—one look of fear and horror, and doubt, and agony—then rushing forward, Amy Heyton caught the arm of Ernest—of Ernest Morden, the object of her deep, fond love—Ernest Morden, to whom she had forgiven so much, for whom she had endured so much—Ernest Morden, who had accused of treachery the gentle being who had proved so well her faithfulness, her loyalty to him,—she caught his arm, looked imploringly in his loved face, tottered as she gazed, and sinking powerless on her knees, ejaculated in a voice, the tones of which were painful in their thrilling touchingness,—

"Ernest—dear Ernest! I—I am Amy—Amy Heyton. What meaning was there in your words—what meaning—what—what?"

She could say no more, she could inquire no further. The mist grew denser before her eyes; the reeling of her brain grew wilder, wilder. It was by the side of Ernest—Ernest, the fondly-cherished idol of her heart, that then she knelt; and his eyes looked not upon her, he did not clasp, as in old time, her pale, cold, clammy hand. She felt that he was changed—that he willed not to have her kneeling so fondly at his side. And when she felt that—when the deadening, numbing truth was understood in all its fearfulness, her tongue became paralysed, her lips motionless. Gently her head sunk upon the arm—his arm, and over that arm fell the trailing sunny tresses which once Ernest Morden had loved to look upon, when admiring their wavy flow.

And still his eyes were averted from her—still he turned his face the other way.

He felt the grasp lessening in its strength, and knew that a fair face rested on his arm. He paused, he deliberated, he looked upon the idiot boy; then, suddenly uplifting his arm—that arm on which she rested, he moved aside, and Amy, senseless stricken—Amy fell prostrate on the floor.

"Man!—murderer! You have slain my sister!" exclaimed Frank Heyton, as, springing at Ernest Morden, he clutched him by the throat.

"Ha! You, too, are a Heyton," cried Ernest, with the voice and manner of a maniac. "I know you; I——."

"Separate them—separate those men!" exclaimed Sir Thomas, his attention being suddenly called to the fray.

The dark hair of Frank Heyton was thrown back from off his forehead; his eyes were fixed upon his foe with a glaring, hideous expression. The countenances of each had assumed a dark, livid hue—dark as were the passions in their bosoms.

"Separate them instantly! There will be murder done!" again exclaimed Sir Thomas.

Gervase Morden and the elder Heyton rushed forward and grasped the arms of the two men. At that moment, the deep breathing of Ernest showed that the hold of his enemy was such as would speedily produce suffocation.

"Take off your hand, Frank!" commanded Mr. Heyton. "Unhand him, boy, or you will commit murder!"

"He has done murder—murder to my sister," returned Frank, madly tightening his hold.

"Gadzooks!" cried Sir Thomas, speedily interposing between the two enemies—"do you dare this? and here too! Loose your hold, young varlet, or I shall commit you to prison for murderous intention. Loose your hold, I command you."

Awed by the stern, rough voice of Sir Thomas, Frank Heyton relaxed his grasp, and moved back a few steps. Still his eyes glared fiercely upon Ernest; still his teeth were locked together in the madness of his rage! The memory of the deep insults he had suffered—the deep wrongs that had been wrought his sister—recurred vividly to his mind. He glanced round the apartment as if in search of some deadly weapon.

Gervase Morden observed the action.

"He is dangerous," whispered the secretary in the ear of his master.

"Remove him. Let him be taken hence immediately," commanded Sir Thomas.

"No, Sir Thomas Warrenton," returned Frank Heyton. "Amy is my sister; and that man has spoken words against her which I can never forgive. See you, he has almost killed her—almost slain her, though she was mad enough to love him. I will not quit this room, Sir Thomas, until I have seen justice done to my poor sister."

"Peace, then, young man—peace, and be silent! Go to your seat and make no further disturbance."

"And he—that man?"

"Lieutenant Morden must be listened to, without interruption from you."

"But Amy—my sister?"

"It is only faintness that has come over the maiden. Let her be taken into the open air."

Lady Warrenton, Constance Ismay, Kate Heyton, and her father had all gathered round the insensate form of poor Amy, and had raised her from off the floor. They were about to obey the instructions of Sir Thomas, and convey her into the open air, when, partially recovering from her fit, the eyes of the poor girl moved, and their glance fell upon the form of Ernest. In a moment, consciousness and memory returned; the accusation of Ernest sounded again in her ears; she remembered the fearful words; she had not forgotten the cold, repellant manner.

"Come, sister—come away," said Kate, in a gentle voice.

Amy still gazed upon Ernest. She saw that he leaned for support against one of the old, high-backed chairs; she saw also that his head was bent down, his face hidden by his hands; his whole appearance that of a person suffering some heartrending agony. Unable to believe that the Ernest whom she loved had really spoken the strange words which still rung in her ears; unable to feel revenge for his slight and cruelty; deeming, in her fondness, that gentle words would soothe his spirit—that the voice which he had once loved to hear would exercise its olden spell over him—recalling, by its tenderness, the memory of by-gone days, assuaging by its gentleness the angry feelings which now agitated his mind; trusting also in the assurances which she had once received from him—had once heard from his own lips—she again threw herself forwards, again clasped his arm, again ejaculated fondly—oh, how fondly!—

"Ernest—dear Ernest! What have I done? Why are you grieved?"

"Away!" thundered Ernest Morden, moving aside, and freeing himself from the gentle clasp of Amy's hand. "Away come not near me."

"Hark you," said Lambert Warrenton to Eugene Dourville, as the two friends gazed upon the scene from a distant corner of the room. "Hark you! It works. He spurns her."

"Sir Thomas Warrenton," said the elder Heyton, in an agitated manner. "I request that you command Lieutenant Morden to explain the accusation which he has made so strangely."

"I will do it, Stephen Heyton," replied Ernest. "Let Amy contradict me, if she can."

"Listen, Kate—listen, dear Kate!" tremulously ejaculated Amy, while resting her head in her sister's lap.

Kate Heyton heard; but her eyes were turned elsewhere, watching still with penetrating gaze the two men in the distant corner.

"Let there be silence," ordered Sir Thomas, "and let Lieutenant Morden give the explanation which is required of him. He has accused Amy Heyton of purloining certain papers; let us hear how he supports that charge."

"I accuse her of more than you have mentioned, Sir Thomas. My accusation against Amy Heyton is, that she has acted treacherously towards her country, by giving the papers just mentioned into the hands of Red Martin, the smuggler."

"What does he mean, Kate—what does he mean, dearest?"

"Be still, good sister—be still, and listen."

"A pretty accusation, truly!" returned Sir Thomas. "But where are your proofs, man? On what grounds do you bring such a charge? What motives do you assign to Miss Heyton for such conduct? What know you of her connection with smugglers? Where are your witnesses, and what have they to say? Have a care, Lieutenant Morden—have a care, young man! This accusation, if not proved, will be of serious consequences to yourself; and, if proved, will not be likely to exonerate you, seeing that the girl is known to be in your confidence—your sweetheart, I believe. It is not feasible that she should have done anything of this kind without authority from you; nor is it probable that by throwing the crime upon her, your own exculpation will be effected.   Have a care, therefore, and speak the truth."

"I thank you for your warning, Sir Thomas," returned Ernest.   "And as to the questions which you have asked me, I reply that, if proofs of that which I assert are wanted, I have proofs ; if witnesses be required, they shall be produced ; if explanations be demanded, they shall be forthcoming."

"At once, Lieutenant Morden—let them be given at once," desired Sir Thomas, testily.

"There shall be no delay.   You, Sir Thomas, have heard from **Amy Heyton's** own lips the story of her obtaining possession of these despatches **unknown to** myself.   There has been evidence given to prove that those despatches, properly sealed and secured, were delivered into Amy Heyton's hands.   A story has been told you of her visit to Mr. Warrenton, and of the delivery of a packet to him, purporting to be the one which she procured at the cottage of Sampson Summers. That it was not the same packet has been fully proved ; though why such a trick was resorted to, and what object the trickster had in view, remains to be made evident. I heard Amy Heyton's story,—I believed that she spoke the truth. She affirmed that she had exerted herself in my behalf, solely because of her affection for me. I believed that statement—and would at that moment—ay, at an hour since, have made any sacrifice to prove my gratitude. Alas! that I have been deceived in where I trusted, that I have been wofully, fearfully deceived!"

"To the point, man—to the point!" interrupted Sir Thomas. "That the maiden became possessed of the papers seems very clear ; but what she did with them is yet to be explained."

"She did this, Sir Thomas :—Two mornings since, Amy Heyton gave those papers into the hands of Red Martin, the smuggler."

"He lies!" exclaimed Frank Heyton. "My sister is no traitor to her country—she holds no acquaintance with outlaws."

"It is you who lie, Frank Heyton," returned Ernest ; "either your sister has deceived you, or you yourself are an accomplice with her in her treachery."

"Unhand me, father!" cried the exasperated Frank, as Mr. Heyton, perceiving the red blood rise to the cheeks of his son, pinioned him firmly, and forbade him to stir. "Unhand me, father, I charge you! It is Amy's brother whom he has insulted now."

"Wait, boy, wait. Ernest Morden will not escape unpunished."

Sir Thomas Warrenton arose from his seat.

"This is a terrible accusation, Lieutenant Morden. What proofs, what witnesses have you to support so grave a charge ?"

"I have one witness, and he is here," replied Ernest. "Archibald, the idiot-boy, will prove that Amy Heyton, and Red Martin, the smuggler, are friends."

"Archy called upon by him!" ejaculated Kate Heyton in an undertone. "Tell me, sister Amy,—what secrets does Archy know ?"

"Secrets ?" returned Amy, musingly.

"Yes ; he must—ha! sister, why that look? Why do you beckon to Archy? You are pale, sister! You tremble in my arms!"

"What—what is the meaning of this ?" stammered Mr. Heyton to his son, as Ernest brought Archy forward. "Look at his countenance, Frank. What has that boy to tell ?"

"Nothing, father—nothing against sister Amy."

"Are you sure of that?" returned the parent, in a hoarse whisper.

"Sure, father! You do not believe his words—Ernest's words ? You do not suspect your child?"

Mr. Heyton was silent.

"Speak, father!" cried Frank—"why that biting of the lip—that wildness of your eyes? What know you of sister Amy?"

Still the parent was silent.

Ernest Morden led Archy towards the table.

"This boy will witness," said he, "that two mornings since, Amy Heyton sought Red Martin, the smuggler, and delivered to him a parcel, which he was in waiting for among the cliffs."

"Amy—dear Amy!" whispered poor Kate, "what does Archy mean?—why are you silent?—why do you not stand up and deny this vile charge?"

Kate felt that her sister's heart was pulsating rapidly.

"The boy is an idiot," said Sir Thomas. "Know you not, Lieutenant Morden, that the evidence of a person who is *non compos mentis*, cannot be admitted in a court of justice?"

"Then," returned Ernest, boldly, "let Amy Heyton contradict, if she can, the accusation which I have made against her."

"She will do it!" thundered Frank Heyton—"she will do it, Ernest Morden, even if it be with her last breath."

There was a silence so deep, so thorough, in that thronged room, that the ticking of the clock in the adjoining apartment could be plainly heard. All eyes—not excepting those of the prisoner—were turned towards the group of which Amy

Heyton formed the centre. A minute passed, and then the pale, trembling girl arose. Supported by her brother and her sister she advanced towards the table. The audience fell back to let her pass.

"Speak boldly, sister," whispered Frank, cheeringly, in her ear. "Take courage, and refute these calumnies in bravely-spoken words."

They led her onwards; her feet tottered as she trod the ground. Nervously she grasped the table's edge; and waved her hand to intimate that her brother and sister were to stand aside.

"Miss Amy Heyton, do you deny or acknowledge having held a conference with the well-known outlaw who bears the name of Red Martin, it having been affirmed that such conference was held by you two mornings since, on the cliffs near this place?"

"I acknowledge it—it is truth," was the clearly-spoken reply.

"Father!" stammered Frank—"she is mad; she is doing it to save him."

"Have we heard aright, Miss Heyton?" exclaimed Sir Thomas. "Do you admit that you held such conference with Red Martin?"

"I own it. I did so."

"Amy Heyton is candid," observed Ernest; "her candour, however, should have led her to this confession before being called upon to make it."

"Amy!" cried Mr. Heyton, as he rushed forward and seized the arm of his daughter, "let nothing but truth be spoken from your lips; confess everything; but utter no falsities with a view to save the guilty."

"I have spoken truth, dear father. Ernest is right in saying I sought Red Martin near the Altar Cliff, and that I carried a parcel to him."

"You, Amy!" ejaculated Frank. "The daughter of Stephen Heyton seeking the acquaintance of one who is her country's enemy?"

"Are you convinced?" whispered Ernest Morden, in the brother's ear.

Frank Heyton grasped the arm of Ernest, and looking threateningly in his face, said,—

"Hear me, Ernest Morden. If she—if Amy, my sister, is telling a falsity in order to screen you from justice, I, her brother, will see that you are doubly punished; but—but if she is confessing truth—if she has really been guilty of this crime, I will disown her—I will thrust her from me; she shall no longer be my sister!"

"Be it so!" replied Ernest Morden.

CHAPTER XLV.

"REJECT—DESPISE—CURSE HER, HE WILL DO IT ALL; AND SHE MUST
REDEEM HER PROMISE!"

AMY continued to stand beside the table, her glances alternately directed to Sir Thomas, Ernest Morden, and poor, anxious, panic-struck Kate, who gazed upon her sister with a look of mingled astonishment and fear.

"This inquiry increases in its importance," observed Sir Thomas. "Captain Charnock, will you hand Miss Heyton a chair?"

The request was complied with. Amy seated herself, refusing the proffered help of those who tendered her their services.

"Miss Amy Heyton," continued Sir Thomas, "you have confessed to the fact of having held an interview with Red Martin, at the time and place specified in the accusation. You have also admitted that you carried a parcel to the smuggler, and delivered the same into his hands. Have you anything to say as to whether that parcel did or did not contain the despatches which you now see before you?"

"I cannot tell, Sir Thomas. I do not know."

" How! you were the bearer of a parcel, yet know not whence it came nor what were its contents?   This, Miss Heyton, permit me to observe, could scarcely have been the case.   I must beg you to be more explicit.''

There was silence for a few seconds.   Then, turning towards her father, Amy clasped his hand, while tears coursed down her cheeks, and her half-opened mouth refused to articulate the words which she wished to utter.

"Speak, girl, speak," said the parent in a stern voice.   Then, relaxing into a milder mood—his heart touched at the dejected, plaintive appearance of poor Amy —he raised his right hand to her head, and stroking her bright hair with affectionate fondness, bade her keep nothing back.

" You will forgive me, father ; oh, you promise to forgive me ?''

" Forgive thee, child !—forgive !   What—what hast thou done to need such a promise from me ?''

'' This, father.   I have kept secrets from you ; I have not confided every thing to you as I should have done.   Red Martin once saved my life, and I never told you of his kindly deed.''

" Ha, girl ! who is it you speak of so familiarly ?   An outlaw—a smuggler—a traitor !''

" He may be all these, dear father ; but listen.   It was towards the close of last autumn that, strolling by myself on the beach, I felt a longing to go out upon the calm, beautiful sea.   Frank's boat was near at hand, and Frank had taught me how to handle an oar ; I moved the boat down to the water's edge, and getting in, rowed myself out towards the middle of the bay.   After remaining in the boat till I was tired, I attempted to make my way back to the shore.   It was flow tide, father, and I had little use for my oars.   Feeling pensive at the moment, I ceased rowing, and neglected to look whither I was going.   The boat drifted inwards ; you know the rocky point that projects into the middle of the bay—the Devil's Spear, father?   I did not perceive that I was nigh it ; I did not notice that the waves were drifting me towards it.   Suddenly, dear father, the boat struck against the Devil's Spear, and I was thrown into the water.   I should have sunk, father— sunk and died, had it not been for one man's kindness.   I felt myself sinking, though I endeavoured to grapple the edge of the rock and cling to it for support ; I did cling, father—I did hold fast by the rock, but my hands grew weary—my strength became exhausted.   Just then, father—just as the water found its way into my ears, and lights began to dance before my eyes, I saw a man swimming towards me ; I took courage ; I grasped the rock again.   In another second the man had caught me in his arm ; he told me not to fear ; he bore me towards the shore.   I was saved, father !   I was saved !—and he who rescued me from death was Red Martin the smuggler !''

" He, child !'

" Yes, father ; he had seen the boat overturn, and had at once plunged into the water to rescue me.   The boat sunk, but Red Martin recovered it, and brought it back to the place whence I had taken it.   He accompanied me to the cottage, father—there was no one at home except Archy.   My preserver refused taking any reward, and when I aked him for his name he told me that every fisherman on the coast knew Red Martin, the dreaded smuggler.''

" And why, child—why have I not heard this story before ?''

" Because, father, I knew that you and Frank hated Red Martin, and that you said hard things of him when his name was mentioned.   Dear father, I did not wish to hear you speak harsh words of the man who had saved my life.''

" A good feeling, Heyton, man,'' observed Sir Thomas, who had been an attentive listener to the story—"a good feeling enough ; though, to be sure, the girl don't seem to have a just and proper horror of such things as smugglers and traitors.''

" But the parcel, sister—the parcel, which you carried to Red Martin,'' hinted Kate.

" Wait, sister, and you shall hear :—two mornings since I went out as usual for a stroll along the beach.   Just as I reached the Altar Cliff—the Eagle's Altar, father—a man darted forth and seized me by the hand. I screamed out, but he bade me to be quiet. He asked me if I had forgotten Red Martin—Red Martin who had saved my life. I answered him, that his kindness would never pass from my memory. He told me that he was watched, that the revenue officers were in search of him, that he dared not leave his place of concealment; after asking me if I was willing to do him a favour in return for that which he had done me, and receiving an answer in the affirmative, he told me he had forgotten a certain parcel, which, having left at a short distance off, he nevertheless dared not to fetch. I hesitated not to fetch him that parcel. I took it, I delivered it into his hands. Archy met me on the beach and saw me do so. Further than as I have said, I know nothing of Red Martin. I returned him kindness for kindness; and even you, father, will not, cannot blame me for having done so."

" No child, no; I do not blame you."

" A pretty story, very prettily told," observed Sir Thomas; " there is one question, however, which it is necessary Miss Amy Heyton should answer, and that is,—where did Red Martin direct you to find the parcel, from what place did you fetch it?"

" Pardon me, Sir Thomas! I may not tell."

" Hey! not tell, indeed! and why not, pray?"

" My so doing might bring harm to others; and I gave my promise to Red Martin that I would keep the secret."

" Tush, girl! Promises to traitors, indeed! The man is an outlaw and a rebel; it is necessary, therefore, that you should tell all you know concerning him. A pretty thing to keep promises made to such kind of gentry!"

" You forget, Sir Thomas," observed Gervase Morden, deferentially, " that Miss Heyton should respect her word, whether passed to Red Martin, or to the vilest il lain in the kingdom."

" Humph! you're right, Morden, man; but a traitor, you know, a rebel to King George,—"

" Has nothing to do, Sir Thomas, with Miss Heyton's plighted word."

Sir Thomas mumbled a few syllables about smugglers and traitors; but, unable to combat the strict logic of his secretary, resumed the legitimate routine of inquiry.

" And you know nothing, Miss Heyton, of what the contents of that parcel were?"

" Nothing whatever, Sir Thomas."

" Then, for aught you can adduce to the contrary, it may have contained these stolen despatches?"

" It may," replied Amy, with a shudder.

Sir Thomas and Mr. Heyton exchanged looks of anxiety at this stage of the proceedings. The worthy knight sat down in his chair, as if, having touched on dangerous ground, he feared to venture further. It was not towards the prisoner, nor towards his secretary, that his gaze was directed; it was poor, pale, shuddering Amy, who alone engaged his attention. And whether he felt for that fair girl because of her firmness, or whether he had cause to take more interest in her welfare than there was reason to suppose, could not be told by his demeanour, suffice it, that he gazed at her with a fixed and sorrowful gaze, that he attempted to speak, but restrained the words which he was about to utter; and that, as thought after thought coursed through his brain, he turned away his face from the fair form before him, while tears gathered in his eyes. Strange enough it was, that Sir Thomas Warrenton should have been thus affected; he, the stout old mariner who had roamed o'er many a sea, borne the brunt of many a battle, and dared death in its wildest and its grimmest shape; what deep-seated feelings could those have been which caused his eyes to trickle with tears! Perhaps in the gentle form of Amy Heyton memory limned to his view the deep outlines of some fondly-loved being, whom he had known in boyhood's days. Perchance, in the sweet face of that poor girl, he traced the shadow of some other countenance, which, though faded from the world, was still present to the old man's mind, radiant with all the golden beauty it had worn of yore. There was evidence, ample evidence, that Sir Thomas Warrenton was undergoing his share of suffering with the rest of those who had cause to weep around him. It may have been that his sorrow was merely caused by his sympathy for the accused girl; it may have been that, perceiving the critical situation in which her own confessions had placed her, he dreaded lest further questioning should result in exposing her degradation, and bringing about the misery of those to whom she was related; or it may have been that at the same time he sympathised with her, and pitied her, he remembered some long-vanished being, who had once been as bright, as fair, as beautiful as was now the Amy Heyton upon whom he gazed. There are few among even the sternest of us, who have not such memories, ever pleasant, yet ever mournful in the re-calling—some glorious visions of a mother tender, a sister kind, or a loved one beautiful—beings to whom the heart paid homage in the past, and whom memory idolizes even when the clay cold earth has long since clasped them to its bosom. Oh! what were life, and what were age, unless it had such memories! To have them not is to be accursed, and yet it seems a curse that the forms themselves were only lent to us for so short a time.

"Sir Thomas," observed Gervase Morden, "you have omitted to ask Miss Heyton if she remembers the shape and appearance of the parcel which she gave into the hads of Red Martin."

"Let her answer the question," replied Sir Thomas.

Amy paused for a moment, as if to recollect herself, and then made answer,—

"It was a small parcel bound round with packthread, and the packthread sealed."

Sir Thomas observed Gervase Morden to turn pale.

"Hey! man, what now—why stare so at Miss Heyton?"

"Sir Thomas," replied the secretary in a solemn manner, and speaking with an effort, "the parcel which fell from Red Martin's pocket, and which was given into my hands, was bound with packthread, and the packthreaad sealed. That parcel contained Captain Charnock's despatches and from Amy Heyton's own confession it is evident that Amy Heyton herself was the agent through whom Red Martin received them."

There was a sudden start, and then a sudden silence. Amy's eyes wandered round the room, vacantly, as if reason had flown from her never to return. She gasped, she made an effort to speak; then sinking down upon the chair, her head fell forwards upon the table, and the silence—the deep silence was deeper still.

"Now, braggart," said Ernest Morden, as he once more laid his hand upon the arm of Frank Heyton, "said I not truly? and will you tell me now that it is I who have wronged your sister? Does her kindness come to this complexion at last?"

Frank Heyton made no reply. He ground his teeth; he clenched his hands; his breathing was performed with difficulty. He was mute, perfectly mute—the brother had not a word to say in defence of the sister!

Amy had heard the words which Ernest had uttered—the bitter, writhing words. As Ernest spoke, she listened; as he taunted, she raised her head. There was stillness for a single second. Then, with one quick movement, Amy cast herself prostrate before Ernest Morden, and clasping his arms, ejaculated—

"Hear me, Ernest—hear me, I implore you! God knows that willingly and consciously I have not done you this wrong! I knew not what that parcel was; I knew not that I was working harm to you! Forgive me, Ernest—forgive me, as —as—I once forgave you!"

"Hypocrite!—liar! Why carry your deception further? Stand from me—stand from me, Amy Heyton, lest I do you harm!"

And again Lambert Warrenton tapped the shoulder of Eugene Dourville.

"Listen!" said he; "it still works bravely—*He has rejected her now!*"

Slowly, and without trembling, Amy Heyton arose to her feet. There was no tottering of her limbs, no unsteadiness of her body. Like Banquo at the banquet-table of the murderer, she arose—like him as sadly, and as solemnly. Sternness had replaced gentleness on her countenance; the timid girl wore the look of a dauntless heroine. No longer the pale face, but the deeply-flushed cheek; no longer the downcast eye, but the glare which reminds the gazer of darkness, and the lightning-flash. She had ceased to be Amy, the despised suppliant; the words which she had heard had transformed her into a woman rejected by the man whom she had loved to madness—who had driven her to madness now.

"Lieutenant Morden has charged me with being a liar. I challenge him to prove that charge!" proclaimed Amy, in a loud unfaltering voice.

"What proof has Lieutenant Morden to bring forward?" demanded Sir Thomas. "Amy Heyton has denied the accusation of conscious treachery, and will he not believe her words?"

"He does not believe her words, Sir Thomas Warrenton!" returned Ernest. "Never till this day did he understand her character thoroughly; never till this day did he believe that she was capable of so mean an act of revenge!"

"Hey! what now, man? Revenge, say you—what had Amy Heyton to revenge?"

"Nothing, Sir Thomas; and I—all. It was not until I paid my last visit to her father's cottage, that I became possessed of a secret, which I cannot communicate, and which I almost wish I had never known—ask me not, Sir Thomas, what that secret is, I have already assured you that I dare not tell it. Previous to making this discovery, I and Amy had been friends, nay—lovers. I had promised Amy that she should be my bride, and I looked forward to the fulfilment of that promise with a feeling of joy. The discovery of that evening dashed from me my cup of happiness, and I knew that Amy Heyton could never become my wedded wife. I was maddened at the time. I fled from her, and hid myself. By her my retreat was discovered. She came to me—came to me with tears—with words of love. I dared not make her acquainted with the secret; but I told her that marriage between us was impossible; yet, although I could not be her husband, I would never become the husband of another, so long as Amy Heyton continued to be my friend. She also made a similar promise, and declared that she would still love me—fondly, fervently as ever. I believed her—fool that I was to do so! I dreamed not that she was playing me the hypocrite—that she remembered the apparent insult which I had offered her, and was silently chewing the cud of her revenge. In an evil hour, she became acquainted with the fact of my having committed a breach of trust, in the matter of Captain Charnock's despatches. She learned that those despatches were still in my possession. Then it was that she conceived the idea of revenging herself—then it was that, recollecting she could never be my bride, she determined upon becoming my destroyer. Still acting the hypocrite, she found means whereby to possess herself of the despatches, and, having made up a fictitious parcel, which she thought would resemble them, conveyed that to Mr. Warrington, and afterwards gave the other into the hands of Red Martin. And still was the character kept up. I fool enough to believe that she had wrought me an act of kindness, and she enemy enough to be working my destruction. Had it not been for a fortunate occurrence, news would have shortly arrived here that, the despatches which had been entrusted to my care, had been handed over to our common foe. Who, save Ernest Morden, would have been suspected of committing the act of treachery? Who, save he, would have been punished for the crime? Doubtless, this discovery of the packet in the possession of Red Martin, was never anticipated by Miss Amy Heyton. Neither is there cause to believe that we should have ever heard anything of her interview with her smuggler-friend, had not this idiot-boy been present at the meeting. We have a story of her going somewhere to fetch the parcel for the smuggler, but she does not tell us where. We have heard that Red Martin thought fit to await her coming on that particular morning; but she does not tell us why. Never did woman, deeming herself injured, seek a deeper revenge; never has a fair face played the hypocrite so well, until Amy Heyton attempted the task. I have no more to say. It is evident who is guilty in this matter. And as for her who has done the evil, much as I loved her once, I am not so far gone in my madness, as to be unable to express a hope, that the ill which Amy Heyton]thought to work me may descend upon her own head!"

And once again did Lambert Warrenton press the arm of Dourville.

"Hear, hear!" he whispered,—"it has worked well—all, all has been effected! Spurned, rejected—hark you! he curses her now!"

CHAPTER XLVI.

HOW THE TRIAL OF LOVE CONCLUDED; AND HOW THE VICTORY OF MADNESS
WAS WON.

ERNEST MORDEN ceased speaking.

With her right hand clasped in the hands of her sister, Amy Heyton listened to every word which was uttered. Not once had she trembled; not once had the slightest tremor passed over her frame. Her eyes had remained fixed upon Ernest; the red flush had deepened gradually upon her cheeks. Kate wondered that her sister moved not—that she stood so statue-like—so still. Nothing could poor Kate detect to indicate to her the effect which the words of Ernest Morden had upon her sister, save that she felt the pulse of the silent listener to beat with increased rapidity, and the muscles of her arm to swell and grow hard beneath her clasp. As, however, Ernest Morden finished speaking, Kate saw that her sister's lips were moving, and felt also that her fingers were writhing convulsively. And as the colour mounted up from Amy's cheeks, higher and higher, until it overspread her brows; and as the fire brightened in her eyes, until from sparks it had risen into flame; and as the beatings of the pulse grew less in number, and increased in strength, until it seemed that the hard, cord-like artery, was about to burst; and as the fearfully-accused maiden strung her muscles and repressed her breathing, until she appeared increased in height and size, so did her fond sister gaze upon her in awe and wonderment, until, as Ernest spoke his last word, she exclaimed,—

"Sister! why do you hold my hand so tightly? Your fingers are piercing my flesh. Sister, dear sister!"

"What has Amy Heyton to say in reply?" demanded Sir Thomas Warrenton.

"Only for a single second was there silence. Then, pushing her sister from her, Amy, with one movement, sprang forward, and again—but more firmly than before—seized the arm of her accuser.

"Man!" said she, in a deep, guttural voice, "you have spoken lies of one who has never entertained evil thoughts of you—one who never knew that she loved you not until this moment. I can bear your hard words. Your evil wishes have been heard by that God who will judge between us both! I have no reproaches for you, and no love. I cannot pardon you, but I do not wish you evil. We part, Ernest Morden—part for ever! I will strive to forget you—to obliterate all memory of one whom I can neither pity nor hate. I—I—I—Give me your hand, sister; let me lean upon your arm. I am faint, sister—very faint. Lead me away, dear sister—lead me to the open air."

Supported by her sister and Gervase Morden, Amy Heyton was led into the adjoining apartment, where there was an open window. And Kate seated herself upon a chair, and placed Amy in her lap. The cool breeze fell upon the younger sister's face, and as she felt its reviving influence, she looked up, and gazing into her sister's dark eyes, said,—

"It was cruel of him, dear sister—more cruel than if he had slain me. He knows not how much I loved him! Dear sister, he will never know!"

Then, sinking back upon the bosom of sweet Kate, Amy Heyton ceased to speak. Her blue eyes were closed over by their lids; her cheeks lost their ruddy flush, and became pale—pale as ever. And all was so still—so silent, there, in th_{at}

antique room, that as Kate bent over Amy, and marked the wanness of her face, and failed to hear her breathing, she almost doubted whether it was the living that she clasped in her arms, and doubted, too, whether those blue eyes would ever open again, and feared to ask herself the question—am I sisterless in this lone, dreary world ?

Gervase Morden returned to the apartment in which the inquiry had been held.

Not once did he glance at his brother, but passed him by, and walked on ; and, taking his seat at the table, covered his forehead with his hands. Those who stood near enough remarked that the breathing of the student was deep and hard, and that his fingers played writhingly with one another, as if in concert with some painful workings of the inward mind.

"Is the girl living ? Will she live ?" inquired Sir Thomas, lowering his head, and whispering the questions in the ear of his secretary.

"She lives, and she will forget him," returned the student, uttering the latter half of the sentence with great effort.

Sir Thomas Warrenton was perplexed, and knew not how to proceed. He had beckoned Amy's father to him, and had conversed with him in whispers. Each appeared equally agitated ; each seemed to share in one common grief. The knight arose from his seat, and in company with Mr. Heyton paced backwards and forwards across the upper end of the room. No one else moved ; there was silence amongst the spectators. Lady Warrenton, Constance Ismay, and Archy, the idiot boy, had stolen away into the next apartment, there to tend on helpless Amy. Thither, too, had Lambert Warrenton retreated. Ernest Morden stood in moody silence, awaiting the conclusion of the inquiry. Opposite to him sat Frank Heyton—the high-spirited, impetuous Frank ; his arms folded on his chest ; his eyes alternately directed towards his sister's accuser, and towards the room in which that sister was.

"Lieutenant Morden," said Sir Thomas, in a voice which betrayed his great mental anxiety, "have you anything further to say which may tend to explain this—this mistake ?"

"I have said all, Sir Thomas. There is nothing that I have to ask, except my right to be tried before a proper tribunal."

"That right will be granted you," replied the knight. "But have you no further suggestions to make—no other suspicions to communicate ?"

"None, Sir Thomas."

"You do not suspect Sampson Summers, the tomb cutter, of having been concerned in this act of treachery, knowing it to be such ? I should not ask the question had I not my reasons for so doing.'

"I do not wonder at your making the inquiry, Sir Thomas. But though Sampson Summers, by his own confession, abstracted the packet from beneath my pillow, and gave it into the hands of Amy Heyton, I have not the least cause to believe that he did so with any wicked intention. On the contrary, it is my belief that Amy Heyton deceived Mr. Summers, equally as much as she deceived me."

"And you continue to assert that you have no knowledge of Red Martin, and that you have in no way or manner held communication with those who are the enemies of our country ?"

"I assert both, Sir Thomas."

"Then," said the knight, "this inquiry is terminated for the present."

Captain Charnock now rose to speak.

"Sir Thomas Warrenton, the instructions which we have each received from London warrant me in demanding that Lieutenant Morden and Miss Amy Heyton be conveyed thither without delay. I trust that you will use measures to that effect."

"Not so, Captain Charnock," returned Sir Thomas. "It is only Lieutenant Morden whom I am authorised so to dispose of, and he must not be sent thither yet. This investigation must be resumed to-morrow. Meanwhile, I do not think it necessary to commit Lieutenant Morden to Darlingham Gaol. There is a strong room in this old building in which he may be confined, and out of which it will be impossible for him to escape. It will be prudent, perhaps, for you to send hither one of your marines, that he may keep watch outside the door during the night. As for Amy Heyton, I myself will be responsible for her appearing whenever and wherever her presence may be required ; that is—if she survive this shock.'

To these propositions and arrangements Captain Charnock somewhat reluctantly gave his consent. The inquiry was brought to a conclusion ; and Sir Thomas Warrenton gave orders that Lieutenant Morden should be confined for the night in a small apartment which nearly adjoined the library. Lambert Warrenton and Gervase Morden were appointed to see that this order was obeyed.

"Give me leave to speak a few words in private to Lieutenant Morden," said the secretary, addressing Lambert Warrenton, as the party stood within the narrow passage which led to the great staircase.

Lambert Warrenton remained at the further extremity of the passage.

There was a deep pause, during which the secretary gazed fixedly upon his younger brother, at the same time drawing in his breath with long, deep inspirations.

"Ernest," at length spoke the student, gravely—"Ernest Morden, I have watched your conduct, and have listened to the words uttered by yourself in reply to the allegations made against you. A few hours ago I believed you innocent—innocent of the great crime laid to your charge. The assurances which you gave me, the solemn protestations which you made, strengthened me in that belief. It was a willing belief—willing, because in accordance with all that I could wish and desire. That belief exists no longer. I, who had a brother two hours since, have none now. Do not interrupt me, Ernest Morden; do not misunderstand my words. Had you confessed your evil deed, had you owned to it openly, I might still have retained a portion of a brother's affection for you. But you have lied, Ernest Morden; you have deceived others, yet not deceived me. Having promised your love to Amy Heyton—having pledged yourself to make that poor girl your wife, you contracted a dislike for her during your long absence, and wishing to rid yourself of the incumbrance, resorted to the most cowardly means—to the most detestable deeds. What is this secret which you profess to have, and which you declare forms a barrier to your union? A mockery, Ernest Morden—a mere, vile mockery! Nay, contradict me not. I hold converse with you for the last time. Your secret is nothing more than your reluctance to redeem your pledge of honour. It may be that some richer beauty is within your grasp, and from that cause poor Amy Heyton is an obstacle in your way. It may be that your conduct arises from baser motives still. That you—you, whose father was Reginald Morden, the man of honour—that you, having committed a misdeed, should have attempted to lodge the punishment upon the shoulders of the fair being whose love had become a nuisance to you; whose love conquered even your coldness; whose love prompted her to dare deeds that scarcely became a timid woman, and all to save you from dishonour: that you should have wrought this injury to her—have brought this disgrace upon her, almost surpasses belief; and stamps you with the character of as great a coward as villain. Repress your rage, Ernest Morden. I fear not those clenched fists, nor that dark countenance. Listen, while I show you that your deep-laid designs have been fathomed to the bottom—that they are known to the man who speaks to you! I heard your accusations. I heard how well, how cunningly you reasoned to prove that Amy Heyton—Amy Heyton, whom you once dared to love, was worthy of the gallows. I was silent, and not a word escaped my ear. Every word to'd its tale—every word had a meaning to me other than you wished it to have. Hark you, Ernest Morden! I believe that the fictitious despatches which Amy Heyton carried to Mr. Warrenton were made up by yourself. I believe that Red Martin the smuggler is known to you; and that he is the agent between you and some one of our enemies, with whom you have agreed to betray your country—to sell your honour for vile gold. I believe, too, that the meeting of Amy Heyton with Red Martin was concerted between you and that man—that you planned the way and manner in which the parcel should be delivered to the smuggler by the hands of unsuspecting Amy, knowing full well that when you came to make your charge against her, she would confess the sad act which in her innocence she committed. All this I believe of you, nor doubt that sooner or later the truth will be made plain. Enough; were your father alive he would disown one of his sons; and from this moment I account myself without a brother. Speak not, Ernest Morden—tell no more lies. I do not wish to hear you; your presence is a torture to me. Go! Mr. Warrenton will conduct you to your prison. God grant that you may never die upon the gallows tree!"

No word spoke Ernest Morden as he accompanied his conductor to the room which had been allotted for his prison. He entered that room, and the door was locked upon him.

Let the scene now change to an old, oaken-walled apartment, in the basement story of Warrenton Hall. It is the same quaintly-decorated room into which Amy Heyton was led by her sister, after Ernest Morden had disowned her for ever. And there, beside the open casement, shaded from the sunbeams by the projection of an adjoining porch, still reclined poor Amy, in the arms of her loving sister. The slight breeze was just sufficient to play with the tangles of her flaxen hair, and to fan lightly her pale, bloodless cheek. Beside her stood the radiant form of Constance Ismay. At her feet knelt the idiot, Archy; whilst, leaning against the back of the old, carven chair, Lambert Warrenton gazed earnestly upon the face of the gentle girl, and appeared wrapped in meditation.

"She wakes!" exclaimed Kate, delightedly, as she observed her sister's eyelids open, and heard her breathing more distinctly. "She wakes—she is recovering!"

"Sissy Amy will not die—she will soon be well?" said Archy, in an inquiring manner.

"She will," answered Lambert Warrenton. "Your fan, Miss Ismay. Air—more air, and she will soon regain her recollection."

As Lambert Warrenton spoke, he pushed the casements further apart, and allowed the perfume of some honeysuckles which clustered round the adjoining porch, to be diffused over the apartment.

"Amy, dear Amy, do you know where you are? Do you know in whose arms you rest?"

"Yes, yes. It is you, sister—it is Kate. But where is *he*—is he gone—has he left the room?"

"Ernest Morden is not here," replied Kate. "Courage, my sister! There is no one in the room, except myself, good Miss Ismay, Mr. Warrenton, and foolish Archy."

"None else?" said Amy, raising her head as she spoke, and gazing tremblingly around her. "You are not deceiving me, sister—you are sure that he is quite gone?"

"Yes, Amy. He is not nigh you now; he will not come here."

"And I shall never see him—never hear him speak again, dear sister?"

"Is such your wish, Amy?"

"Yes, sister, yes." And Amy raised herself upright, and looked with her blue sorrowing eyes into the dark, beamy orbs of her sister. "You know, Kate, that we are not lovers now—not now, sister. Love is dead—dead and cold, dear Kate. We must never see—never speak to one another more."

Kate looked tearfully at her sister, unable to answer a word.

The idiot boy drew nearer, and laid his hand upon Amy's arm.

"Then Sissy Amy hates Ernest. She will not go with him to the great ship now?"

"Ernest will never come to the cottage again, Archy; and I shall never see him more."

A gleam of joy glistened upon the idiot's countenance. He arose, strode towards the opposite end of the apartment, and, seating himself upon an ottoman, chuckled with inward glee.

"Sissy Amy will not go now," he repeated to himself. "She will stay at home with Archy—she would have gone—she would have gone, but Archy would not let her."

It was because Lambert Warrenton had changed his position, and had half concealed himself within the dark window curtains, that Amy had as yet not perceived his presence. Now, however, as hearing a slight movement behind her, she turned her glance in that direction, her eyes rested upon the form of the man to whom she had paid her memorable midnight visit. One sudden start she gave, and then remained gazing, but motionless. She could not turn her eyes away; she lisped words that were inaudible to those around her. Suddenly, there had flashed across her mind the memory of that strange meeting in the moonlit library—that meeting at the midnight hour. The scene stood again as a vision before her; the words then spoken were whispered again in her ears. She saw the pale moonlight streaming in through the painted window, as distinctly as she had before seen it

in its reality. The picture was clear and vivid ; the scene was played over again.
And memory recalled to her the promise she had given—that strange promise, the
conditions of which were stranger still. Yet now those conditions were fulfilled.
The events which, in her faithfulness and love, she had once believed eternity
would never give birth to, had happened in the short space of one single week.
Ernest Morden had cast scorn upon her ; Ernest Morden had rejected her with
violence ; Ernest Morden had cursed her with his own lips ! And she, too, had
disavowed all love of him—had cast him from her, and expressed her hope that
she should never see him more. No wonder that poor Amy half fancied that it
was all a dream ; no wonder that she raised her weak hand to her cold, clammy
brow, and, in an incoherent manner repeated the words,—

"Scorn—reject—curse me ! Yes, yes, he has done it all !"

"He has, Amy Heyton," said Lambert Warrenton, stepping forward and
clasping the fair girl's hand. "The conditions are fulfilled. Nothing remains but
for you to be faithful to your promise."

"Promise !" repeated Kate, gazing strangely at Lambert Warrenton. "Ha !
sister, what is this ? What have you hidden from me ?"

"Nothing, sister—nothing, but——"

"I must leave you, sister—I must leave you for awhile. I will return presently :
I shall be back soon, sister."

So saying, Kate Heyton started up, and still continuing to gaze wildly at Lambert
Warrenton, moved quickly towards the door, and in haste quitted the apartment.

"Where is she gone ? What has Sister Kate left me for ?" asked Amy of
Miss Ismay.

"I do not know—I cannot tell you. She has remembered something—something, perhaps, which she has gone to fetch."

Again the scene changed ; and pacing backwards and forwards within the hall of
the old mansion, are Sir Thomas Warrenton and Gervase Morden, his secretary.
The pale figure of a woman glided across the planked floor, and Kate Heyton
seized the hand of Sir Thomas Warrenton.

"Quick—quick, Sir Thomas ! I have words to say to you—to you alone !"
The knight led the maiden towards the doorway of the Hall.

"What is it, girl ? Tell me—is your sister dying ? Come you to tell me of that ?"

"Not of her—not of Amy, Sir Thomas."

"Of whom, then ?"

"Of—listen to me, Sir Thomas. Neither Sister Amy, nor Ernest Morden are
guilty of this crime. Both are innocent—both are deceived !"

"Would that it were so, my poor girl !"

"It is—it is ! Listen to me, and I will tell you who is guilty. I have sought
you for that purpose."

"You tell me !"

"Yes ; hear me—listen to me, Sir Thomas ! I fear to tell you ; but I must—
I must."

And in a tremulous, whispering voice, Kate Heyton confided to Sir Thomas
Warrenton the strange knowledge which she had already declared herself to possess.
In silence, and with many manifestations of the deep interest which he took in
the story, the knight listened to the relation. Once or twice he started suddenly
as some strange piece of information was communicated to him. Once or twice he
interrupted the speaker, and turned aside his head to muse. Then, as he heard
further, his cheeks paled ; his eye-balls rolled wildly in their sockets ; he listened
with opened mouth ; and compressed nervously and involuntarily the hands of
poor Kate.

The communication was made—the speaker had finished speaking. Speechless,
motionless, abstracted, stood Sir Thomas ; his gaze fixed upon the countenance
of Kate ; his mind occupied with the new idea which it had recently received,
and which were as strange as they were novel.

"You will not believe it, Sir Thomas—you do not think it likely ?" inquired Kate.
The knight started, moved aside, and for some minutes paced backwards and

forwards, apparently deeply absorbed in thought. Presently, however, he made a sudden stop, turned towards Kate, grasped her hand, drew a deep inspiration, and with much difficulty of utterance, said,—

"It shall be seen to, Kate Heyton—it shall be seen to. Let such prove to be the case, and I will be just—very just," he added, with much emphasis. "And now go—go to your sister! She is waiting for you. Be careful of her. Watch her well. She must not die. Not for all the wealth which the broad world holds would I have harm happen to her whom you call your sister. There —do nt wonder. Go—go at once."

Kate Heyton obeyed the command. No sooner was she gone, than striking his clenched hand to his brow, Sir Thomas ejaculated,—

"This is frightful—maddening! Fooled—fooled so easily! By Heaven if it prove so, there shall be justice—terrible justice!"

Then, after taking a few steps, the knight paused, and again assumed a moody attitude. He was disturbed by the entrance of a domestic.

"Robson, man, come here," commanded Sir Thomas. "Are the men who came with me from the ship still in the house—have they finished their repast?"

"They will be gone presently, Sir Thomas."

"Quick, then—quick. Inquire for the man who picked up the parcel on the cliff, and send him hither immediately."

Many minutes had not passed before the seaman presented himself in obedience to the summons.

"The parcel which fell from out of Red Martin's pocket was picked up and given by you to my secretary, was it not?" demanded the knight.

"It was, your honour. Seeing as how it was something that had to do with that sea-shark of a Frencher, and thinking as how it might be something of vally, I gived it into Mr. Morden's care."

"And when you did so, it was enclosed in a sealed cover, which Mr. Morden tore off. Do you know what became of that cover?"

"I can't say as how I do, your honour; though, now I come to think of it, I remember seeing it flying away along the cliff, when Mr. Morden threw it from him. There was a smart breeze at the time, your honour."

"Then, it is likely, that by means of a careful search, in the proper direction, that cover may be found?"

"I should say as how it might, your honour."

"Hark you, then! You shall have five guineas if you bring me that cover to-night. Go and search for it without delay. If you find it, fold it up carefully, bring it here with all speed, tell your business to no one, but inquire for me, and say that I desired you should at once be shown into my presence."

The man bowed and departed.

"Let but that cover be found," said Sir Thomas to himself, "and, doubtless, this dark mystery will be made clear."

What had the cover to do with the mystery?

CHAPTER XLVII.

THE STERN BROTHER AND THE DARK BEAUTY.—HOW LOVE LAID SIEGE TO HONOUR.

THE time was evening, and the stars were shining, and the fair moon had just made her appearance in the distant heaven.

Seated in the bay-windowed drawing-room of Warrenton Hall were three individuals, each silent, each pensive, each meditating on the strange occurrences which had happened within the last few hours. These three individuals were Lady Warrenton, Constance Ismay, and Gervase Morden.

And the casements of the old window were open; and the starlight and the moonlight shone upon the painted glass; and the perfume of honeysuckles and of jessamine were wafted into the antique, sombre chamber by the soft, soothing breeze of evening. All was beauty and serenity without, all was gloom and anxiety within.

Lady Warrenton arose from her seat.

"Constance, darling!" said she, "it is late in the evening, and the air is becoming chilly. Will you not come with me to my own room? Doubtless a fire has been lighted there."

"I am not cold, dear Lady Warrenton," returned Miss Ismay. "And I love to sit here at the open window, and gaze upon the pale, bright moon, and watch how the stars come out, one after the other, and how the deep shadows fall across the distant fields, so darkly—so very darkly."

"But, dearest, you forget that Mr. Morden may wish to be alone."

The student heard the observation and arose from his seat.

"I thank you, Lady Warrenton," said he, "but, if Miss Ismay prefers remaining here, I have no desire to dispense with her company. Indeed, she will confer a kindness by staying."

"Lady Warrenton paused for a moment, and afterwards said,—

"Then, Constance, darling, I shall expect you in my own room some half hour hence. You had better ring for lights, dearest."

So saying, Lady Warrenton quitted the apartment. As she did so, Gervase Morden resumed his seat.

And the moon rose higher in the heavens, allowing its rays to stream into the quaint, old room more fully and more brightly; and the silence had become deepened; and evening was verging into night.

"Still at the stained window, her fair cheek resting on her hand, sat Constance Ismay. But it was not at the moon that fair Constance gazed, nor was it at the silvery stars; her eyes were turned towards the stern brother—the silent student; and she marked, as the moonbeams played around the place where he sat, that his head was bent down, and that he breathed deeply and heavily. Yet did not his breathing break the solemn silence—it was not loud enough to interfere with the faint sound emitted by the distant sea, as its waves gurgled upon the pebbly beach, falling hushingly upon the ear of the listener, far, far away.

But this silence was becoming irksome to the maiden; it was so solemn that she feared to break it; it was so oppressive that the tap, tap of her beating heart was to her a source of pain. At length, rising slowly from her seat, she crept towards the moody student, and laying her soft fingers upon his head, said,—

"You are sad, Mr. Morden, and you have cause to be so. Do not let my presence be an annoyance to you. I would have gone before, but—" Miss Ismay paused.

"I do not wish you to leave me. I pray you not to let me be alone!" returned the student, in a low and hollow voice.

"But why do you wish me to stay, Mr. Morden? What assistance can I be to you? What solace can I render you?

"Much, Miss Ismay—much. Your voice soothes me; your presence calms me; the very consciousness of your being nigh me acts as a charm to chase away the gloomy thoughts which come crowding to my brain—to dispel the dark broodings in which my spirit would otherwise indulge."

Constance was silent for a few moments; then, placing her fingers again upon the student's hand, she said,—

"I thank you, Mr. Morden, for having spoken so nobly, so bravely of your poor brother, when you were called upon to state what you knew. I was afraid that you were not friendly, and that some harsh word would escape your lips. But I was happy when I heard you speak so kindly of Mr. Ernest,—when I heard you declare your belief that your brother would not tell a lie, and would not commt an act of dishonour."

"And yet, Miss Ismay, he has done both," said Gervase, after a pause, and uttering the words with much effort.

"Both, Mr. Morden?"

"Would to God that he had done no more! Would to God, Miss Ismay, that my—that Lieutenant Morden were only a liar and a traitor!"

"Mr. Gervase," exclaimed Constance, in affright, "you do not know what you say; you are unconscious of what fearful words you uttered."

"No, Miss Ismay. The wish that I expressed came from my heart, ay—from my soul! Would to God, I repeat, that in becoming the liar and the traitor, Ernest Morden had never become also the mean, despicable coward that he has shown himself to be. To have turned traitor to his country was infamy enough, without seeking to make that infamy greater by traducing a fair and innocent girl, who has long loved him with a love of which he has proved unworthy—a love that he has repaid with bitterest cruelty."

Poor Constance was transfixed with astonishment and terror. That terror was increased, when, rising from his seat, Gervase Morden said, in a hasty and angry voice,—

"Miss Ismay, I must beg you to remember that Lieutenant Morden is no longer any brother of mine. The relationship is at end; and there will be no further correspondence between that man and myself."

"Mr. Morden! Mr. Gervase!" exclaimed Constance, grasping the hand of the excited student, "this is unjust—this is cruel—this is wicked of you. What has your poor brother done? What is proved against him? What is really known? You wrong him; you wrong him very much. He is not what you think him to be—he is not so base, so mean, so dishonoured as you fear he is. Oh, believe—believe that he is not!"

"Believe him to be guiltless, Miss Ismay?"

"Yes; believe it—hope it—wait for its being made evident."

"But what of Amy Heyton, Miss Ismay? Would you have me put faith in the accusation which Lieutenant Morden has made against the gentle girl who trusted in his love?"

"No, Mr. Morden; it would be cruel to do so. Your brother is mistaken. He has not meant that which he has said; he cannot—he does not believe poor Amy to be so vengeful—so wicked."

"He does not, Miss Ismay. He knows that he has uttered falsehoods this day in the matter of accusing that poor girl. Ernest guiltless, and Amy innocent! Why, to whose charge, Miss Ismay, would you lay the crime?"

"Do not ask me, Mr. Morden; I cannot answer you that. It is not for me to explain the mystery which has puzzled Sir Thomas and yourself."

"Your pardon, Miss Ismay. To me the mystery has ceased to be one. Amy Heyton I know to be innocent, and Ernest Morden is the villain which I have declared him to be."

"Oh! do not say so; do not use such words, I conjure you, Mr. Morden. Wait, wait awhile. Something tells me that you are mistaken—that Amy and your brother will in a short time be proved guiltless of all that has been alleged against them. Wait, and God will bring it about. Do not accuse your poor brother; but wait—wait."

Gervase placed a chair near the centre of the room, and begged fair Constance to be seated.

"Miss Ismay," said he, in a voice the tone of which was unusually grave and solemn, "neither my precipitation nor my delay in deciding the question of Lieutenant Morden's guilt or innocence, will do aught towards hastening or averting the retribution which justice exacts, and which the laws of his country will decree. That you wish well to the man who was once my brother I have every reason to believe; that you desire to see him acquitted of this charge does honour to the kindly feelings of your heart. But, Miss Ismay, what bitter mockery it would be, did I attempt to delude myself by cherishing hopes which I know can never be realised; and how poor an occupation would be that which could bring no other

rewards than disappointment, vexation, and regret! I tell you,—and God wit-
nesses to the deep sorrow with which I make the affirmation—that the guilt of
Lieutenant Morden is certain, and that time will only make that certainty greater.
Why, then, should I hope? Why caress a delusion? Why believe in that which
it is impossible can ever happen? Do not call me harsh nor uncharitable, Miss
Ismay. Saw I the least reason to think otherwise than I do of Lieutenant Morden,

how gladly would I alter my opinion! how readily would I put faith in all that
you have wished me to believe."

"And there is such reason, Mr. Gervase," replied fair Constance. "In the
gloomiest hour, and amidst the darkest prospects, there is still reason to hope—
still reason to cherish that one bright gift which Heaven has granted unto man.
Oh! never should we lightly disregard that holy gift; never should we cease to
hope while life is with us, and time has not passed on into eternity! Hope all—

hope everything; hope that the future will clear up mysteries in a manner otherwise than you have ever dreamed as possible; hope that the shadows are not so dark as they seem to be, and that they will be dispersed before long; hope that you yourself are deceived, and that all which you now think to be most certain will prove eventually to be fallacies and fancies. Oh! do not relinquish hope; do not shut hope out—never, never!"

"Not when he—the traitor—is being led to the gibbet, Miss Ismay. Would you have me to hope even then?"

"To—to the gibbet, Mr. Morden!" ejaculated fair Constance, with a sudden start—"your brother to the gibbet!"

"Ay; of what avail would all my hopes be there?"

Minutes passed, and Constance Ismay remained silent, gazing wildly at the stern man who was her companion in that lone apartment. Suddenly she bent forward, and resting her hand upon the student's arm, said,—

"You do not—oh! you cannot believe that so fearful a doom will ever happen to your poor brother?"

"It will! it must!" was the reply, uttered in a voice of anguish.

"'Will,' 'must,'" repeated Constance, relapsing again into brooding silence.

The conversation had become painful to both parties. Gervase Morden arose in order to leave the room.

"Not yet—do not go yet, Mr. Morden!" exclaimed Miss Ismay, detaining the student by tremblingly grasping his arm.

"You have something further to say, Miss Ismay?"

"I have—I——"

The student led the fair girl to her chair.

"Do not blame me, Mr. Morden—do not think unkindly of me for what I am about to say."

"Unkindly of you, Miss Ismay!" replied the student, with some warmth of expression. "Alas! you know not how much it has pained me to speak to you as I have had occasion to do this evening!"

"I—I fear that I have been interrupting you. I fear that I have stayed too long in this apartment. I——"

Constance paused. The moonlight fell through the stained window, and played round the form of her whom once before, on a night almost as beautiful as the present one, the pale student had gazed upon with admiration and with silent ecstasy. One beam, brighter and more pure than all the rest, illuminated the fair white forehead of the maiden, and played amongst her jetty tresses So white was the forehead, and so pure was the moonbeam, that, as the one lay stretched out upon the other, it was difficult to tell which had the most pearly whiteness, and whether the fair brow or the pure beam lost by the comparison.

"Miss Ismay," said the student, clasping gently the soft hand of her to whom he spoke, "a time has arrived when it becomes me to confess the truth on a subject which has occasioned me much mental anxiety. Only this minute you pained me by saying you were afraid that your company had been disagreeable to me. Miss Ismay—Constance, did you really believe that of which you expressed your fear?"

"I was afraid—I thought—I supposed that you wished to be alone—that I was troublesome," stammered poor Constance.

"Have I ever given you cause to think that your society was unpleasant to me, Miss Ismay?" asked the student.

"No, Mr. Morden. I—I—pardon me! I did not know what I was saying," replied the fair girl, with much embarrassment.

"Let me assure you, Miss Ismay, that, if at any time you have entertained such suspicions, you have done so without cause. I have long waited for an opportunity to disclose my sentiments to you—to tell you of a passion which has been cherished in secret, and which has given birth to many hopes of future happiness now, alas! destroyed for ever."

"This room is warm, the air is close," said Constance, moving towards the window.

"Listen to me, Miss Ismay!" continued the student, again renewing his clasp of the soft hand; "I came into this house a poor friendless boy, one upon whose forlorn state Sir Thomas Warrenton had taken pity when I knew not where to turn for shelter, nor where to seek for subsistence. Ardent to attain knowledge, willing to exert myself, and anxious to repay the kindness of my generous benefactor, I took the path of industry, and neglected no opportunity of testifying my gratitude to Sir Thomas by attending to his interests; while at the same time I endeavoured to prove myself worthy of the favour which he had shown me by an unremitted application to such studies as were most likely to prove of service to my benefactor and myself. My exertions were not in vain. Years passed, and Sir Thomas Warrenton took the poor orphan boy into his confidence, and, making him his secretary, treated him at the same time as his friend. Miss Ismay, I have abused that confidence—I have acted treacherously towards my friend."

"Mr. Morden!" exclaimed Constance.

"Yes, Miss Ismay. Listen still further, and I will tell you how I have so acted. I will tell you how, when a fair and beauteous girl came to reside in this same house, in my admiration of her rare beauty, I forgot my duty to my patron—forgot that I was a man dependant on his bounty—forgot that I owed all which I possessed to his generosity and benevolence. Miss Ismay—Constance! it was your coming which beguiled the student from his duty; you it was who charmed him from his studies, and caused him to forget his position; you have been the one sole object of his thoughts throughout the busy day and in the dreaming night-time. Forgive him—forgive me for this confession! I have loved you, Constance Ismay, loved you with a deep and fervent passion. When midnight has stolen upon me, it has found me with the opened book before me, my eyes fixed upon that, but my lips muttering your name; and if the grey, chill morning came, and found me still bending over the same book, still found me at my task, it found me there with fevered brow and pallid cheeks, toiling for position and renown in order that I might be worthy of you. Yes, dearest Constance—for such I must call you—the hope which has led me on has not been the mere dreamy ambition of my boyhood, but a fond belief that at some future day, by dint of unremitted toil, I might become a fitting suitor for your fair hand. And all this time, dear Constance, I have been ignorant as to whether the poor student was scorned or esteemed by her whom he had thus presumed to love. Sometimes I have cherished a fond suspicion of being loved in return. I have watched you, Constance, marked every glance of your sweet eyes, and dwelt on every word which has fallen from your tongue, thus hoping to read the secrets of your heart in glances and in words. This has been a task of pain as well as of pleasure. At times, when your beaming eyes were directed towards me, I fancied that it was love which gave to them their softness and their beauty. Then again, when I have sat near you in the same room for hours together, and remarked that never once during the whole time your gaze was turned towards me, and that your lips forbore to mention my name, I have experienced a feeling of cold death-like despair; and as my heart has sunk within me, I have said, "Why am I so foolish? What am I to her that she should regard me, or take any notice of my presence? She cares not for me; she has no pity, no affection, no love for the poor student, and dreams not of the deep passion which is burning within his breast." And then, Constance, came the dreadful suspicion of your having detected the existence of that passion—of your having become aware of the poor student's daring, and treated it with contempt and silent derision—treated it as a theme for your amusement and your ridicule—treated it as a subject for your merriest moods, when feeling disposed for laughter you thought of the presumption of the dependant secretary in aspiring to the hand of Sir Thomas Warrenton's niece!: thus I thought, and thus——"

"Gervase—dear Gervase!" ejaculated Constance, as she laid her weeping face upon the student's arm, "you have thought cruelly of me—thought as I have never thought of you!"

Gervase Morden clasped the fair girl to his heart.

"Then, Constance—then, I have not been mistaken—my hope has not been falsely grounded—I have not deceived myself by trusting in your love? You have loved me—you own it—you have said it with those sweet lips. Oh! say it again, my Constance! Let me hear you confess that you have loved me—loved me as fondly as I have loved you!"

"I love you now, dear Gervase, more fondly, more dearly than aught else in this wide world."

"And I to doubt—I to think that it was otherwise!"

Then followed confessions, affirmations, assurances, and all the score of other forms of speech which have to do with a first avowal of love. It needs not to be told how Constance blushed, and how Gervase embraced her: it needs not to be told that there were kisses and smiles mingled with tears of joy. Calmly and peacefully as ever the moonbeams played around the lovers, the same broad ray falling upon each, the same pale beam resting upon the student's face and mingling with the maiden's tresses. Heart to heart, cheek to cheek, arm entwined round arm, and breath interfused with breath—so stood they in the old apartment, while the painted figures in the bay-window through which the moonbeams fell, seemed to laugh for very joy that the stern student had been conquered by love, and that wisdom had paid its homage to beauty, as ever wisdom should.

"Constance—dear Constance! how happy should I have been if I had with certainty known that which your sweet lips have now confessed."

"And I, Gervase—I, too, should have been happy," answered Constance.

"But you are happy now, my love—my own heart's love?"

"I am."

"And I—but, Constance,—Miss Ismay, this is foolishness—this is madness!" cried Gervase Morden, suddenly moving aside and detaching the fair girl from his embrace.

"Madness, dear Gervase!—what—what is madness?"

"This talk of love—these foolish confessions—this hoping for that which may never—can never be."

Constance Ismay threw her fair arms around the student's neck, and looking plaintively upwards towards his averted face, asked, in a quivering voice,—

"What may never be, dearest? I do not know the meaning of your words."

"Hear me, Constance! I have acted foolishly, nay wickedly, in forgetting my true position in this house; and in venturing to love the niece of Sir Thomas Warrenton, unmindful of my being a poor dependant on his bounty."

"Why grieve because of that, dear Gervase? Believe me—believe your Constance, when she tells you that your sorrow is without cause. My uncle respects you; he admires your noble nature, and your devotion to study. Do not call yourself his servant, dear Gervase; he esteems you as his friend."

"And I to be undeserving of that friendship—I to think of stealing from him his niece—his darling, she whom he loves and fondles as if she were his own child! Constance, I have done wrong. This foolish affection must cease to be; this love must be subdued."

"Oh! why—why do you say so, dearest Gervase? You are talking wildly—strangely! Sir Thomas will consent to our love; he will consent, dear Gervase—he will consent!"

"Consent to what, Constance? To see you, his favourite, his fondling, become the bride of a man whose brother will ere long hang upon the gibbet? No, Constance Ismay; even you must never consent to that."

"The gibbet—Ernest hung on the gibbet?"

"Ay; knowst thou not that such will be his doom? It must be, Constance Ismay; the traitor will be hung, and I—I am his brother."

And once more there was silence in the moonlit room—a silence that was broken only by the deep breathing of fair Constance, and the noise produced by the grating of the student's teeth.

Suddenly the maiden fell upon her knees and clasped the stern brother's hand.

" Gervase—Gervase Morden," said she, " is that which you have told me truth ? Have I been loved by you so long, and do you love me now ?"

"I do. Heaven witnesses to it that I do ! and yet such love is madness—worse than madness."

"Not so, dear Gervase. You have assured me that your love is real. Let me ask of you one proof; let me ask of you, on my bended knees, to make me one promise."

" Rise, Miss Ismay—rise, I beg of you. The niece of Sir Thomas Warrenton should not kneel to her uncle's vassal."

" I will not rise, dear Gervase ; I will not relinquish your hand until you have made me this promise."

" And the promise is—what ?"

" Your brother is a prisoner ; you have said that his guilt is certain, and that he will be hung for the crime which he has committed. Gervase—dear Gervase, that must never be ! It must never be said that your brother met the doom of a traitor ; it must never be said that he was executed on the gibbet. You must save him, dear Gervase, you must save him speedily ! There must be no delay. In virtue of that love which you have professed for me, I demand that you do this. He is your brother—your own brother ! Promise me that you will save him ; promise your poor Constance that the brother of the man she loves shall be saved from the disgrace which awaits him. Promise me, dear Gervase—promise me !"

" How am I to make you such a promise, Constance ? Is it in my power to prove Ernest an honest man ? What word of mine will save him from the gibbet ?"

" Not your word, dear Gervase. I know that he cannot be saved by that, or I should not fear for his safety. Your hand must do it, dear Gervase—your strong hand. There are a thousand ways in which you can help him to escape."

" And if I did so assist him, Constance Ismay—if I betrayed that trust which your uncle reposes in me, by aiding the escape of a man who is his prisoner, would you respect me then ? Would you give your hand to a man who had sacrificed his honour by allowing his feelings to get the better of his sense of duty ?"

" You reason wrongly, dear Gervase. Your honour—your father's honour would be saved by your so doing. What honour would there be in hearing it said that your brother died upon the gibbet—that he died a traitor's death ? Listen to me, Gervase Morden ! it is your duty to preserve your father's name stainless ; will that duty be the better performed by permitting his son to be hung ?"

" No, Constance, no. He must not—Ernest must not meet that death ; he must not bring upon the name of Morden that ignominy."

" Then you consent to save him ? You promise me that you will help him to escape."

" And what is to be my reward for keeping that promise, if I make it ?"

" My love, dear Gervase, if that be of value to you—the love of a poor orphan girl. It shall be yours, dear Gervase—all yours !"

" And you will not object to wed the traitor's brother ?"

" I will not, dear Gervase. My hand shall be your guerdon for this deed."

The student hesitated for a few seconds, and then replied,—

" The reward be mine, sweet Constance ! Ernest Morden shall be saved."

"My love—my own heart's love !" ejaculated the fond girl as she clasped the hand of the student, and pressed it to her warm, ruby lips.

And as the two lovers embraced each other, and as the pale moonlight shone upon them both, the door of the apartment opened, and Sir Thomas Warrenton became a witness to their love. The old knight started, gazed for a few seconds, then closed the door, and summoning one of the domestics, gave orders that Gervase Morden should be bidden to wait upon his master in the library.

CHAPTER XLVIII.

THE CAUTION.—THE COVER OF THE PACKET.—FATHER AND SON.—THE SECRET
PANEL AND THE GLIDING SHADOW.

THE old dial upon the mantel of the library proclaimed that it was within two
hours of midnight as Sir Thomas sat waiting the arrival of his secretary.

Gervase Morden entered.

Some few preliminaries were gone through ; then, bidding the student to listen
attentively, Sir Thomas said,—

"It is needless, Mr. Morden, that I should assure you in words of that which
my behaviour towards you has long since proved. You know that I have taken an
interest in your welfare, and that I have in every possible way striven to aid you,
and to promote your happiness."

"You have, Sir Thomas. Would that my poor thanks fully expressed the deep
gratitude which I feel for every kindness which you have shown me."

"Your actions have been your best thanks, Morden, man. No more on that
subject. I have called you here to give you a caution, which I have omitted
giving you before, but which I should have given you some years since. Everything
depends on how you pay attention to this caution."

"To do so, Sir Thomas, I shall consider a duty."

"Ay, man—a duty to yourself. Hark ye ! there is in this house a fair maiden
whose name you know, and whose beauty might warm a colder heart than your
own. Beware, Morden, man ! let not that beauty snare you ! Beware, I say !
Friends you may be if you will, but let there be no love-passages between you, no
softly-spoken words, no squeezing of hands, no giving away of hearts. Such doings
would bring misery to you both; such misery, Morden, man, as you little dream
of and cannot divine."

The student hung down his head, and was silent.

"Mr. Morden !" exclaimed the old knight, "why, what does this mean ? I—
I—God pardon me !—have I given you the caution too late ?"

"Forgive me, Sir Thomas !" ejaculated the student, falling on his knees as he
spoke, "forgive me ! I love your niece."

"And the girl——"

"Constance loves me in return."

Strange was the expression which the countenance of Sir Thomas Warrenton
suddenly assumed. No flush of anger rose to his cheeks. On the contrary, his
face assumed a deadly paleness. Consternation and horror were displayed in his
upraised eyebrows, and fear in his fallen under lip. He clutched the hand of his
secretary ; his voice was hoarse and deep.

"Fool !" he ejaculated—"you know not what folly—what crime you have
committed. Go—go to the girl at once. Tell her that you love her not—that you
cannot love her—that—that—O God ! that I should not have foreseen this !"

"Pardon me, Sir Thomas. I am guilty—I have abused your trust. Yet, perhaps, in a few years—years, Sir Thomas, for Constance will wait—I shall have
done something in the world to make me worthy of this honour, and you will then
consent to our union."

"Hush, Morden ! Fool ! It is madness you are talking. There can be no
wedding between the son of Reginald Morden and the daughter of——Enough !
I give you warning. I warn you to cease this madness at once. Go—go to the
girl. Bid her come to me quickly. Tell her that——Ha ! go, see who knocks at
the door."

"One of the seamen who were here to-day is waiting below, and says that he
must see Sir Thomas at once," said the domestic who had knocked at the library
door.

"Send him up—show the man in here," replied Sir Thomas. Then, turning to the student, he grasped his arm, and, looking at him wildly, bade him retire to his own room, telling him that before the night was over, he would see him again.

Gervase Morden departed, and the seaman entered.

" Well, man, what success ?"

" I've had a long hunt for it, your honour, stars and moon and a lantern to help me. But somehow or other I think this is just the little article which you wanted me to lay hands on," said the man, as he pulled a piece of paper out of his jacket pocket, and presented it to Sir Thomas.

The knight took the paper and carried it to the lamp. Scrutinising it narrowly for a few moments, his eyes suddenly rested upon something which rivetted his attention, caused his hands to tremble, his face to turn pale, and the paper to fall from his grasp.

"I arnt made no mistake, have I, your honour?" asked the man.

" No ; it is right—it is the paper I wanted. I—here, take your reward ; take it, and be silent."

" Your honour won't be angry with me for asking if the bit of paper is likely to set all things square ? It's a hard thing for a poor gal to have such a serious charge made again her."

" Go, fellow, go ! To-morrow you will know all."

Five minutes after the seaman had departed, Sir Thomas Warrenton passed out of the library, and made his way towards the staircase leading to the upper apartments. In the gallery he saw the marine keeping guard at the door of the room in which Ernest Morden was confined.

Gently and nervously the old knight ascended the oaken stairs, bearing with him a small lamp, the light of which he shaded with his hand. On reaching the upper gallery his step became more cautious, and he took pains to shade the lamp-light more completely as he advanced. He passed by the door of the first chamber—it was that occupied by his secretary ; he trod lightly as he approached the second door—it was that which led to the apartment of his son ; at the third door he came to a pause, raised his hand to the lock, turned back the latch, and entered a room where all was darkness and silence.

Eugene Dourville, the Frenchman, and the friend of Lambert Warrenton, had left the Hall at an early hour of the evening. Sir Thomas knew not whither his guest was gone, but had received intimation that he would be absent until the following day.

It was the chamber allotted to Eugene Dourville's use in which the old knight now stood. Cautiously, and with a tip-toe step, he approached a table, on which was the writing-desk of his guest. He paused, placed the lamp upon the table, and drew from out his pocket a small chisel.

There was a slight trembling of the hand as the knight inserted the chisel into the crevice between the lid of the desk and the lock with which it was fastened ; there was a marked compression of the lips, as having fixed the instrument in its place, he caught up an old dressing-gown and wrapped it round the desk to dull any noise which he might have cause to make.

One grasp, one wrench, one slight movement of the hand, and the desk was broken open. The chisel was laid aside—the lamp raised.

Drawer after drawer was opened—recess after recess was pryed into. Sir Thomas examined the written papers ; there were letters, and he read them— memoranda, and he scanned them over. Still was the secret hunter at fault— still had his perquisitions failed in accomplishing the object which he had in view.

In one corner of the desk lay a handkerchief, loosely folded up. As the knight removed this from the place into which it had been thrust, a small bunch of seals dropped out from amongst the folds, and fell upon the floor.

Sir Thomas stooped, picked up the seals, examined them by the aid of the lamp, and as one of them more particularly attracted his attention, his hands trembled and his countenance altered in its expression. Silently, and carefully was that seal scrutinised ; then, the scrutiny over, everything else was restored to its place ;

the desk closed, the hasp fitted into the lid, the dressing-gown hung upon its peg, and all traces of the past deed carefully obliterated. Sir Thomas took up the lamp, stepped cautiously towards the door, and quitted the apartment, bearing with him the seal which he had removed from off the bunch.

The chamber of the guest had been entered; the object of the search was found.

Retracing his steps along the gallery, Sir Thomas Warrenton stole noiselessly towards the door of his son's apartment. He placed his hand upon the lock, thrust open the door, and perceiving the young man to be engaged in writing, said in a low, husky voice,—

"What! up so late, Lambert? that is well. Follow me to the library."

Lambert Warrenton started on hearing the door open; and his pen fell from his hand when he perceived that the visitor was his father. Something there was in the strange expression of that father's countenance—something in the deep, husky tone of his voice, that caused a tremor to pass through the nerves of the young man, as with a pale countenance and faltering limbs he arose to obey the command which he had thus abruptly received.

"Hist! boy. Tread the stairs lightly—the house sleeps."

"Why go to the library now, Sir Thomas?"

"I'll tell thee—I'll tell thee, presently. Gently—step gently!"

Father and son stood together in that olden, gloomy library. It was moonlight without, but the heavy curtains were drawn across the stained window—that window, standing by which Amy Heyton had given her promise to Lambert Warrenton. The faint rays of the lamp but dimly illuminated the apartment; and the ancient suits of armour, as they hung upon the rusty pegs, had the appearance of grim and frowning spectres, keeping watch amidst the silence and the gloom.

"Lambert," said Sir Thomas, fixing his gaze upon the pallid countenance of his son, "I have brought you here to answer me questions which are of the utmost importance, and which concern yourself in such a manner that your answers must be explicit and without reserve."

"What—what questions, Sir Thomas?"

"Hark ye! There is a man whom you have taken into your friendship, whom you have made your associate, with whom your leisure hours are now generally spent—that man is by birth our country's foe; his very name is, in these troublesome times, sufficient to excite suspicion. Yet you have introduced this man as your friend, you have caused him to become a guest beneath this roof, you have admitted him to your confidence, and behaved towards him as if he were your brother. Lambert Warrenton, I ask of you who is this Eugene Dourville? What know you of him? Why is he, a Frenchman, a resident in this country? What is his business here? What guarantee have you of his not being a spy—an enemy to King George?"

"Mr. Dourville is my friend, Sir Thomas. I have already told you, on the occasion of my introducing him to you and Lady Warrenton, that, having once enjoyed riches and large possessions in his native land, and having been deprived, unjustly, of those possessions, as well as of a portion of that wealth which came to him as his heritage, he conceived a dislike to remaining longer in the country which had witnessed his misfortunes; and having collected together the remnants of his patrimony, abjured the land of his birth, and determined to make this island his home. Surely, Sir Thomas, you do not object to England offering a shelter to the unfortunate, come they from what country or clime they may?"

"Ay, ay, boy; a pretty story, and one of easy fabrication. I ask you, Lambert Warrenton, what voucher you have for the truth of this account, or what testimony you have to prove the verity of Mr. Dourville's story?"

"His word, Sir Thomas—I have Mr. Dourville's word."

"No more than that, my boy—nothing more than that? Then you know not whether this Eugene Dourville be a mere liar, or whether he be both liar and foe?"

"Pardon me, Sir Thomas—my father," said Lambert Warrenton, rising from his seat. "I cannot sit here and listen to such unjust accusations made against a gentleman whom I have the pleasure of calling my friend."

"Keep your seat, boy—keep your seat, Lambert Warrenton," exclaimed the knight, wrathfully. "You have called this man your friend. As a friend, you should have Eugene Dourville's confidence. What know you, then, of him? With what secrets of his are you acquainted? Know you who *his* friends are, and with whom he corresponds?"

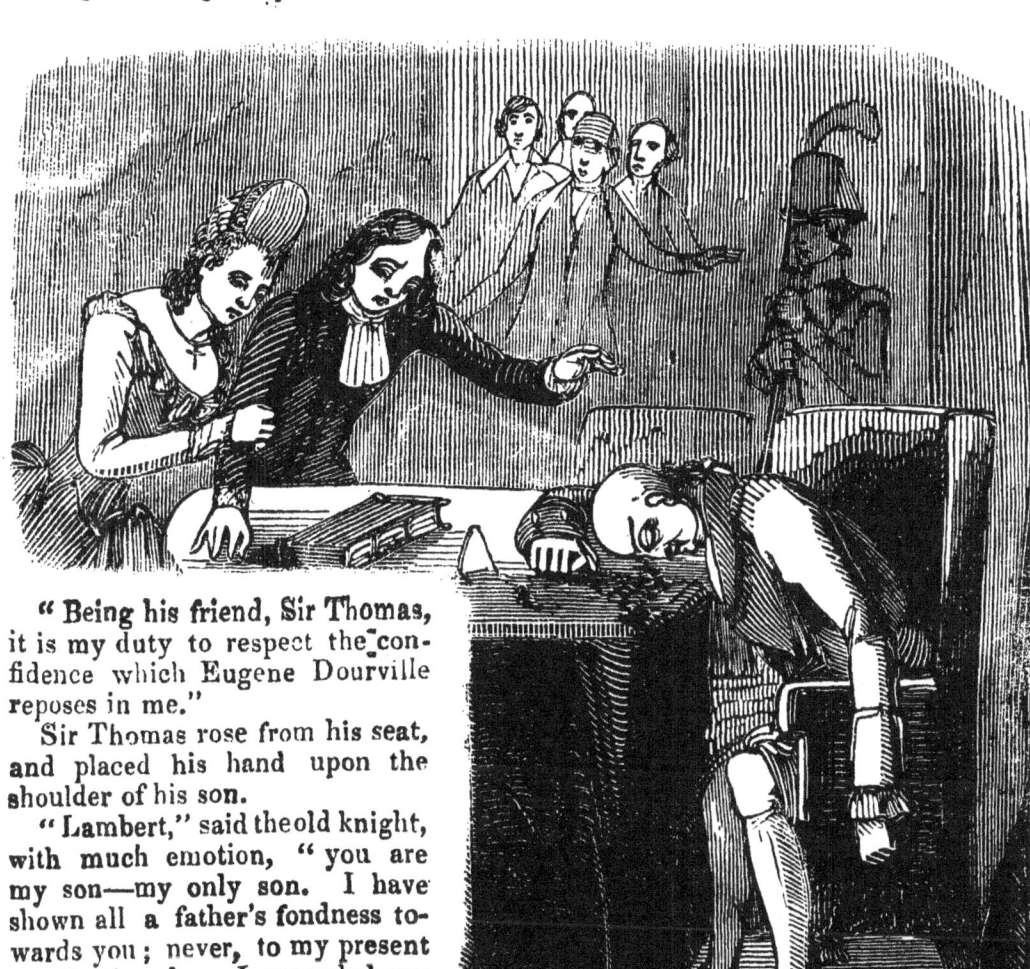

"Being his friend, Sir Thomas, it is my duty to respect the confidence which Eugene Dourville reposes in me."

Sir Thomas rose from his seat, and placed his hand upon the shoulder of his son.

"Lambert," said the old knight, with much emotion, "you are my son—my only son. I have shown all a father's fondness towards you; never, to my present recollection, have I exceeded my parental duties by the use of harsh measures or an over-strictness of discipline. Your entrance into the world was an event which wrought me much anxiety, and your after conduct therein has occasioned me the most painful solicitude. I have watched you, boy; and while petitioning to Heaven for your welfare, have had the sorrow of noticing various irregularities in your conduct which I have neglected to censure. God knows, boy, whether I have erred in withholding that censure. It may be that I shall find cause to reproach myself for my neglect. London and Warrenton Hall are many miles distant from each other; nevertheless rumours have found their way here of your having misconducted yourself in the metropolis. Lambert Warrenton, I will not name to you what those rumours have been; but I ask you to answer me, truly and unreservedly, whether any improprieties committed by you in moments of excitement have placed you in difficulties, to escape from which you have had resort to deeds derogatory to your own honour and to mine?"

The countenance of the young man was of an ashen paleness, as he replied,—

"I know not to whose kindness, Sir Thomas, I am indebted for the origin of these most pleasant rumours, nor who has had the obliging impertinence of troubling themselves with my affairs. As to the question which you have asked me, my only reply is, that it is too vague for me to comprehend it clearly, and is evidently too absurd to require from me an answer in the negative."

The brows of the parent became contracted, and he threw a stern glance at his son, as he rejoined,—

"Be careful, Lambert Warrenton. There is a levity in your reply which ill accords with the occasion. Once more I ask you, have you by any overt act of your own placed yourself within the power of any individual who may use that power to your destruction? The question is plain—let your answer be plain also."

"Father, I cannot understand why these interrogatories are addressed to me. What do you suspect? What answer do you require?"

"Your cool, your serious answer, Lambert Warrenton. No trifling, boy—no evasive replies. Have you or have you not so committed yourself, in selling your honour to any man living?"

"I have not, Sir Thomas."

"You speak glibly, boy. Hark you! This book is a Bible: take it in your hand, Lambert Warrenton, and, while God witnesses to your words, repeat the assertion which you have just made."

"What would you have me say, father?"

"That your honour, boy, is intact; that you have not placed your future peace and happiness in the power of any living man."

"On my oath I have not!" replied Lambert Warrenton, in a faltering voice.

"Not even in the power of your friend—in the power of Eugene Dourville?"

The young man started to his feet, thrust aside the chair on which he had been seated, and making a movement towards the door, replied,—

"I know not what reason you have to disbelieve my words, Sir Thomas, nor from what motives you offer these insults to my friend. My answer has been given—has been sworn to—what occasion is there for my further stay?"

"None. Return to your chamber, boy. To-morrow I may have further inquiries to make."

Pale and trembling, Lambert Warrenton quitted the presence of his father. No sooner was he gone, than clasping one hand to his forehead, and placing the other upon the table for support, the parent bent down his head, and ejaculated,—

"God grant that others have deceived me, and that my child has told me truth!"

Then, after musing for a few minutes, Sir Thomas opened a drawer, took thence the torn cover which the seaman had brought him, and placed beside it the seal which he had removed from the writing-desk of his guest. He drew the lamp nearer, and compared the engraved seal with the impression upon the wax with which the cover had been secured.

The dial upon the mantel proclaimed that the hour of midnight had arrived.

Sir Thomas Warrenton relit the smaller lamp, took it in his hand, and again passing out of the library, proceeded towards the chamber in which Ernest Morden was imprisoned.

"Know you if your prisoner be asleep?" inquired the knight of the marine who kept guard at the door.

"He may be, your honour—I haven't heard him move."

Sir Thomas turned the key, and entered the chamber. Ernest Morden was seated upon the bed's edge, his head bent, his forehead resting on his hands.

"Lieutenant Morden," said the knight, as he tapped the shoulder of the moody man, "I have somewhat to say to you. Ask no questions here, but follow me."

The guard made some objections to this unseasonable removal of the prisoner, and was disposed to act the part of escort. He was silenced, however, by Sir

Thomas, who bade him to rest quietly in his chair, and have no fears about being called upon to answer for his so doing.

Seated in the same old gloomy library, the conference between Sir Thomas Warrenton and Lieutenant Morden was of long continuance. The particulars of the conversation need not be recorded here. Suffice it to say, that the knight placed before his companion the torn cover, together with the stolen seal; and afterwards, as he led Ernest Morden to the door, bade him have no fear, but bide the coming morrow with a stout heart and a repentant soul.

Ernest Morden returned to the room which had been selected for his prison. The guard was sleeping at his post; so, without caring to wake him, the prisoner entered the room, and reclosed the door.

No disposition for sleep did Sir Thomas Warrenton evince that night; but when Ernest Morden had departed, and silence once more reigned in the old library, he resumed his seat at the table, placed the cover and seal again before him, reclined his head upon his hands, and gradually passed into a state of abstraction and reverie.

And now it was—now while the owner of Warrenton Hall was absorbed in reverie, and while the light grew dimmer and dimmer in the oilless lamp, that a panel in the oaken wall of the old library was moved aside, a dark figure emerged into the apartment, and stepped with noiseless step upon the polished floor.

The dial ticked—the lamp flickered. Onwards crept the dark figure towards the table where sat the musing man.

One minute did the figure pause—ere that minute had expired the light went out, and the figure upraised its arm in the darkness.

A deep sleep was that which Sir Thomas Warrenton that night slept!

There is a sleep deeper than that of slumbering infancy, deeper than that which opium produces, deeper than that which mesmerism is said to effect. What name do men give to that strange sleep?

The dark name—Death!

CHAPTER XLIX.

HOW THE PHANTOM APPEARED IN WARRENTON HALL FOR THE LAST TIME.

The time was the dead of night, the place was the sleeping chamber of Lady Warrenton. Her ladyship had long since retired to rest, and lay wrapt in slumber. A taper was burning on an adjoining table. There was no sound to break the stillness, save the soft breathings of the sleeper.

Suddenly the door of the chamber was thrown open; a figure attired in white, and having a pale bloodless countenance, entered, and glided across the floor.

The figure approached the bed, drew aside the curtains, and placed its hands upon the shoulder of the fair sleeper.

Lady Warrenton awoke.

"Constance!" exclaimed her ladyship, recognising in the trembling figure by her side the features of Miss Ismay. "Constance, darling! what do you here? Why have you left your bed?"

"I—I. It has come again—I have seen it again."

"Seen what, dearest?" asked her ladyship, in surprise.

"The—the shadow—the man. Oh, I know not what it is—I cannot tell!"

"But what, darling? explain to me what you mean. Your hands are cold, your cheeks are blanched, there is a strange wildness in your eyes. What have you seen? What frightful dream has disturbed your sleep?"

"No dream—no dream. The figure—the dark figure. I saw it cross my room again."

" Ha !" exclaimed Lady Warrenton ; " has that returned ? Wore it the same aspect as before ?"

" The same—the very same."

Lady Warrenton sat upright in the bed, and folded her arms around the neck of the timid girl.

" Tell me, Constance—tell me, child—how did the figure appear, and what did it do or say to you?"

" It did not come near me—it did not speak one word. It was late when I retired to bed, and my thoughts prevented me from sleeping. I had lain awake for more than an hour, and had heard the turret clock strike ' one.' Suddenly my ear caught the sound of something moving in my apartment. I listened—I trembled. Again I heard the sound, and knew it to be a footstep. My tremor became so great that I could not cry out, I could not move a finger. There was a sensation as of cold water trickling down my back, though I was covered with profuse perspiration. After a time I raised my head, and drew aside the curtains. I looked forth into the room, but nothing was there—no living thing that I could see. I did not lose my fear. I was not inclined to think that my ears had deceived me. In vain I tried to turn away my eyes, or cover them with the bed-clothes—I could not do so. I remained gazing into the deep gloom at the farther end of my chamber. Minutes after minutes passed, and then I closed my eyes, for they were weary. Scarcely had I closed them before I again heard the noise which I had heard before. I listened—the footfall was repeated. I unclosed my eyes—I looked forth—I saw a shadow flitting across the room—I followed it with my eyes—I heard its garments rustle—I saw it glide towards the wall; and —and——"

" Well, dearest ?"

" I know nothing more. What it was, or where it went, I cannot say. All became silent. I dared not close my eyes again in that room. I lay for some minutes without moving ; then, feeling the loneliness to be insupportable, I sprang out of bed, threw round me this covering, and, without looking to the right or to the left, hastened out of the room. Never, Lady Warrenton, will I sleep there again. I could not do so were it for the worth of worlds."

Lady Warrenton smoothed the dark hair of the agitated girl, and bidding her take courage, hinted a suspicion that the whole affair had been nothing but a dream.

" Did I dream before, Lady Warrenton ? How came the blood there then ?" demanded Constance.

The question was one to which her ladyship was unwilling to make any reply. What her own thoughts really were, and why she herself shuddered as she pressed the head of fair Constance to her bosom, cannot be explained here. It was after a considerable pause that she at length said,—

" I know not, my dear child, what course to take. Sir Thomas warned me that, as he had business of importance, which required his attention, he should not retire to rest until an early hour in the morning. He is doubtless in the library now. I do not like to disturb him. The morning has already advanced, and it is probable that he will soon be here. Meanwhile, dear Constance, dress yourself with clothes out of yonder wardrobe, and I will rise and sit with you at the window. The air is very warm, and it scarcely wants an hour to daybreak."

Constance Ismay obeyed the desire of her ladyship, and having put on some loose attire, took a seat within the recess of the window ; she was joined by Lady Warrenton, who placed her own chair next to that of the fair girl. The curtains were drawn aside, disclosing the thick greenwood and the distant meadows bathed in silvery light ; but the moon had disappeared round one of the angles of the old building, and not one of its rays fell upon the casements of that antique window, at which sat the fair ward of Sir Thomas, with her head resting upon the swelling bust of the courtly Lady Warrenton.

Slowly crept the weary minutes on. The moonlight became fainter, the shadows deeper, the sounds of the waking morning more distinct. Grey streaks dappled the eastern sky, and white mists curled up from off the ground, and dissolved away like airy spirits fleeing from the sun.

So still was fair Constance that Lady Warrenton thought she had at last fallen asleep. As, however, the faint light of early morning fell upon the maiden's face, her ladyship perceived that the eyes of Constance Ismay were still open, though the eyeballs were fixed, and that the lips were of a deadly whiteness, while the murmur of respiration could scarcely be heard.

" Constance !" she cried.

There was no answer.

" She is ill—she is dying !" exclaimed Lady Warrenton, as she placed her fair charge upon a couch, and rushed towards the bell-pull.

Somewhat more than ten minutes passed before the summons was answered.

" Martha," said her ladyship, as the servant, on entering the room, started on beholding Constance there, " go quickly, and bid Sir Thomas come hither. You will find him in the library. Tell him that Miss Ismay is unwell—very unwell. Hasten, good Martha, hasten !"

The servant departed to obey the command of her mistress, and Lady Warrenton busied herself in administering medicaments to poor Constance, and in chafing her cold, pallid hands. Her ladyship was thus occupied when a sudden shriek, accompanied by the noise of a falling body, resounded through the gallery.

" What is that ?" ejaculated her ladyship, overcome by sudden terror.

Trembling and affrighted, Lady Warrenton stood listening for a repetition of the sound, and wondering that neither Sir Thomas nor Martha came to her assistance. She was about to move towards the door, when loud cries of " Help !" uttered in a male voice, caused her to draw back for a moment, and then to rush precipitously into the gallery, and hasten towards the library-door.

At the entrance to the library she was met by the soldier who had been put as a guard over Lieutenant Morden.

" My lady—my lady !" exclaimed the affrighted man.

" Why do you cry help ? What has happened ?" demanded Lady Warrenton.

" Do not go in, my lady—do not look into that room !" implored the man, as her ladyship was about to step into the library.

" Not enter ! Why—why—what—what—" And, unable to finish the sentence, Lady Warrenton thrust open the door.

" Help ! help !" exclaimed the terrified soldier.

" Help ! help !" echoed a faint voice from the interior of the room.

Many minutes had not passed before Gervase Morden, together with some halfdozen of affrighted domestics, entered the gallery.

" Why is this outcry ?" asked Morden of the trembling man.

" Oh, sir ! his honour—his honour !"

" What of Sir Thomas ?"

" Murdered, sir !—murdered !"

" Murdered !" ejaculated the student, dashing forward, and entering the library.

A strange, sad sight was that which presented itself to the view of Gervase Morden. Still seated in his chair, but with his head fallen forward upon the table, sat Sir Thomas Warrenton, with a pool of clotted gore at his feet, and a spring of liquid blood oozing out from a hole in his left temple. Leaning against the same table for support, her eyes wildly glaring at the murdered man, was the dead knight's widow ; while prostrate upon the floor lay the insensate domestic who had been sent by Lady Warrenton to apprise Sir Thomas of Miss Ismay's illness.

When Gervase Morden had partially recovered from the consternation and fear into which his first glance at the dreadful spectacle had thrown him, he approached the still bleeding man, and attempted to upraise his face. Then it was that Lady Warrenton crept forward, and placing her hand upon the student's arm, asked in a hollow whisper,—

" What—what does it mean ?"

" Wait. I cannot tell," was the reply.

" Is he—is he dead ?" asked the same hollow voice.

" I know not. Lady Warrenton, I must beg you to leave this room."

" No—no—I—I must not go, I——"

" Walters," said Morden, in a stern voice, addressing a domestic, " I give Lady Warrenton into your charge. See that some of her maids wait upon her at once; and let her be taken to her own apartment. You, Thwaites, hasten to Dr. Cosgreave and to Dr. Raynton. Bid them both speed hither immediately. Where is Mr. Lambert—why is he not here ? Go, Richards, and waken Mr. Warrenton. Tell him to lose no time, but hasten at once to this room. Some of you must go and keep guard until the house can be searched. Let every one be on the alert lest the murderer—the man who has done this deed—should escape."

In vain came the doctors—in vain brought they their plaisters and their medicines. Sir Thomas Warrenton was beyond the reach of human aid; his heart had stilled its beating; his eyes were shrouded with the glazy film of death.

There were secret consultations, diligent searchings, and careful inquiries. Still nothing could be discovered; no one could point to the murderer, and say— " That is he!"

The soldier who had kept guard at the door of Lieutenant Morden's room was examined. His answers went to prove that, in the early part of the evening, he had seen Mr. Gervase Morden enter, and afterwards leave the library; but at a subsequent period of the same evening, Sir Thomas Warrenton had passed out, and afterwards returned in the company of his son; that he—the soldier—had also seen Lambert Warrenton make his exit from the library ; and that, towards the middle of the night, Sir Thomas had sought the apartment of Lieutenant Morden, had taken him thence, and again, as before, returned to the library.

" And you saw Lieutenant Morden safe again in his own room?" inquired the student.

" I did," replied the man, falteringly.

" Did you see Sir Thomas again after that ?" continued Gervase Morden.

" I did," answered the soldier, after some hesitation. " He opened the door of this room, looked out in the gallery, and then went back again, shutting the door after him. That was the last time of my seeing him, till the shriek of that young woman there made me rush into the room this morning."

It was evident that Sir Thomas Warrenton's death had been caused by a bullet having fractured his skull, and passed into his brain. Strange to say, there lay upon the floor at his feet a small pistol, which was identified by Gervase Morden, and by the deceased's son, as having belonged to Sir Thomas Warrenton himself.

" Gentlemen," said Lambert Warrenton, addressing in a voice of agony the medical attendants, " tell me—tell me—do you think that my poor father destroyed himself by his own hand ?"

" If no murderer be discovered, that will be the most probable supposition," replied Doctor Cosgreave.

" Mr. Warrenton," said Gervase Morden, " I have been submitting this soldier to a further examination, and have just elicited from him the extraordinary assertion that, though on guard but a few yards off, he heard no shot fired in this room, nor any sound that resembled the discharge of a pistol or a musket."

" That is decidedly a very strange assertion," replied Doctor Cosgreave. " Nothing can be more evident than that by some hand a shot was fired, and that by means the death of Sir Thomas Warrenton has been occasioned. Nor is it less strange that this man should make such a declaration, than that the report of a pistol, during the silence of night, should not have been heard by some of the indwellers of the house, notwithstanding that they were not asleep at the time."

Mystery followed mystery the more that the party assembled in that room of death cogitated upon the sad and inexplicable tragedy—the more that they endeavoured to account for all the strange facts which, one by one, rose up to confound them. Sir Thomas Warrenton was dead ; but whether his life had been rashly taken by his own hand, or by that of another person, formed the one great mystery which remained to be discovered.

The doors and windows of the library were all examined, but none presented the appearance of having been broken open. There was nothing to indicate that any one had surreptitiously entered the apartment—nothing, except the secret panel in the oaken wall, and that escaped every eye.

The house was searched, the adjacent premises were pried into; but no murderer could be discovered, no hider in secret was to be found.

"This is strange, inexplicably strange!" ejaculated Gervase Morden, as he threw himself into a chair, and bent his head upon his hands.

One strange occurrence had happened of which, however, Gervase Morden knew nothing. Sir Thomas Warrenton had placed the torn corner of the despatches, and the seal belonging to Eugene Dourville upon the table before him on the previous night; and when morning came, and the first ray of daylight shone upon the self-same table, neither the cover nor the seal was there!

CHAPTER L.

THE MAN WITH THE SECRET.

THE day passed on, and preparations were made for holding an inquest concerning the manner of Sir Thomas Warrenton's death. Meanwhile, an interview occurred between Gervase Morden and Constance Ismay; the student hearing from the lips of the fair girl a full account of the visit of the phantom to her sleeping-chamber, and pondering thereon in order, if possible, to discover some connection between that strange recountal, and the still more mysterious and lamentable event which had occurred on the same night.

"Say you, dear Constance, that the figure twice visited your bed chamber?"

"Yes, twice."

"The first time you heard, but did not see it; the second time you saw it, I believe. Now, do you remember in what direction it moved, and where it seemed to disappear?"

"I—I know not how it went, dear Gervase; but I saw it glide towards the wall, first where the picture of the old knight on horseback is hung in the recess; and there it seemed to pass away."

"There is something very marvellous in this story of yours, dear Constance," observed the student, after meditating for a while.

"I will once more go and make an examination of your chamber, and of the adjoining rooms. Perchance a careful scrutiny may bring about some strange revelation."

So saying, the student proceeded at once to the execution of his self-assigned task. Every nook and corner of the chamber in which the fair girl had that night lain was peered into, and subjected to a strict search. There was the bed from which the terrified maiden had hastily arisen; there was an ancient wardrobe with its doors locked and otherwise secured; there was the picture of the knight on horseback hanging in its oaken frame; and there was the toilet-table of fair Constance, with its mirror and customary paraphernalia. Nothing else, save a few chairs and other smaller articles of furniture, did the chamber contain. No footmarks could be traced upon the soft carpet, no spot of blood was this time to be seen upon the polished floor; nothing there was to reward the student's search, or in any way help towards an explanation of the mystery. Even Gervase Morden himself was now inclined to believe that the figure which Constance Ismay averred to having seen, had been nothing else than the mere phantasm of a dream.

The student was returning to the drawing-room in which he had left Miss Ismay, when he was met by the soldier who had kept guard during the night at the door of Ernest Morden's room.

"I beg pardon, sir," said the man, with a faltering voice, and with much nervousness of manner; "there is a something that sits uneasy on my mind, which I want to tell you about. Only, sir, I can't speak about it here."

"Is the door of Lieutenant Morden's room fastened?" inquired the student.

"It is," replied the soldier.

"Come with me, then, I will take you to a room where we can talk together without being overheard."

The student led the way, followed by the soldier. Both entered the bay-parlour, and Gervase Morden closed and fastened the door.

"What is it you have to say, my good fellow? Know you anything concerning the matter of last night, which you have yet refrained from communicating?"

The soldier hesitated, made sundry attempts at a commencement, and at length falling upon his knees said, in an imploring voice,—

"You will forgive me, sir, and will promise to say nothing about it to Captain Charnock? I know I've done wrong, but Lieutenant Morden has always been a kind officer, and I shouldn't like to see him get into any harm if I could help it."

"Lieutenant Morden!" exclaimed the student. "Why, what have you got to say concerning him?"

"Last night, sir—— But you'll promise not let me get into trouble about it, sir—you'll promise to keep it from Captain Charnock?"

"Keep what—promise what? My good fellow, it is folly to ask me such questions, before I know what the nature of your communication is to be. Use no reserve in making your confession ; and you may rely upon it, that, if it be in my power to shield you from any punishment likely to fall upon you from misdeeds of your own, I will exert myself to the utmost in your behalf."

"Well, sir, I don't know that you can say fairer, so I'll make a clean breast of it at once, and tell you all I know, and what I've done wrong. You know, sir, I was asked this morning if I saw Lieutenant Morden go back to his room last night, and if I saw Sir Thomas afterwards. I said yes to both questions, sir; but I told lies, and I ask Almighty God to forgive me for telling 'em."

"You told lies!" repeated Gervase Morden, in a breathless voice. "What mean you—why did you tell such lies?"

"I told them, sir, because when I came to know of Sir Thomas's death this morning, and saw that he was murdered, I thought—I——"

The man hesitated, and appeared unwilling to finish the sentence.

"Speak! Tell me what you thought. What was it—what?" asked the student, his lips losing their colour as he spoke.

"Why, you see, sir, the truth is I had a hard day's work of it yesterday, aboard-ship, and wasn't very well fitted to keep watch all night. I saw Sir Thomas take Lieutenant Morden out of his room, and his honour told me not to follow them. I don't know how it was, sir ; but somehow or other I fell asleep, and when I woke up, and opened the door of the room, Lieutenant Morden was there, and must have gone in while I was asleep. You see, sir, if this should come to the ears of Captain Charnock I should get a flogging. Of course, sir, when I woke up, I took care to shake off all my drowsiness, and mind my duty for the rest of the night. And when, sir, I saw the young woman go into the library in the morning, and afterwards heard her cry out, and went in myself and saw the blood on the floor, and Sir Thomas dead ; and heard everybody say he'd been murdered, I could not help thinking, sir, there'd been a quarrel between him and Lieutenant Morden."

"Ha!" ejaculated the student, huskily, "and—and you have not mentioned this suspicion—you have not said a word about it to any one except myself?"

"No, sir. Knowing as how Lieutenant Morden is your own brother, I though it would be best only to tell you about it. And as Lieutenant Morden has always been very kind to us, I was willing to do him a service in saying what I did to the gentleman this morning."

Some time elapsed before the student uplifted his head, or spoke a single word. At length, rising from his seat, he grasped neruously the hand of the soldier, and in a deep, but scarcely articulate voice, said,

"You have done rightly. Say not a word of this to any one. Remember, your confession proves nothing, and were it made public, you yourself would be punished for sleeping at your post. Go—go back to your place. Fear nothing. I—I will reward you well. Go—go!"

"I hope, sir, I'm wrong in what I've hinted about your brother, but——"

"Go—go!" exclaimed the student, as, leading the soldier to the door, he watched him pass into the gallery. No sooner was the man gone, than, reclosing the door, Gervase Morden staggered towards a couch, threw himself upon it, and clasping his hands to his brow, ejaculated,—

"Ernest—Ernest a murderer ! Yes, yes, I can easily believe it ! I—oh, God ! that I should have lived till now !"

And hour after hour passed away with heavy and with weary pace, while the student remained in the same position, meditating upon the terrible discovery which he now believed that he had made. What motive Ernest Morden could have had in taking the life of Sir Thomas Warrenton was not easily to be conceived ; nevertheless, the high principles of action which swayed the mind of the student taught him to believe that man as capable of committing murder who had already maligned the character of an innocent girl, and caused sorrow to take up its abode in the same fond heart which had once beat with the truest love for him. Oh ! it was a soul-withering belief—that fearful belief of the student, that the brother of his youth—the brother who bore the same name with him—the brother whom he had regarded with kindness, with affection, and with honest pride, was a murderer—the worst, the vilest of murderers ! Yet such was the belief of Gervase Morden ; nor saw he aught to cause him to waver in that faith. The hours passed, and as they went they wrought strange changes on the student's countenance ; for when day waned, and the evening came, and the stern, sorrowful man arose from the couch upon which he had thrown himself, there were traces upon that face of the workings of no common agony, there were marks—such deep-sunken, immoveable marks, that it seemed as if not a few hours of torture, but long years of mental sorrow had fled by, and engraven the records of their visits upon that downcast brow, that lean and ashen cheek, that head depressed as if for evermore. The stern man trembles ; the iron heart is pierced by the barb of sorrow,—Gervase Morden, the man of honour, is the brother of one whose hands are dyed with blood !

So thought the student, but he locked his sad thoughts in his tortured breast, and told to no one of his sorrow.

The dusky evening came, and with it a messenger from Captain Charnock, with his commands, that as Sir Thomas Warrenton was dead, Lieutenant Morden should be sent the same night to London as a prisoner, there to answer to every charge which might be preferred against him.

"What did that man want—on what errand did he come, dear Gervase?" inquired Constance Ismay, as she clung to the student's arm.

"Nothing, Constance ; his errand was but—but trivial."

"No, Gervase, no—it was not as you say; your looks declare it to have been of serious import. He came from Captain Charnock. Tell me—did he—did he bring news about your brother ?"

"I have received orders that Lieutenant Morden be sent to London this night. Under present circumstances, Miss Ismay, I need hardly remind you that the inquiry cannot be continued here."

"But—but—you will not let him go—you will not send him—you will not be so harsh, so cruel ! He must not go, dearest Gervase—he must not go !"

"Pardon me, Constance. You forget what position I hold in this house, and what my duties are. You forget also that I have no power in this matter, other than to obey the instructions which I have received."

"But your promise, Gervase—your promise !"

"Remind me of nothing, I beg of you, Miss Ismay, that may induce me to swerve from the path of duty. Painful as are the tasks which I am compelled to perform, I would not shrink from the performance were they a thousand times more torturing. It must be, dear Constance—it must be."

"No, Gervase. The promise—the solemn promise which you gave to your poor Constance, you must not break—you will not do so, I am sure you will not. Dearest, we are both desolate now ; there is the same lone world around us each. Last night I was not quite friendless, I did not even feel that I was an orphan ; but now—now, Gervase, the one friend which I had I have no longer, the kind hand which has protected me from my childhood is lost to me for ever ; and I feel

—I feel now how fatherless and motherless I am. It was only last night, too, that we were speaking of love, and yet a whole year seems passed away, and all things seemed changed, and our love seems old—old and forgotten——"

"Not forgotten, Constance Ismay. Say not that!" exclaimed the student, passionately. "Deep as ever—deep as in those by-past times which I have told you of, that love exists now. Yes, Miss Ismay, it is true, as you say, that we are desolate and friendless—God knows how desolate the world appears unto me now. We want friendship, we want some remnant of the wretched ship of our youthful happiness. Let us keep them together, let us continue our love ; let us, friendless as we are, face the cold world, and walk the weary earth united. We need courage, Constance, and we need mutual sympathy; our sympathies must not be suffered to die, our courage must be exerted to the utmost—to the utmost, Constance Ismay, for there will be much to withstand."

"I will be brave, dear Gervase ; I will not fear."

"Neither will I," returned the student ; "and yet, Constance, you guess not, you have not the remotest conception how difficult the task is—how great the exertion of wearing a front of bravery while the heart is playing the coward within."

"Yes, dearest, I know the difficulty. I comprehend your feelings. The situation of your poor brother distresses you. You must help him, dear Gervase ; you must keep your promise to me, and assist poor Ernest to escape."

"I, Constance ; I——"

"Yes, indeed, yes. You know what you said his doom would be; you know that you assured me of his being really guilty, that his guilt will be proven, and that if he be not rescued, the law will punish him. Gervase—dear Gervase, let your heart rule you in this matter ; let your affection save poor Ernest."

"Would you have me to be a participator in his guilt, Constance Ismay ?"

"No, Gervase—no. It will be no guilt to save him ; no guilt to assist a brother in escaping from the gibbet. Never—oh, never let me have cause to reproach you for allowing your brother to be hung."

"Hung!" repeated the student, in a husky voice, pressing his hands to his brow.

"You said so ; you said that his crime is one for which men meet the gibbet. It must not be, Gervase Morden—the gibbet must not be your brother's doom! This night he must be saved—you yourself must save him. It is your promise, dear Gervase—your promise which you must not break. If there be truth in your words—if you really love me as you have said that you do—if you wish to make your poor Constance happy, you will do this, dear Gervase—you will do it without delay. Do not refuse me ; do not say that you retract your promise. Go at once to your brother and consult with him how his escape may be effected. Lose no time—not an hour—not a minute. Hasten, dear Gervase, hasten !"

The student paced the room moodily for a few seconds, then coming to a pause, he laid his hand upon the arm of fair Constance, and in a strange, guttural voice, said—

"It shall be. I will keep my promise. Ernest Morden shall be saved from the gibbet."

"Oh ! that is brave—that is noble of you, dearest Gervase !" exclaimed the fair girl, flinging her arms around the neck of the student. "But why do you avert your face ? Why do your arms quiver as I touch them ?"

"Leave me, Constance—leave me. I must away to Ernest. I will see you again soon."

"Not till you have saved your brother, dear Gervase; do not let it be till then."

He shall be saved from the gibbet, Constance Ismay; he shall be saved this night."

"Heaven prosper you in the attempt !" ejaculated the fair girl, as she left the apartment, after watching the student take his way towards the chamber in which Ernest Morden was imprisoned.

The stern brother and the weaker one were again together ; again they stood in one room ; again they looked upon each other's countenance, as they had done in their childhood's days.

"Hear me, Ernest, said the student. "Sir Thomas Warrenton—as you have already heard—is dead ; he was your friend, and can befriend you no longer. I have this evening received an order from Captain Charnock, desiring that the instructions brought from London by Mr. Lambert be acted upon immediately, and that you forthwith be sent to the metropolis. Once there, Ernest, and your doom is certain. Be your guilt or innocence what it may, there is sufficient evidence to convict you in the present excited times. You will not escape by attempting to cast the blame upon others. Amy Heyton will confess that she gave a certain parcel into the hands of the French smuggler—but what of that ? It is known that you were the lover of that poor girl, and it will at once be agreed upon that she was your agent. Then, as to your after attempt at casting the whole blame upon her shoulders, the perfidy of that very deed will be accounted sufficient proof of the blackness of your character and actions. Think not that I speak other than the truth, when I say that everything is against you. The fact of your long hiding in the cottage of the tombcutter would be construed as an act of treachery, and then again there are those who know well that Sampson Sumners and Red Martin are more friendly than they should be. I warn you, Ernest, that death—the felon's death will be yours ; I give you no hope ; for it would be deception on my part to do so."

" But I am innocent, Gervase—I am innocent !"

" It is not the question of your innocence or guilt which I wish to discuss. You know full well the state of parties in this country ; you know that at the present moment the mere suspicion of treachery—the mere rumour of his being a friend to France—is sufficient to send a man to the gibbet. You know this, Ernest Morden ; and you know also the position in which you are placed."

" I do. I fear."

" And you dare to meet your fate—you dare to stand the issue of a trial ?"

Ernest Morden was silent.

" Coward !—coward in his very nature !" ejaculated the student to himself, as his dark eyes flashed indignant glances at the crouching form before him.

Still the silence continued.

" Listen, Ernest !" said the elder brother; " I would save you from this fate ; I do not wish my father's son to meet such ignominy. It is now nine o'clock; at midnight the coach will call here as it passes by, in order to convey you to London. Are you willing in the meantime to attempt effecting your escape ?"

" I am, brother. But how ?"

" I will prepare all for you. That casement is locked—here is the key. There are some thirty feet between it and the court-yard below—here is a cord by which you can descend. Wait until you hear the turret-clock strike ten, and then commence your enterprise. A whistle will be the announcement of my being in waiting for you in the court-yard below."

" But whither shall I flee—where make my retreat, dear brother ?"

" I have already arranged that," replied the student, gravely. Then, placing pen, ink, and paper upon the table, he motioned his brother to take a seat.

" What am I to write ?" asked Ernest, as the student dipped the pen in the ink, and gave it into his hand.

" Words that will exonerate me from suspicion," replied Gervase Morden. " Your flight effected—your escape made, who will be suspected of having been your abettor ?"

" Not you, brother Gervase—they will not suspect you."

" I know not that. There is paper. Write as if you were addressing me."

" And I am to say—what ?"

" Say, that, unwilling to bring dishonour upon your father's name, unwilling to have it said that a Morden died upon the gibbet, you resolved attempting an escape. In making a confession of your guilt, say also that Amy Heyton is innocent, and that your accusation was——"

" Never, brother !" exclaimed Ernest, starting to his feet and flinging down his pen. " I will not—cannot write that !"

"Write then, as you will," replied the student, in the same grave tone as that in which he had before spoken. "Make mention of your crime in the manner which you think best; and confess to your escape having been effected by your own hands."

Ernest Morden resumed the writing of his letter; when he had wrote all that he wished to write, he submitted the paper to his brother's inspection.

"That will do," said the student, as he glanced over it with his dark moody eyes. "Now add, by way of a postscript, that as your escape is attended with many difficulties, and as the way which you have chosen to effect it is a dangerous one, there is a possibility of your meeting with some accident which may frustrate your plans, and, perchance, prove fatal to yourself."

"What is your meaning, brother? What cause is there for my writing such words?"

"Were there no cause I should not press you to do so. Why do you object?"

"I have no objection brother, none; but——"

"Then write."

Ernest Morden complied with the dictation, and wrote accordingly.

"Some one may enter your room in the course of the present hour, therefore keep the paper hidden," said the student. "When, however, the time for attempting your escape shall arrive, place that paper open upon the table, and leave it there. Remember to be in readiness when the turret-clock strikes ten!"

CHAPTER LI.

HOW THE ESCAPE WAS EFFECTED, AND WHERE THE ELDER BROTHER LED THE YOUNGER.

It wanted but ten minutes to the appointed hour, and the student was busy in his own room. Spread out upon the table before him lay the coils of a large rope, to the middle, and not to either of the ends, of which he was engaged in affixing a large iron hook.

The hook was of the grapnel description: it had two strong prongs, and its attachment to the rope was effected by passing the latter through a ring made for the purpose.

It was to the middle of the rope that this hook was fastened.

Five minutes to the hour, and the student, had placed the rope in a bag, and placed therein also a large clasp-knife, which he had taken the precaution of whetting upon a hone.

It was strange with what systematic precision—with what cool collectedness of manner the student made these preparations. Only once did his hand tremble, and that was—when he placed the clasp-knife in the bag.

One minute to the hour, and the student's feet were on the stairs; he descended them cautiously, passed through the stone passage, drew back the bolts of the old creaking door, and stood in the court-yard without. As the cool evening air met his cheek, he heard the clock strike the first stroke of the hour of ten.

The clock had finished striking. Gervase Morden heard the unclosing of a casement. The whistle was given; he looked up; a rope was slowly let fall from the open window; a dark body dangled against the wall; and in a few seconds the brothers stood together in the court-yard.

"Quick, Ernest! I have a key which will open this small gate. We will lock it after us; and then make our way to the wood."

Through the dark wood the brothers went; and not a word did the stern student speak —not one word of congratulation, hope, or consolement. Once or twice Ernest called upon his brother by name, but his call remained unanswered; it was not noticed even by a look. And Ernest wondered why his brother was so silent, and why he accompanied him so moodily ; for drear and noiseless, and full of gloom was the old forest—so full indeed of sombre gloom that Ernest trembled, and his heart misgave him, as he saw the dark form which he believed to be his brother gliding so phantom-like by his side.

Through the wood, and out upon the open upland. It was a dark night; there was no moon-rays, and a dense, heavy mist was seen loitering over the deep dells, and spreading itself out like a shroud over the dusky sea.

"Gervase, whither are you going?" asked Ernest, placing his hand upon his brother's arm.

" On !" was the only reply.

They were nearing the cliffs. There were paths which led down to the beach but the student did not go towards them ; there was a high cliff, the upper part of which overhung its base, and it was toward the topmost verge of that the fugitive accompanied his brother, wondering at the strangeness of their way.

" Where are you leading me, brother Gervase ? Why not turn down towards the beach ?"

"On !" was the word of answer.

" Why go up to the edge of this rock, Gervase, my brother ?"

" On," was the reply.

And now the stern student and the erring fugitive stood upon the verge of the precipice ; before them was the swelling ocean—below them was the craggy shingled beach. Yet nothing of that beach could they see ; for the creeping, crawling mist was down there among the shingies, writhing about them like some huge monster that had floated up from the deep, entwining its damp arms around the points of broken rock, and resting upon them, as upon an uncouth couch of its o n choosing, whereon it best liked to linger and lie.

" Again I ask you, brother, why have you brought me here ?"

"Hark you, Ernest!" answered the student, in a husky, hollow voice ; "I told you there would be danger in your escape—that danger you behold. To have descended to the beach by the ordinary way would have been still more dangerous ; for the revenue-officers keep watch there, and it would not be easy to elude their vigilance. This way is open to you. In this bag I have the means by which you may descend to the beach, at a point where no eyes are watching. You must be bold, Ernest Morden ; it is no time to play the coward now."

" I am no coward, brother. Tell me what you will have me to dare."

" The means of your further escape are on the beach below. Look over, Ernest Morden. It is far from where you now stand to that mist-hidden beach. Will you dare to reach it by the means of a rope?"

" Who will hold the rope, brother ?"

" Myself."

" Give it me, let me see its length."

And as the student stooped to draw the rope out of the bag in which he had brought it, a dark shape that had hitherto stood upright at some distance behind him, threw itself upon the earth, and glided upwards towards the cliff's edge. That dark shape had followed the brothers through the wood ; it had been near them in the gloomy silence there ; it had crept behind them as they journeyed over the open upland ; it had played shadow to them as they ascended the cliff-top ; it was near them now—now as the stern brother took the rope from the bag, and placed the clasped-knife on the ground beside him.

" Why is this hook here ?" asked Ernest, as he examined the rope.

"It has its use," replied the student.

"And is there a boat in waiting for me below, brother ?" asked Ernest.

" All is ready for you there," replied the same husky voice which Ernest Morden had heard speak before, and wondered at the strangeness of its tone.

"I am ready, brother. Let me press your hand, let me pray you to pardon me for the errors of which I have been guilty, and express a hope that you will not contiue to think worse of me than I really am. You have thought harshly of me, dear Gervase—very harshly; I forgive you. Why do you refuse me your hand?"

"Take it, Ernest, if you wish it."

"Wish it, brother! Why, who but God can tell whether this may not be the last time of my so doing."

"It may," answered the student.

"So strange your voice! Brother, why do you speak so coldly?"

"Quick!—quick and take the rope! The time hastens."

Gervase Morden gave the end of the rope to his brother and assisted him in fastening it around his waist. Ernest again pressed his brother's hand, advanced to the verge of the cliff, glanced downwards at the misty beach below, crept over the brink of the precipice, and clung for a moment to its sharp edge.

"Brother; how strangely your eyes seem to glisten to-night!" ejaculated poor Ernest.

"Hold by the rope, Ernest Morden—the rope!" returned the student.

And over—over in the misty air, and down—down towards the dusky beach, dangled and descended the fugitive. Above crouched the elder brother, grasping the rope in his hand, and slowly letting it out, inch by inch, and foot by foot. Behind, undefined in the darkness, lay outstretched upon the ground, the shadow which had followed the brothers. High, high above the beetling precipice— higher than the hidden stars, watched the God—the God alike of the stern man and of the erring fugitive.

Slower and slower did the student let out the rope; more and more did his dark eyes glisten as the black moving line passed over the precipice. Another foot, another inch, and he struck the grappling hook in the earth, and felt that it took hold in the rock.

"Brother!" cried a voice from the depth below, "why do you not let out the rope?"

The student—his dark eyes glistening yet more strangely—advanced to the end of the cliff, and bent over, so that he might see the dangling man.

"Ernest," he said, speaking in a deep though faltering voice, "I have a few words to say to you. Can you hear me?"

"Speak louder, dear brother. The dashing of the waves upon the shingles almost drowns your words."

"Pray to your God, Ernest Morden," continued the student. "I have this night promised to save you from the gibbet, and I will do it. I will do it to save the name of my father from disgrace. You have brought disgrace enough upon it already; you have played traitor to your country; you have treated with base- ness a poor girl who trusted in your love; you have uttered falsehoods innume- rable; you have done deeds of utmost villany. You, Ernest Morden, are the murderer of Sir Thomas Warrenton—deny it not; for falsehoods will not serve you now! Why I brought you to this place you wished to know. I have brought you, Ernest, to the place of expiation—the place where your life must pay the forfeit of your crimes, where your death must shield you from further disgrace. Ernest Morden, your brother is your executioner! no other hangman shall you have. Do you hear me, Ernest? Do you understand me?"

"Draw me up, brother. My arm is weak with my wound, and I cannot climb the rope. Draw me up, and let me answer your words."

"Answer them where you are."

"Brother, I am no traitor; I have betrayed no trust!"

"Go on."

"I have not wronged Amy Heyton. I could not marry her; I could not, did I love her still."

"Why?"

"Brother, you know not; our father never told the secret to you. I dare not marry her who bears that mark."

"Tush! Go to the murder, man—what of the murder?"

"Murder! dear Gervase! You do not think your brother to be a murderer?"

"Answer, man! Say you that you are neither villain, traitor, nor murderer?"

"Neither, dear Gervase, neither."

"Liar!" exclaimed the student, as he laid the open knife across that part of the rope which rested on the rocky edge of the precipice.

"Brother, do not keep me here; my arm is weak. Let out the rope."

"Hear me for the last time, Ernest Morden," said the student, while his dark eyes glistened more fearfully than ever. "Once before, on an occasion which you well remember—your brother told you, that if you disgraced the name he bore, he himself would be your murderer. You have disgraced that name. I am the brother who gave you that caution. To make your crimes secrets for ever—to prevent your disgracing any further the name I bear, I have taken this step. Pray, Ernest! Ask your God for pardon. I have cut the strands of the rope, all but one—that one is chafing against the rock's edge. Struggle not, the strand is straining—is becoming weaker. Farewell, brother! farewell for ever!"

"Gervase, dear Gervase!"

The student heeded not the call, but rushed down the steep, and sought the distant wood.

Then it was, that the shape which had crouched behind in the gloom glided forwards—forwards to the very edge of the cliff.

And one strand, one strand of feeble hemp was all that intervened between Ernest Morden and death.

One strand to hold a life!

CHAPTER LII.

A SHORT CHAPTER, WHICH TELLS OF MANY CHANGES.

WHEN the coach stopped at the gate of Warrenton Hall, a servant went to the apartment of Gervase Morden to apprise him of the circumstance, and to ask him if his brother was in readiness. The student was seated beside the window. He arose and accompanied the domestic. As they passed along the gallery, a soft, trembling hand was laid upon the student's arm.

"The promise, Mr. Morden!"

"It is kept, Miss Ismay.

The party proceeded towards the room in which Ernest Morden had been imprisoned. A soldier was guarding the door, and many of the domestics attached to the hall had gathered around to witness the removal of the prisoner. No prisoner, however, was found. There was the empty room, there the open window, there the letter on the table. It was plain that Ernest Morden had made his escape; but no one hinted a suspicion that in that escape he had been assisted by his brother.

There was a fruitless search; and after Gervase Morden had duly performed his part in the mockery, he again sought his own chamber. As he was about to enter it, a light form glided to his side, and the fair arms of Constance Ismay embraced his neck.

"Dear—dear Gervase!" ejaculated the gladdened girl, "oh, how I thank you for this kindness. You have saved your poor brother; and your own good heart will recompense you for the noble deed on many a future day. Never will you regret what you have this night done, never—never."

The student took the maiden's hand, and looking with his dark moody eyes upon her countenance, said, huskily,—

"Go, Constance—go pray to Heaven that it pardon me for the deeds of this night."

"Heaven wants no such prayer, dear Gervase."

"I do, girl. Go—go and pray!"

Fair Constance was about to seek her chamber, but ere she did so, she turned back, and again placing her soft hand upon the student's arm, said—

"Tell me, dear Gervase—Is Ernest, is your brother in safety?"

"Yes," was the reply, uttered in so hollow a voice that it seemed spoken by some unearthly form.

On the following 'day the coroner held his inquest upon the body of Sir Thomas Warrenton. Many conjectures were hazarded as to the cause of the old knight's death, but the mass of evidence went to prove that he had destroyed himself by his own hand. Lambert Warrenton called Mr. Chartrey, his legal adviser, aside, and asked him why he appeared to take such pains to rebut the evidence, and assert his opinion that Sir Thomas had been murdered,

"Do you not know the law of the land?" returned Mr. Chartrey. "Let a verdict of *felo de se* be returned, and all the goods and chattels of your father are forfeit to the king; his body also would be buried with disgrace."

"And cannot this be helped?" asked Lambert Warrenton, turning pale as he spoke.

"We must wait and see."

It was strange that without any previous manifestations of dejectedness, or mental anguish—that without any apparent assignable cause—that without leaving a single written line in explanation of the deed, Sir Thomas Warrenton should have lifted his hand against his own life. So thought the jury; and yet, to them, the evidence appeared conclusive, and fully sufficient to warrant them in returning a verdict of suicide. That verdict was accordingly returned; and the coroner gave orders that the body of Sir Thomas Warrenton, of Warrenton Hall, should have a stake driven through it, and, according to custom, be buried in the nearest cross-road at the hour of midnight.

"Sandy," said Glib Griffiths, whispering in the tombcutter's ear, "you've lost a good job this time. I did think, man, you'd have to carve a new tablet for the old church, seeing as how the family stone is pretty well covered over with black letters."

"Humph!" returned the tombcutter. "See you! this is the pistol with which they say Sir Thomas shot himself. I rub my little finger round the inside of the barrel, and see! it comes out as clean as it was before. What does that mean?"

Glib Griffiths could not answer him. They walked away together, and as they passed down the staircase, they met a domestic hastening to her ladyship's apartment with Dr. Cosgreave following close behind.

Sir Lambert Warrington seemed to dislike the old hall after his father' death; and spent the most of his time in London. Eugene Dourville continued to be his friend, and was constantly to be found in his company. As for Gervase Morden, the whole affairs of the estate were entrusted to his management and care; while the fair girl whom he loved remained a dweller in the same house with him, apartments having been allowed to her use and that of the Lady Isabel.

Ernest Morden having disappeared, Captain Charnock, and those under whose directions he acted, thought fit to drop all further proceedings with regard to the despatches. Amy Heyton was therefore at liberty; though the imputation still remained as a stain upon her character. The death of Sir Thomas visibly affected Mr. Heyton, and caused him, as it seemed, to behave with more tenderness to poor Amy than he had even hitherto done. Frank was strictly prohibited by his father from saying a reproachful word to his younger sister; while blooming Kate manifested all the kindness which formed the very ground-work of her nature, in soothing pale Amy's anguish and in picturing to her happy days which were yet to come—happy days of serenity, peace, and joy.

Perhaps the happiest of the party inhabiting that sea-side cottage was now Archy, the idiot boy.

Our story hastens to its *denouement*; and twelve months pass away and are forgotten, before the events related in the next chapter occur. Twelve months! and during those twelve months strange changes are being wrought—strange circumstances are evolving in mysterious succession; as if under the sway of some supernatural hand, and as if obeying some imperative law. Crime is hastening to tell of its own criminality; the wicked are working out their own overthrow; the hidden things that were drowned in secrecy are one by one floating up, and rising to the light. So the twelve months pass away; while love continues to illuminate the dreary earth, and madness stalks onward through the maddened world!

CHAPTER LIII.

THE FESTIVAL AT GILLCROSS.—THE DARK STRANGER AND THE IDIOT BOY.

IT was festival day in the pretty village o fGillcross, and brightly shone the sun upon the merry villagers, as they tripped to and fro on the green sward, joined hands in the mirthful dance, and with unr strained gestures of glee expressed the happiness they felt in thinking of the p nteous harvest which they had just gathered in, and the many preparations they had made to meet the coming winter, whenever it should arrive with its storms and frosts, its snow and hail and icicles. Laughing, buxom girls, whose joyousness of heart was told by their sparkling eyes ; gay and gallant swains, whose joviality caused the welkin to ring with the the shouts of rollicking mirth ; old men and grandames who had come out to see the sports which reminded them of their own youthful years, all dressed in their best attire, and adorned with their humble finery, were there to enjoy the holi-day, and take what part they cold in the general revel. Gillcross had never shown a better collection of smiling faces, nor had so many happy hearts even before met together on the village green. Glib Griffiths told neighbour Seymore that the number of people was greater than had ever been known at " Bartlemy Fair;" and that as to show and splendour, the dresses beat anything and everything that could be seen in St. James's Park. But Glib Griffiths was never very accurate in his statements ; and in the present instance he was fairly led away by his enthusiasm.

Still, it was a grand *fete* indeed for Gillcross, and every one was right in saying so. The sun was so bright, the air was so balmy, the trees were so green, the people were so merry. Talk about ribbons ! why, the whole town of Darlingham had been rifled to furnish the requisite supply. The girls had ribbons round their waists, and ribbons about their bonnets ;—of course we know how they came to get them. The lads had ribbons round their knees, ribbons round their hats, and bows of ribbon fastened to their jackets ;—of course we know who made them up the bows. Then the old people had new ribbons to their caps ; and the very dogs that were gambolling about the green had pieces of red ribbon round their necks. Then there were ribbons tied to poles, and ribbons fastened to ale-barrels, and rib-bons flaunting everywhere in the air whenever there was a breath of wind to stir them. From what mysterious place all the fine dresses had come, and where and when and how they had been made up, was a puzzle to some old heads that ought to have been wiser. Such troops of merry faces, such varieties of gay costumes, such barrels of beer, such baskets of cakes, such buckets of new milk, such bunches of fresh flowers, were never before seen by any Jack of Jill among the company ; and it followed that the unanimous belief of the villagers was, that the whole was a very glorious affair, and one which ought never to pass out of remembrance and be forgotten.

Well, it was a glorious affair—there was no doubt about that. Then, as to its ever being forgotten, there were many grounds on which to doubt that it ever would be. For there were very many kisses given, and those who gave them were not likely to forget the taste of the sweet lips which had come in contact with their own ; then there were very many kisses taken, and those who took them—slyboots that they were—remembered pretty accurately from whom they received them. Of course, as there was dancing, many pretty waists got squeezed, and it isn't to be supposed that the waists were so dull and stupid as to forget who were the squeezers. Many little presents were made, and the givers of them were not for-gotten ; many soft hands were pressed, and the owners of them were not troubled with bad memories. Some ears had tender vows whispered in them which they could not possibly forget ; some listened to delicate proposals that they determined to think about and remember. It need scarcely be told that events did occur which the parties concerned wished to forget, but never could ; and, then again, other

occurrences took place, which produced results that ever after kept them in remembrance. Thus, there were causes sufficient to dispel all doubts about the festival
being forgotten, arising out of the festival itself; but, besides these, there occurred
one other event which was of such a character, the recollection of it could not
easily pass from the memory of those who were witnesses to its occurrence. What
that event was, the present chapter will show.

Evening was approaching; the last rays of the setting sun were painting in gold
and crimson tints the cloud-land of the west, and a light breeze which had just
sprung up invigorated those who had become fatigued through the merriment which
they had carried on during the heat of the day. The game of "kiss-in-the-ring"
was now proposed by one of the villagers, and the proposition meeting with general
approbation, the sport was at once commenced in right earnest. Hardly had the
parties arranged themselves in the proper order, before the eyes of each individual
were directed towards a dark figure that had taken up its position against the trunk
of an old beech tree which flourished on the green. The figure was that of a man
enveloped in a large coarse cloak. His hat was drawn down over his forehead, and
his head was bent forward so as to conceal his countenance from view. None
knew who he was nor whence he came, for none had marked his coming.
There was nothing in his appearance to attract general attention, except the contrast afforded by his attire when compared with that of the gay group near which
he stood, and the fact of his being a stranger, concerning whom no one could
give his neighbour any information.

Merrily the game proceeded, and right hearty was the spirit in which it was
kept up. When, however, a challenged maiden took her flight from the ring, she
especially avoided passing near the tree where stood the silent stranger, and when
her captor gallantly brought her back to claim his reward, he obeyed the maiden's
request, and took care not to lead her under the shadow of the beechen boughs.
After the sport had been indulged in for a full hour, the ring was broken up, and
the various lads and lasses who had composed it separated themselves into groups,
some pacing the green arm-in-arm, and others collected together in little knots
upon the ground, or on the surrounding benches, to rest themselves, and get rid of
their weariness, previous to the commencement of the dancing which was to
terminate the amusements of the day.

One of these knots was composed of three young girls, and a sprucely-attired
rustic to whose care they had been committed by their parents. As the maidens
were very pretty, and by no means bad-tempered, their company had been courted
during the day by more than one or two of the gallant swains who had participated
with them in their sports. Unfortunately, however, the youth who had been
entrusted with their safe keeping, feeling rather proud of his charge, and being in
love with the whole three, took upon himself to show his greediness by quarrelling
with every other amorously-disposed lad who ventured to offer his services to any
one of the maidens. Whether they liked to be so chivalrously protected is a matter
of doubt. But their guardian had contrived to isolate them from the rest of their
admirers, and secure their company to himself by leading them to a retired part of
the green, where, remote from the laughing, chattering throng, he could discourse
with them at his pleasure, and say all the score of pretty things which he had laid
in store for that express purpose some weeks previous. The maidens, however,
had grown tired of their prosy friend, and were chatting amongst themselves upon
a subject which at that very time was furnishing a theme for discourse to some
twenty or thirty other pretty mouths besides their own.

"I'm sure, Margaret," said the youngest of the three, "I shall be afraid to go
near that old beech tree again, for I don't know how long. You may think, and
you may say, that he is a man, but if you had seen what I saw, when I ran past
him as Hugh Grantham was running after me, you would think and say different."

"Goodness gracious, Alce!" ejaculated the eldest maiden, "why, what do you
mean—what did you see?"

" Oh, don't tell—don't tell it here !" interposed the third beauty. "We are so lonely ; and I shall be so frightened."

Hearing this, the gallant rustic who was the guardian and lover of all the three damsels, looked up staringly in the face of the last speaker, and said,—

" You beant lonesome, be you, Miss Betsy ?"

" Yes, I am, Mr. Roger ; and so is Margaret, and so is AliceIt makes us feel so to sit here alone. I think we'd better go over to the tent."

" He ! he ! he !" returned the gallant guardian. "Why, you must be silly ones ! Only to think of your saying the place be lonesome. Beant I here, and beant I a man ?"

The beauties returned no answer to this tender inquiry, but the eldest renewed her entreaty for Alice to tell her what it was she saw when passing the dark stranger, as he stood against the trunk of the old beech.

" Oh, such eyes !" answered Alice, with a shrug.

" Eyes !" echoed Betsy, with a shudder.

" Yes, such eyes—so dark, so hollow, so terrible, and death-like, that I shall dream of them for many nights to come."

" And his face, Alice—did you see his face ?"

" Only a part of it. But as to what it was like, I'm sure I can't say. It didn't at all look as if it were the face of a Christian ; for the skin was of such a pale blue colour, and the eyebrows such dark, black, bushy ones, that I declare it put me in mind of the naughty man's picture in granny's old Bible. I'm not certain that I saw fire coming out of his mouth, but——"

" Patience me, Alice !" ejaculated Betsy, "how cold you make one's blood feel ! I'm really afraid to open my eyes, or move my fingers."

" Suppose, Betsy," suggested Margaret, "that when we are standing up for the dance, this horrible, I-don't-know-what-to-call-him should come and ask one of us to be his partner ?"

" Oh, good Heavens, Margaret !" shrieked Betsy, " how can you think of such a thing ? I should drop down dead on the green, I'm quite sure. I shall be afraid to dance this evening, that I shall !"

" Doant you think, Miss Betsy," asked the gallant guardian, "we'd better get up and go away home ? You be fearsome—beant you ?

" Go home, Mr. Roger !" returned Margaret. "What, before the sports are half over, and without waiting to see Sir Lambert Warrenton, who promised he'd come down from the hall, and be present at the merry-making ?"

" I'm sure I shall stay," declared Alice, "if it's only to see whether Sir Lambert brings Miss Amy Heyton with him. Everybody says he will."

" And quite proper that he should," observed Margaret. "Isn't it well known that he is going to make Amy Heyton his wife ? I'm sure she ought to think herself very fortunate, and be very proud, too.—I should if I were in her place."

" So should I, Margaret. Only to think of being made a lady—to be called ' My lady !' Oh dear me ! my poor head would be quite turned. And yet they say Amy Heyton is not proud about it at all, and she don't hold her head up a bit the higher, and she hasn't put on any fine-lady airs, and she's just the same good-natured thing that she ever was. I always liked her ; but I should have envied her good fortune, and hated her a little, I think, if she had become proud and stuck-up because of her being made my Lady Warrenton, and going to live at the hall."

" You mustn't judge in a hurry, Alice. Now what I think of Amy is, seeing she's been deceived once, she's very cautious, and won't say too much till the wedding is over, and she finds herself Lady Warrenton. Stay till that is all over and done with, and see how high she will hold her head up then."

" She'll have no occasion to, I'm sure," remarked Betsy ; "I wonder how Sir Lambert can think of marrying her when he remembers how wickedly she behaved to poor Mr. Morden in stealing his papers and bringing all his trouble upon him, till at last he had to make his escape in the best way he could, and is either dead, or will never be heard of again. Mr. Gervase, at the hall, declares that his poor brother killed himself by falling off the cliffs, and certainly there was the rope to be seen by which he tried to get down, and there was some blood on the shingles beneath, but the tide had been high in the night and might have washed away the body. Well, how Sir Lambert can think of marrying that girl, or how Amy Heyton can forget her own wickedness and dare to be so bold as she is, astonishes me; one twelvemonth after his father's death Sir Lambert is about to have a wedding at the hall, and he hasn't been able to find a better person to make 'my lady' than Amy Heyton. Welladay! I wish I had the cunning to catch such a husband, but Sir Lambert will find his mistake before long; such marriages never turn out happy ones—never."

"I don't know why they shouldn't, Betsy," observed Alice, "but as to what you say about Amy, I think you have not judged quite rightly: the poor girl does not seem so happy nor so proud as she ought be, especially as the wedding is so soon to take place."

"How soon?" asked a hollow voice behind the last speaker.

The maidens looked up, and beheld the dark stranger whom they had seen beneath the beech tree. A simultaneous shriek escaped from the lips of each, and too terrified to take to flight, they bent down their heads and buried their faces in their hands.

"May be, sir, you wouldn't mind my asking you to go a little way off the lasses," said the gallant Roger, after a short pause; "they be fearsome sort of girls, and I shouldn't like to see them come to any harm, because they be sweethearts of mine."

"Well, I'm sure, Mr. Roger! What impudence!" exclaimed Margaret. "It's a very great story of yours, to say that we care for you; and I'm certain that I'm not afraid of the—the—the gentleman."

"You have no reason to be, Margaret Morland," returned the unknown. "So fair a face as yours should ever protect you from injury."

Feeling the full force of the compliment, wondering how the dark stranger had become acquainted with her name, and beginning to think that she was not amongst such bad company as she had at first supposed herself to be, the maiden took courage, and looking up, said,—

"Were you asking, sir, about the weddings that are to be at the hall?"

"Yes," replied the unknown; "say you that Sir Lambert Warrenton is about to marry Amy Heyton?"

"He is, sir, and on the same day Mr. Gervase Morden, who also lives at the hall, is to be married to Miss Ismay, Sir Lambert's cousin, I believe."

"When, say you, the weddings are to be?"

"In two days from this time, sir, they are to take place in Darlingham church."

"So soon!" ejaculated the stranger; "and has Amy Heyton really consented to this match?"

"Oh yes, sir! she is to be Lady Warrenton, and go and live at the great hall. Lady Lambert Warrenton, or Lady Amy Warrenton, I suppose she will be called, because the real Lady Warrenton—Sir Thomas's widow, I mean, is living there still."

The stranger buried his face in the folds of his cloak and mused for a few seconds.

"Say you the wedding is to be in Darlingham church?" asked he. "Have the banns been published there?"

"Every Sunday, sir, for the last three weeks."

"And has no one forbidden them—no one stood up and said the marriage should not be?"

"Oh, sir! nobody would be so wicked. What! forbid Sir Lambert's marriage?"

"Ay; has no one done so?"

"Mercy me, Mr. Roger! Do you hear what the gentleman says? I—but here, sir, comes Sir Lambert and Miss Amy. That is Miss Amy Heyton, sir, who is holding Sir Lambert's right arm; and the lady on the other side is Miss Kate Heyton. Miss Kate, sir, doesn't seem to like her sister marrying Sir Lambert, but that is of course a little jealousy on her part, Miss Kate being the elder sister, sir. The gentleman and lady walking behind Sir Lambert are Mr. Morden and Miss Ismay, sir. And there too is Lady Warrenton, dressed in mourning still. The gentleman she is walking with is Mr. Dourville, the foreigner, sir, who is often staying at the hall."

So chatty had the maiden become that she had failed to observe how little attention had been paid to her words by the stranger to whom they were addressed. Silent and motionless, he stood with his eyes directed towards the gay party that had just arrived upon the green. His gaze followed Sir Lambert and his fair companions whithersoever they wandered. One by one the timid girls, amongst whom he had intruded, rose up, and tripped stealthily away. The villagers had all gathered around the young owner of Warrenton hall; the shades of evening had descended, and the stranger found himself unnoticed and alone.

"So soon—a wedding so soon !" he ejaculated, as he clasped his hands to his pale forehead. "She has consented to wed him, has she ? She gives her hand to be the mistress of that titled villain, when she would not have given it to be the wife of —— No matter! How well she remembers her vow in the tomb cutter's cottage! How well she bears in mind the solemn pledge she gave there ! But she shall suffer for her cursed ambition; she shall meet a worse shame than she has met yet ! And for him also there is a doom preparing of which he but little dreams. It will come, however—it will come! To the church—to the bridal let them go, and they shall find one to meet them there !"

Just then, a slim delicate figure glided to the spot where the dark stranger stood, and placed its hand upon his arm.

"You have come, Archy," said the stranger, recognising in the figure by his side the form of the poor idiot boy.

"Archy is here," was the response.

"It is well," rejoined the stranger. "I waited for you beneath yon beech for a full hour, and I have sought you on the green since then. Let us walk over to the shade of those high trees, and we will talk together."

The stranger took the hand of the idiot boy, and led him towards the secluded spot which he had pointed out. Arrived there, the two entered into conversation; and the subject upon which they conversed, was the marriage of Amy Heyton with Sir Lambert, of Warrenton Hall.

"You promised Archy," said the idiot, addressing his companion, "Sissy Amy should not go away from home ; and now she is going to the great wedding."

"She will go, boy, but she shall return again. She will not leave you and live at the large hall, but will come back to the cottage, and stay at home."

"And she'll never go away in the big ship with Mr. Morden, will she ?"

"Never, boy. But why, Archy, do you ask these questions ? You have never told me why you wish Miss Amy to stay with you, and yet you seem to wish it very much."

The idiot boy was silent. He hung down his head, pressed his fingers to his eyes, and reclined motionless against the trunk of one of the large trees, under which the conference was held.

"Does not Archy wish Miss Amy to stay with him at the cottage ?" repeated the unknown.

"Sissy Amy must stay," replied the idiot, lifting up his head and grasping the hands of the stranger. "They think poor Archy cannot love Sissy Amy like Mr. Morden and Sir Lambert can; but Archy loves Sissy Amy more, and he will not let her go away."

"What does Archy mean when he says, ' love ?' " asked the stranger.

The idiot looked up at the face of the inquirer ; and made answer,—

"Archy would die if Sissy Amy wished him to, and Archy could kill any one who took away Sissy Amy."

"Right, boy," returned the stranger. "And have you told Miss Amy herself this pretty tale ?"

"Sissy Amy laughs at poor Archy," was the reply; "but Sissy Amy is kind, and Archy feels."

Fixing his ghastly eyes upon the countenance of the youth who stood before him, the unknown mused for some minutes upon the strange confession which he had just heard. Then, returning to the subject of the approaching marriage, he asked,—

"Does Miss Amy seem happy that she is about to go to the grand wedding with Sir Lambert of the Hall?"

"Archy has seen Sissy Amy crying, but Sissy Amy will not tell Archy why she cries," was the reply.

"Ha! boy! Cry, say you? Does she not seem happy, and glad, and merry-hearted? Does she not show her gay clothes, and her golden finery? She does, boy!—you are mistaken."

"Archy means what he says. Sissy Amy is not so merry as she used to be—not so merry as Archy would like her to be."

"And Kate Heyton—what of her, boy?"

"Sissy Kate tells Amy not to go to the great wedding. Archy likes Sissy Kate, now."

"And Kate's father, boy, and Frank—what of them?"

"Frank is wicked, he wants Sissy Amy to go and live at the great hall. But Frank's father will not let him tease Amy; and Frank's father will not promise Archy to keep Sissy Amy from going to the wedding."

"You have observed well, boy," said the stranger. "Now, hear me!—You want Miss Amy to stay at the cottage, and you tell me you are ready to do anything that will prevent her going away. I have work for you. Meet me at this same spot, just as the moon is rising, to-morrow night; and you shall help me in the work I have to do. Tell me, Archy, will you promise to be here?"

"Archy will promise anything to——"

"Hush! boy. My name must not be spoken till the night-time comes. None in this village must know yet who it was that came amongst them in their sports to-day. Be silent, Archy; meet me here as I have told you; and Amy shall never marry Sir Lambert, but stay at home, and be ever with you, as you wish she should be."

"For that, Archy will do all—anything!" ejaculated the idiot, joyfully. Then, creeping forward, he grasped nervously the stranger's arm, and in a whisper asked,—

"Will Archy have to kill?"

"What mean you, boy?—why ask such a question?"

"See!" returned the idiot, drawing out a glittering object from the folds of his dress. "They will not let Archy have a sword like Frank has, but Archy's knife is very sharp."

For a moment the stranger was startled, and regarded the idiot boy in silent amazement. "Fool!" he exclaimed, snatching the weapon from him, and flinging it to a distance. "So young, yet ripe for murder! Not for that I want you. The blood-work is for others to do."

"Archy will be here," said the idiot, as parting from the dark stranger, he loitered in the shade of the old trees till his late companion had left the spot, and then crept out upon the green sward to hunt for his lost weapon.

The bright steel glittered as the moonbeams fell upon it. It met the glance of the searcher; he picked it up, and restored it to the place where before it had been hidden.

"Archy may want this," said he. "Archy will never let any one else love Sissy Amy."

CHAPTER LIV.

THE WEDDING EVE.

ANOTHER day had passed, and on the following morning Sir Lambert Warrenton was to lead Amy Heyton to the alter. It was now night. The preparations for the bridal were going on in Warrenton Hall, and in the cottage of Stephen Heyton, where dwelt the fair maiden who was destined for the bride.

The scene is again that antique library in which Amy held her midnight meet'ng with Lambert Warrenton. Two of the actors who were present then are present now, for, seated by the same bay window, with the same pale moon beaming in upon them, are Sir Lambert himself and his friend, Eugene Dourville.

" Warrenton," said the Frenchman, raising a glass of wine to his lips, " I drink to your success. May the plot work well to its termination, an I to-morrow's sun change the clever bachelor into the fortunate bridegroom !"

Sir Lambert acknowledged the toast; and throwing himself back in his chair, indulged in a hearty laugh.

"To think," said he, "that the game should be won with so much ease; and the pretty bird fancy that her fine feathers have gained her a mate. Gad's me! Dourville, the little jade should seem prouder than she does at what she thinks to be her good fortune"

"Tush, Warrenton! I thought you understood the game better. The girl is proud enough at heart, I warrant you; but being somewhat sentimental, she wishes you to understand that she loves Lambert Warrenton and cares nothing about the owner of Warrenton Hall. A very noble sentiment, truly, and very honourable to the sex, who usually receive praise for their ingenuousness. My word for it, your loving bride, that is to be, would curl her lip at her old sweetheart, the lieutenant, were he to come back from the grave, where they say he is gone, and pay her a visit."

"I have thought otherwise," said Lambert Warrenton. "I have seen cause to doubt whether she forgets him so entirely, and whether no mouldering embers of the old passion still remain in her bosom."

"Done again, Warrenton! The girl is playing her cards well, and yet you cannot perceive the game. She wishes you to think she has a heart with which to love, and in order to convey that impression, induces you to believe it is with extreme difficulty she can obliterate the memory of an object on which her affections have been once fixed. My word again for it, she thinks as much about Lieutenant Morden, as she loves Sir Lambert Warrenton. She will marry you to be mistress of this mansion, and for nothing besides. Wisdom comes with experience. The girl has loved once, and having been cured of that nonsense, turns her attention to the more solid things of life, and very wisely preferred a title to anything that would be more sentimental, but more foolish."

"But afterwards, Dourville—after the wedding, when the revelation is made?"

"Why, she will have had more experience, and, as a matter of course, be wiser still. At present she only knows how to lay the snares—by this time to-morrow she will have learned how to be caught in them. The biter bit, my friend; a very common occurrence in every day life, yielding often, as in the present instance, an excess of amusement."

"Humph!" returned Sir Lambert, "as regards the girl, there is much probability in your guess-work. But how, Dourville, will the case stand with respect to old Heyton and this Mr. Netherby, who is a sharp hand, and with whom I shall have to transact all the more important affairs?"

"Trouble not yourself about them, my dear Warrenton. Both knew their duties too well to interfere with the present arrangements; and the ceremony over, the knot once tied, what matters how wide they open their eyes then?"

Sir Lambert mused for a few seconds. Then, springing up, and grasping the hand of his companion, he laughed heartily, though in a chuckling manner,—

"Gad's me! Dourville, the game does honour to its players. We have tricked them after all; to-morrow, we count our winnings!"

"Some would think it strange, if they heard Sir Lambert Warrenton talk of having achieved a victory in gaining for his bride no *belle* of better renown than she who is to be Lady Amy Warrenton on the coming morrow," remarked Dourville.

"They would," said the young baronet; "there are those under this roof who make a wonder of the matter at the present moment. The girl herself, Dourville, and those who are deeper in the secret, are doubtless wondering likewise. To-morrow then, for the explanation of the mystery! to-morrow for the triumph and the treasure!"

"Where are you going, Warrenton?" asked Dourville as Sir Lambert moved towards the door.

"Know you not that there are others who have their anticipations of the happiness which the morrow will yield? Excuse me, Dourville; I have an appointment to keep with Mr. Morden, who is here to speak with me concerning is marriage."

So saying, Sir Lambert passed out of the library, and descended the oaken staircase, entered an apartment in which he found Gervase Morden and Miss Ismay, who had been apprised of his coming, A conference ensued; in the course of which, Sir Lambert informed fair Constance that, as he had already intimated to her, she was entirely mistaken in supposing herself to be any relation to the late Sir Thomas Warrenton. Miss Ismay," said he, "I know not why my father chose to call you his neice. The inquires which I have made result in the few simple facts that you were adopted by an aunt as her child, and that at her death you were transferred as a ward to Sir Thomas. I have acquainted Mr. Morden with these discoveries, and he has in all probability talked with you n the snbject. I have heard that he wished such an event not to take place; but his motives for so wishing were probably only those which arose from a reluctance to part with one whom he always regarded with an excess of fondnes."

" And whom I will ever love as fondly in testimony of my gratitude, and still more fondly for her own intrinsic wort h,'ite rposed the student, as he pressed the soft hand of fair Constance, and looked upon her blushing face with eyes that were radiant with affection's eloquence.

"There is one more communication which I have to make," said Sir Lambert' "and which, under present circumstances, concerns you both. Some years prior to his death, Sir Thomas invested a certain sum of money in the purchase of an annuity for Miss Ismay. The first payment is to be made to her on her attaining her twenty-first year. Now, as that event happens in two days hence, the sum which will then be paid, must be considered by you, Mr. Morden, as the dowry of your bride, and, hoping that the reception of it will increase your mutual happiness, I wish you both the realisation of all the joy you have anticipated, and a bright sun to shine upon you on your wedding day."

The lovers thanked Sir Lambert for his compliment, and wished him a similar one in return. The baronet was about to leave the room, when he was detained by Constance, who politely inquired from whom she was to receive the annuity of which Sir Lambert had spoken.

" It will be paid to you by Mr. Netherby, rhe rich merchant of Darling-hane. He and Sir Thomas were intimate friends, and this arrangement was made many years previous to my father's melancholy death."

"Shall I see Mr. Netherby?" asked Constance, eagerly.

" He will be present at your bridal to-morrow."

The hour was late, and Constance Ismay received a summons from Lady Warrenton to attend upon her in her dressin-groom. As the lovers embraced each other, and parted for the night, Constance looked up into the dark eyes of the student, and in a musing manner said,—

" I wish, dear Gervase, we could see Mr. Netherby at once. I think, dearest, my uncle, Sir Thomas, I mean, must have confided to him the secret of my birth."

" Care not for that, sweetest," replied Gervase. " Whatever Mr. Netherby may know, he has not thought fit to contradict our marriage. Then, as to his affording the information which you refer to, it is, perhaps, as well that he has refrained from so doing, if, indeed, he have the power. Those dear eyes might beam less gently upon me, if their owner knew herself to be the daughter of some proud noble of the land."

" Gervase, you cannot think so," ejaculated the fair girl, as tears rose to her eyes, and she laid her head fondly upon the shoulder of her beloved. " I should still be the same poor Constance, who has ever loved you, and who loves you dearly now. But—" and the voice of the maiden became fainter, " it may be, dear Gervase, that I am the child of some parent who blushed to own her daughter, the child of a beggar or criminal."

" And if you are, my sweet Constance, why should the discovery give you cause to grieve? There is one, at least, who would—who will love you as he loves you now; one who would still prize the beggar's child as his choicest treasure, one who would forget the parents, criminality in idolizing the daughter's purity. Will not my sweet Constance believe that her Gervase loves her for her own inherent worth, and that the addition of fortune or of rank, would not, cannot enhance her value to him? Will she not believe that he, whose passion has been cherished so long, whose affection has been the growth of years, would lead her to the altar to-morrow with equal joy if he knew her to be an earl's daughter, or a foundling whom charity had rescued from death? Will not fair Constance believe that?"

"I will, I do believe it!" ejaculated the enraptured maiden, as she hid her face upon the student's bosom, and as he pressed his treasure to his joyous heart.

Leaving Warrenton Hall and its inmates, we now change the scene to the cottage of the Heytons. There also it is night; and there, in one apartment, seated side by side, and surrounded with all the finery and paraphernalia appertaining to a bridal, was Kate Heyton, holding the warm hand of her, who on the morrow was to become a bride. Tears were on the countenance of each, and Kate was looking imploringly into the blue eyes of her gentle sister.

"Amy—dearest Amy!" said she, "you are weeping on your wedding eve. Oh! why should this marriage be, when your own heart chides you for it, as I am sure it does?"

"No, Kate, you are mistaken, dear sister. I am not happy as I should be on such an occasion; but my heart does not accuse me of doing wrong. The promise which I made it is my duty to fulfil."

"Yes, Amy. But you have never told me the conditions under which you made that promise to Lambert Warrenton. Tell me now, dearest—tell me!"

Amy was silent for a few seconds; then casting her arms around her sister's neck, she ejaculated,—

"Oh! dear Kate, believe me—believe me when I made that promise, I deemed all things to be more possible than that I should ever be called upon for its fulfilment. The condition was one which your poor sister believed from her heart that time and circumstances would never produce."

"And the condition, sister Amy, was—what?"

"That Ernest, sister—Ernest Morden should reject the love of the poor girl whose whole happiness consisted in the love she bore to him; that he should reject, despise, contemn her; that he should curse her sister—that he should curse her!"

"He did so, Amy. But listen. I would speak to you of Ernest."

"Of Ernest, sister Kate! speak not of him now—not at this time. They say he is dead; and if such be the case, Amy Heyton has forgiven him, and would forget his name."

"But supposing he were not dead, sister; supposing he were still living, and had discovered that he was deceived in the accusation he made against you, and repented of the wrong he did you; and were desirous of soliciting your forgiveness; you would grant it him, Amy—would you not?"

"Grant it, sister! Why do you ask me these questions?"

"Because, Amy, I do not believe Ernest Morden to be dead; because I do believe he has discovered the falsity of those accusations, and is deeply repentant for all the wrong he wrought you. Sister, I ask you if you would not forgive him if he were now suing his pardon at your feet? You would, sister, I am sure you would. Nay, I think I am too well acquainted with the gentleness of sister Amy's heart to doubt that she would refuse him even her love."

"This from you, Catherine!" exclaimed Amy, rising from her seat and looking indignantly at her sister. "It is strange for you to use such words when speaking of a man whose truth and honesty you yourself so often doubted! Ernest Morden and Amy Heyton must never meet again. There is no love remaining for the man who could curse where he had once professed to love!"

"Sister Amy, make no promise which at some future day you may wish to break!" said Kate in a serious voice. Then after a short pause, she again looked in her sister's face, and said,—"Tell me Amy, when was it that you made this promise to Lambert Warrenton,—tell me, sister, the occasion on which it was made?"

"It was made sister, Kate, when I, believing in Ernest Morden's truth and love, conveyed what I thought to be the dispatches of his captain, to the only individual whose assistance I could solicit in saving Ernest Morden from dishonour and from punishment. Then it was I gave Sir Lambert Warrenton the promise which is binding on me now, and which on the morning of the morrow I am about to fulfil."

" Ha !" exclaimed Kate, a light seeming to break suddenly in upon her mind,— " you made this promise then !—you made it to him !"

" Why this astonishment, Kate ? Why does your countenance turn pale ?"

" Sister,—dear sister ! Answer me this question,—did he—did Sir Lambert Warrenton require you to give him such a promise, or was it of your own freewill ?"

" With my own free will, Sister Kate, but at his own request."

" Then listen to me, sister,—listen and think ! Sir Lambert is about to make you his bride ; Sir Lambert leads you to the altar on the morrow to wed you there. Twelve months ago dear Amy, Lambert Warrenton knew you to be betrothed to Ernest Morden. Then it was you went to him in Ernest Morden"s behalf ; then was he extorted from you this promise. Oh, Amy !—dearest Amy, if Lambert Warrenton loved you then, do you think he would have exerted himself to save the honour of his rival ? No, sister ! I have watched and I have thought, I have observed and I have reflected ; listen, Amy, while I declare to you that Lambert Warrenton was the cause of Ernest Morden's disgrace, that he it was who worked Ernest Morden's downfall ! You gave him your promise upon certain conditions, and he so worked that those conditions should be soon fulfilled. Sister, Ernest Morden was guiltless,—the criminal is Lambert Warrenton, whom you are now about to wed !"

" Kate—Sister Kate !" ejaculated Amy, in astonishment and indignation.

" I speak the truth, sister,—Lambeth Warrenton has deceived you—is deceiving you now !"

For a moment Amy Heyton stood still and statue-like. Her countenance was pale, her bosom elevated ; her eyes fixed glaringly upon her sister. " No, Kate—no," she stammered ; " not now—he cannot be deceiving now. I—I am to be his wife on the morrow ; and must not—will not hear such words spoken of him who is to be my husband ?"

" His wife, Sister Amy, and why his wife ? He loves you not, sister, your own heart tells you that he does not. Why, then, is it that he—that Sir Lambert Warrenton, whose station and title privilege him to choose his bride from amongst the court beauties of the land,—why does he descend to seek the hand of one so humble and so lowly as yourself ? Why, in order to win you, has he used such art, practised such deception, and displayed such baseness ? Why, not loving you himself, should he have wished to supplant Ernest Morden in your love, and why, not loving you now, sister—for Catharine Heyton would tell him to his face that love lives not within his dark breast—why does he exult in having gained your consent, and why has he exerted himself to hasten this union ? Oh, sister—dearest sister ! there is a mystery—a strange fearful mystery in this marriage ! You have not read the heart of him to whom you give your hand ; you have not learned the motives of that man whom you would marry to your misery. Marry him not—wed him not—go not to the altar with him ! Wait, sister, but for one ——"

" Girl ! do you dare to disobey me ?" exclaimed Mr. Heyton, in a voice of anger, as he entered the room, and hastily laid his hand upon the arm of his elder daughter. " You have been warned and commanded—have you forgotten ?"

" No, dear father ; but I cannot see my sister preparing for this wedding—I cannot part with her to-night without telling her how anxious I am for her happiness, and what fear I have that she will repent the bridal of the morrow. I ——"

" Silence !" commanded the parent ; and Kate Heyton accompanied her father into the next apartment. Mr. Heyton closed the door which communicated between the two rooms, so that Amy might not hear anything which he was about to say.

Kate looked up; she saw that there were tears in the eyes of her parent, and that his countenance was sorrowful—sorrowful even as her own.

" Dear father!" said she, in an imploring voice, "you fear—oh, I know you fear this wedding advantageous though it seems, bodes not well for poor Amy's happiness. My sister will wed Sir Lambert, to keep the promise she has made him —she will wed him because she has not been forbidden to do so by you. Here me, dear father! Do not let this marriage take place yet; say that it must not be; tell Sir Lambert that he must wait—that my sister cannot be his bride to-morrow morn; tell——"

" Cease, child! it is us less for you to make such requests. Amy has of her own free will chosen to become the wife of Sir Lambert Warrenton, and I have no power to prevent her from giving him her hand."

" No power!—father!—is she not your child?—Have we not both ever been obedient to your wishes, and think your Sister Amy would disobey you even in this?"

"I have no such thought, my child. Amy has never been undutiful even when my wishes have been opposed to her own."

" Then why not interpose now, dear father? You are not certain that Sir Lambert loves my sister; you doubt his love, his truth, his honour. Ay, father, I am sure you do! I have seen you regard him with suspicion, I have watched your eyes when they have been fixed upon him, and in them I could read distrust. I have marked the expression of your lips when Sir Lambert has been speaking, and I saw doubt seated there. Father, you are not happy, you grieve that this marriage should take place. You suspect that Sir Lambert has not love for his motive in seeking the hand of my sister, and yet you fear to declare your suspicions."

" No, Kate. All that I have thought I have communicated; every suspicion which I have had I have fulfilled my duty in mentioning."

" But to whom, dear father—to whom?"

" To Mr. Netherby."

" But why to him, father? Who is Mr. Netherby that you should tell to him that which you withhold from your child? Twelve months ago, dear father, Sir Thomas Warrenton possessed your confidence, and since his death it has been enjoyed by Mr. Netherby. I have seen you closeted together, father; I have heard you speak to him of Sister Amy; I have remarked that when looking sorrowful you have sought him—that when Sir Lambert has made any proposal concerning my sister you have immediately conferred with Mr. Netherby, and not with Amy—not with your child. Why has this been so, dear father? Why do you say that you have spoken to Mr. Netherby concerning my sister's marriage?"

" You will learn soon, Kate, my child."

" But how soon, father, and why not now?"

" To-morrow, child—to-morrow at the bridal—Mr. Netherby will be there."

" The bridal, father!" ejaculated Kate, in a faint voice. "And will you not forbid it—will you not say this night there shall be no bridal on the morrow?"

" Peace, child! Ask me not why I act as I do. I have told you before now that your sister's will in this matter must not be opposed; and I again tell you that I have no power to forbid this wedding."

" But why no power, father?"

" Silence! child. Be satisfied."

" No, father, I am not satisfied. Your words imply a mystery, and I have learned that such mystery exists. Whatever that mystery may be, it is bringing misery on Amy—it is bringing sorrow to yourself. It caused Ernest Morden once to lift up a knife against her whom he had loved; it induced Lambert Warrenton to extort the sad promise from Amy which she feels to be binding on her now; it will lead her to the altar to-morrow, and cause her to give her hand where I know she cannot bestow her heart. Father, there is a secret which you have not told your children—there is a mystery with which they are unacquainted."

Mr. Heyton took the hand of his daughter, and looking seriously in her face for a few moments, said in a grave voice,—

"There is a mystery, my child. Would that the secret had not been entrusted to my keeping!"

"Ha, father! you own it! What is it, dear father—tell me—tell me!"

"No, Kate, not to-night."

"When then, father—when—when?"

"To-morrow—to-morrow, at your sister's bridal."

"Not till then, dear father; but what if——"

Abruptly Kate Heyton ceased from speaking. Her father had taken his seat upon a chair near the wall. There was a small window behind him; and looking up, Kate saw outside that window a man dressed in sailor's clothes, who held up a sealed letter against the glass. Gently, and without making any noise, the maiden unclosed the casement, took the letter from the man's hand, and after speaking with him in a whisper, pressed her fingers against her heart as if to still its beating; then reclosed the window, and stole lightly towards the opposite side of the apartment.

All was silent. Kate glanced at her father, and saw that his head was bent down in a musing attitude, and that he was not observing her actions. So placing herself between him and the candle, she drew from her bosom the letter which she had just received, and, after assuring herself that her father was still deeply buried in thought, broke the seal with trembling fingers, unfolded the paper with much care, and for a moment suspended her breathing.

There were two letters within the same envelope. On the back of one was written the words:—"Carry this to Hilson so soon as you receive it. Two hours after midnight the Daredevil will be in the bay; and Red Martin will walk its deck for the last time." Kate replaced this letter in her bosom, and opened its companion.

Quick and deep became the breathing of the maiden as her eyes glanced over the written words. Those eyes lost their look of misery, parted with their tears, and beamed in joyful radiancy. The pallor gave place to the flush on the cheeks of the gentle reader. Eagerly did she peruse every line; carefully did she dwell upon every syllable. And when the whole was thrice read, and when the contents had been fully learned, and when blooming Kate was convinced that the letter was a real letter, and that the communication which it contained was truth, she pressed the paper to her heart with rapture, kissed it again and again, reopened it, glanced at this word and at that, folded it up with care, scanned once more the superscription with sparkling eyes, then, hiding it in her bosom, she rose from her seat, moved across the room with steps that were no longer timorous, but firm, and placing her hand upon her father's shoulder, and bidding him look up, and gazing at him when he did so, with a gaze that told of exultation and triumph, she said,—

"No bridal now, dear father—there will be no bridal on the morrow now."

"What mean you, my child?" asked the astonished parent.

"This, father. There are more mysteries than one. You have your secret, and I have mine. The morrow will disclose both."

"I do not understand your words, Catherine, my child," said Mr. Heyton. "The secret of which I have spoken cannot—must not be revealed by me till Amy stands to-morrow at the altar."

At that moment Amy, accompanied by the idiotboy, entered the room.

"You have hinted to me already, dear father, that you have something which you will confide to me on the morrow, and I have promised you to wait patiently till then," said Amy; "but will it not be told me here, father—will it not be told me before I go to the church!"

"It will be told you at the altar. child, and not till you stand there as a bride!"

Kate laid her hand upon her sister's arm.

"At the altar be it, Amy. There shall be one to meet you there."

In vain did poor Amy and Mr. Heyton endeavour to extract from Kate the meaning of these words. She had nothing further to communicate. Towards her stole the idiot-boy, and whispered in her ear,—

" Then Kate will promise Archy Sissy Amy is not to go and live at the great hall ?"

" She will not, Archy; Kate promises you she will not."

Midnight approached ; the sisters retired to their chamber, and when, fatigued with anxiety, Amy fell asleep, Kate arose from her feigned slumber, attired herself in silence, and placing the letter which she was to convey to Hillson in her bosom, stole out of the house, and took her way towards the seashore.

" Quick !" said she, as she gave the letter into the hands of the captain of the coast-guard—"quick ! The vessel will be in the bay in less than two hours, and he expects you there. The object is accomplished, and he has kept his promise."

Hillson knew the secret of who the individual was to whom Kate Heyton referred.

CHAPTER LV.

THE GUESSERS ON THE GRAVE-STONE, AND THAT WHICH WAS BEHIND THEM THERE.

THE time was the dusk of evening. Seated upon an old tombstone in the churchyard of the village was Sandy Sumners and his friend Glib Griffiths. Sandy wore a dispirited air, and Glib appeared less jovial than usual. The conversation in which they were engaged was concerning the death of Sir Thomas Warrenton— a subject, by-the-by, which had furnished Mr. Griffiths with ample matter for talk during the whole of the last winter.

" It was a sad affair, Sandy; there's no saying that it wasn't," observed Glib ; " though to be sure it looked like a sort of punishment upon him ; and punishments will come, Sandy, to gentlemen as well as to common people. Neither I nor one clergyman can explain the way in which it is done ; but it's awfully beautiful, Sandy, and awfully solemn. Do what hurt to anybody you may, you're sure to get paid back for it somehow or other. And that's how I say it was with old Sir Thomas."

" There's no denying the truth of some of the things you have said, Glib," returned Sandy ; " but I don't quite comprehend you, when you talk of Sir Thomas being punished, because I'm not clear as to what he ever did that deserved punishment."

" I'll tell you, Sandy. If you've forgotten it, I haven't; and I thought at the time old Sir Thomas would never come to a good end. I couldn't believe he ever would."

" But why, Mr. Griffiths ?"

" Mayhap, Sandy, you remember he ordered me to be put in the stocks once, for nothing more than making use of my rights and privileges, as a free-born Englishman, and according to what is laid down in a straightfor'ard manner in Magnay Carter. Now, if you can say that he didn't do hurt to an innocent man, why I'll say he didn't deserve to come to the dreadful end he did. I never wondered at it, for I expected it all along. Of course, it took a good many by surprise, and a good many wondered at it, but it was a sort of thing I looked for'ard to, the very day I sat in the stocks, in Darlingham market, and it was just the very thing that I knew would come about. I shouldn't wonder but that his heart was atwitching him for what he did in that little affair of mine, when he was a ramming down the powder into the pistol with which he shot himself."

" Then you think he did shoot himself, Mr. Griffiths?" observed Sandy inquiringly.

" Why, wasn't there the hole in his head, and the pistol lying at his feet, Mr. Summers? Didn't every one of us see the blood? And didn't I put some of it in a bottle and bring it home with me? To be sure, I did; and I've got it now among my curiosities, properly labelled, and properly dated. It's a curious fact

about what I'm now going to tell you, Mr. Summers, and it's what I haven't yet liked to say a word about to anybody. That blood, you know, was quite of a bright red when I first put it in the bottle ; and, of course, blood is red, there's nobody who'll dispute that. Well, the bottle was put away in my cupboard, and six month afterwards, when I went to take it out and look at it, I thought I should have fallen back upon the floor. I was never so astonished in all my life.

Mr. Summers, never, I may say it to a certainty. I've heard of mirrycles, and one knows mirrycles do happen at times; but I never had a mirrycle happen under my own roof before, never."

"But what is that which has happened, Mr. Griffiths?" asked the tombmaker.

"The blood, Sandy—that very blood I put in the bottle. It's changed its colour; and what colour do you think it is now?"

"Perhaps it would be better for you to tell me than for me to make a wrong guess, Glib. What colour is it?"

"The very colour of the old stocks in the market-place—a sort of blackish brown as one may say. The thought struck me when I took the bottle out of the cupboard, and the very next morning I got up early, went to Darlingham, took the bottle with me, and compared the two colours. There wasn't a shade of difference, Sandy—not a shade!"

"Then you are convinced, Mr. Griffiths, that Sir Thomas shot himself with his own hand, and so came by his death?"

"Convinced, Sandy! Why, body o' me, man! didn't I say so when I were on the jury! and didn't the cor'ner say he hadn't a doubt but what we'd given a very good judgment—our best, I think he said. There was the blood, Sandy—there the pistol. We gave our verdict to the cor'ner, and I saw with my own eyes the cor'ner write his own name to it; which was just as much as saying he approved of what we did, and would n't mind coming and asking one's opinions in any concern of his own at any time. And I don't suppose he would either; for, let me tell you, Mr. Summers, cor'ners are sensible men. They beant spoken about in Magney Carter; but the circumstance of his putting his name to our verdict was enough to convince any man about the cor'ner for our part of the county being a a real, practical, sensible sort of man. As to Sir Thomas shooting himself, which was committing suicide on himself, to speak lawyer-like, you known Sandy—why, there it was all plain enough; and the cor'ner ordered him to be buried in the cross-road; and we saw him, you know, with our own eyes buried by Gaveston turnpike, without any coffin, or any proper Christian sort of burial. That was enough to convince any one he did suicide on himself—wasn't it?"

"It's the opinion of Mr. Griffiths; but I can't say I'm in that way of thinking. It was a strange affair, and I've had my thoughts about it."

"Well, Sandy, man; and what have your thoughts been, if a body may know?"

"Just what I'm going to tell you, Mr. Griffiths. You see every Warrenton who has yet died in the hall, except Sir Thomas, has been buried here in our old church. There's Sir Ralph, and Sir Redmond, and the first Sir Thomas, and second Sir Ralph, and the last Sir Thomas's father, and grandfather, besides the Lady Warrentons, and the children, all lie together in the old vault under the communion table. There are monuments to them in the church, and there's a large tablet on the north wall which bears the names of the last four, but which is all filled up, and knowing Sir Thomas would want a stone to his memory when he died, I've always thought the job would be mine, and I as much as bespoke it of Sir Thomas himself. It isn't for you, Glib, to understand—seeing that you are only a barber and postman—the kind of feelings I've had about the making of that stone. I've always set it down for being the grand work of my life, and the only piece of chiseling which I should wish to see bearing my name just before I died. I meant to cut " S. SUMMERS," deeper on that stone than ever I did on any other before. Days and nights I've thought over that work; and many are the designs I've made for it. All my best ideas, Glib, and all the smoothest chiseling I ever did in my life, were to be carried out on that stone; there wasn't to be an edge but what was properly squared, and there wasn't to be a figure but what was to be carved like life itself. And, after all, Sandy—after all these thoughts and intentions, I saw Sir Thomas buried where he now lies, and, nothing put up to his memory in the old church, but his mere name and the day of when he died. I've thought about this, Mr. Griffiths, though it's not for you to comprehend what my thoughts have been like."

" But I can, Sandy, I can. I had a similar kind of feeling myself, when Will Blatchley came to live in the village, and was carried to his grave just one month afterwards. Will had the best head of hair I ever saw on mortal man ; and I used to think what a pleasure I should have in trimming it one day or other. But he died, Sandy, and I never had the job. That was much the same as your being cheated out of Sir Thomas's monyment. I can feel for you, Sandy ; the sorrows which have made their way into your heart took up their lodgings in mine just two years and three months ago—that was when Will Blatchley died. But I couldn't make poor Will come to life again, though, to be sure, I got more by his death than you did, Sandy, by Sir Thomas Warrenton doing suicide to himself."

" How so, Glib ? "

" Why, I wouldn't tell everybody, Sandy ; it wouldn't do, you see. But Will Blatchley, if you remember, had no wife, and lived along with his poor mother. When he died, she was too ill to follow him to his grave, and as I was a sort of friend of his, they asked me to be chief mourner. Of course, I couldn't refuse. So being chief mourner, I claimed a right to taking the last look at the body before the coffin-lid was screwed down. I had my scissors with me, and I couldn't help it ; that fine hea of hair you've seen among my curiosities, Sandy, was poor Will's, though I haven't put on any label to it as yet. Now, Sandy, as I've told you all I have to tell you on that head, perhaps you'll go on to state your opinions about how Sir Thomas died."

" You shall hear, Mr. Griffiths, if you'll pay attention. I've pondered and pondered about losing the making of that stone, until I've asked myself how it was that I came to lose it, and whether it was lost fairly. First I had one thought, and then another, but it was a long time before I could put two together, so as to make them fit. At last, Glib, as I was sitting upon this very stone on a Sunday night, and thinking of the sermon I had heard, all of a sudden-like the death of Sir Thomas came into my mind, and the different thoughts I'd had about it, all arranged themselves together in proper order ; and I saw what had puzzled me before all as plain as possible, though I couldn't make out the great secret which I can make out now."

" Well, Sandy ; but the thoughts—what did they amount to ? "

" To conviction, Mr. Griffiths ; to a certainty of that which I had only suspected before."

" And what is that, Sandy ? "

" Neither more nor less than that Sir Thomas Warrenton did not die by his own hands ; but was murdered—murdered in cold blood."

" Body o' me ! Mr. Summers. Murdered, do you say ? and—and you think so ? Well, I should like to talk to you about it, but not here—not where we are now."

" Why not, Mr. Griffiths ? "

" Because, Mr. Summers, I'm not timorsome, you see ; but a man like you, who has been cutting gravestones all his life mayn't fancy such things as another one does, when he finds himself in a churchyard at this hour of the night. We can't say for certain neither what there is under us in this old tomb, which we are sitting upon."

" Bones, and dust, and murdered men, who were thought to have died peaceably upon their beds, Mr. Griffiths. There may be such beneath us, as no doubt there are beneath half of the other stones of this ground. It's a thought of mine, Glib, that if all the people who are buried here could start up again to life just now, they'd tell strange tales, which they hadn't time to tell before they died."

" Hush ! Sandy. I thought I heard something moving behind us."

" And so there is, Mr. Griffith's ; there's the long grass that's waving to and fro, and talking to itself about the dead men ; but we don't mind it, Glib, we cannot understand what it's saying."

Glib Griffith's arose from his seat, and moved towards the pathway, leading from the churchyard.

"I'm not timorsome, Sandy," said he, "but I don't think it proper to talk about such things in a place like this. It's not showing respect to the dead, Sandy; it's not doing as we would wish to be done by, Mr. Summers."

"Sit down, Glib—sit down and listen," said the tombmaker, imperatively; "I've often thought of speaking to you about the way by which Sir Thomas came to his end, and there'll never be a better opportunity than the present, perhaps, for letting you know my thoughts upon the subject."

"Yes, yes, Sandy; its very kind of you. We'll—we'll go to the cottage, and talk about it there."

"The best place is where we now are, Glib; for Fan is at home in the cottage, and I shouldn't like Fan to hear what I have to say. Sit down, man, and be still. If you're not timorous, what are you fidgeting about so for, and looking this way and that?"

"No, Sandy; I'm not timorsome—I never was in my life. The very last time I met a ghost and shook hands with it, was when ——"

"If it was any time afore you learned to tell lies, Glib, I dare say it was longer ago than you can recollect. I was talking to you about Sir Thomas, and I was going to let you into a secret or two if you hadn't got frightened and wanted to run away."

"Run away, Mr. Summers! Did you say 'run away?' I'm afraid you've made a mistake, and don't understand my character, which isn't to be wondered at, as you hadn't an opportunity of seeing me when I was out in the 'Merikin war, and Lord Cornwallis finding there were two hundred rebels coming against him, and having none of his troops near by at the time, put a sword into my right hand and another larger one into my left hand, and asked me to go out and fight them."

"Did you go, Glib?"

"Go! Mr. Summers. What, do you think I hung back? No, no, Sandy, I'm not timorsome. So, just let me hear what you have to say about Sir Thomas, and how you think he died. But speak low; there's no occasion to talk in a loud voice in such a place as this."

"Listen then, Mr. Griffiths. When I heard about the death of Sir Thomas, I went up to the old hall at once. There were many people together in the room; there was the dead body in the chair, and the blood all in a stream upon the floors. Mr. Morden pointed to a small pistol, and said he had no doubt it was with that Sir Thomas had shot himself, and of course everybody else thought the same. I took up the pistol, and put my little finger down the barrel to feel if it was still warm. I pulled back the trigger too, and looked at the pan. At the time, Mr. Griffiths, I can't say that I had my thoughts completely about me; but since then I've remembered two things which I've thought about a great deal. In the first place, when I drew my finger out of the barrel, I can positively swear it came out as clean as it went in; and secondly, I have a clear recollection that when I looked at the pan, I saw the rust upon it of the same reddish-brown colour that rust always is. Now, it's not necessary for me to tell you, Mr. Griffiths, as you've been a bit of a soldier, that a fire arm can't be discharged without blackening the barrel and the pan. There was no black in the barrel or the pan of that pistol—I can swear to it there wasn't; and as that was the case, I come to the conclusion that the pistol had never been discharged—that Sir Thomas did not shoot himself with it—that it was placed on the floor to mislead those who saw it, by another person, and that the person who put it there was the murderer of Sir Thomas Warrenton."

"Body o' me! Sandy; but that's quite a lawyer-like sort of conclusion. You don't mean to say though, Sir Thomas wasn't shot in the head, because I'm clear upon that point myself, as I saw the hole, and placed my finger in it to feel out the way the bullet had gone."

"Ha !" exclaimed the tombcutter—"you did that, Mr. Griffiths—you placed your finger in the hole."

"I did, Mr. Summers."

"Which finger, man—can you tell me which finger ?"

"This one, Sandy—the one next the thumb. I never use the others for such jobs, they've all of 'em got a touch of the gout."

"That's proof, Mr. Griffiths—that's real proof !" ejaculated the tombmaker. "My fingers are smaller than yours. I could only get my little one into the barrel of the pistol, and you say you put your index one into the bullet-hole. Dosen't that show the bullet never came out of that barrel ?"

"It does, Sandy. And to think no one thought of looking to that at the time ! But, Sandy, if Sir Thomas didn't do suicide to himself with that pistol, as you say, how came the bullet-hole in his head ? I'm clear as to its having been a bullet-hole, though if you remember, Sandy, it couldn't be accounted for at the time why nobody in the house had heard the report of a gun, or anything of the kind." I

"That was the riddle, Mr. Griffiths; and now you understand what e wa puzzled at for so long a time. At last, however, as I sat on this grave stone one Sunday night—and as I told you before, a thought struck me of a sudden, which explains the riddle in a way which you'd never think of. I'll tell you what that thought was."

"Hist ! Sandy. I'm sure I heard something more behind us just then. Speak lower, and don't use more horrible words than you can help, Mr. Summers."

"The words are no worse than the subject, Griffiths, man. What I was going to observe to you was—You know Mr. Lambert Warrenton—Sir Lambert as he now is—was always fond of meddling in doctoring matters, and has a turn for chemistry, and other things of that kind, which are just like magic doings. Well, one day, a long time ago, he came into my workshop, and shewing me a kind of gun he had in his hand, told me he hadn't got a bullet-mould which would make a bullet to fit it, and asked me if I could cut a mould out of two pieces of stone. I promised him I would; and observed to him it was a queer-looking sort of a gun which he had in his hand. He told me it was an air-gun, which would discharge without any powder or flint. Of course I wished to see how a thing of that kind was done; and he squeezed some air into a round ball at the top of it, and rammed a marble into the barrel to show me the way. I had never seen anything so strange in my life. He sent the marble into the wood-work of my shop-door without the gun making any noise, or there being any smoke, or anything else that was like the discharge of a proper fire-arm. I made the bullet mould, and cast Mr. Lambert about two score of bullets. The whole circumstance had passed out of mind, till, as I say, I was sitting on this stone one Sunday night. You see, Glib, Sir Thomas was shot, and no one heard the report—how could that have been done without the murderer using an air-gun ?"

"I see, Sandy—I see. But you don't—you can't mean to say as how Sir Lambert shot his own father ?"

"I don't say so, Mr. Griffiths, and God forbid I should. But I'm pretty strong in the opinion that some one murdered Sir Thomas, and used an air-gun to do it with. I can't say whether it was the one Sir Lambert has got; but that's a point I should like to know."

"Then know it, Sampson Summers ! said a strange voice behind the tomb-maker. And the next moment a tall figure emerged from the shadow of the grave-stone, and confronting the mason and his friend, disclosed to their view the form of the dark stranger who had been present at the village festival on the preceding evening.

"Did you speak, sir ?" asked Sandy in a faultering voice, while Glib Griffiths crouched down and hid his face behind his friend's back.

"I spoke to you Sampson Summers," returned the unknown, "I am aware what the subject of your conversation has been, and I heard you say it was your wish to learn if Sir Thomas Warrenton was killed with the weapon which you know to be in possession of his son. To gain that knowledge is an easy matter, and I as well as you wish to be certain on the point."

" I—I can't say I'm over curious," replied Sandy, "and I don't think my friend Mr. Griffiths is."

' 'No, Sandy, I'm not, I don't care anything about it; I haven't got any wish to be kind," declared Glib, in a quivering voice.

"Hark ye both," resumed the stranger, seating himself on the stone as he spoke, " this matter is of interest to you. If it were proved that Sir Thomas was murdered, and did not kill himself by his own hands, you, Mr. Summers, would no doubt get the job which you have been disappointed in obtaining ; and you, Mr. Griffiths, would get your reward if you helped your friend in making the discovery. Now if you are both bold men, there will be no difficulty in settling the point at o nce.'

" My friend, Glib Griffiths, is a sort of man who is noted for his boldness," replied Sandy, "and as for myself, I must say that it's a subject about which I should like to know a little more than I do."

" Look you here then, Mr. Summers," said the stranger, as he held up a small object to the view of the tombmaker, " here is a bullet-mould which you made for Lambert Warrenton, and in the head of Sir Thomas, where he lies in a cross-road yonder, 'tis the bullet by which he died. If that bullet fitted this mould, what would you say then ?"

" And does it ?" asked the tombmaker, eagerly.

" That is left for you to discover," was the answer.

The stranger, Glib Griffiths, and Sandy Summers conversed together for some minutes. Then rising up to depart, the unknown said—

"In three hours hence, then, I shall be waiting for you by the finger-post. I have a lantern that will serve your purpose ; and you promise to provide a pickaxe, spades, and a saw ?"

" Yes," answered Sandy.

" Be ready, then, I will meet you there."

Leaving the stone-mason and his friend in the churchyard, the stranger departed, and took his way towards the chump of trees, under which he had held converse with the idiot boy on the preceding night. Scarcely had he reached their shadow, before a hand was laid upon his arm, and a voice said,—

" Archy is here."

"This is well of you, Archy. Now for the work which we have to do. Are you afraid to go with me, where there is likely to be danger?"

" Arch y is not afraid to go anywhere with you," was the reply.

" Then look you, Archy. In yonder hall is the bedchamber of the ma, who is to marry Amy on the morrow—Sir Lambert's bedchamber. You must go with me there, you must hide yourself with me in that room. We can enter by the secret passage from the old fort ; and when there, you will have to do as I bid you."

" But why must Archy go there ?"

The stranger drew a roll of white cloth from under his cloak, and telling the idiot to unfold it, and hold it up by two of its corners, he placed a light in a lantern, and threw the rays which passed through the glass bull's-eye upon the extended cloth. Immediately, a painted transparency became apparent ; and the idiot boy starting at the sight, exclaimed,—"

" Archy sees the picture."

" Yes, boy ; and when I hold up the cloth, as you are now doing, in the sleeping-room of Sir Lambert, you must throw the light from this lantern upon it as I throw it now. Do you understand ?"

" Archy knows what he is to do. But what does the picture mean? It is like a murder."

The unknown rolled up the cloth, and taking the boy's hand, said—

" It represents that which you say it does. You have heard, Archy, that Sir

Thomas who died at the hall killed himself, but he was murdered, boy—murdered as he sat in his own chair."

"Archy was never told that," said the idiot with some surprise.

"There are none who could have told you, boy. I know that he was murdered, but I cannot tell you yet, Archy, who it was who killed him. We go to find out that to-night, and by means of this picture."

The idiot took the painting, unrolled it again, and held it up, so that the moonlight shone through it.

"Was not Sir Thomas killed by a pistol ? Archy thinks so," said he.

"He was shot, Archy."

"Then why is the man in the picture killing him with a knife ?"

"Because, Archy—but no matter. There is meaning in that, more than I can explain to you now. It is time—come, Archy, come."

"Where must Archy go ?" asked the idiot.

"To Warrenton Hall, boy; to the chamber where Sir Lambert sleeps to-night.

The idiot and his companion took their way together towards the old fort which stood by the sea.

CHAPTER LVI.

THE BRIDAL EVE IN THE CHAMBER OF SIR LAMBERT.—THE STRANGER AND THE IDIOT AT THEIR WORK.

MIDNIGHT had passed, but it was the dead of night still. All was silent in the chamber where slept Sir Lambert Warrenton; the lamp was extinguished; the timepiece ticked but faintly ; the flies had ceased to hum around the bed curtains, and had betaken themselves to sleep upon the oaken ceiling.

Sir Lambert slept—slept in the same chamber and upon the same bed which he had occupied in his careless boyhood, and in his dreaming youthtime. The slumber was deep, for exhausted nature willingly courted repose, and the wearied mind felt the necessity of rest.

Sir Lambert slept, to wake on the morrow as a bridegroom, to lead on the approaching morn fair beauty to the altar, kneel beside her there, and utter the words of that vow which should be binding through time, and find its echo in eternity.

Already had the bridal couch been prepared, and damsels were waiting to strew it with fresh flowers on the morrow ; already had the maiden put off the virgin attire, and the ringers were preparing to send forth the chimes from the old belfry, to hail the blushing bride. Many were they, who were thinking of the coming morn, and wishing to themselves that the time would soon arrive, when the church-bell would ring out a peal for them, and the sun shine brightly on their own glad marriage-day.

Sir Lambert slept — oh! pleasant should be the dreams of the slumberer when sleeping on his bridal eve! Visions of beauty, and pictures of delight should be present to him then ; and dreamland should disclose every magic scene of that enchanted realm. No horrible phantoms should disturb the happy sleeper, no terrors of the night-time should he know, Then, if ever, should angels whisper in his ear of a future full of joy; and imagination exert its wondrous alchemy in changing this common earth into a golden land, with flowers by every pathway, and jems on every tree.

But are such the dreams of Sir Lambert Warrenton? Watch him as he sleeps see with what restlessness he presses his couch ! Watch him in his dreamings; why does he start, and tremble. and mutter words which have a fearful meaning ? Look ! what means that convulsive movement ? Why is his hand outstretched as if to bid back phantoms from his pillow ? Watch him—watch him well !

And see again ! He bites his lip; the red blood stains the corners of his mouth. He clasps his hands over his eyes, and his nails imprint themselves upon his forehead. Ha! did you mark how he sprung upward in his bed—how he started as if to elude the grasp of some demon—how the muscles of his neck became rigid as carven marble, and then how they played beneath the pale skin like electric wires ? Oh, watch him—watch him well !

What can his dreams be ? What mean those groans of agony—those mutterings of pain ? Will he sleep like that when married to his gentle bride ? will he startle her in the night-time with such wild gestures, and will she wake to listen to such groans ? There must be meaning in those movements ; there must be cause for those writhings, and that pain. It is not imagination only ; it is not fancy's work alone which you see there. And that is he who is to be Amy's bridegroom ! Oh, watch him—watch him well !

Watch him well—watch him now !—take not your eyes off him ! See— see—he struggles—he writhes—he wrestles with some foe ! and hark ! he laughs, but the laugh is hollow ; he chuckles, but the chuckle is dying away into a groan. .d now—ha! watch him—now see! he rises up- right in his bed, his hands are put forth to keep the demons at a distance, his eyes open -they open wider still—he shrieks—he starts—he stares !

What is it that has woke the sleeper from his sleep ? What is that which he beholds before him now ?

Look at it—what is its meaning ? It represents an old man sitting in his chair, and a murderer standing behind him with a knife uplifted in his hand. Is it a picture ? and if so, how came it there ? and whence comes the light which shines upon it ?

Why does Sir Lambert Warrenton stare so fixedly at that picture—his eyes bulging from their sockets, his hands stretched out, his fingers expanded ?

Watch him ! His lips are working—his eyeballs roll ; there's a gulping movement about his throat, as if words are there struggling for utterance—an utterance which they cannot win.

But look again ! the lips open—the chest heaves ; a scowl of derision has arisen on the face of the startled man. He speaks now—he springs forward— he speaks !

" It is false !" he cries, " it is false ! It was not a knife. I did not kill him with a knife—I did not stab him ! Away, I say—away. It is my bridal eve, and I have won her ! Away—away ! What—no ! Dourville—Dourville, I say !"

See ! he springs from off the bed—he shrieks—he staggers—he falls upon the floor. The picture is no longer there ; and the stranger and the idiot have accom- plished their work !

" Quick, Archy ! We must not stay here. Through the passage, boy. The panel is open—haste !"

In less than twenty minutes after this scene had come to its conclusion, the dark stranger and the idiot boy stood together on the glacis outside the old fort.

" Archy wants to be told the meaning of what he saw," said the idiot, touching the arm of his companion, and looking upwards inquiringly

" It meant, boy, all that I wished to know. The secret is mine now, and I will turn it to its use."

" But Archy does not know what the knife was painted on the picture for."

" To do the work it has done, boy—to make the secret-holder betray his secret."

" Then Amy will not be married to Sir Lambert, and will not go with him to the great hall !"

" Never, Archy—never !"

" Then Archy is happy—Archy is quite happy now," said the idiot, as, obeying the instructions of his companion, he departed, and took his way towards the cottage of the Heytons.

At the hour appointed, the stranger met Sandy Summers and Glib Griffiths by the finger-post on the road-side.

"Are you prepared?" he asked.

"Quite," answered the tombmaker.

"And have you brought with you a saw, as I told you to?"

"It is here," replied Glib Griffiths. "'Tisn't a very good one, though I set

the teeth of it this morning. But Mr. Summers and myself have been trying to guess what we shall want a saw for; perhaps you won't mind enlightening my friend Sandy on that point?"

"You will know presently," returned the stranger. "If you are ready, and are both of you bold enough to undertake this work, come with me at once. The roads are silent, and the night is dark."

"We'll go, Sandy," said Glib. "May be you'll have the making of the tomb yet, man ; and may be you'll want me for a witness by-and-by. I'll make a speech, Sandy. Dang it, man! I'll make a speech."

With this declaration, Glib Griffiths shouldered a pickaxe, and set off in company with Sandy Summers and the stranger to the cross-road, where twelvemonths before the body of Sir Thomas Warrenton had been interred.

CHAPTER LVII.

AMY AT THE ALTAR, AND THE MYSTERY OF THE MARK EXPLAINED.

A GLOOMY, lowering morning was that which ushered in the day appointed for Sir Lambert's bridal. Dark clouds moved heavily across the sky ; the sun had risen of a red colour, with black stripes intermingled with its rays ; and a sharp, whistling wind, which turned up the white backs of the leaves, indicated that a storm was approaching, and that there would be much rain.

And early that morning fair Amy was awake, but when she awoke, she looked around and found that her sister had arisen before her. She listened, but all was silence in the cottage ; no sound of moving footsteps could she hear ; no voice, no merry troll like that which she had been accustomed to hearken to from the lips of mirthful Kate, on mornings that were past and gone. Wondering why her sister had risen so early, and curious to know how she was at present engaged, Amy rose from her bed, dressed herself hastily, and stole on tiptoe down the stairs. She peeped into the sitting-room, but Kate was not there ; she opened the door of the adjoining apartment, but still she saw not her sister. It was very strange. There was no one in the flower garden, no one in the bower, and no one sitting on the seat beneath the old apple-tree. Amy was about to awaken her father and Frank, when at that moment the cottage-door was thrown open, and Kate herself, attired in the same dress which she had worn on the preceding day, entered, and stood in the presence of her sister.

"Kate—dear Kate!" exclaimed Amy.

"Why are you down stairs so early, sweet sister?" returned Kate. "You should have slept later considering the fatigue you will have to undergo during the day."

"Rather let me ask you, dear Kate, why you have risen so early, and whither you have been?"

"Been, sister?" Why, to see the bright sun rise, to be sure—to see if it rose brightly on the morn of your wedding-day."

"My wedding-morn, dear sister," echoed Amy half-mournfully.

"Ay, that which you think to be such, sweet sister mine. But come, we will return to the bedroom. I am to be your bridesmaid this day, and a merry bridesmaid I shall be. Come, sister, come. You have to dress ; you have to don your marriage finery, that you may glow to-day in all your beauty, and stand at the altar in fitting guise, when gay groups are there to look upon you, and the wedding bells chime merrily their gladsome peal of joy."

Amy returned to her chamber in company with Kate. The morning progressed, and Frank Heyton paid a visit to his sister, to wish her a happy day, and inform her that Miss Atherleigh, who had consented to be bridesmaid along with Kate, would arrive in the course of an hour.

Kate stood beside her sister's dressing-table, holding in her hand the wreath which Amy was that day to wear.

"Sister," said she, "Once upon a time I heard Amy Heyton say that orange blossoms would never be worn upon her poor, pale brow. Look you how true a propet that Amy Heyton is. The orange-blossoms are here, and the pretty bride elect is waiting to put them on·"

Amy arose from her seat, and approaching, wound her arm around her sister's neck.

"You are merry—you are very very merry, dear Kate. Tell me, do you wish that this marriage should be? Why is your behaviour so changed from what it was last night?"

"Do you think me changed, dear sister?"

"I spoke of the alteration in your behaviour, good Kate. You are not changed, I know. But do you approve now of my being married to Sir Lambert? Is it your wish that I kneel at the altar with him this day?"

"Yes, sister. Go thither; kneel at the altar; take Sir Lambert's hand! You have consented to do so—wherefore should I object?"

"But you have expressed your objection, dear Kate. You think, sister, that I am willing to marry Sir Lambert to win a title and a name thereby; but you are wrong, sister—very wrong to hold that thought. And you think, too, that when Ernest loved me, if Sir Lambert had offered me his hand, I should have taken it, that I might be the lady of yonder hall, instead of being the wife of Lieutenant Morden. There too you are mistaken, and you wrong me, sister. Had I never given to Sir Lambert that promise—that promise which I fully, firmly believed I should be called upon to fulfil, I should not have consented to be his bride; I would not have received these gifts from him which I am to wear to-day. You think me happy, sister, but I do not feel so; though why should I be otherwise—what reason have I to be sad at accepting Sir Lambert Warrenton for my husband?"

Kate Heyton did not reply for some seconds. At length, putting down the orange-wreath, which she had hitherto held in her hand, she said,—

"There is happiness in store for you yet, sister Amy. It may meet you at the altar where you go to wed Sir Lambert Warrenton."

"You speak strangely, sister Kate! What meaning is there in your words?"

"Sister, this sandal is loose on your shoe; give me a needle that I may fasten it on," said Kate, changing the subject of conversation.

And the hours flew by, and the bridesmaids busied themselves at their work. Gay groups collected in the adjacent village, the ringers took their way to the church, to send forth the peal from the merry bells, and Sir Lambert himself arrived in his carriage, at the cottage of the Heytons, to claim her whom he had chosen for his bride, and escort her to that sacred place wherein he was to plight to her his vows.

"You are not looking so well this morning, as beseems a bridegroom to look at such a time, Sir Lambert," observed Mr. Netherby, who was waiting to join the party in their way to the church.

"Nothing has occurred to cause me to appear unwell, the excitement of the occasion excepted," replied the young baronet. "By-the-by, Netherby, have you heard the news which has just been told me? They say that a sea-fight took place last night, and that that rascal Red Martin the smuggler has been captured at last."

"No," answered Mr. Netherby, "I have not been informed of the occurrence till now, though I have heard that Mr. Hargreave, of the Grange, has received a summons to attend somewhere in his magisterial capacity, and that he was seen a few minutes since going towards the church, attended by Ruggles, the tipstaff, and another man."

"Towards the church!" repeated Sir Lambert, with some surprise.

"So I was told; and—but your bride is waiting, Sir Lambert. Be not wanting in gallantry on your marriage morn."

It is needless to describe how fair Amy looked and blushed as Sir Lambert led her to the carriage; it is needless to relate how she demeaned herse'f as that carriage rolled on its way to the church, arriving there amid the loud huzzas of the villagers, and heralded by the merry chimes which rang out joyfully from the old ivy-mantled tower.

Passing on up the gravelled pathway which led to the entrance porch, Sir Lambert and fair Amy were greeted with many happy wishes by the assembled group which had congregated to receive them. All were arrayed in their best attire, and the maidens had brought flowers to strew over the path.

Amy and Sir Lambert entered the church. As they stepped upon the threshold, a loud peal of thunder suddenly rolled along the heavens, and the storm, which had been gathering for some hours past, burst forth in all its violence.

"This is a strange omen for Sister Amy's wedding," observed Frank Heyton to Kate.

"It is," was the reply.

But the eyes of Kate wandered round the church, and, seeing not what she thought to see, the countenance of the gay bridesmaid suddenly became pale, and she muttered to herself,—

"Not here! Why are they not here?"

A large party had collected in the church. Gervase Morden and Constance Ismay were there, waiting for the marriage of Sir Lambert to be completed, that they too might plight their vows before the same altar. Eugene Dourville was there, to grace the bridal of his friend. The acquaintances whom Sir Lambert had invited were there; and there, also, were those who took an especial interest in the fortunes of fair Amy. Strangely enough, Mr. Hargreave, the gentleman whose name had been mentioned by Mr. Netherby, and who was the magistrate for the district, stood amongst the crowd that had assembled near the altar. In one of the aisles stood the tipstaff Ruggles; while, remote from the rest, and partly concealed by one of the large columns, was the dark stranger of the festival, accompanied by Archy, the idiot boy.

Glib Griffiths and Sandy Summers had also taken their places in the church, and near them was Mr. Leybridge, the principal surgeon of the town of Darlingham.

Loudly rolled the thunder through the heavens; fiercely beat the rain against the windows of the old church. The storm was increasing in its strength; the commotion of the elements was becoming greater every moment.

And now the clergyman had taken his place within the railing which surrounded the communion-table, and the prayer-book was open from which the service of the ceremony was to be read.

"Where is Kate?" exclaimed Mr. Heyton, suddenly.

Amy had been accompanied to the church by two bridesmaids, one of whom was standing by her side now; the other, who was Amy's sister, could not be seen.

"How is, Frank?" said Mr. Heyton. "Where is your sister gone?"

Frank Heyton could not answer the question. In vain he cast his eyes round the church, and made inquiries of those about him. He was proceeding towards the porch, when Kate herself entered by a side door, and, with a flushed face, and eyes that glistened with a strange meaning, advanced quickly, and took her place beside her father.

"We were wondering at your absence, Kate," said Mr. Heyton.

The maiden made no reply.

All was now in readiness. Sir Lambert, leading Amy by the hand, advanced towards the altar. When, as he took his place there, a flash of lightning, bursting from a thunder-cloud, swooped through a window of the old church, and struck the brass railing near which the bride and bridegroom stood. Both started back, and Amy trembled with a sudden fear, which she found it impossible to subdue.

"Be not afraid of the storm, my child," said Mr. Heyton.

The places were again taken, and the clergyman cast his eyes upon the book to commence reading the service.

"Not yet, Dr. Overton," exclaimed Mr. Netherby, suddenly stepping forwards, to the astonishment of the clergyman, and of those assembled around. "Not yet.

There is a duty which I have to perform, preparatory to your uniting these two people."

"Whatever you may have to say, Mr. Netherby," replied Dr. Overton, "had better not be spoken here. Let us retire to the vestry."

"It must be said at this place," answered Mr. Netherby. "Amy Ormsby—for such, Amy Heyton, is your real name—I now undertake the performance of a task, which was assigned to me and Mr. Heyton many long years ago. There was a gentleman, whose name was Everard Ormsby ; he was my friend, the friend of Stephen Heyton, and cousin to the late Sir Thomas Warrenton. He was possessed of large estates, and much property. Early in life he married a woman, whose station in society was much lower than his own, but whose beauty attracted his attention, and won his heart. That woman—that wife—afterwards proved false to him. He made the discovery that she had married him solely for his riches, and not for any love that she had even felt for him, or for any affection that she for him had ever known. By that wife Everard Ormsby had one daughter. Full well he loved his child ; full well he enjoyed her infant prattle, and her infant smiles. But the thought haunted him that, as his daughter would inherit his wealth, she might, also, be deceived, by her hand being sought for the winning of her riches, while a false tale of love was whispered in her ear. To prevent such an occurrence ever taking place, Everard Ormsby applied to his friend Stephen Heyton, and, agreeing with him, committed his daughter to Stephen Heyton's care. The arrangement was, that she was to be brought up by him in the belief that she was his own child ; that she was to receive a good education ; and that she was not to be acquainted with the true secret of her birth. Many years had not passed, before Everard Ormsby lay on his death-bed. Sir Thomas Warrenton, Mr. Heyton, and myself, attended him there, and became the trustees of the property which he bequeathed to his child. A sister of his wife had been forced by her parents to marry against her will. Like Mrs. Ormsby, that sister also proved false to her husband. Everard Ormsby remembered the circumstance when framing the will by which he made his daughter his heiress. In that will, a copy of which I now produce, he ordered that his daughter should remain ignorant of her true parentage, and of the wealth which she was destined to inherit, until the day and hour when she should stand before the altar to give her hand to the husband of her choice. No such husband was to be forced upon her, and no objections were to be raised against her giving her hand to whomsoever she should choose, provided that his moral character stood good. You, Amy, are the daughter of that Everard Ormsby ; the wealth which he left in trust for you will yet be yours. And if you have, of your own free will, chosen Sir Lambert Warrenton for your husband, and if Sir Lambert consents as readily to wed you, now that he finds you a heiress, as he did when he knew you only as Amy Heyton, then do both of you join hands, and let this marriage proceed."

It would not be easy to describe the astonishment with which these revelations were listened to by all who heard them ; neither would it be easy for the pen to tell how many and what various emotions agitated the breast of gentle Amy, as the strange news struck upon her ear, explaining one, at least, of the mysteries with which she had long felt her life to be surrounded. The poor maiden was nearly overpowered by her feelings, and had it not been for the support afforded her by the kind arms of Mr. Heyton and his daughter Kate, she would have sank upon the altar-step, unable to bear up under the sudden surprise.

Fiercer beat the rain against the windows ; louder and with increasing nearness pealed the thunder along the sky. Every moment the storm seemed adding to its strength ; every moment the elemental commotion became heightened and more terrific.

Mr. Netherby advanced, and took the hand of the maiden in his own.

"Amy Ormsby," said he, "is it still your wish to be the wife of Sir Lambert Warrenton ?"

"It is," she replied, faintly.

"And you, Sir Lambert—do you consent to accept this fair, soft hand in marriage, now that its owner appears before you in her true character?"

"I do," replied the baronet. "Would that she had always remained that which she thought herself to be, that she might have been convinced of my loving her for herself alone!"

"And will you declare that you have such true and sincere love for her whom you are about to wed, Sir Lambert Warrenton?" asked Mr. Heyton.

"Indeed, indeed, I have! Heaven witnesses to its truth and to its fervency! Dearest Amy! had you continued to be the humble yeoman's daughter, instead of proving to be the heiress that you are, my love for you and my desire to win your hand, could not have been greater—could not have been more pure than it is now. Believe me, dearest; believe me!"

"Liar!" cried a loud, but hollow voice, which resounded throughout the church. "Hypocrite and liar!"

The company were startled; Sir Lambert turned hastily round, and his eyes rested upon the form of the dark stranger who had conversed in the churchyard with the tombmaker and Mr. Griffith's on the preceding night.

"Whence come you, sir? And why this unseemly interruption?" inquired Mr. Netherby.

"Whence I came matters not," replied the unknown; "but my business here is to unmask that hypocrite—that more than villain—who stands there, and whom you call Sir Lambert Warrenton!"

Kate Heyton started, and murmured to herself, "This is not he! Why is he not here himself?"

"Your words are strange, sir; and your behaviour is highly indecorous, be you who you may," observed Dr. Overton.

"Not more indecorous than that that man should kneel beside yon altar!" replied the unknown, extending his hand as he spoke to indicate that his words had reference to Sir Lambert. "I am here to disclose the treachery and perfidy which has been used towards that fair girl, and the villany of him to whom she has consented to give her hand. Let all who are here assembled listen to that which I have to tell."

Suddenly, but with a violent effort, Sir Lambert moved from the place where he had yet remained standing; and in a faltering voice said,—

"Come, Amy! Let us retire until this intruder is removed."

"Stir not—take not another step, Lambert Warrenton!" exclaimed the unknown. "And you, too, Eugene Dourville, move from where you are at your peril! Listen to me, Dr. Overton; and let me be heard by those around."

Sandy Summers took up his position before Sir Lambert. Eugene Dourville was prevented from moving by Glib Griffith's planting himself by his side. As for poor Amy, she had fallen back into the arms of Frank Heyton, and with her eyes wildly fixed upon the stranger, listened to his words with open mouth.

Silence reigned in the church.

"Amy Ormsby," said the deep, hollow voice of the unknown, "it is to you that I will reveal the scheme of villany which has been carried into effect by Lambert Warrenton, the man whom you have promised to wed. He has declared that were you a cottager's daughter, instead of the heiress which you are, he would still accept your hand. That declaration is a lie; the words are those of a hypocrite! Lambert Warrenton was acquainted with the secret of your birth; he knew, ere he sought your hand, that he wooed no dowerless maiden, but one whose wealth was worth the winning, and only whose wealth he cared to win!"

"There is some mistake here," interposed Mr. Heyton, "the secret of Amy Ormsby's birth and fortune was known only to the late Sir Thomas Warrenton, Mr. Netherby, and myself. To us alone it was committed, and by us it has been faithfully kept."

"Not so, Mr. Heyton," replied the unknown. "It is you who are mistaken. The secret you speak of was long ago known to Lambert Warrenton yonder,

Eugene Dourville, and to him who addresses you now. Everard Ormsby, Amy's father, had a servant in his house who overheard as he listened in an adjoining room, on the night his master was dying, the arrangement which he made with his executors concerning the disposal of his property, and the education and future treatment of his child. In after years, the servant of whom I speak availed himself of the secret which he had learned, by wooing Everard Ormsby's daughter. But not because of her wealth only did he woo her—he loved her, deeply as ever woman has been loved by man. She rejected that love—she despised the humble, moneyless wooer; she treated him with scorn; she looked upon him with contempt. Scorn and contempt which he never forgot—which is not forgotten by him now. I am he who was that wooer; I am he whom she scorned in her pride, and despised in her haughtiness. You that stand around look at me and wonder who I am; but *she* knows me; my name is upon her lips. Look! I throw off my disguise; I appear before you as one whom all of you have seen before. Ha! ha! Who knows not Luke Masters? Who knows not the man whose parents here have taught their children to shun? You, too, know me Lambert Warrenton; you know how much I have the power to tell—what secrets I can disclose!"

"It is Black Luke—Black Luke, the reprobate," exclaimed Sir Lambert "What man of you would believe a word spoken by him?"

"All of them shall believe me!" returned Luke Masters, "all of them shall hear my story. Lambert Warrenton and Eugene Dourville, the man whom I point out to you now, have long been acquainted with each other. To Dourville, Lambert Warrenton long ago lost large sums of money at the gaming-table. This friendship was unknown at that period to the late Sir Thomas, who had obtained for his son a situation of trust in the Admiralty office, at London, and who believed that son to be leading a life of a far different description than that which was in reality the case. A strict disciplinarian himself, Sir Thomas was not disposed to countenance any extravagance, or any irregularity of conduct on the part of his son; and of this fact Lambert Warrenton was well aware. Still continuing to frequent the gaming-house, his losses became greater and greater, and having taken me into his confidence, I was employed by him to cause false representations of his manner of living to reach his father's ears, in order that all suspicion of his conduct might be lulled at home. I have said that he became acquainted with Mr. Dourville, who not only won money from him, but introduced him to gamesters whose skill, in the practice of their art, was far greater than his own. And when all that he had was lost—when his bonds had been given to money-lenders, and all the property which he expected to inherit mortgaged to Jews, Eugene Dourville made known to him that he was a spy in this country on the part of France; that he was desirous of gaining information as to all the secret movements of the government, and that if Lambert Warrenton would be a traitor to his country, and betray his trust—if he would take advantage of the office which he held, to glean what information he could, and confide it to the enemy of his native land, he should be well rewarded for his treachery. Lambert Warrenton consented; but as he was already in debt to Dourville, and owed sundry large sums to other persons, a plan was contrived to arrange these difficulties. I had confided to Lambert Warrenton the secret which I knew regarding Amy Ormsby, and he had told the story to his friend Dourville. The latter proposed that Lambert Warrenton should at once attempt to gain Amy's hand in marriage, and by winning her wealth repay a certain sum which Dourville proposed to advance. One difficulty lay in the way of carrying out this scheme; Amy had chosen to love Mr. Ernest Morden, and by the terms of her father's will, she was to be permitted to marry whomsoever her hoice should select. To supplant Ernest Morden in her favour was now the great object to be accomplished. Little did Amy, herself, dream at the time, and little does she imagine even now, the plan which was resorted to in order to bring about hat event. The mark which twelve months ago she bore upon her neck, witnessed to the truth of that part of my story which I have now to reveal."

"Ha!" exclaimed Kate Heyton, grasping the arm of Black Luke; "do you know what that mark meant, and how it came?"

"I know and will explain," answered Luke Masters, "ay, frown not at me in that manner, Lambert Warrenton. Your frowns will not make me fear to tell that which I have come here to disclose. You remember the meeting which you had with Mr. Dourville there, when he proposed to you this scheme. You remember his letting you into a portion of his past history, by informing you that previous to becoming a spy, he had been a Roman Catholic priest. Yes, Eugene Dourville— and a priest too who has betrayed the secret confided to him in the confession of a dying man! The dying man was Mr. Reginald Morden, the father of your Ernest, fair Amy; your own father, Mr. Gervase. When dying, he called for a priest, and that priest's name was Dourville. To him Mr. Morden confessed his sins, and confessed also that, having been abroad for a time, he returned, and found his wife the mother of a child of which he knew that he was not the father. That wife he punished in no other method than by removing the child from her, and conveying it away. A sailor's superstition had taught him that no harm could happen to man or child whose skin bore the imprint of the cross; and not wishing that harm should come to the hapless infant which he had cast out, he branded on its skin, between the shoulders, the mark of a Maltese cross. There stood beside the bed of the dying man when he made this confession, not only yonder traiterous priest, but Ernest Morden also, the dying man's own son. Both heard the tale. That one of the two would refrain from telling it, Reginald Morden had a right to expect; to the other—his own son—he gave a charge that the story of his mother's infamy should never escape his lips. The whole of these circumstances were recounted by Eugene Dourville to Lambert Warrenton, and the latter devised a plan, whereby, through the agency of a chemical compound, which stains, a short time after application, the skin to which it is applied, he should effect the placing of a mark upon Amy Ormsby's neck, similar to that which Mr. Morden had branded on the neck of the cast-out child; that afterwards Ernest Morden should be led to see that mark; that he should then be reminded of the secret confided to him by his dying father; and that, by such a plan of action, an eternal separation between Ernest Morden and Amy Ormsby should be brought about. Lambert Warrenton prepared himself for the achievement, and waited his opportunity. One day he found Amy seated by the sea side, where she had fallen asleep over her book. Then it was that he stole behind her, and imprinted the stamp upon her neck. It was not apparent at once, but became so in the course of a few hours. Lambert Warrenton had learned that this poor idiot boy, who is an orphan, whom Mr. Heyton had brought up, cherished an affection for Amy, and wished that she should never leave the cottage; from him he got information of Ernest Morden's arrival, and of the time when he and Amy would be together, and from him he derived his knowledge of the proceedings in the cottage. To that cottage, disguised as an old and wearied traveller, Lambert Warrenton went. He played his part well, and, selecting a fitting opportunity, reminded Ernest Morden of the date of the day on which his father died, and challenged him to look at the neck of his sweetheart. What Ernest saw there; how he acted at the time; and how the traveller disappeared, you already know. Lambert Warrenton was afterwards pursued by Ernest; a combat ensued, in which Mr. Morden was wounded. There is, at the summit of the old fort which stands by the sea, a passage closed over by a stone, which leads to the vaults below, and thence, by a subterranean path to Warrenton Hall. It was by means of this passage Lambert Warrenton escaped his pursuers, when nearly overtaken by Frank Heyton. The passage is continued within the old hall. Of its existence none were aware but Lambert Warrenton, who had discovered it through turning over some old papers, among which he found an ancient plan of the building. It was used by him on the occasion to which I allude, and doubtless has been used by him since. The wall of his chamber is provided with a sliding panel giving admission to the next apartment, the opposite wall of which is provided with a similar panel communicating with the secret passage. The apartment last men-

tioned, was Miss Ismay's bedchamber; and it was in crossing it on the night of which I have spoken that Lambert Warrenton so much alarmed that young lady; leaving behind him on the floor a blood-spot, which had dropped from a wound in his arm, received during his combat with Ernest Morden. Hitherto I have disclosed the villany of yon two men; it is now time that I speak of my own. Inasmuch as Amy Ormsby had scorned me, I sought revenge; inasmuch as Ernest Morden had gained her favour, I hated him because he enjoyed that privilege. Therefore was it, that learning on the occasion of a visit which Amy paid to Ernest at the cottage of Sampson Summers, she still retained her affection for him, was willing to forgive him his insult, and hesitated not to vow eternal love for him, I resolved to join in a common cause with Lambert Warrenton, and by seeking Ernest Morden's ruin, satisfy at once my hatred and my revenge. An occasion presented itself. Assisted by Archy, I learned that Ernest Morden was in possession of certain despatches which might be of use to Eugene Dourville, the French spy; and acquiring some information respecting Amy's intention of carrying those despatches to the hall, met her on her way, contrived to abstract the packet from her basket, and substitute another in its place. With Lambert Warrenton I had previously made my arrangements; he received the fictitious packet of despatches from Amy, took care to point out to her notice the circumstance of the single seal; and knowing what would be the issue to Ernest Morden, won from Amy that promise by virtue of which he has now claimed her for his bride. The true despatches were committed by Eugene Dourville to the care of Red Martin, the smuggler; and I received my reward for the part I had taken in the affair. How or by whom it was contrived that Amy herself should deliver a similar packet to Red Martin I do not know. All that I can tell of the matter— all that I can confess relating to my own misdeeds, and those of Lambert Warrenton which have borne reference to Amy Ormsby, I have now told. My reasons for appearing here, and making these disclosures, are first—that having once loved Amy I did not wish to see her become married to a blacker villain than myself; and secondly, being as you see me a disease-stricken man, whose limbs have become feeble, whose eyes are sunken, whose cheeks are hollow, and whose hours are numbered, I have wished to make this atonement to those whom I have wronged; so that when in a short time I shall have become one of the dead, my soul may meet with mercy from a just yet merciful God. Lambert Warrenton, of you I ask no pardon for having made these disclosures. I have told the truth, I have spoken that which as a dying man I could keep secret no longer."

Luke Masters ceased from speaking; there was a slight bustle in the church, and all eyes were turned from the accuser, and directed towards the accused.

"This man has uttered falsities," stammered forth the baronet. "There is no evidence to support a single affirmation which he has made."

"Yes, Lambert Warrenton, there is evidence!" exclaimed a loud voice, and a man advanced from behind the crowd, and stood in the open space before the altar.

"Lieutenant Morden!—Ernest Morden here!" ejaculated a score of individuals at once.

Gervase Morden turned pale as his eyes met those of his brother. Ernest observed the change in his countenance, and stepping towards him, whispered in his ear,—

"Be not afraid, brother! Kate Heyton followed us to the cliff that night. Her hands saved me from destruction when you had turned your back upon me. She knew that I yet lived—that I should be here to-day."

"What has Lieutenant Morden to disclose?" inquired Mr. Netherby.

"His innocence—your innocence, dear Amy! Said I not there would be some one to meet you at the altar?" exclaimed delighted Kate.

"Speak, Ernest Morden!—what have you to tell?" said Mr. Heyton.

"Much, Mr. Heyton, that it will please you, as well as many else present, to hear," replied Ernest. "A twelvemonth has passed since I made my escape from Warrenton Hall. On the night of that escape—but where or under what circumstances I need not reveal—I had an interview with Miss Catherine Heyton. She endeavoured to impress my mind with a conviction of Amy's innocence, and the wrong which I had done her in accusing her as I had. She urged me to seek out Red Martin, learn from him how the despatches had come into his possession, and how Amy had happened to be the bearer of a packet to him which so nearly resembled them. I gave her my promise to do according to her wish; I told her that I would seek out Red Martin, learn his true character, do if possible a service to my country by capturing one whom I believed to be a traitor and a spy, and finally clear up the mystery which was alike a perplexing puzzle to us both. Th pledge which I made to Kate Heyton I have redeemed. The words which Luk

Masters has spoken I have listened to.   Red Martin was captured last night through a stratagem which I thought fit to employ, and through the bravery of those who assisted me.   His vessel is lying in the bay; he himself is a prisoner without. Let him be brought in."

Ernest Morden's command was obeyed.   Red Martin, with gyves upon his wrist, was brought into the church.   At that moment Eugene Dourville was seen to turn pale, and endeavour to slink out of the crowd.

"Stop that man from escaping!" cried Ernest.   "Eugene Dourville, you it was who gave those despatches, which I accused most wrongfully this fair girl of stealing,—you it was, I say, who gave them into the hands of Red Martin, who is here a prisoner.   Those same despatches afterwards passed through the hands of Amy; but it was an accidental occurrence, they having been left by the smuggler at a place where he dared not go to fetch them, but to which place he requested Amy, whom he met upon the beach, to proceed and procure them for him.   She did so, not knowing what it was that she was really doing.   Thus is the whole matter explained; and of the prisoner, Red Martin himself, I ask if the account which I have rendered be not true?"

"It is," replied the smuggler.

Ernest Morden turned to Amy, and fell upon his knee at her side,—

"Forgive me, Amy! forgive me!   There is much to be forgive!   You have heard why I acted so strangely towards you, as I once did; you have heard how woefully I was deceived—how much I was mistaken.   It was in a moment of passion—a moment of madness I suffered my lips to open in accusation against you.   Oh, you know not how great was the frenzy under which I laboured; you guess not what feelings rived my bosom after that fearful scene was past, and my heart chided me for the cruel words which I had uttered!   You, Amy, have ever been great, ever been noble, ever been that pure and perfect being which in my first fond dream of love I fancied you to be!   Would to Heaven I could atone for the deep wrongs I have done you!   Would to Heaven I could efface from your memory and mine the remembrance of the dark periods of the past!   I have sought and obtained proof of your purity of conduct; I have exculpated myself from the grave crimes which were laid to my charge; I have served my country in capturing her enemies; I have won back my good fame by deed of bravery and perilous adventure; and now, Amy, I ask not for your love—I am not worthy that.   But if you can forgive one who cannot forgive himself for wronging you; if you can pardon the past, and say that you feel no ill-will towards him who once was happy in your love, I will ask no more; I will pray for blessings on your head, I will not let my presence call up painful remembrances to your mind; but I will depart to some distant scene, I will fight bravely for the cause of my fatherland, and in my death-hour, when my life-blood shall be ebbing fast, my last prayers shall be to Heaven that it rain down blessings upon you."

"No, Ernest, dear—ever loved Ernest!" ejaculated Amy, throwing herself upon the breast of him who had so strangely returned; "you must not—shall not go!"   I have nothing to forgive in you, and if I had, it is forgiven all.   I have never forgot you—never thought otherwise but kindly of you.   My love is all your own; it was yours long, long ago."

"Ernest Morden," said Kate Heyton, laying her hand upon the shoulder of him whom she addressed, "my prophecy is accomplished.   I told you when I parted from you on that terrible night, that this day would come at last.   It has come; and Kate is happy in having been the means of bringing happiness to her whom she finds to be no longer her sister.   Oh! Amy—sweet Amy, you know not what joy Kate Heyton at this moment feels!"

And as the brave girl spoke, the storm ceased, the clouds separated, and the bright sun shining forth shed its beams upon the happy party then assembled together in the old church.

"Sir Lambert Warrenton, and you, Mr. Dourville, stand both alike accused of treachery and conspiracy against his majesty the king, and against the country in which you have resided for some years past," said Mr. Hargreave, the magistrate.

"It is my duty to see that each of you is immediately arrested on those charges' and that you are both forthwith committed to custody."

"What! am I to suffer such an indignity, merely because of the falsities which that man—that reputed villain has thought fit to come here and tell?" demanded Sir Lambert, pointing as he spoke to Luke Masters.

"Say you that I have uttered falsities, Lambert Warrenton?" asked Black Luke, in a bold voice.

"You have, villain! you have come here with a strangely-concocted tale, not one word of which is truth. At another place and at another time I will make evident who and what you are, and will show what reliance is to be placed in any one affirmation made by Black Luke."

"But here and at this time, Lambert Warrenton," exclaimed Masters, "I will make evident what you are,—so evident, indeed, that all who stand around shall believe, and you yourself shall tremble as I speak. I, Luke Masters, have accused Sir Lambert Warrenton of being a traitor; to that accusation, I add the charge of murder."

"Murder!" ejaculated the voices of the assembled group.

"Ay," continued Black Luke, in a yet louder tone, "of the murder, Lambert Warrenton, of your own father, whom you killed in cold blood."

"My—my father committed suicide," stammered the baronet; "his death was wrought by his own hand."

"Liar! He was slain by you. In your own chamber is an air-gun, armed with which you stole along the secret passage opening into the library, where, on the night of his murder your father sat; you slew him with a bullet discharged from that gun; you it was who placed the pistol at his feet; you it was who took away his life. That such was the case Black Luke has long suspected—he has proofs and certainty now!"

"It is untrue—it is false!" faintly exclaimed the baronet. "Who will believe this man?"

"They shall all believe me! The proofs shall be theirs. Look you here, Lambert Warrenton."

And as Black Luke spoke, he entered the space around the communion-table and plucking away the crimson cloth which covered the altar, revealed to view the body of a corpse partially wrapped up in a white sheet. Consternation and horror seized the whole assembly; every face turned deadly pale; every mouth was open with affright."

"Here, Lambert Warrenton—ay, in this holy place, is the body of Sir Thomas' your father—within that fleshless skull is the bullet by which the murder was effected. In your chamber will be found the gun from which it was discharged; and here is a mould which there are those present who can witness belongs to you. Sampson Summers, you have brought with you mallet and chisel; let them be handed to me.

"What profanity would you commit?" hastily asked Dr. Overton, seizing the arm of Black Luke.

"No profanity; nothing but an act which will win the proof I seek!" replied Luke Masters. "See you here, Lambert Warrenton, this is the skull of your own father. It has been partially sawed round already. I place this chisel in the same curve—I strike it with this mallet; the bone separates—the skull is opened—the bullet is here, in my hand! Ha! ha! it fits the mould—it will fit the gun! It is no pistol-bullet. It is the one with which you slew your father—the one with which you took his life! Ha! ha! you are pale now, Lambert Warrenton! you cannot speak; you do not call me liar! Where, where are your taunts for Black Luke now? Ha! ha! ha! Hypocrite! traitor! murderer!"

"Murderer!" echoed the by-standers, as they closed around the fallen baronet, and as the constables fastened the fetters upon his wrists.

CHAPTER LVIII.

HOW LOVE AND MADNESS WORKED TO THE END OF THE JOURNEY.—CONCLUSION

ON the arrival of the whole party at Warrenton Hall, whither they took their way, Mr. Netherby sought the apartment to which Gervase Morden and Constance Ismay had retired. He found the latter in tears, and the pale student bending over her, and making solicitous inquiries as to the cause of her grief.

"Miss Ismay," said Mr. Netherby, "I have this day to pay over to you the first dividend of an annuity settled upon you by the late Sir Thomas Warrenton, and to give into your hands a sealed letter which Sir Thomas entrusted to my care."

Fair Constance started, sprung up from her seat, grasped the hand of Mr. Netherby, and in a breathless, choking voice, ejaculated,—

"Give me that letter! Oh, give it—give it to me quickly!"

"It is here, Miss Ismay."

Constance took the letter, broke it open, and exclaimed,—

"Look, see who I am—see who it is whom you were about to wed."

The student looked. On the neck of fair Constance he saw the indelible mark of a cross. He started, caught up the letter from the floor, and read, its contents.

That letter told that Constance Ismay was the daughter of Reginald Morden's wife; that Sir Thomas Warrenton had been her father; and that she had been brought up by, in her younger years, his sister.

Gervase Morden flung the letter upon the floor, threw one look at poor, prostrate Constance; then, rushing from the apartment in mute agony, he took his flight, never to return. None knew what became of him; none were ever able to tell the end of the man who, strong in his sense of honour, and strict in his love of justice, was, nevertheless, twice led to the verge of committing two of the most heinous crimes. The stern man's end is unchronicled—his death-place unknown.

Sir Lambert Warrenton was tried for the murder of his father, but was found "Not guilty," on the ground of insufficient evidence. He was also tried on the accusation of treachery; but, as Ernest Morden refused to give evidence against him, as Black Luke had died many days before, and as Eugene Dourville had effected his escape from prison, and could not be found, a long trial terminated in the prisoner being set at liberty, and being allowed to retain his title of Sir Lambert Warrenton, of Warrenton Hall.

Red Martin was hung in the market-place at Darlingham, and, previous to his execution, the discovery was made that he was a brother of Sampson Summers, who had played a reckless part from his youth, but towards whom the poor tomb-maker had always behaved with kindness, and more than once had effected his rescue, when in the midst of danger.

And now many months rolled by, and one fine morning in spring Amy Ormsby again appeared in bridal attire, preparatory to giving her hand and heart and fortune to Ernest Morden—Ernest, her first, fond love. As, however, the procession was setting off to the church, and as Ernest stopped to whisper something in the ear of Kate, who was again a bridesmaid, Archy, the idiot boy, stole behind them, and, uplifting a knife which he held in his hand, aimed a blow at Ernest. The blow was misdirected; Ernest escaped; the knife entered the bosom of Kate Heyton. The idiot saw the evil work which he had wrought; again he seized the weapon, and struck it into his own chest. One simultaneous shriek escaped from the lips of all present. Kate Heyton and the idiot boy were carried into one room.

In vain was all surgical aid. A fatal wound had in each case been inflicted. But when the idiot boy was in the pangs of his last agony, and the end of the murderer and the suicide was near, he crept from his bed, crawled noiselessly to the couch where Amy was bending over poor dying Kate, and grasping the hands of each, said, in a faint voice,—

"Archy is dying—Archy will be dead soon. He did not mean to hurt Sissy Kate, but he loved Sissy Amy, and could not bear to see her go to the old church to marry Ernest. Archy meant to kill Earnest, but Archy did not mean to harm Kate. Will Kate forgive Archy before Archy dies?"

"I do forgive you, poor boy," replied the once-blooming Kate. "Yours has been a strange passion ; it has brought about a sad result. From my heart, poor boy, I pardon you ; and pray to Heaven that it may do the same."

"And will Sissy Amy pardon Archy, too?"

Amy answered in words similar to those used by Kate.

"Then Archy will die ; Archy can die now. Archy ought to die," rejoined the idiot boy, as he sank upon the floor, never again to rise from it alive.

But death was also at work with the beauteous Kate. She pressed fair Amy's hand ; she turned her sunken eyes towards the face of her whom she had long been used to term her sister.

"Amy—Sister Amy," said she, the death-drops cling to my brow, sister ; the blood trickles cold through my heart. Never more shall we walk the fields to-gether—never more till we walk the broad fields of heaven ! The sun is sinking in the sea, sister. I love to gaze at the golden sunset. Lift me up that I may look at it ; lift me up that I may behold it for the last—last time !"

Amy did so. The dying girl clasped her hands together in admiration, and as the bright orb passed away into the distant wave, so passed the spirit of noble-hearted Kate to its home in the halls of heaven !

* * * * * * *

A twelvemonth glided by ; the bells chimed merrily from the tower of the old church. Dr. Overton again stood with his prayer-book open at the altar, and Amy Ormsby gave her hand to Ernest Morden, and became Amy Morden for ever more.

But no wedding ring ever shone on the finger of Constance Ismay ; she lived in solitude, loved by all who knew her, and loving all in return, and when she died, children strewed white blossoms on her grave.

* * * * * * *

This was the story contained in the papers which I received from the old man in the haunted house. He did not die so soon as I at first expected. I had time to look them through before his last breath was drawn.

"Who are you," I asked, " that this story should be in your hands?"

"I," he said, " am Lambert Warenton ! I am he who slew his own father!"

"You that parricide!"

"I am. I have lived in the world too long, but have not till now had the courage to die. In the room beneath are blood-marks on the wall; it is the blood of Eugene Dourville, the villain who first lured me to crime. He sought me here, he sought me in this house ; and I availed myself of the occasion, and took my re-venge. Parricide and murderer, I am both! It was a fair and gentle maiden whom I once wronged ; and in reparation for that wrong, I would now bequeath all the property I possess to some maiden as gentle and as fair. Say you that lovely girl is your cousin? Let me know her name, and give me pen and ink that I may write it to my will. Quick, quick !"

"No," replied I, urging my cousin away. "That property was bought by you with blood, it cannot be transferred to her. Let it waste, let it be dissipated ; let it be destroyed ! Old man, your hour of death is nigh."

"It is, I feel it is. Go, go ! Remain not in this room when the evil one comes to claim his own. He is coming now ! Depart, I say—depart !"

Whether the parricide struggled much in his last moments I know not, and cannot tell.

FINIS.

London : Published by E. Lloyd, 12, Salisbury Square, Fleet Street.